ALWAYS HUMAN

ARI NORTH

YELLOW
JACKET

To my parents, I love you all the way
around the universe and back again.

—A.N.

YELLOW JACKET glaad

an imprint of Little Bee Books
yellowjacketreads.com | glaad.org

ISBN 978-1-4998-1109-4 (pb) 10 9 8 7 6 5 4 3 2 1 | ISBN 978-1-4998-1110-0 (hc) 10 9 8 7 6 5 4 3 2 1

251 Park Avenue South, New York, NY 10010 | Copyright © 2020 by Ari North | Characters used with permission:
Ch6. Sarah Dallas C/O of Dreamerouthere, Aerith C/O Symone Holmes (@owletskies), Thane C/O Stephanie Schevis and
Alice Thomas | Ch16. Jörgen from *ShootAround* on Webtoon C/O Suspu, Nokia from *Immortal Nerd* on Webtoon C/O H-P
Lehkonen, Landon from *Where Tangents Meet* on Webtoon C/O instantmiso | Ch20. Blair from *Noah's Game* on Webtoon
Canvas C/O ROEL | Ch21. Triss and Connie from *Rock and Riot* C/O Chelsey Furedi | Ch29. Abielle and Miel from *Love not
Found* C/O Gina Biggs, Elena C/O LeAzeri | Ch32. @radvelii C/O @radvelii, Warrick and Fred from *Namesake* published
by Hiveworks C/O Isabelle Melançon and Megan Lavey-Heaton, Lori and Dahlia from *Sundaze* C/O Hale, Celeste C/O
Madeleine Adams | Title font: ISL Jupiter by Derik Schneider | Lettering by Paige Pumphrey | All rights reserved, including
the right of reproduction in whole or in part in any form. | Yellow Jacket and associated colophon are trademarks of
Little Bee Books. | Manufactured in China TPL 0420 | First Edition | Library of Congress Cataloging-in-Publication
Data is available upon request.

For more information about special discounts on bulk purchases, please contact Little Bee Books at sales@littlebeebooks.com.

1- I GUESS THAT'S WHY I ADMIRE HER

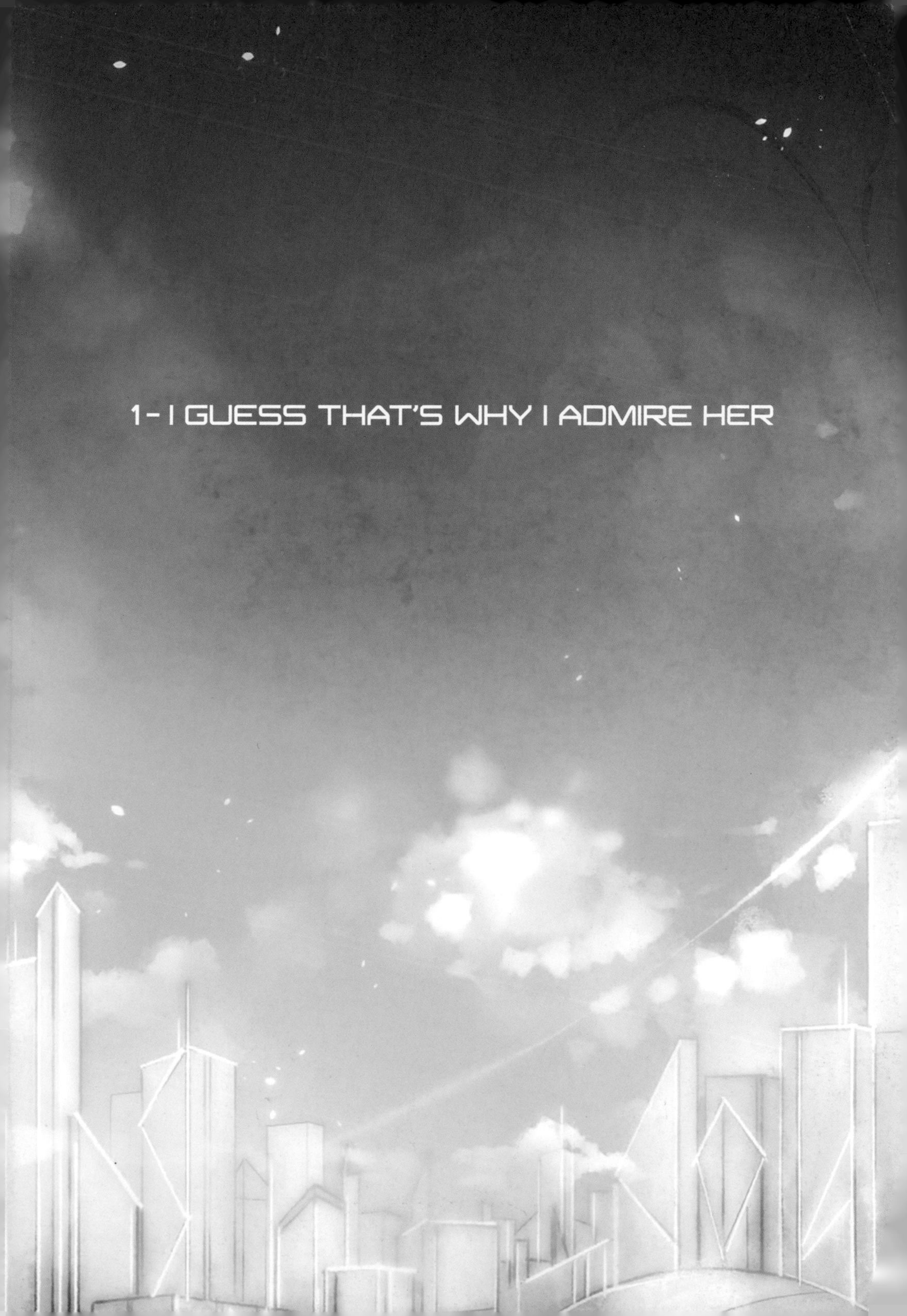

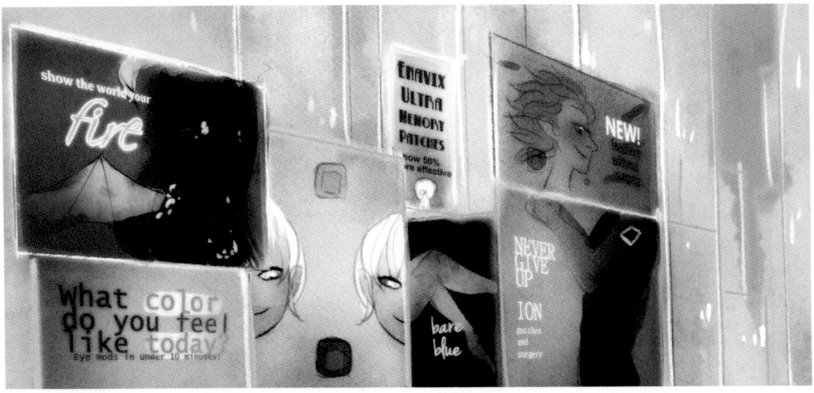
show the world your
fire
What color do you feel like today?
Eye mods in under 10 minutes!
ENAVIX ULTRA MEMORY PATCHES
now 50%
bare blue
NEW!
NEVER GIVE UP
ION
patches and surgery

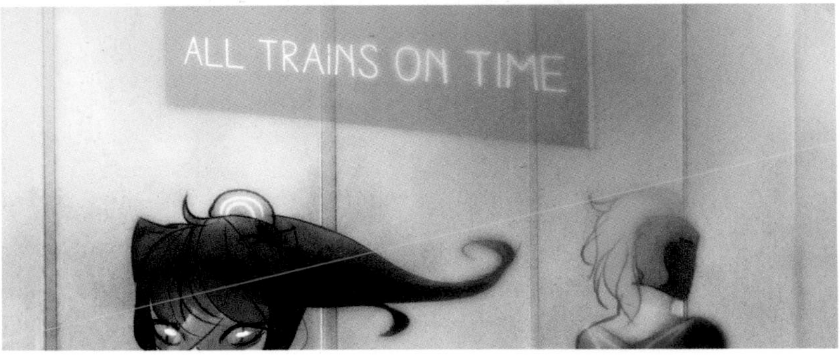
ALL TRAINS ON TIME

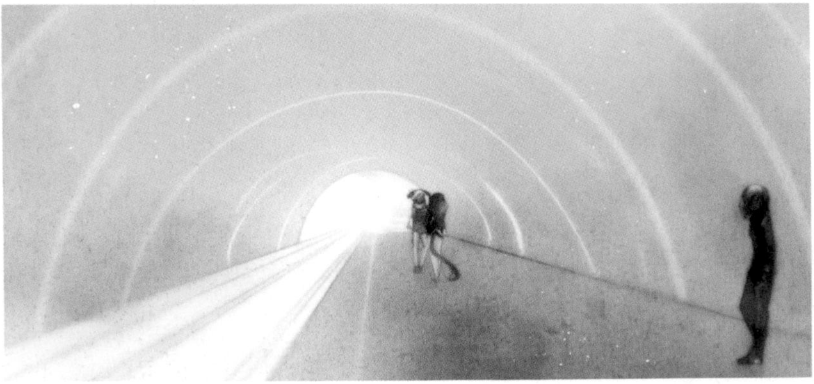

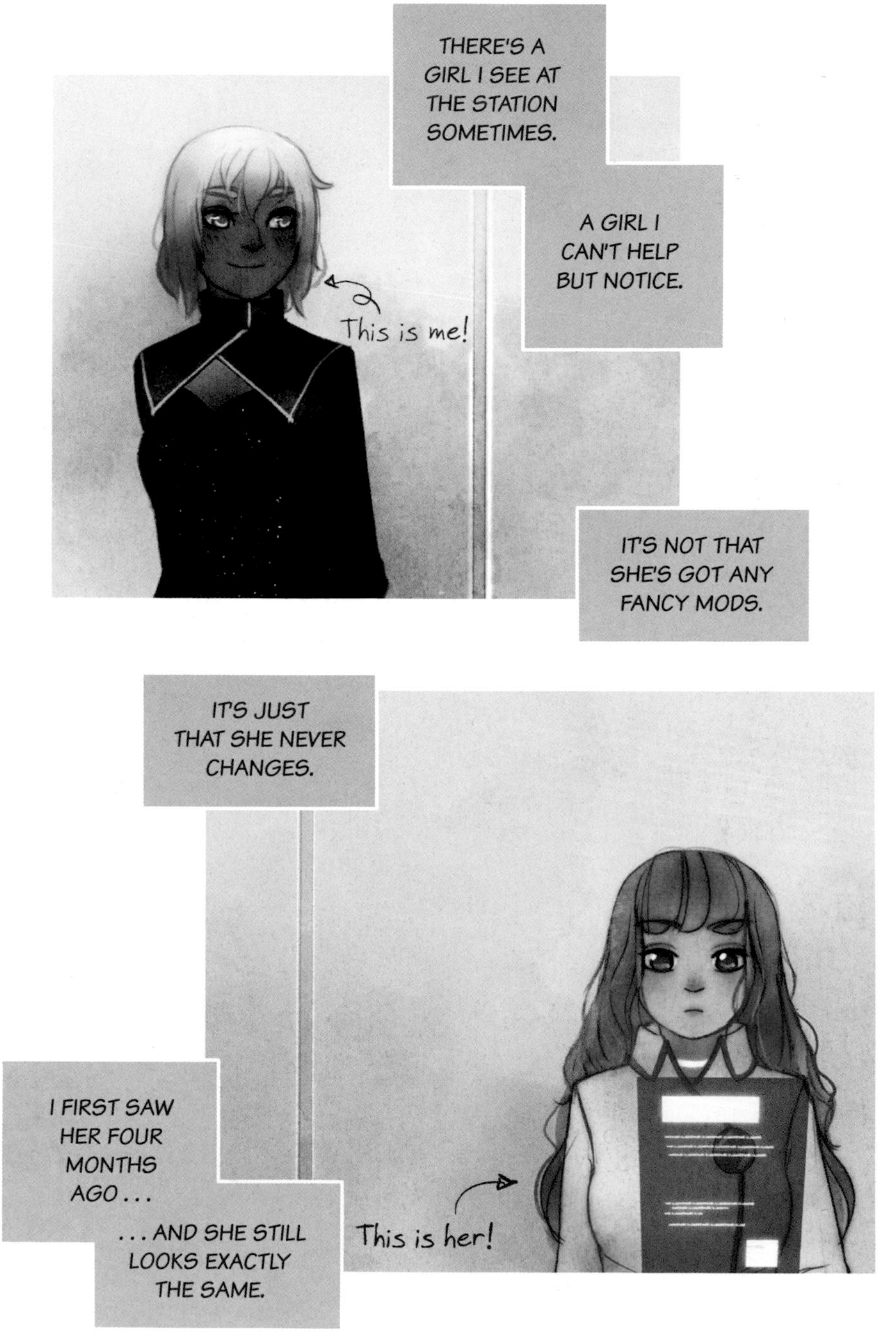
THERE'S A GIRL I SEE AT THE STATION SOMETIMES.
A GIRL I CAN'T HELP BUT NOTICE.
This is me!
IT'S NOT THAT SHE'S GOT ANY FANCY MODS.
IT'S JUST THAT SHE NEVER CHANGES.
I FIRST SAW HER FOUR MONTHS AGO . . .
. . . AND SHE STILL LOOKS EXACTLY THE SAME.
This is her!

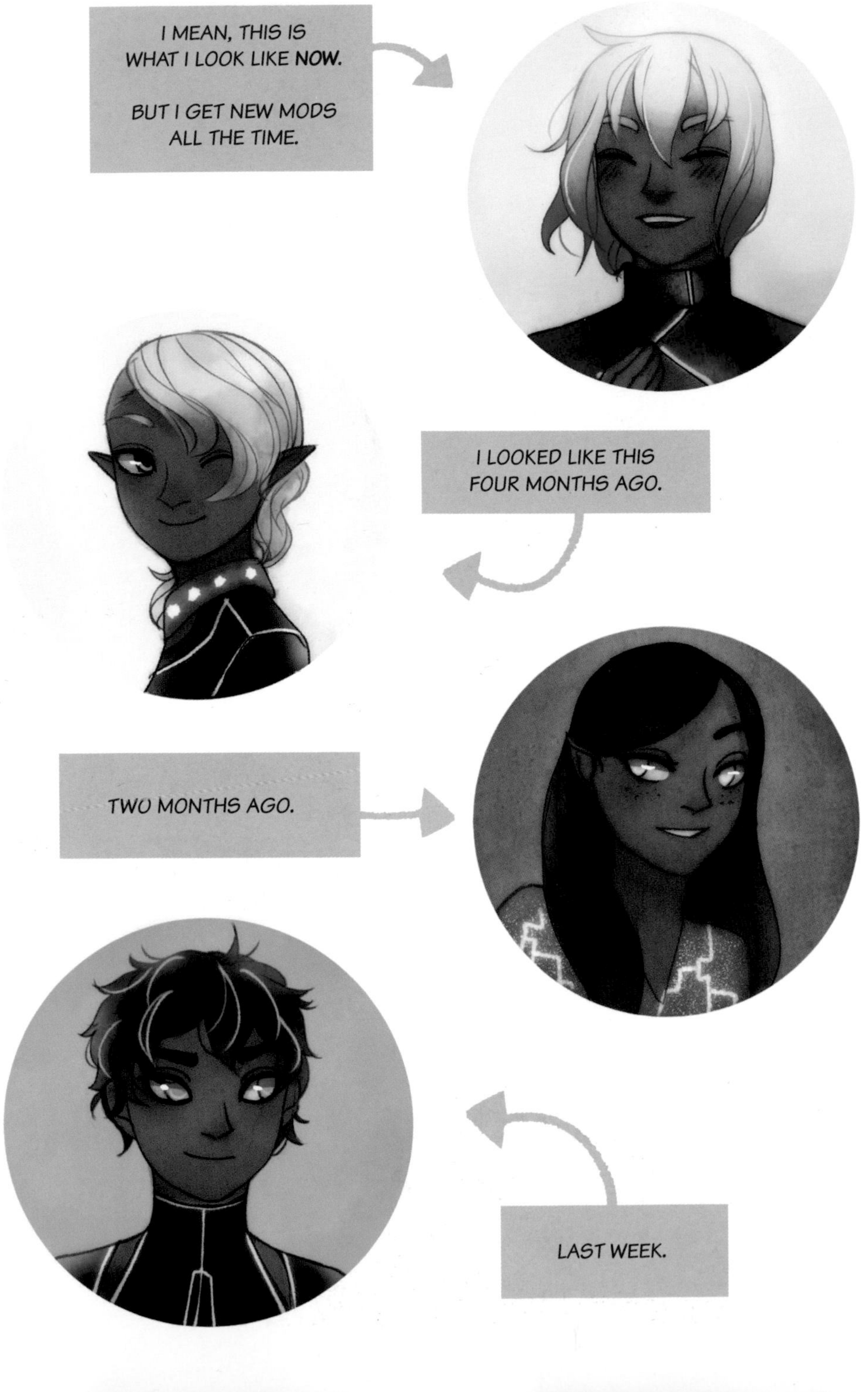
I MEAN, THIS IS WHAT I LOOK LIKE NOW.
BUT I GET NEW MODS ALL THE TIME.
I LOOKED LIKE THIS FOUR MONTHS AGO.
TWO MONTHS AGO.
LAST WEEK.

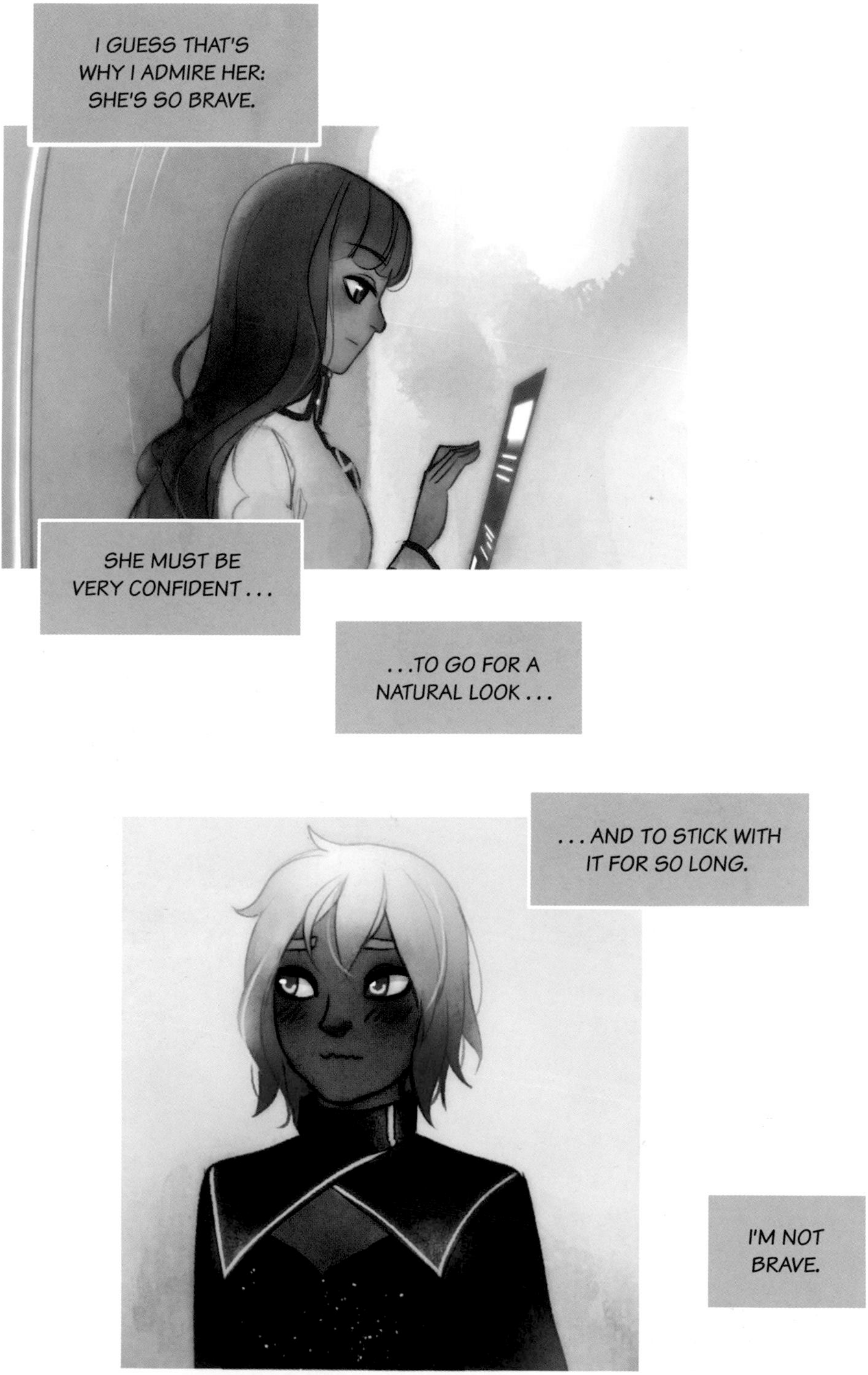
I GUESS THAT'S WHY I ADMIRE HER: SHE'S SO BRAVE.
SHE MUST BE VERY CONFIDENT . . .
. . .TO GO FOR A NATURAL LOOK . . .
. . . AND TO STICK WITH IT FOR SO LONG.
I'M NOT BRAVE.

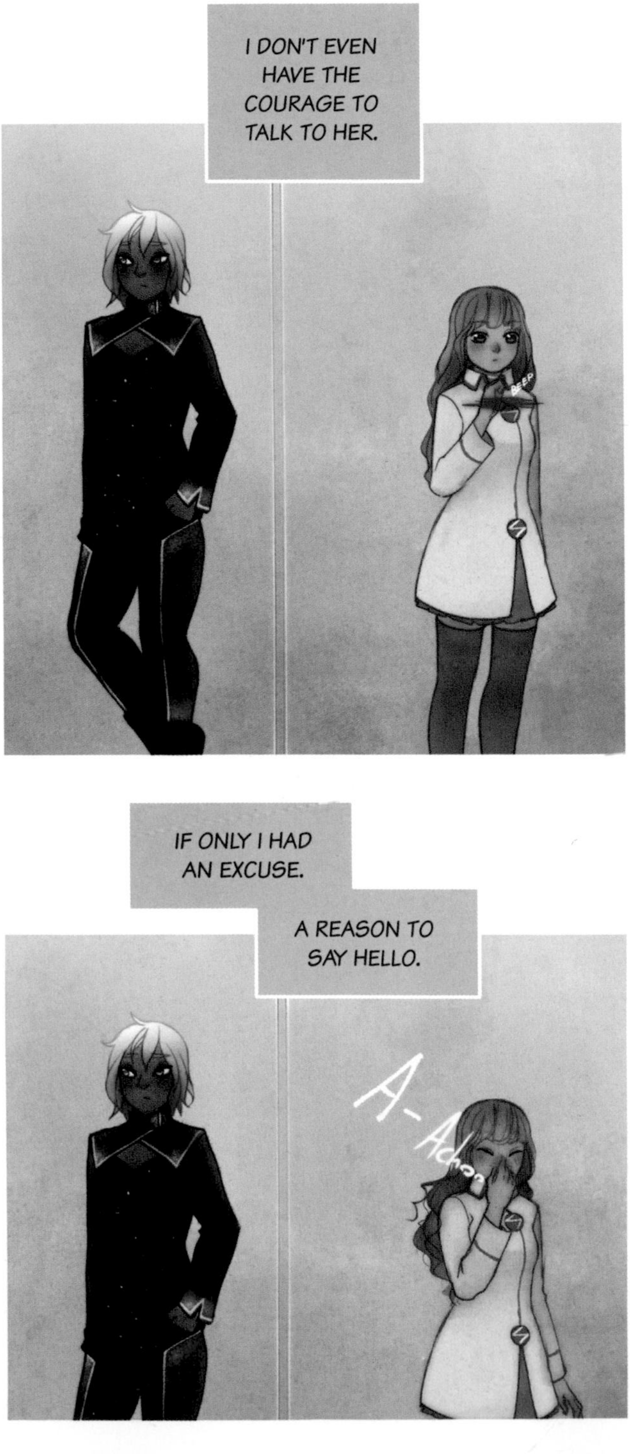
I DON'T EVEN HAVE THE COURAGE TO TALK TO HER.
BEEP
IF ONLY I HAD AN EXCUSE.
A REASON TO SAY HELLO.
A- Achoo

Achoo!
Achoo!
CHANCE!
sniff
HERE.
IT'S A HAY FEVER MOD.

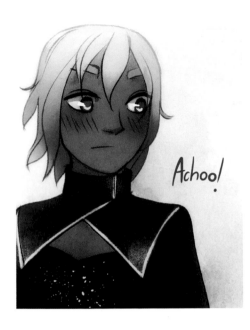

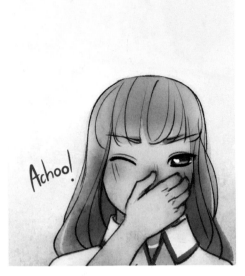

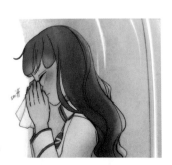

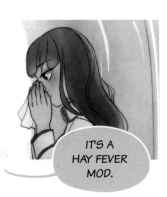

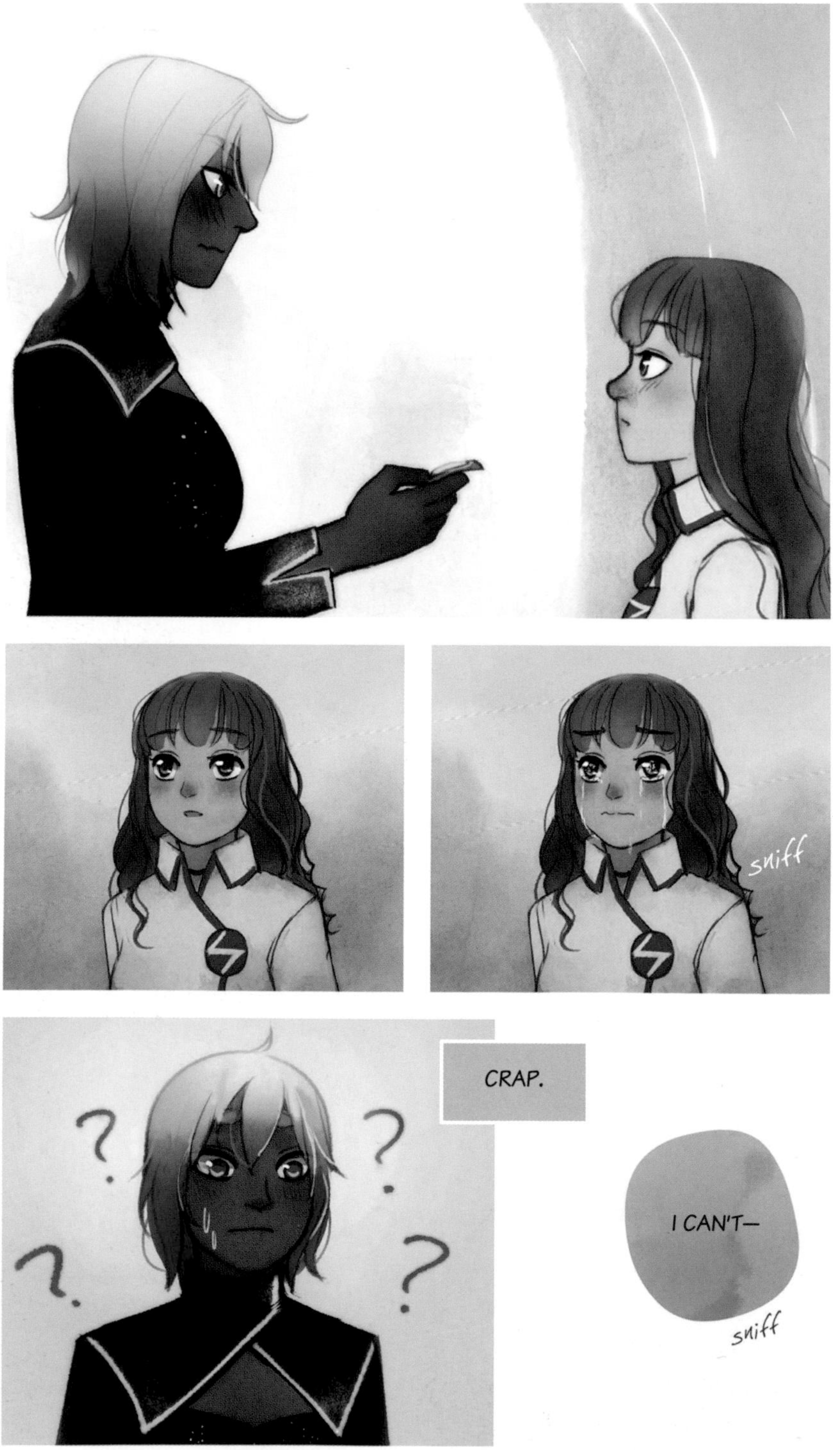
sniff
CRAP.
I CAN'T—
sniff

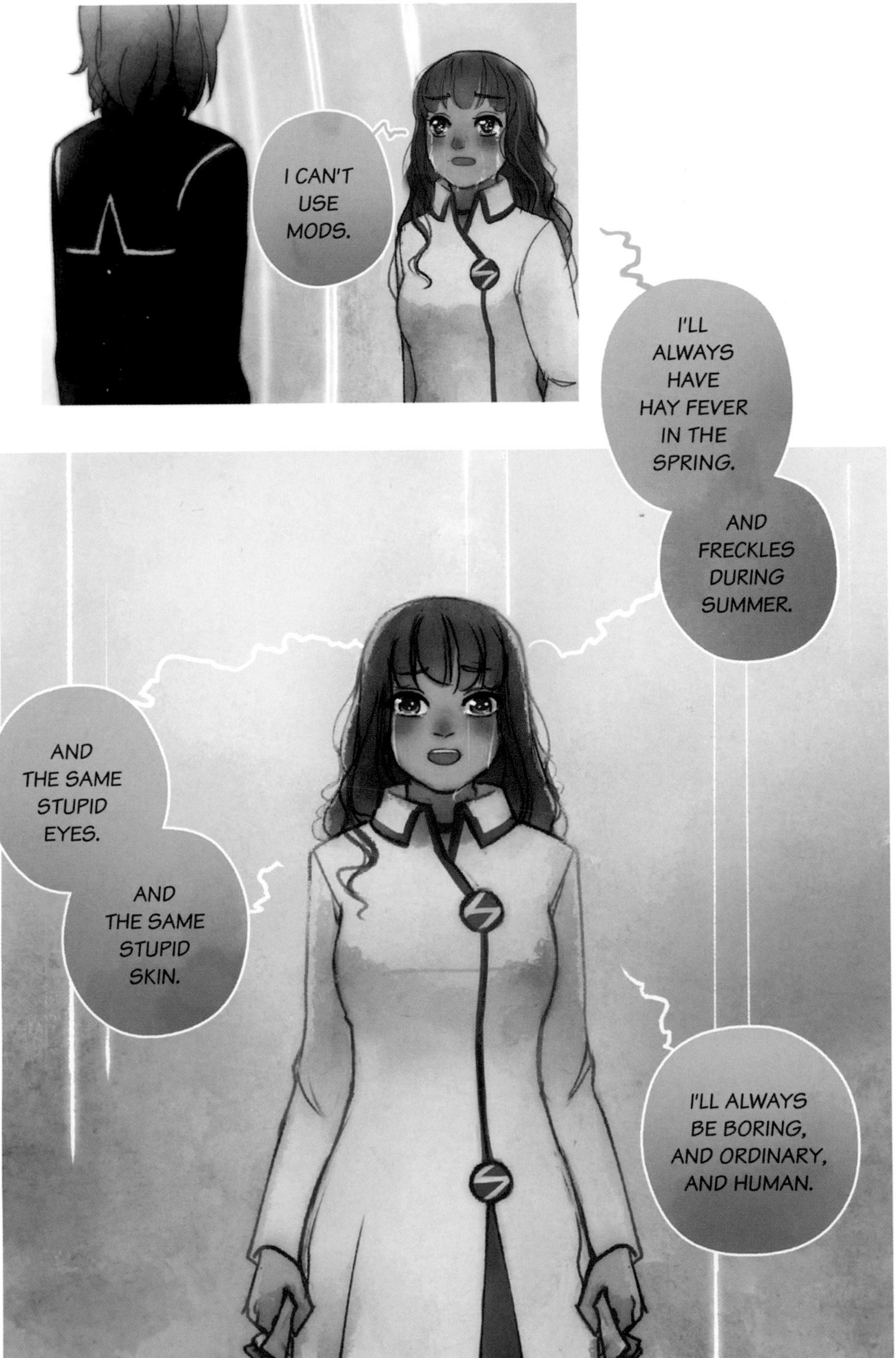
I CAN'T USE MODS.
I'LL ALWAYS HAVE HAY FEVER IN THE SPRING.
AND FRECKLES DURING SUMMER.
AND THE SAME STUPID EYES.
AND THE SAME STUPID SKIN.
I'LL ALWAYS BE BORING, AND ORDINARY, AND HUMAN.

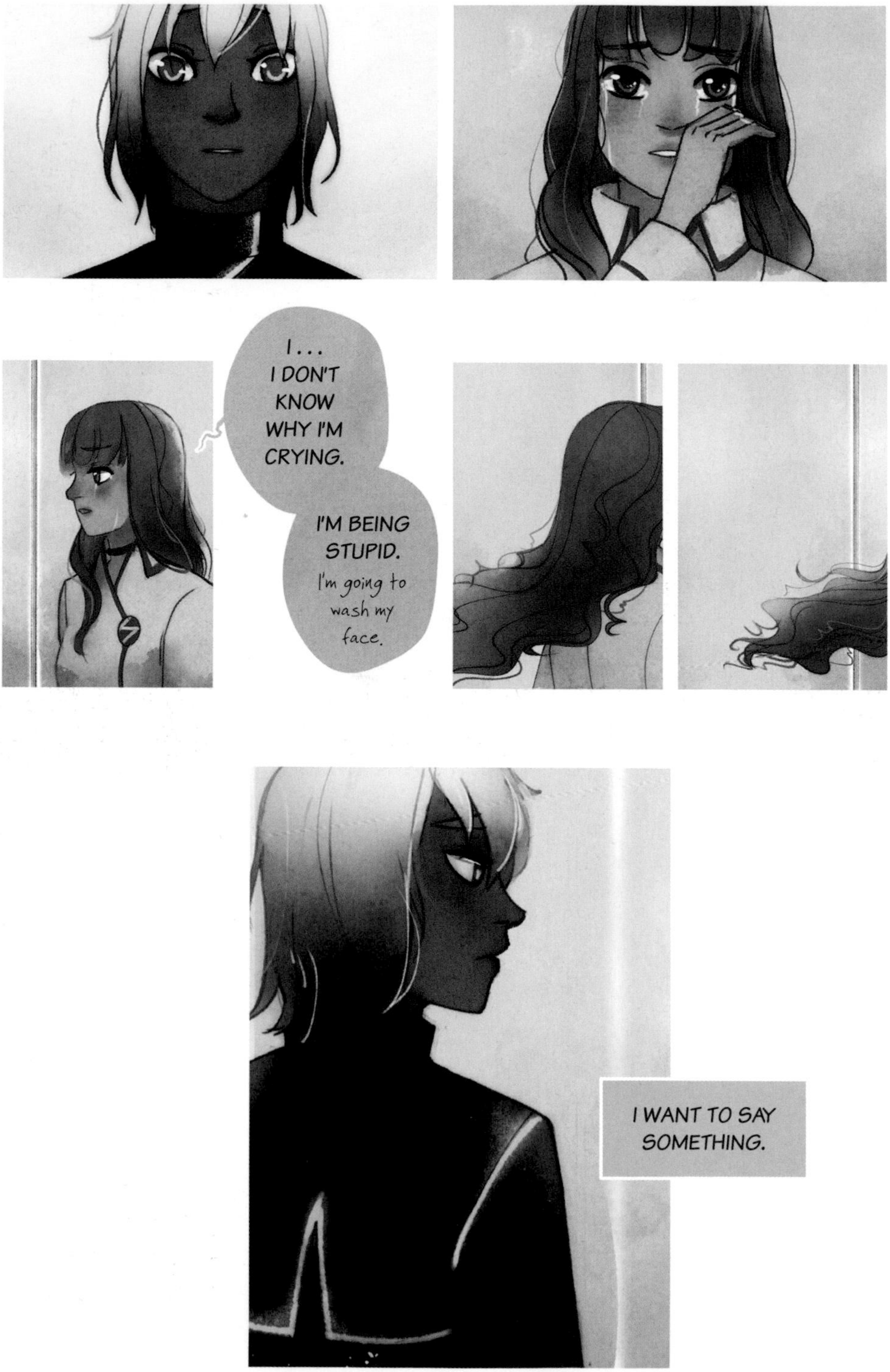
I . . .
I DON'T KNOW WHY I'M CRYING.
I'M BEING STUPID.
I'm going to wash my face.
I WANT TO SAY SOMETHING.

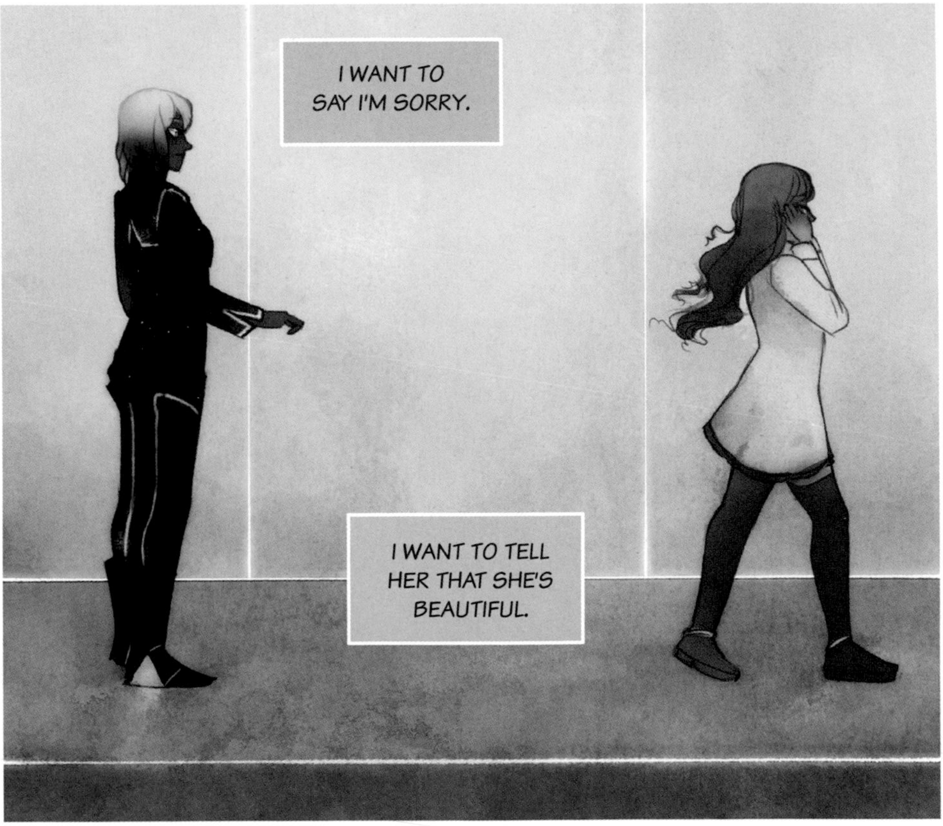
I WANT TO SAY I'M SORRY.
I WANT TO TELL HER THAT SHE'S BEAUTIFUL.

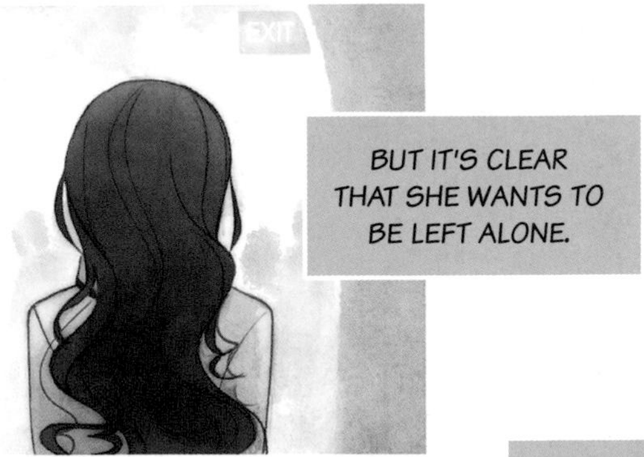
EXIT
BUT IT'S CLEAR THAT SHE WANTS TO BE LEFT ALONE.

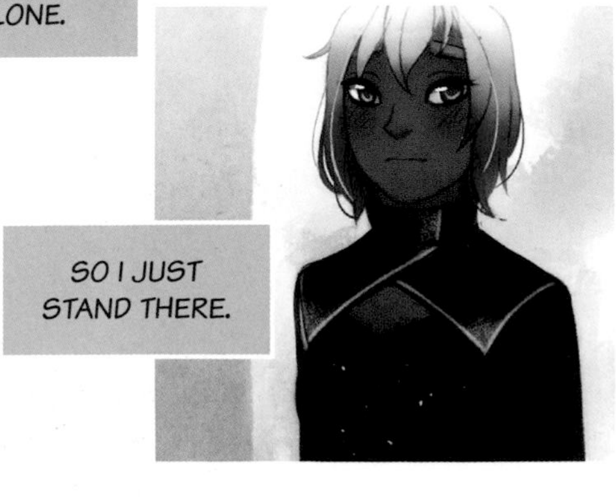
SO I JUST STAND THERE.

AND WATCH
HER GO.

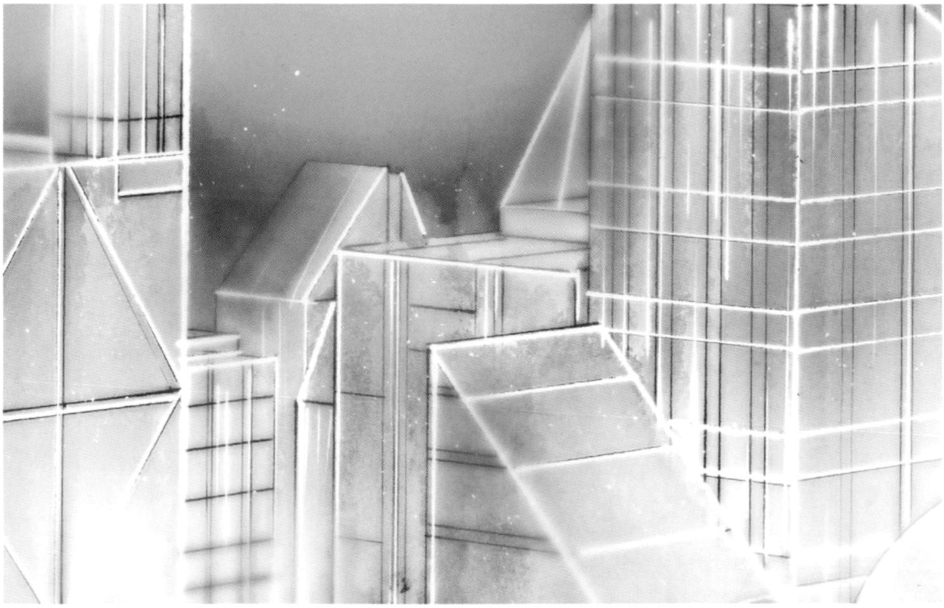

2 - WELL, THAT SUCKS

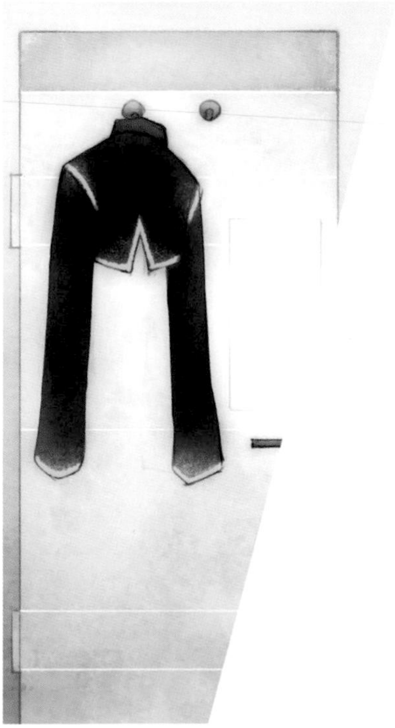

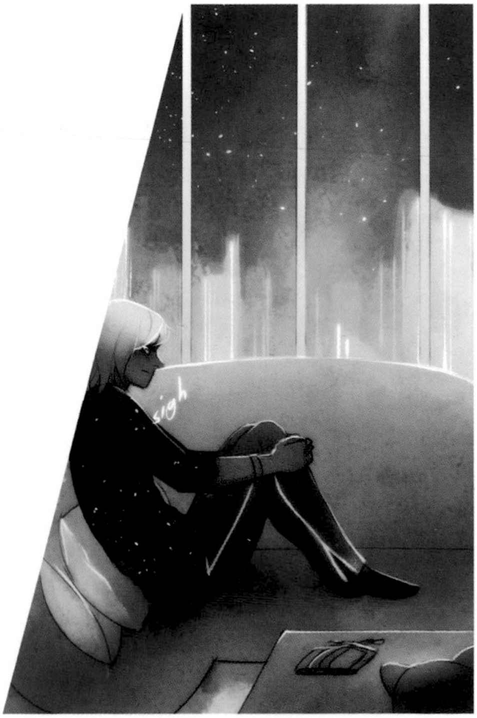
sigh

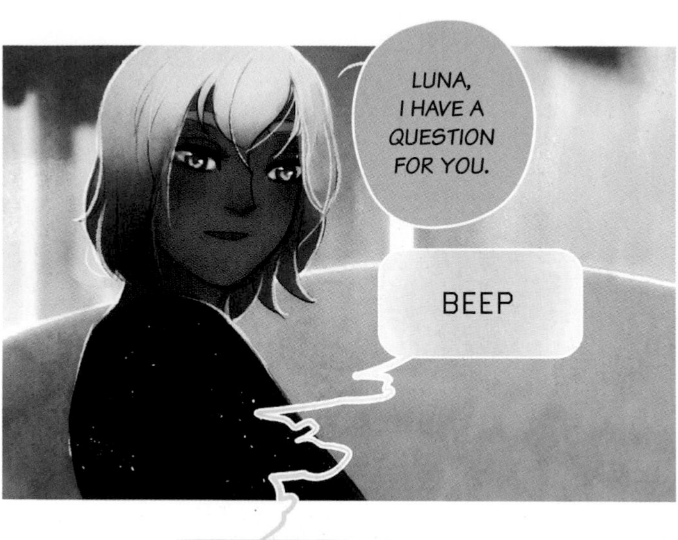
LUNA, I HAVE A QUESTION FOR YOU.
BEEP

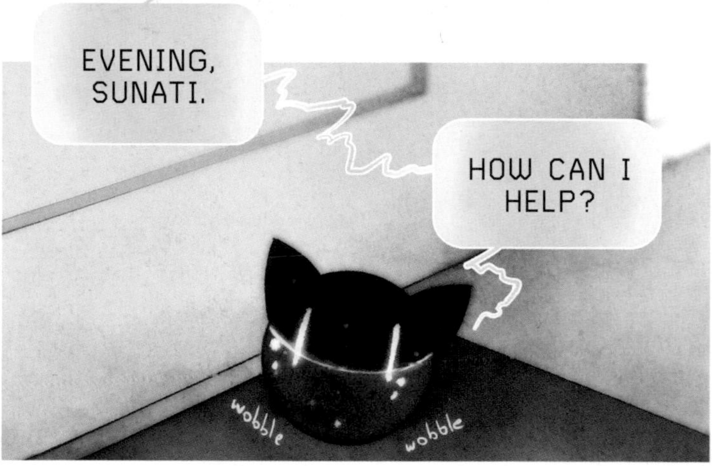
EVENING, SUNATI.
HOW CAN I HELP?
wobble
wobble

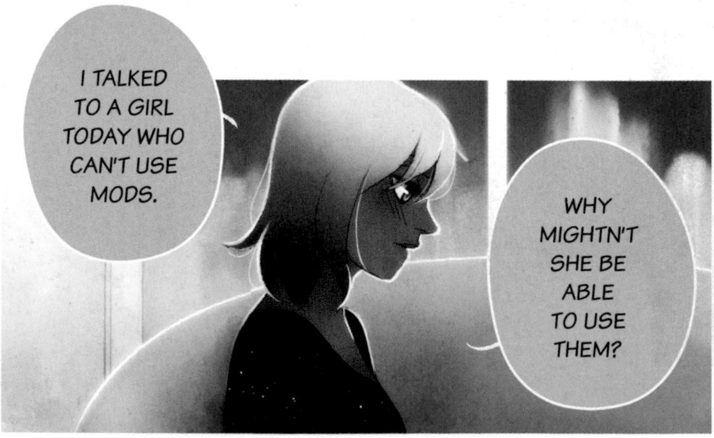
I TALKED TO A GIRL TODAY WHO CAN'T USE MODS.
WHY MIGHTN'T SHE BE ABLE TO USE THEM?

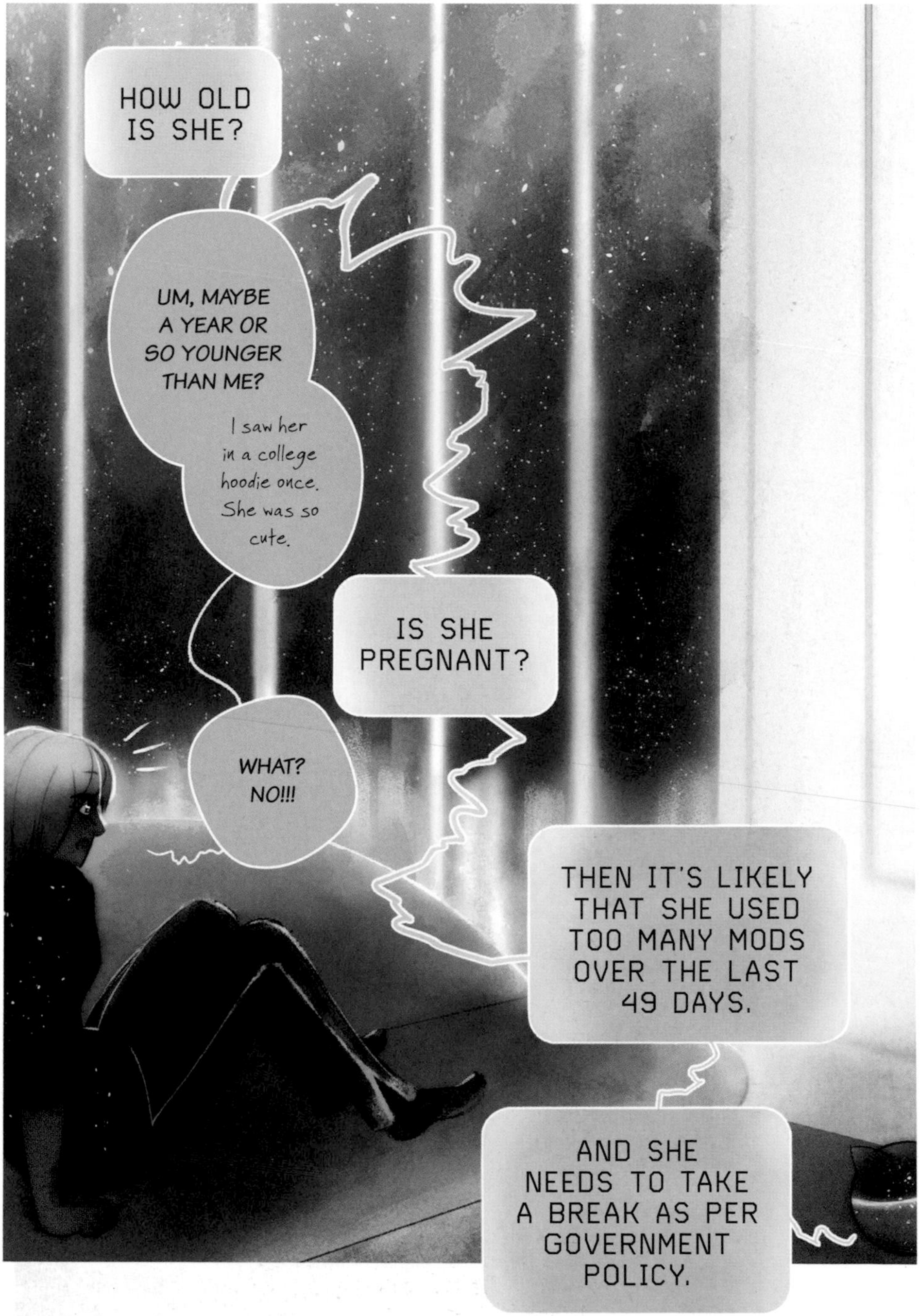
HOW OLD IS SHE?
UM, MAYBE A YEAR OR SO YOUNGER THAN ME?
I saw her in a college hoodie once. She was so cute.
IS SHE PREGNANT?
WHAT? NO!!!
THEN IT'S LIKELY THAT SHE USED TOO MANY MODS OVER THE LAST 49 DAYS.
AND SHE NEEDS TO TAKE A BREAK AS PER GOVERNMENT POLICY.

...

NO, I DON'T THINK THAT'S IT.

I DON'T THINK SHE'S EVER BEEN ABLE TO USE MODS.

LUNA, ARE THERE PEOPLE LIKE THAT?

PEOPLE WHO CAN'T USE MODS AT ALL?

OF COURSE.

PEOPLE WITH EGAN'S SYNDROME.

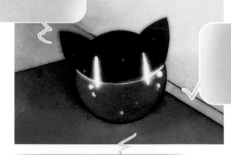

THESE PEOPLE HAVE HIGHLY SENSITIVE IMMUNE SYSTEMS.

AND THEIR BODIES REJECT THE NANOBOTS THAT ARE USED TO TRANSFER MODS.

SO, SHE CAN'T USE MODS BECAUSE HER IMMUNE SYSTEM IS TOO GOOD?

POSSIBLY.

WELL, THAT SUCKS.

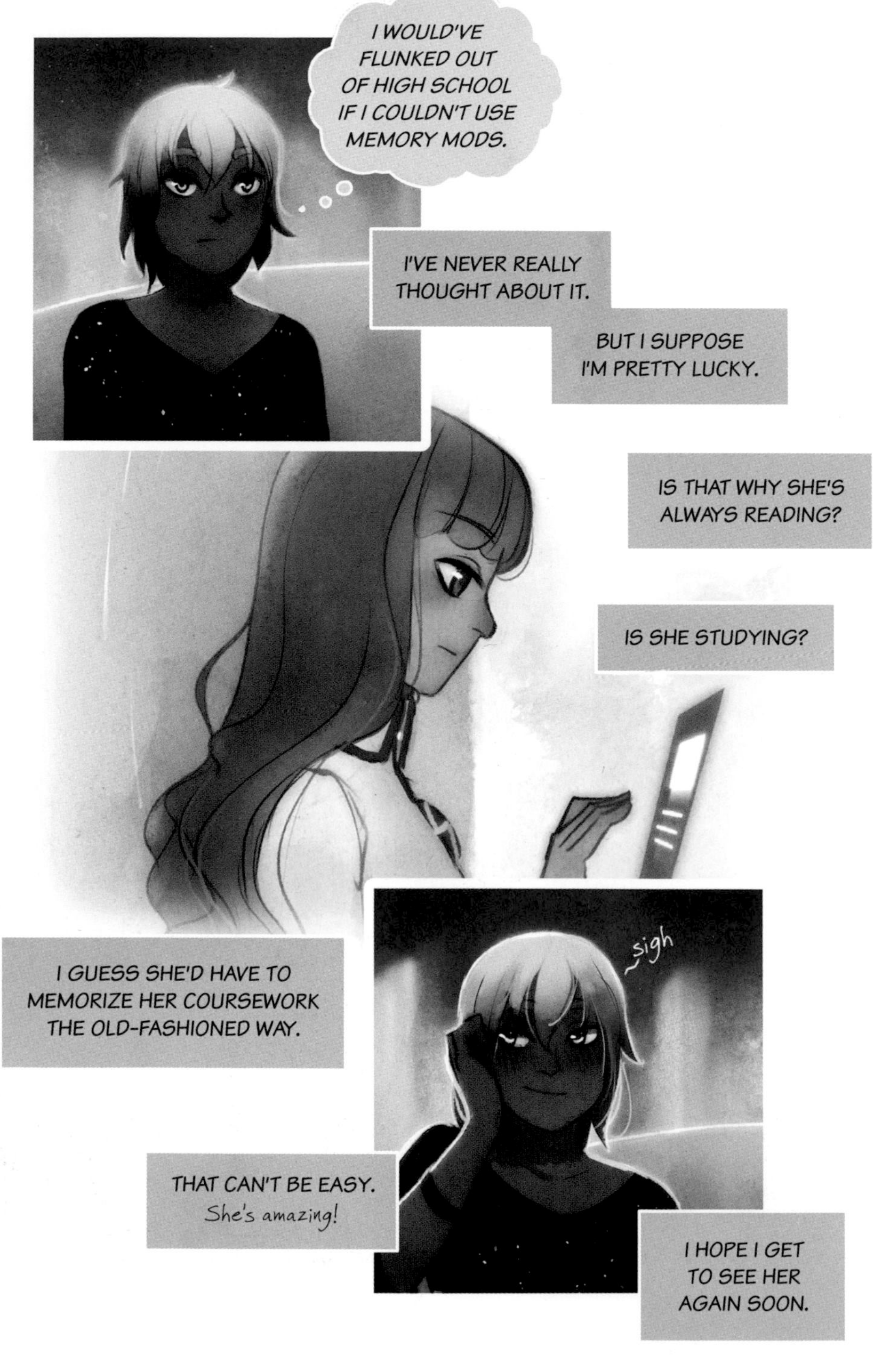
I WOULD'VE FLUNKED OUT OF HIGH SCHOOL IF I COULDN'T USE MEMORY MODS.
I'VE NEVER REALLY THOUGHT ABOUT IT.
BUT I SUPPOSE I'M PRETTY LUCKY.
IS THAT WHY SHE'S ALWAYS READING?
IS SHE STUDYING?
I GUESS SHE'D HAVE TO MEMORIZE HER COURSEWORK THE OLD-FASHIONED WAY.
~sigh
THAT CAN'T BE EASY.
She's amazing!
I HOPE I GET TO SEE HER AGAIN SOON.

BUT I DON'T SEE HER AT THE STATION THE NEXT DAY.

OR THE DAY AFTER THAT.

IT'S ONLY ON FRIDAY THAT I FINALLY SEE HER AGAIN.

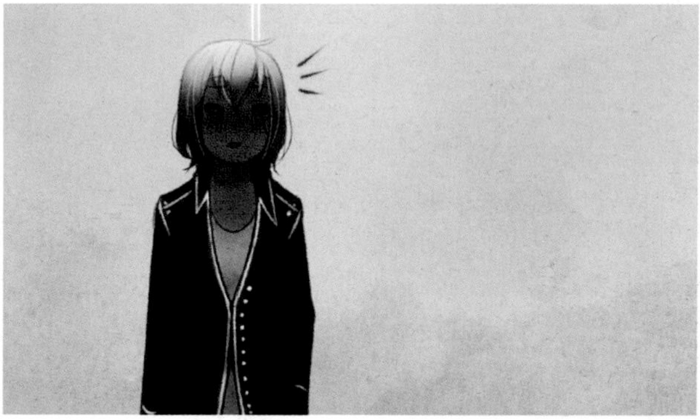

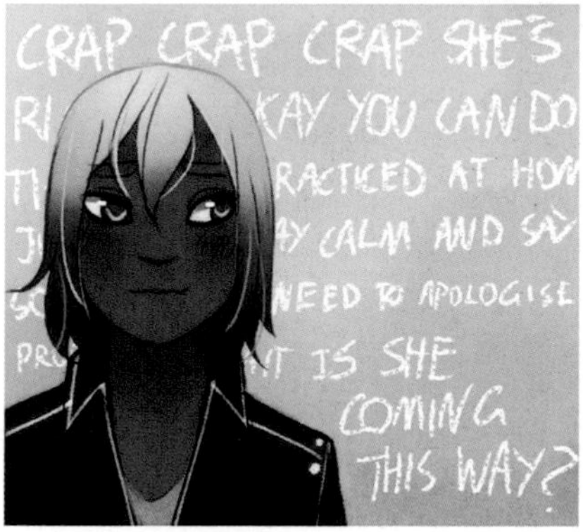
CRAP CRAP CRAP SHE'S
NEED TO APOLOGISE
IS SHE
COMING
THIS WAY?

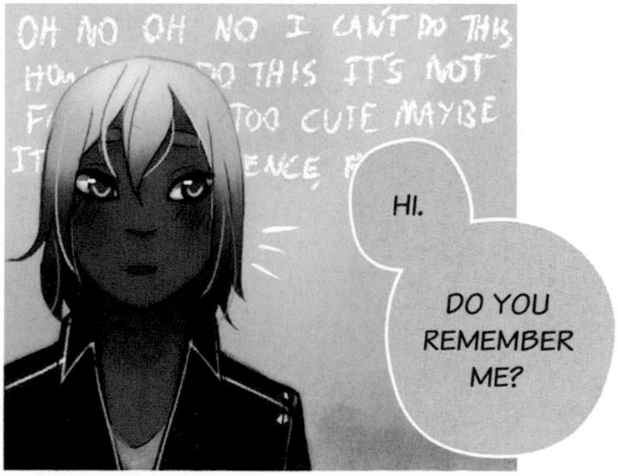
OH NO OH NO I CAN'T DO THIS
DO THIS IT'S NOT
TOO CUTE MAYBE
HI.
DO YOU REMEMBER ME?

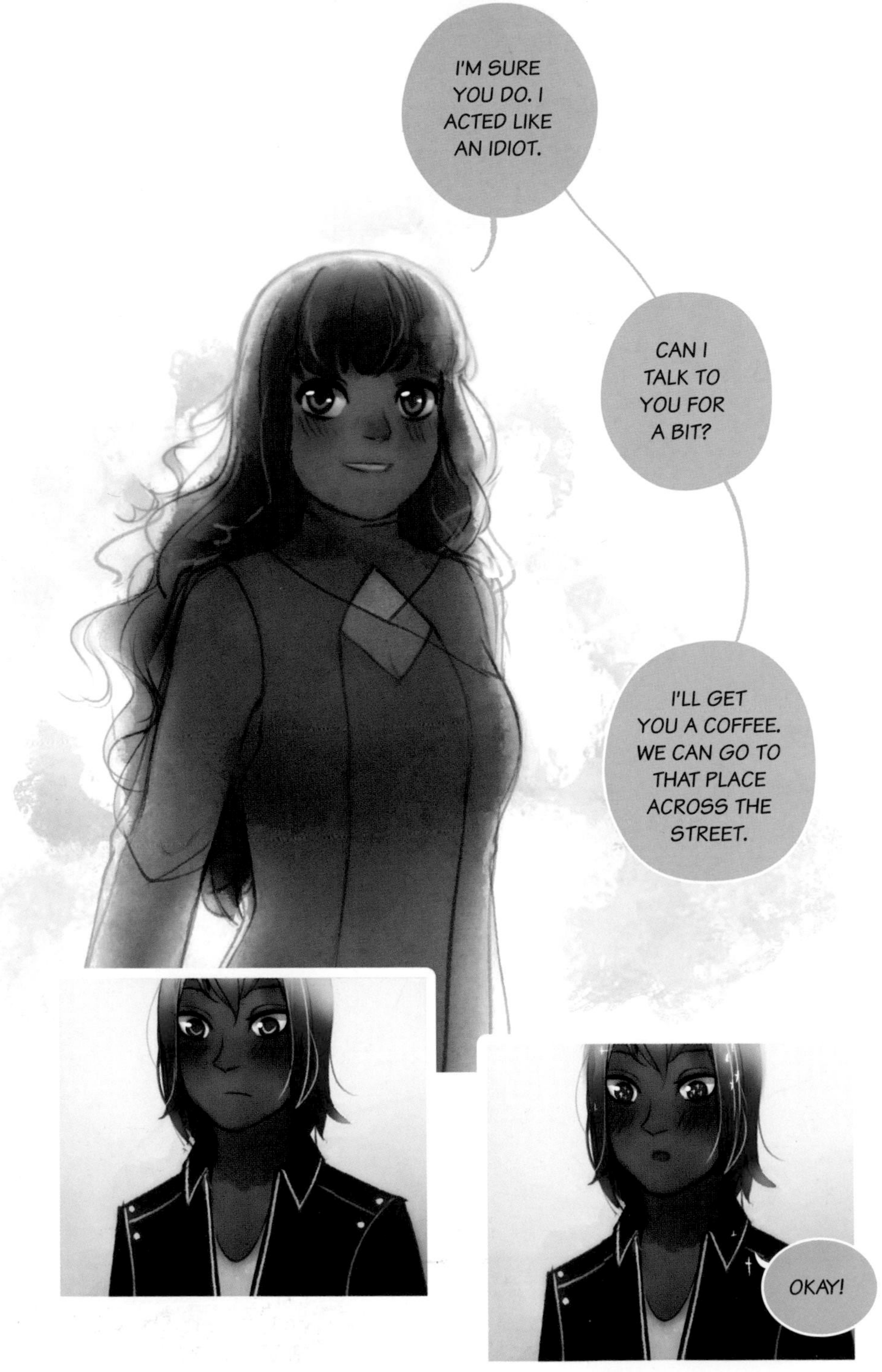
I'M SURE YOU DO. I ACTED LIKE AN IDIOT.
CAN I TALK TO YOU FOR A BIT?
I'LL GET YOU A COFFEE. WE CAN GO TO THAT PLACE ACROSS THE STREET.
OKAY!

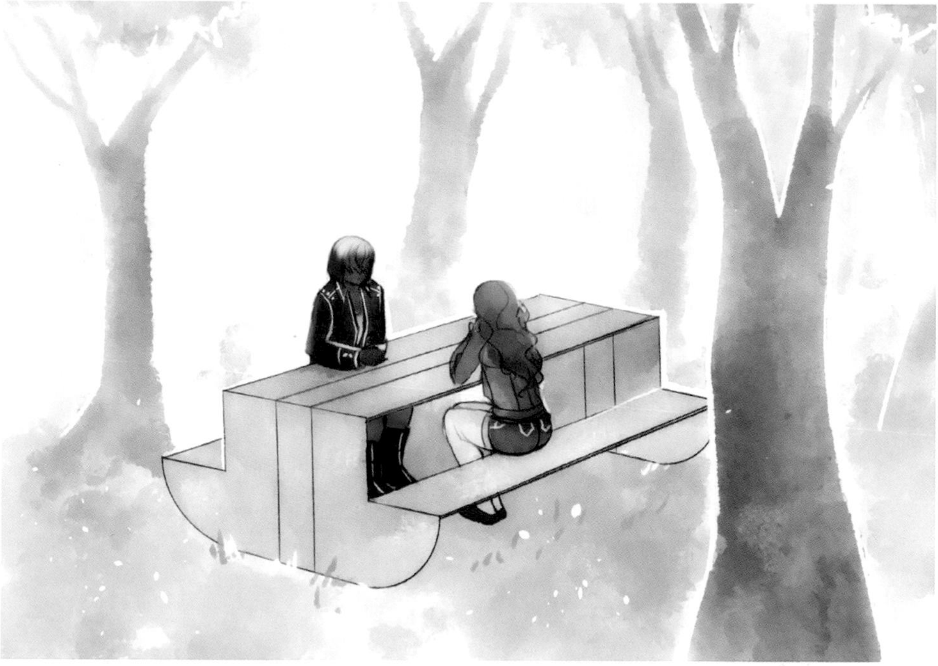

3 - BUT I'M NOT JUST SAYING IT

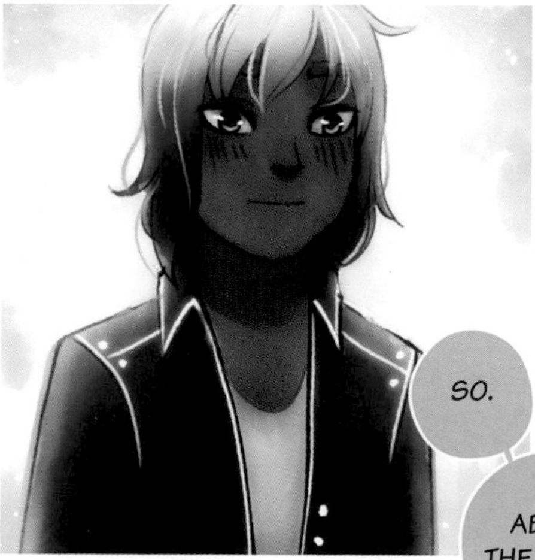
SO.
ABOUT THE OTHER DAY.

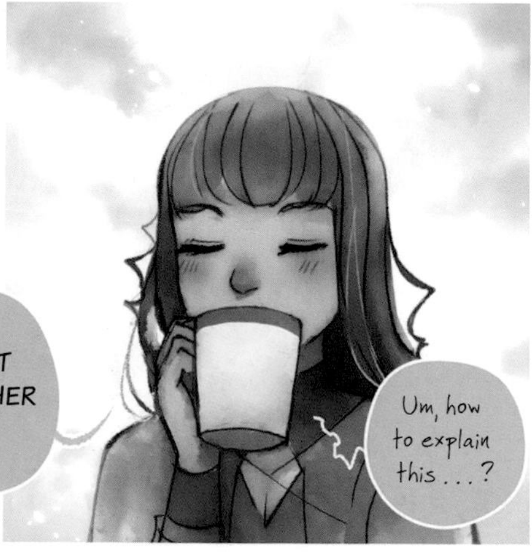
Um, how to explain this . . . ?

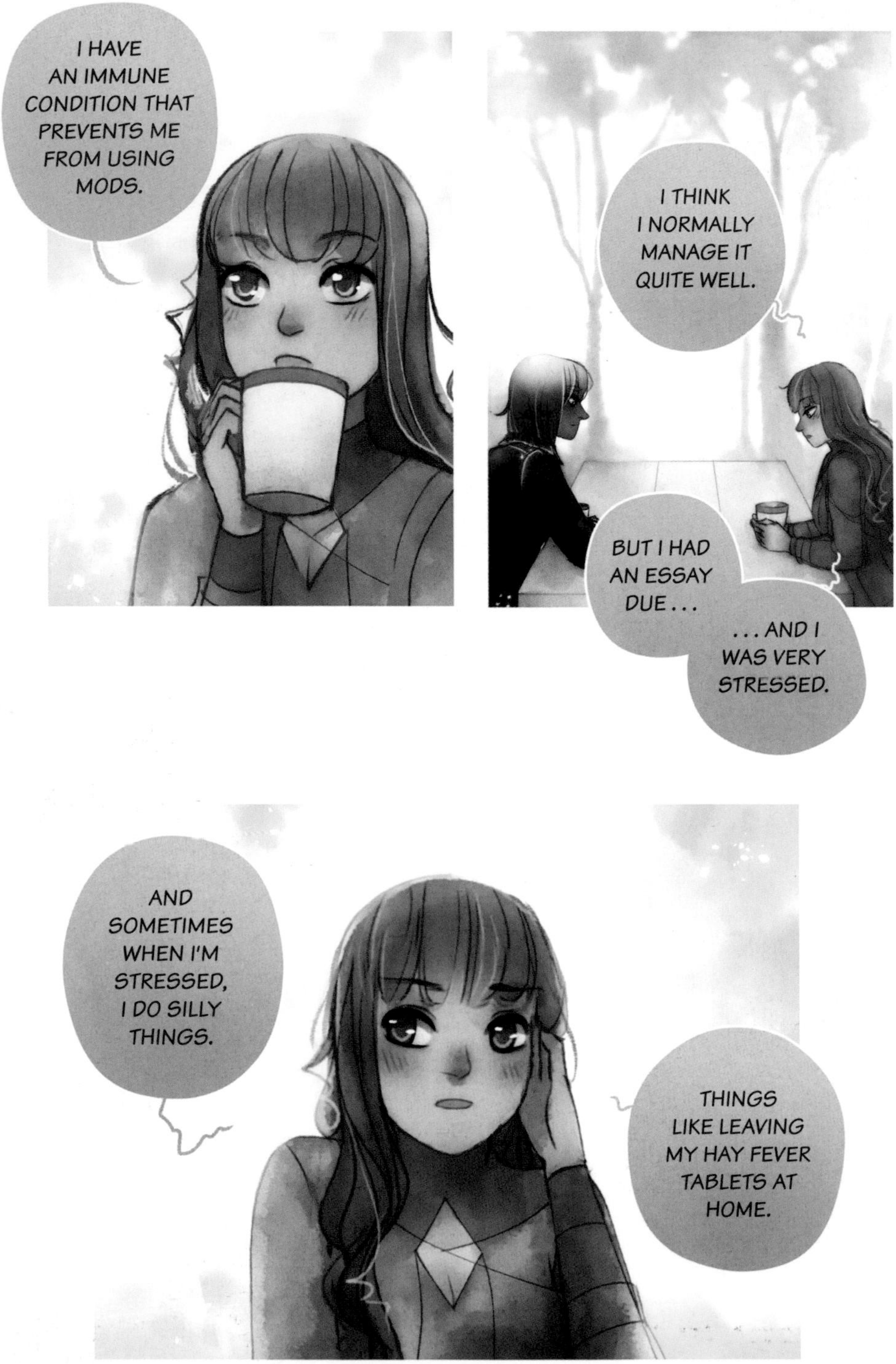
I HAVE AN IMMUNE CONDITION THAT PREVENTS ME FROM USING MODS.
I THINK I NORMALLY MANAGE IT QUITE WELL.
BUT I HAD AN ESSAY DUE . . .
. . . AND I WAS VERY STRESSED.
AND SOMETIMES WHEN I'M STRESSED, I DO SILLY THINGS.
THINGS LIKE LEAVING MY HAY FEVER TABLETS AT HOME.

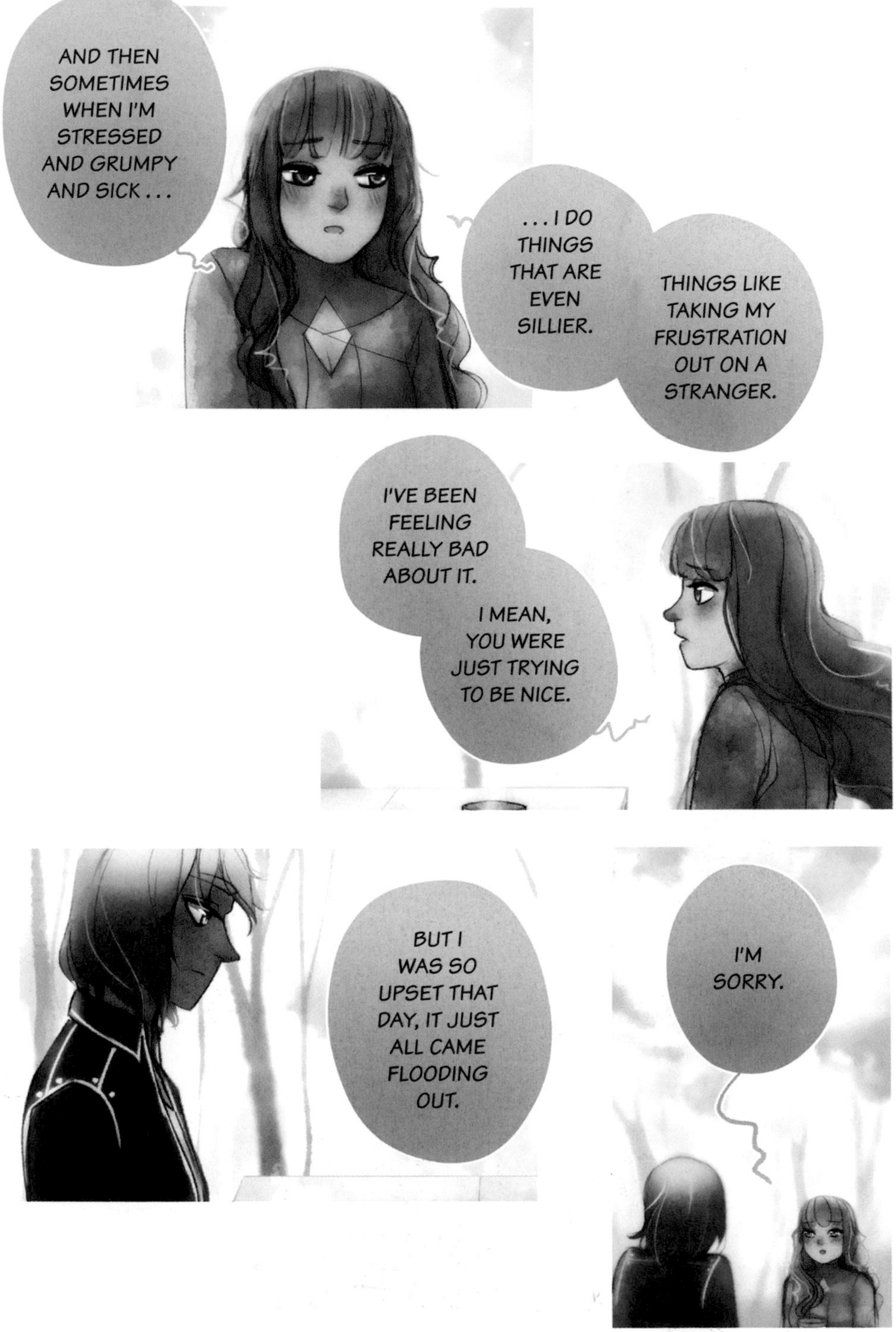
AND THEN SOMETIMES WHEN I'M STRESSED AND GRUMPY AND SICK . . .
. . . I DO THINGS THAT ARE EVEN SILLIER.
THINGS LIKE TAKING MY FRUSTRATION OUT ON A STRANGER.
I'VE BEEN FEELING REALLY BAD ABOUT IT.
I MEAN, YOU WERE JUST TRYING TO BE NICE.
BUT I WAS SO UPSET THAT DAY, IT JUST ALL CAME FLOODING OUT.
I'M SORRY.

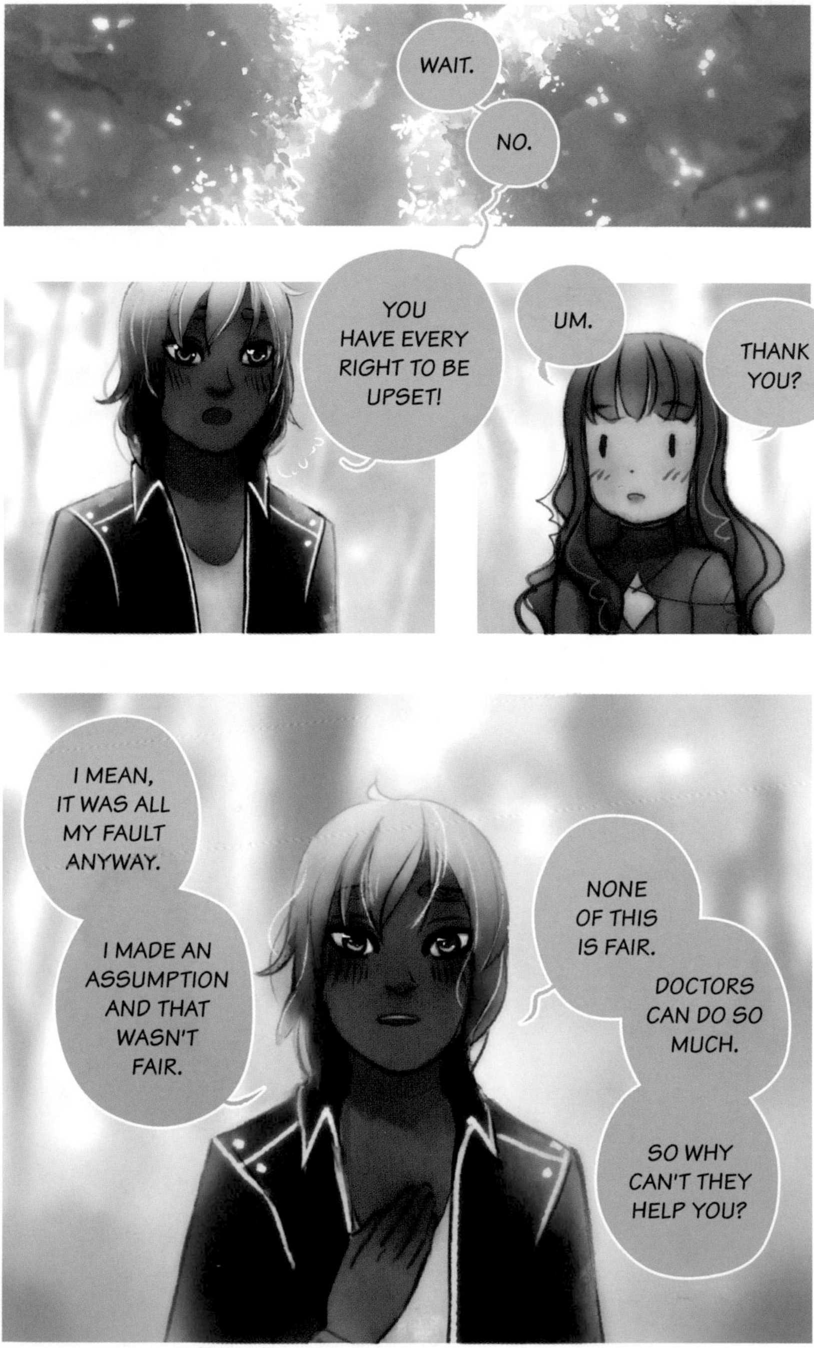
WAIT.
NO.
YOU HAVE EVERY RIGHT TO BE UPSET!
UM.
THANK YOU?
I MEAN, IT WAS ALL MY FAULT ANYWAY.
I MADE AN ASSUMPTION AND THAT WASN'T FAIR.
NONE OF THIS IS FAIR.
DOCTORS CAN DO SO MUCH.
SO WHY CAN'T THEY HELP YOU?

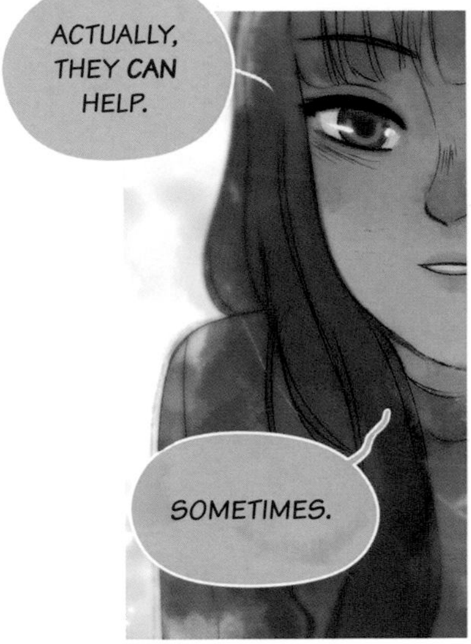
ACTUALLY, THEY CAN HELP.
SOMETIMES.

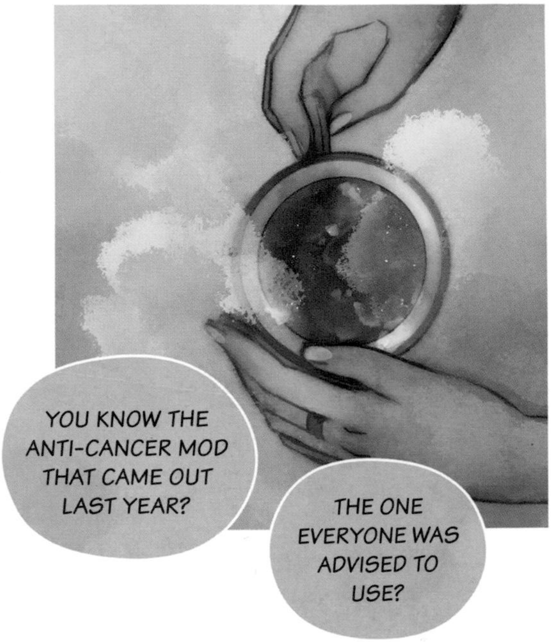
YOU KNOW THE ANTI-CANCER MOD THAT CAME OUT LAST YEAR?
THE ONE EVERYONE WAS ADVISED TO USE?

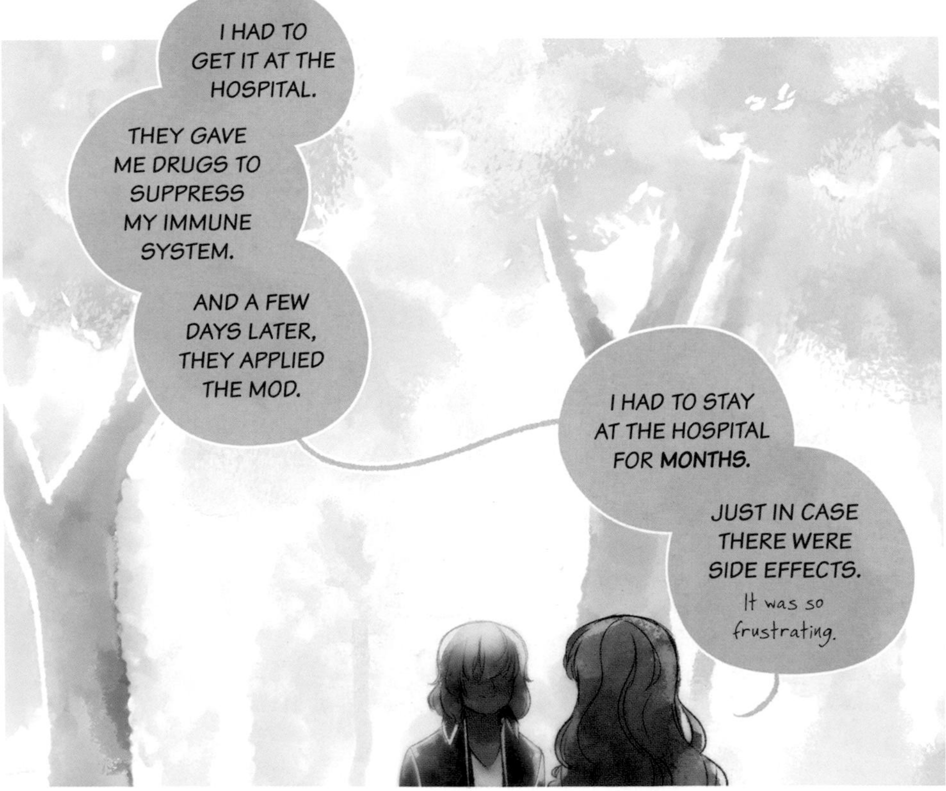
I HAD TO GET IT AT THE HOSPITAL.
THEY GAVE ME DRUGS TO SUPPRESS MY IMMUNE SYSTEM.
AND A FEW DAYS LATER, THEY APPLIED THE MOD.
I HAD TO STAY AT THE HOSPITAL FOR MONTHS.
JUST IN CASE THERE WERE SIDE EFFECTS.
It was so frustrating.

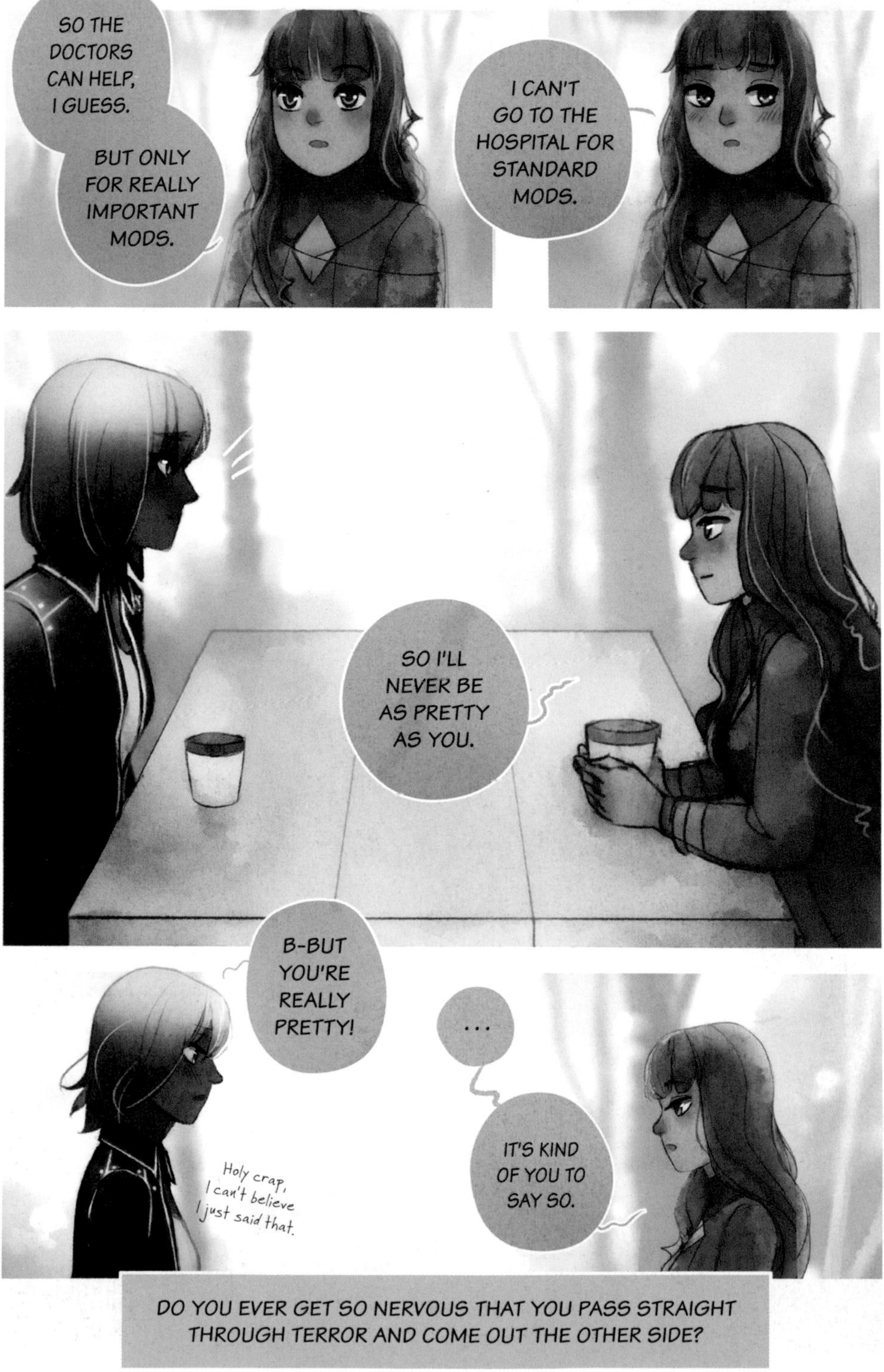
SO THE DOCTORS CAN HELP, I GUESS.
BUT ONLY FOR REALLY IMPORTANT MODS.
I CAN'T GO TO THE HOSPITAL FOR STANDARD MODS.
SO I'LL NEVER BE AS PRETTY AS YOU.
B-BUT YOU'RE REALLY PRETTY!
...
IT'S KIND OF YOU TO SAY SO.
Holy crap, I can't believe I just said that.
DO YOU EVER GET SO NERVOUS THAT YOU PASS STRAIGHT THROUGH TERROR AND COME OUT THE OTHER SIDE?

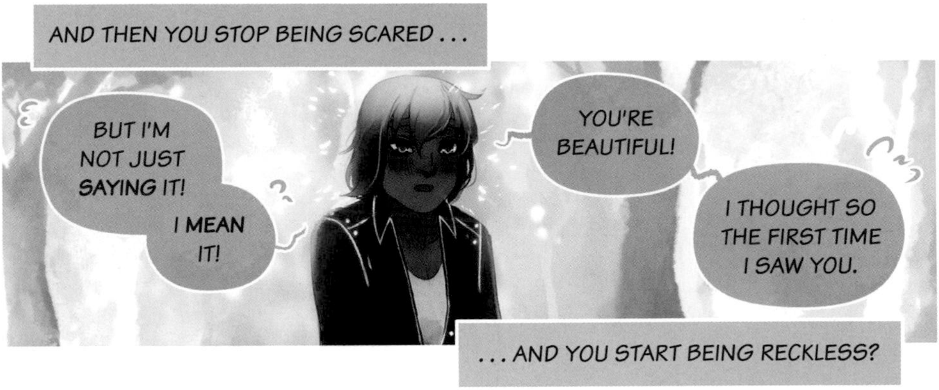
AND THEN YOU STOP BEING SCARED . . .
BUT I'M NOT JUST SAYING IT!
I MEAN IT!
YOU'RE BEAUTIFUL!
I THOUGHT SO THE FIRST TIME I SAW YOU.
. . . AND YOU START BEING RECKLESS?

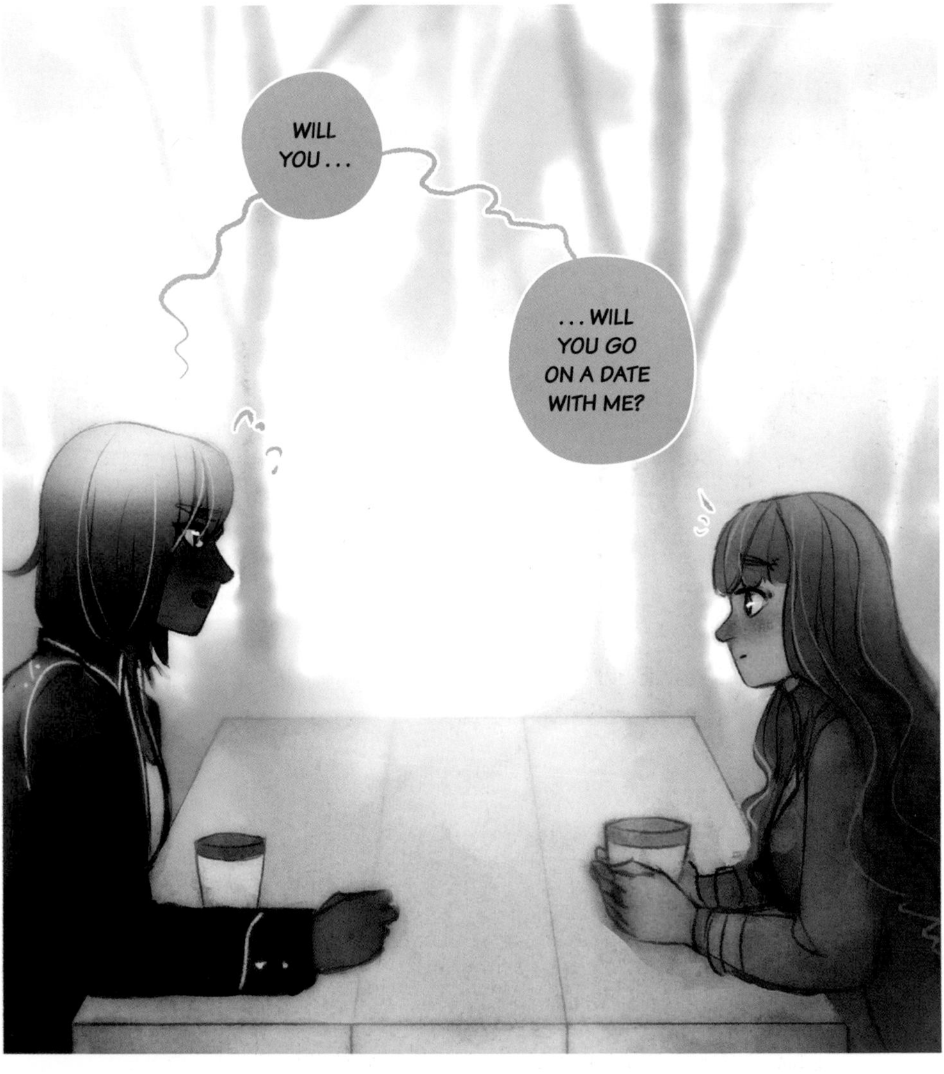
WILL YOU . . .
. . . WILL YOU GO ON A DATE WITH ME?

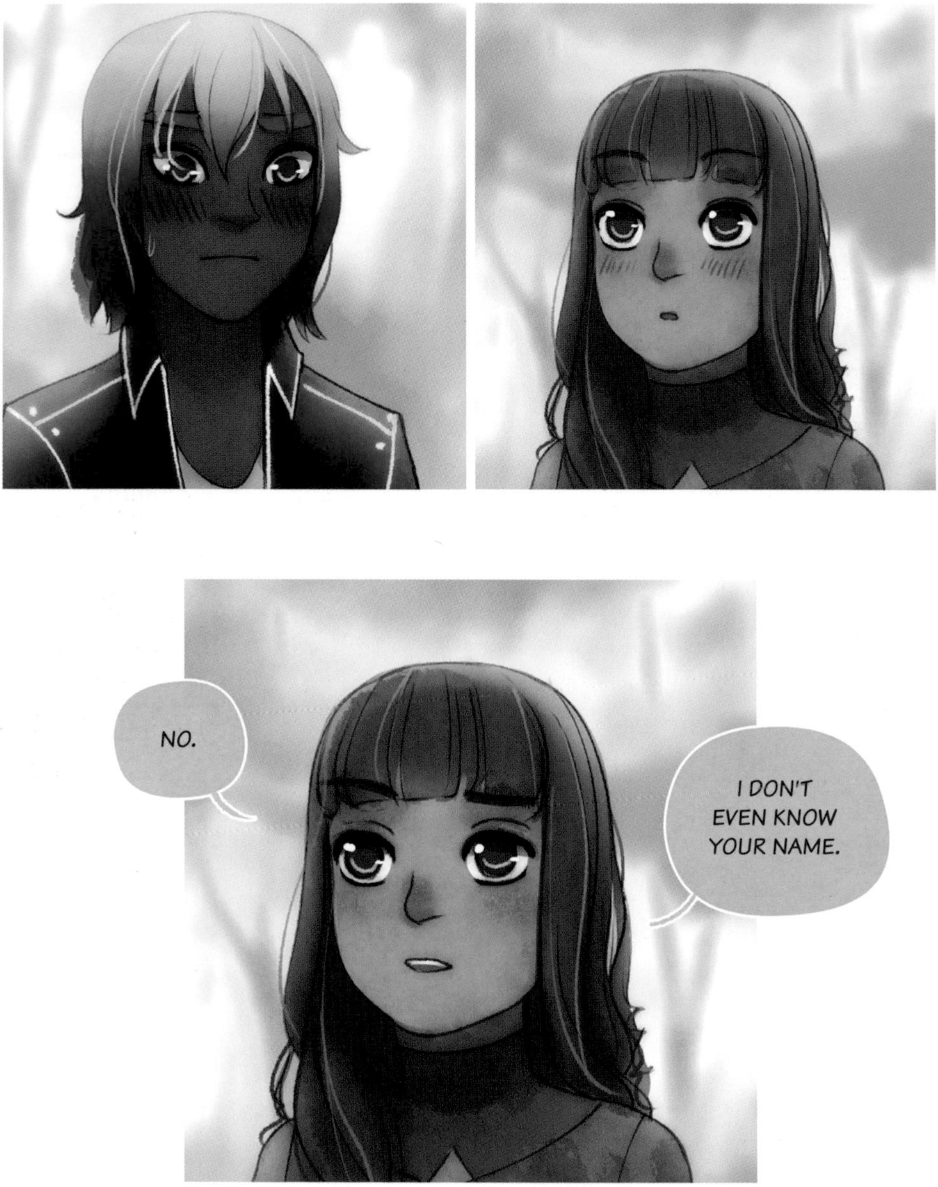
NO.
I DON'T EVEN KNOW YOUR NAME.

4 - ISN'T THAT WHY PEOPLE GO ON DATES?

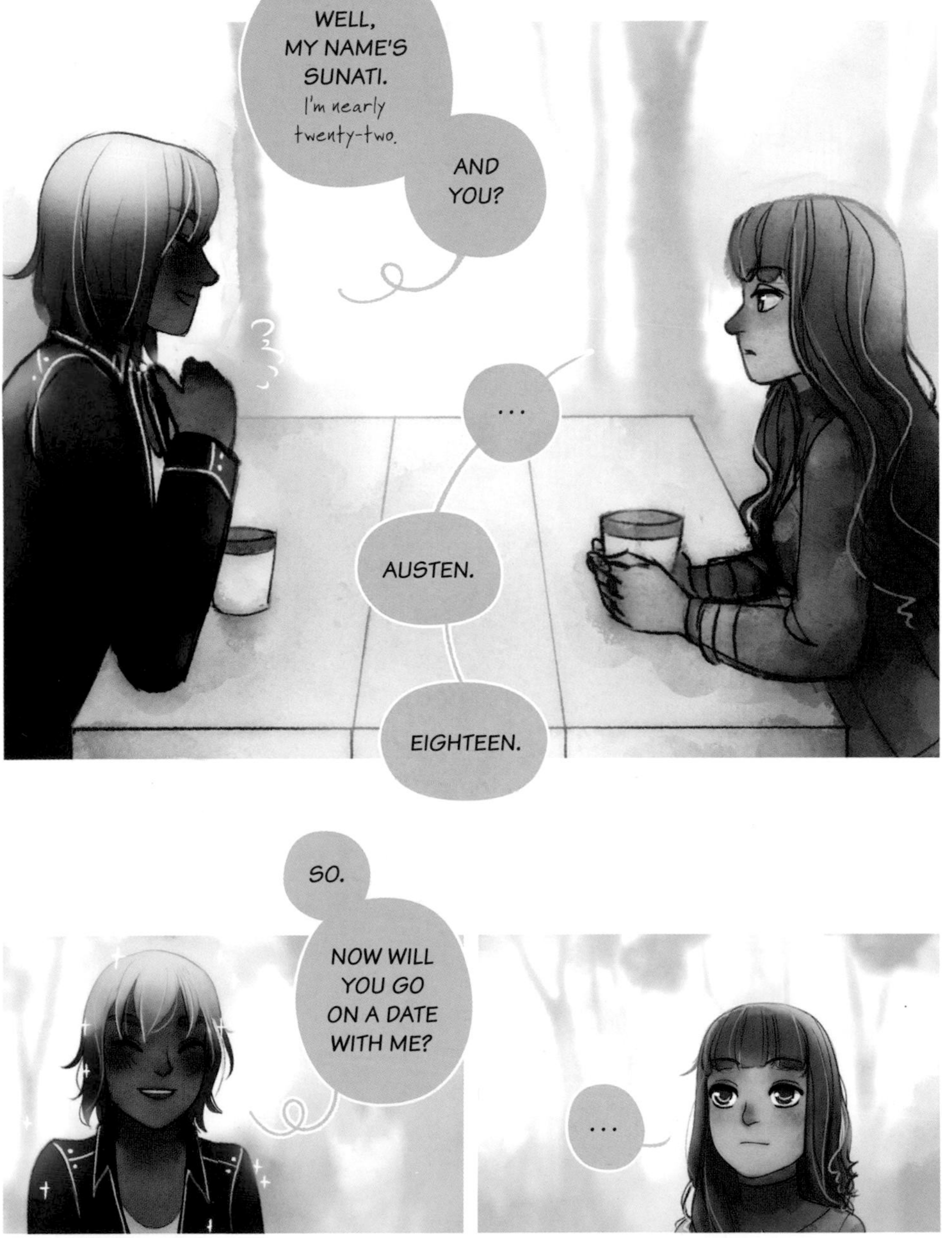
WELL, MY NAME'S SUNATI.
I'm nearly twenty-two.
AND YOU?
...
AUSTEN.
EIGHTEEN.
SO.
NOW WILL YOU GO ON A DATE WITH ME?
...

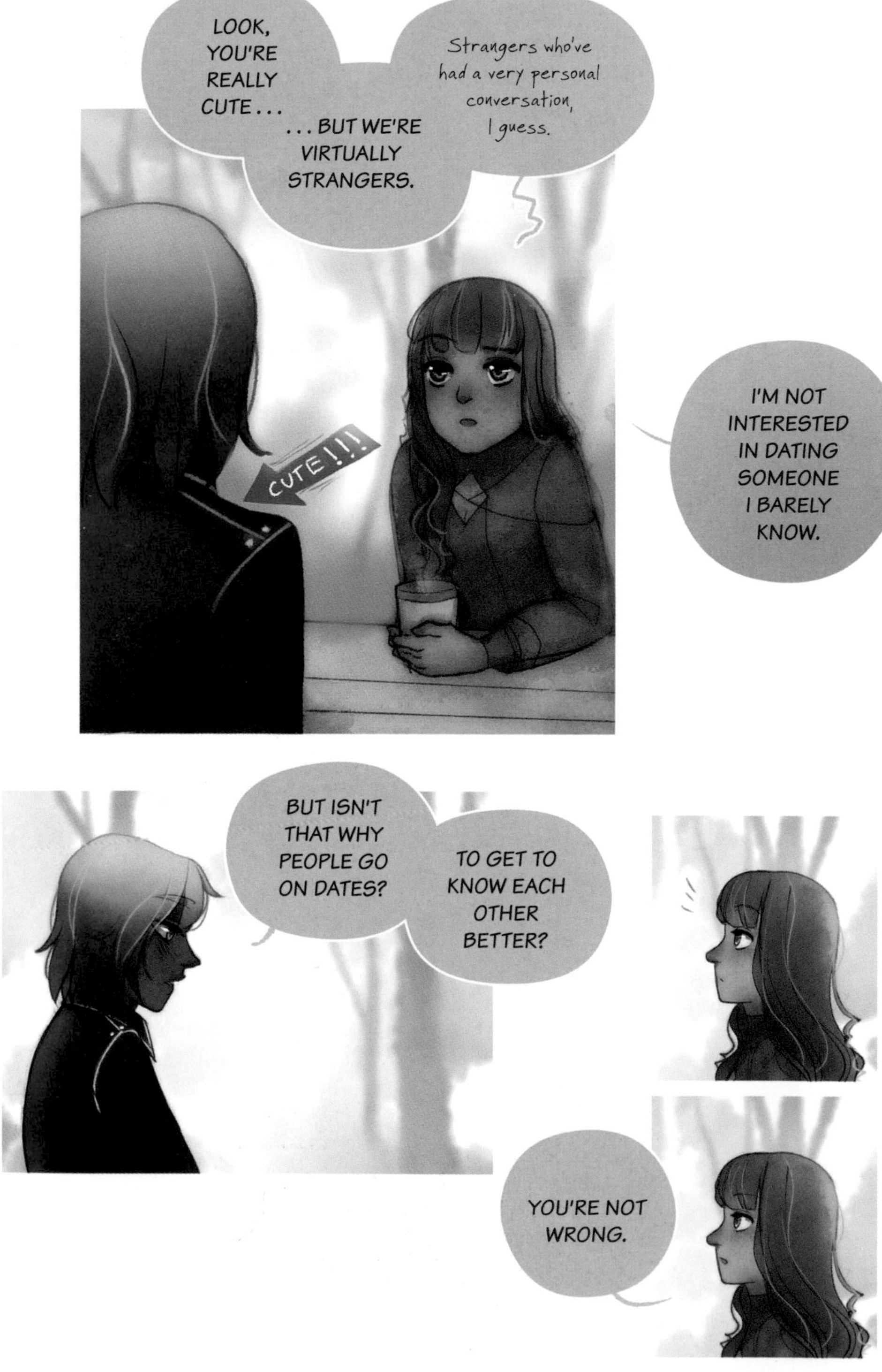
LOOK, YOU'RE REALLY CUTE . . .
. . . BUT WE'RE VIRTUALLY STRANGERS.
Strangers who've had a very personal conversation, I guess.
CUTE!!!
I'M NOT INTERESTED IN DATING SOMEONE I BARELY KNOW.
BUT ISN'T THAT WHY PEOPLE GO ON DATES?
TO GET TO KNOW EACH OTHER BETTER?
YOU'RE NOT WRONG.

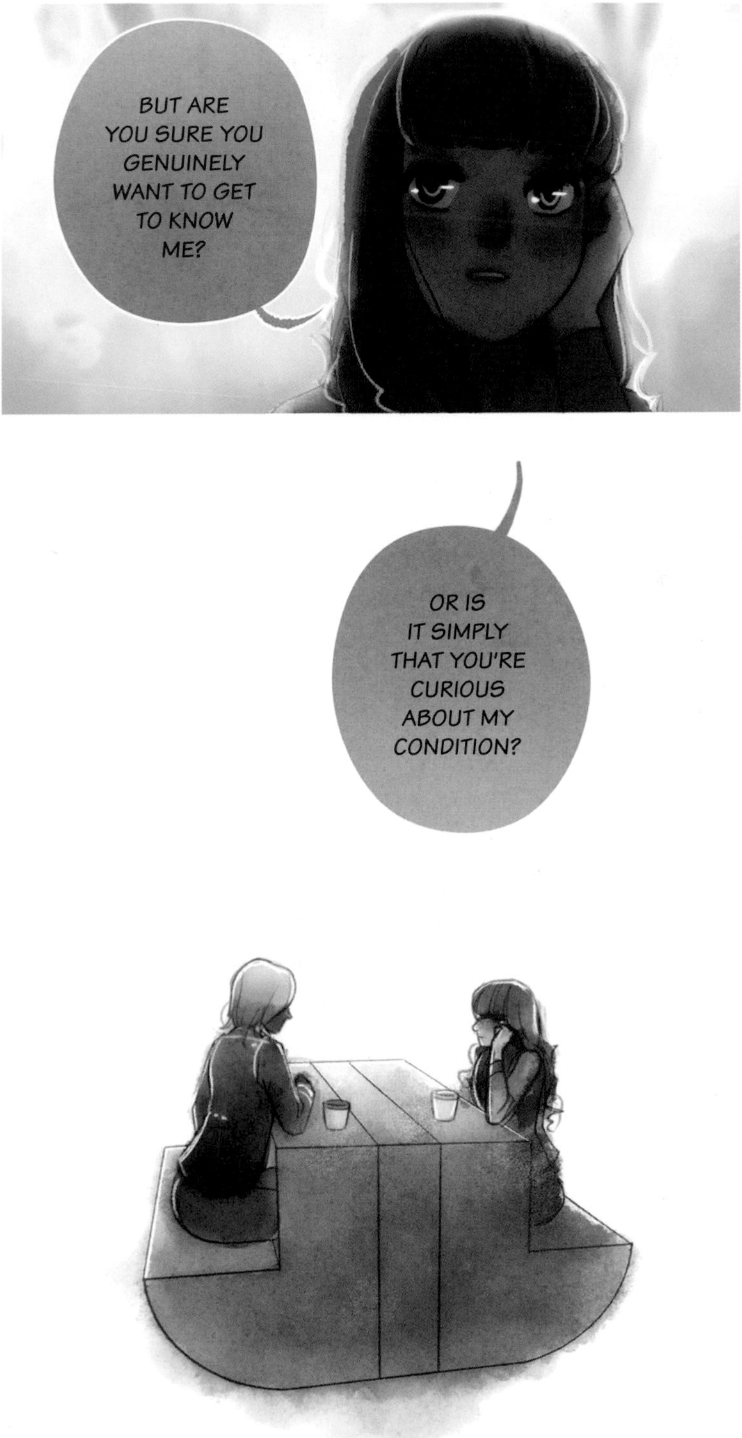
BUT ARE YOU SURE YOU GENUINELY WANT TO GET TO KNOW ME?
OR IS IT SIMPLY THAT YOU'RE CURIOUS ABOUT MY CONDITION?

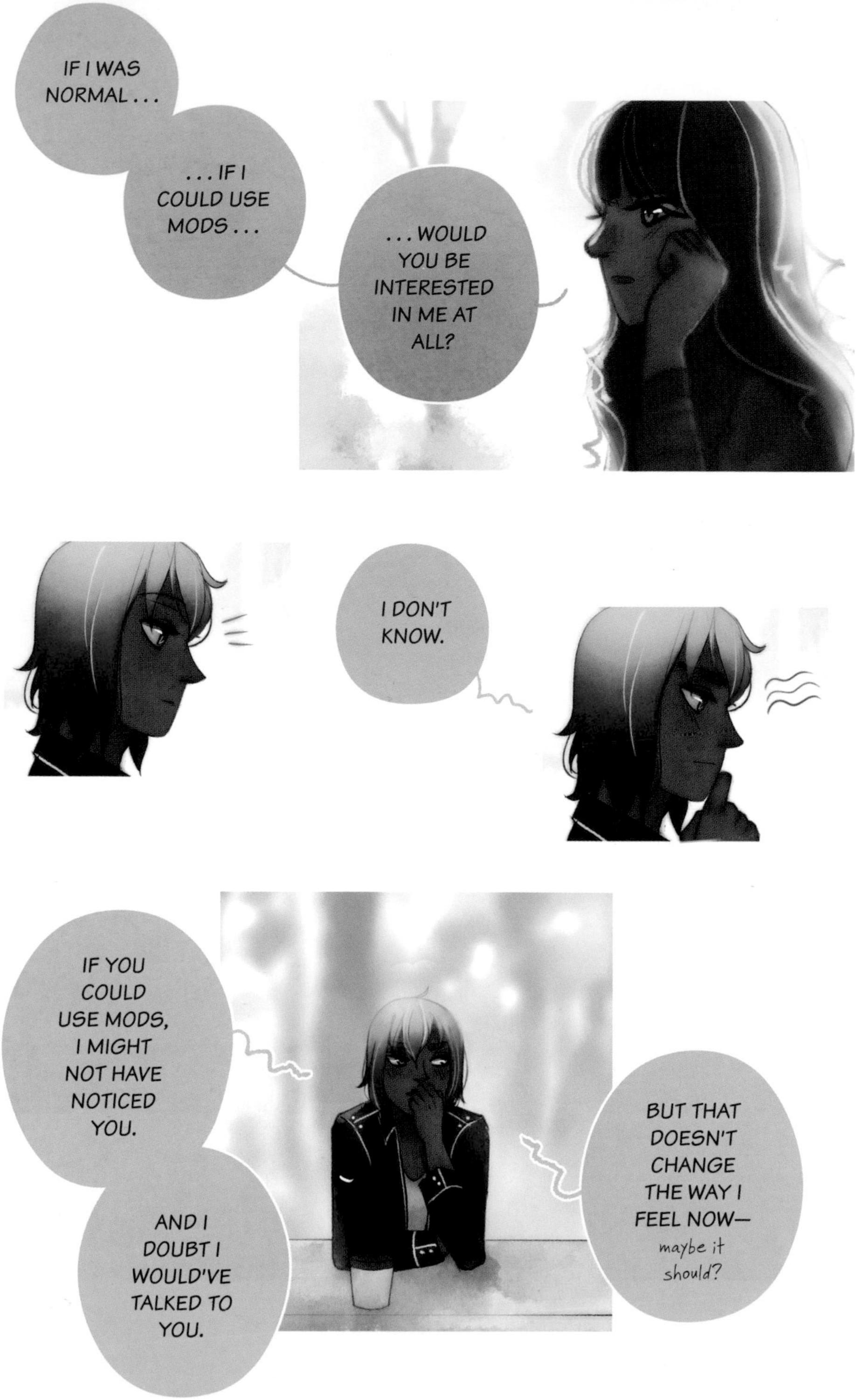
IF I WAS NORMAL . . .
. . . IF I COULD USE MODS . . .
. . . WOULD YOU BE INTERESTED IN ME AT ALL?
I DON'T KNOW.
IF YOU COULD USE MODS, I MIGHT NOT HAVE NOTICED YOU.
AND I DOUBT I WOULD'VE TALKED TO YOU.
BUT THAT DOESN'T CHANGE THE WAY I FEEL NOW—
maybe it should?

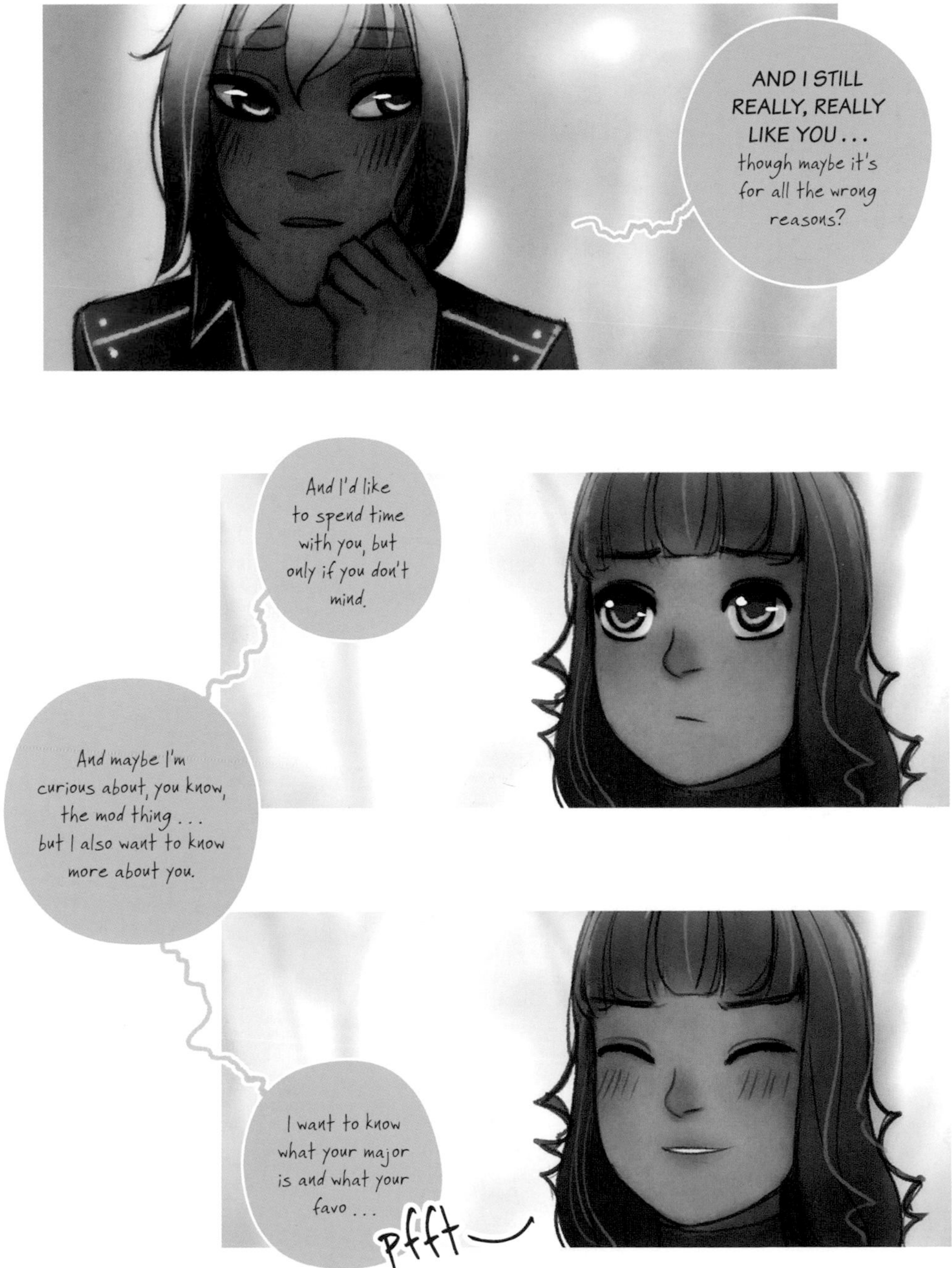
AND I STILL REALLY, REALLY LIKE YOU . . . though maybe it's for all the wrong reasons?
And I'd like to spend time with you, but only if you don't mind.
And maybe I'm curious about, you know, the mod thing . . . but I also want to know more about you.
I want to know what your major is and what your favo . . .
pfft

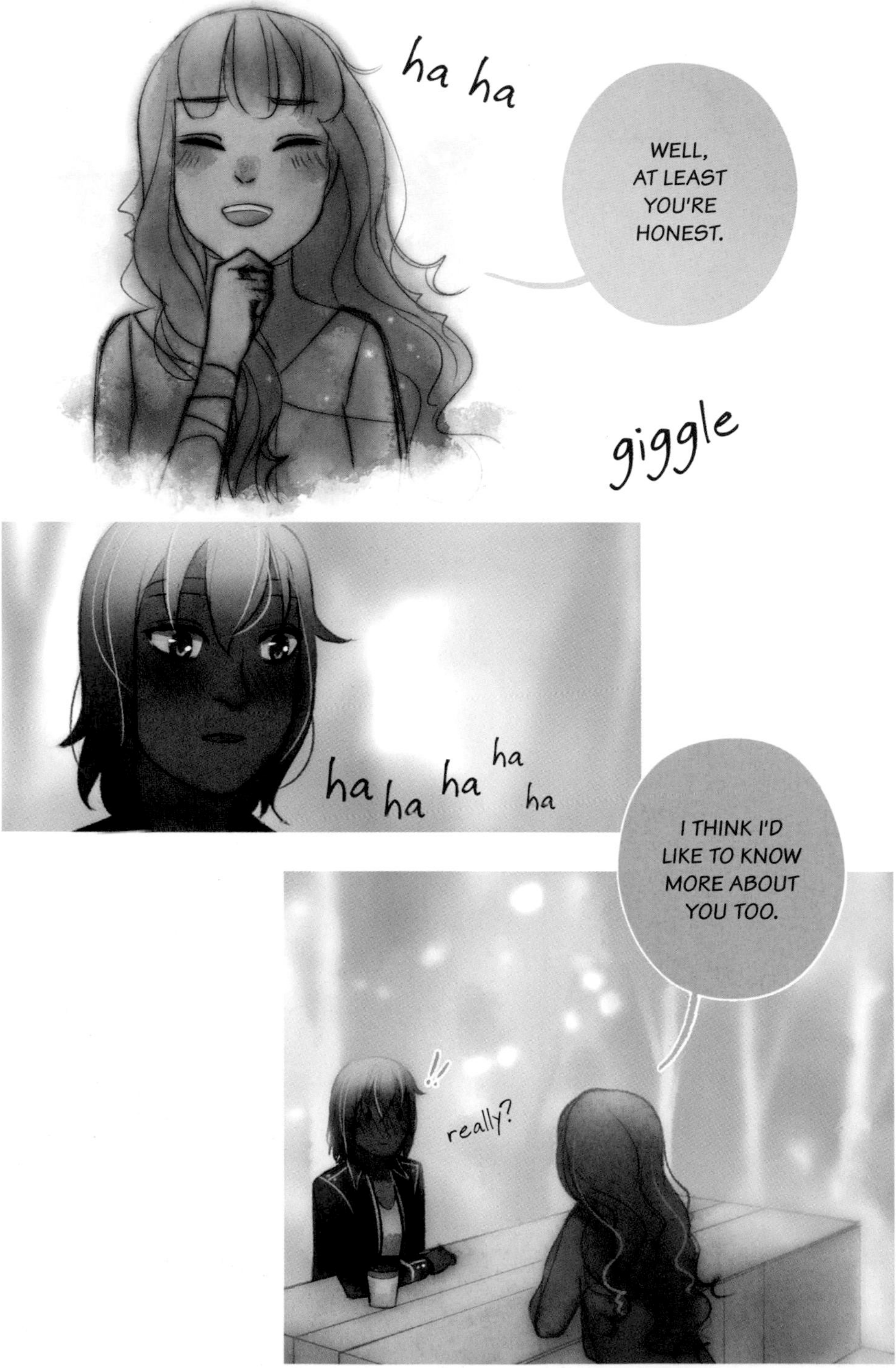
ha ha
WELL, AT LEAST YOU'RE HONEST.
giggle
ha ha ha ha ha
I THINK I'D LIKE TO KNOW MORE ABOUT YOU TOO.
!!
really?

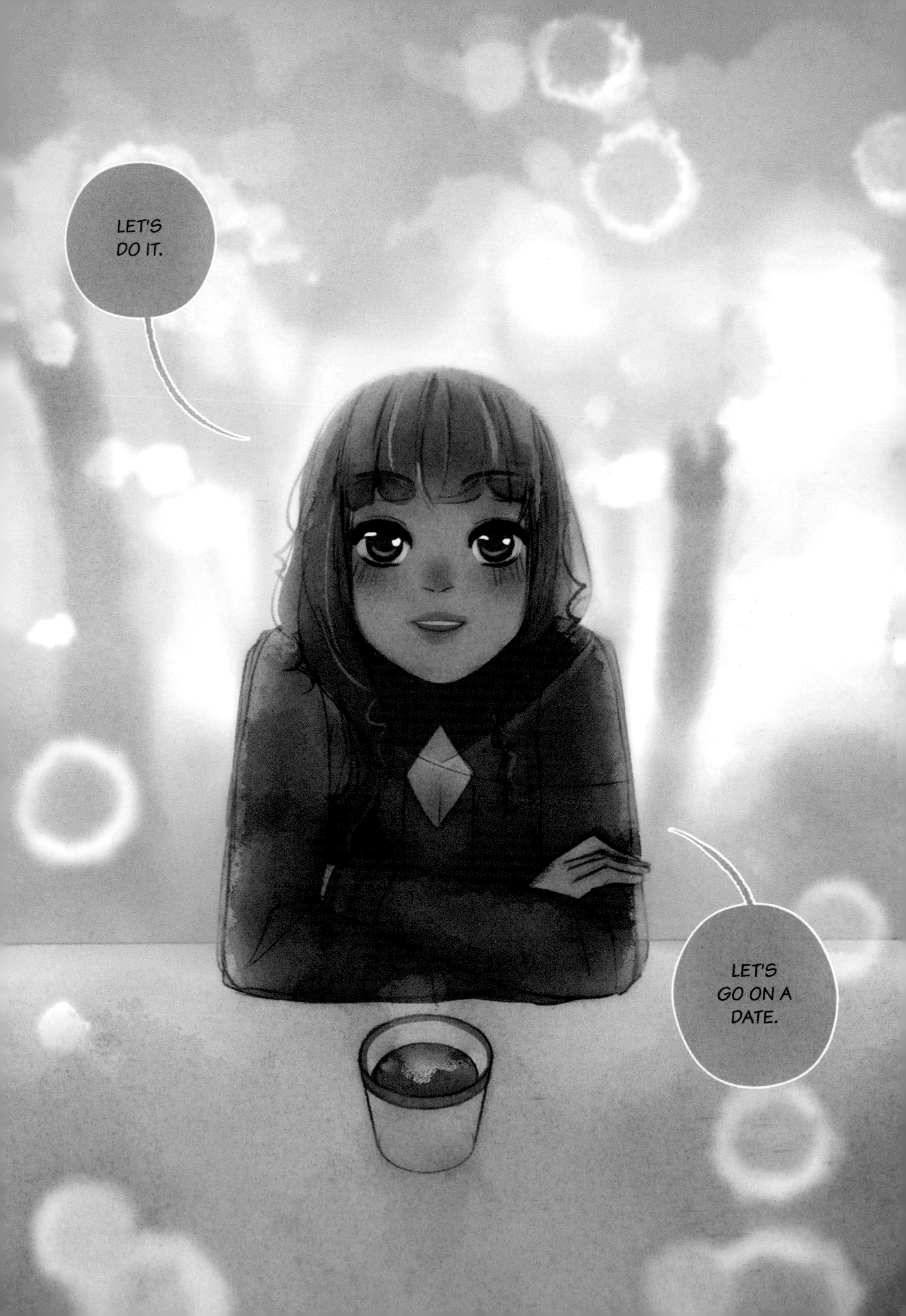
LET'S DO IT.
LET'S GO ON A DATE.

5 – THIS IS IMPOSSIBLE, I CAN'T THINK STRAIGHT

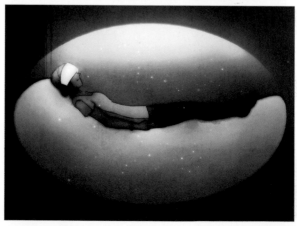

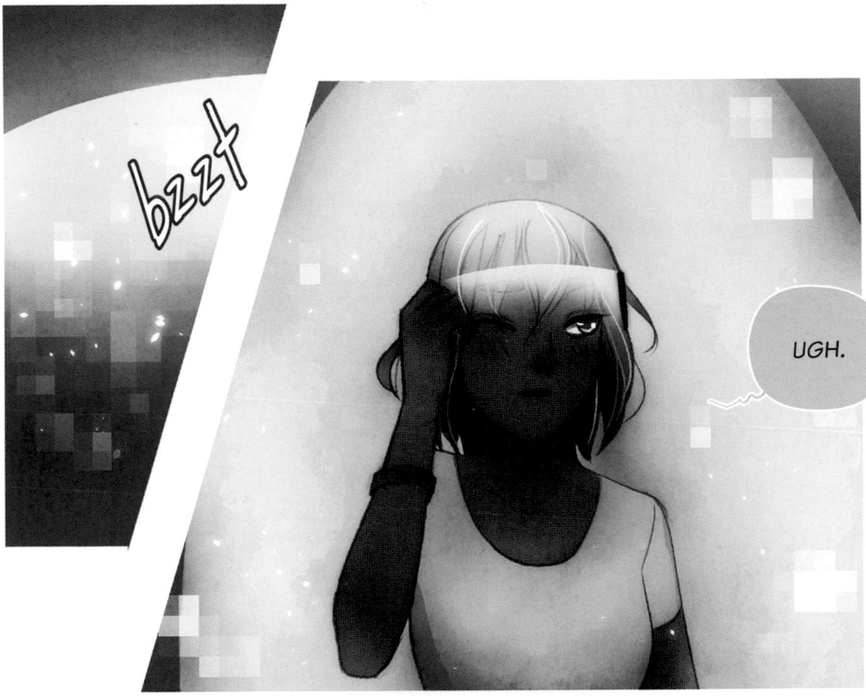
bzzt
UGH.

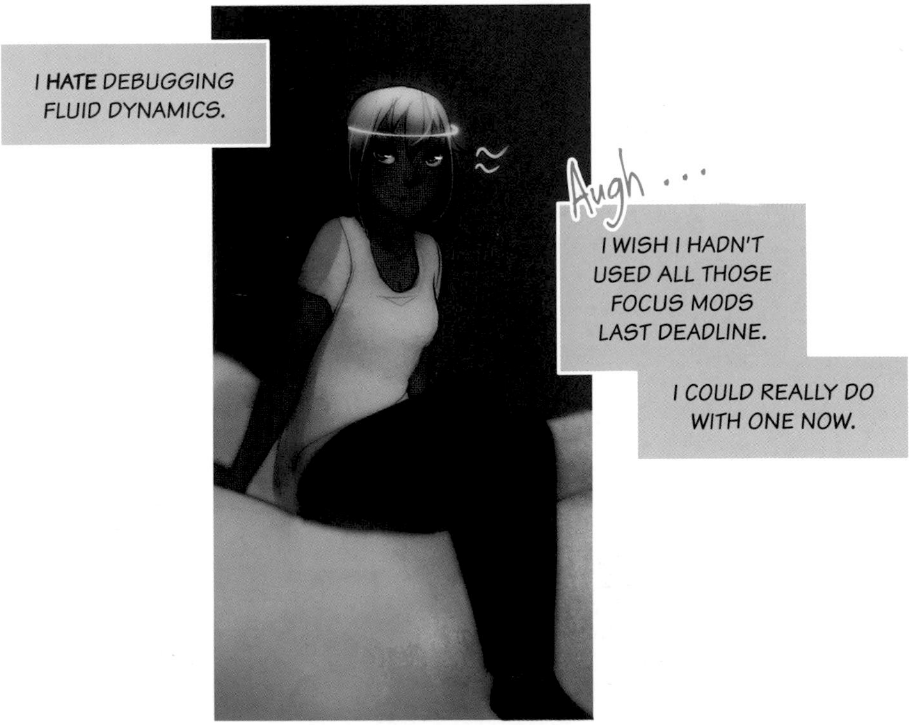
I HATE DEBUGGING FLUID DYNAMICS.
Augh . . .
I WISH I HADN'T USED ALL THOSE FOCUS MODS LAST DEADLINE.
I COULD REALLY DO WITH ONE NOW.

sigh

ahahah~

THIS IS IMPOSSIBLE,
I CAN'T THINK STRAIGHT.

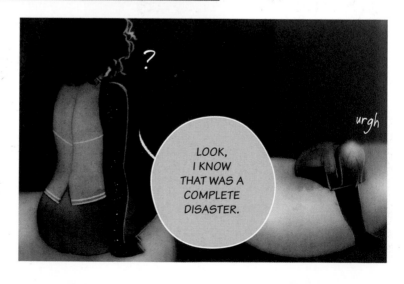

?

urgh

LOOK,
I KNOW
THAT WAS A
COMPLETE
DISASTER.

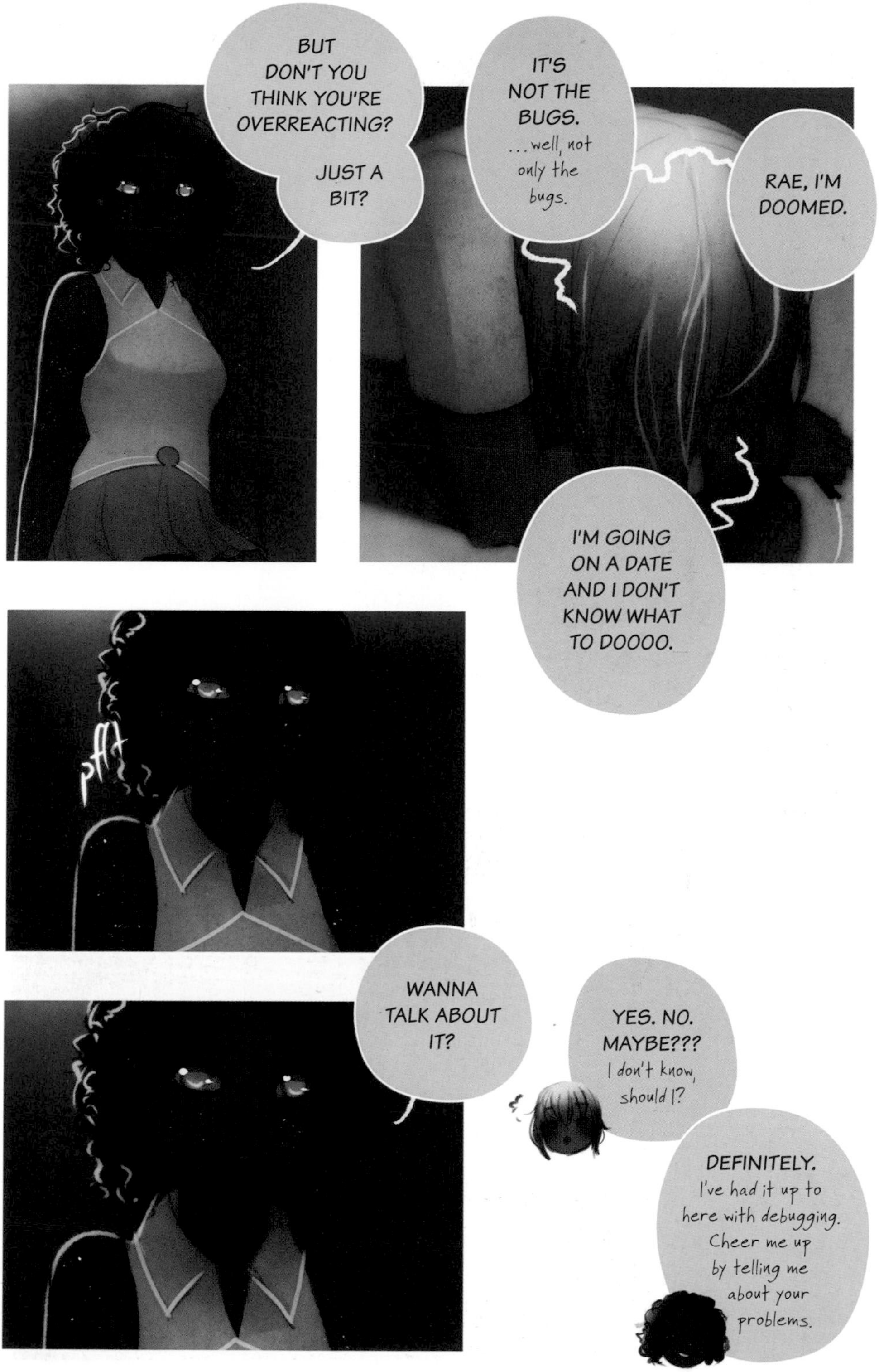
BUT DON'T YOU THINK YOU'RE OVERREACTING?
JUST A BIT?
IT'S NOT THE BUGS.
...well, not only the bugs.
RAE, I'M DOOMED.
I'M GOING ON A DATE AND I DON'T KNOW WHAT TO DOOOO.
pfft
WANNA TALK ABOUT IT?
YES. NO. MAYBE???
I don't know, should I?
DEFINITELY.
I've had it up to here with debugging. Cheer me up by telling me about your problems.

THAT POOR GIRL.

IMAGINE NOT BEING ABLE TO USE MODS.

MAKES ME FEEL LUCKY.

. . .

IT MAKES ME FEEL SELFISH, ACTUALLY.

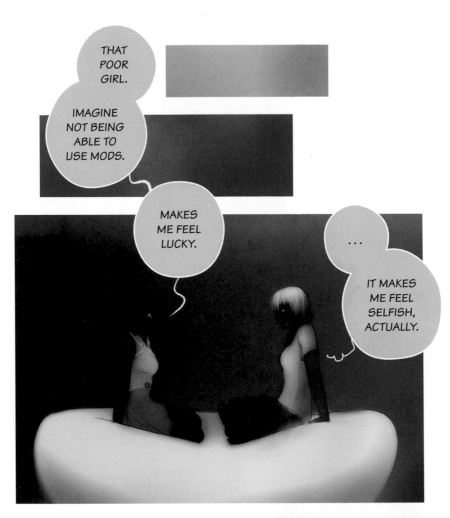

IT DOESN'T SEEM FAIR TO SHOW UP FOR A DATE LOOKING LIKE THIS.

Since she can't use mods, it just feels wrong.

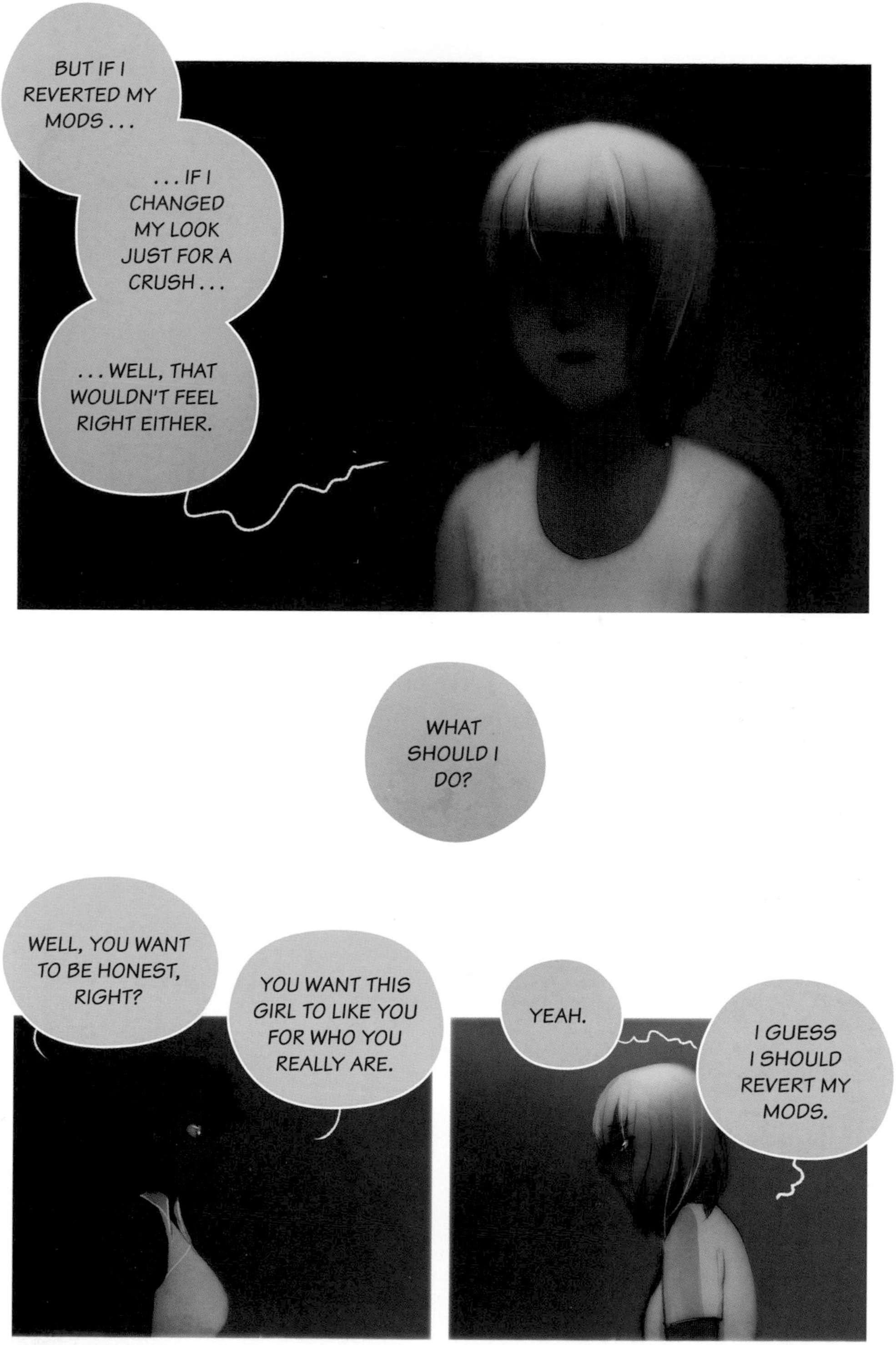
BUT IF I REVERTED MY MODS . . .
. . . IF I CHANGED MY LOOK JUST FOR A CRUSH . . .
. . . WELL, THAT WOULDN'T FEEL RIGHT EITHER.
WHAT SHOULD I DO?
WELL, YOU WANT TO BE HONEST, RIGHT?
YOU WANT THIS GIRL TO LIKE YOU FOR WHO YOU REALLY ARE.
YEAH.
I GUESS I SHOULD REVERT MY MODS.

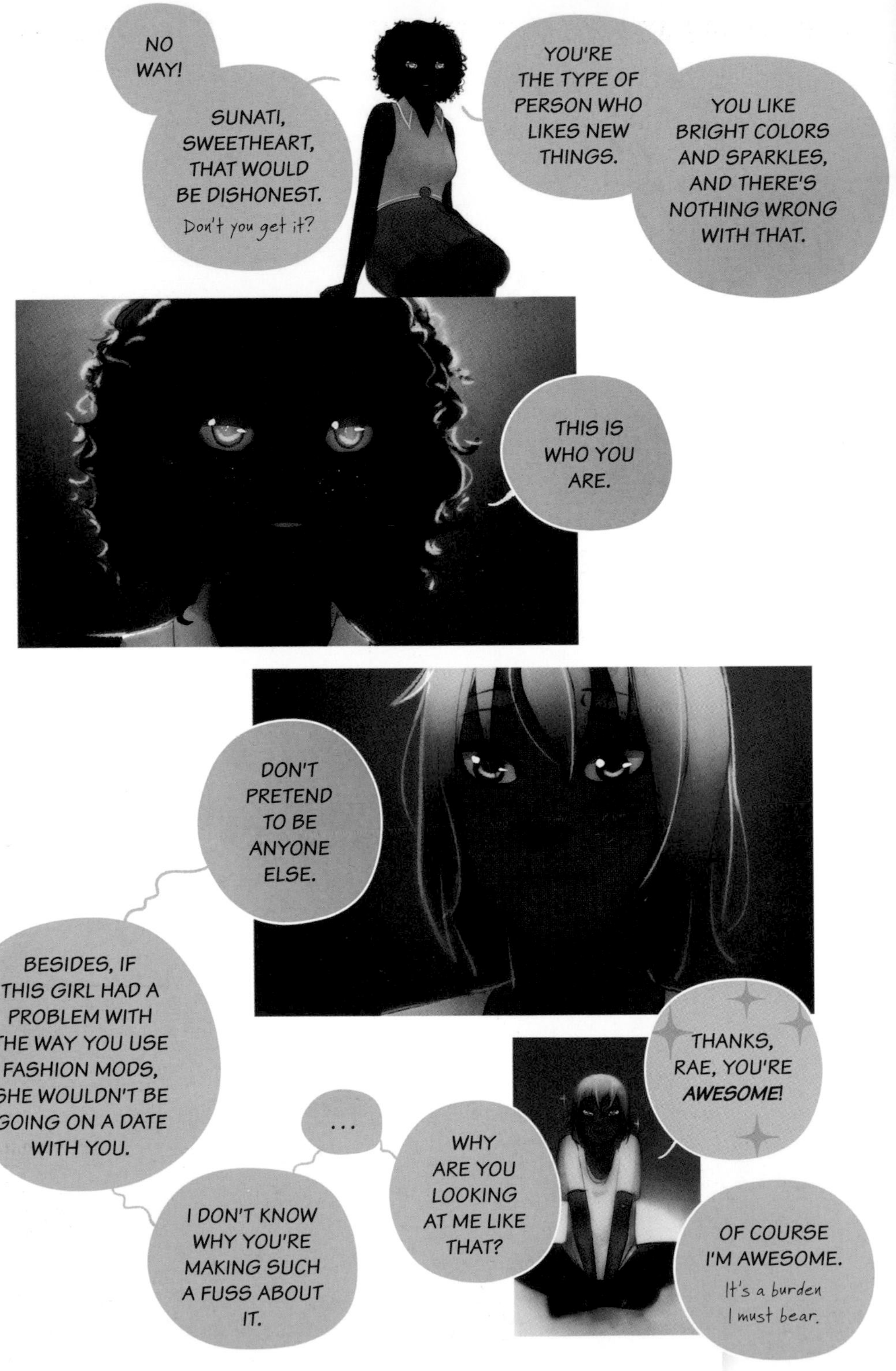
NO WAY!
SUNATI, SWEETHEART, THAT WOULD BE DISHONEST. Don't you get it?
YOU'RE THE TYPE OF PERSON WHO LIKES NEW THINGS.
YOU LIKE BRIGHT COLORS AND SPARKLES, AND THERE'S NOTHING WRONG WITH THAT.
THIS IS WHO YOU ARE.
DON'T PRETEND TO BE ANYONE ELSE.
BESIDES, IF THIS GIRL HAD A PROBLEM WITH THE WAY YOU USE FASHION MODS, SHE WOULDN'T BE GOING ON A DATE WITH YOU.
I DON'T KNOW WHY YOU'RE MAKING SUCH A FUSS ABOUT IT.
...
WHY ARE YOU LOOKING AT ME LIKE THAT?
THANKS, RAE, YOU'RE AWESOME!
OF COURSE I'M AWESOME. It's a burden I must bear.

6 - I'M NOT QUITE SURE HOW TO EXPLAIN IT WITHOUT IT SOUNDING STUPID

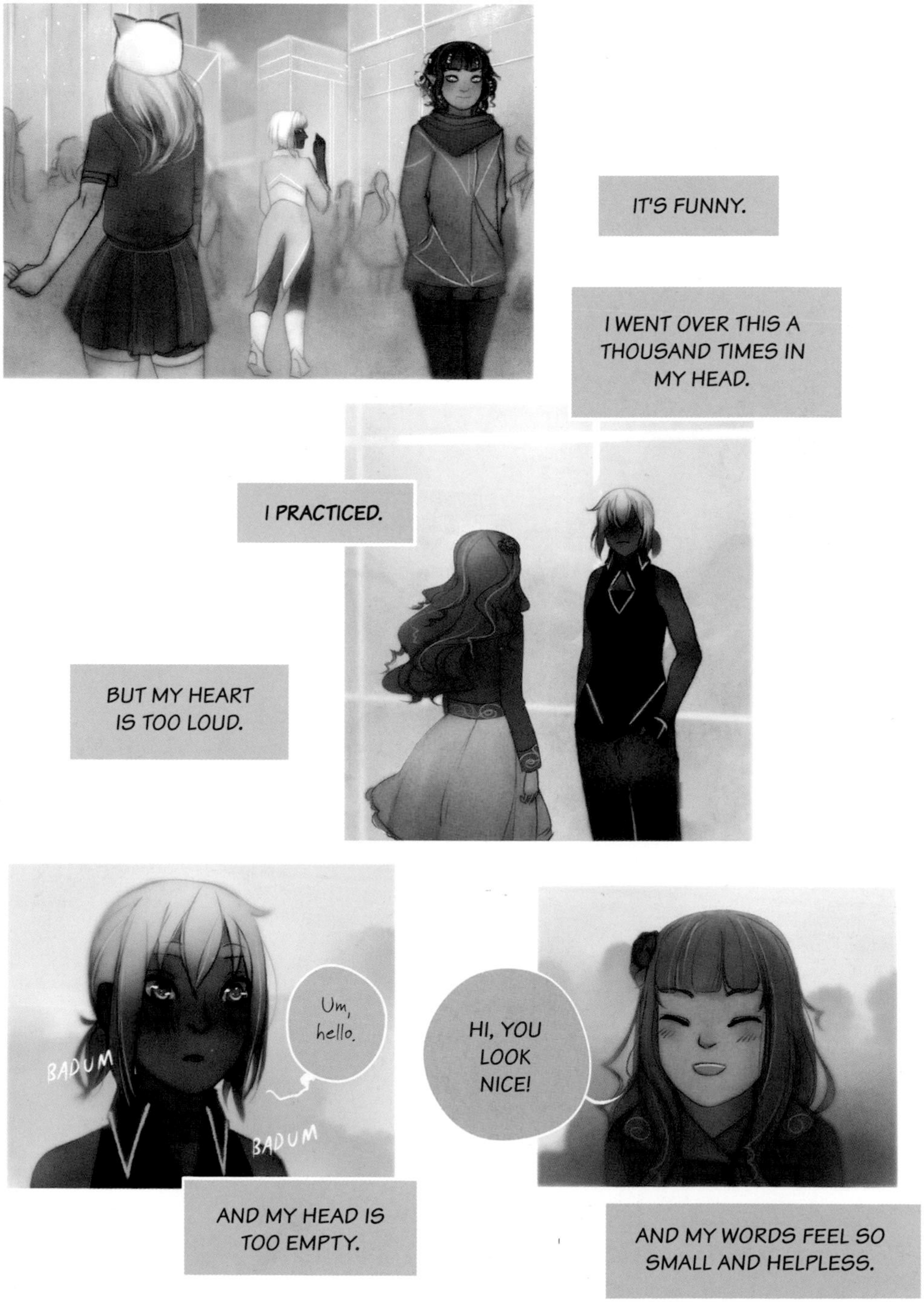

IT'S FUNNY.
I WENT OVER THIS A THOUSAND TIMES IN MY HEAD.
I PRACTICED.
BUT MY HEART IS TOO LOUD.
Um, hello.
BADUM
BADUM
AND MY HEAD IS TOO EMPTY.
HI, YOU LOOK NICE!
AND MY WORDS FEEL SO SMALL AND HELPLESS.

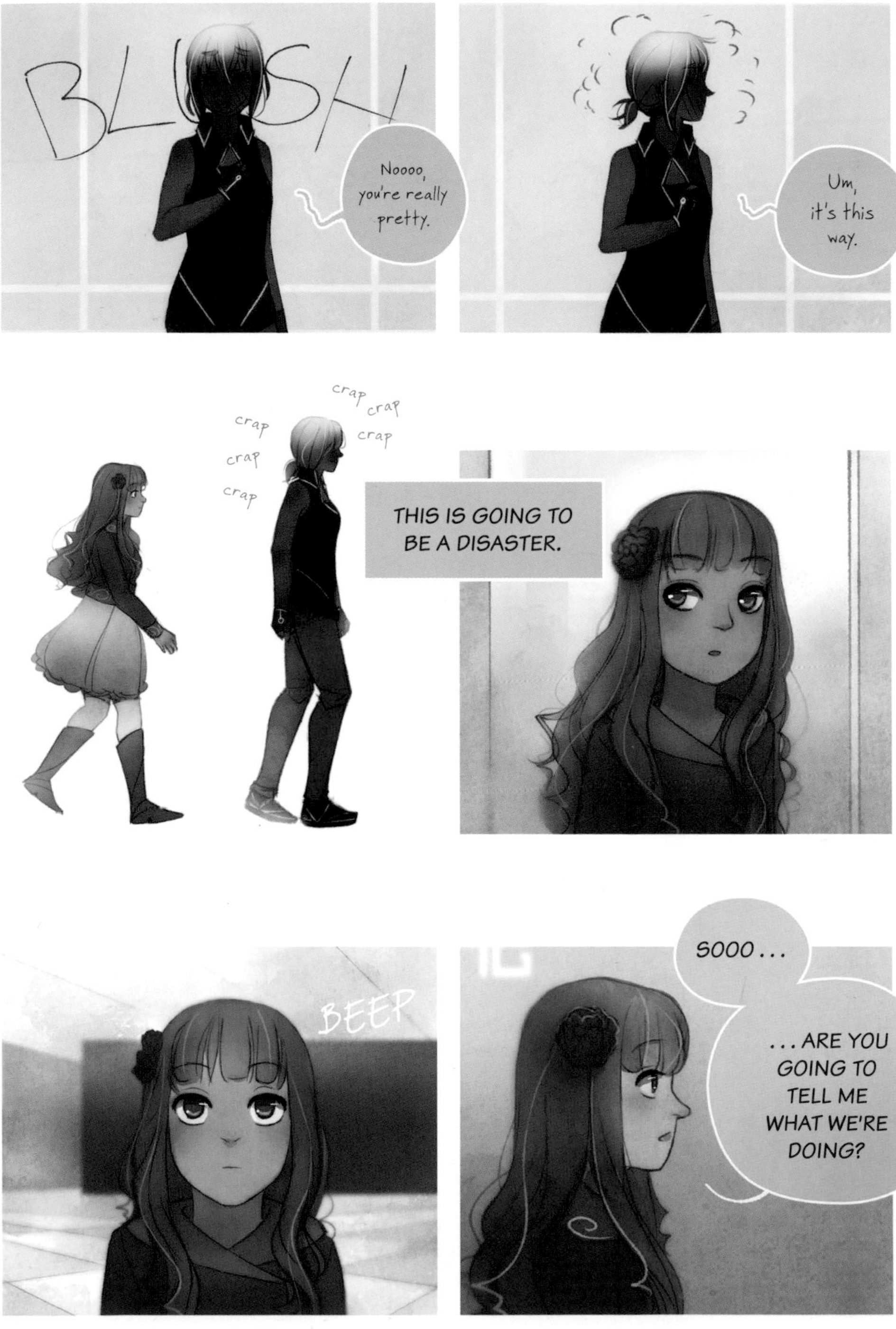
BLUSH
Noooo, you're really pretty.
Um, it's this way.
crap
crap
crap
crap
crap
crap
THIS IS GOING TO BE A DISASTER.
BEEP
SOOO . . .
. . . ARE YOU GOING TO TELL ME WHAT WE'RE DOING?

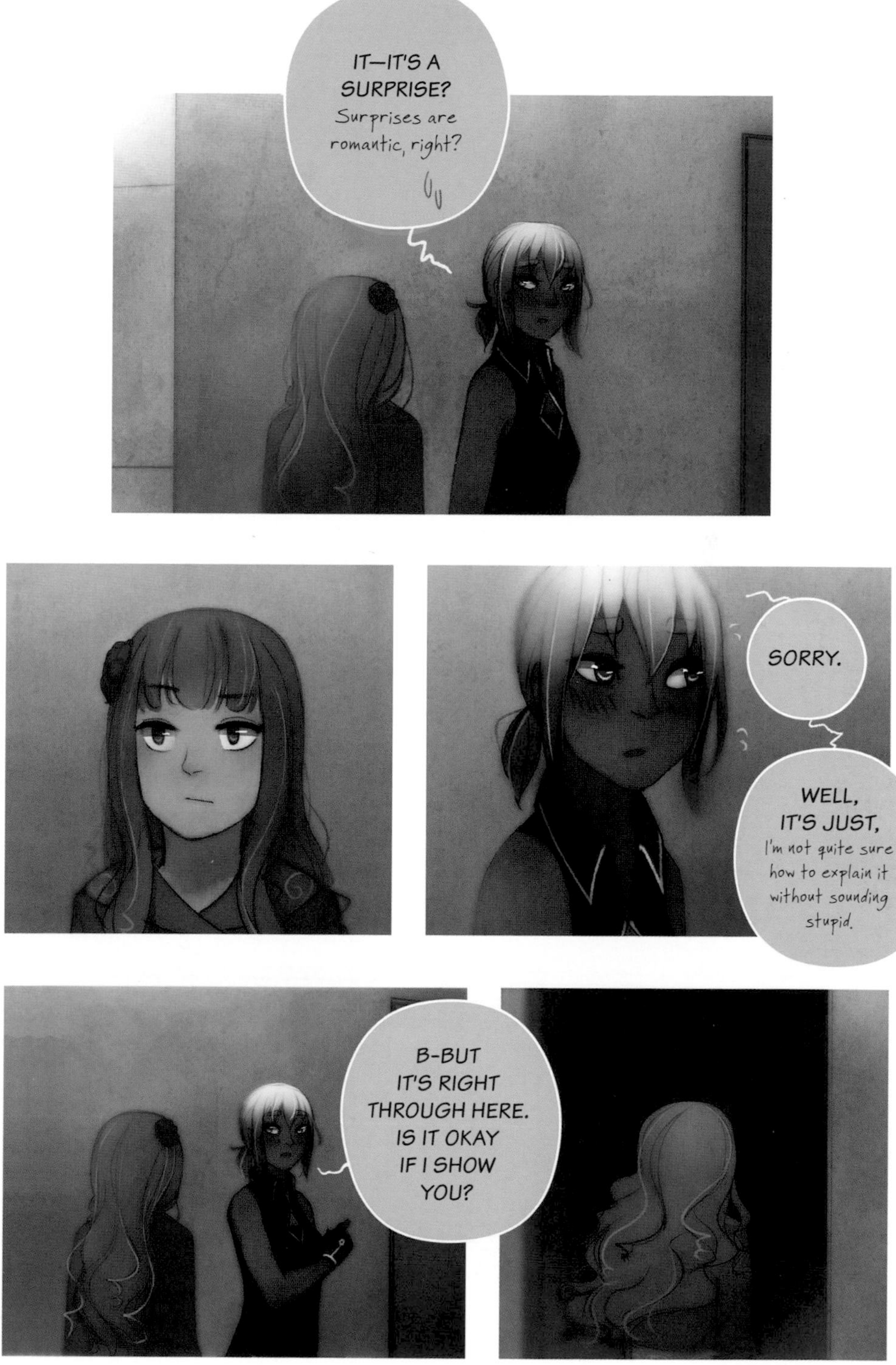
IT—IT'S A SURPRISE? Surprises are romantic, right?
SORRY.
WELL, IT'S JUST, I'm not quite sure how to explain it without sounding stupid.
B-BUT IT'S RIGHT THROUGH HERE. IS IT OKAY IF I SHOW YOU?

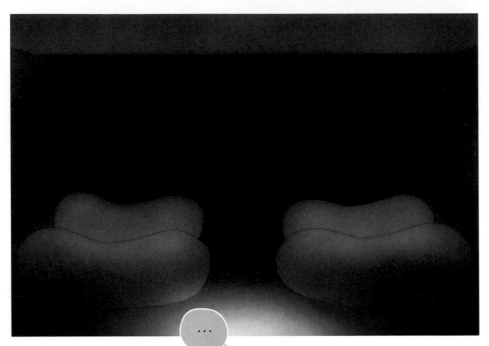

...

WE'RE GOING ON A VIRTUAL REALITY DATE?

That's very twenty-third century.

WELL...

...

THIS IS WHERE I WORK.

I DO VR ENVIRONMENT DESIGN.

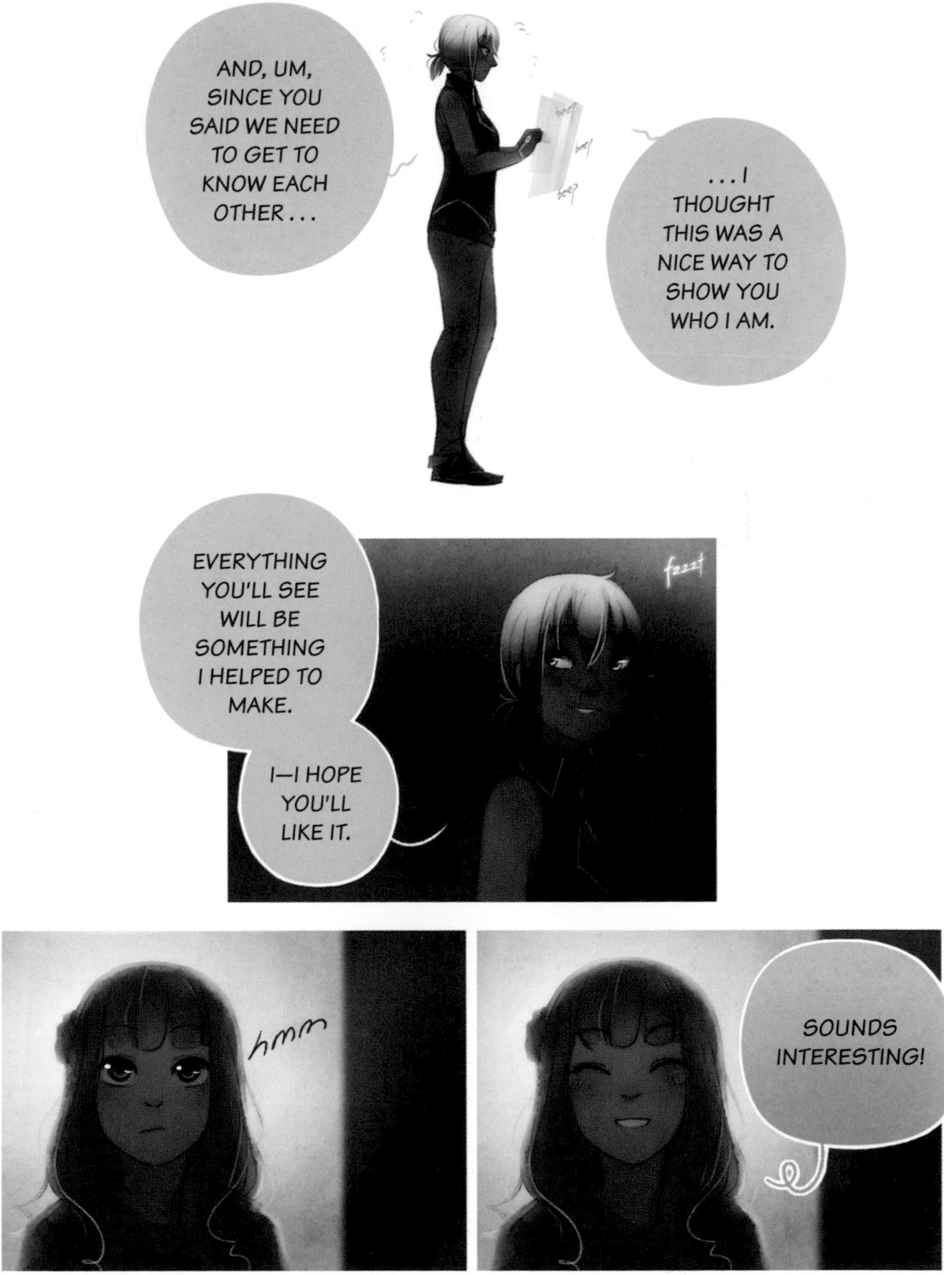
AND, UM, SINCE YOU SAID WE NEED TO GET TO KNOW EACH OTHER . . .
. . . I THOUGHT THIS WAS A NICE WAY TO SHOW YOU WHO I AM.
fzzzt
EVERYTHING YOU'LL SEE WILL BE SOMETHING I HELPED TO MAKE.
I—I HOPE YOU'LL LIKE IT.
hmm
SOUNDS INTERESTING!

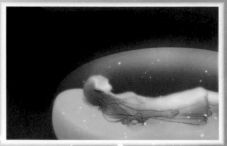

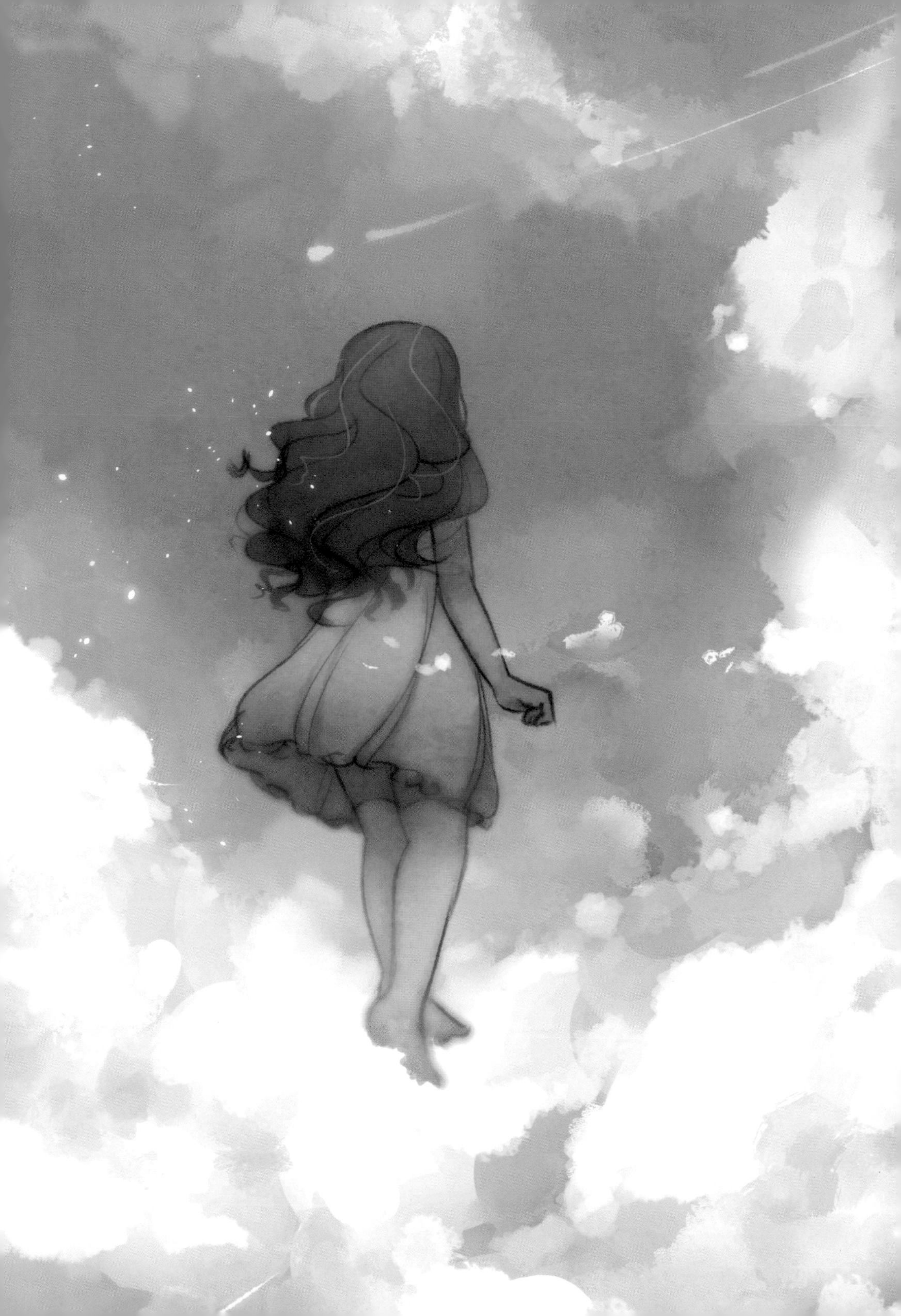

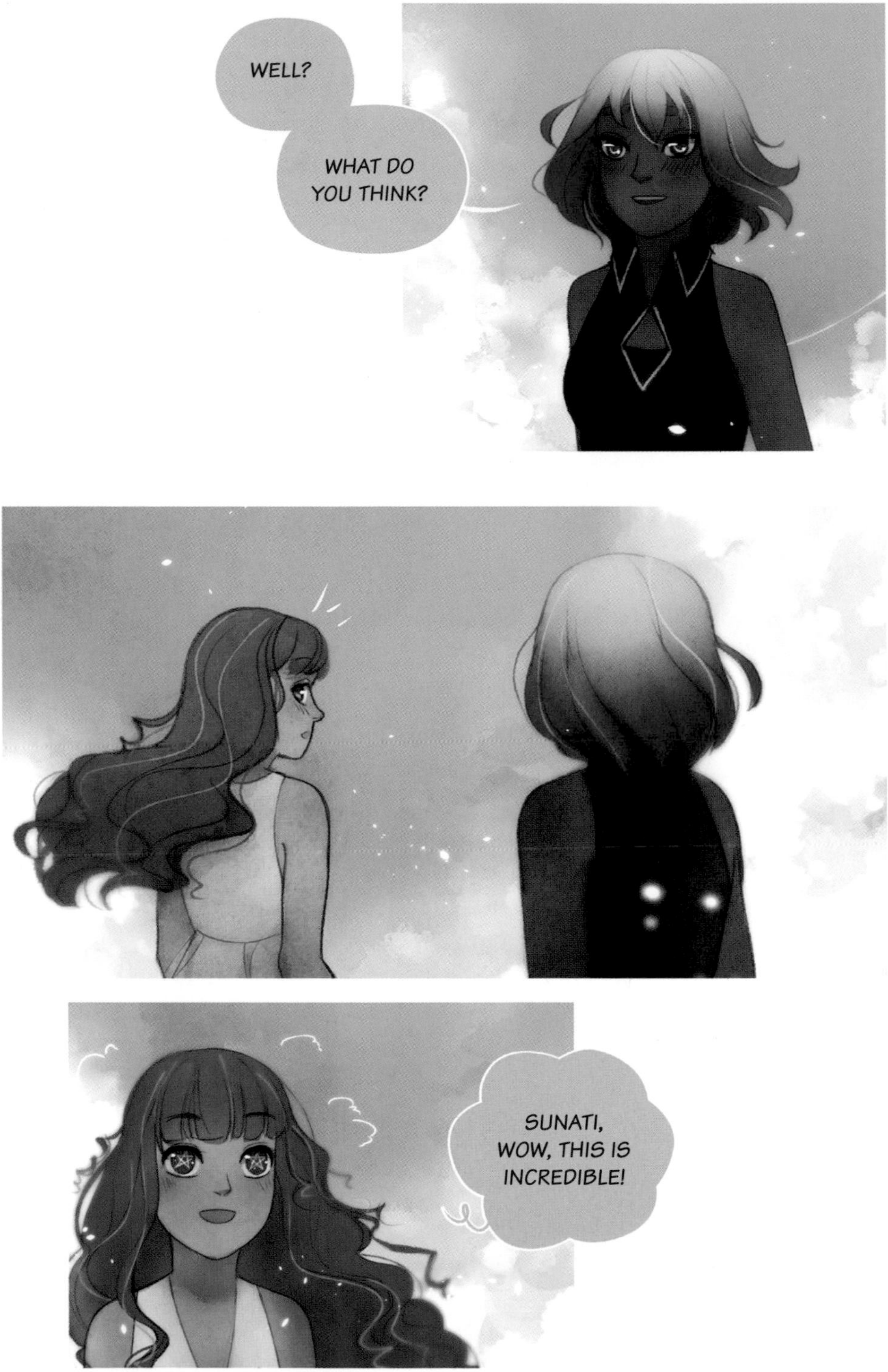
WELL?
WHAT DO YOU THINK?
SUNATI, WOW, THIS IS INCREDIBLE!

SO TELL ME, WHICH PARTS DID YOU WORK ON?

OH, UM, MOST OF IT, everything but the avatar software.

THIS WAS MY INTERNSHIP PROJECT.

I ONLY FINISHED IT IN JUNE.

I DON'T KNOW HOW OR WHEN IT HAPPENED.

BUT I'M THINKING CLEARLY NOW.

TALKING TO HER IS SO EASY.

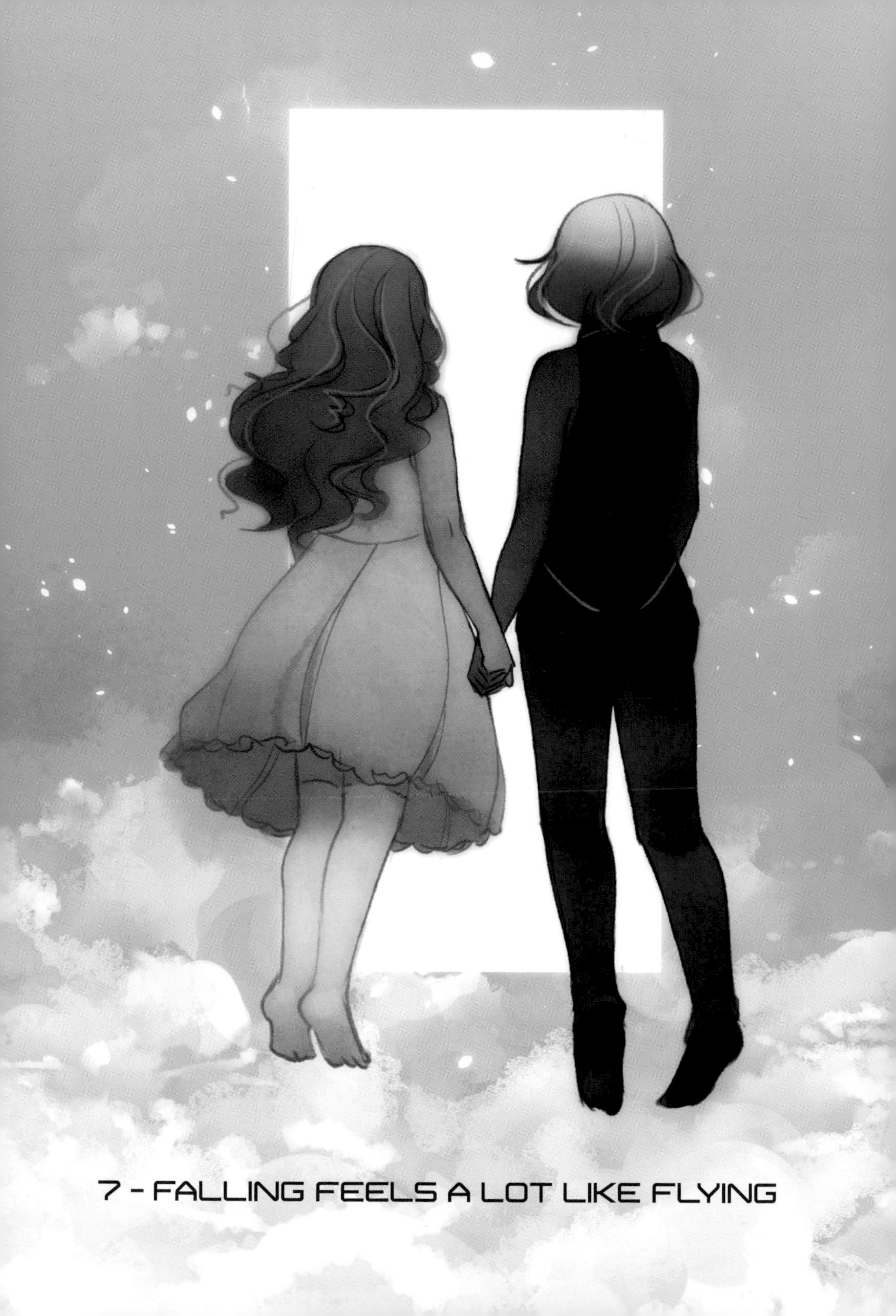

7 - FALLING FEELS A LOT LIKE FLYING

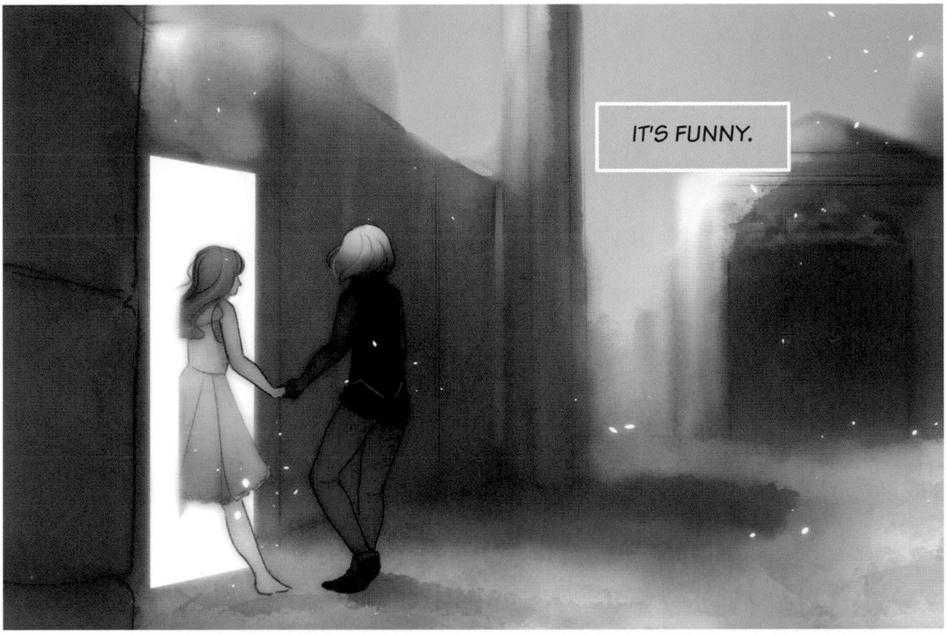
IT'S FUNNY.

I THOUGHT I NEEDED TO PREPARE FOR THIS.

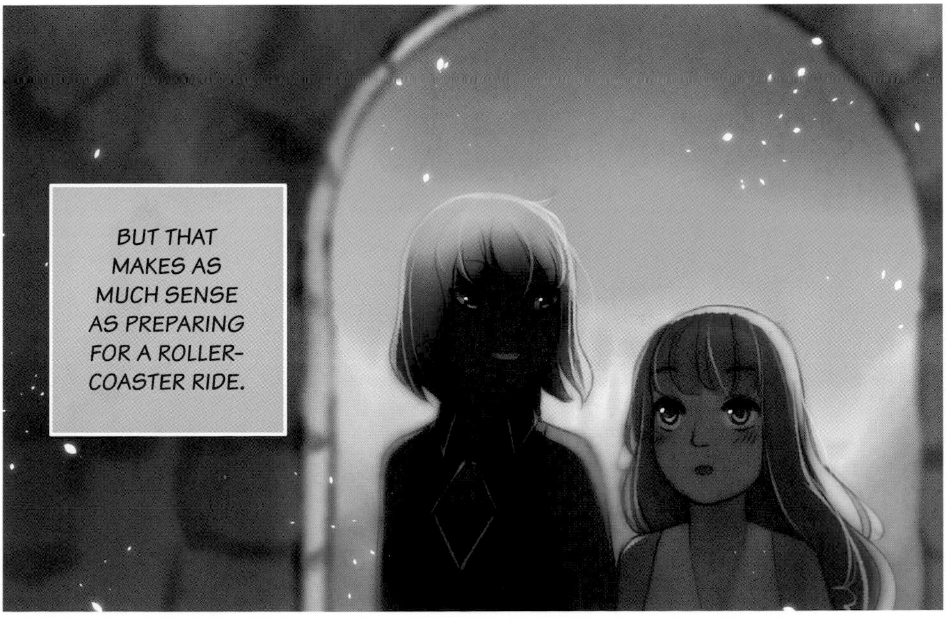
BUT THAT MAKES AS MUCH SENSE AS PREPARING FOR A ROLLER-COASTER RIDE.

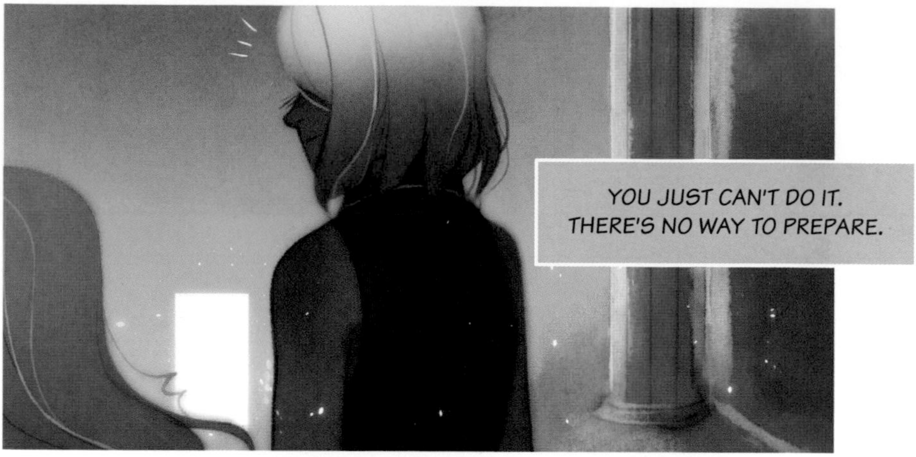
YOU JUST CAN'T DO IT.
THERE'S NO WAY TO PREPARE.

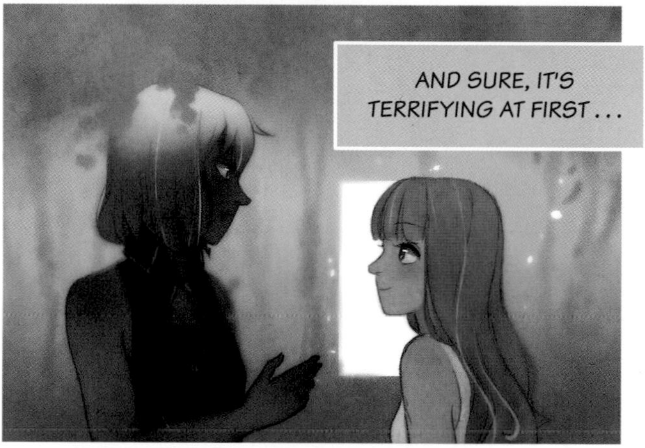
AND SURE, IT'S
TERRIFYING AT FIRST . . .

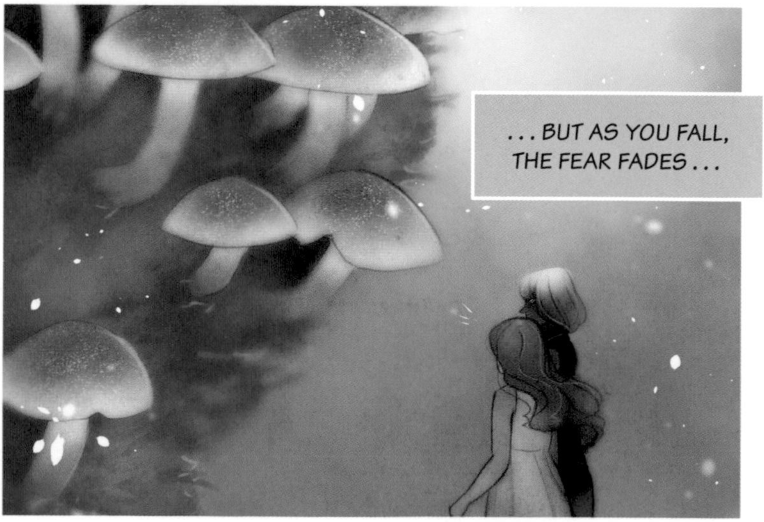
. . . BUT AS YOU FALL,
THE FEAR FADES . . .

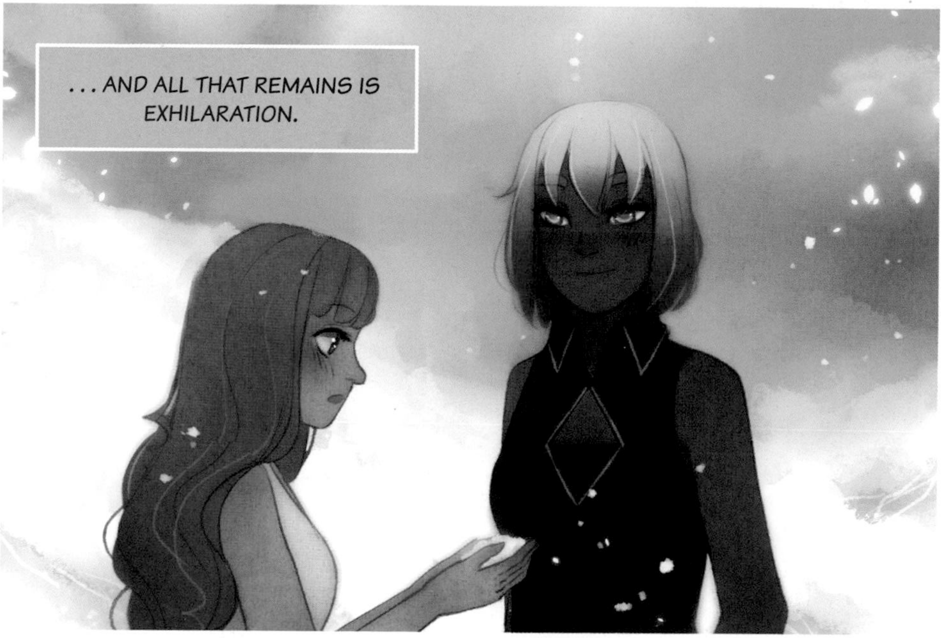
. . . AND ALL THAT REMAINS IS EXHILARATION.

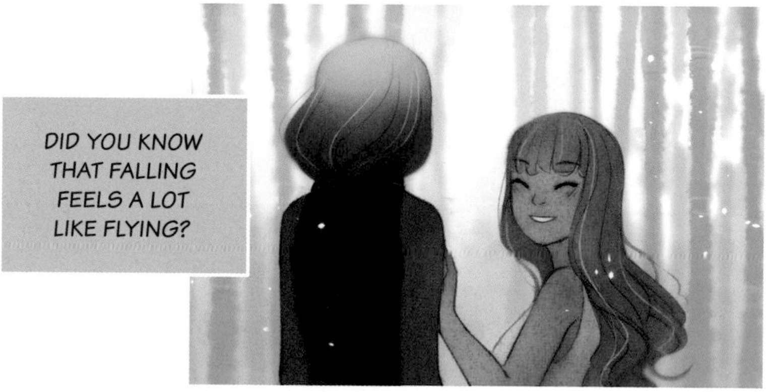
DID YOU KNOW THAT FALLING FEELS A LOT LIKE FLYING?

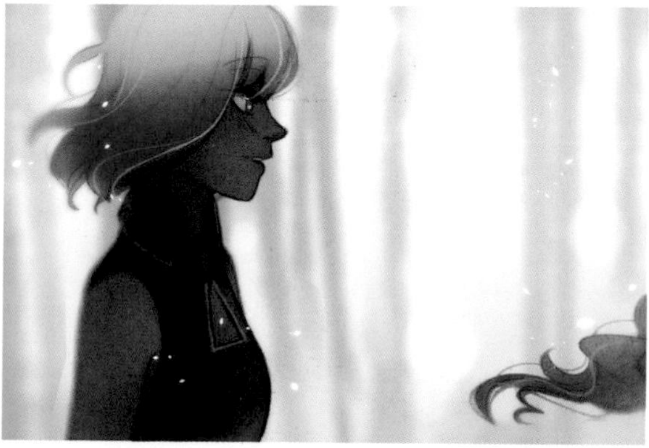
I'M FALLING SO FAST RIGHT NOW.

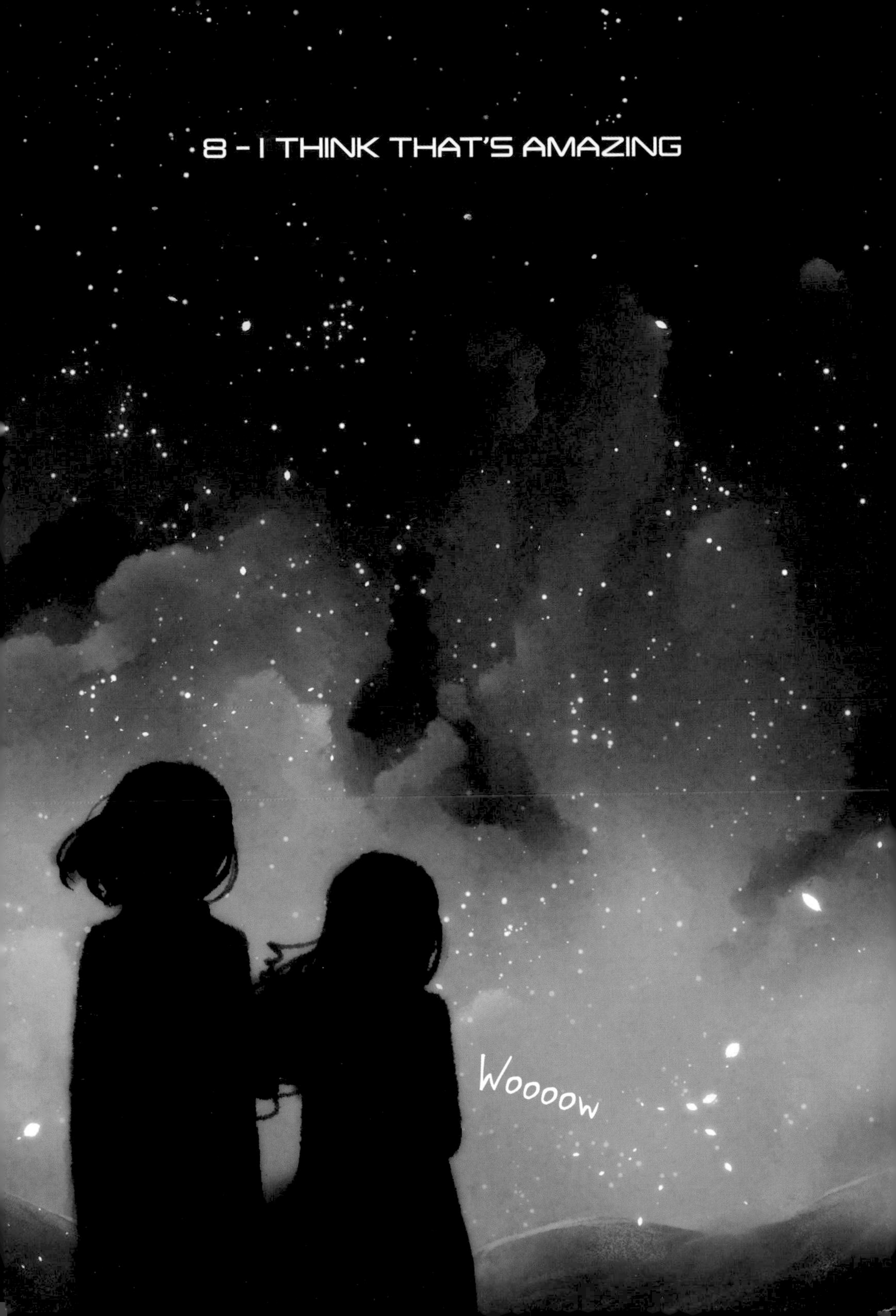
8 - I THINK THAT'S AMAZING
Woooow

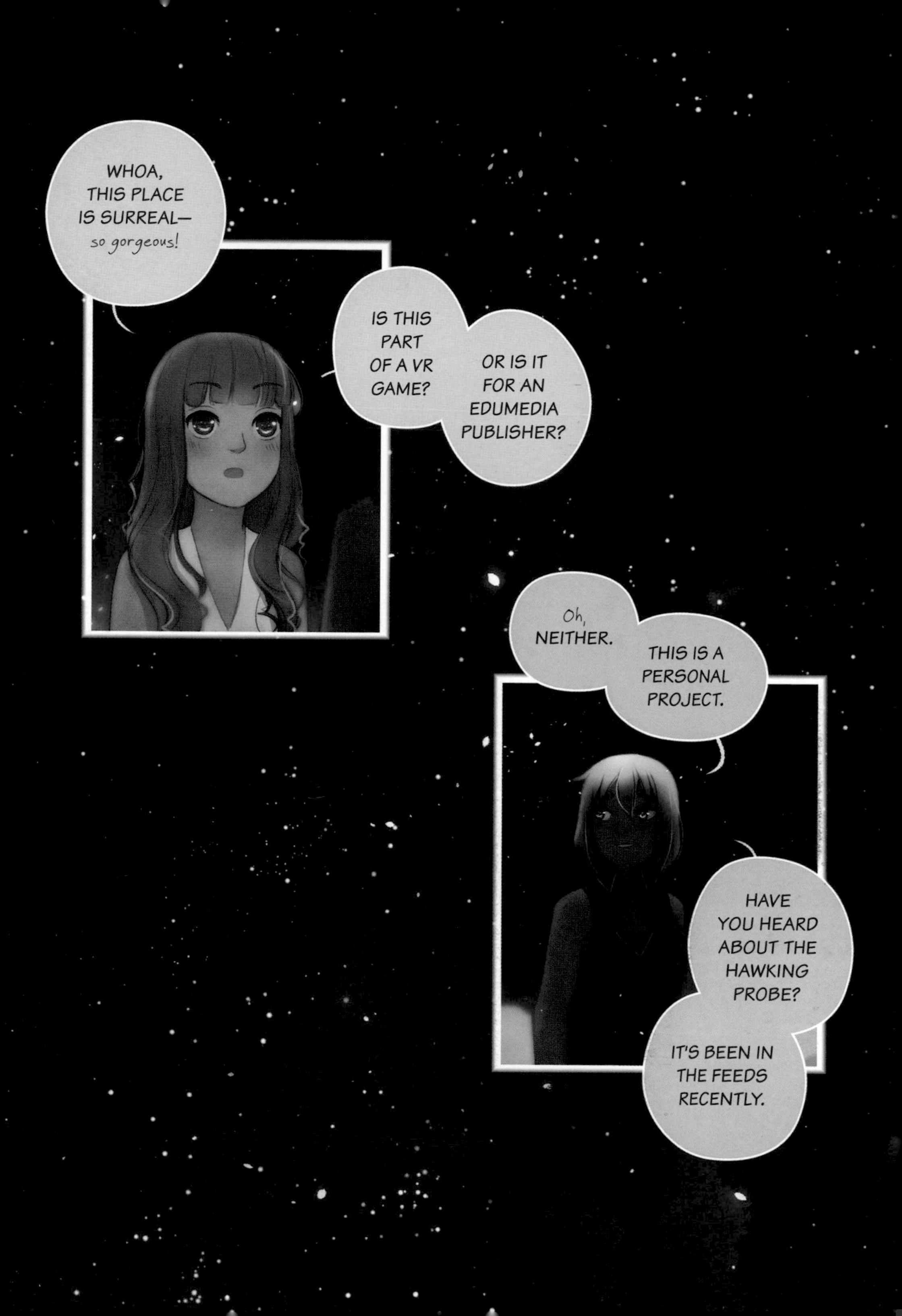
WHOA, THIS PLACE IS SURREAL— so gorgeous!
IS THIS PART OF A VR GAME?
OR IS IT FOR AN EDUMEDIA PUBLISHER?
Oh, NEITHER.
THIS IS A PERSONAL PROJECT.
HAVE YOU HEARD ABOUT THE HAWKING PROBE?
IT'S BEEN IN THE FEEDS RECENTLY.

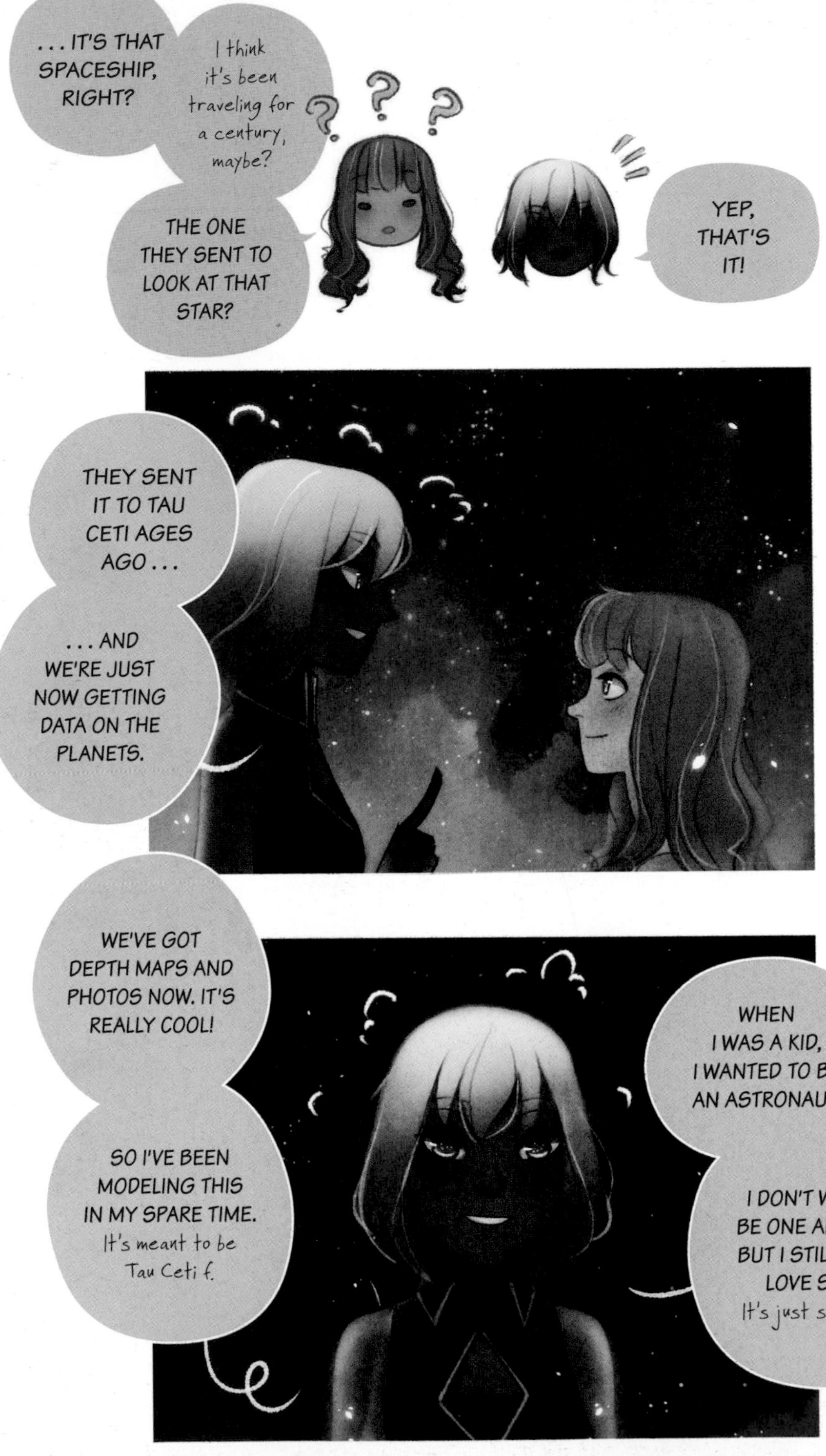
. . . IT'S THAT SPACESHIP, RIGHT?
I think it's been traveling for a century, maybe?
THE ONE THEY SENT TO LOOK AT THAT STAR?
YEP, THAT'S IT!
THEY SENT IT TO TAU CETI AGES AGO . . .
. . . AND WE'RE JUST NOW GETTING DATA ON THE PLANETS.
WE'VE GOT DEPTH MAPS AND PHOTOS NOW. IT'S REALLY COOL!
SO I'VE BEEN MODELING THIS IN MY SPARE TIME. It's meant to be Tau Ceti f.
WHEN I WAS A KID, I WANTED TO BE AN ASTRONAUT.
I DON'T WANT TO BE ONE ANYMORE, BUT I STILL REALLY LOVE SPACE. It's just so coooool!

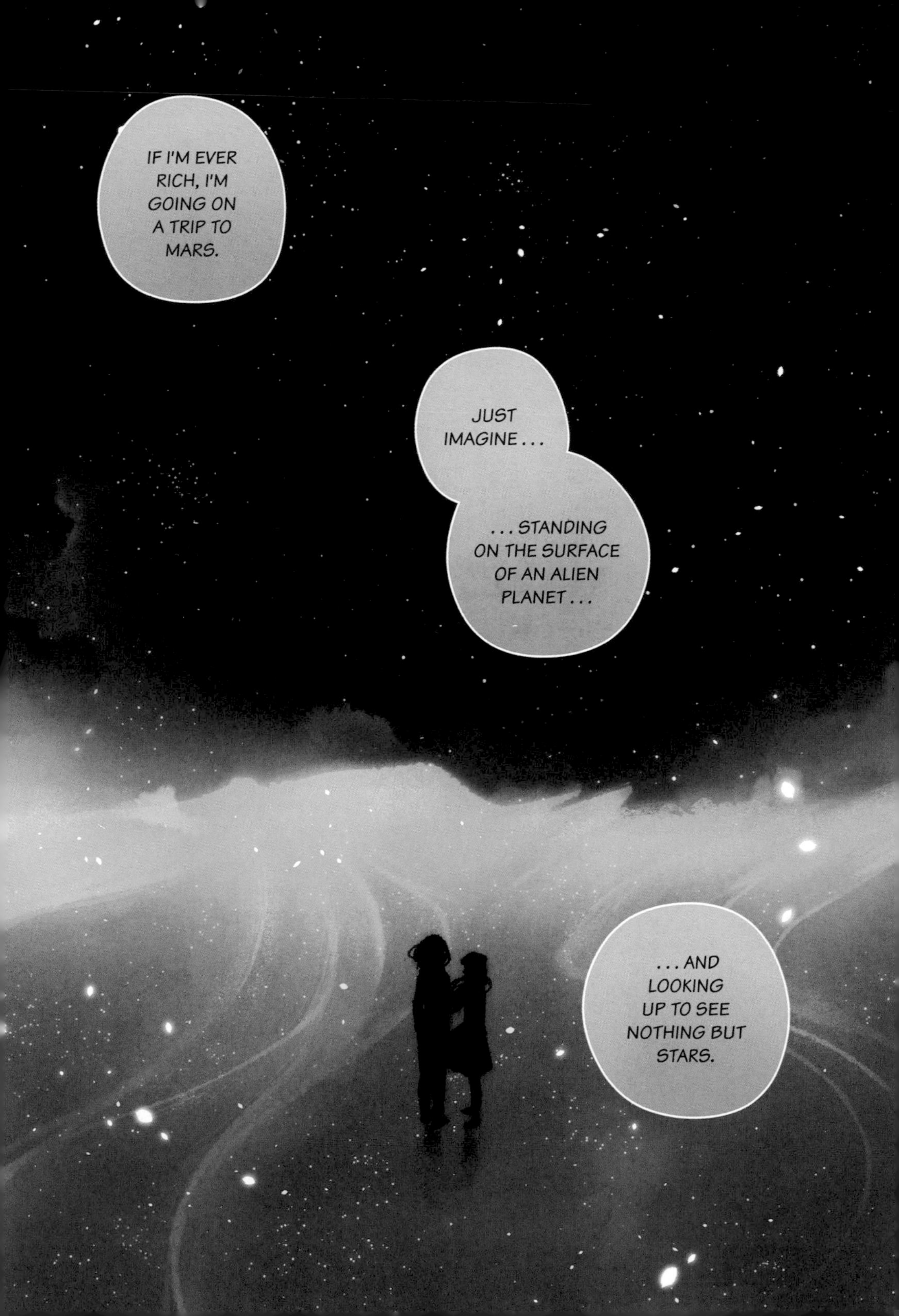
IF I'M EVER RICH, I'M GOING ON A TRIP TO MARS.
JUST IMAGINE . . .
. . . STANDING ON THE SURFACE OF AN ALIEN PLANET . . .
. . . AND LOOKING UP TO SEE NOTHING BUT STARS.

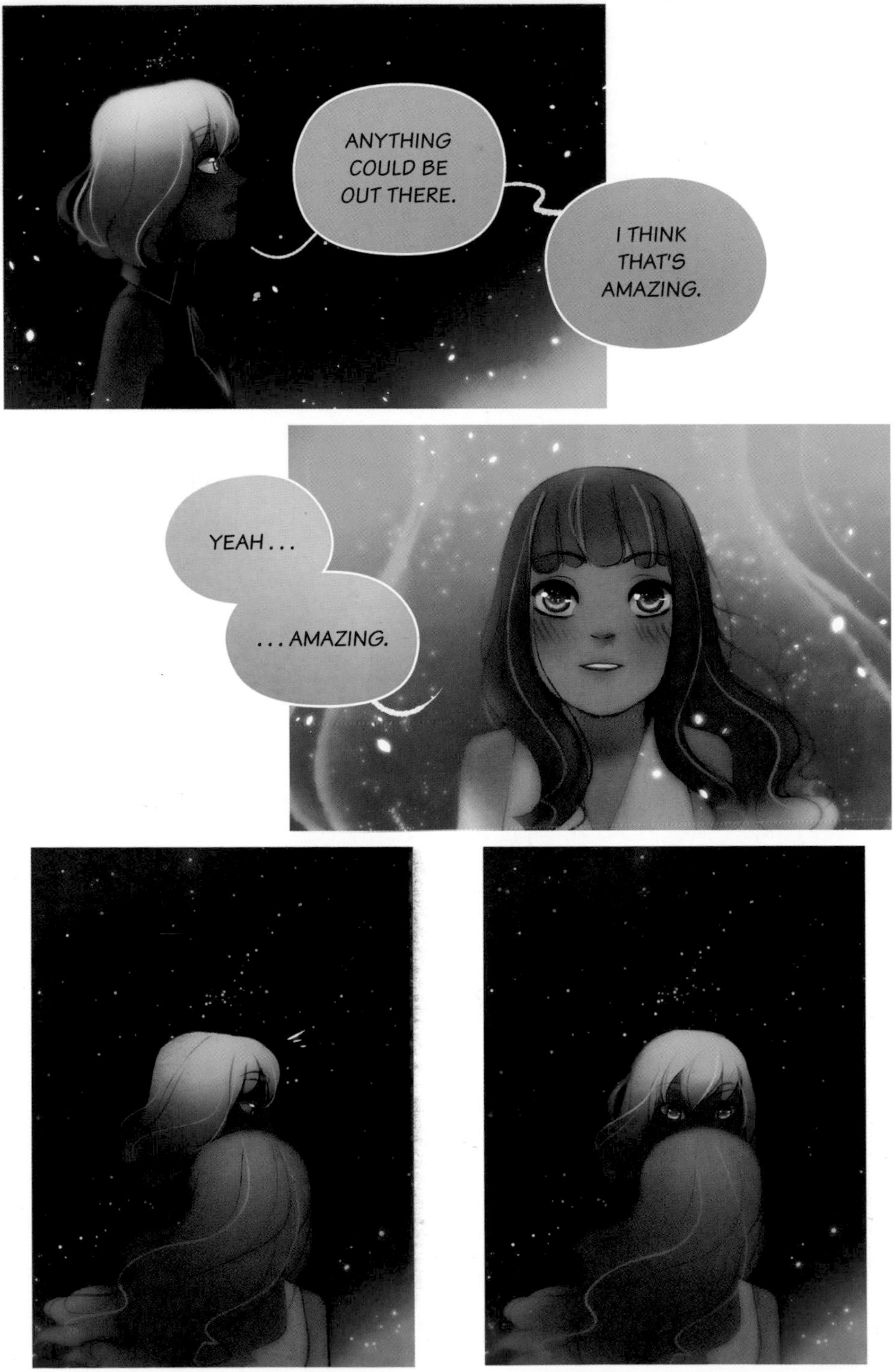
ANYTHING COULD BE OUT THERE.
I THINK THAT'S AMAZING.
YEAH . . .
. . . AMAZING.

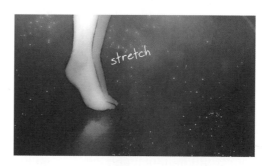

stretch

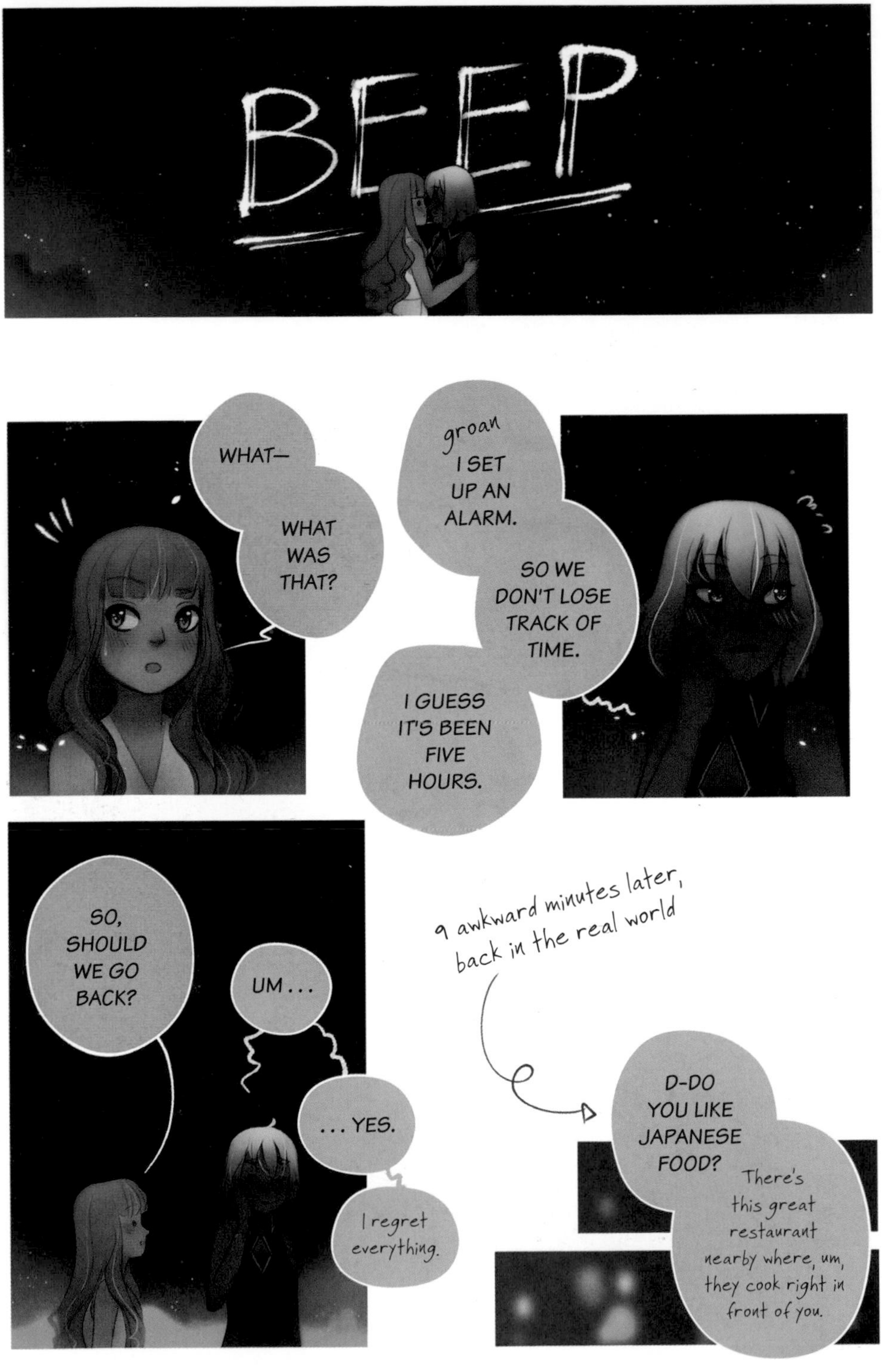
BEEP
WHAT—
WHAT WAS THAT?
groan
I SET UP AN ALARM.
SO WE DON'T LOSE TRACK OF TIME.
I GUESS IT'S BEEN FIVE HOURS.
SO, SHOULD WE GO BACK?
UM . . .
. . . YES.
I regret everything.
9 awkward minutes later, back in the real world
D-DO YOU LIKE JAPANESE FOOD?
There's this great restaurant nearby where, um, they cook right in front of you.

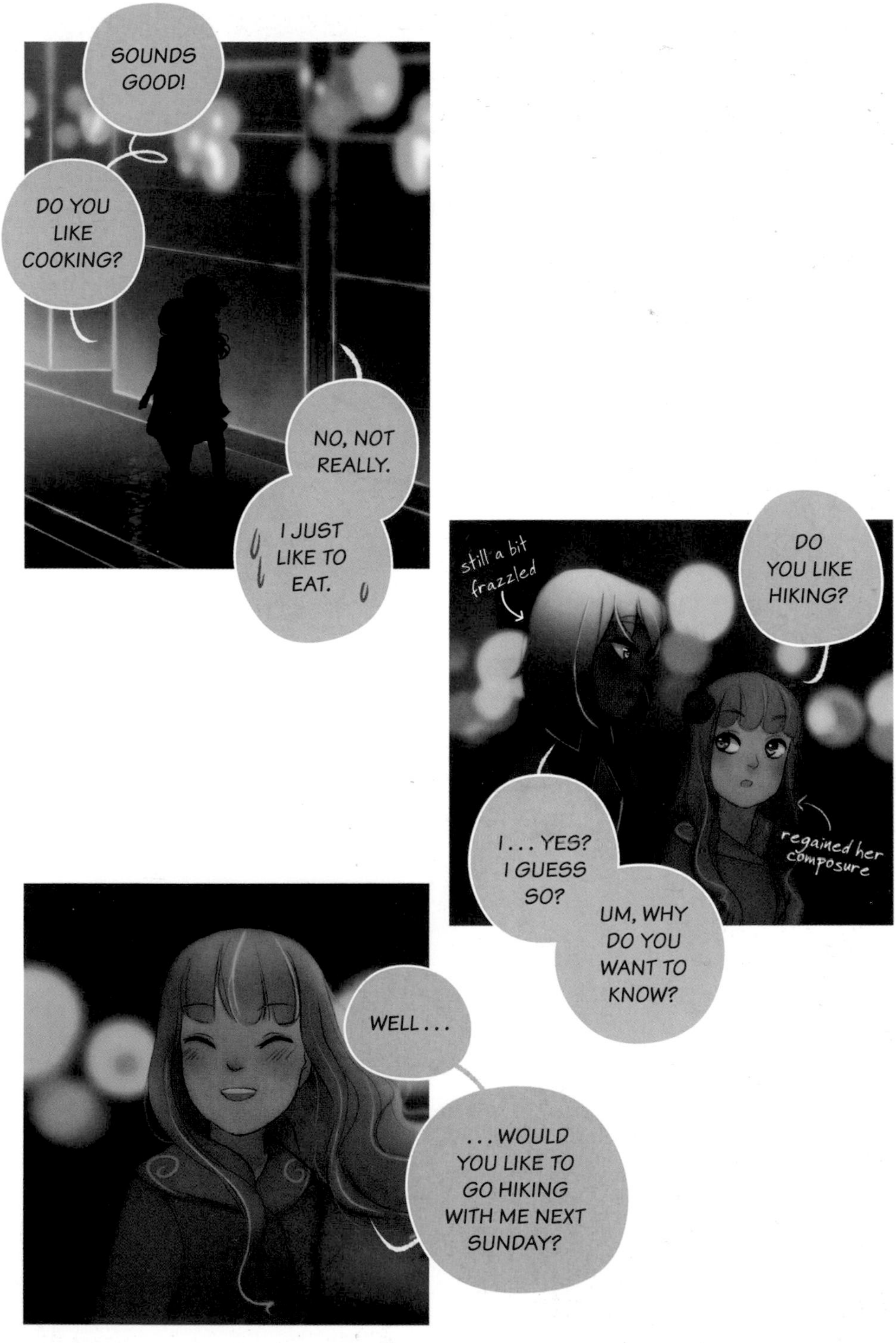
SOUNDS GOOD!
DO YOU LIKE COOKING?
NO, NOT REALLY.
I JUST LIKE TO EAT.
still a bit frazzled
DO YOU LIKE HIKING?
I . . . YES? I GUESS SO?
UM, WHY DO YOU WANT TO KNOW?
regained her composure
WELL . . .
. . . WOULD YOU LIKE TO GO HIKING WITH ME NEXT SUNDAY?

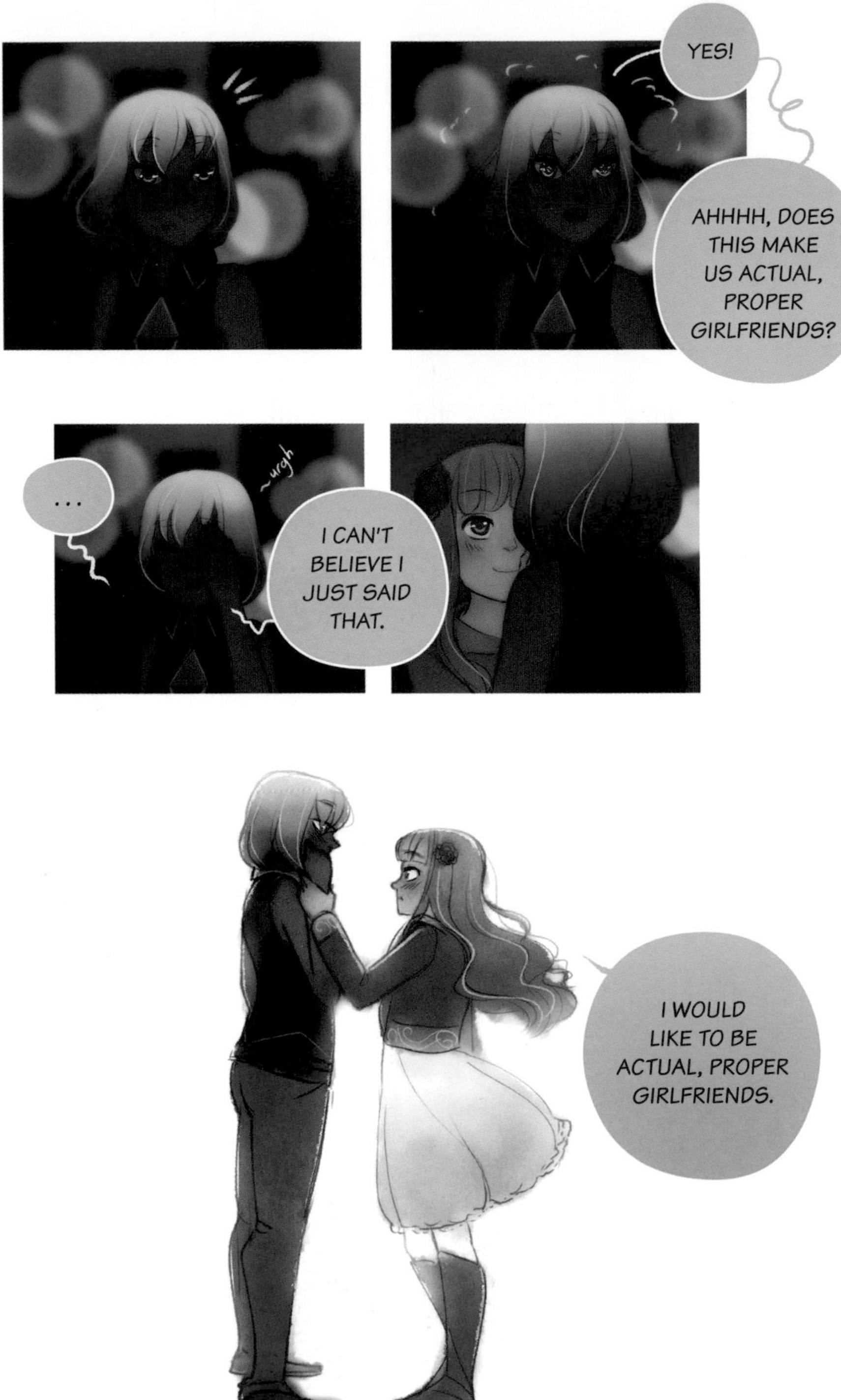
YES!
AHHHH, DOES THIS MAKE US ACTUAL, PROPER GIRLFRIENDS?
...
~urgh
I CAN'T BELIEVE I JUST SAID THAT.
I WOULD LIKE TO BE ACTUAL, PROPER GIRLFRIENDS.

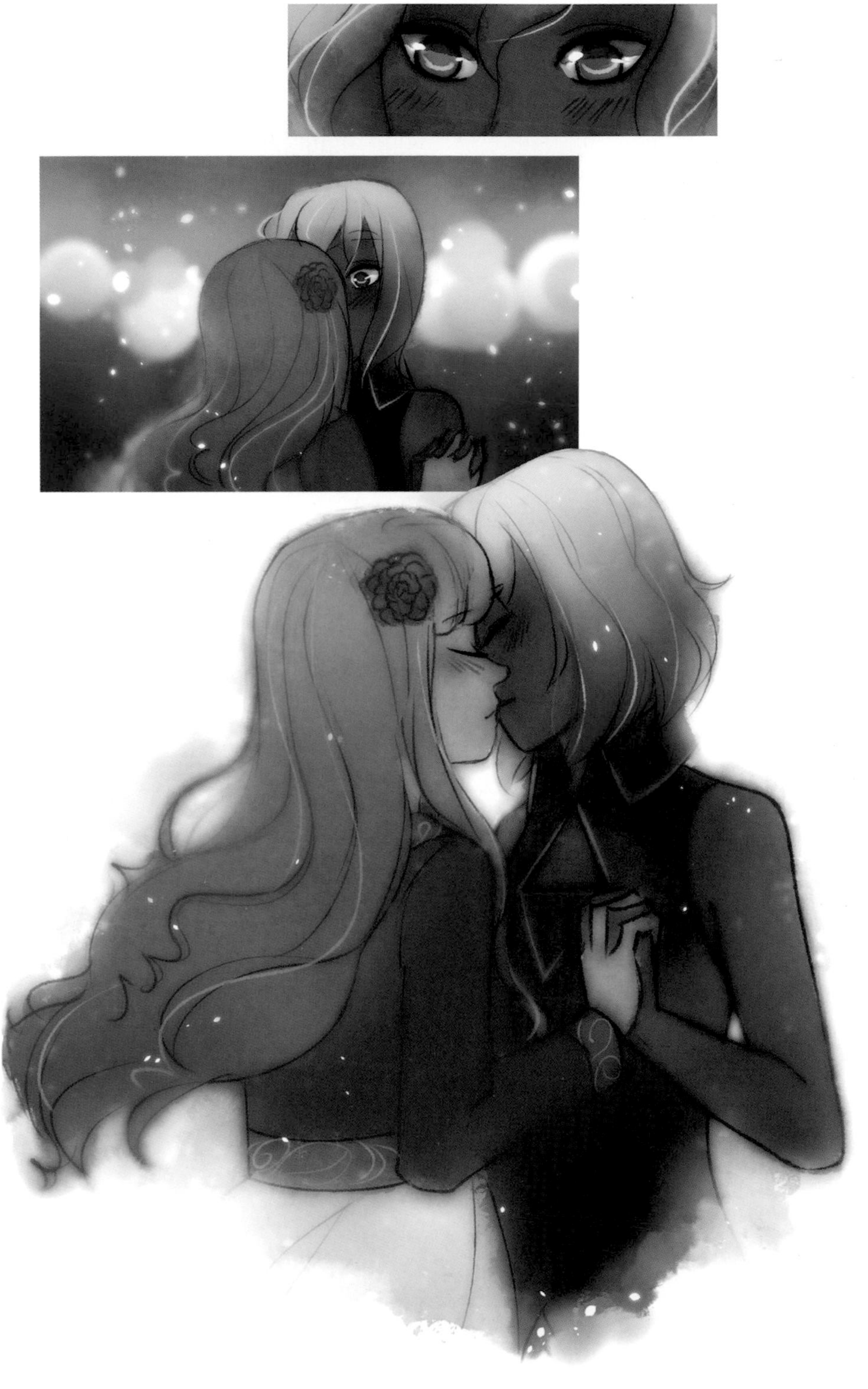

9 - FIRST IMPRESSIONS

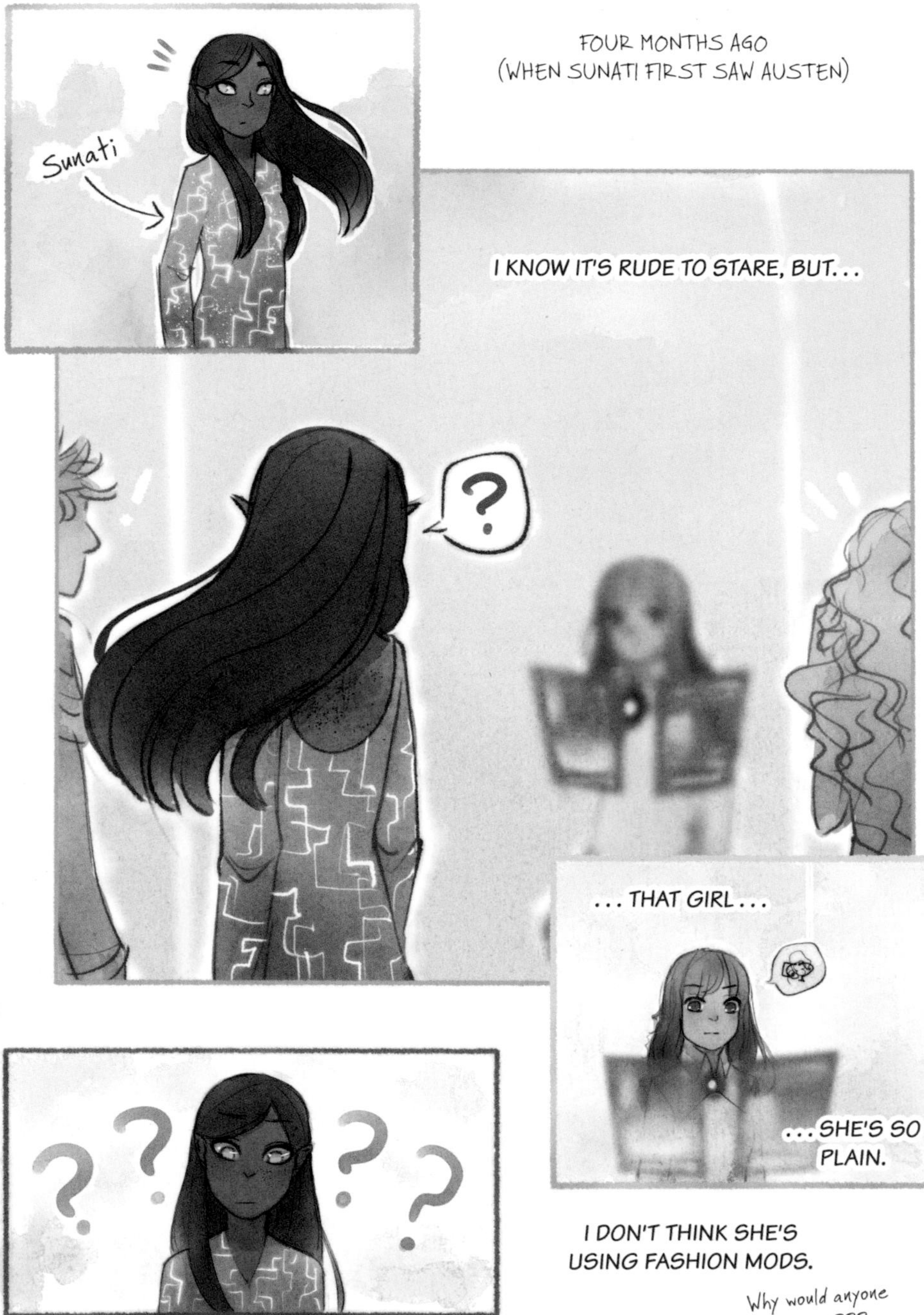
FOUR MONTHS AGO
(WHEN SUNATI FIRST SAW AUSTEN)
Sunati
I KNOW IT'S RUDE TO STARE, BUT...
?
...THAT GIRL...
...SHE'S SO PLAIN.
I DON'T THINK SHE'S USING FASHION MODS.
Why would anyone do that???

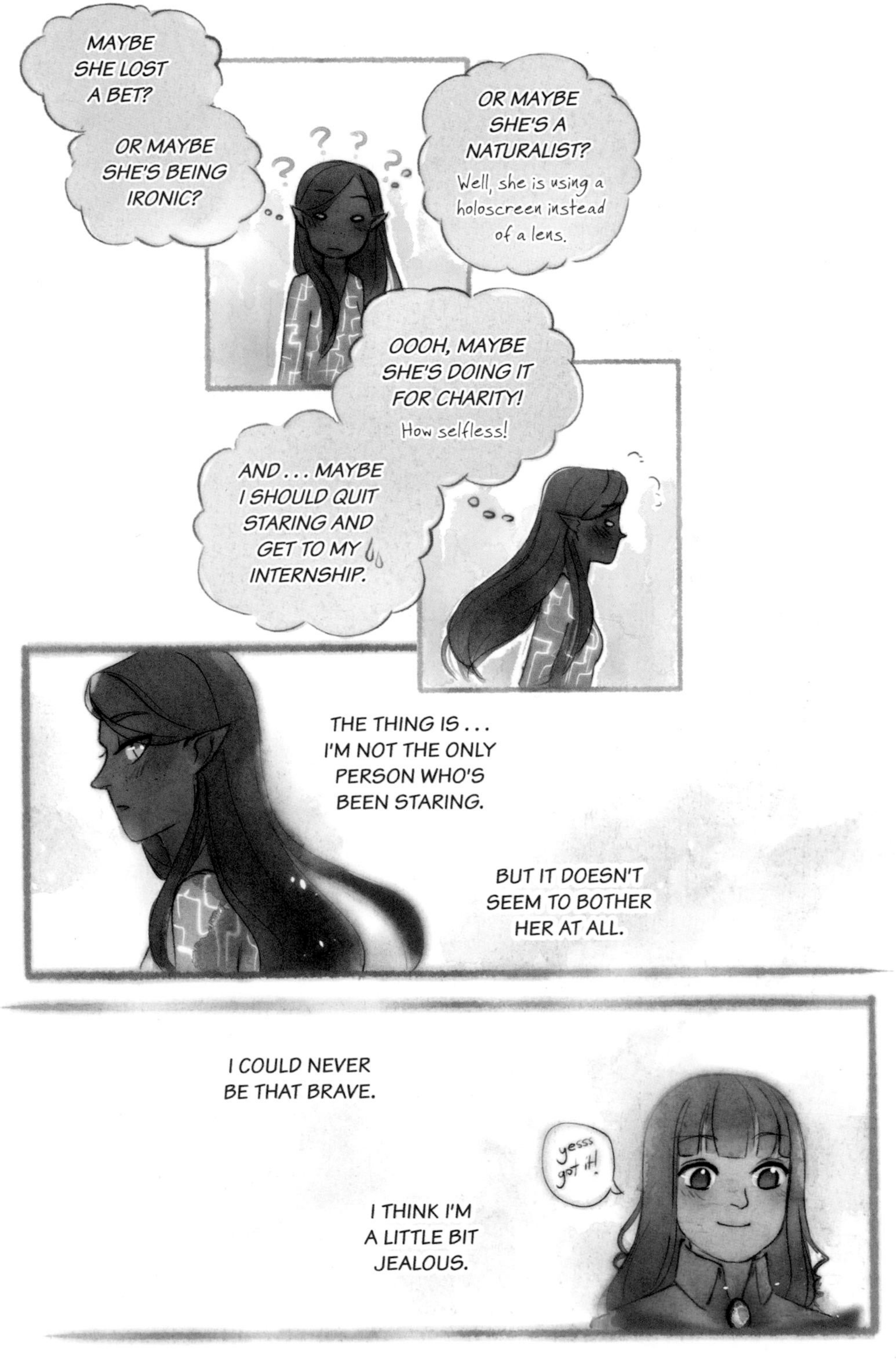
MAYBE SHE LOST A BET?
OR MAYBE SHE'S BEING IRONIC?
OR MAYBE SHE'S A NATURALIST?
Well, she is using a holoscreen instead of a lens.
OOOH, MAYBE SHE'S DOING IT FOR CHARITY!
How selfless!
AND . . . MAYBE I SHOULD QUIT STARING AND GET TO MY INTERNSHIP.
THE THING IS . . . I'M NOT THE ONLY PERSON WHO'S BEEN STARING.
BUT IT DOESN'T SEEM TO BOTHER HER AT ALL.
I COULD NEVER BE THAT BRAVE.
yesss got it!
I THINK I'M A LITTLE BIT JEALOUS.

THE NEXT DAY:

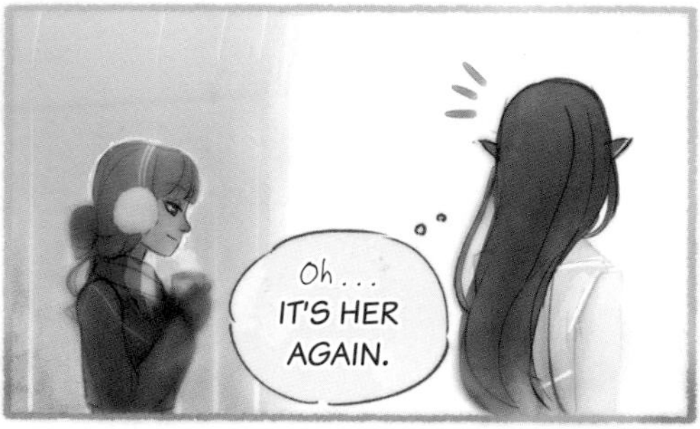
Oh . . .
IT'S HER AGAIN.

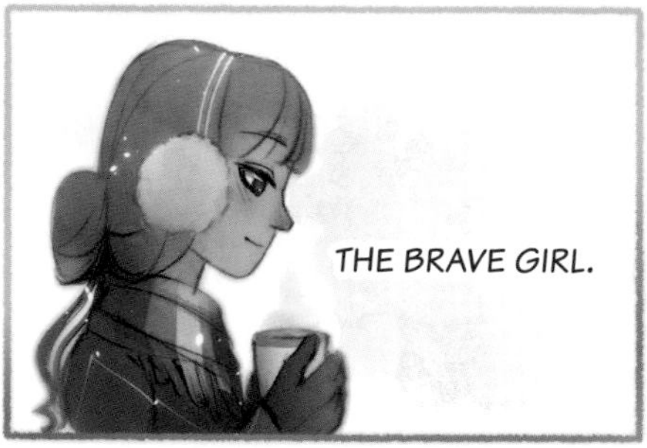
THE BRAVE GIRL.

I STILL DON'T UNDERSTAND WHAT SHE'S DOING.

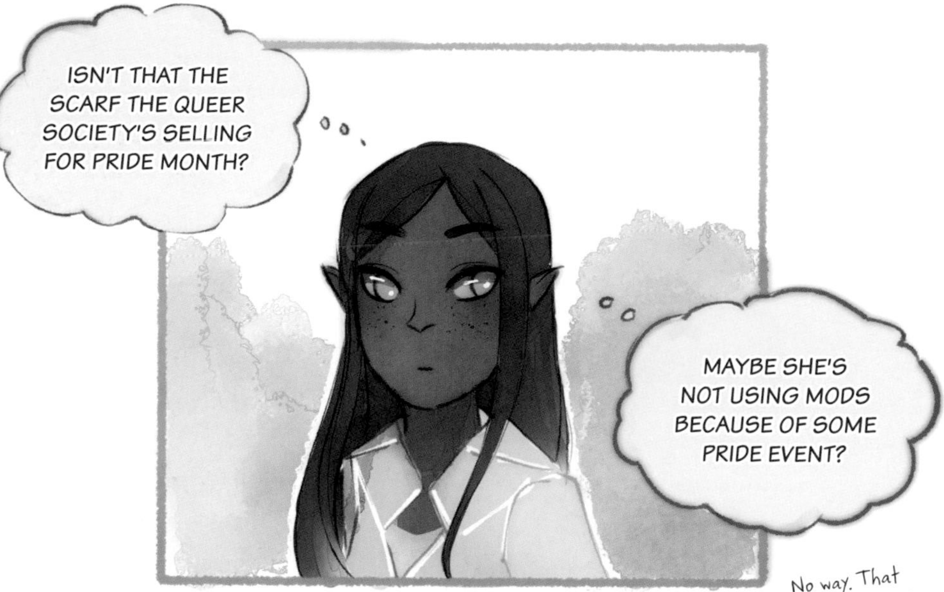
ISN'T THAT THE SCARF THE QUEER SOCIETY'S SELLING FOR PRIDE MONTH?
MAYBE SHE'S NOT USING MODS BECAUSE OF SOME PRIDE EVENT?

No way. That makes absolutely no sense.

WELL, WHATEVER THE REASON, GOOD FOR HER.

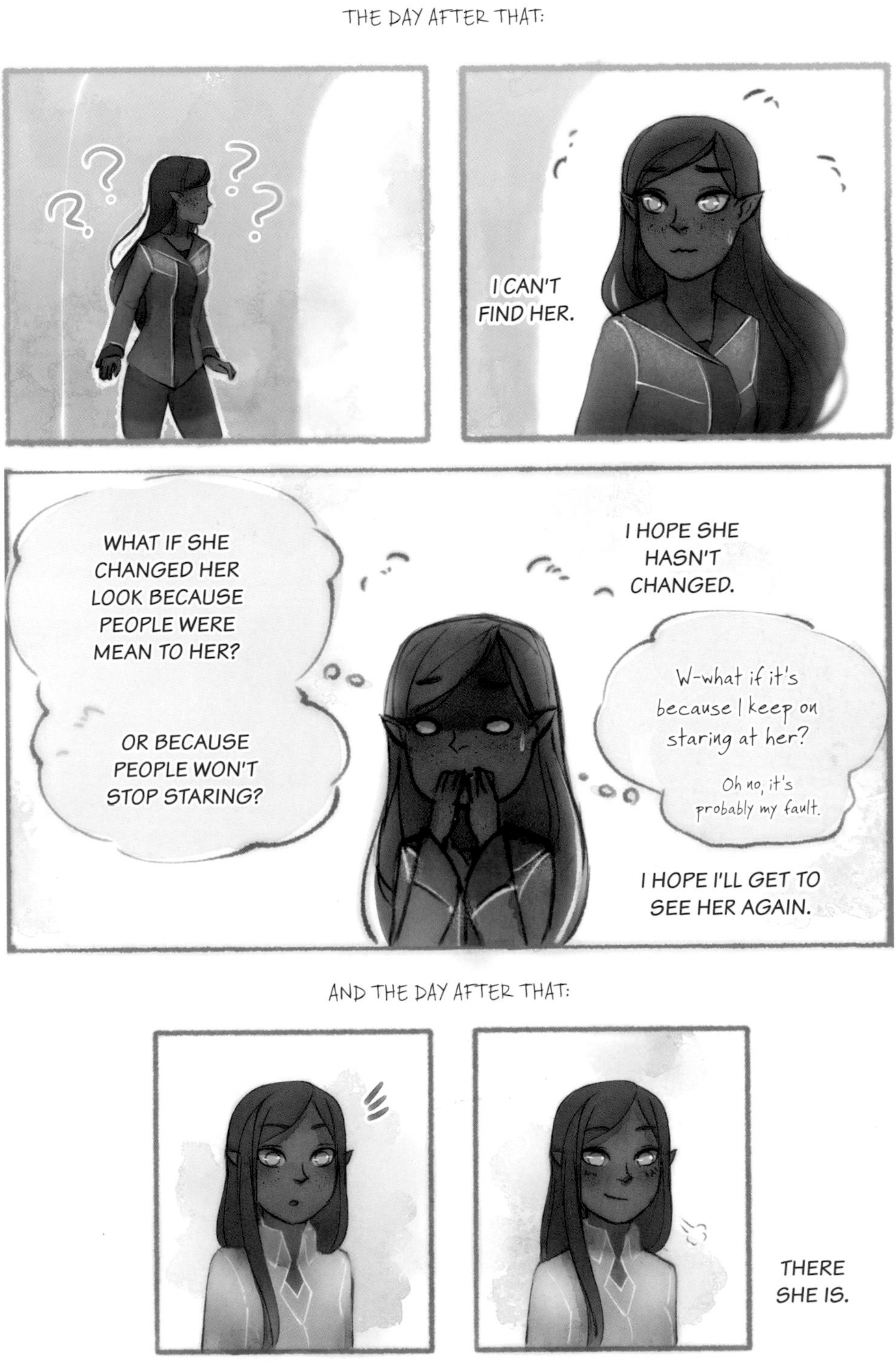
THE DAY AFTER THAT:
?
I CAN'T FIND HER.
WHAT IF SHE CHANGED HER LOOK BECAUSE PEOPLE WERE MEAN TO HER?
OR BECAUSE PEOPLE WON'T STOP STARING?
I HOPE SHE HASN'T CHANGED.
W-what if it's because I keep on staring at her?
Oh no, it's probably my fault.
I HOPE I'LL GET TO SEE HER AGAIN.
AND THE DAY AFTER THAT:
THERE SHE IS.

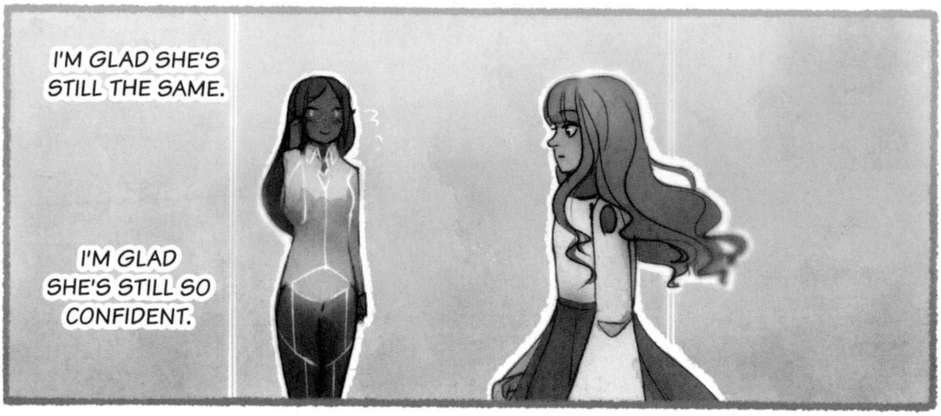
I'M GLAD SHE'S STILL THE SAME.
I'M GLAD SHE'S STILL SO CONFIDENT.

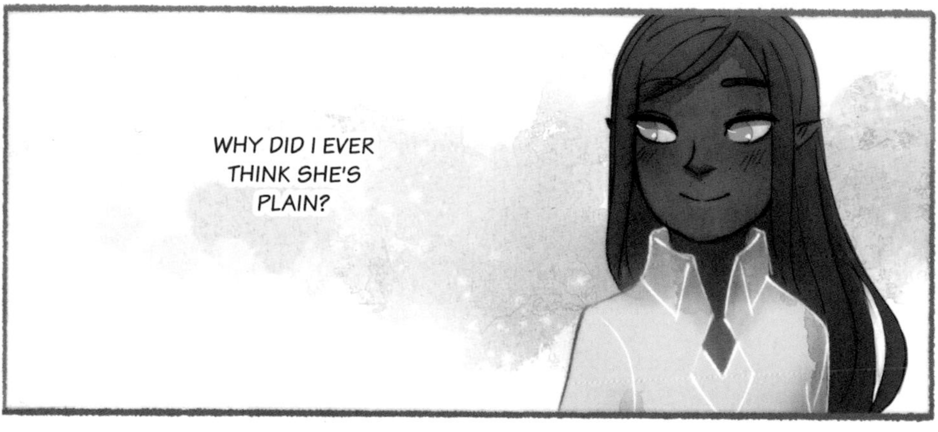
WHY DID I EVER THINK SHE'S PLAIN?

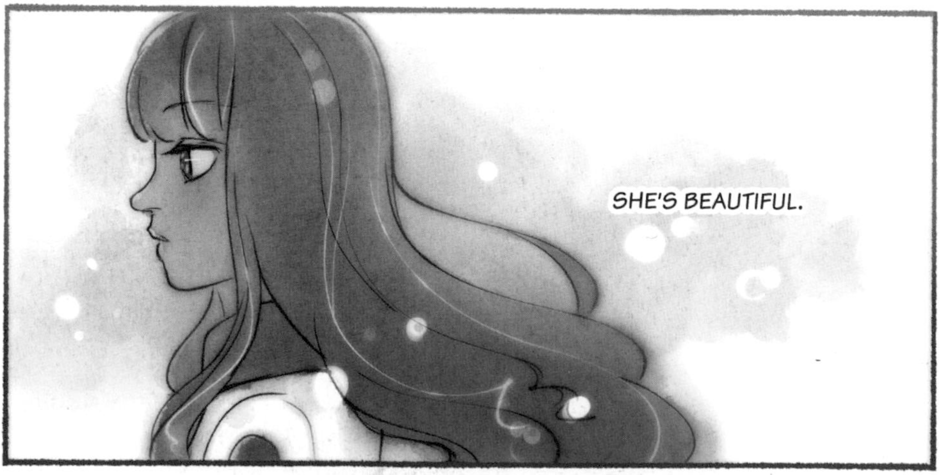
SHE'S BEAUTIFUL.

10 - YOU REALLY LIKE HER, DON'T YOU?

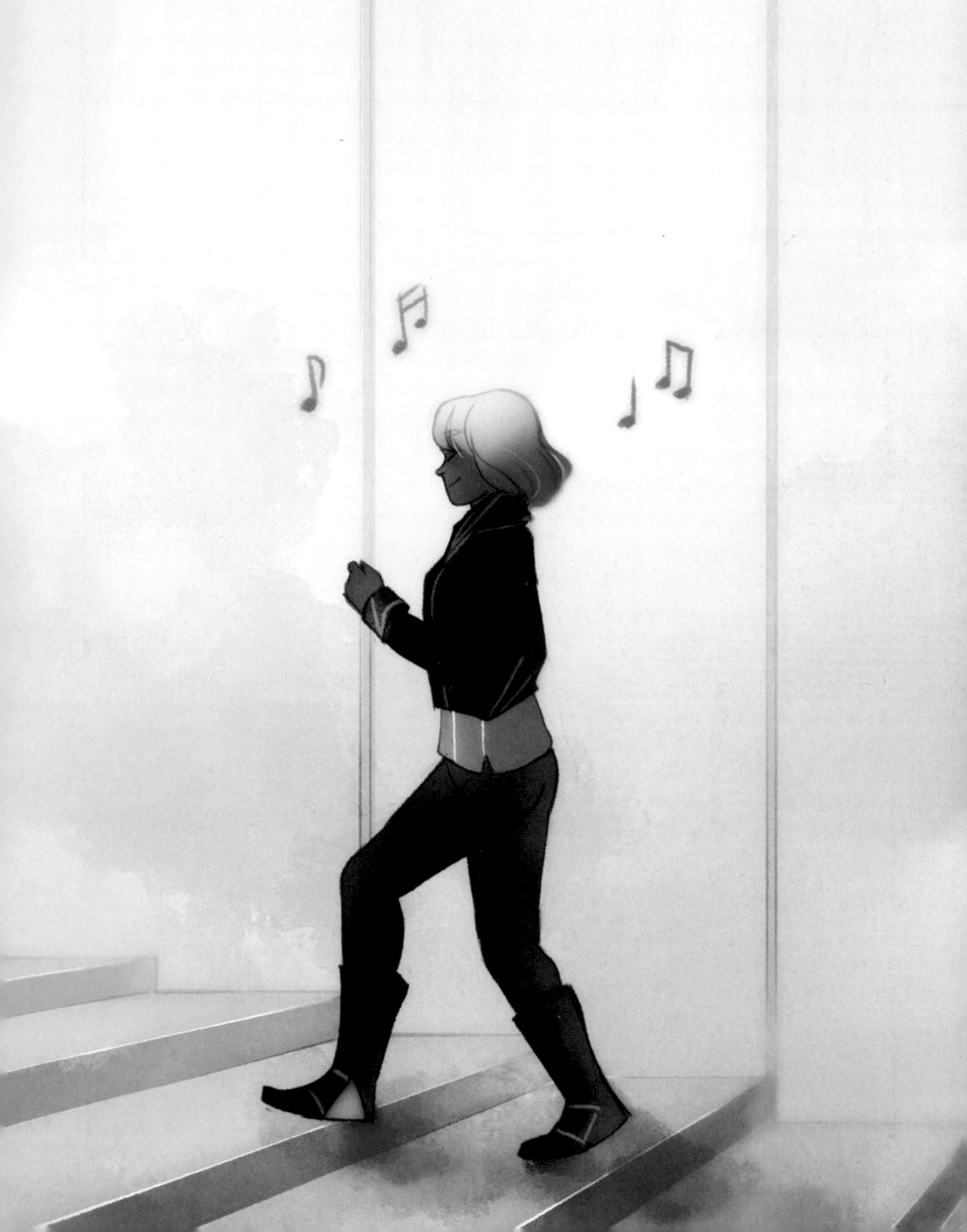

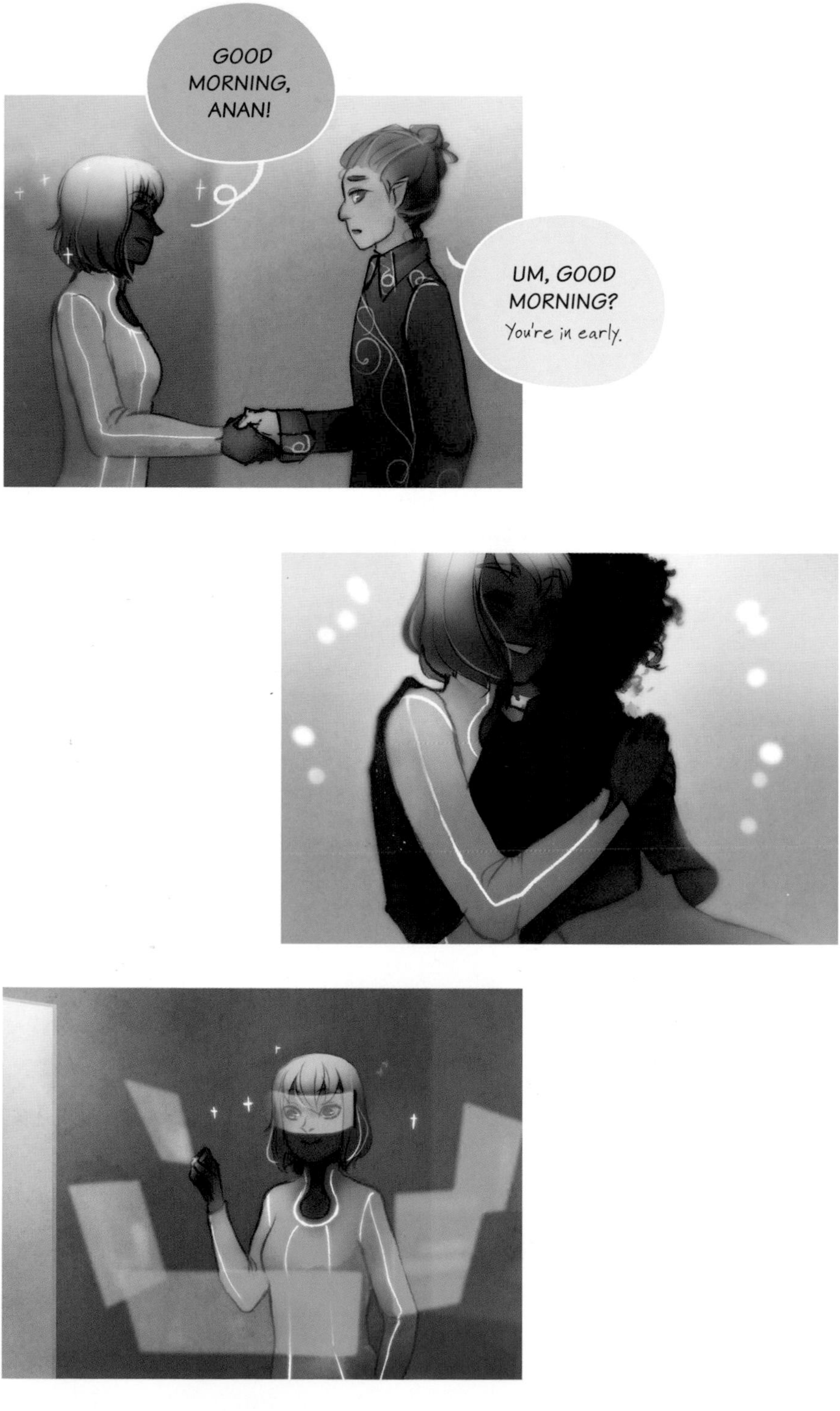
GOOD MORNING, ANAN!
UM, GOOD MORNING? You're in early.

HEY, SUNATI.
SOME OF US ARE COMING IN ON SUNDAY TO FINISH THE JNC PROJECT.
CAN YOU JOIN US?
SURE, OF COURSE, ORION!
WAIT, CRAP . . .
. . . SUNDAY ?????
OH NO OH NO ***OH NO.***

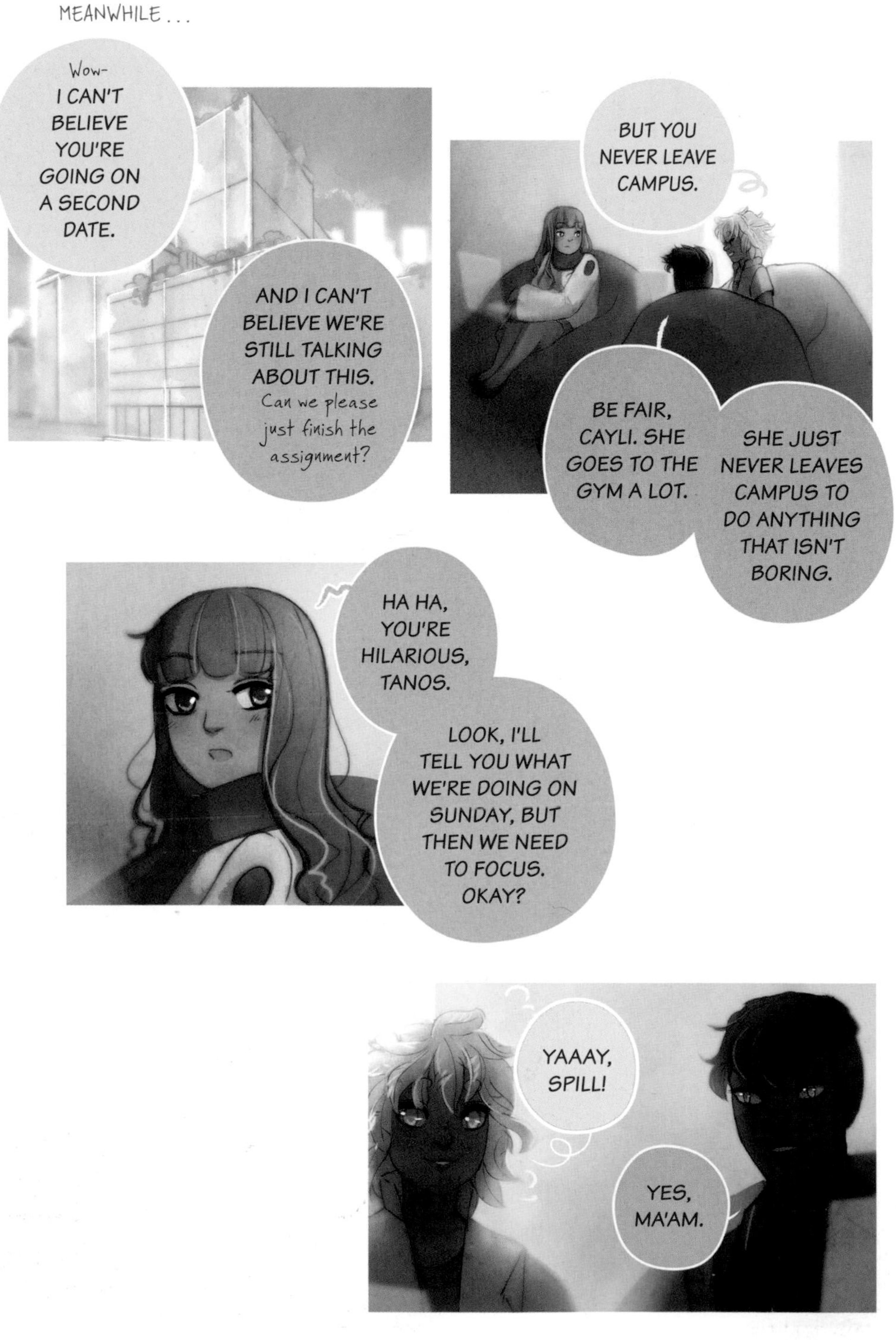
MEANWHILE . . .
Wow- I CAN'T BELIEVE YOU'RE GOING ON A SECOND DATE.
AND I CAN'T BELIEVE WE'RE STILL TALKING ABOUT THIS. Can we please just finish the assignment?
BUT YOU NEVER LEAVE CAMPUS.
BE FAIR, CAYLI. SHE GOES TO THE GYM A LOT.
SHE JUST NEVER LEAVES CAMPUS TO DO ANYTHING THAT ISN'T BORING.
HA HA, YOU'RE HILARIOUS, TANOS.
LOOK, I'LL TELL YOU WHAT WE'RE DOING ON SUNDAY, BUT THEN WE NEED TO FOCUS. OKAY?
YAAAY, SPILL!
YES, MA'AM.

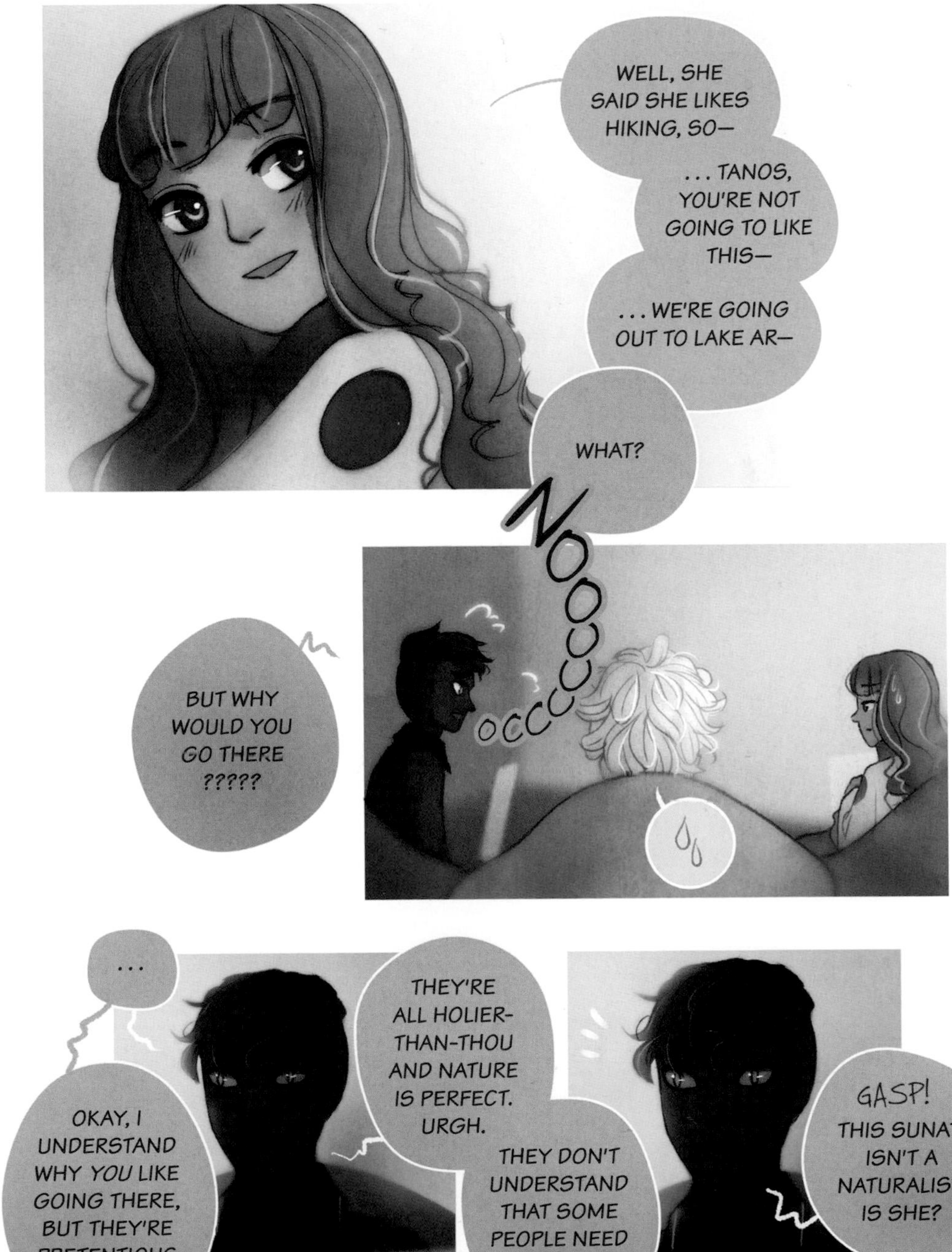
WELL, SHE SAID SHE LIKES HIKING, SO—
. . . TANOS, YOU'RE NOT GOING TO LIKE THIS—
. . . WE'RE GOING OUT TO LAKE AR—
WHAT?
NOOOOCCCCCC
BUT WHY WOULD YOU GO THERE ?????
. . .
OKAY, I UNDERSTAND WHY *YOU* LIKE GOING THERE, BUT THEY'RE PRETENTIOUS JERKS.
THEY'RE ALL HOLIER-THAN-THOU AND NATURE IS PERFECT. URGH.
THEY DON'T UNDERSTAND THAT SOME PEOPLE NEED MODS.
GASP!
THIS SUNATI ISN'T A NATURALIST, IS SHE?

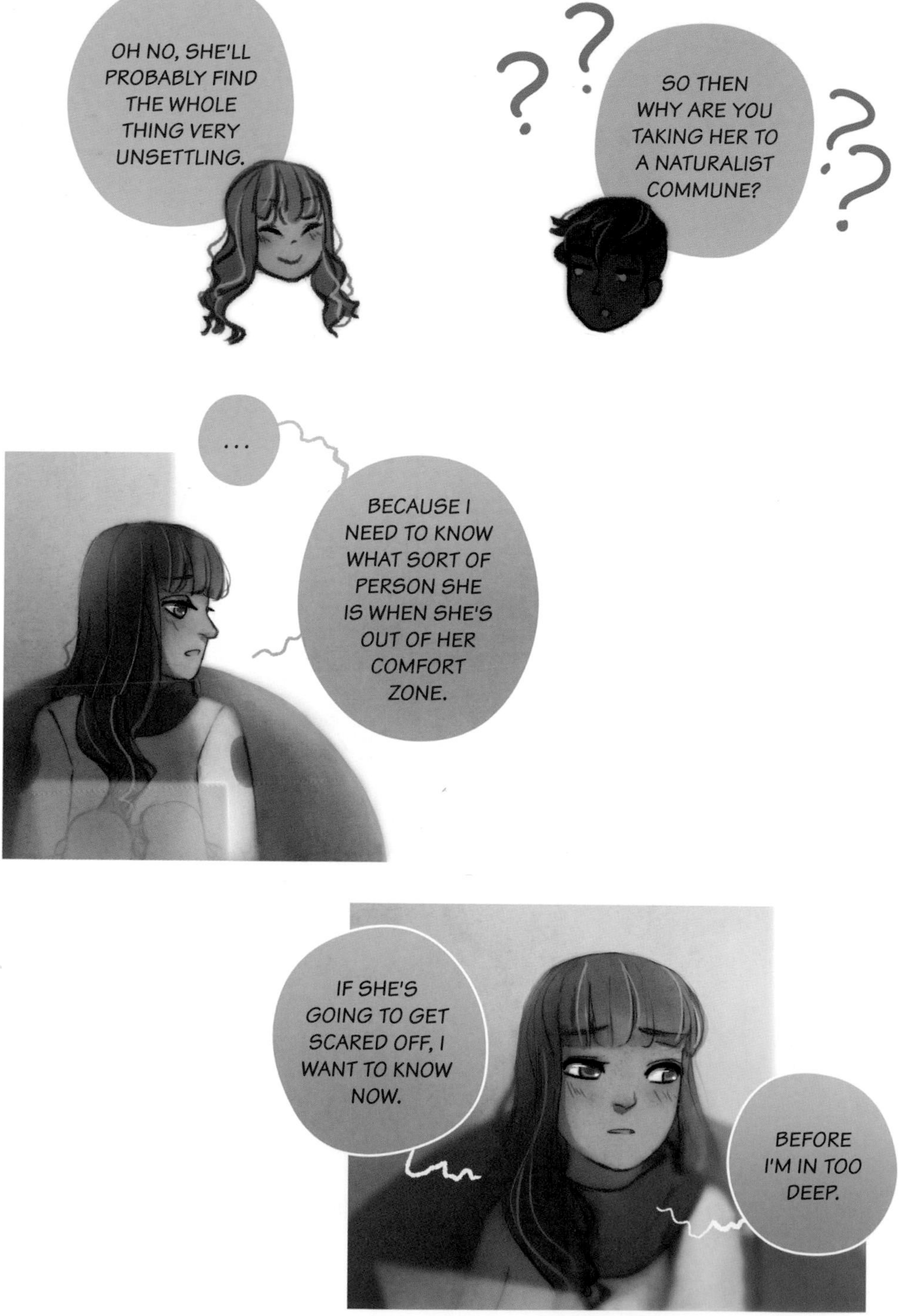
OH NO, SHE'LL PROBABLY FIND THE WHOLE THING VERY UNSETTLING.
SO THEN WHY ARE YOU TAKING HER TO A NATURALIST COMMUNE?
...
BECAUSE I NEED TO KNOW WHAT SORT OF PERSON SHE IS WHEN SHE'S OUT OF HER COMFORT ZONE.
IF SHE'S GOING TO GET SCARED OFF, I WANT TO KNOW NOW.
BEFORE I'M IN TOO DEEP.

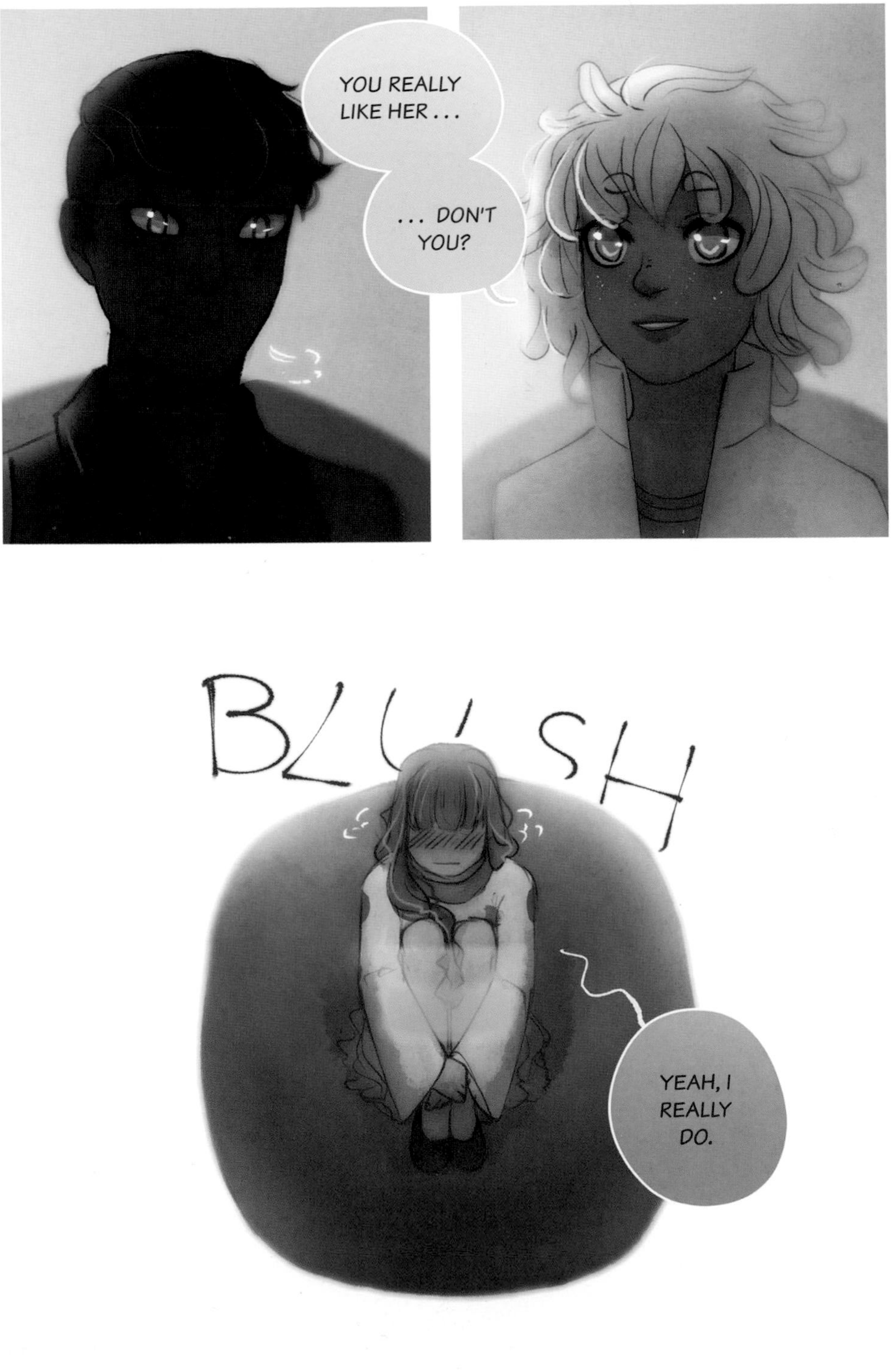
YOU REALLY LIKE HER . . .
. . . DON'T YOU?
BLUSH
YEAH, I REALLY DO.

CRAP CRAP CRAPPITY CRAP, WHAT SHOULD I DOOOOO?

WHAT SHOULD I SAY?

"WHOOPS, SORRY. I KNOW I SAID YES AND I KNOW THIS IS A REALLY IMPORTANT PROJECT, BUT I WANT TO GO ON A DATE INSTEAD"?

Nooo, I can't do that. That's so selfish.

I COULD ASK RAE FOR HELP?

...Augh, THAT WOULD BE MORE SELFISH.

MAYBE I SHOULD TRY TALKING TO AUSTEN?

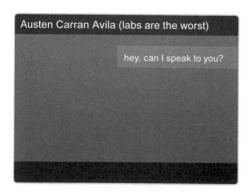

Austen Carran Avila (labs are the worst)

hey, can I speak to you?

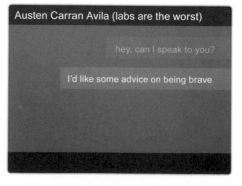

Austen Carran Avila (labs are the worst)

hey, can I speak to you?

I'd like some advice on being brave

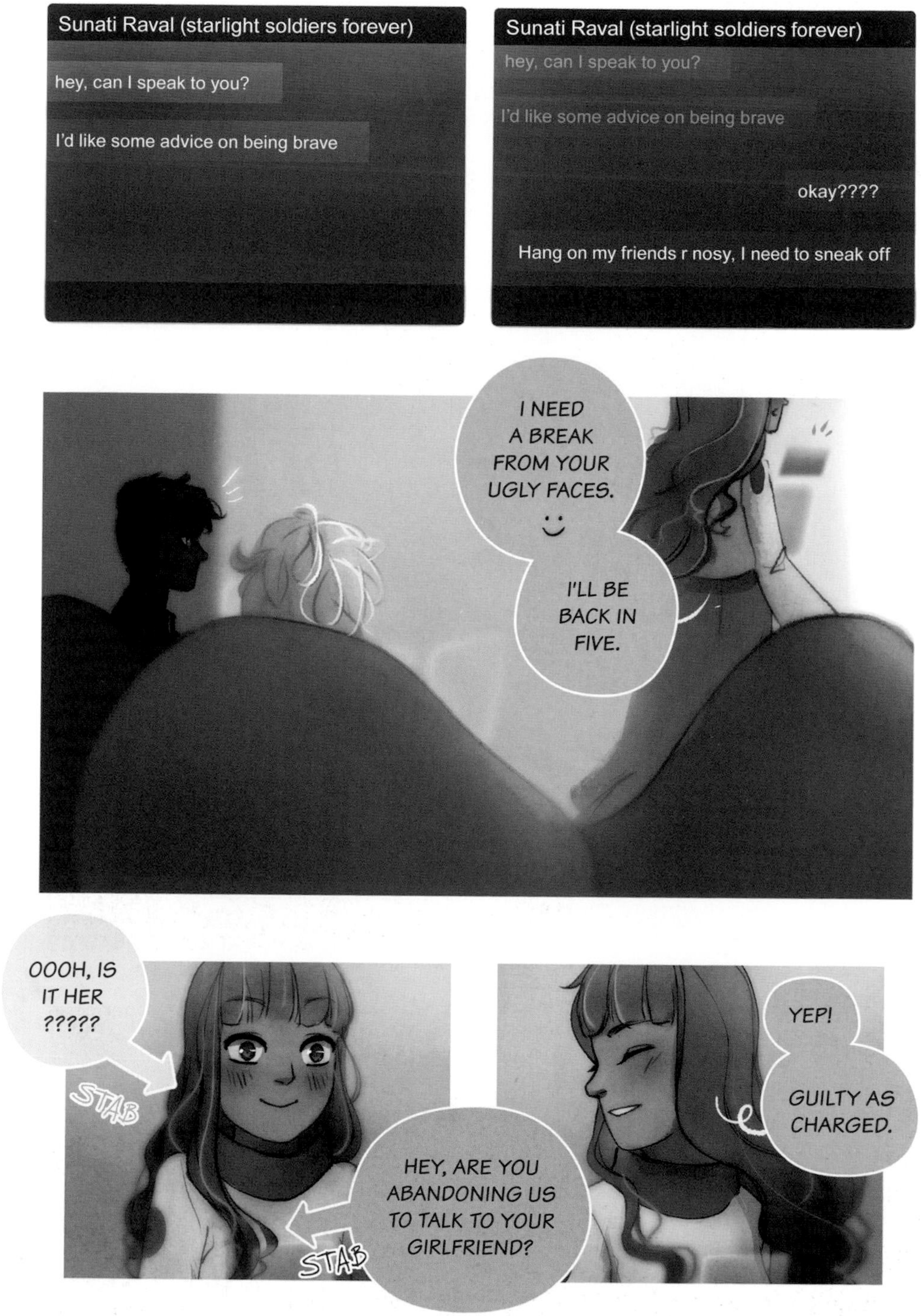
Sunati Raval (starlight soldiers forever)
hey, can I speak to you?
I'd like some advice on being brave
Sunati Raval (starlight soldiers forever)
hey, can I speak to you?
I'd like some advice on being brave
okay????
Hang on my friends r nosy, I need to sneak off
I NEED A BREAK FROM YOUR UGLY FACES. :)
I'LL BE BACK IN FIVE.
OOOH, IS IT HER ?????
STAB
HEY, ARE YOU ABANDONING US TO TALK TO YOUR GIRLFRIEND?
STAB
YEP!
GUILTY AS CHARGED.

11 - I GIVE YOU PERMISSION TO BE SELFISH

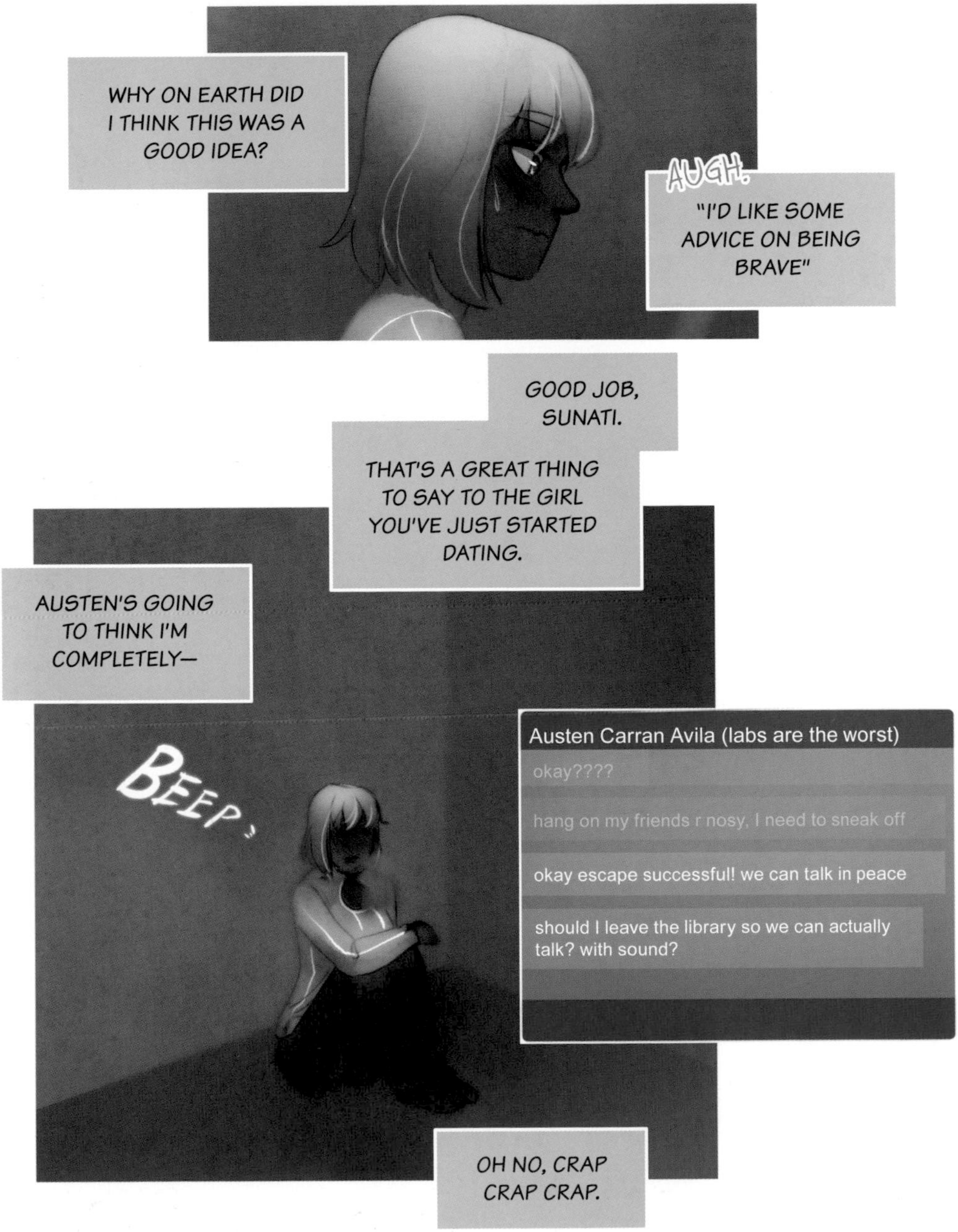

WHY ON EARTH DID I THINK THIS WAS A GOOD IDEA?
AUGH.
"I'D LIKE SOME ADVICE ON BEING BRAVE"
GOOD JOB, SUNATI.
THAT'S A GREAT THING TO SAY TO THE GIRL YOU'VE JUST STARTED DATING.
AUSTEN'S GOING TO THINK I'M COMPLETELY—
BEEP
Austen Carran Avila (labs are the worst)
okay????
hang on my friends r nosy, I need to sneak off
okay escape successful! we can talk in peace
should I leave the library so we can actually talk? with sound?
OH NO, CRAP CRAP CRAP.

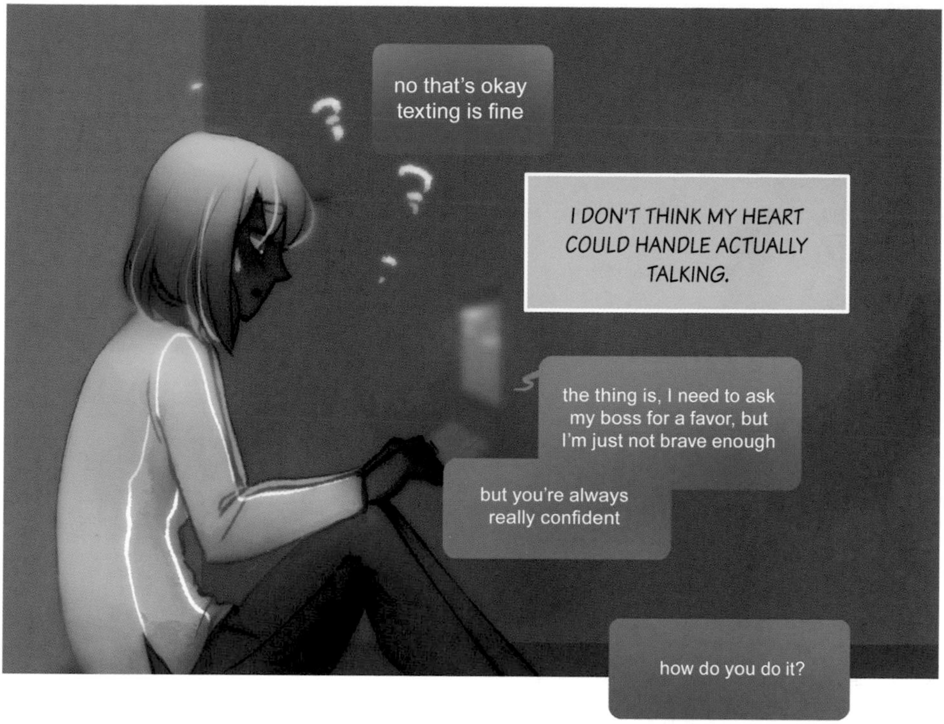
no that's okay
texting is fine
I DON'T THINK MY HEART COULD HANDLE ACTUALLY TALKING.
the thing is, I need to ask my boss for a favor, but I'm just not brave enough
but you're always really confident
how do you do it?

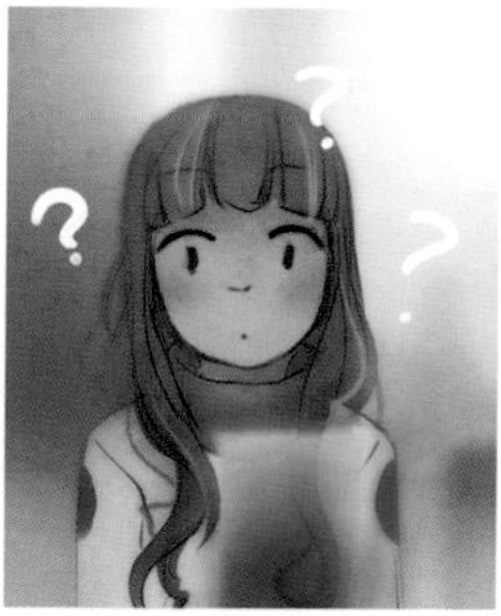

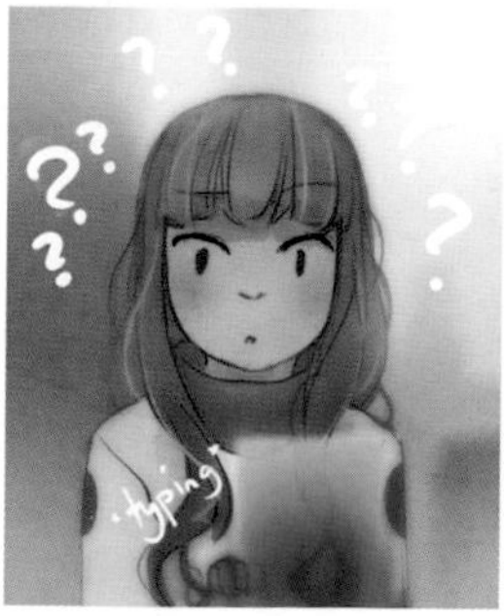
typing

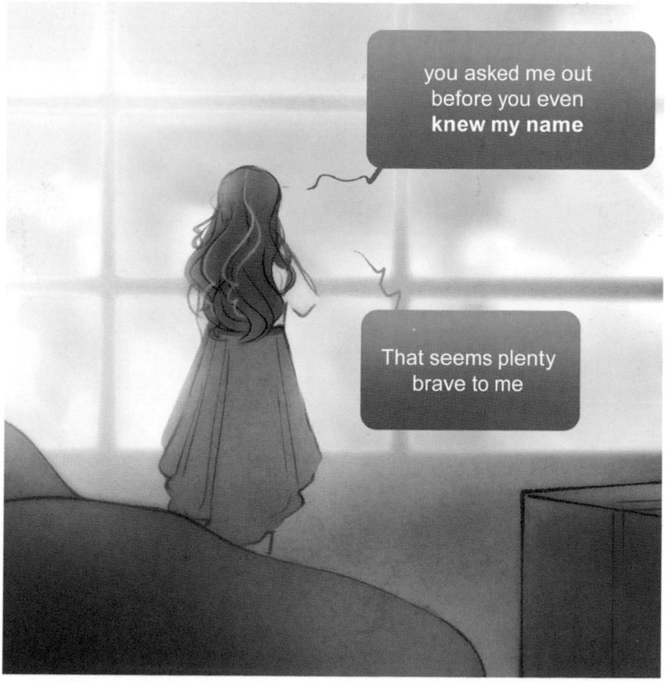
you asked me out before you even **knew my name**
That seems plenty brave to me

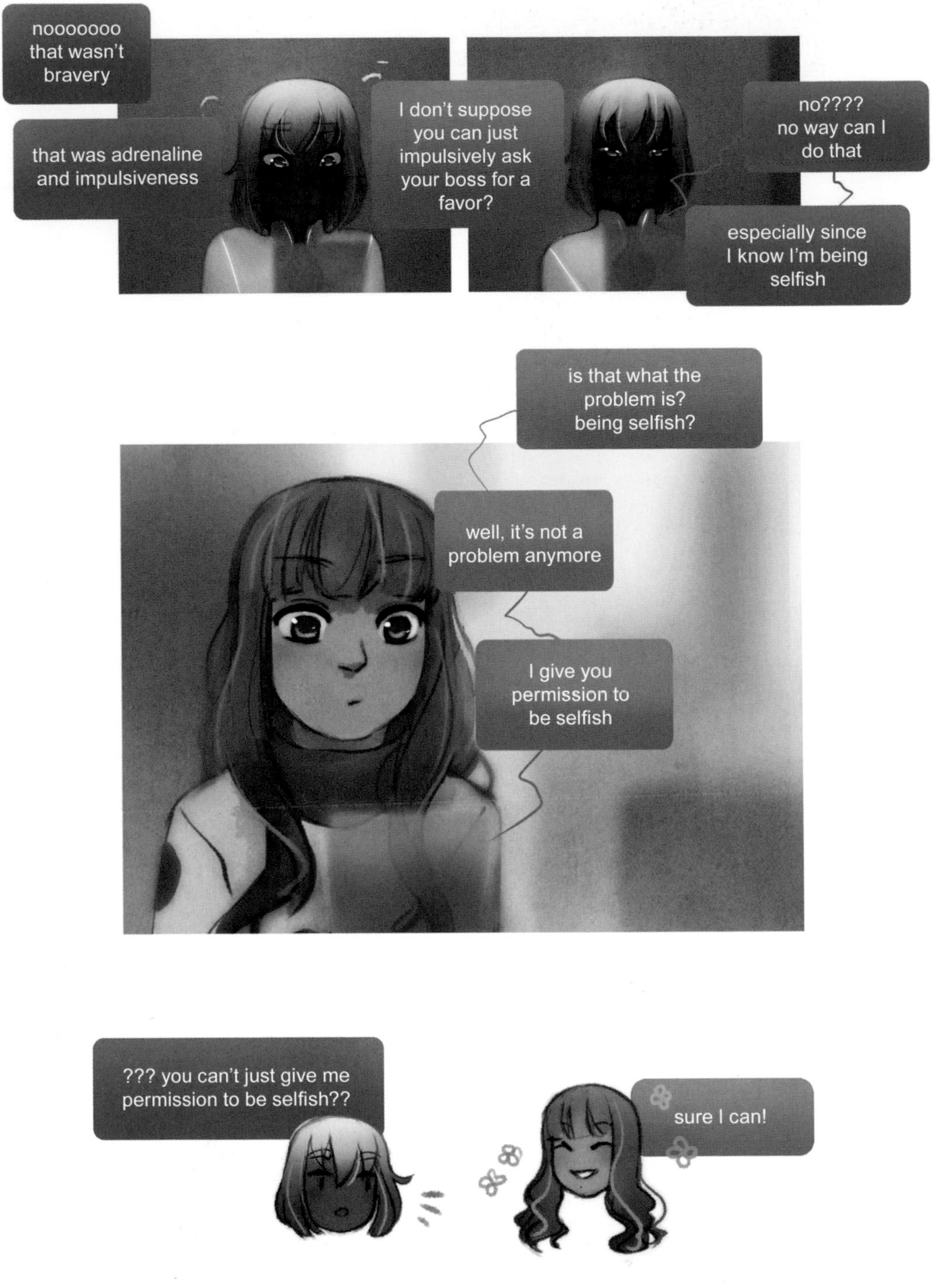
nooooooo that wasn't bravery
that was adrenaline and impulsiveness
I don't suppose you can just impulsively ask your boss for a favor?
no???? no way can I do that
especially since I know I'm being selfish
is that what the problem is? being selfish?
well, it's not a problem anymore
I give you permission to be selfish
??? you can't just give me permission to be selfish??
sure I can!

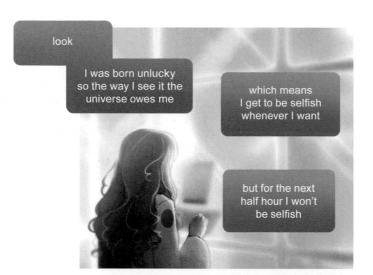

look

I was born unlucky so the way I see it the universe owes me

which means I get to be selfish whenever I want

but for the next half hour I won't be selfish

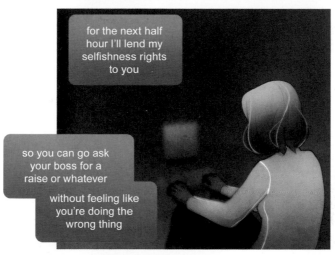

for the next half hour I'll lend my selfishness rights to you

so you can go ask your boss for a raise or whatever

without feeling like you're doing the wrong thing

can you do that?

yeah, I think I can!

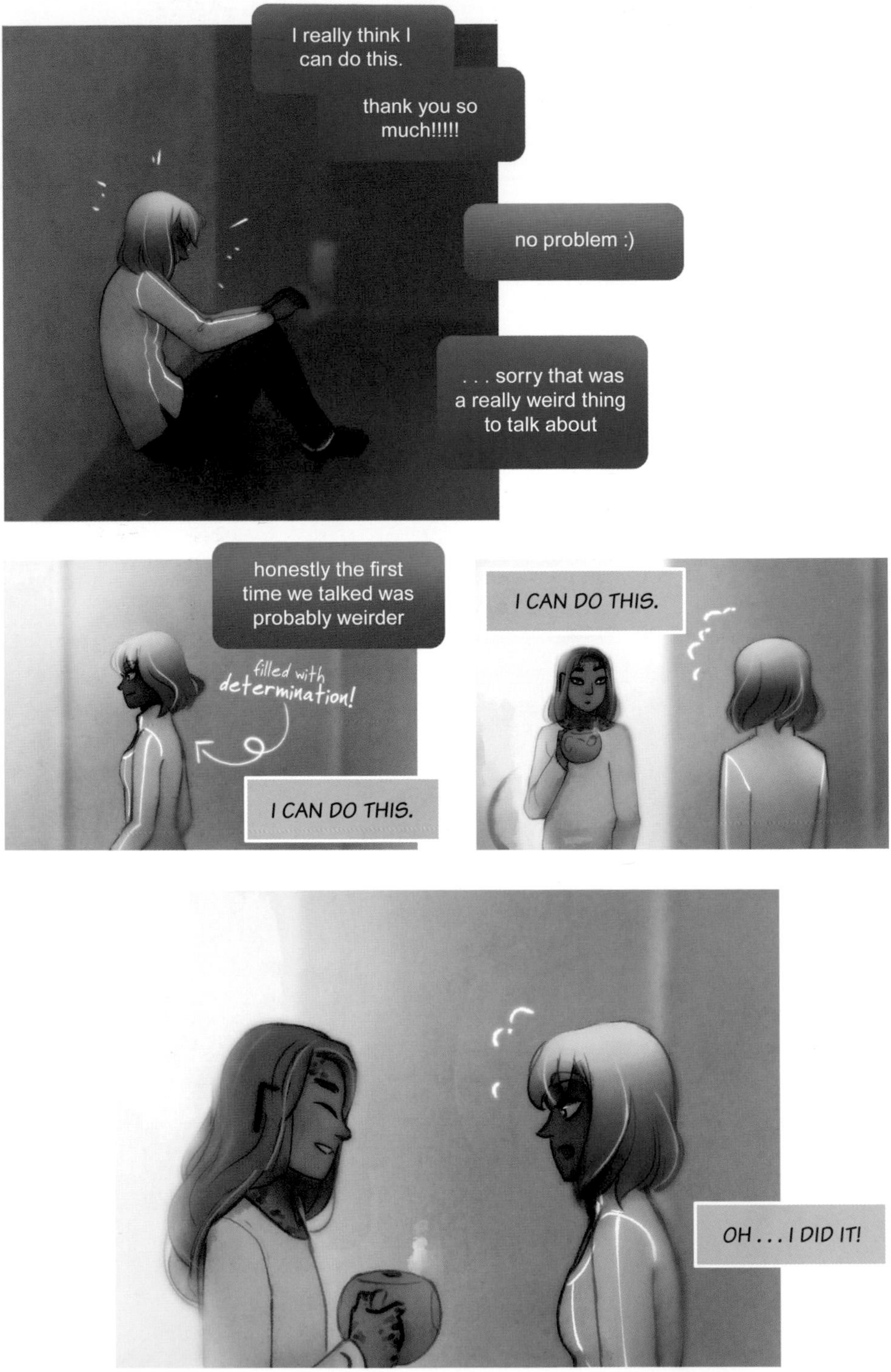
I really think I can do this.
thank you so much!!!!!
no problem :)
. . . sorry that was a really weird thing to talk about
honestly the first time we talked was probably weirder
filled with determination!
I CAN DO THIS.
I CAN DO THIS.
OH . . . I DID IT!

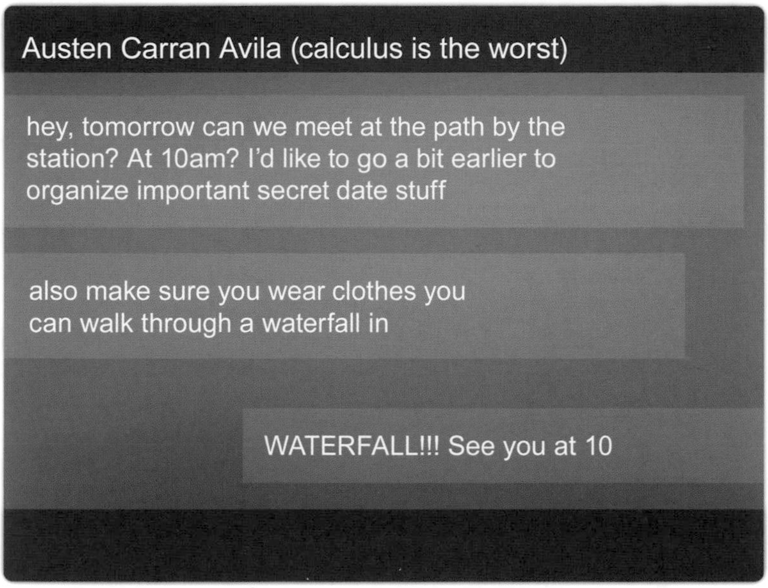
Austen Carran Avila (calculus is the worst)
hey, tomorrow can we meet at the path by the station? At 10am? I'd like to go a bit earlier to organize important secret date stuff
also make sure you wear clothes you can walk through a waterfall in
WATERFALL!!! See you at 10

12 - HOW LITTLE I KNOW

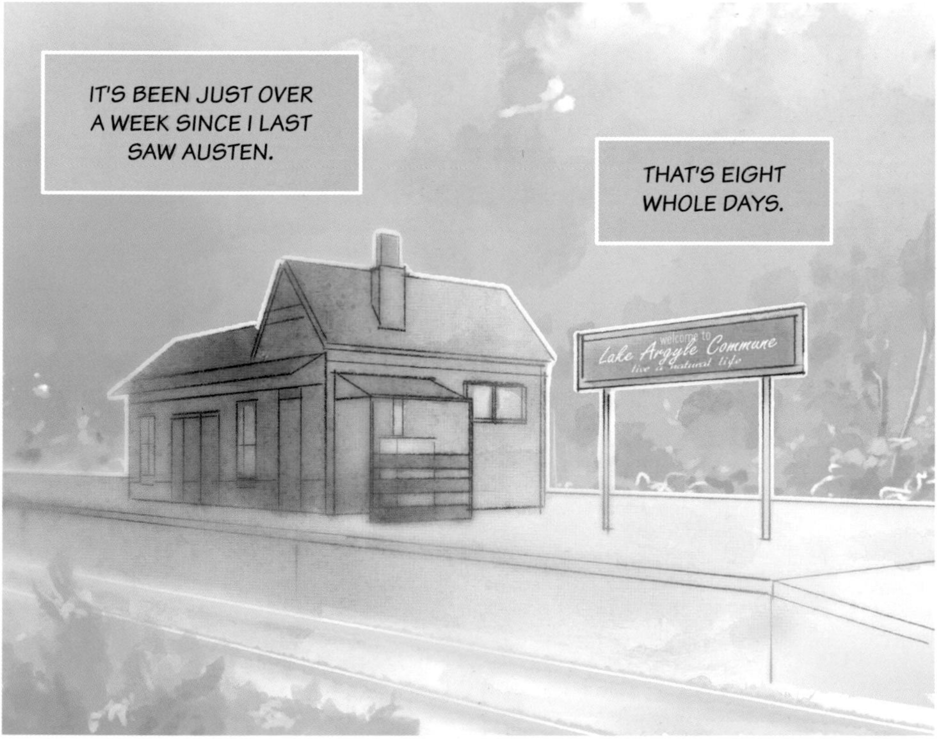
IT'S BEEN JUST OVER A WEEK SINCE I LAST SAW AUSTEN.
THAT'S EIGHT WHOLE DAYS.
welcome to
Lake Argyle Commune
live a natural life

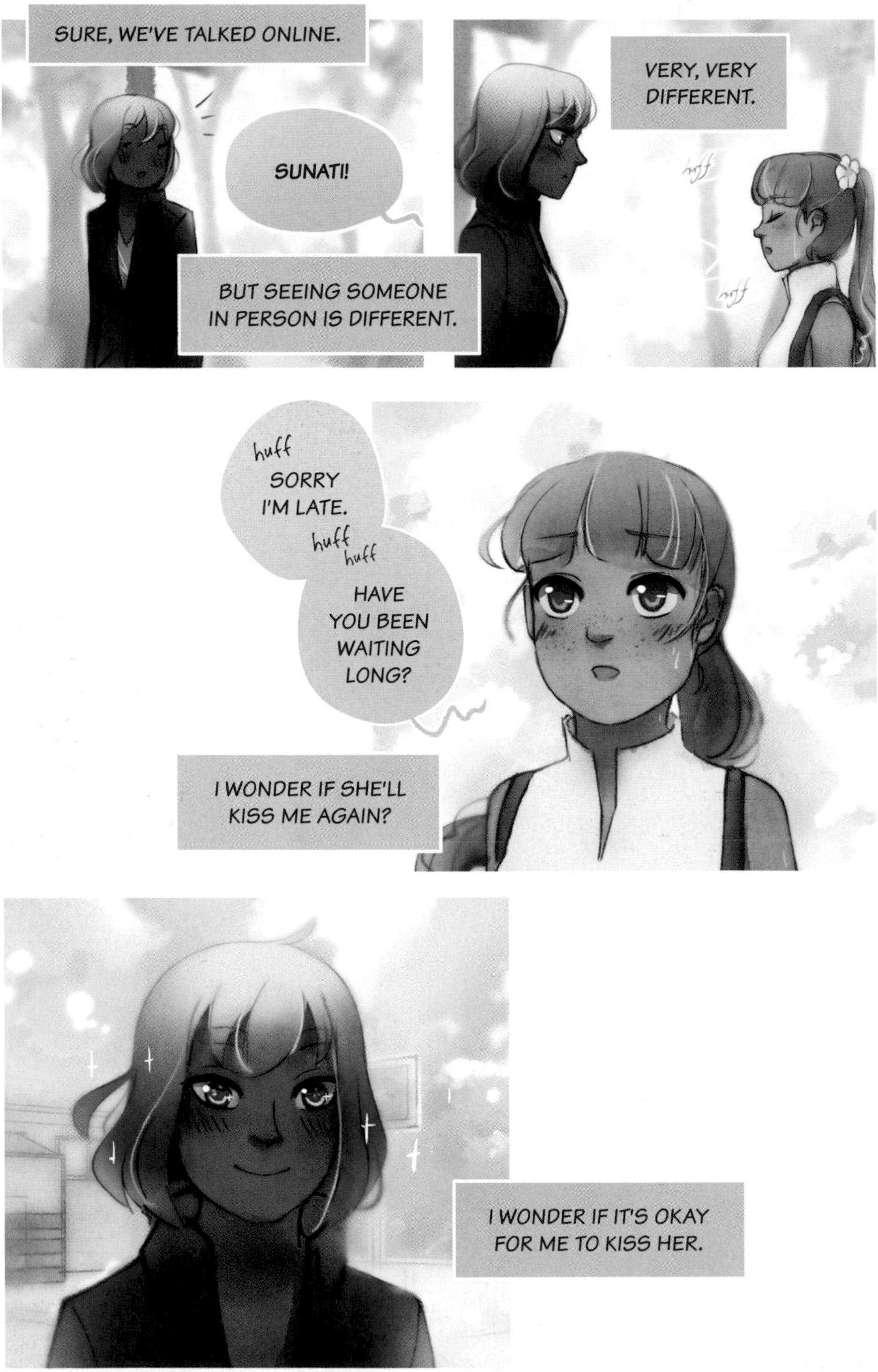
SURE, WE'VE TALKED ONLINE.
SUNATI!
BUT SEEING SOMEONE IN PERSON IS DIFFERENT.
VERY, VERY DIFFERENT.
huff
huff
huff SORRY I'M LATE.
huff huff HAVE YOU BEEN WAITING LONG?
I WONDER IF SHE'LL KISS ME AGAIN?
I WONDER IF IT'S OKAY FOR ME TO KISS HER.

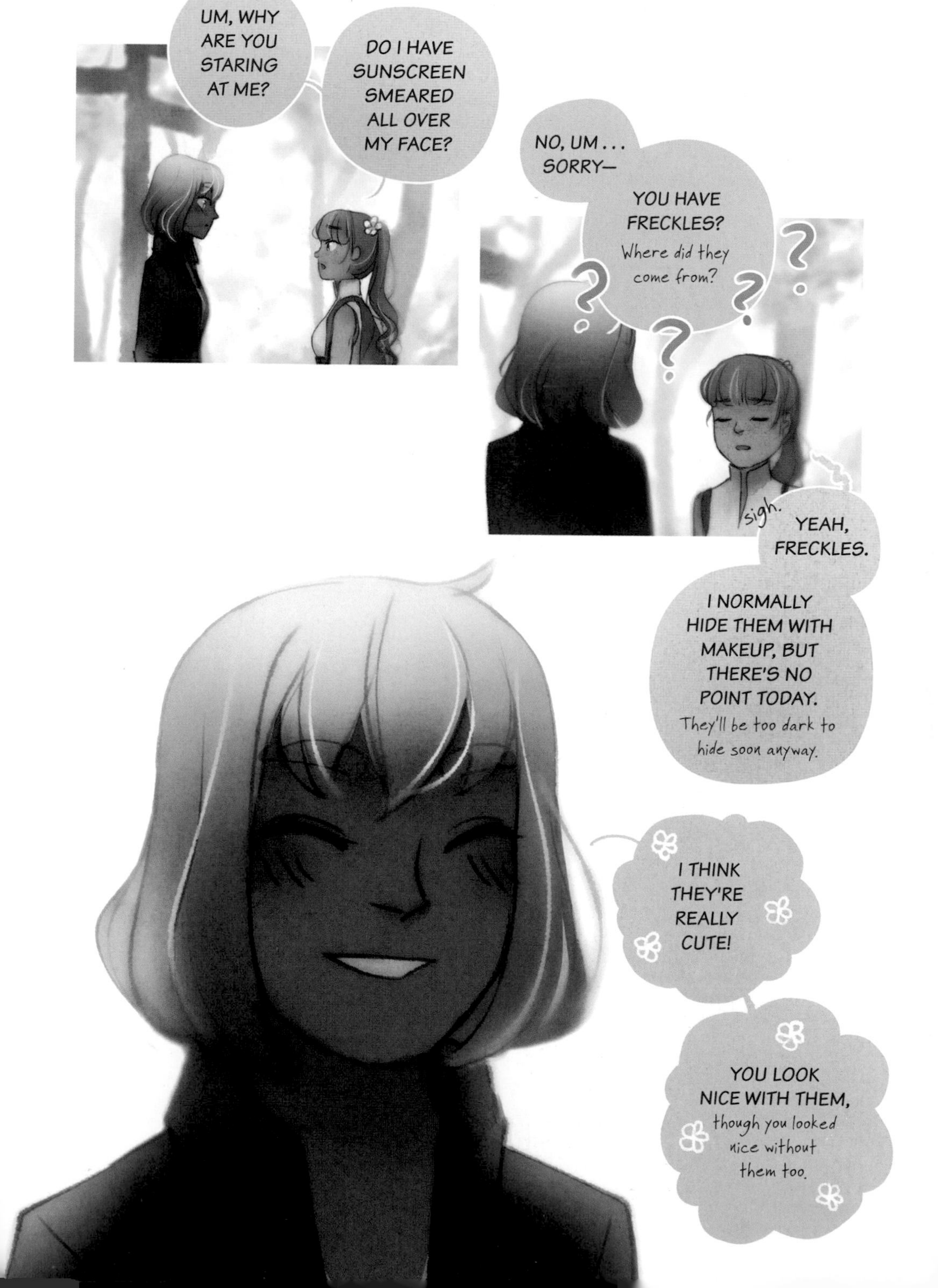
UM, WHY ARE YOU STARING AT ME?
DO I HAVE SUNSCREEN SMEARED ALL OVER MY FACE?
NO, UM . . . SORRY—
YOU HAVE FRECKLES? Where did they come from?
sigh.
YEAH, FRECKLES.
I NORMALLY HIDE THEM WITH MAKEUP, BUT THERE'S NO POINT TODAY. They'll be too dark to hide soon anyway.
I THINK THEY'RE REALLY CUTE!
YOU LOOK NICE WITH THEM, though you looked nice without them too.

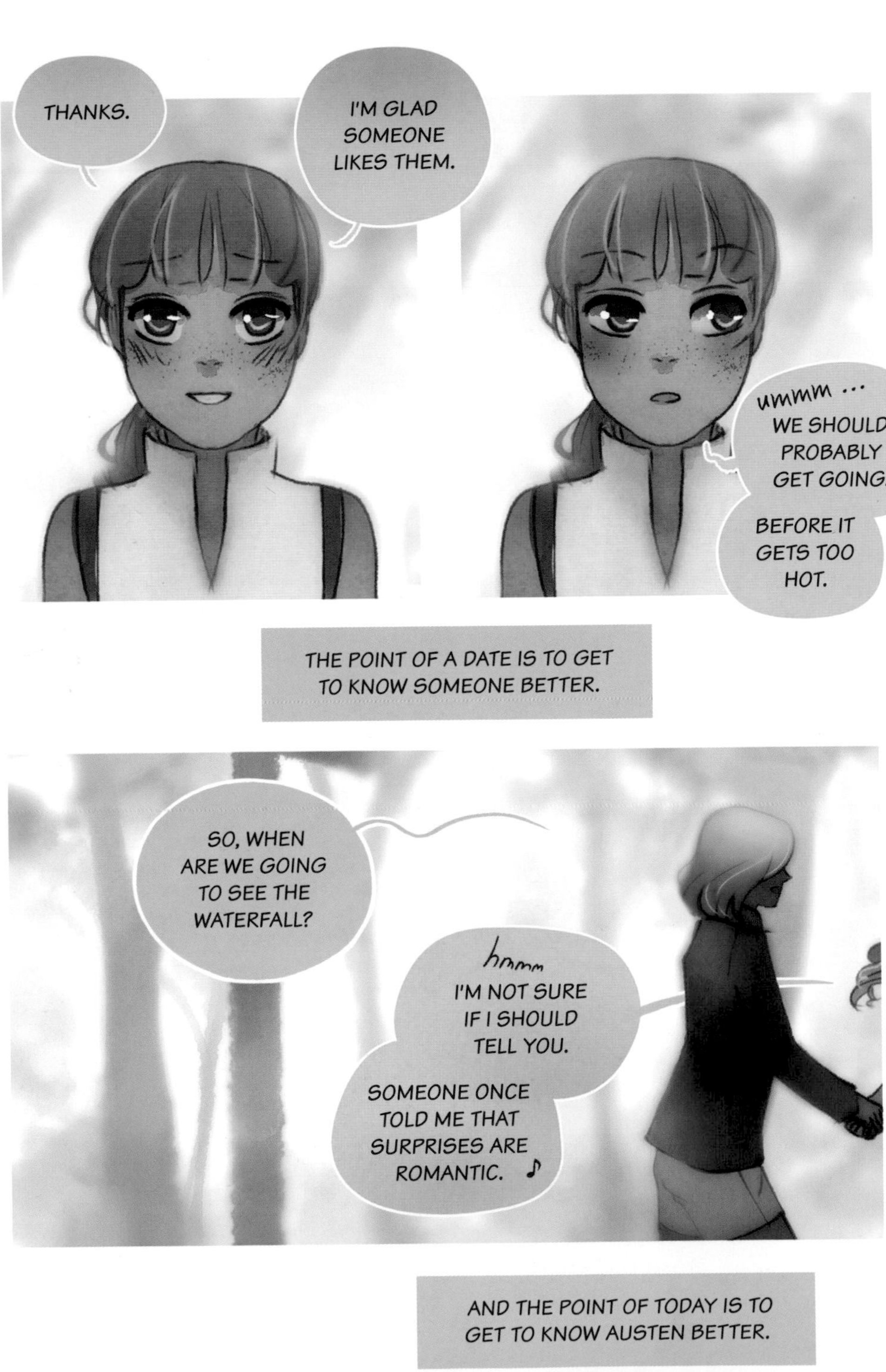
THANKS.
I'M GLAD SOMEONE LIKES THEM.
ummm ... WE SHOULD PROBABLY GET GOING.
BEFORE IT GETS TOO HOT.
THE POINT OF A DATE IS TO GET TO KNOW SOMEONE BETTER.
SO, WHEN ARE WE GOING TO SEE THE WATERFALL?
hmmm I'M NOT SURE IF I SHOULD TELL YOU.
SOMEONE ONCE TOLD ME THAT SURPRISES ARE ROMANTIC. ♪
AND THE POINT OF TODAY IS TO GET TO KNOW AUSTEN BETTER.

AND I'M ACUTELY AWARE
OF HOW LITTLE I KNOW.

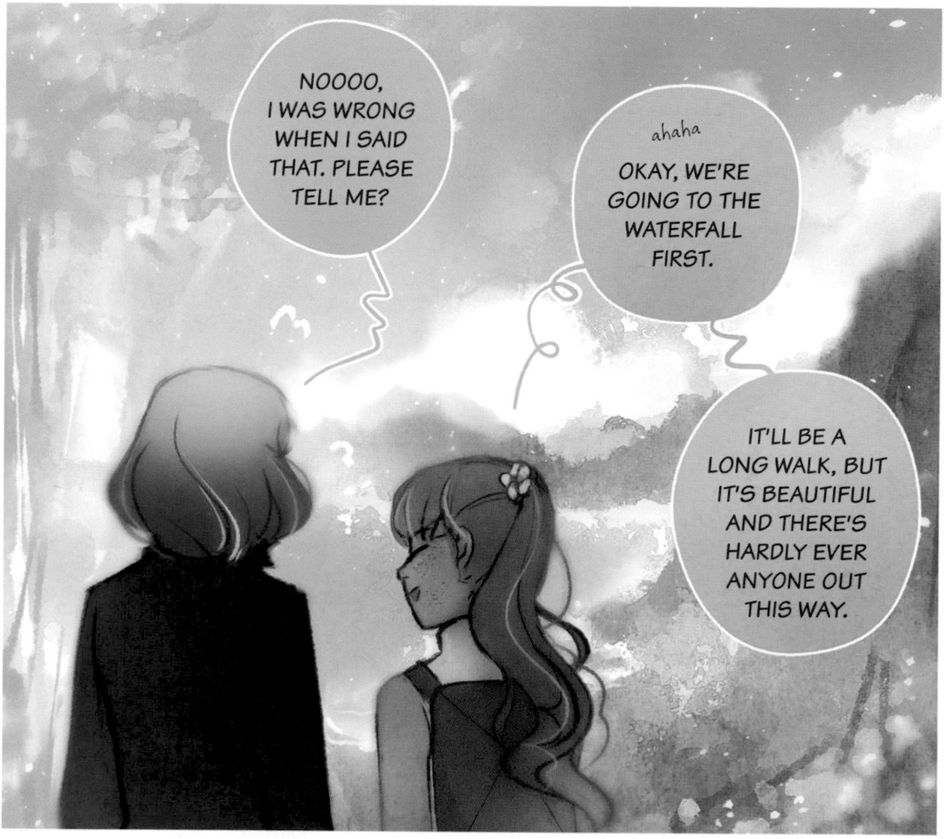
NOOOO, I WAS WRONG WHEN I SAID THAT. PLEASE TELL ME?
ahaha
OKAY, WE'RE GOING TO THE WATERFALL FIRST.
IT'LL BE A LONG WALK, BUT IT'S BEAUTIFUL AND THERE'S HARDLY EVER ANYONE OUT THIS WAY.

THERE ARE SO MANY THINGS I'VE NEVER
REALLY THOUGHT ABOUT BEFORE.

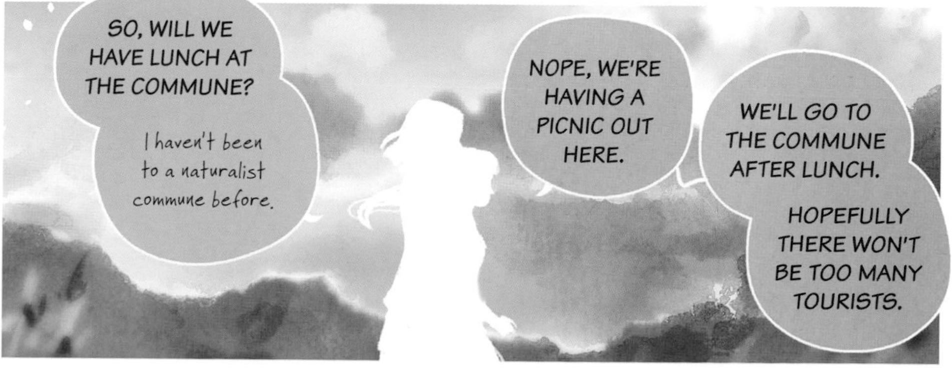
SO, WILL WE HAVE LUNCH AT THE COMMUNE?
I haven't been to a naturalist commune before.
NOPE, WE'RE HAVING A PICNIC OUT HERE.
WE'LL GO TO THE COMMUNE AFTER LUNCH.
HOPEFULLY THERE WON'T BE TOO MANY TOURISTS.

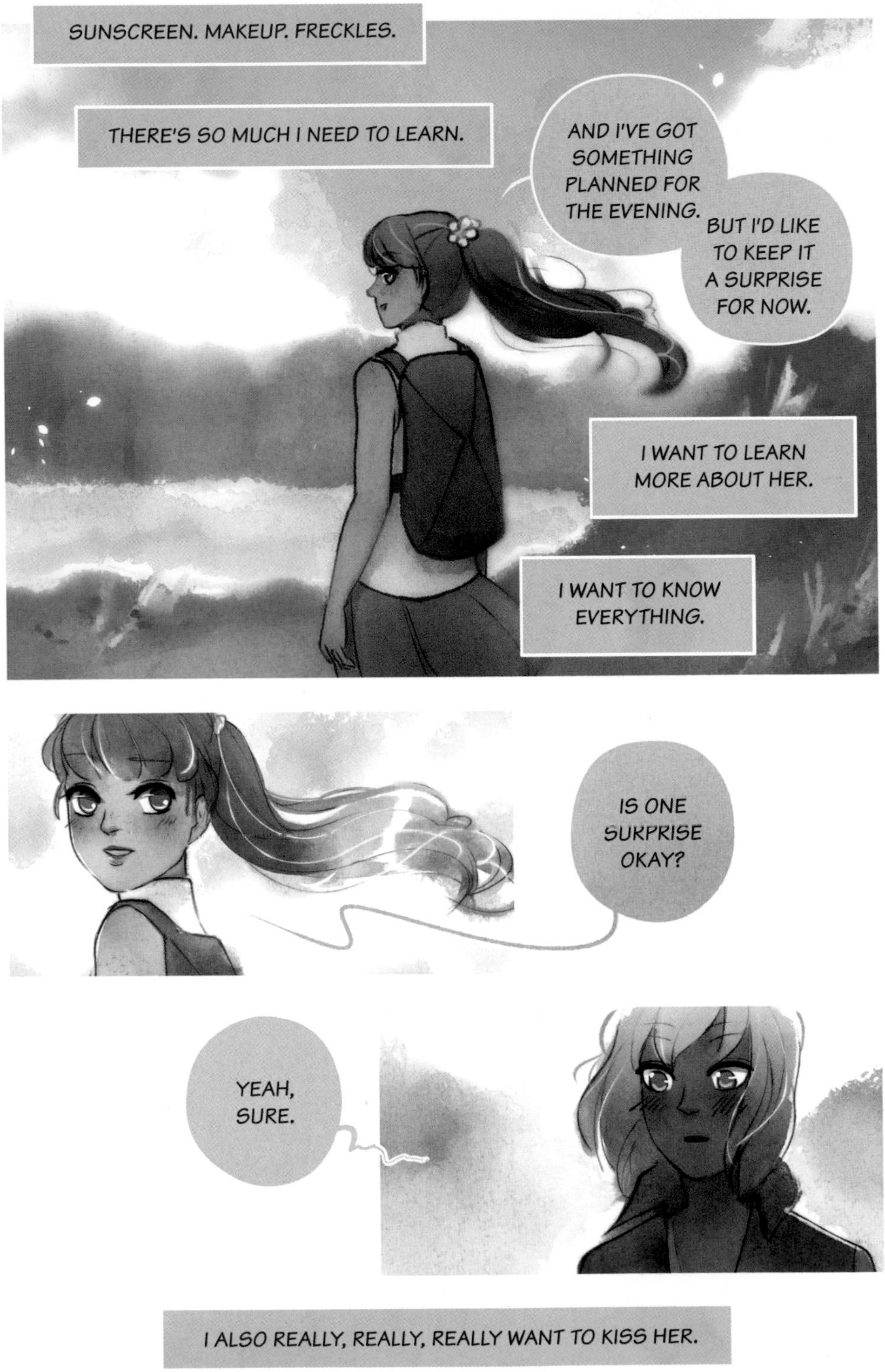
SUNSCREEN. MAKEUP. FRECKLES.
THERE'S SO MUCH I NEED TO LEARN.
AND I'VE GOT SOMETHING PLANNED FOR THE EVENING.
BUT I'D LIKE TO KEEP IT A SURPRISE FOR NOW.
I WANT TO LEARN MORE ABOUT HER.
I WANT TO KNOW EVERYTHING.
IS ONE SURPRISE OKAY?
YEAH, SURE.
I ALSO REALLY, REALLY, REALLY WANT TO KISS HER.

13 - TO LIVE A NORMAL LIFE

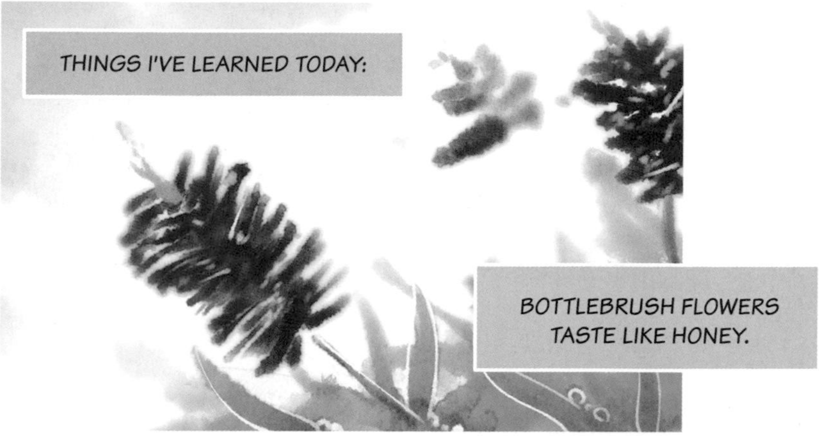
THINGS I'VE LEARNED TODAY:
BOTTLEBRUSH FLOWERS TASTE LIKE HONEY.

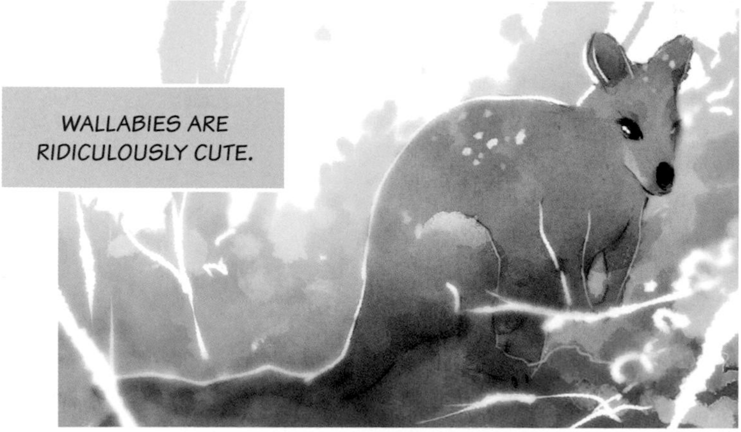
WALLABIES ARE RIDICULOUSLY CUTE.

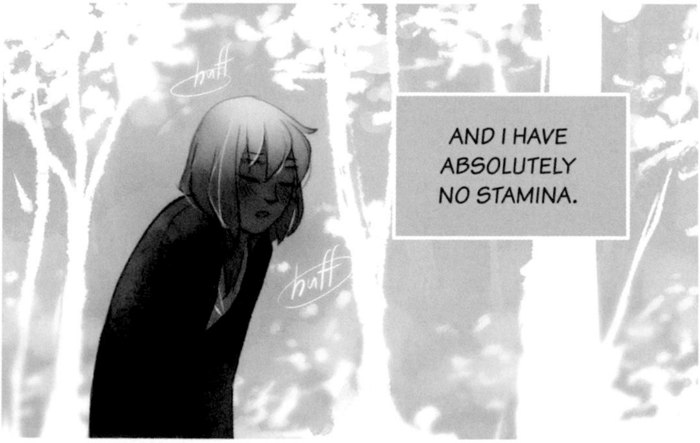
huff
AND I HAVE ABSOLUTELY NO STAMINA.
huff

HERE, WATER WILL HELP.

haff haff haff haff

WHY ARE YOU SO TIRED?

AREN'T YOU USING ENDURANCE MODS?

ERRRR . . . NO. I DIDN'T THINK I'D NEED TO SINCE—

haff

haff

SINCE I CAN'T USE MODS?

. . . YEAH.

HOW ARE YOU SO GOOD AT THIS?

ahaha

I LIKE TO STAY FIT, SO I SPEND A LOT OF TIME AT THE GYM.

Pounding away on a treadmill is therapeutic.

HAVE A COOKIE. GET YOUR ENERGY BACK.

OOOOH, THANKS!

PLOP

SNATCH

FWOOOSH

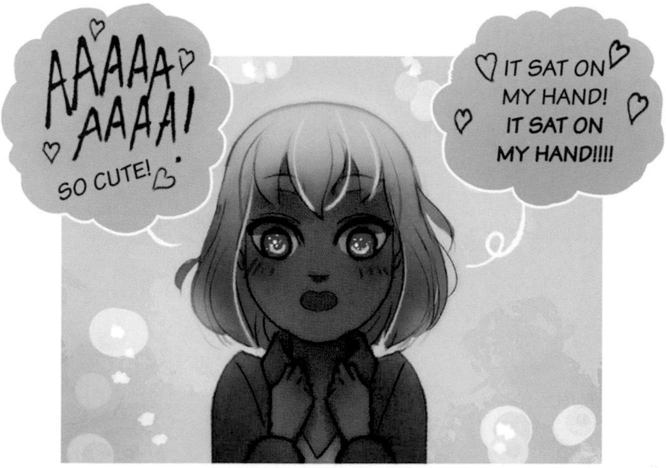
AAAAA AAAA!
SO CUTE!
IT SAT ON MY HAND! IT SAT ON MY HAND!!!!

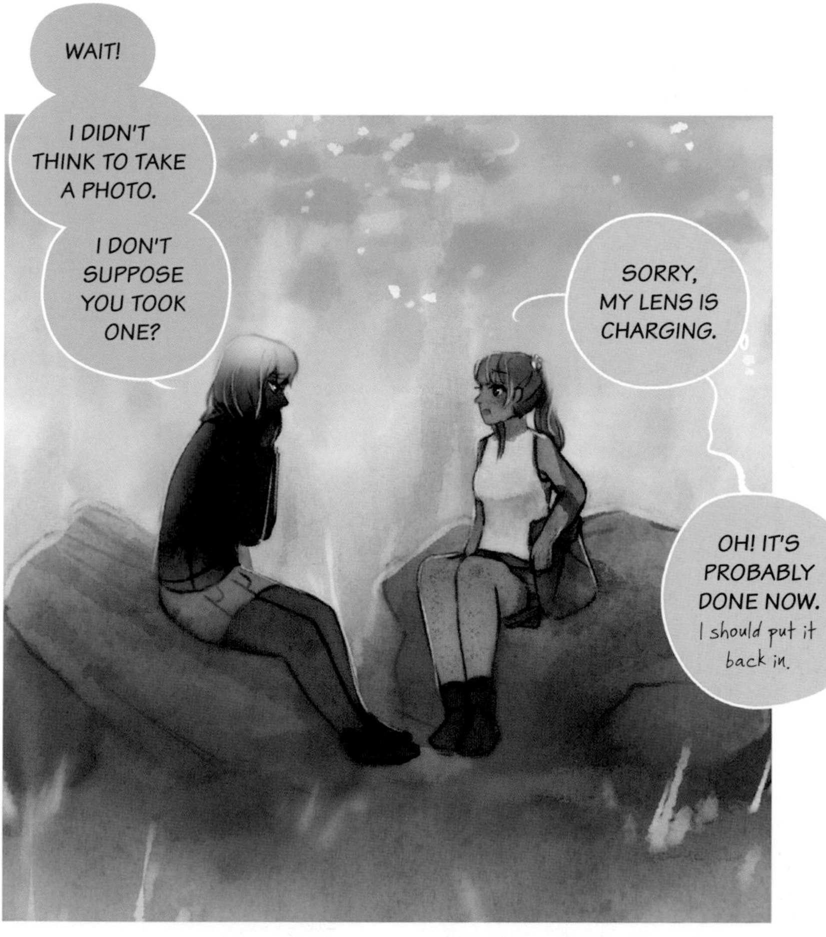
WAIT!
I DIDN'T THINK TO TAKE A PHOTO.
I DON'T SUPPOSE YOU TOOK ONE?
SORRY, MY LENS IS CHARGING.
OH! IT'S PROBABLY DONE NOW. I should put it back in.

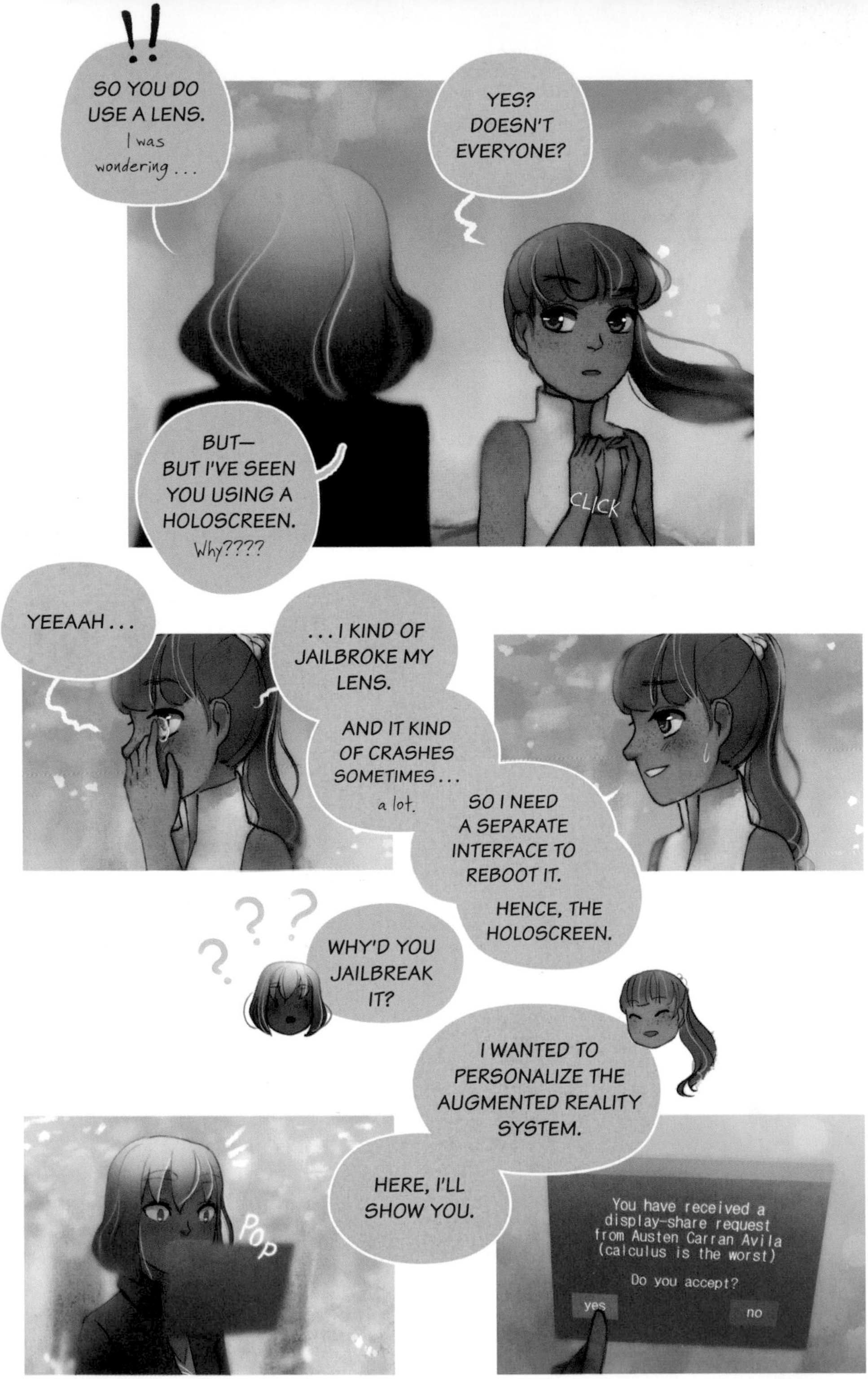
!!
SO YOU DO USE A LENS. I was wondering . . .
YES? DOESN'T EVERYONE?
BUT— BUT I'VE SEEN YOU USING A HOLOSCREEN. Why????
CLICK
YEEAAH . . .
. . . I KIND OF JAILBROKE MY LENS.
AND IT KIND OF CRASHES SOMETIMES . . .
a lot.
SO I NEED A SEPARATE INTERFACE TO REBOOT IT.
HENCE, THE HOLOSCREEN.
? ? ?
WHY'D YOU JAILBREAK IT?
I WANTED TO PERSONALIZE THE AUGMENTED REALITY SYSTEM.
HERE, I'LL SHOW YOU.
Pop
You have received a display-share request from Austen Carran Avila (calculus is the worst)
Do you accept?
yes
no

I USE INFORMATION OVERLAYS TO COMPENSATE FOR NOT BEING ABLE TO USE MEMORY MODS.

I'VE TAUGHT THE AUGMENTED REALITY SYSTEM TO GIVE ME INFORMATION I MIGHT NEED, BASED ON THE THINGS I SEE.

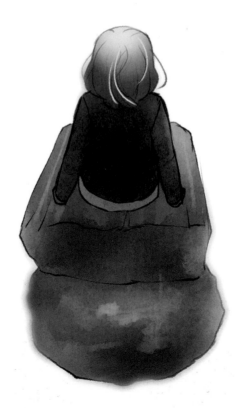

IT'S A BIG HELP WHEN DOING COURSEWORK.

IT'S NOT MUCH USE OUT HERE THOUGH. I haven't taught the AI how to respond to this sort of environment.

Golden Wattle 80"

more ✓ ✗

OOOOH.

Lake Argyle 5.6 m

HEY, IT'S ONLY A HALF MILE TO THE WATERFALL!

Am I reading that overlay right?

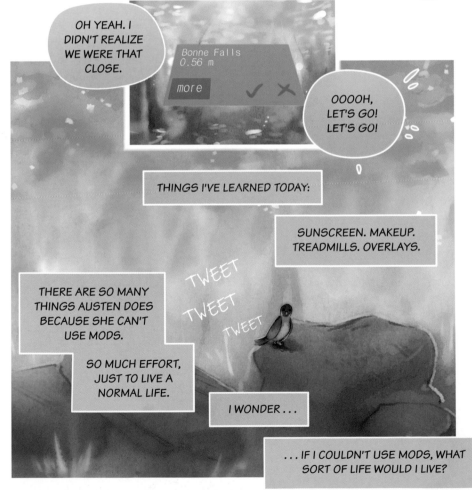

OH YEAH. I DIDN'T REALIZE WE WERE THAT CLOSE.

Bonne Falls 0.56 m

more ✓ ✗

OOOOH, LET'S GO! LET'S GO!

THINGS I'VE LEARNED TODAY:

SUNSCREEN. MAKEUP. TREADMILLS. OVERLAYS.

TWEET TWEET TWEET

THERE ARE SO MANY THINGS AUSTEN DOES BECAUSE SHE CAN'T USE MODS.

SO MUCH EFFORT, JUST TO LIVE A NORMAL LIFE.

I WONDER . . .

. . . IF I COULDN'T USE MODS, WHAT SORT OF LIFE WOULD I LIVE?

14 - DO YOU BELIEVE ME?

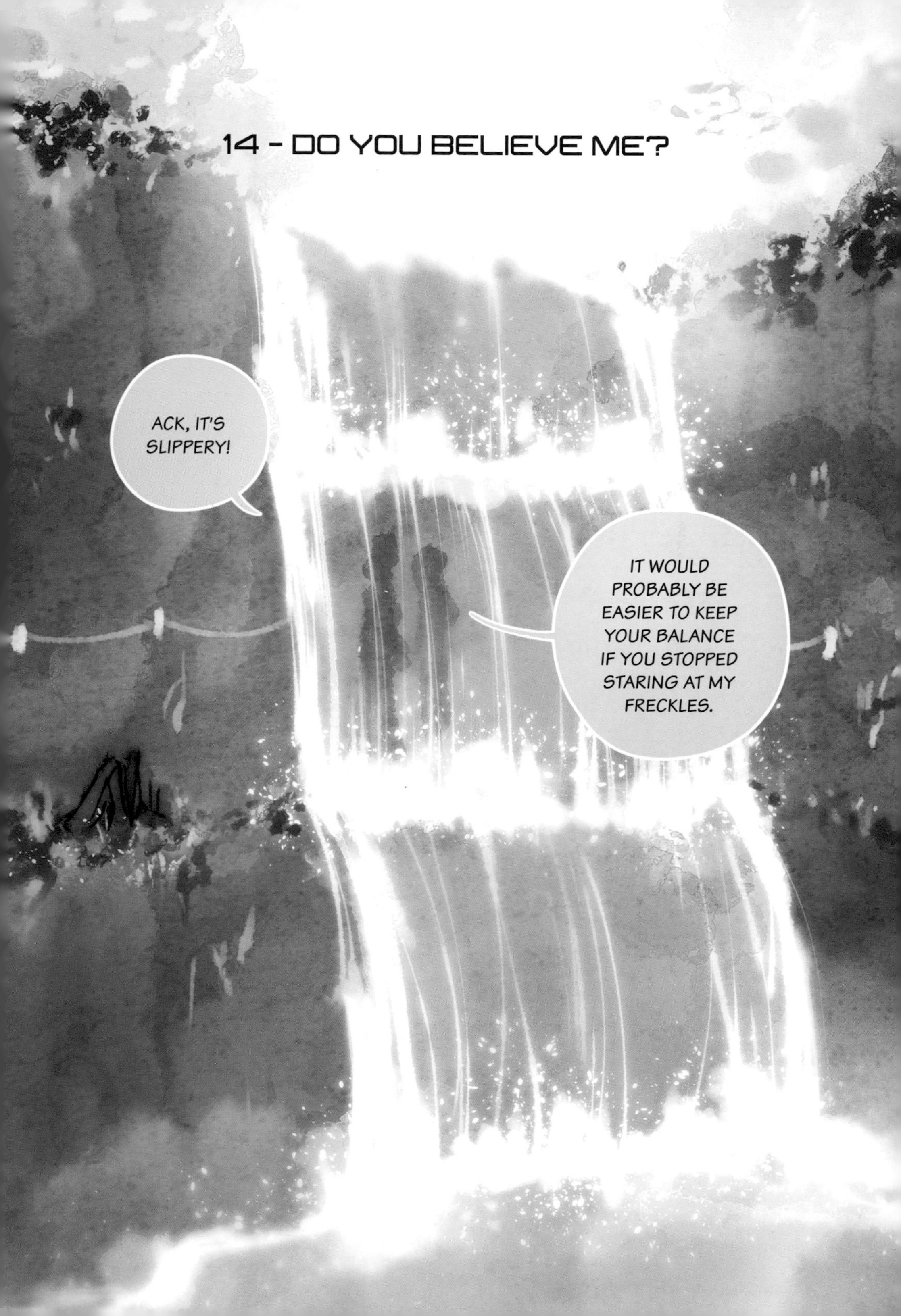
ACK, IT'S SLIPPERY!
IT WOULD PROBABLY BE EASIER TO KEEP YOUR BALANCE IF YOU STOPPED STARING AT MY FRECKLES.

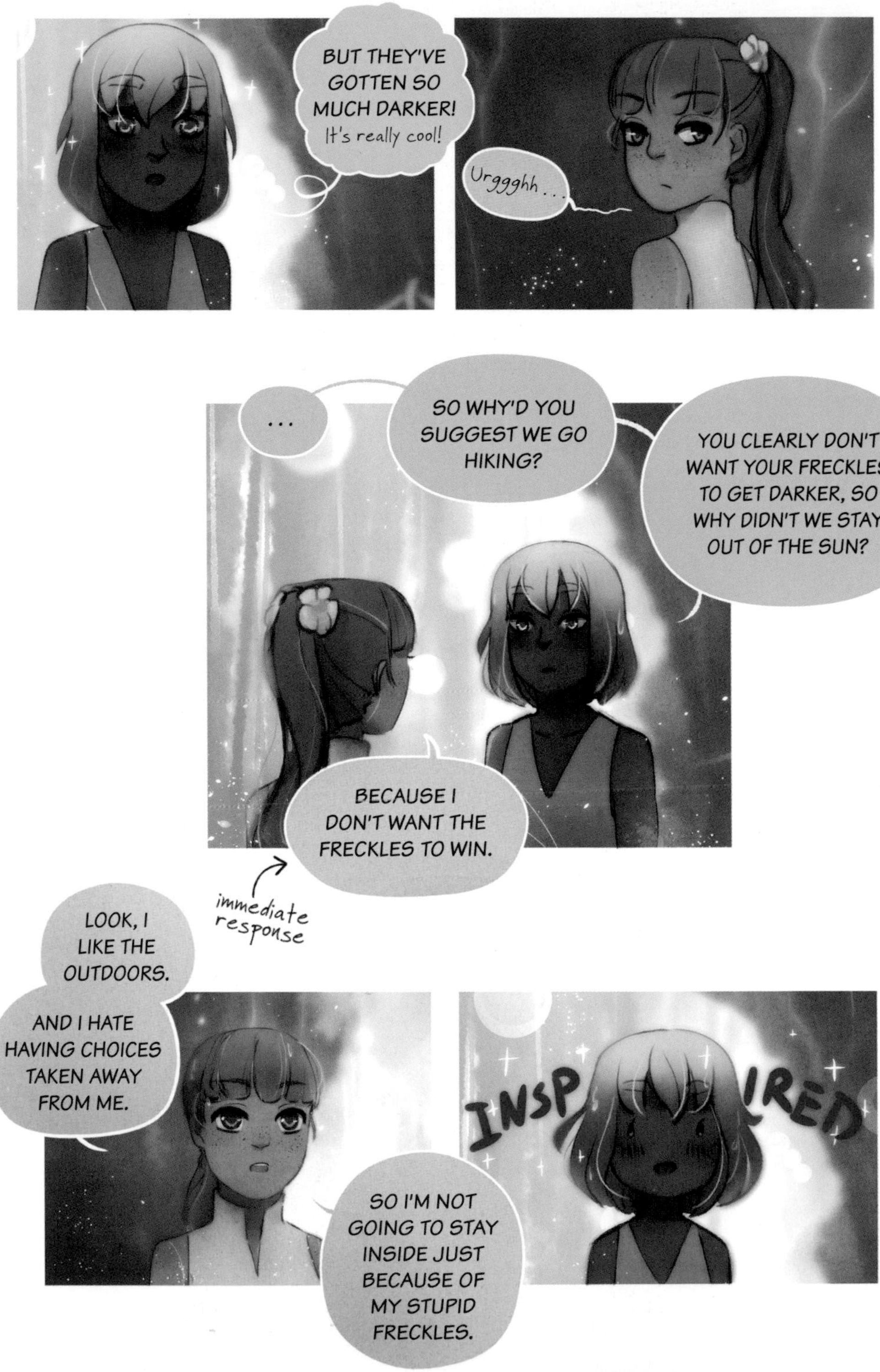
BUT THEY'VE GOTTEN SO MUCH DARKER!
It's really cool!
Urggghh...
...
SO WHY'D YOU SUGGEST WE GO HIKING?
YOU CLEARLY DON'T WANT YOUR FRECKLES TO GET DARKER, SO WHY DIDN'T WE STAY OUT OF THE SUN?
BECAUSE I DON'T WANT THE FRECKLES TO WIN.
immediate response
LOOK, I LIKE THE OUTDOORS.
AND I HATE HAVING CHOICES TAKEN AWAY FROM ME.
SO I'M NOT GOING TO STAY INSIDE JUST BECAUSE OF MY STUPID FRECKLES.
INSPIRED

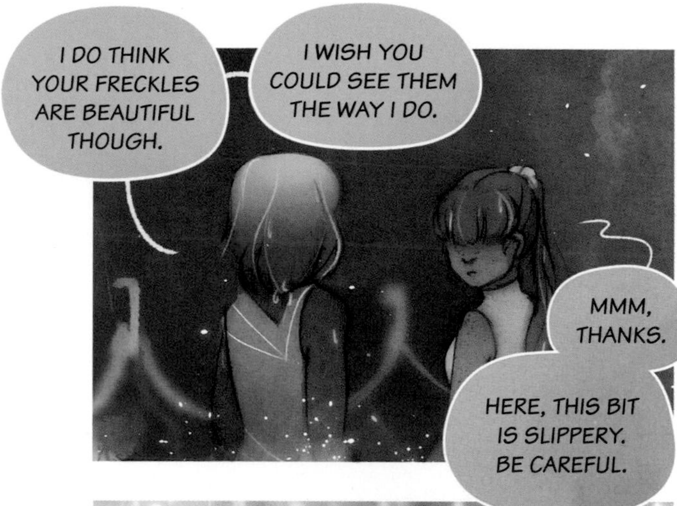
I DO THINK YOUR FRECKLES ARE BEAUTIFUL THOUGH.
I WISH YOU COULD SEE THEM THE WAY I DO.
MMM, THANKS.
HERE, THIS BIT IS SLIPPERY. BE CAREFUL.

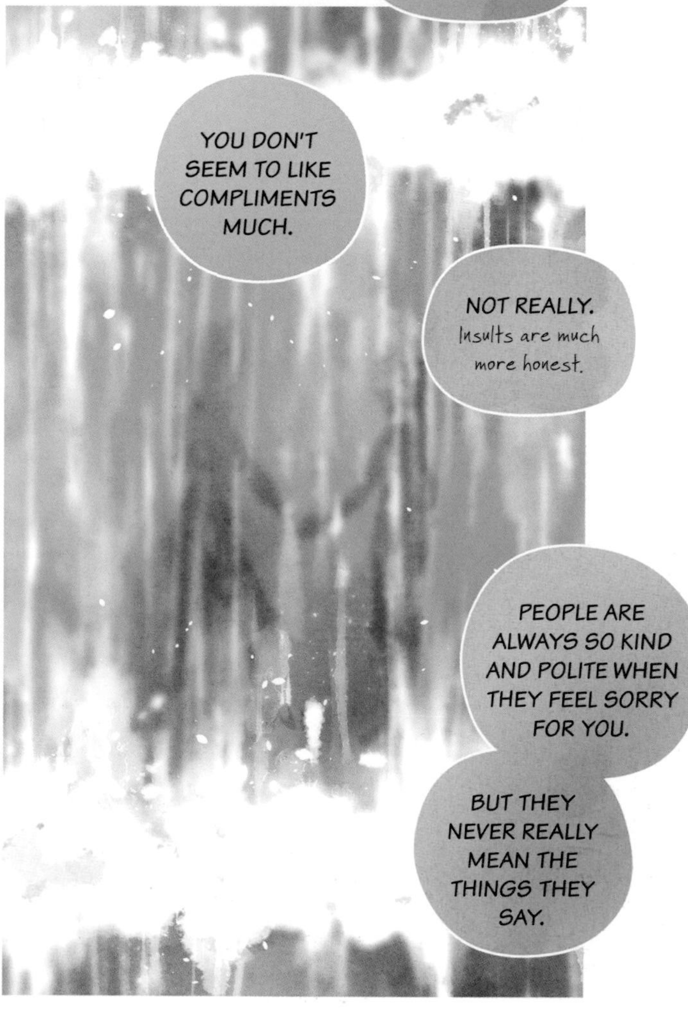
YOU DON'T SEEM TO LIKE COMPLIMENTS MUCH.
NOT REALLY. Insults are much more honest.
PEOPLE ARE ALWAYS SO KIND AND POLITE WHEN THEY FEEL SORRY FOR YOU.
BUT THEY NEVER REALLY MEAN THE THINGS THEY SAY.

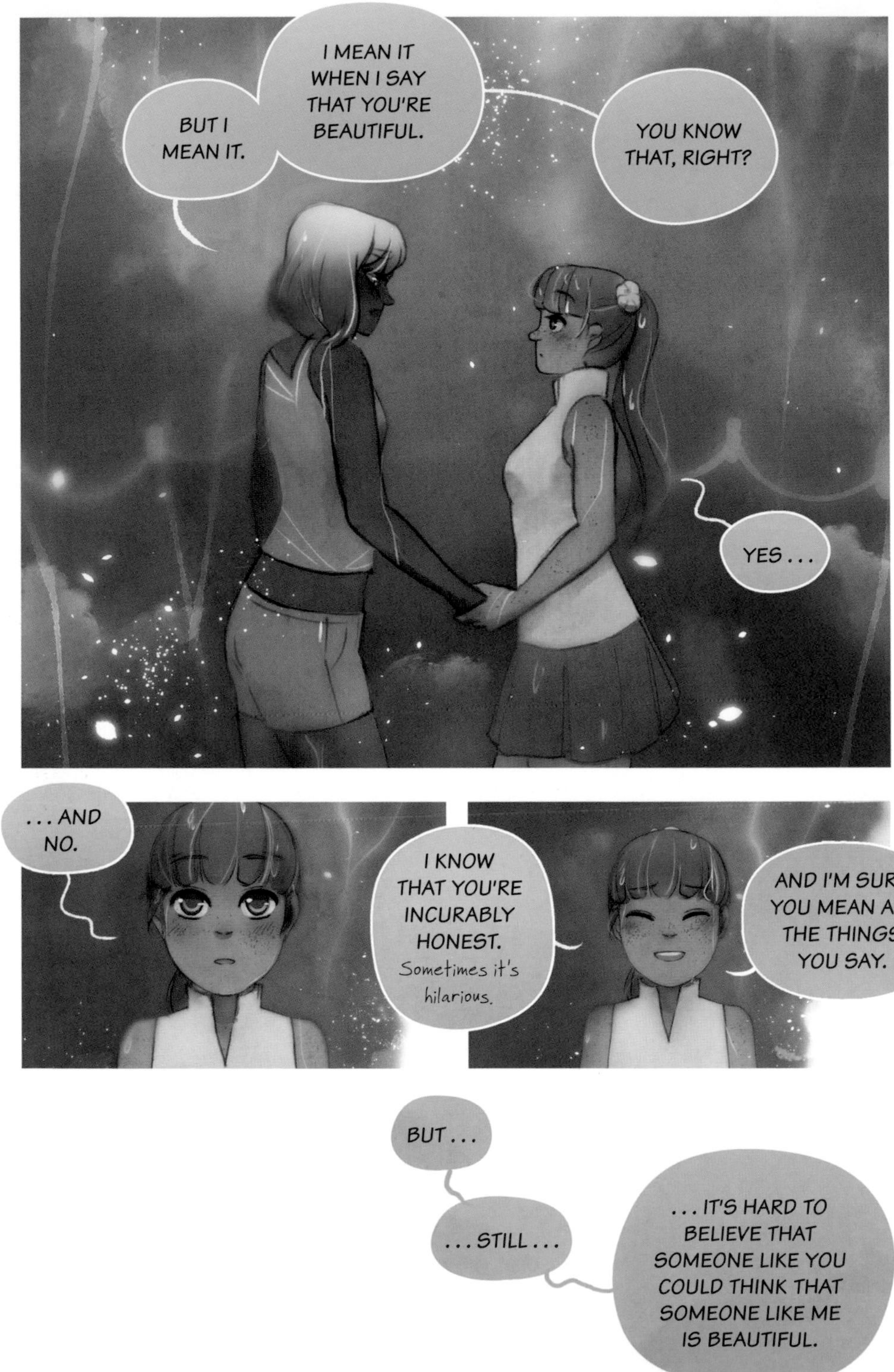
BUT I MEAN IT.
I MEAN IT WHEN I SAY THAT YOU'RE BEAUTIFUL.
YOU KNOW THAT, RIGHT?
YES . . .
. . . AND NO.
I KNOW THAT YOU'RE INCURABLY HONEST. Sometimes it's hilarious.
AND I'M SURE YOU MEAN ALL THE THINGS YOU SAY.
BUT . . .
. . . STILL . . .
. . . IT'S HARD TO BELIEVE THAT SOMEONE LIKE YOU COULD THINK THAT SOMEONE LIKE ME IS BEAUTIFUL.

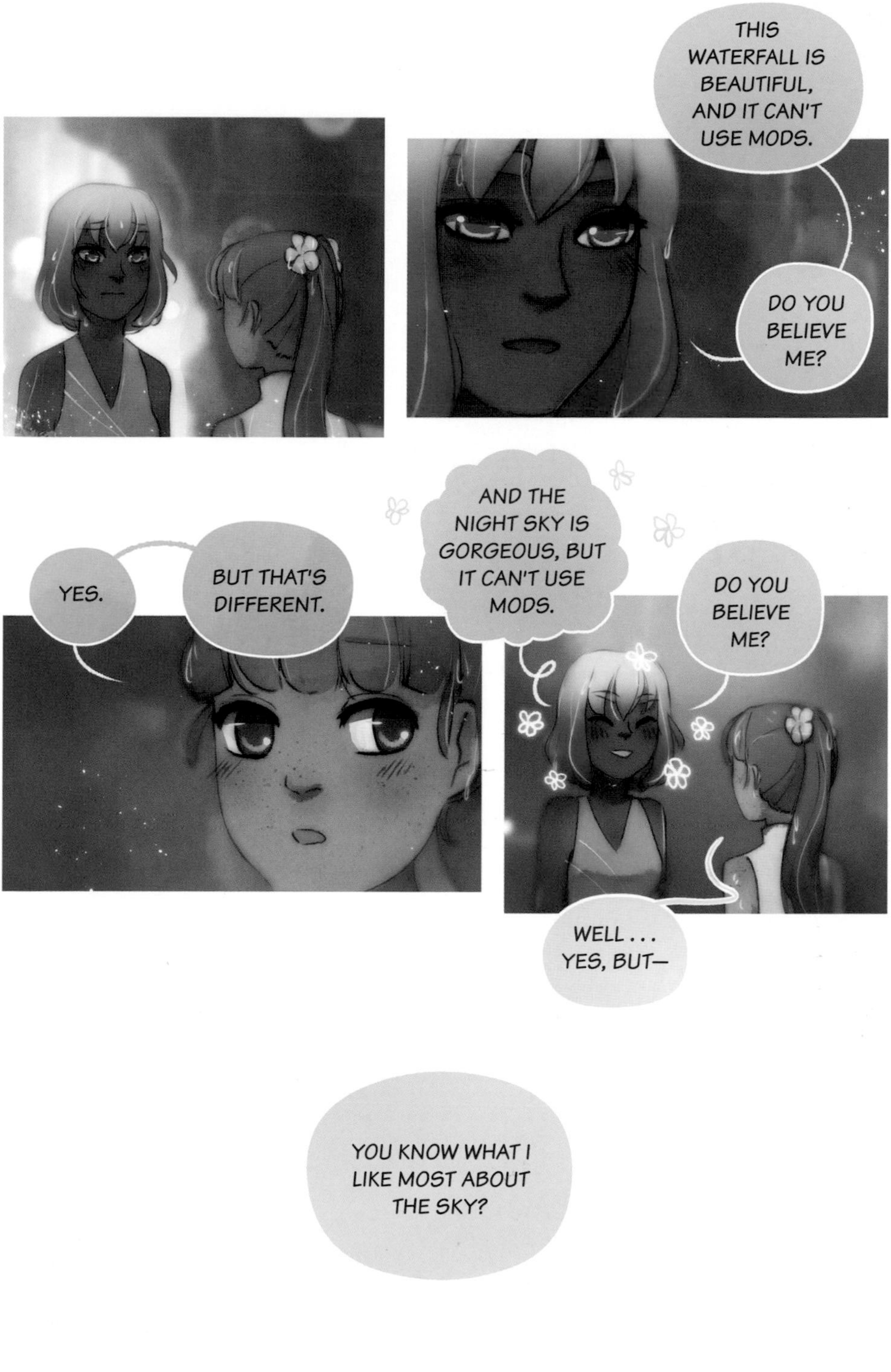
THIS WATERFALL IS BEAUTIFUL, AND IT CAN'T USE MODS.
DO YOU BELIEVE ME?
YES.
BUT THAT'S DIFFERENT.
AND THE NIGHT SKY IS GORGEOUS, BUT IT CAN'T USE MODS.
DO YOU BELIEVE ME?
WELL . . . YES, BUT—
YOU KNOW WHAT I LIKE MOST ABOUT THE SKY?

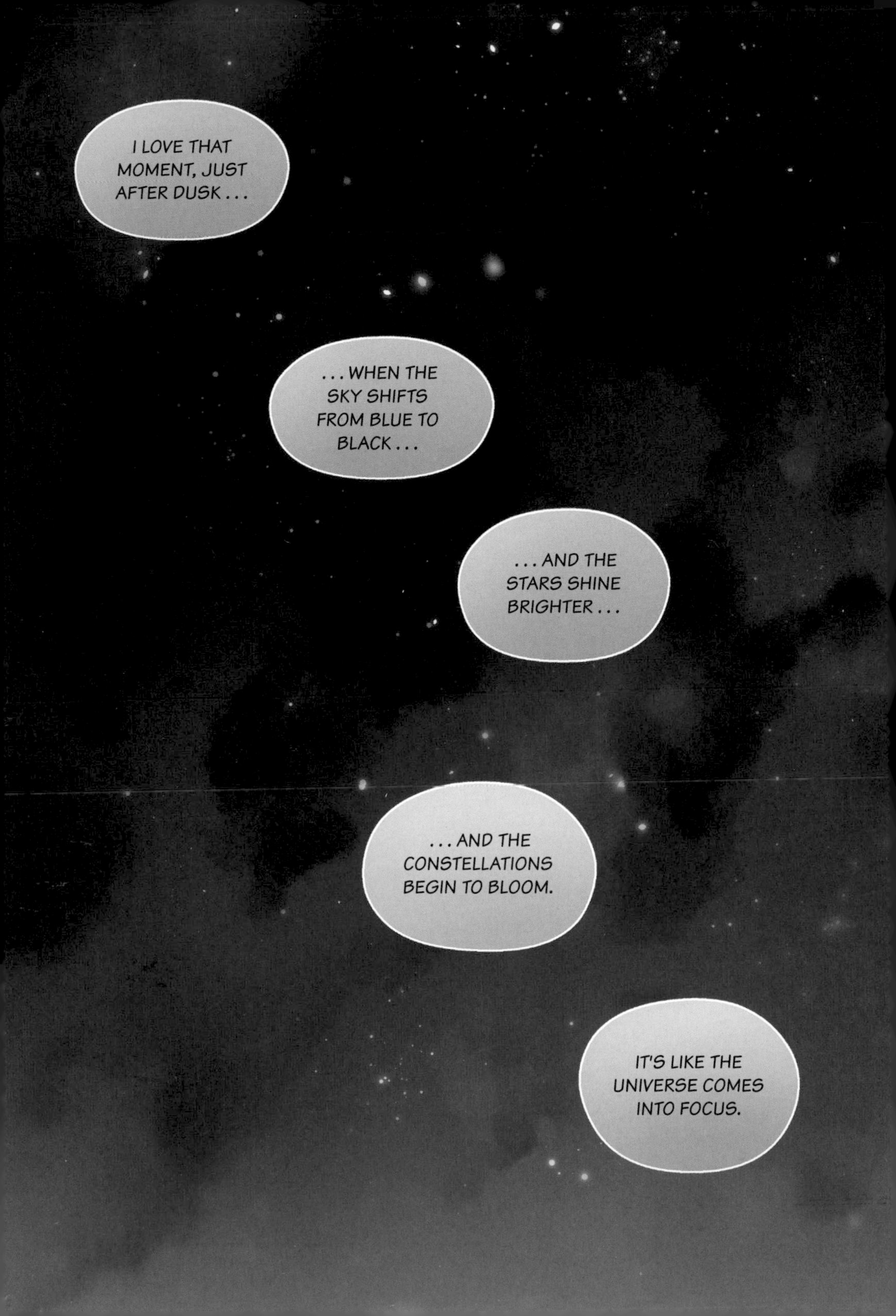
I LOVE THAT MOMENT, JUST AFTER DUSK . . .
. . . WHEN THE SKY SHIFTS FROM BLUE TO BLACK . . .
. . . AND THE STARS SHINE BRIGHTER . . .
. . . AND THE CONSTELLATIONS BEGIN TO BLOOM.
IT'S LIKE THE UNIVERSE COMES INTO FOCUS.

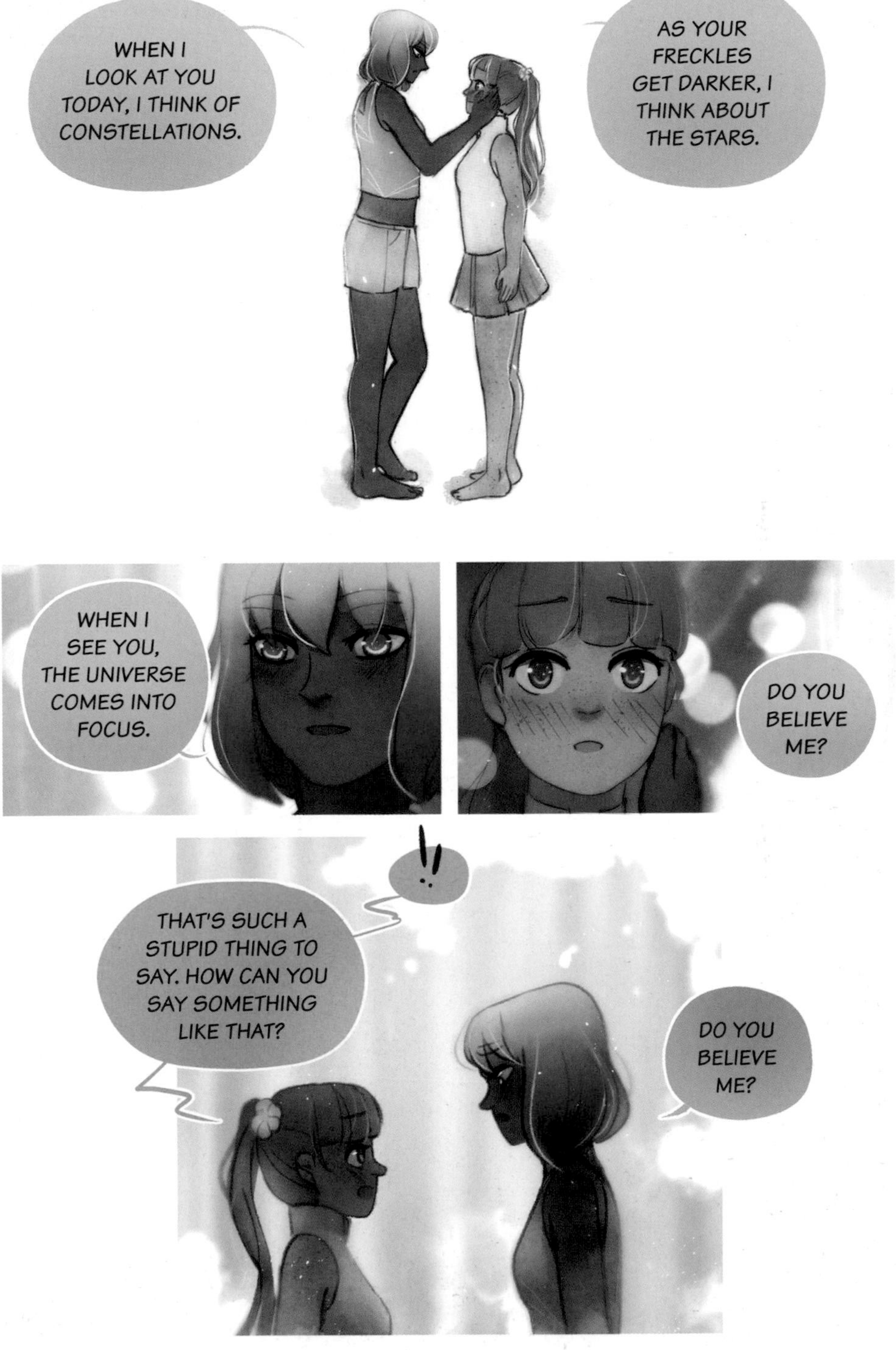
WHEN I LOOK AT YOU TODAY, I THINK OF CONSTELLATIONS.
AS YOUR FRECKLES GET DARKER, I THINK ABOUT THE STARS.
WHEN I SEE YOU, THE UNIVERSE COMES INTO FOCUS.
DO YOU BELIEVE ME?
!!
THAT'S SUCH A STUPID THING TO SAY. HOW CAN YOU SAY SOMETHING LIKE THAT?
DO YOU BELIEVE ME?

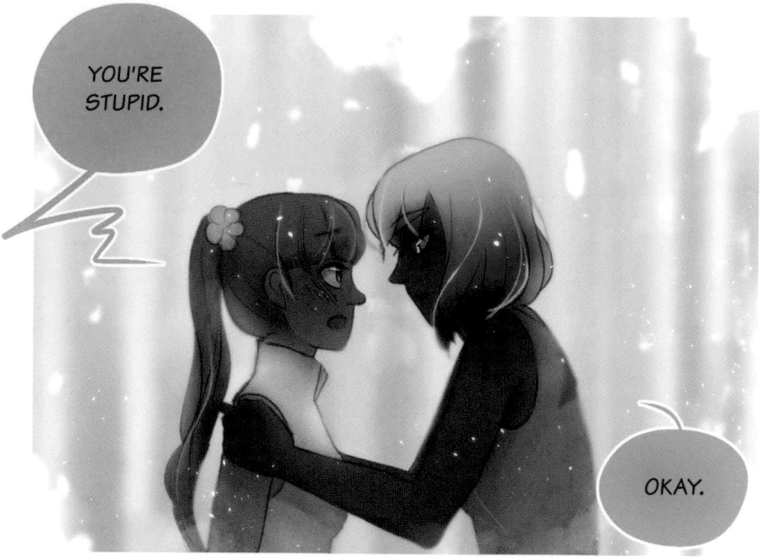
YOU'RE STUPID.
OKAY.

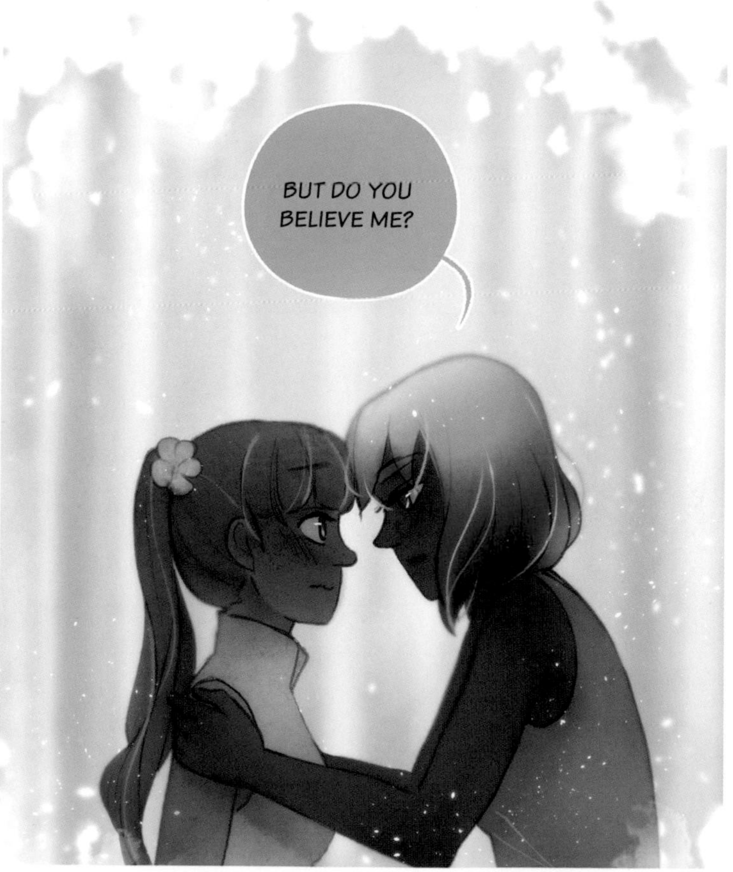
BUT DO YOU BELIEVE ME?

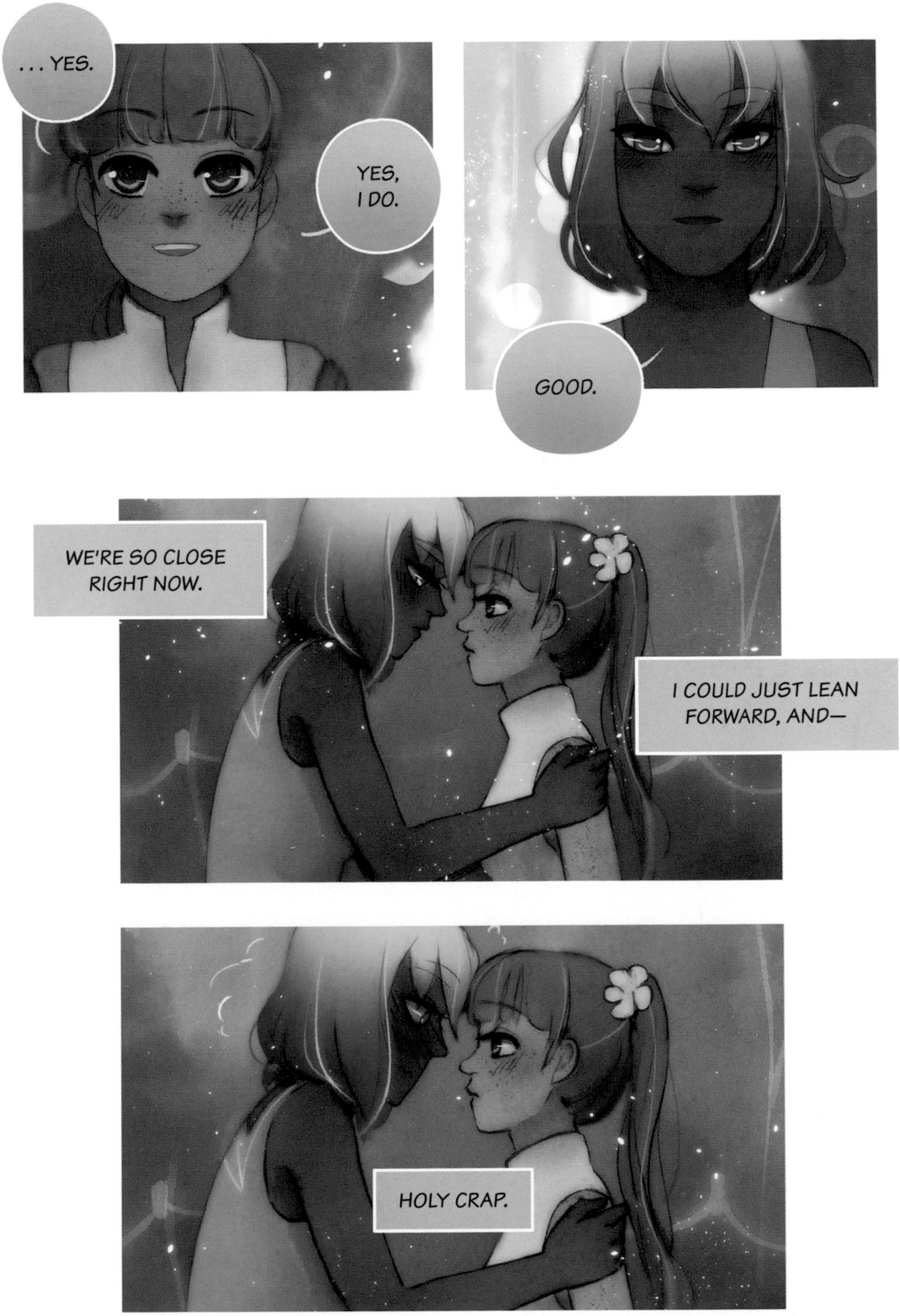
. . . YES.
YES, I DO.
GOOD.
WE'RE SO CLOSE RIGHT NOW.
I COULD JUST LEAN FORWARD, AND—
HOLY CRAP.

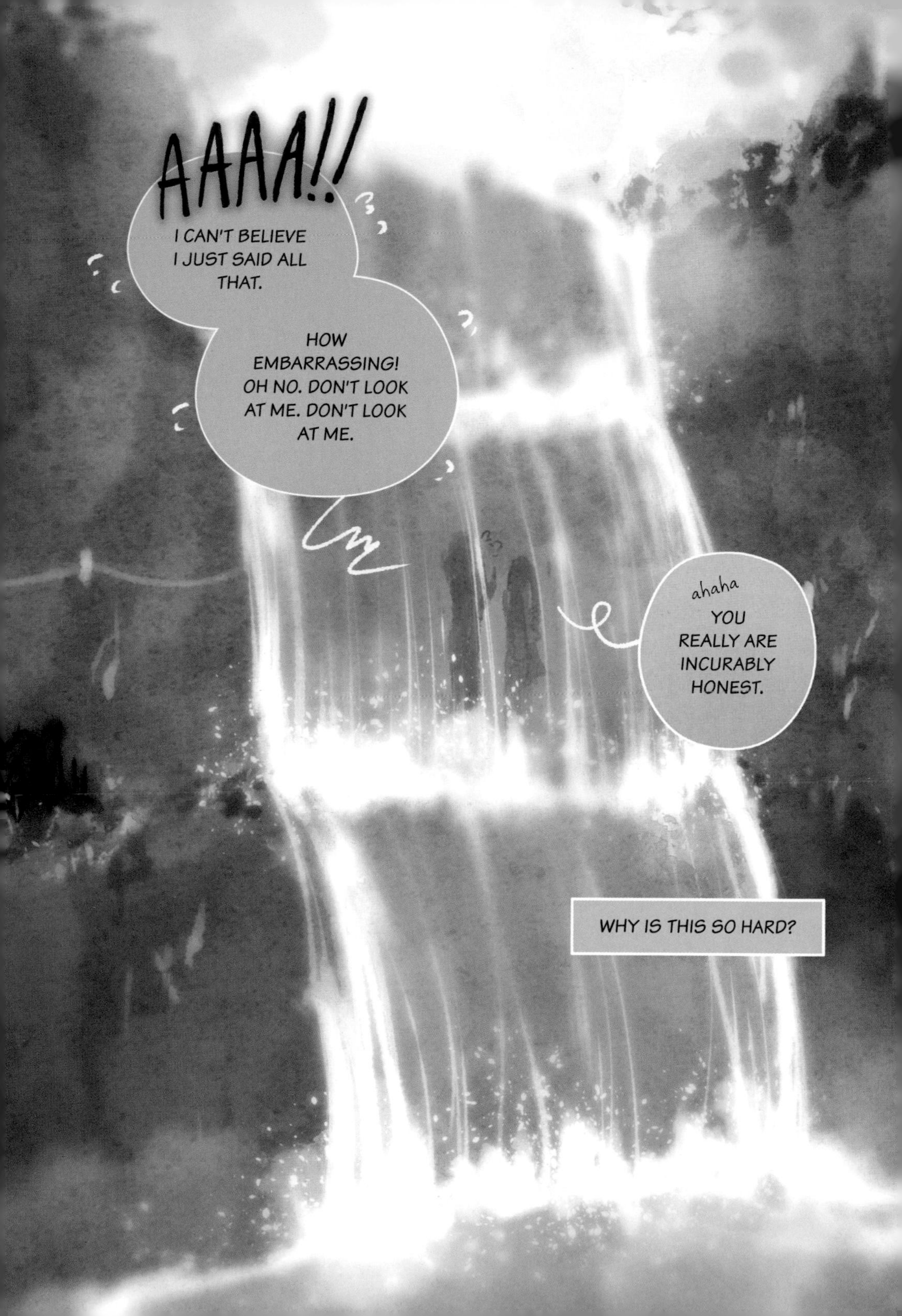
AAAA!!
I CAN'T BELIEVE I JUST SAID ALL THAT.
HOW EMBARRASSING! OH NO. DON'T LOOK AT ME. DON'T LOOK AT ME.
ahaha
YOU REALLY ARE INCURABLY HONEST.
WHY IS THIS SO HARD?

15 - A NICE SORT OF AWKWARD

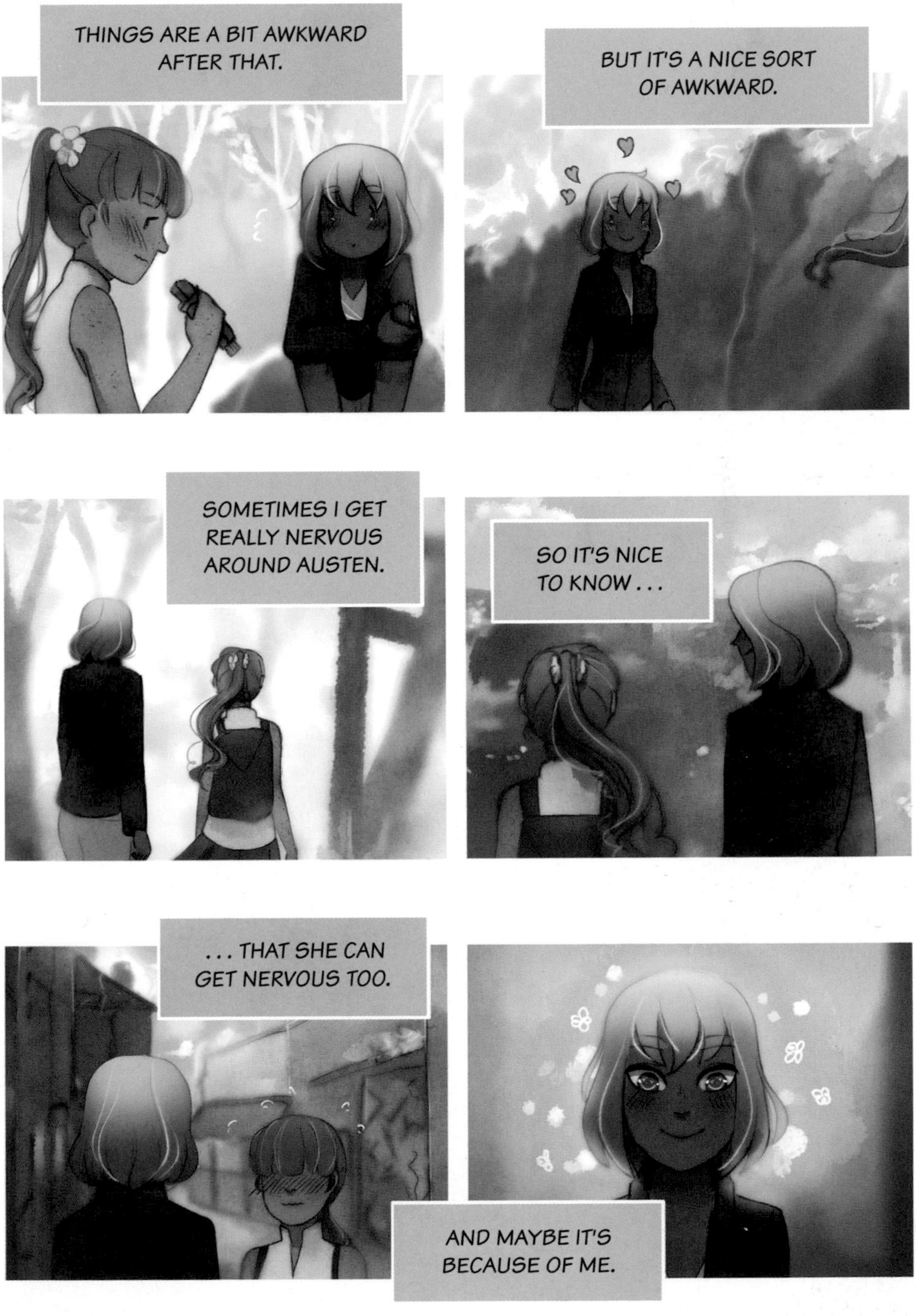
THINGS ARE A BIT AWKWARD AFTER THAT.
BUT IT'S A NICE SORT OF AWKWARD.
SOMETIMES I GET REALLY NERVOUS AROUND AUSTEN.
SO IT'S NICE TO KNOW . . .
. . . THAT SHE CAN GET NERVOUS TOO.
AND MAYBE IT'S BECAUSE OF ME.

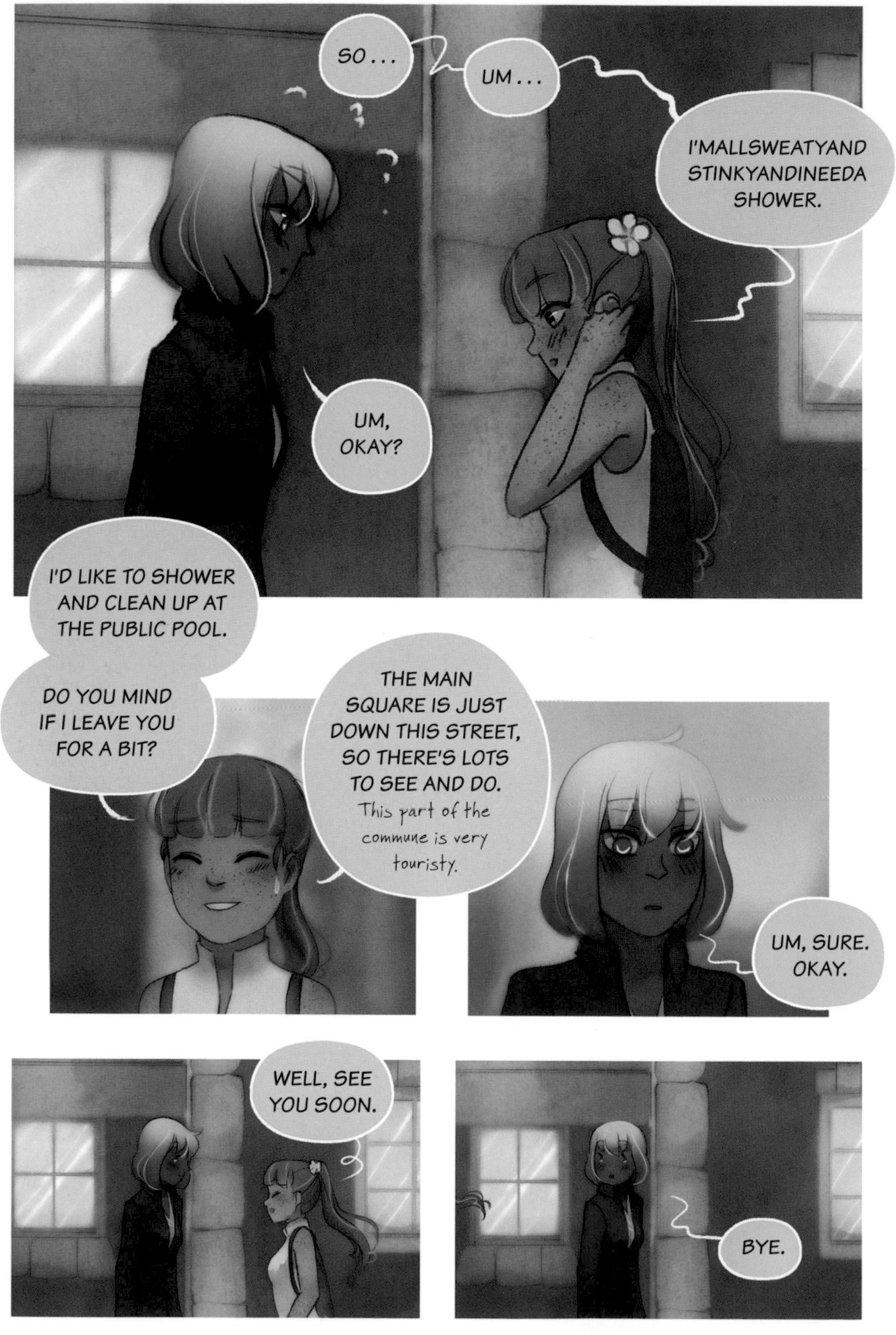
SO . . .
UM . . .
I'MALLSWEATYAND STINKYANDINEEDA SHOWER.
UM, OKAY?
I'D LIKE TO SHOWER AND CLEAN UP AT THE PUBLIC POOL.
DO YOU MIND IF I LEAVE YOU FOR A BIT?
THE MAIN SQUARE IS JUST DOWN THIS STREET, SO THERE'S LOTS TO SEE AND DO.
This part of the commune is very touristy.
UM, SURE. OKAY.
WELL, SEE YOU SOON.
BYE.

Soooo...
I GUESS
I'LL GO LOOK
AROUND?

EVERYTHING
HERE LOOKS SO
ANCIENT. IT'S
LIKE I'VE GONE
BACK IN TIME.

I WONDER IF THE
BUILDINGS ARE
AS OLD AS THEY
LOOK . . .

. . . OR IS
IT ALL TO
IMPRESS THE
TOURISTS?

WOW.

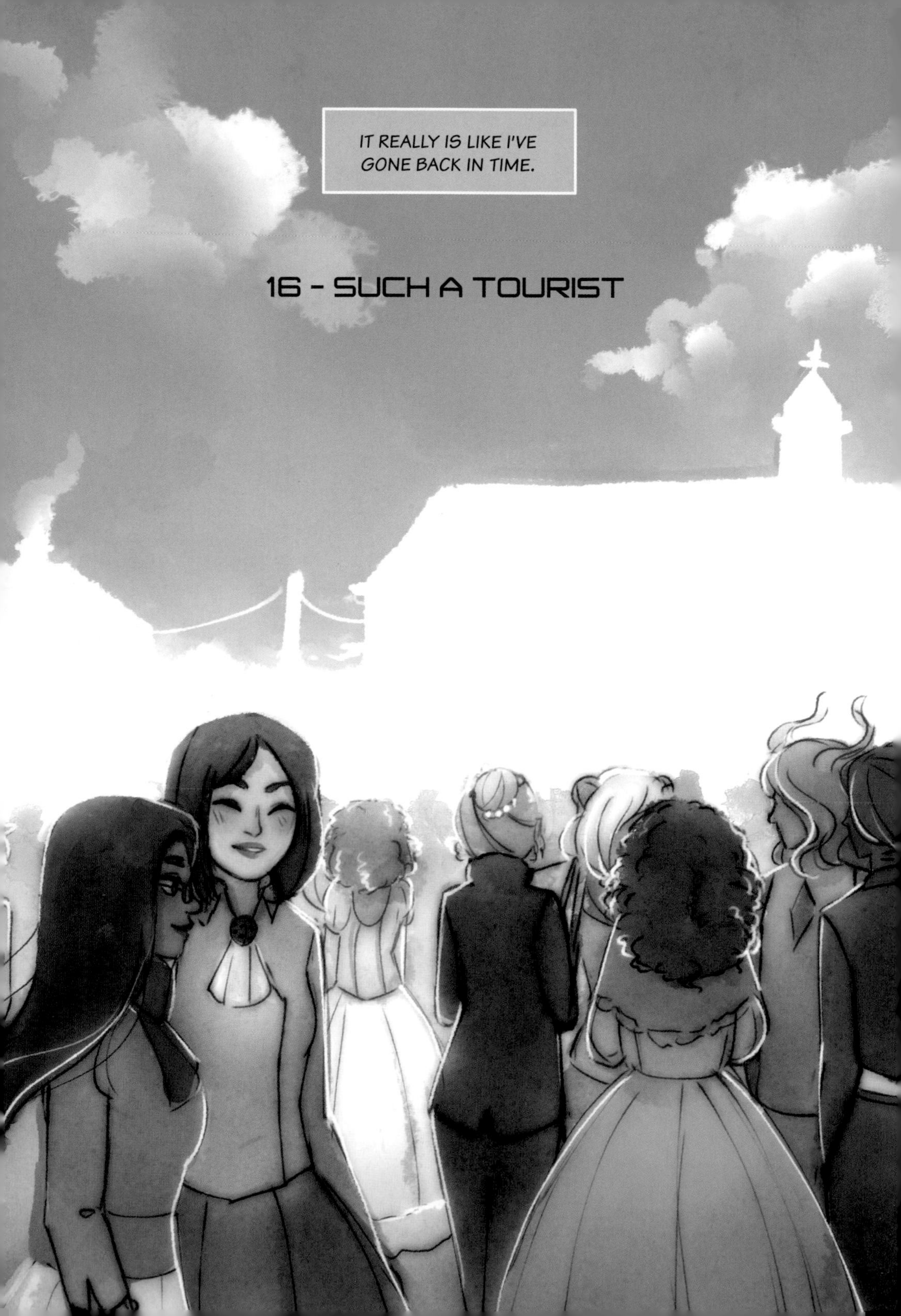
IT REALLY IS LIKE I'VE GONE BACK IN TIME.
16 - SUCH A TOURIST

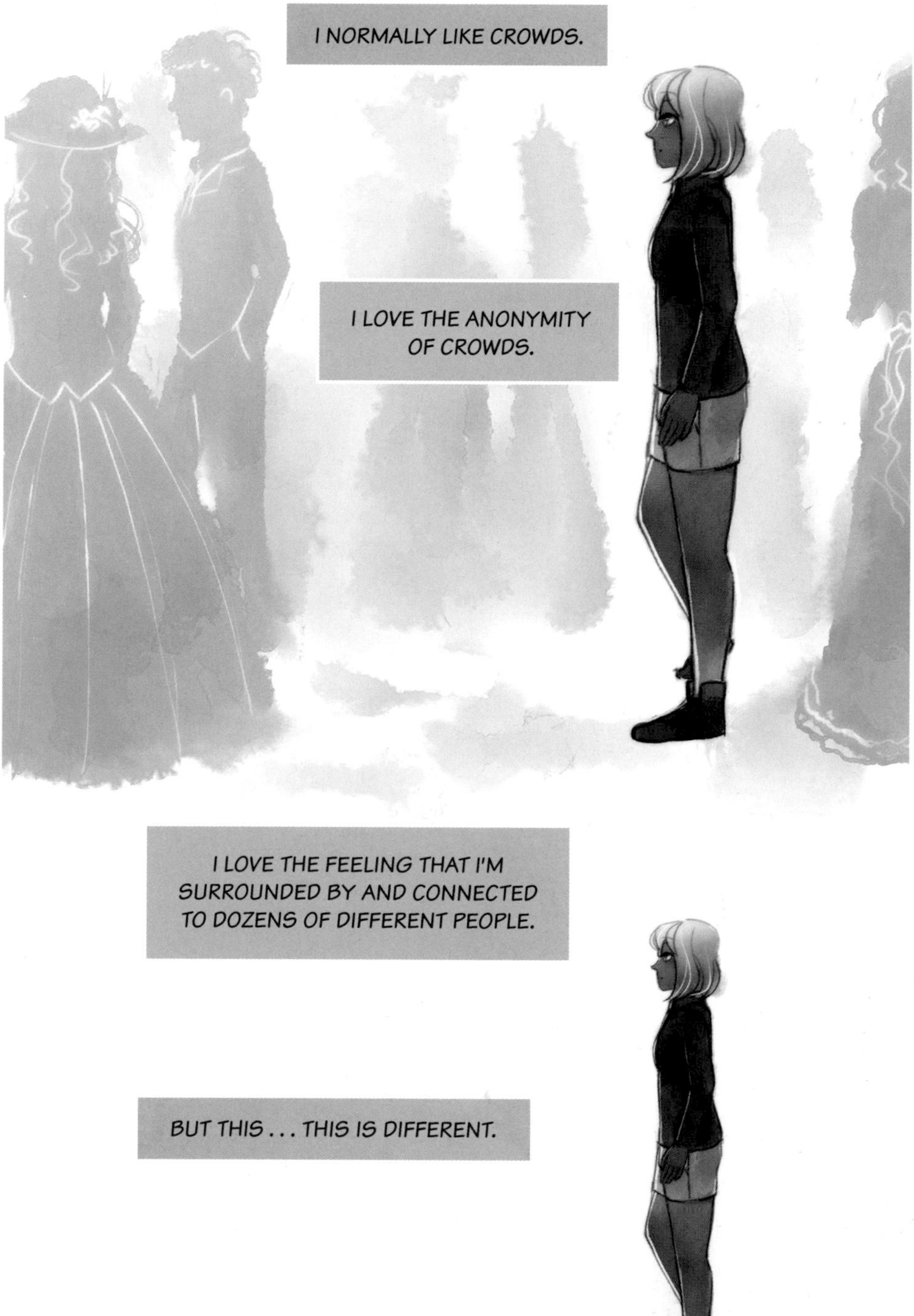
I NORMALLY LIKE CROWDS.
I LOVE THE ANONYMITY OF CROWDS.
I LOVE THE FEELING THAT I'M SURROUNDED BY AND CONNECTED TO DOZENS OF DIFFERENT PEOPLE.
BUT THIS . . . THIS IS DIFFERENT.

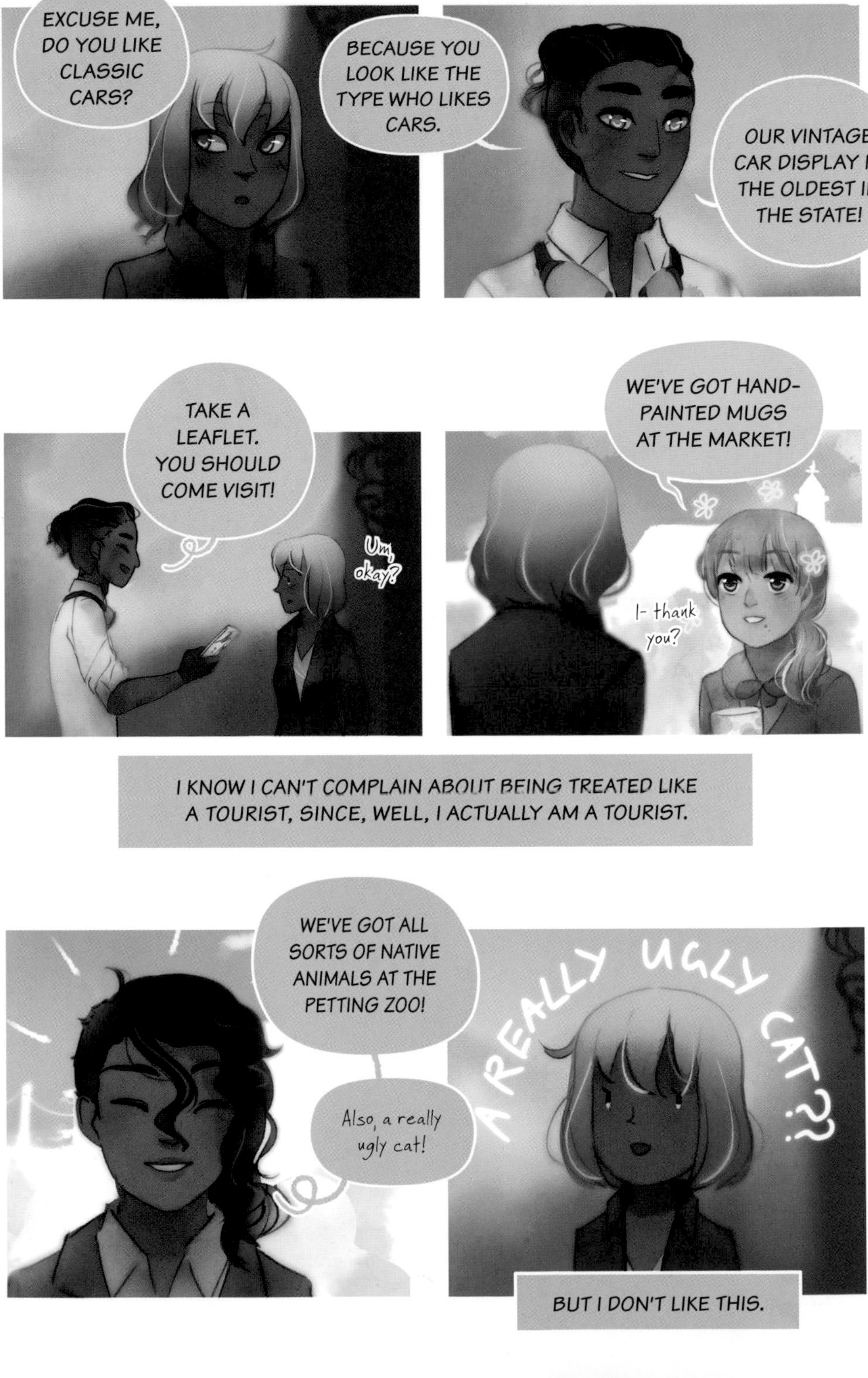
EXCUSE ME, DO YOU LIKE CLASSIC CARS?
BECAUSE YOU LOOK LIKE THE TYPE WHO LIKES CARS.
OUR VINTAGE CAR DISPLAY IS THE OLDEST IN THE STATE!
TAKE A LEAFLET. YOU SHOULD COME VISIT!
Um, okay?
WE'VE GOT HAND-PAINTED MUGS AT THE MARKET!
I- thank you?
I KNOW I CAN'T COMPLAIN ABOUT BEING TREATED LIKE A TOURIST, SINCE, WELL, I ACTUALLY AM A TOURIST.
WE'VE GOT ALL SORTS OF NATIVE ANIMALS AT THE PETTING ZOO!
Also, a really ugly cat!
A REALLY UGLY CAT??!
BUT I DON'T LIKE THIS.

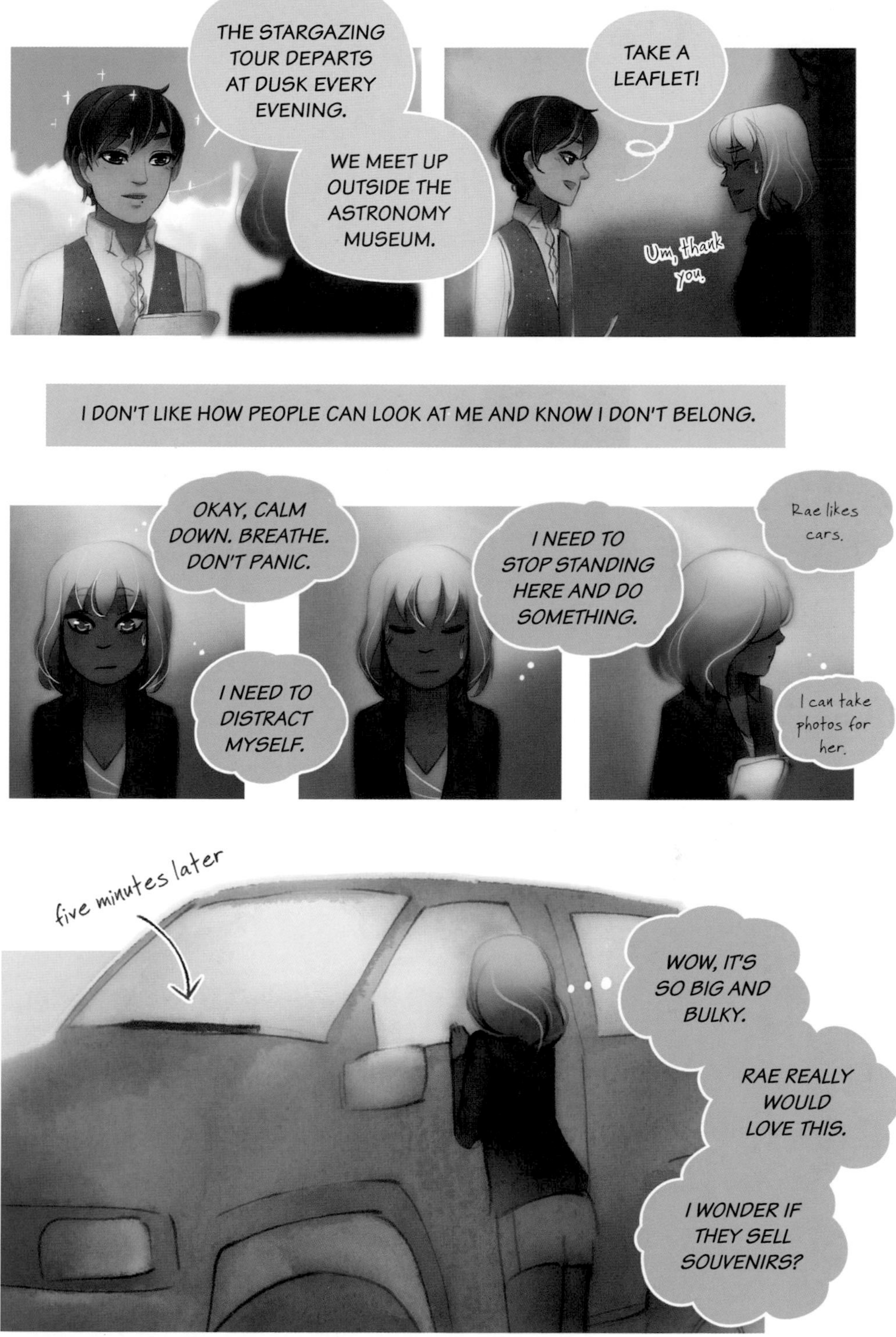
THE STARGAZING TOUR DEPARTS AT DUSK EVERY EVENING.
WE MEET UP OUTSIDE THE ASTRONOMY MUSEUM.
TAKE A LEAFLET!
Um, thank you.
I DON'T LIKE HOW PEOPLE CAN LOOK AT ME AND KNOW I DON'T BELONG.
OKAY, CALM DOWN. BREATHE. DON'T PANIC.
I NEED TO DISTRACT MYSELF.
I NEED TO STOP STANDING HERE AND DO SOMETHING.
Rae likes cars.
I can take photos for her.
five minutes later
WOW, IT'S SO BIG AND BULKY.
RAE REALLY WOULD LOVE THIS.
I WONDER IF THEY SELL SOUVENIRS?

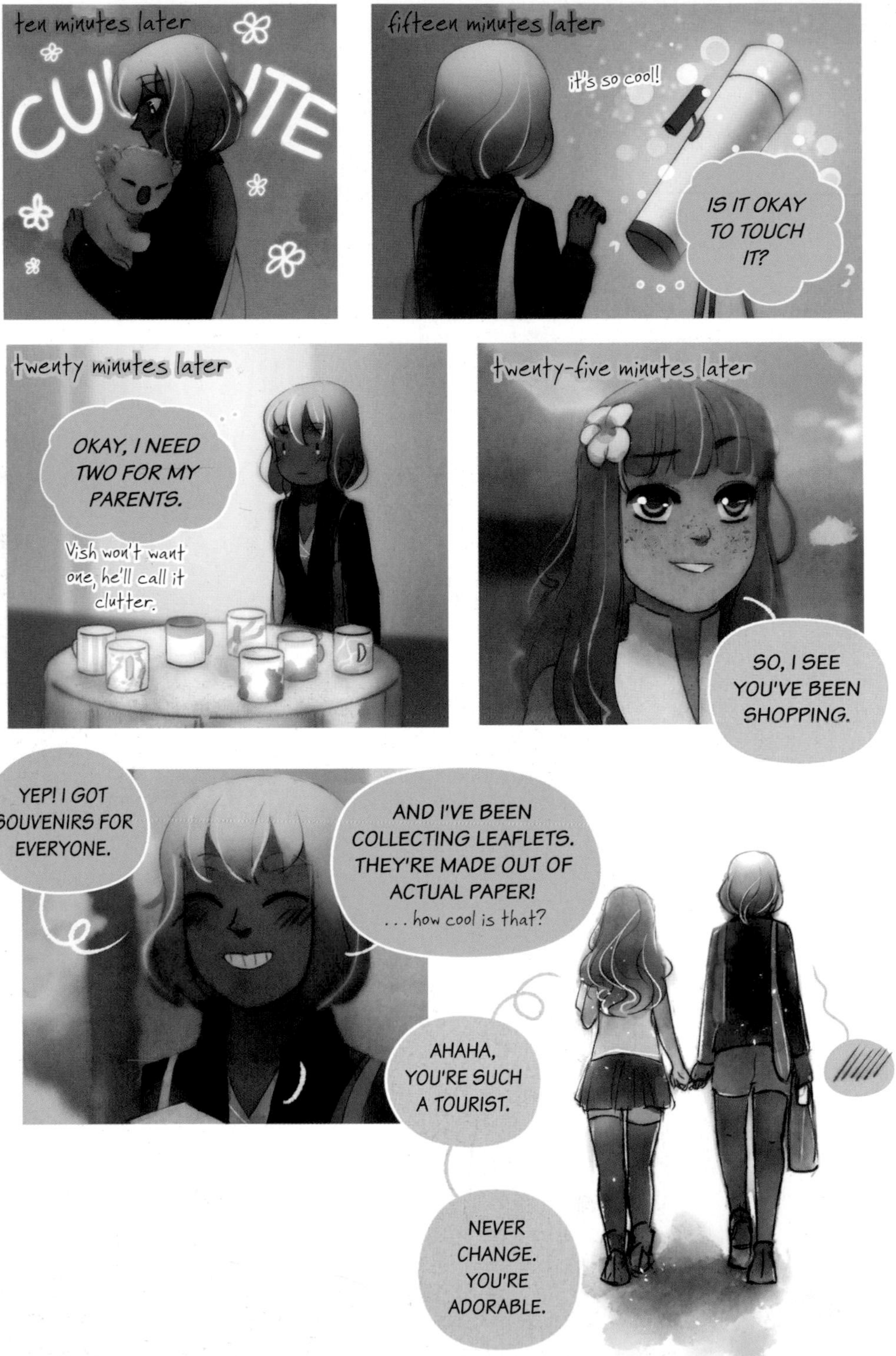

ten minutes later
CU TE
fifteen minutes later
it's so cool!
IS IT OKAY TO TOUCH IT?
twenty minutes later
OKAY, I NEED TWO FOR MY PARENTS.
Vish won't want one, he'll call it clutter.
twenty-five minutes later
SO, I SEE YOU'VE BEEN SHOPPING.
YEP! I GOT SOUVENIRS FOR EVERYONE.
AND I'VE BEEN COLLECTING LEAFLETS. THEY'RE MADE OUT OF ACTUAL PAPER! . . . how cool is that?
AHAHA, YOU'RE SUCH A TOURIST.
NEVER CHANGE. YOU'RE ADORABLE.

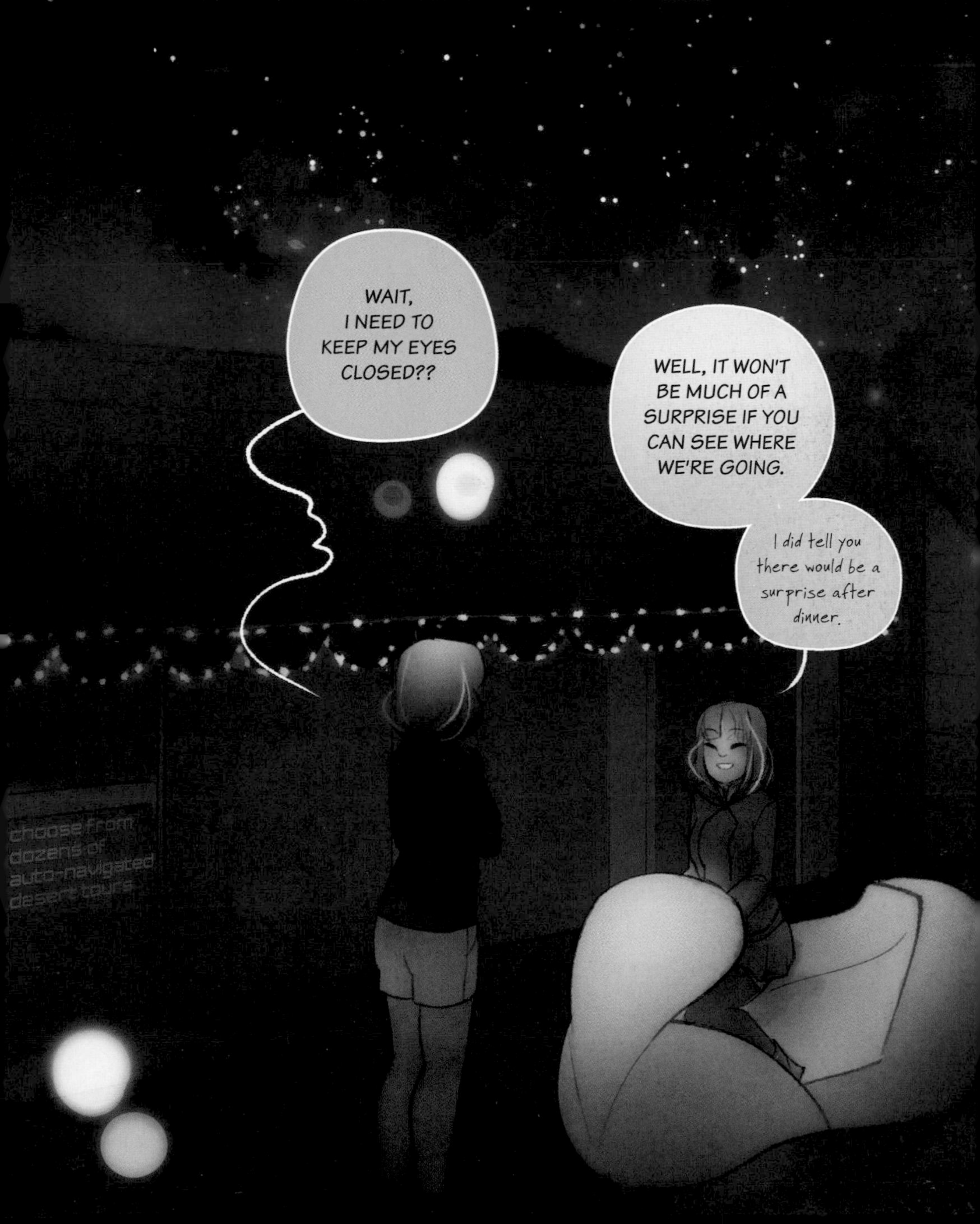
WAIT, I NEED TO KEEP MY EYES CLOSED??
WELL, IT WON'T BE MUCH OF A SURPRISE IF YOU CAN SEE WHERE WE'RE GOING.
I did tell you there would be a surprise after dinner.
choose from dozens of auto-navigated desert tours

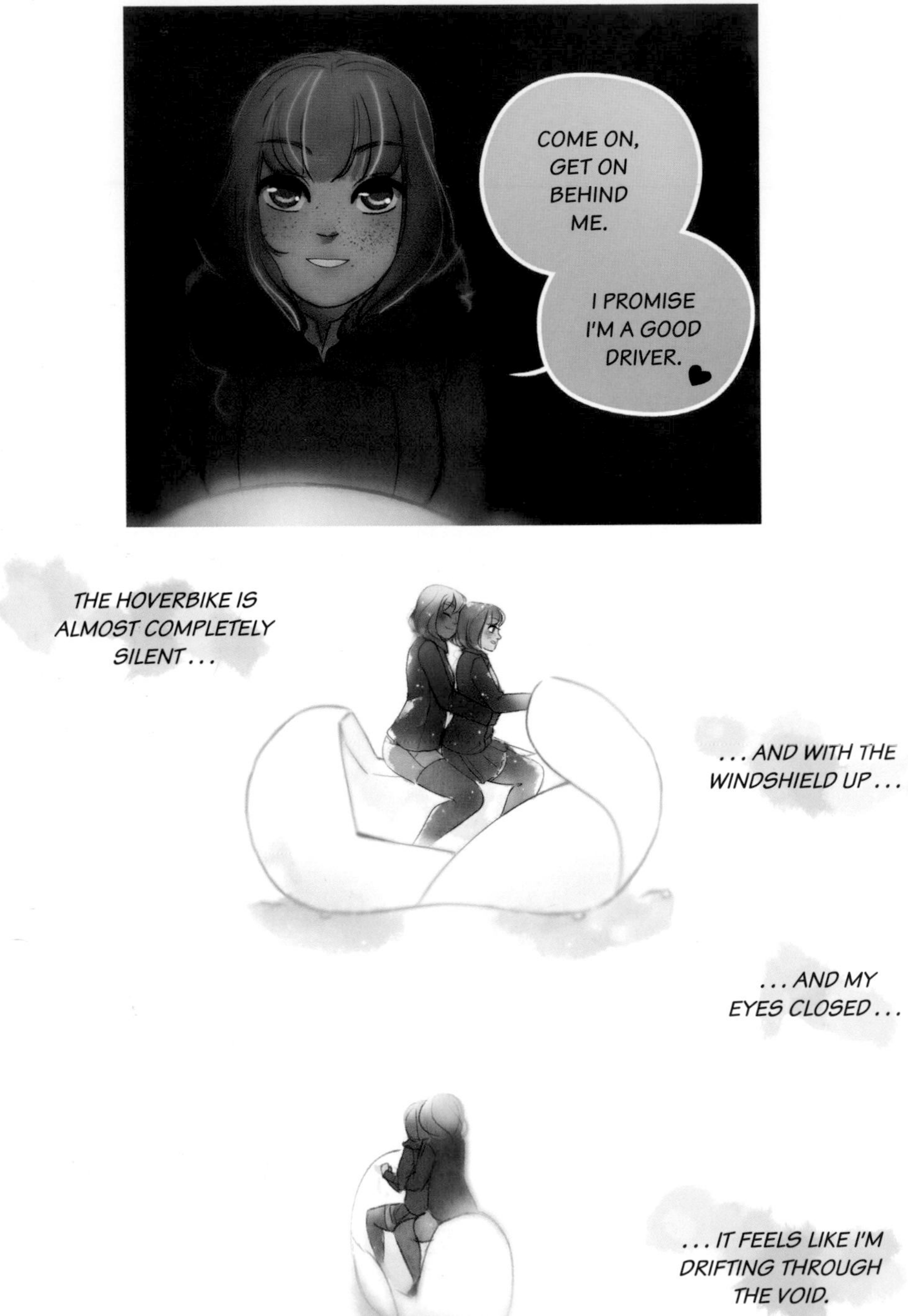
COME ON, GET ON BEHIND ME.
I PROMISE I'M A GOOD DRIVER.
THE HOVERBIKE IS ALMOST COMPLETELY SILENT . . .
. . . AND WITH THE WINDSHIELD UP . . .
. . . AND MY EYES CLOSED . . .
. . . IT FEELS LIKE I'M DRIFTING THROUGH THE VOID.

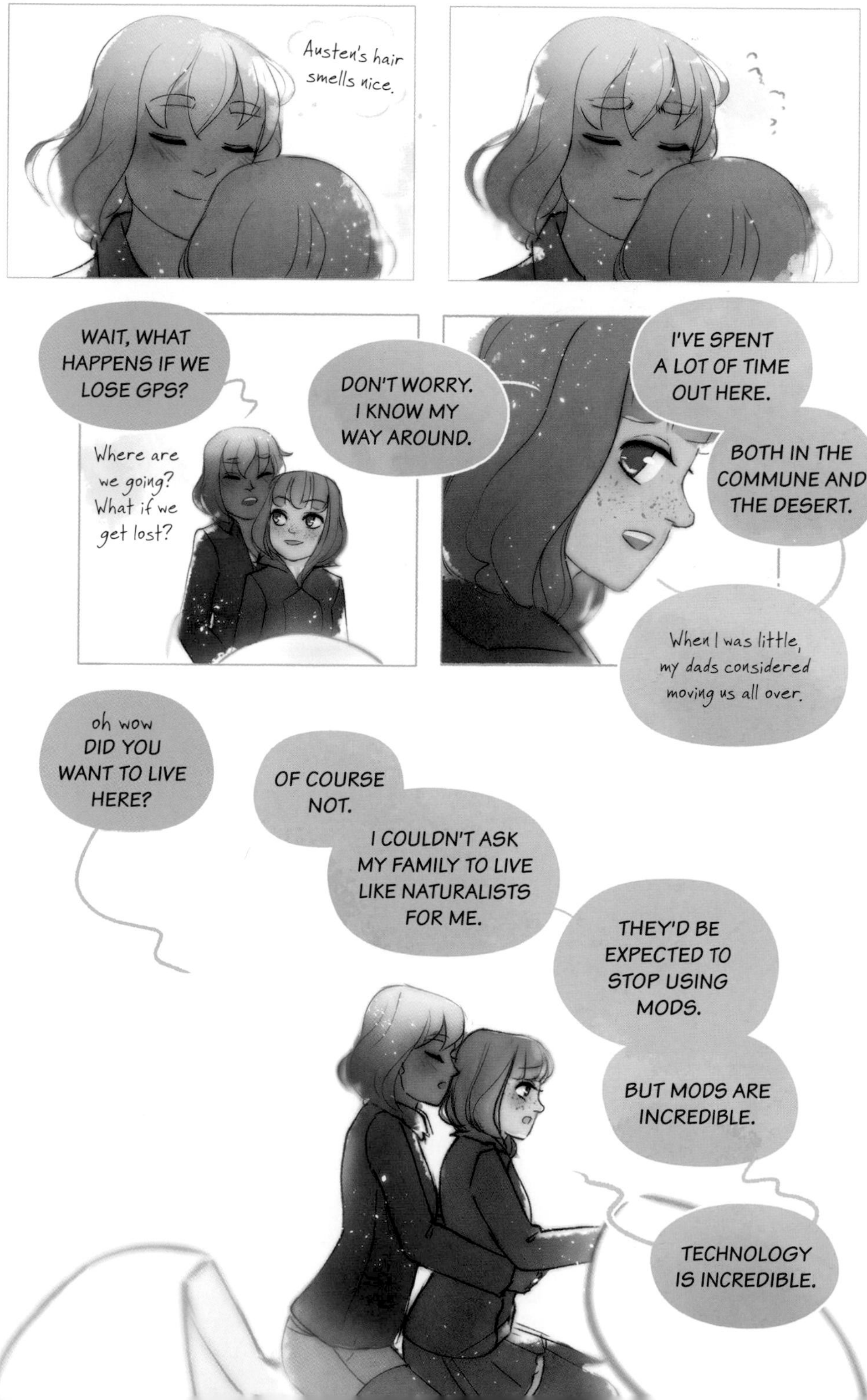
Austen's hair smells nice.
WAIT, WHAT HAPPENS IF WE LOSE GPS?
Where are we going? What if we get lost?
DON'T WORRY. I KNOW MY WAY AROUND.
I'VE SPENT A LOT OF TIME OUT HERE.
BOTH IN THE COMMUNE AND THE DESERT.
When I was little, my dads considered moving us all over.
oh wow DID YOU WANT TO LIVE HERE?
OF COURSE NOT.
I COULDN'T ASK MY FAMILY TO LIVE LIKE NATURALISTS FOR ME.
THEY'D BE EXPECTED TO STOP USING MODS.
BUT MODS ARE INCREDIBLE.
TECHNOLOGY IS INCREDIBLE.

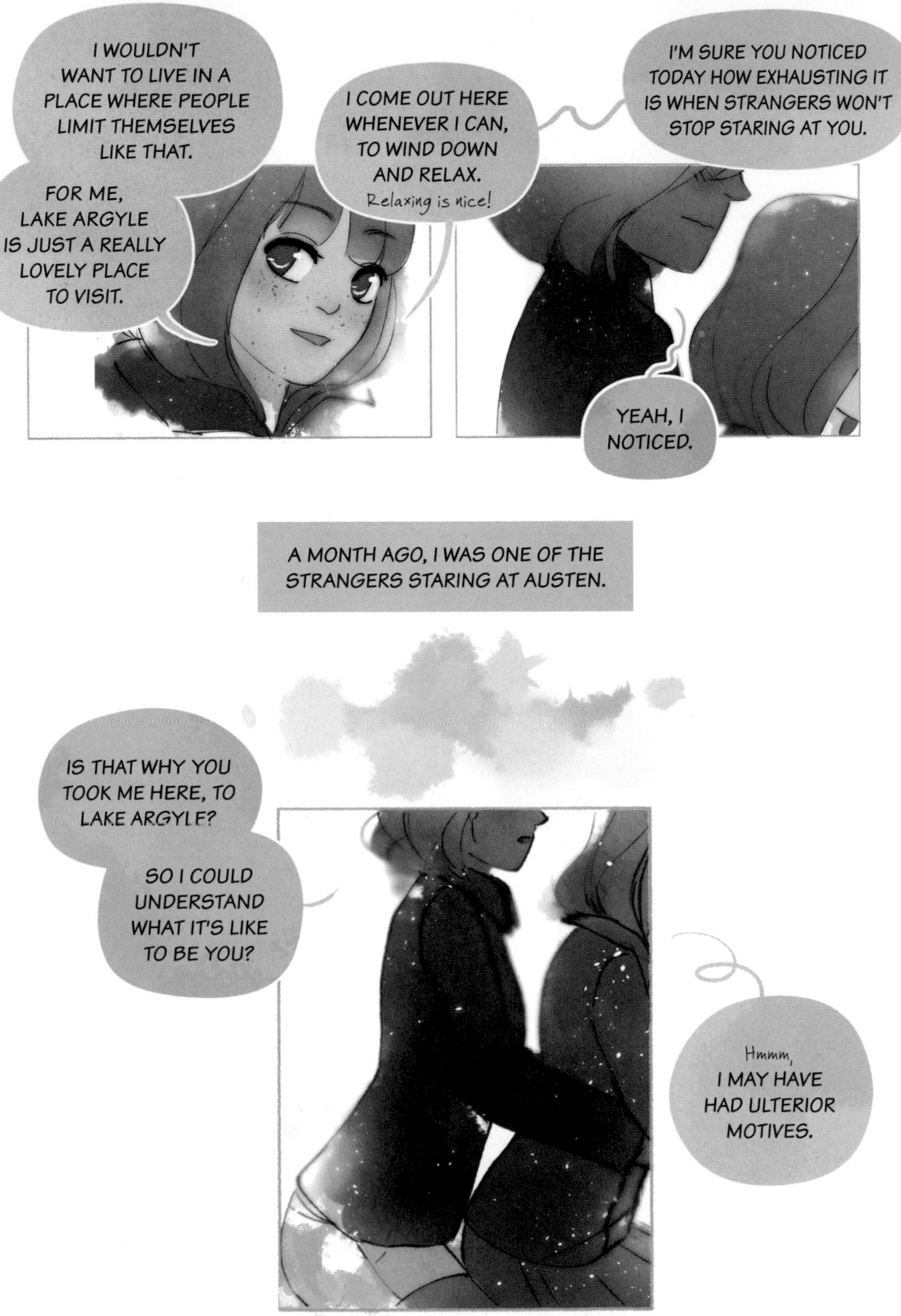
I WOULDN'T WANT TO LIVE IN A PLACE WHERE PEOPLE LIMIT THEMSELVES LIKE THAT.
FOR ME, LAKE ARGYLE IS JUST A REALLY LOVELY PLACE TO VISIT.
I COME OUT HERE WHENEVER I CAN, TO WIND DOWN AND RELAX.
Relaxing is nice!
I'M SURE YOU NOTICED TODAY HOW EXHAUSTING IT IS WHEN STRANGERS WON'T STOP STARING AT YOU.
YEAH, I NOTICED.
A MONTH AGO, I WAS ONE OF THE STRANGERS STARING AT AUSTEN.
IS THAT WHY YOU TOOK ME HERE, TO LAKE ARGYLE?
SO I COULD UNDERSTAND WHAT IT'S LIKE TO BE YOU?
Hmmm,
I MAY HAVE HAD ULTERIOR MOTIVES.

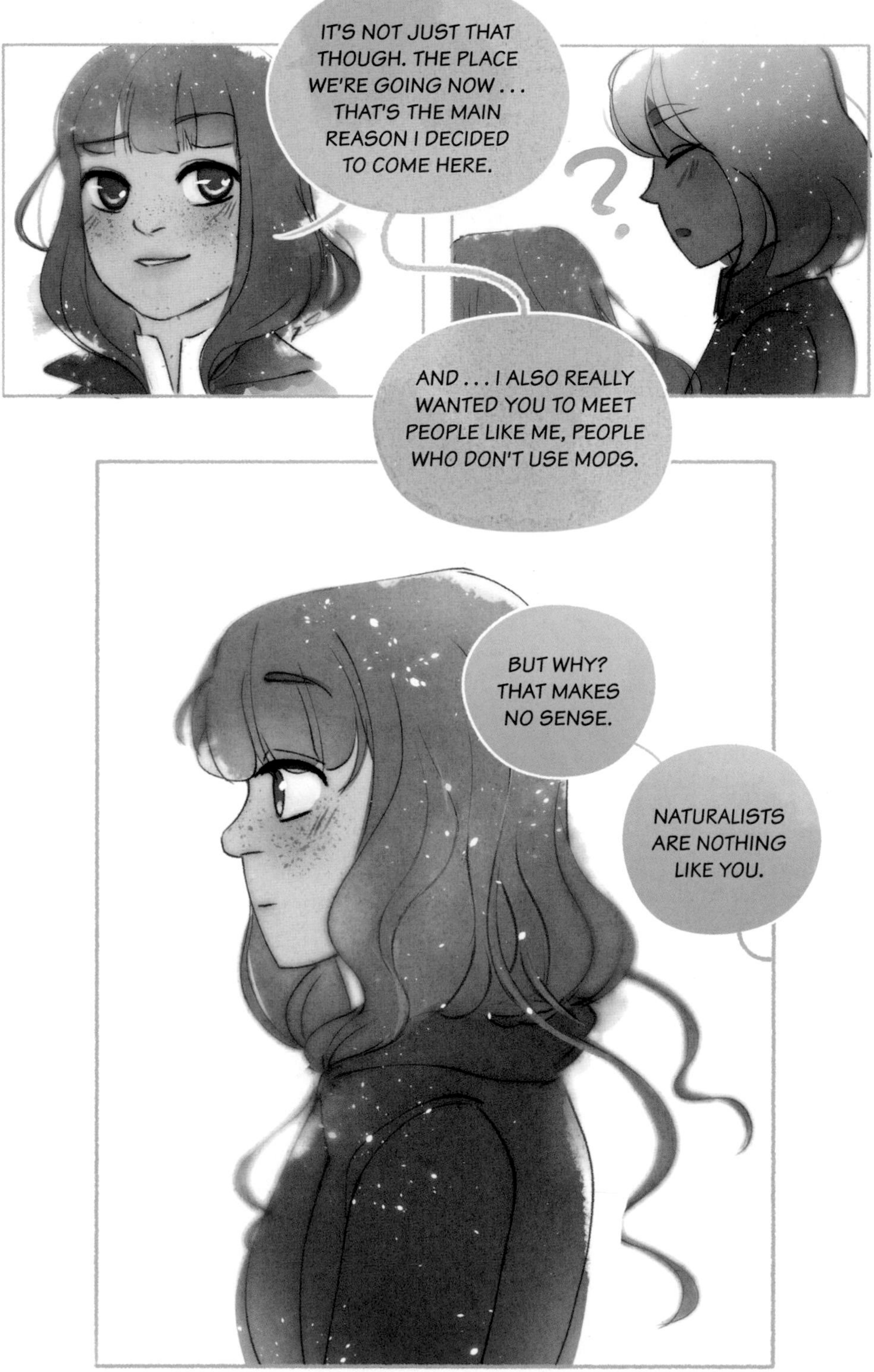
IT'S NOT JUST THAT THOUGH. THE PLACE WE'RE GOING NOW . . . THAT'S THE MAIN REASON I DECIDED TO COME HERE.
?
AND . . . I ALSO REALLY WANTED YOU TO MEET PEOPLE LIKE ME, PEOPLE WHO DON'T USE MODS.
BUT WHY? THAT MAKES NO SENSE.
NATURALISTS ARE NOTHING LIKE YOU.

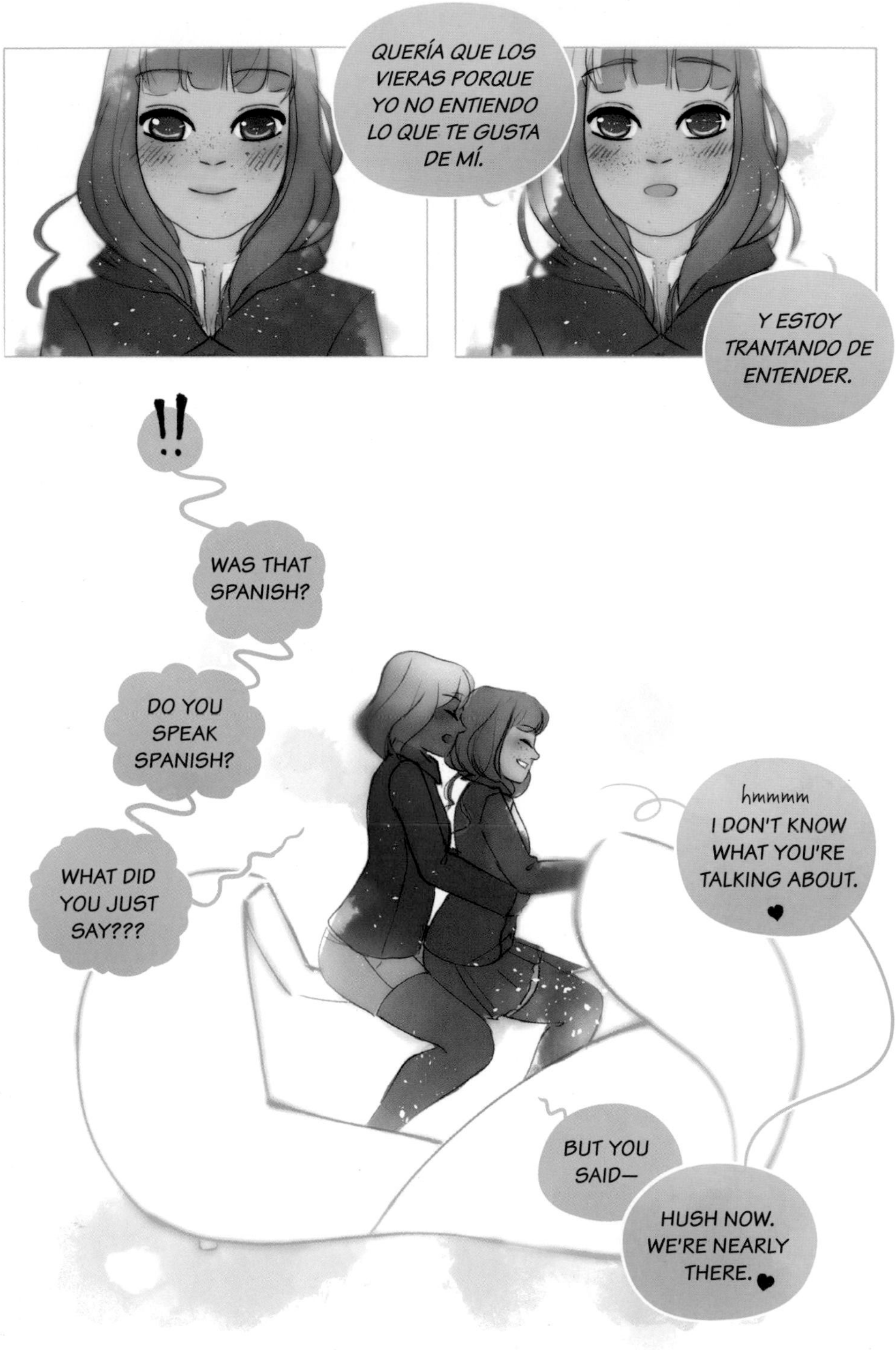
QUERÍA QUE LOS VIERAS PORQUE YO NO ENTIENDO LO QUE TE GUSTA DE MÍ.
Y ESTOY TRANTANDO DE ENTENDER.
!!
WAS THAT SPANISH?
DO YOU SPEAK SPANISH?
WHAT DID YOU JUST SAY???
hmmmm I DON'T KNOW WHAT YOU'RE TALKING ABOUT. ♥
BUT YOU SAID—
HUSH NOW. WE'RE NEARLY THERE. ♥

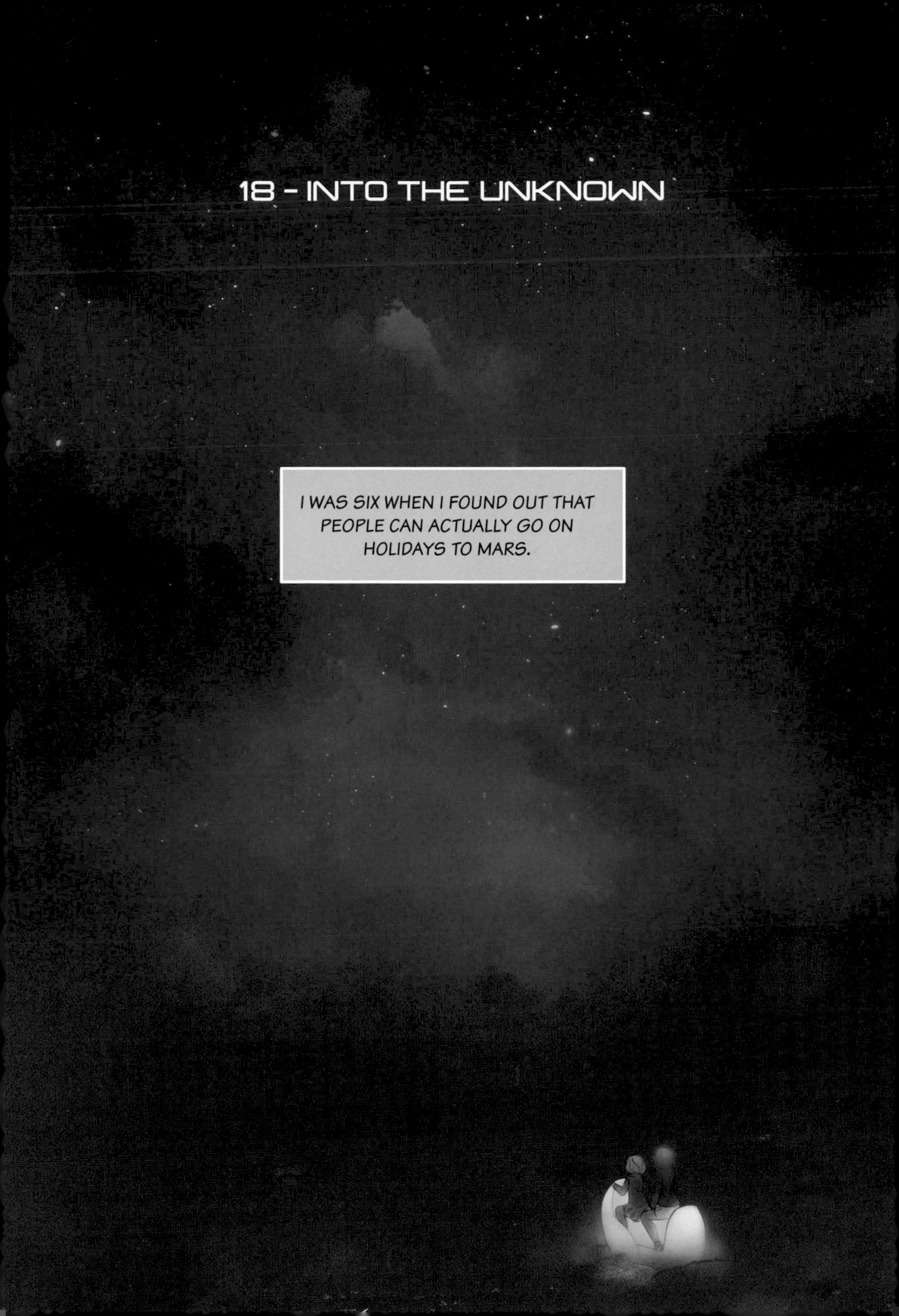
18 - INTO THE UNKNOWN
I WAS SIX WHEN I FOUND OUT THAT PEOPLE CAN ACTUALLY GO ON HOLIDAYS TO MARS.

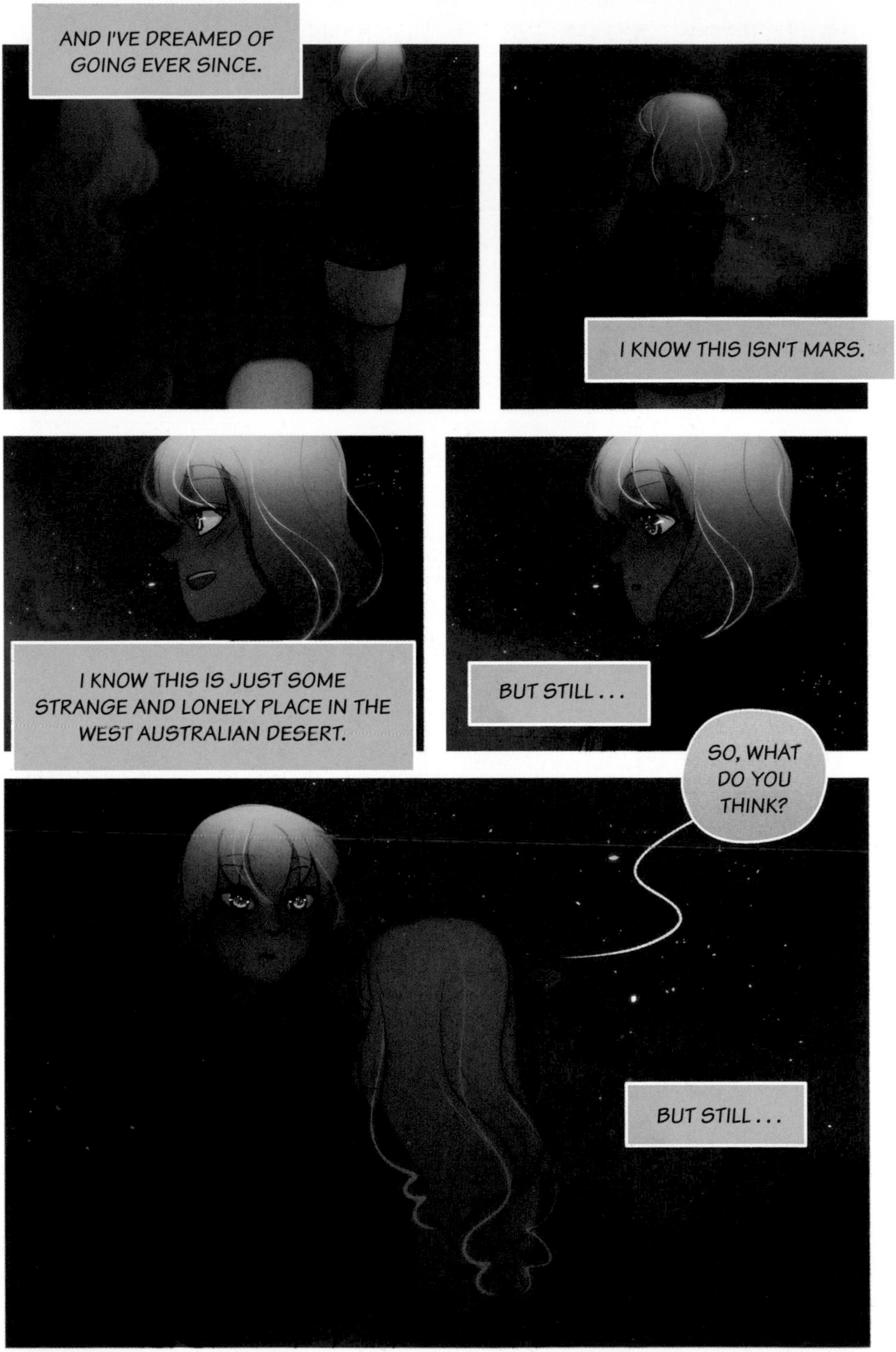
AND I'VE DREAMED OF GOING EVER SINCE.
I KNOW THIS ISN'T MARS.
I KNOW THIS IS JUST SOME STRANGE AND LONELY PLACE IN THE WEST AUSTRALIAN DESERT.
BUT STILL . . .
SO, WHAT DO YOU THINK?
BUT STILL . . .

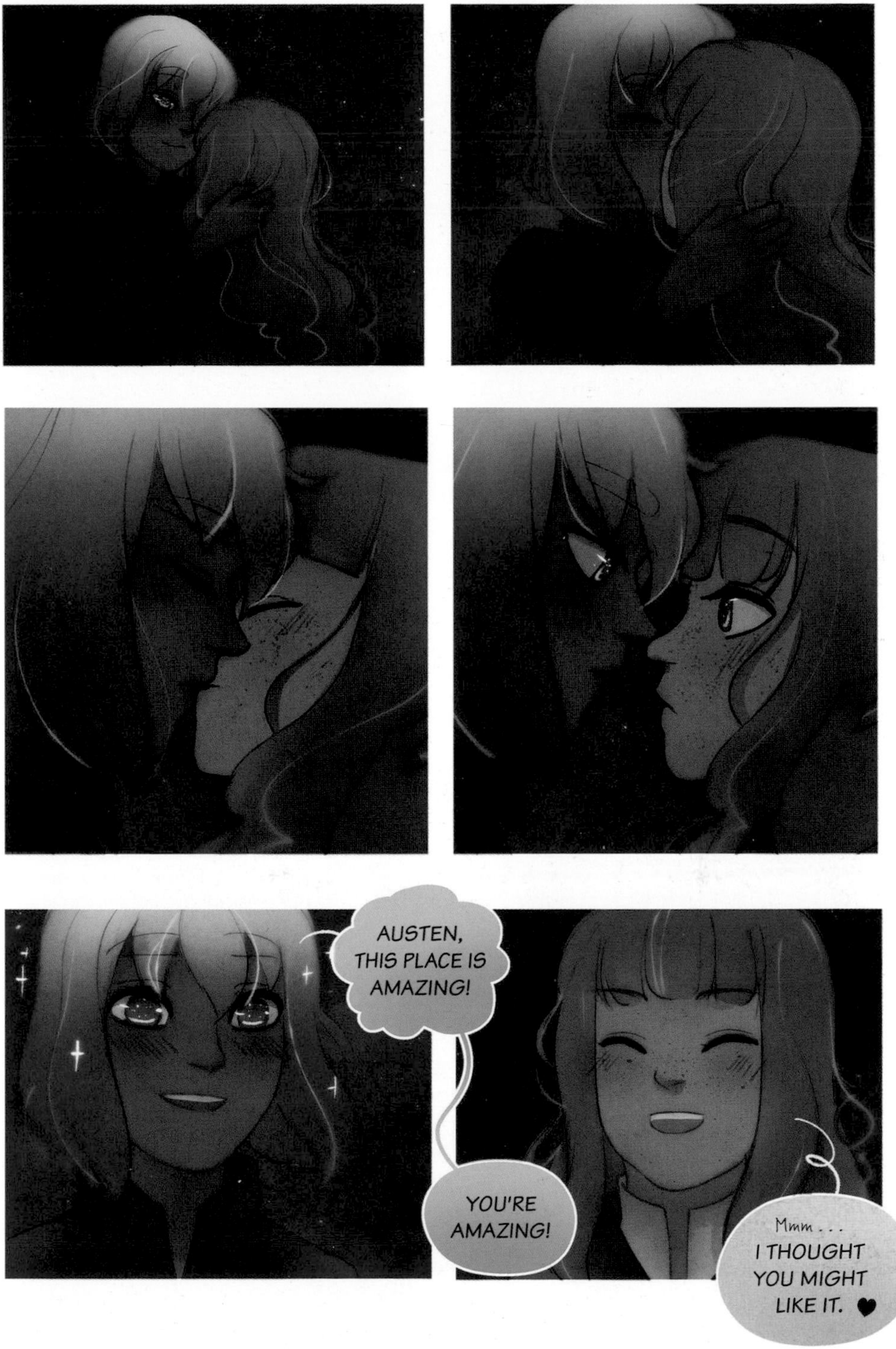
AUSTEN, THIS PLACE IS AMAZING!
YOU'RE AMAZING!
Mmm . . . I THOUGHT YOU MIGHT LIKE IT. ♥

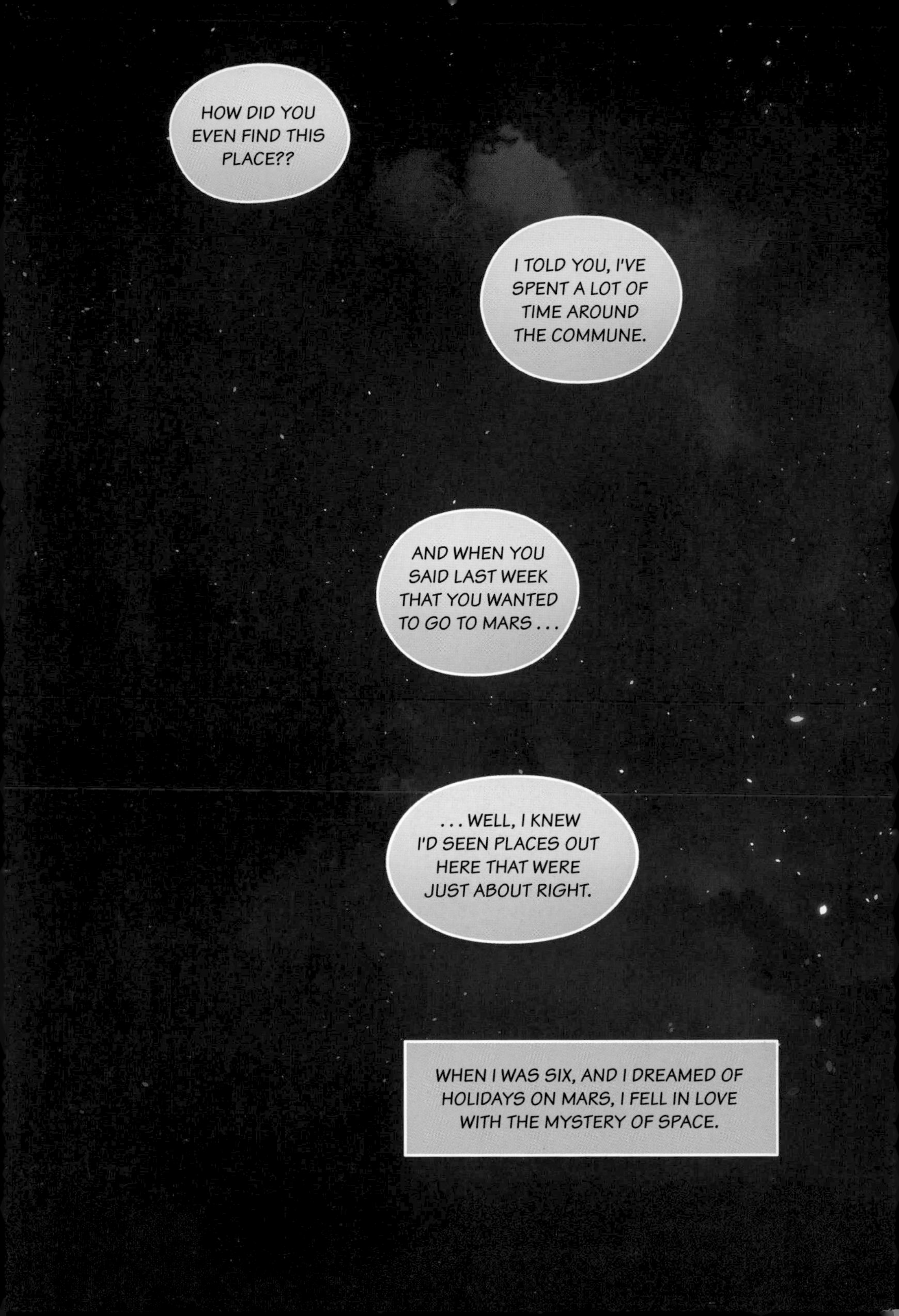
HOW DID YOU EVEN FIND THIS PLACE??
I TOLD YOU, I'VE SPENT A LOT OF TIME AROUND THE COMMUNE.
AND WHEN YOU SAID LAST WEEK THAT YOU WANTED TO GO TO MARS . . .
. . . WELL, I KNEW I'D SEEN PLACES OUT HERE THAT WERE JUST ABOUT RIGHT.
WHEN I WAS SIX, AND I DREAMED OF HOLIDAYS ON MARS, I FELL IN LOVE WITH THE MYSTERY OF SPACE.

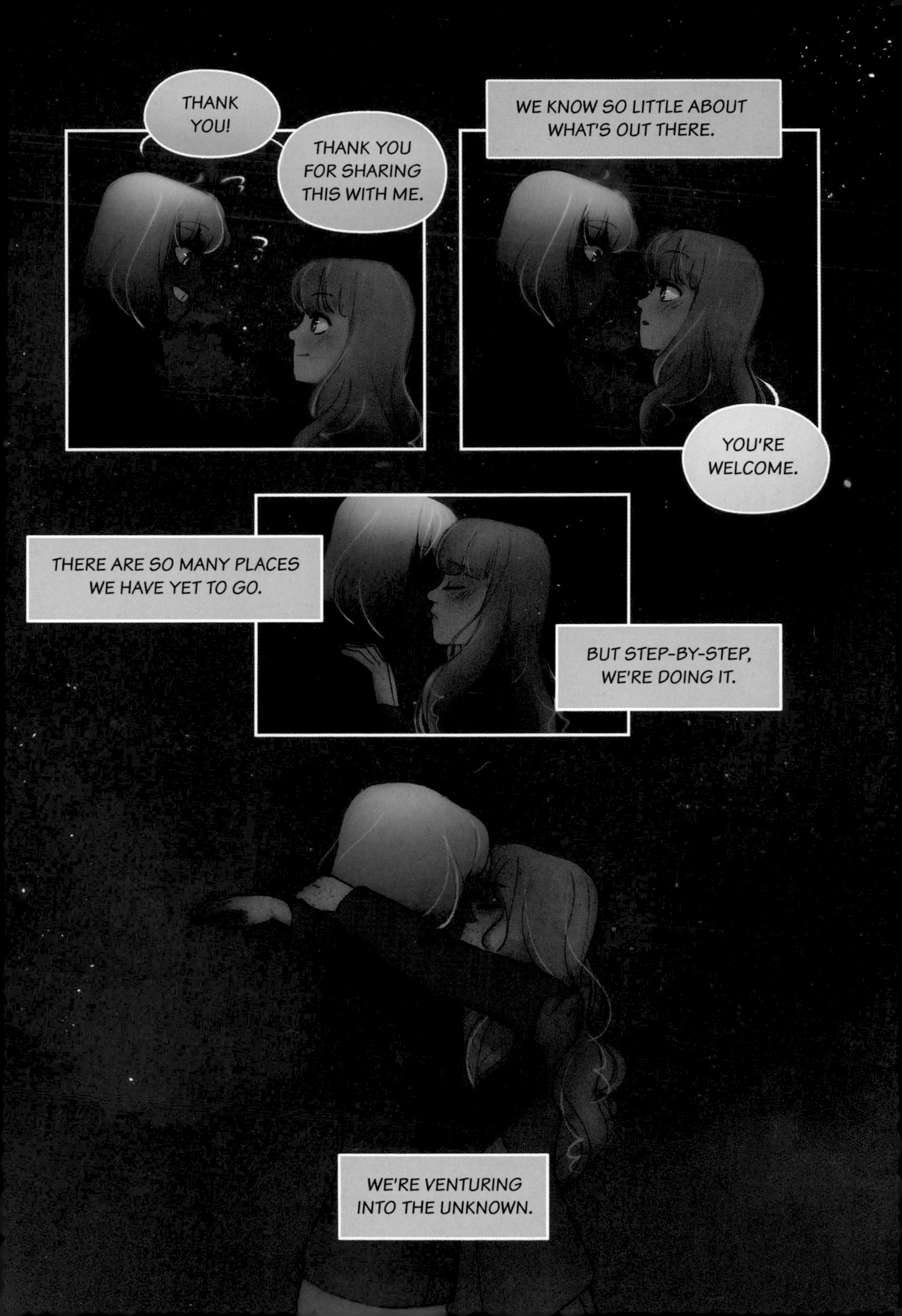
THANK YOU!
THANK YOU FOR SHARING THIS WITH ME.
WE KNOW SO LITTLE ABOUT WHAT'S OUT THERE.
YOU'RE WELCOME.
THERE ARE SO MANY PLACES WE HAVE YET TO GO.
BUT STEP-BY-STEP, WE'RE DOING IT.
WE'RE VENTURING INTO THE UNKNOWN.

19 - FIRST IMPRESSIONS

THREE WEEKS AGO (WHEN AUSTEN FIRST SAW SUNATI):

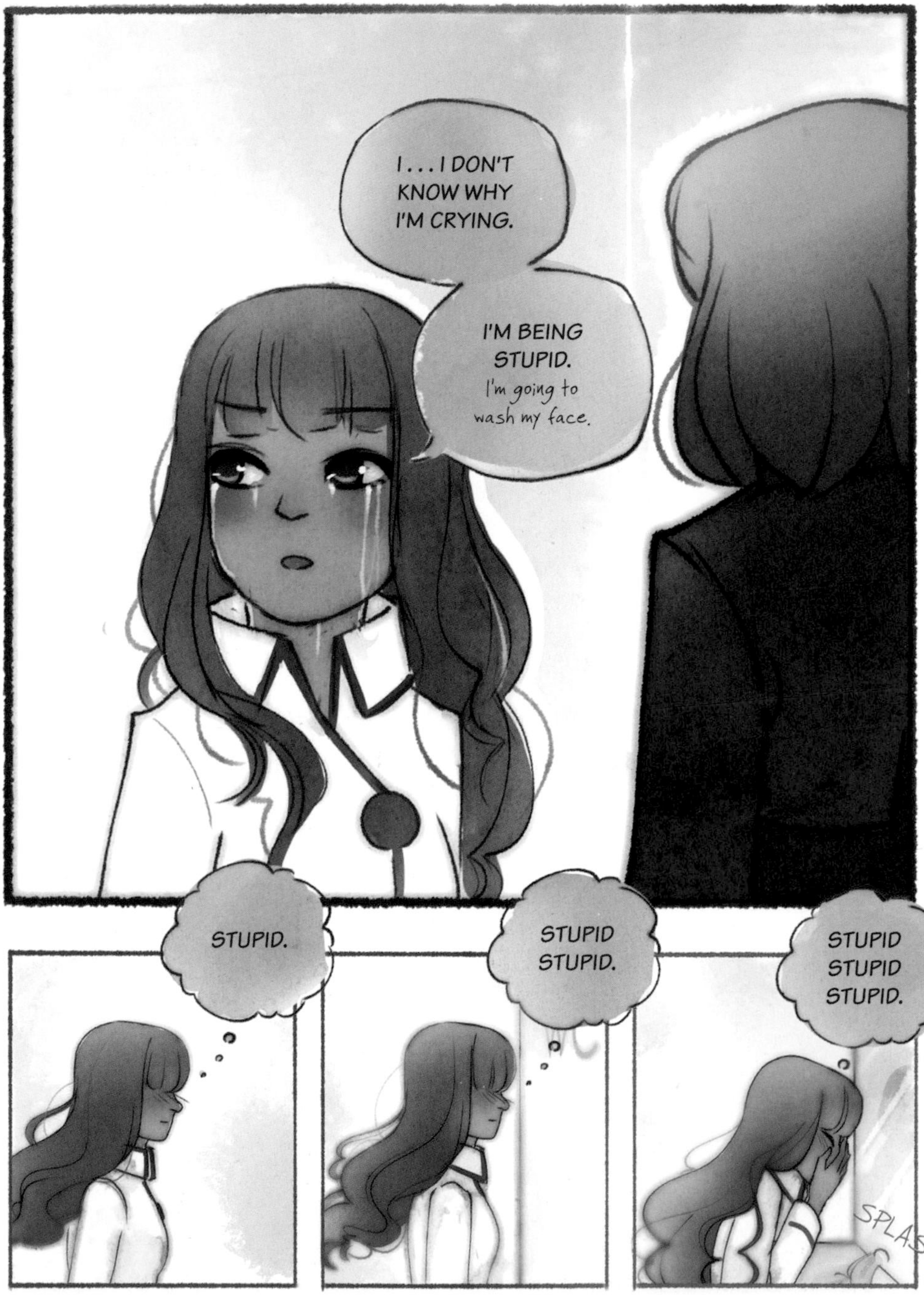
I . . . I DON'T KNOW WHY I'M CRYING.
I'M BEING STUPID.
I'm going to wash my face.
STUPID.
STUPID STUPID.
STUPID STUPID STUPID.
SPLASH

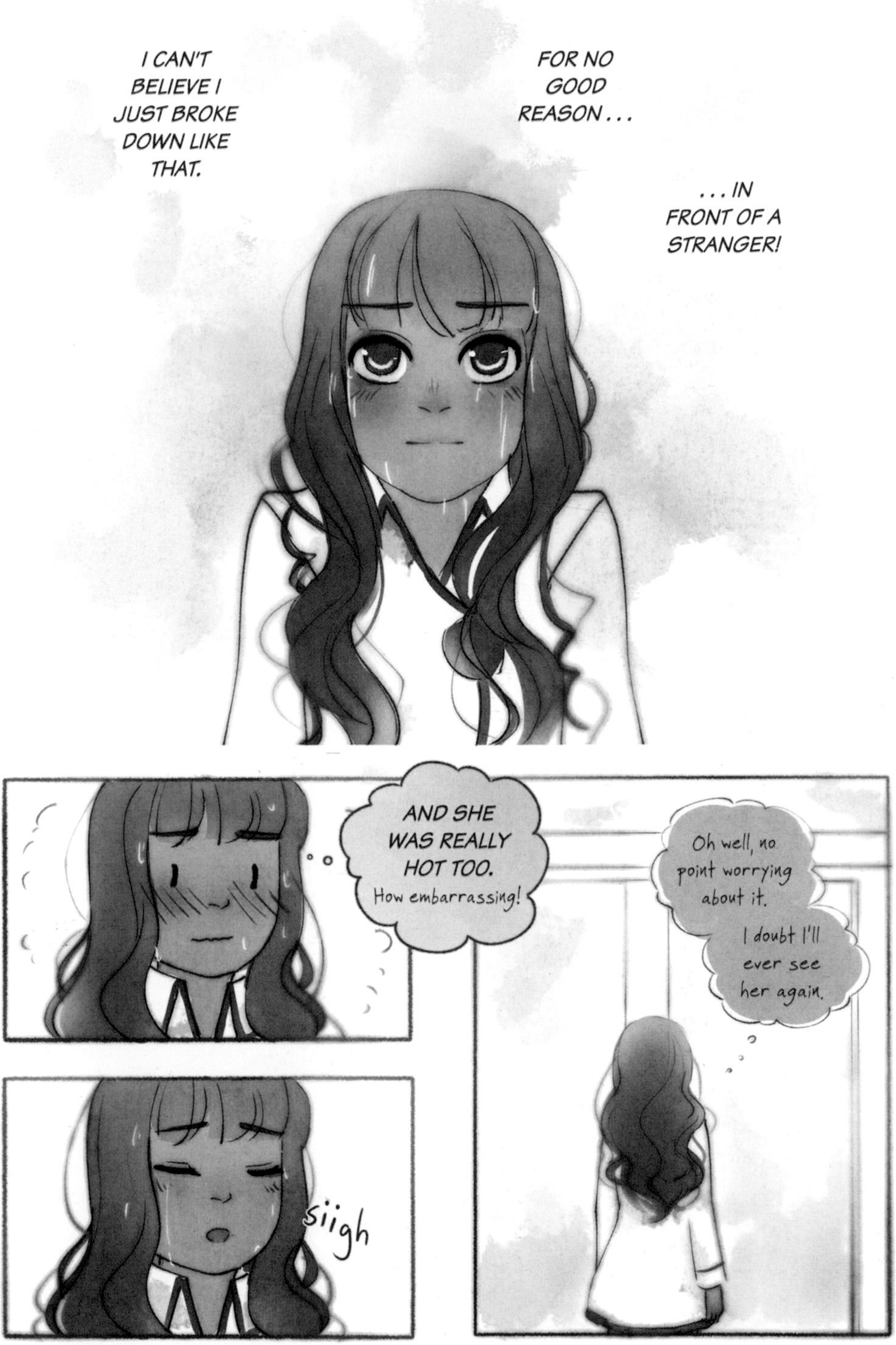
I CAN'T BELIEVE I JUST BROKE DOWN LIKE THAT.
FOR NO GOOD REASON . . .
. . . IN FRONT OF A STRANGER!
AND SHE WAS REALLY HOT TOO. How embarrassing!
siigh
Oh well, no point worrying about it.
I doubt I'll ever see her again.

THE NEXT DAY:

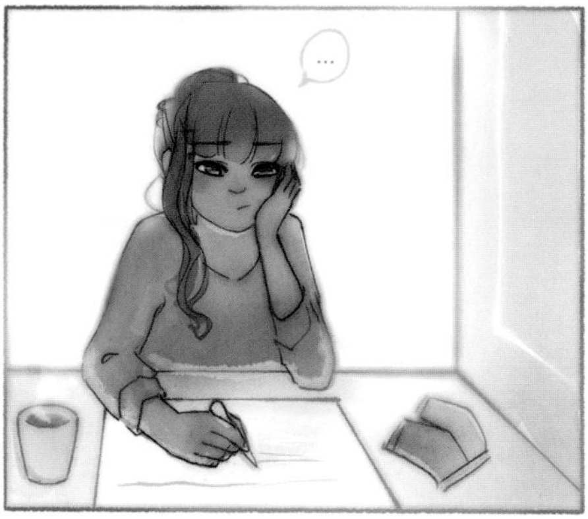
...

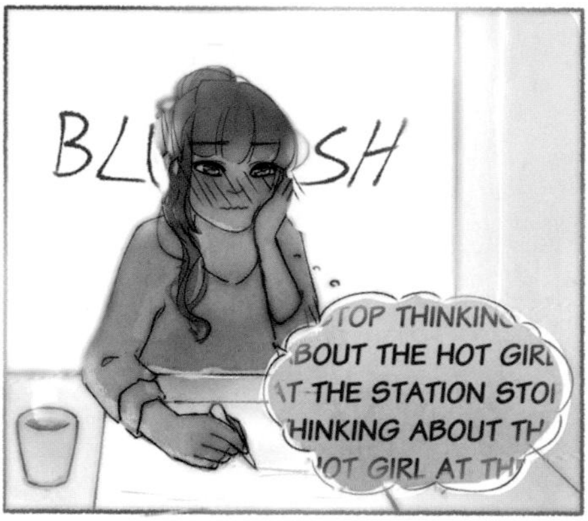
BL SH
TOP THINKING
BOUT THE HOT GIRL
T-THE STATION STO
HINKING ABOUT TH
OT GIRL AT TH

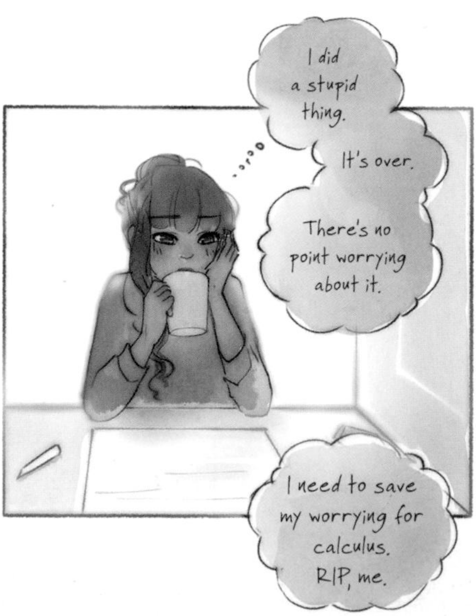
I did a stupid thing.
It's over.
There's no point worrying about it.
I need to save my worrying for calculus. RIP, me.

THE DAY AFTER THAT:

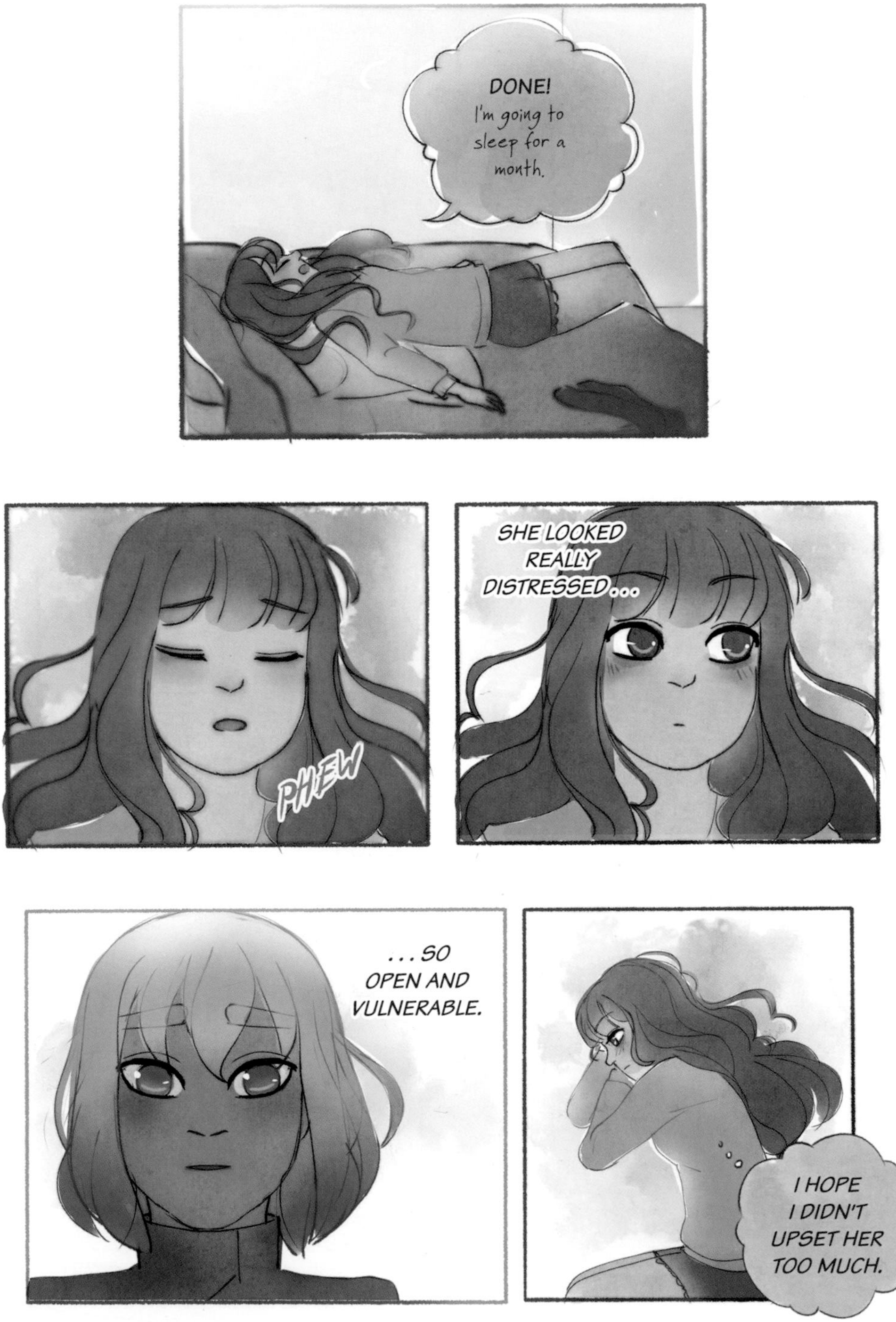
DONE! I'm going to sleep for a month.
PHEW
SHE LOOKED REALLY DISTRESSED...
...SO OPEN AND VULNERABLE.
I HOPE I DIDN'T UPSET HER TOO MUCH.

AND THE DAY AFTER THAT:

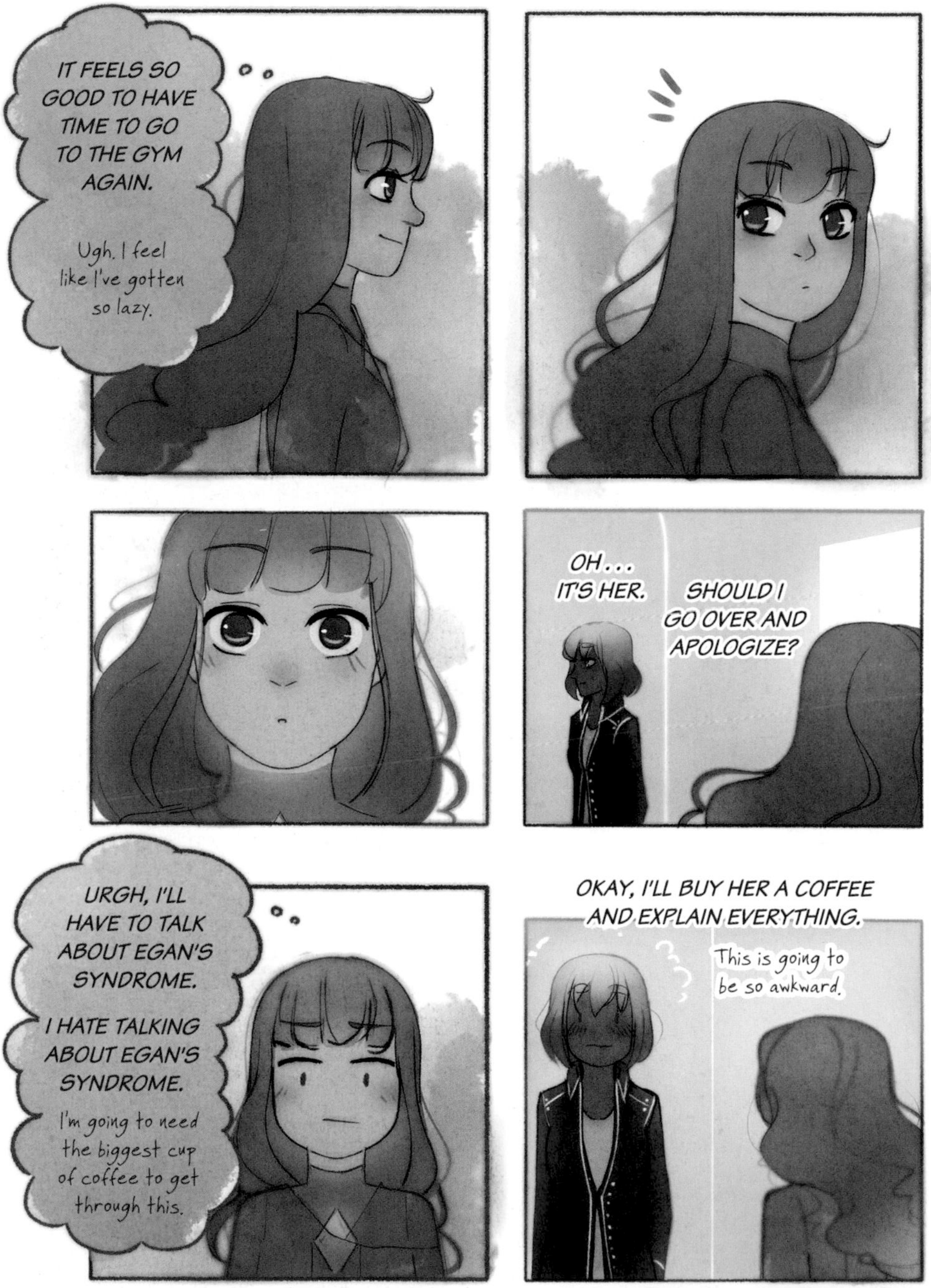
IT FEELS SO GOOD TO HAVE TIME TO GO TO THE GYM AGAIN.
Ugh. I feel like I've gotten so lazy.
OH... IT'S HER.
SHOULD I GO OVER AND APOLOGIZE?
URGH, I'LL HAVE TO TALK ABOUT EGAN'S SYNDROME.
I HATE TALKING ABOUT EGAN'S SYNDROME.
I'm going to need the biggest cup of coffee to get through this.
OKAY, I'LL BUY HER A COFFEE AND EXPLAIN EVERYTHING.
This is going to be so awkward.

OH WELL, AT LEAST I'LL NEVER SEE HER AGAIN.

20 - A BIT OF A JERK

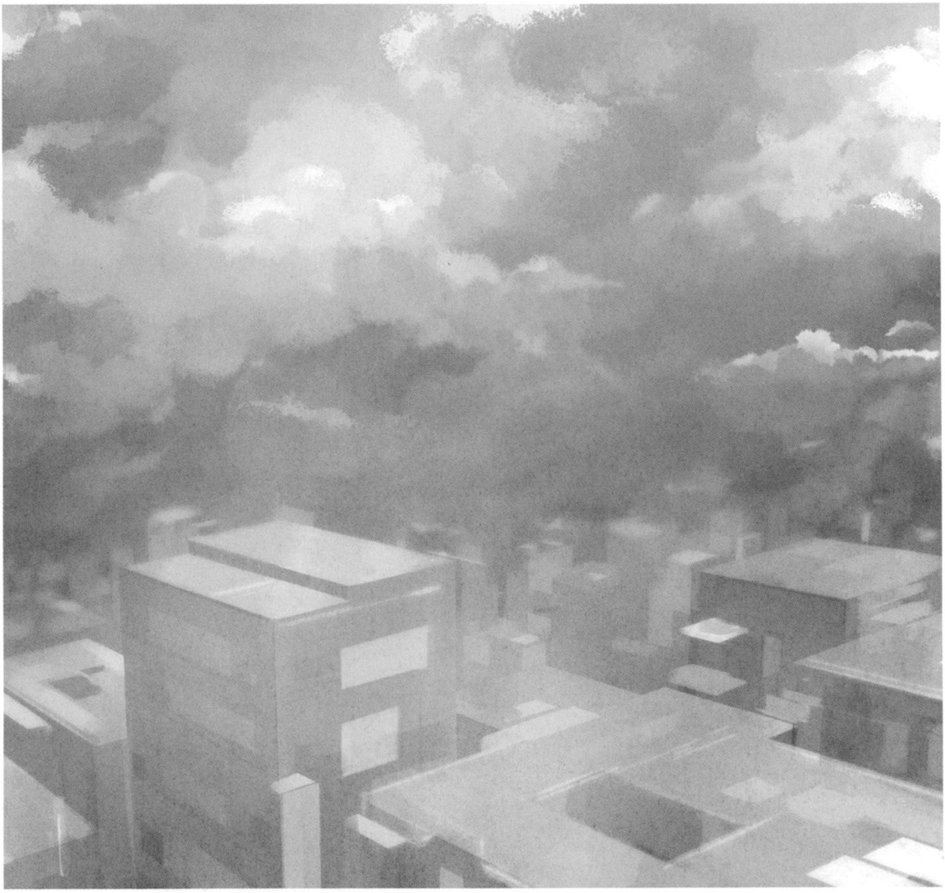

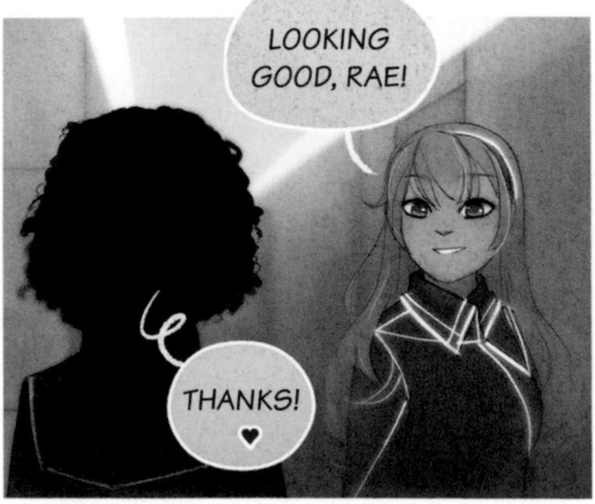
LOOKING GOOD, RAE!
THANKS! ♥

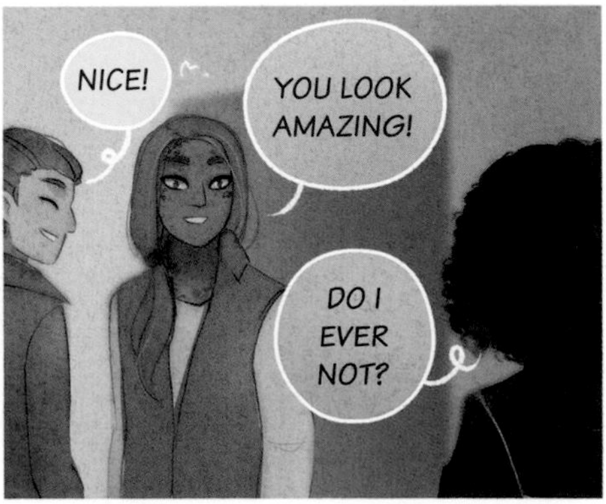
NICE!
YOU LOOK AMAZING!
DO I EVER NOT?

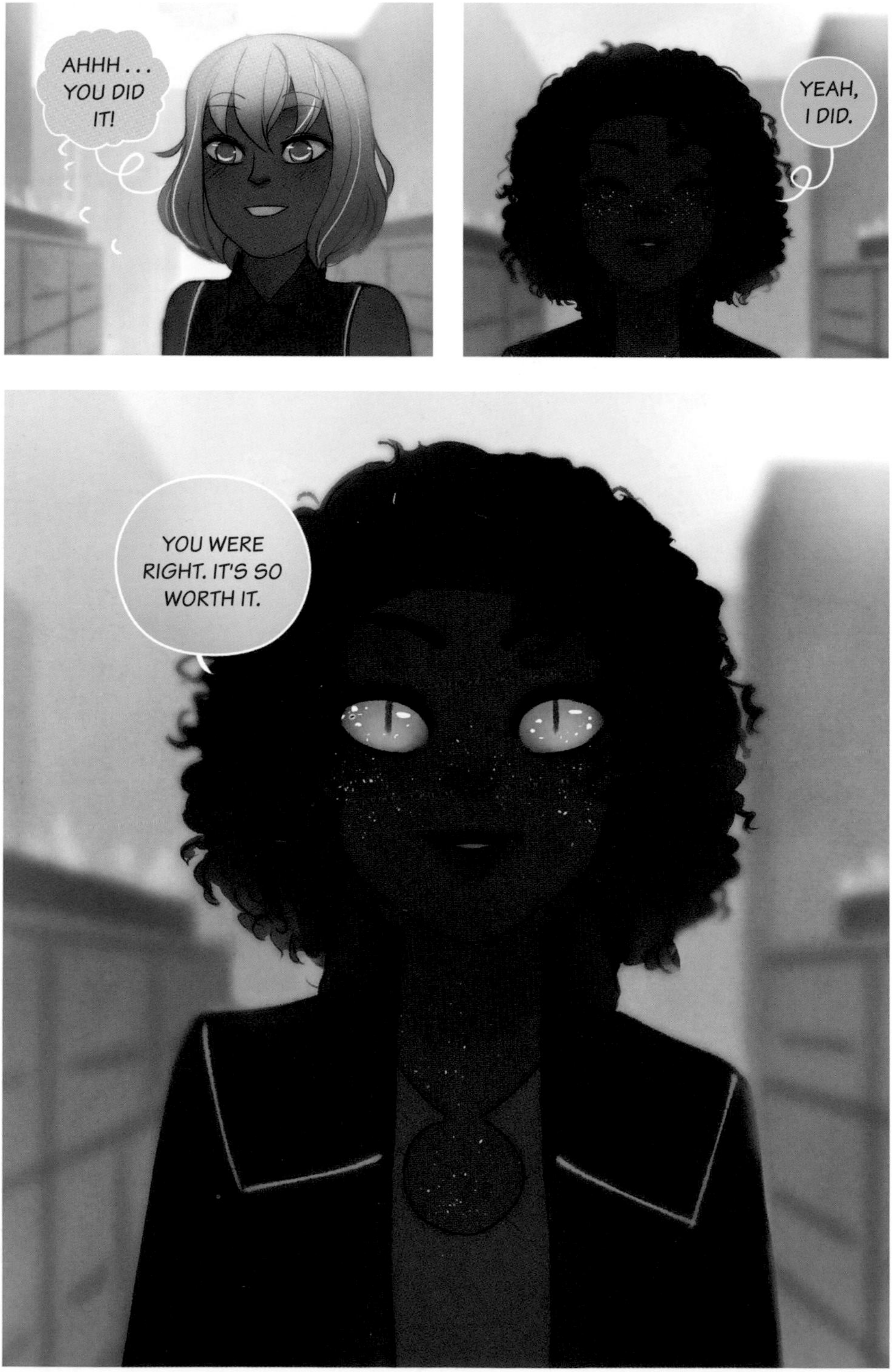
AHHH . . . YOU DID IT!
YEAH, I DID.
YOU WERE RIGHT. IT'S SO WORTH IT.

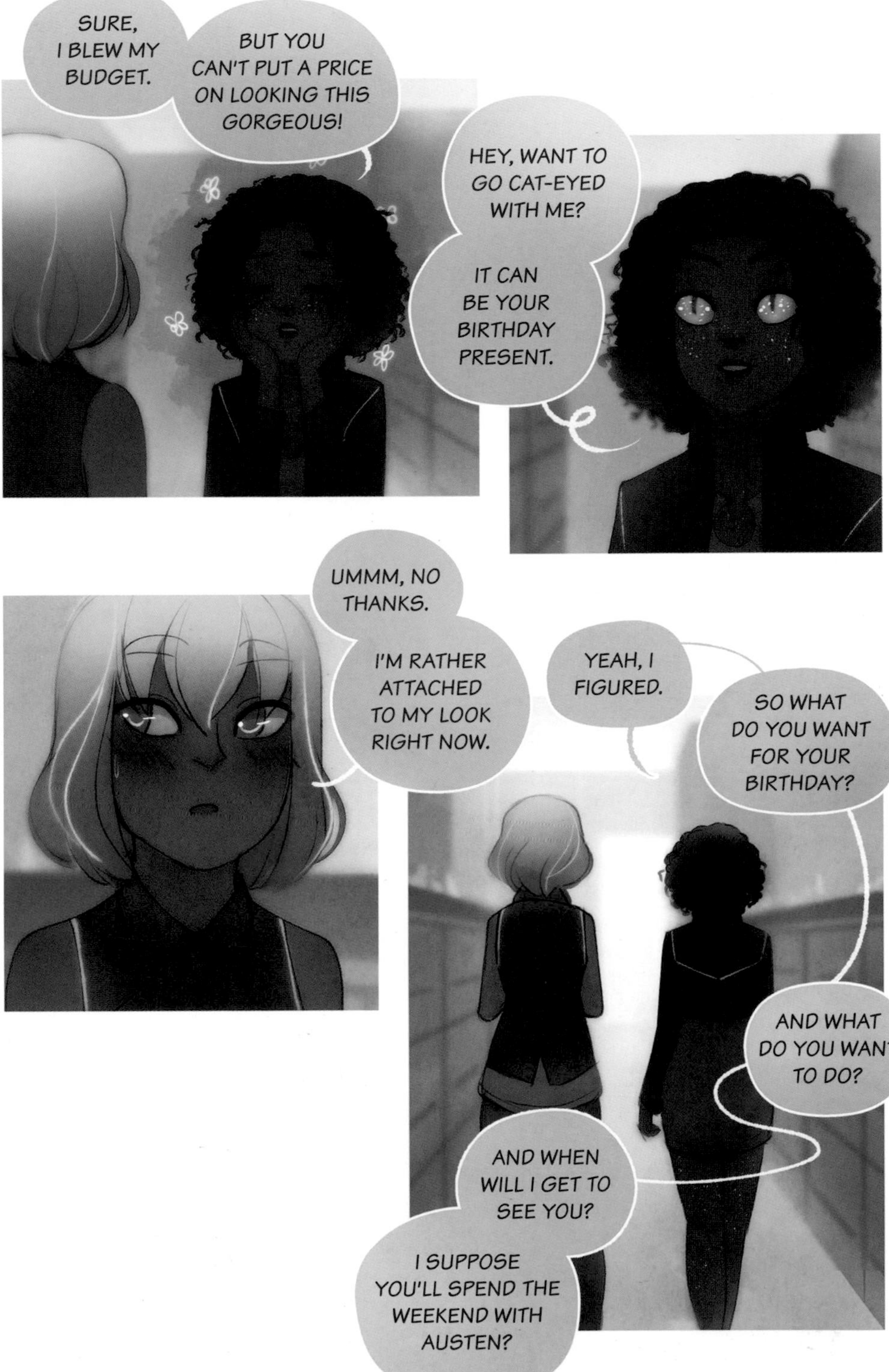
SURE, I BLEW MY BUDGET.
BUT YOU CAN'T PUT A PRICE ON LOOKING THIS GORGEOUS!
HEY, WANT TO GO CAT-EYED WITH ME?
IT CAN BE YOUR BIRTHDAY PRESENT.
UMMM, NO THANKS.
I'M RATHER ATTACHED TO MY LOOK RIGHT NOW.
YEAH, I FIGURED.
SO WHAT DO YOU WANT FOR YOUR BIRTHDAY?
AND WHAT DO YOU WANT TO DO?
AND WHEN WILL I GET TO SEE YOU?
I SUPPOSE YOU'LL SPEND THE WEEKEND WITH AUSTEN?

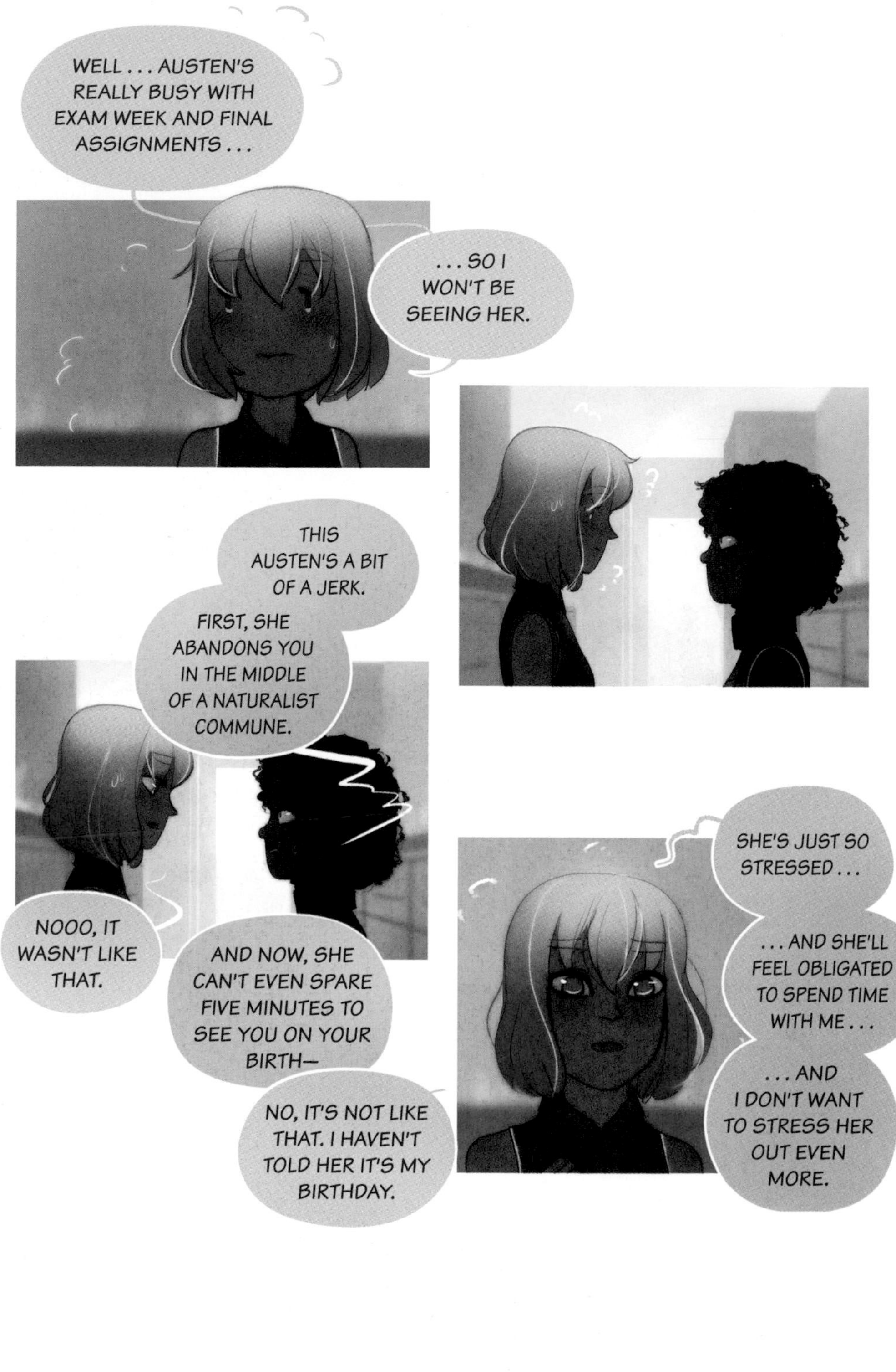

WELL . . . AUSTEN'S REALLY BUSY WITH EXAM WEEK AND FINAL ASSIGNMENTS . . .
. . . SO I WON'T BE SEEING HER.
THIS AUSTEN'S A BIT OF A JERK.
FIRST, SHE ABANDONS YOU IN THE MIDDLE OF A NATURALIST COMMUNE.
NOOO, IT WASN'T LIKE THAT.
AND NOW, SHE CAN'T EVEN SPARE FIVE MINUTES TO SEE YOU ON YOUR BIRTH—
NO, IT'S NOT LIKE THAT. I HAVEN'T TOLD HER IT'S MY BIRTHDAY.
SHE'S JUST SO STRESSED . . .
. . . AND SHE'LL FEEL OBLIGATED TO SPEND TIME WITH ME . . .
. . . AND I DON'T WANT TO STRESS HER OUT EVEN MORE.

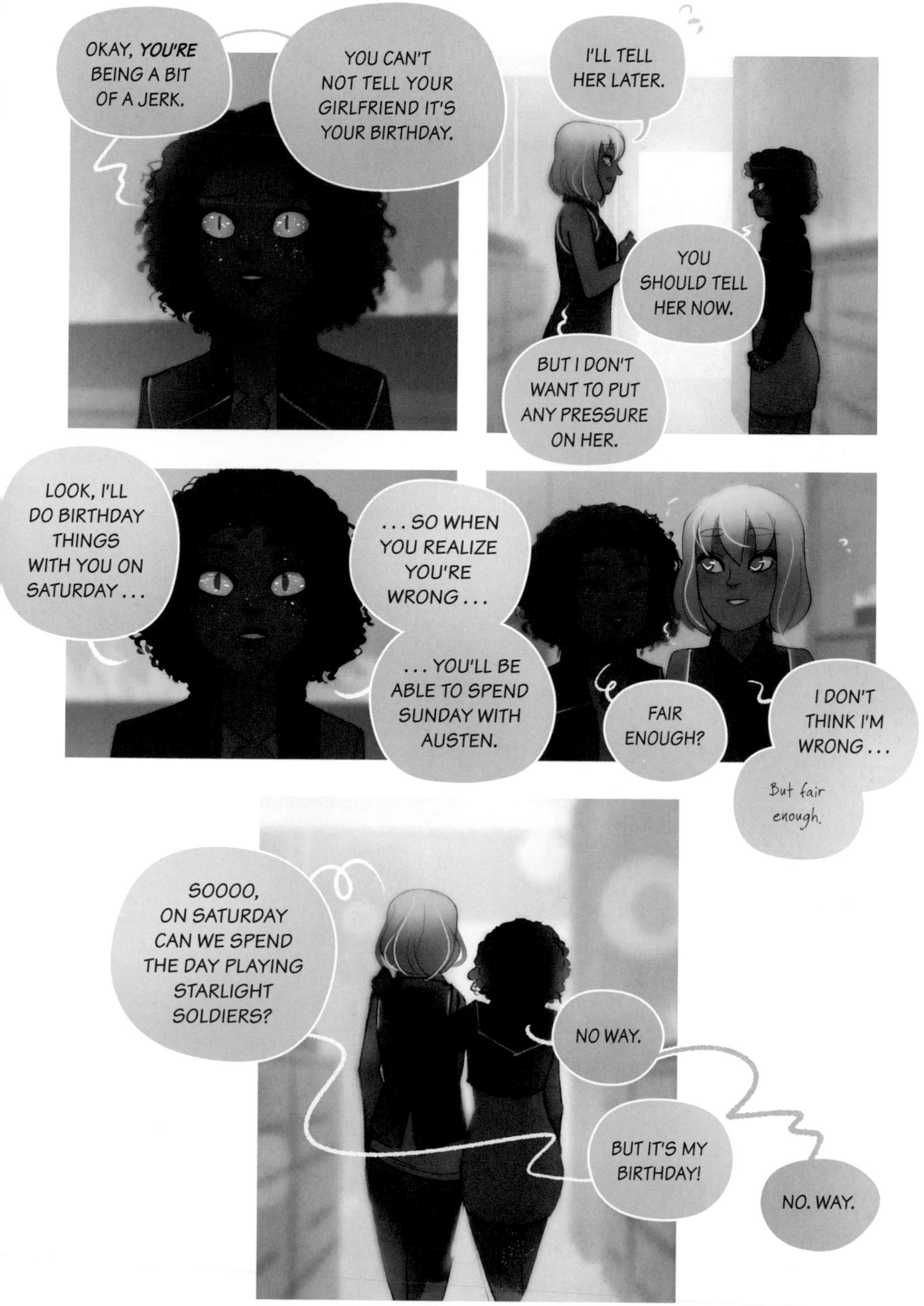
OKAY, **YOU'RE** BEING A BIT OF A JERK.
YOU CAN'T NOT TELL YOUR GIRLFRIEND IT'S YOUR BIRTHDAY.
I'LL TELL HER LATER.
YOU SHOULD TELL HER NOW.
BUT I DON'T WANT TO PUT ANY PRESSURE ON HER.
LOOK, I'LL DO BIRTHDAY THINGS WITH YOU ON SATURDAY . . .
. . . SO WHEN YOU REALIZE YOU'RE WRONG . . .
. . . YOU'LL BE ABLE TO SPEND SUNDAY WITH AUSTEN.
FAIR ENOUGH?
I DON'T THINK I'M WRONG . . .
But fair enough.
SOOOO, ON SATURDAY CAN WE SPEND THE DAY PLAYING STARLIGHT SOLDIERS?
NO WAY.
BUT IT'S MY BIRTHDAY!
NO. WAY.

21 - A COMPROMISE

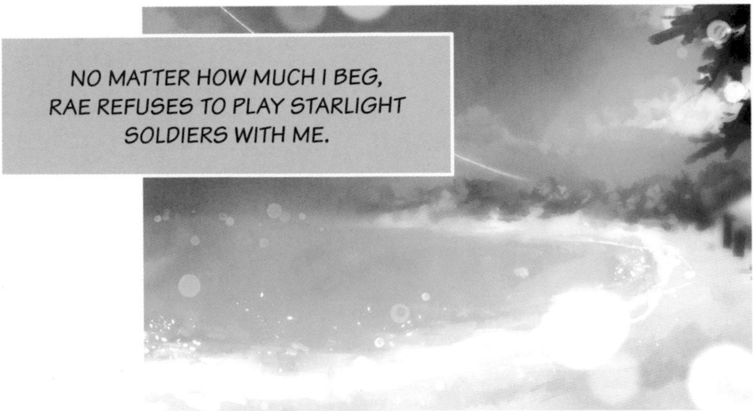
NO MATTER HOW MUCH I BEG, RAE REFUSES TO PLAY STARLIGHT SOLDIERS WITH ME.

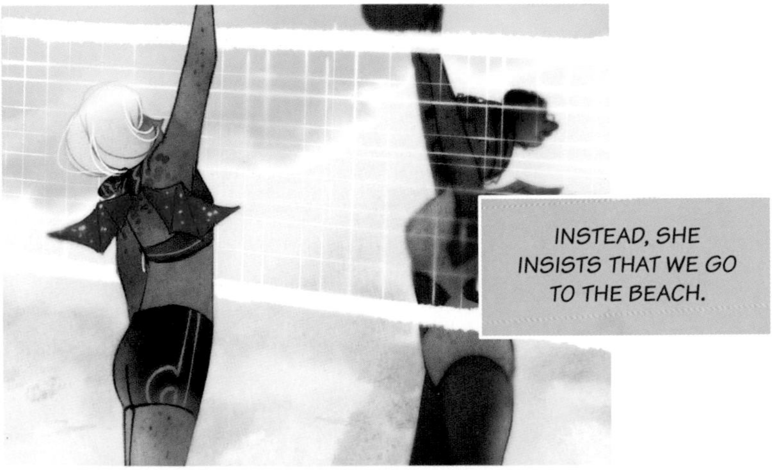
INSTEAD, SHE INSISTS THAT WE GO TO THE BEACH.

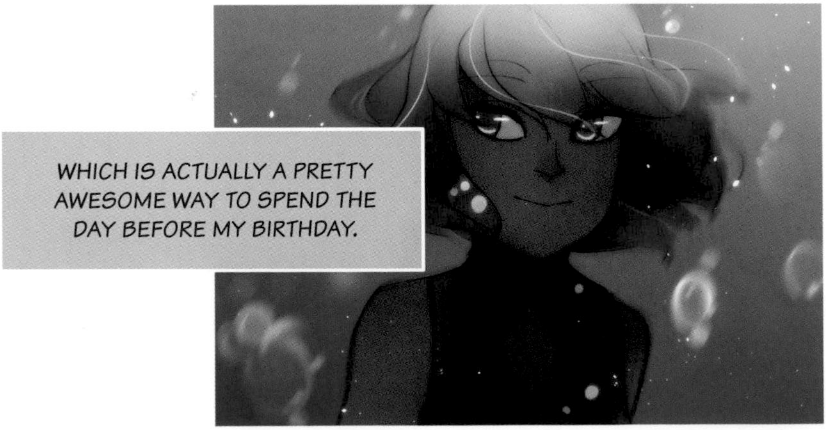
WHICH IS ACTUALLY A PRETTY AWESOME WAY TO SPEND THE DAY BEFORE MY BIRTHDAY.

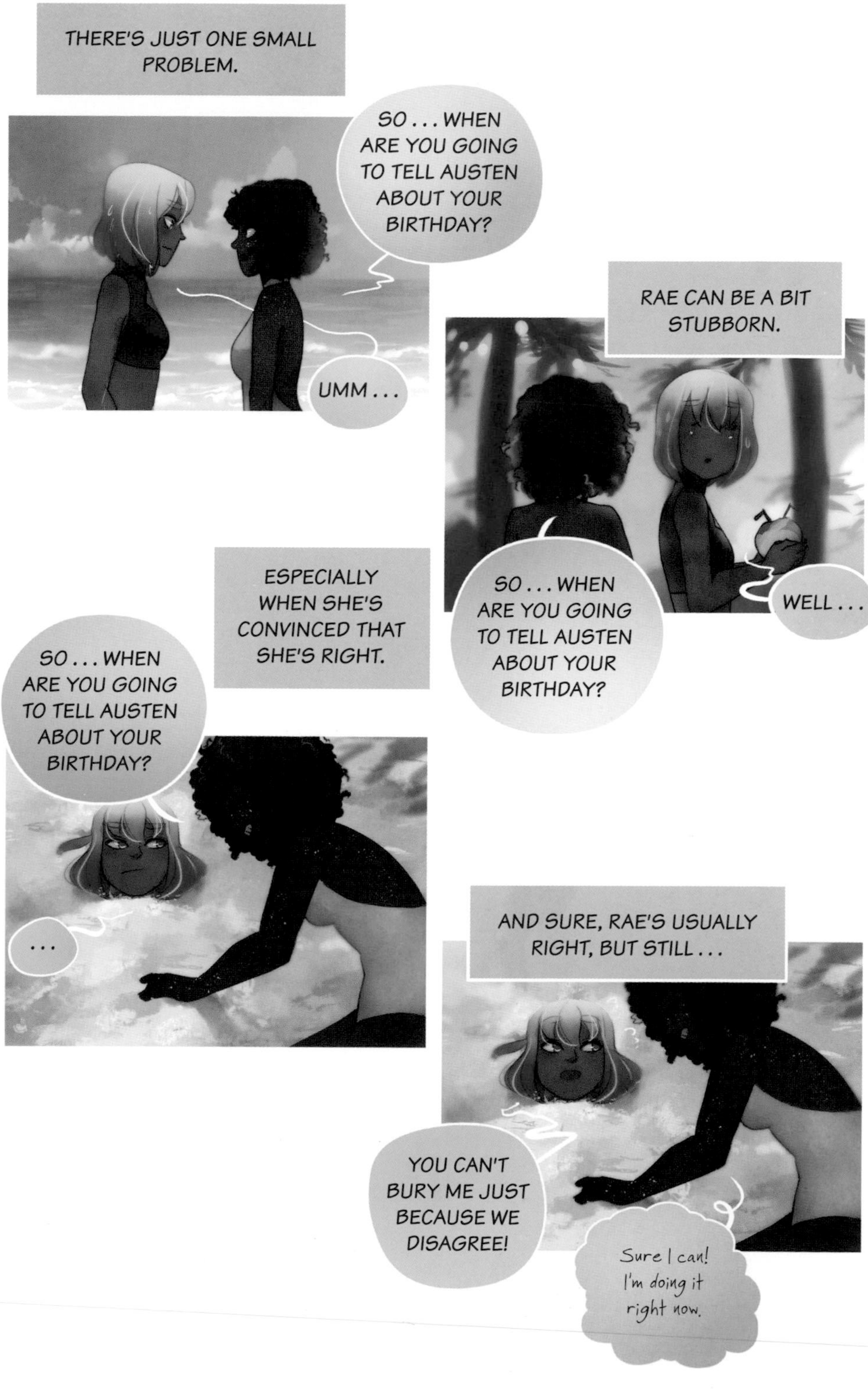
THERE'S JUST ONE SMALL PROBLEM.
SO . . . WHEN ARE YOU GOING TO TELL AUSTEN ABOUT YOUR BIRTHDAY?
UMM . . .
RAE CAN BE A BIT STUBBORN.
SO . . . WHEN ARE YOU GOING TO TELL AUSTEN ABOUT YOUR BIRTHDAY?
WELL . . .
ESPECIALLY WHEN SHE'S CONVINCED THAT SHE'S RIGHT.
SO . . . WHEN ARE YOU GOING TO TELL AUSTEN ABOUT YOUR BIRTHDAY?
. . .
AND SURE, RAE'S USUALLY RIGHT, BUT STILL . . .
YOU CAN'T BURY ME JUST BECAUSE WE DISAGREE!
Sure I can! I'm doing it right now.

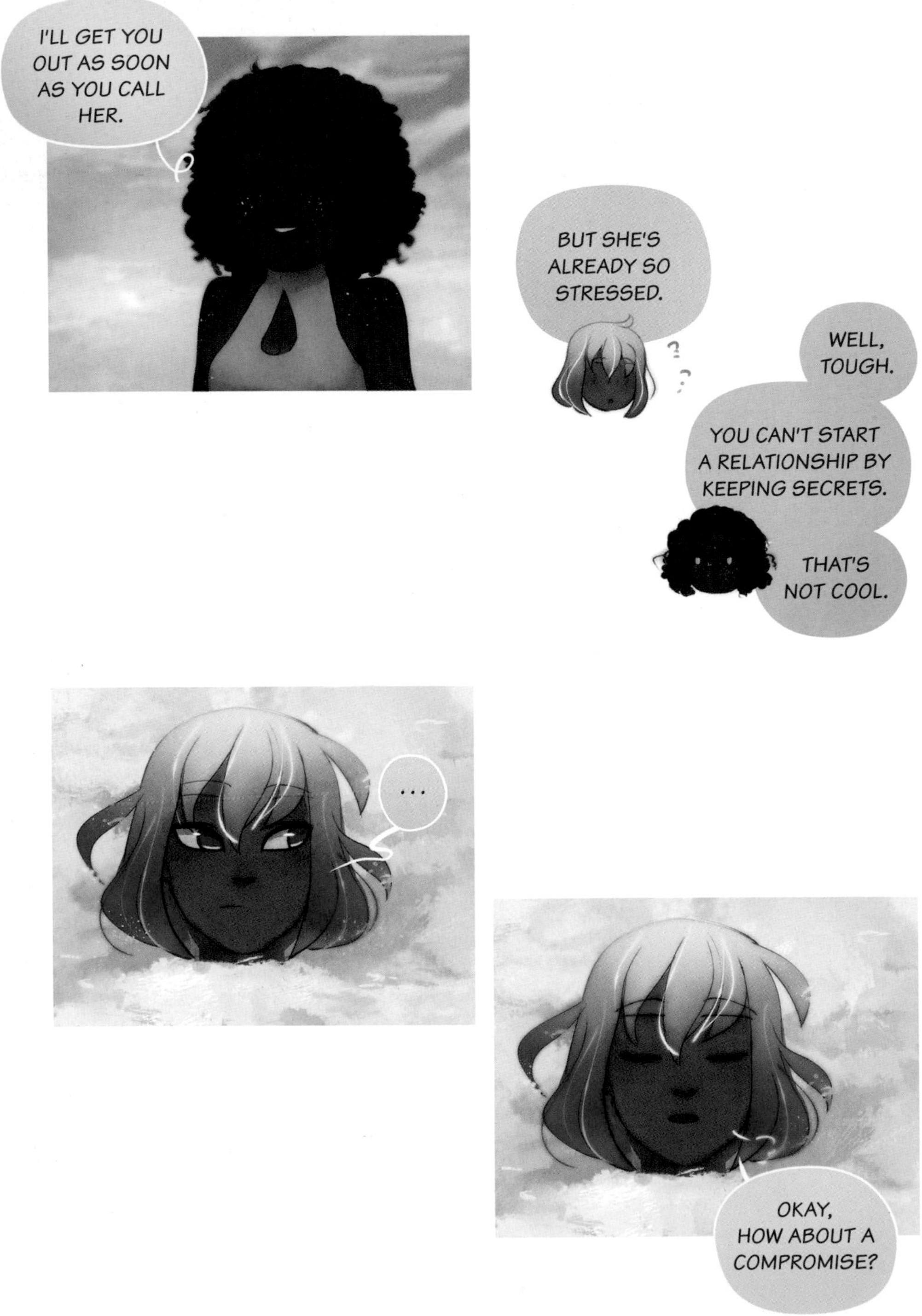
I'LL GET YOU OUT AS SOON AS YOU CALL HER.
BUT SHE'S ALREADY SO STRESSED.
WELL, TOUGH.
YOU CAN'T START A RELATIONSHIP BY KEEPING SECRETS.
THAT'S NOT COOL.
...
OKAY, HOW ABOUT A COMPROMISE?

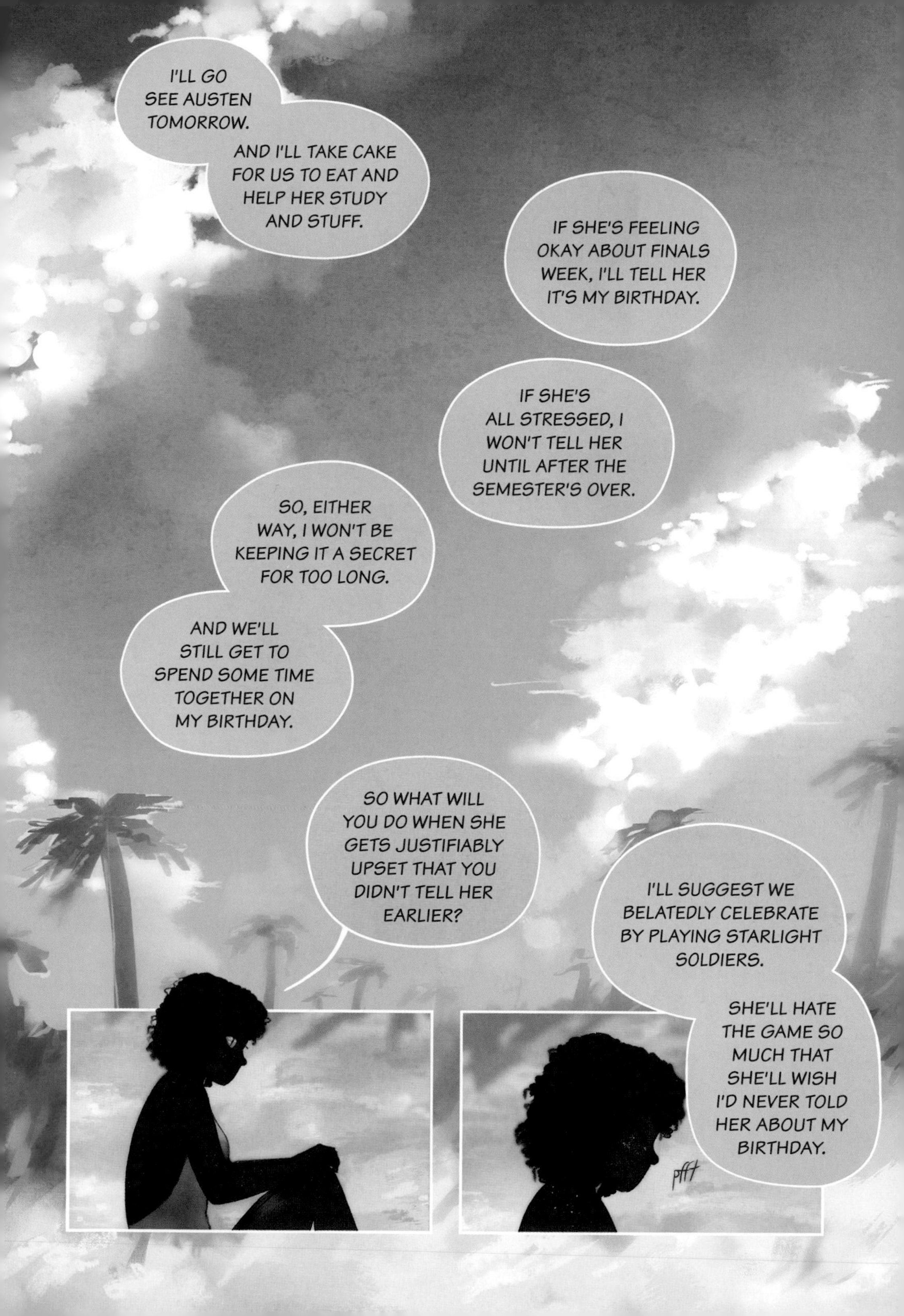
I'LL GO SEE AUSTEN TOMORROW.
AND I'LL TAKE CAKE FOR US TO EAT AND HELP HER STUDY AND STUFF.
IF SHE'S FEELING OKAY ABOUT FINALS WEEK, I'LL TELL HER IT'S MY BIRTHDAY.
IF SHE'S ALL STRESSED, I WON'T TELL HER UNTIL AFTER THE SEMESTER'S OVER.
SO, EITHER WAY, I WON'T BE KEEPING IT A SECRET FOR TOO LONG.
AND WE'LL STILL GET TO SPEND SOME TIME TOGETHER ON MY BIRTHDAY.
SO WHAT WILL YOU DO WHEN SHE GETS JUSTIFIABLY UPSET THAT YOU DIDN'T TELL HER EARLIER?
I'LL SUGGEST WE BELATEDLY CELEBRATE BY PLAYING STARLIGHT SOLDIERS.
SHE'LL HATE THE GAME SO MUCH THAT SHE'LL WISH I'D NEVER TOLD HER ABOUT MY BIRTHDAY.
pfft

THAT'S NOT A COMPLETELY TERRIBLE IDEA.

DOES THAT MEAN I CAN COME OUT?

I really need to pee.

I STILL THINK YOU SHOULD TELL AUSTEN IT'S YOUR BIRTHDAY NOW.

BUT I GUESS I'LL ALLOW IT.

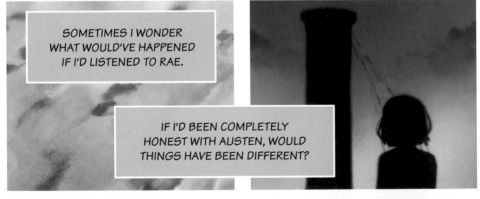

SOMETIMES I WONDER WHAT WOULD'VE HAPPENED IF I'D LISTENED TO RAE.

IF I'D BEEN COMPLETELY HONEST WITH AUSTEN, WOULD THINGS HAVE BEEN DIFFERENT?

AND DOES IT EVEN MATTER?

IT'S NOT LIKE I CAN GO BACK AND CHANGE THE PAST.

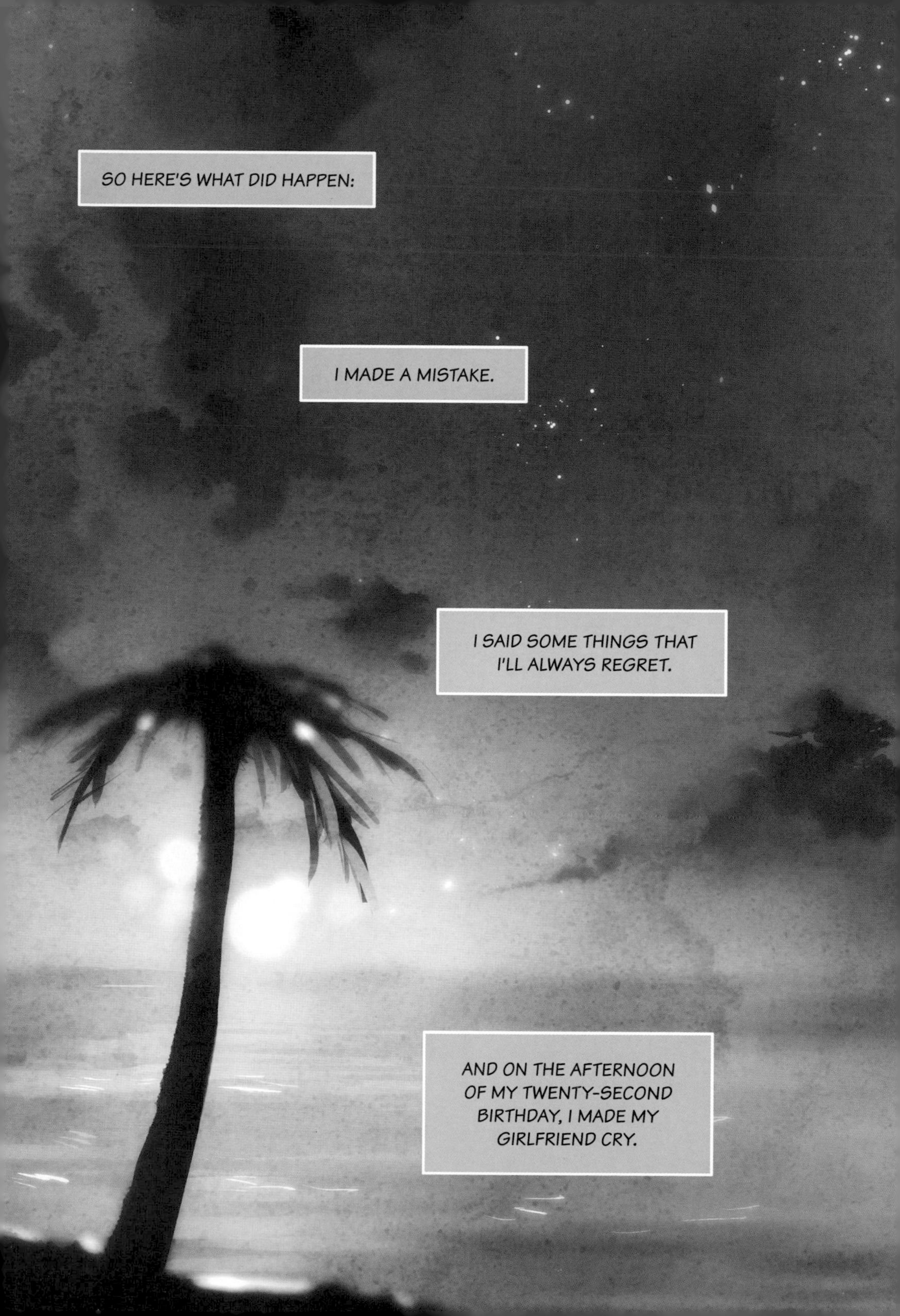
SO HERE'S WHAT DID HAPPEN:
I MADE A MISTAKE.
I SAID SOME THINGS THAT I'LL ALWAYS REGRET.
AND ON THE AFTERNOON OF MY TWENTY-SECOND BIRTHDAY, I MADE MY GIRLFRIEND CRY.

22 - TIRED

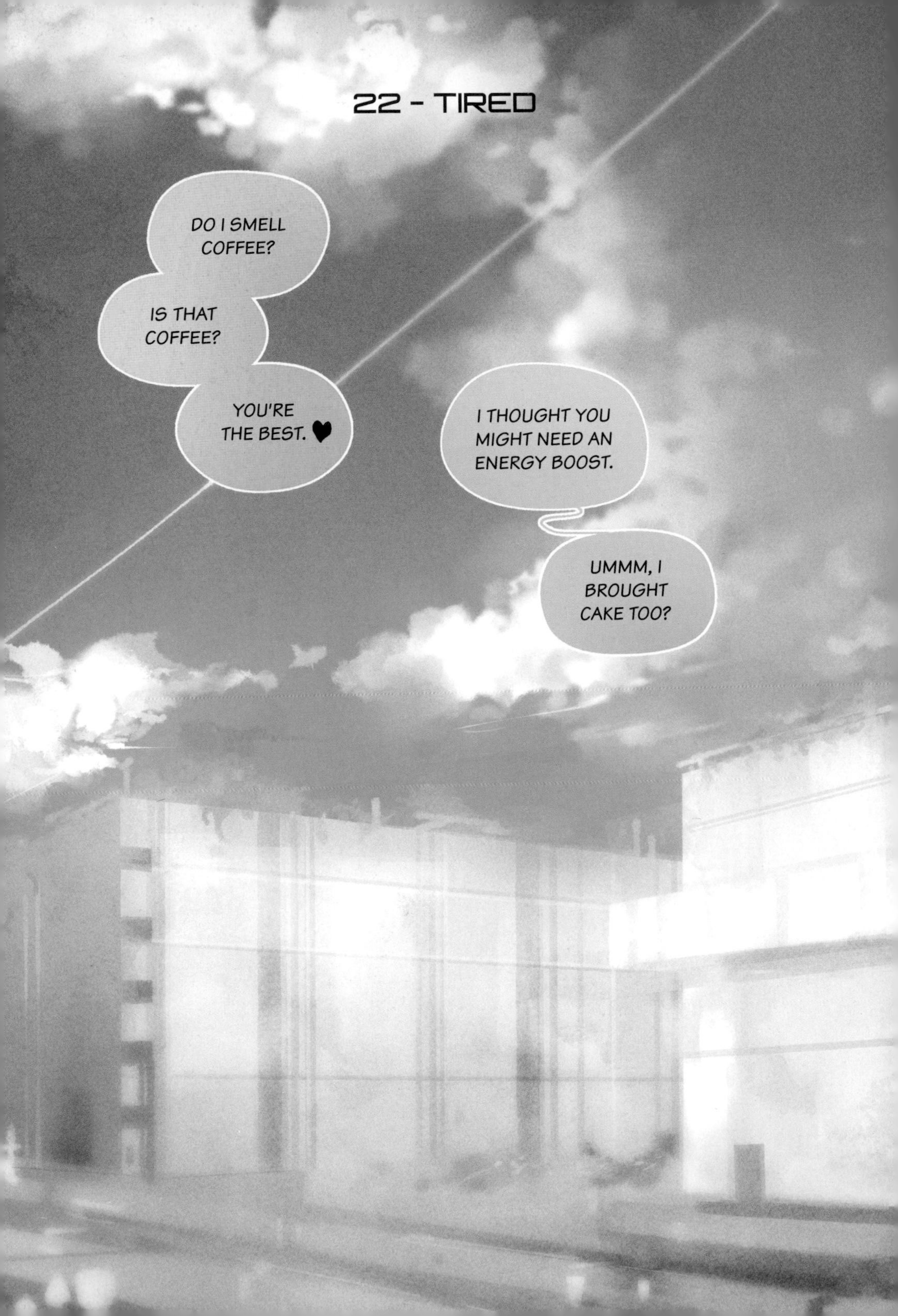
DO I SMELL COFFEE?
IS THAT COFFEE?
YOU'RE THE BEST. ♥
I THOUGHT YOU MIGHT NEED AN ENERGY BOOST.
UMMM, I BROUGHT CAKE TOO?

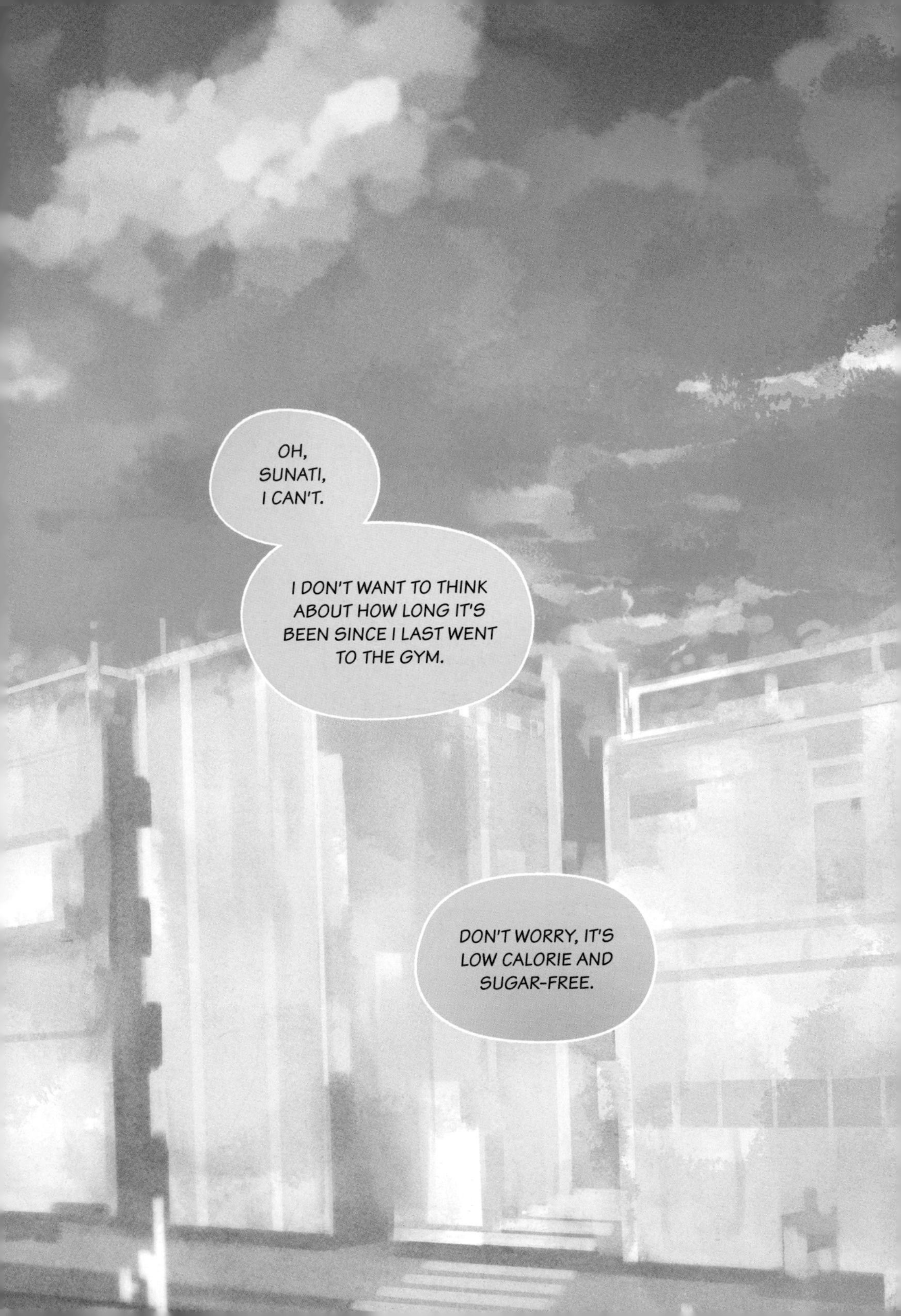
OH, SUNATI, I CAN'T.
I DON'T WANT TO THINK ABOUT HOW LONG IT'S BEEN SINCE I LAST WENT TO THE GYM.
DON'T WORRY, IT'S LOW CALORIE AND SUGAR-FREE.

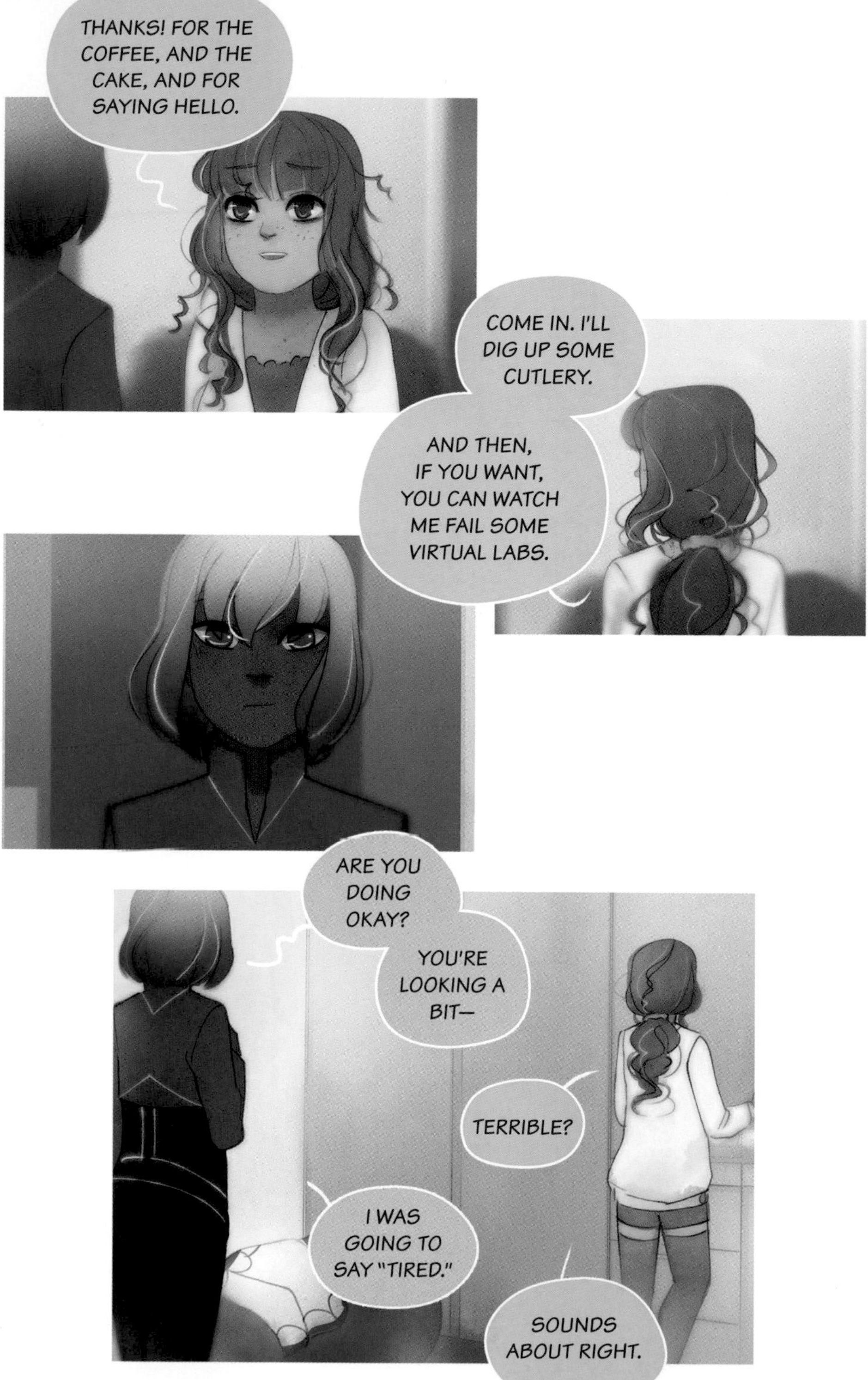
THANKS! FOR THE COFFEE, AND THE CAKE, AND FOR SAYING HELLO.
COME IN. I'LL DIG UP SOME CUTLERY.
AND THEN, IF YOU WANT, YOU CAN WATCH ME FAIL SOME VIRTUAL LABS.
ARE YOU DOING OKAY?
YOU'RE LOOKING A BIT—
TERRIBLE?
I WAS GOING TO SAY "TIRED."
SOUNDS ABOUT RIGHT.

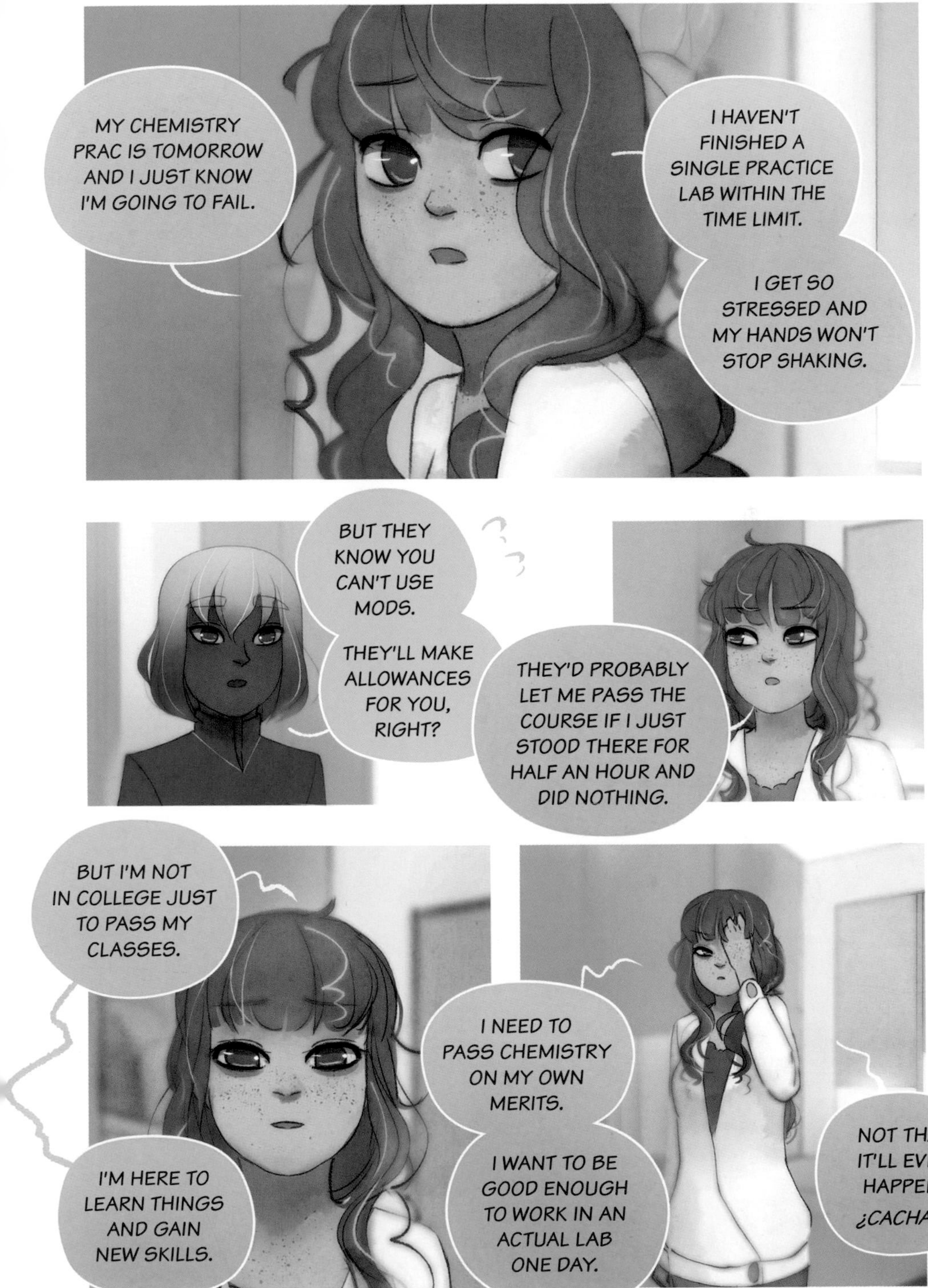
MY CHEMISTRY PRAC IS TOMORROW AND I JUST KNOW I'M GOING TO FAIL.
I HAVEN'T FINISHED A SINGLE PRACTICE LAB WITHIN THE TIME LIMIT.
I GET SO STRESSED AND MY HANDS WON'T STOP SHAKING.
BUT THEY KNOW YOU CAN'T USE MODS.
THEY'LL MAKE ALLOWANCES FOR YOU, RIGHT?
THEY'D PROBABLY LET ME PASS THE COURSE IF I JUST STOOD THERE FOR HALF AN HOUR AND DID NOTHING.
BUT I'M NOT IN COLLEGE JUST TO PASS MY CLASSES.
I'M HERE TO LEARN THINGS AND GAIN NEW SKILLS.
I NEED TO PASS CHEMISTRY ON MY OWN MERITS.
I WANT TO BE GOOD ENOUGH TO WORK IN AN ACTUAL LAB ONE DAY.
NOT THAT IT'LL EVER HAPPEN.
¿CACHAI?

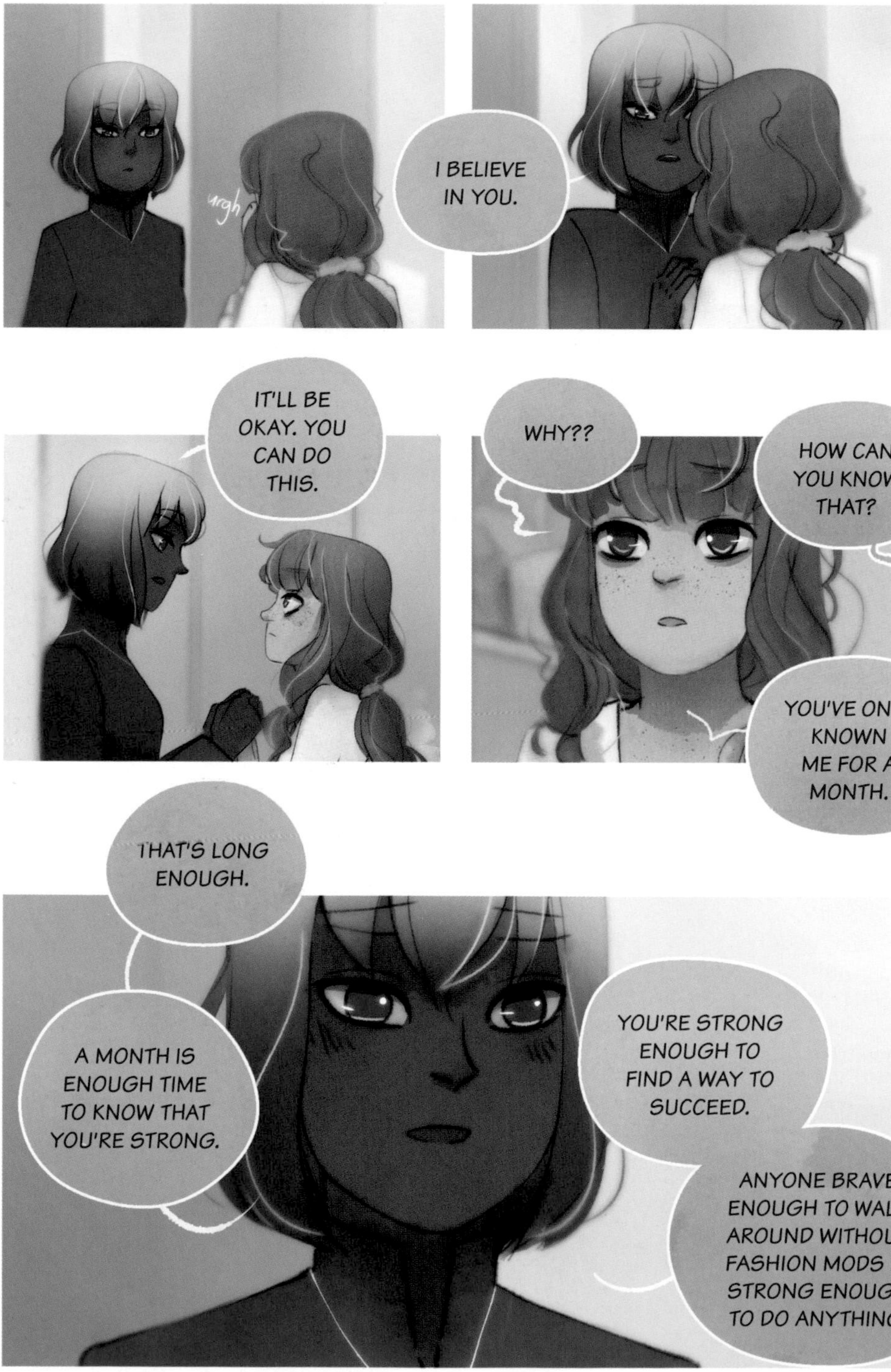

urgh
I BELIEVE IN YOU.
IT'LL BE OKAY. YOU CAN DO THIS.
WHY??
HOW CAN YOU KNOW THAT?
YOU'VE ONLY KNOWN ME FOR A MONTH.
THAT'S LONG ENOUGH.
A MONTH IS ENOUGH TIME TO KNOW THAT YOU'RE STRONG.
YOU'RE STRONG ENOUGH TO FIND A WAY TO SUCCEED.
ANYONE BRAVE ENOUGH TO WALK AROUND WITHOUT FASHION MODS IS STRONG ENOUGH TO DO ANYTHING.

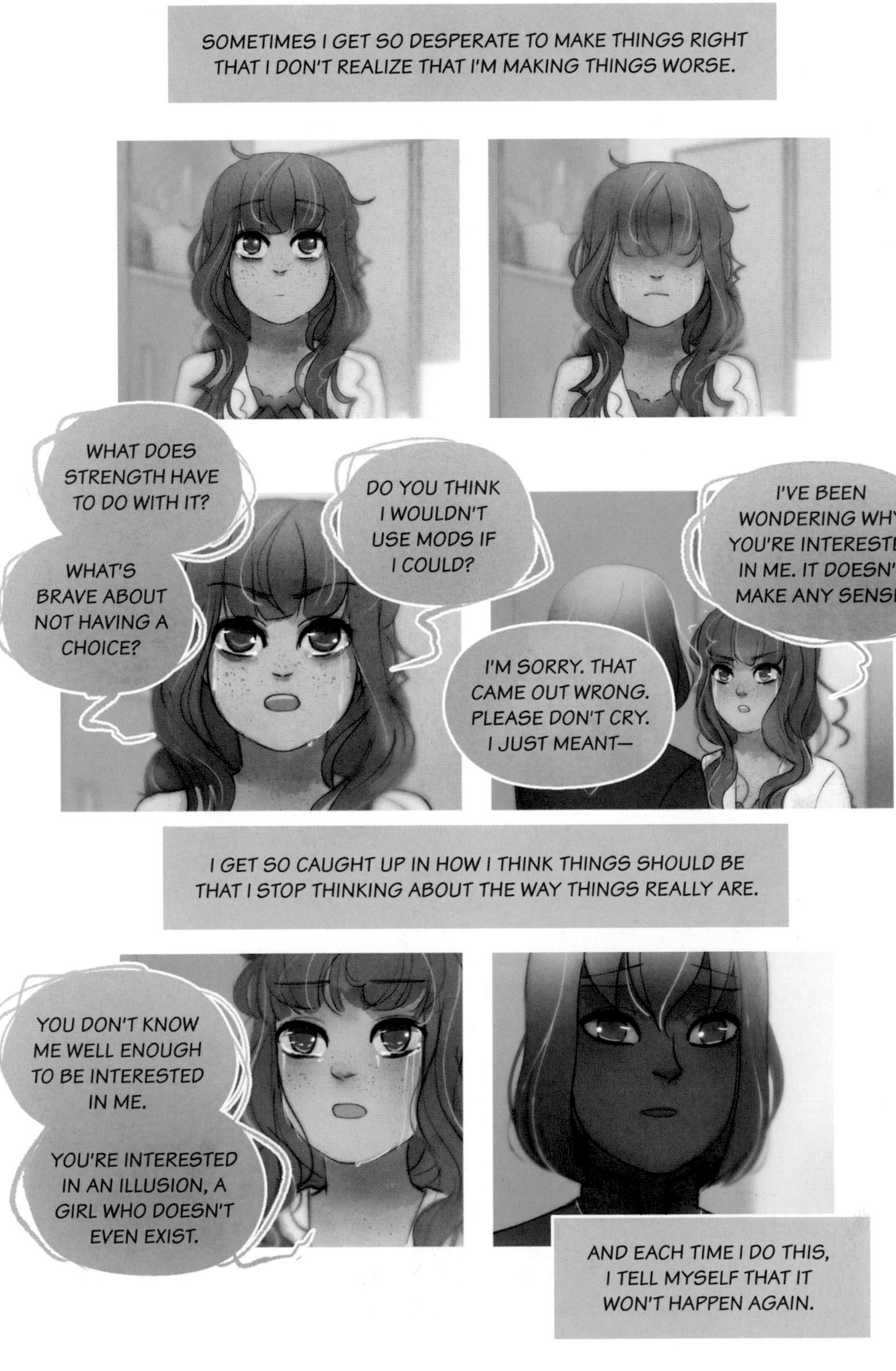
SOMETIMES I GET SO DESPERATE TO MAKE THINGS RIGHT THAT I DON'T REALIZE THAT I'M MAKING THINGS WORSE.
WHAT DOES STRENGTH HAVE TO DO WITH IT?
WHAT'S BRAVE ABOUT NOT HAVING A CHOICE?
DO YOU THINK I WOULDN'T USE MODS IF I COULD?
I'M SORRY. THAT CAME OUT WRONG. PLEASE DON'T CRY. I JUST MEANT—
I'VE BEEN WONDERING WHY YOU'RE INTERESTED IN ME. IT DOESN'T MAKE ANY SENSE.
I GET SO CAUGHT UP IN HOW I THINK THINGS SHOULD BE THAT I STOP THINKING ABOUT THE WAY THINGS REALLY ARE.
YOU DON'T KNOW ME WELL ENOUGH TO BE INTERESTED IN ME.
YOU'RE INTERESTED IN AN ILLUSION, A GIRL WHO DOESN'T EVEN EXIST.
AND EACH TIME I DO THIS, I TELL MYSELF THAT IT WON'T HAPPEN AGAIN.

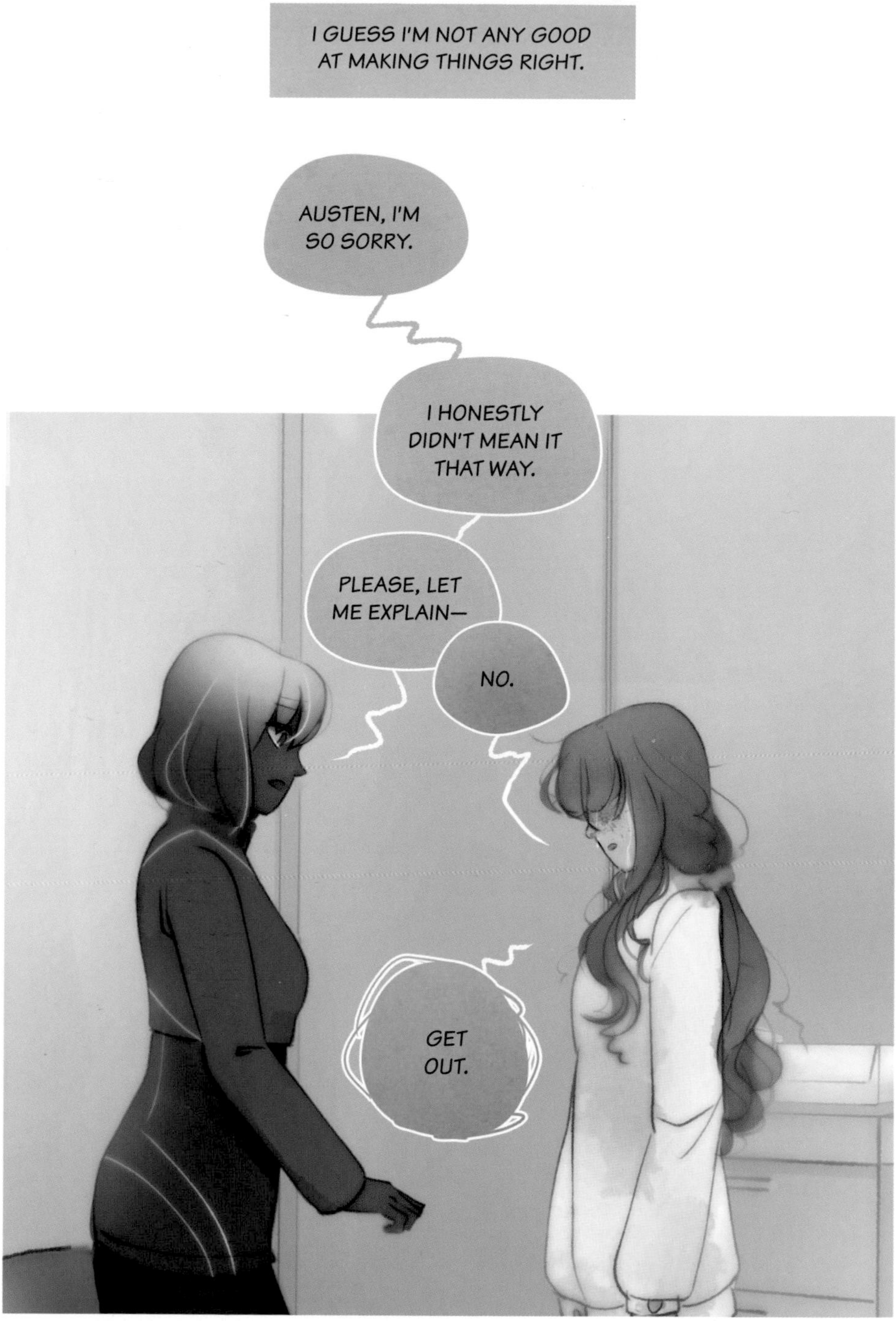
I GUESS I'M NOT ANY GOOD AT MAKING THINGS RIGHT.
AUSTEN, I'M SO SORRY.
I HONESTLY DIDN'T MEAN IT THAT WAY.
PLEASE, LET ME EXPLAIN—
NO.
GET OUT.

23 - NOT NOW

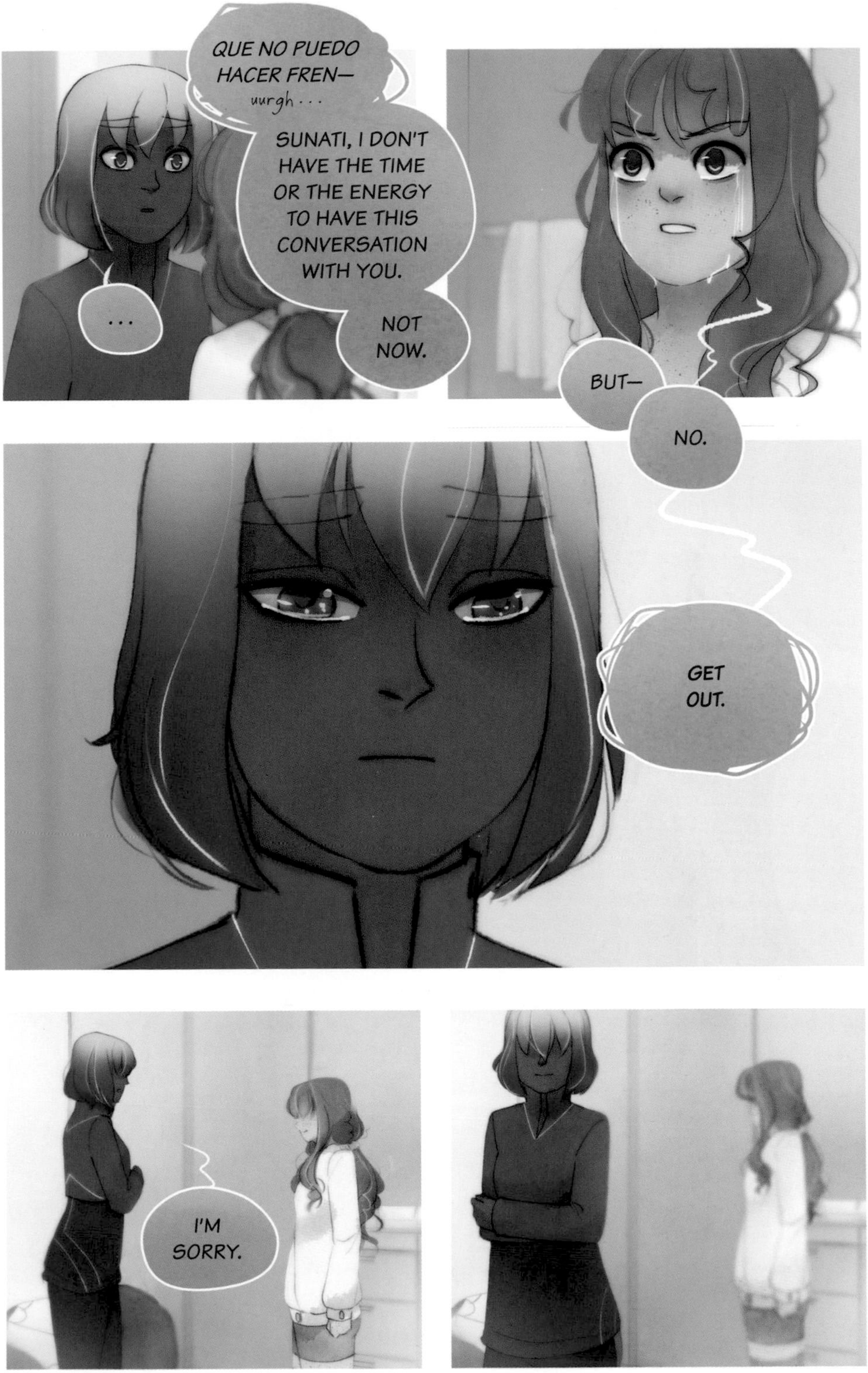
QUE NO PUEDO HACER FREN—
uurgh . . .
SUNATI, I DON'T HAVE THE TIME OR THE ENERGY TO HAVE THIS CONVERSATION WITH YOU.
NOT NOW.
. . .
BUT—
NO.
GET OUT.
I'M SORRY.

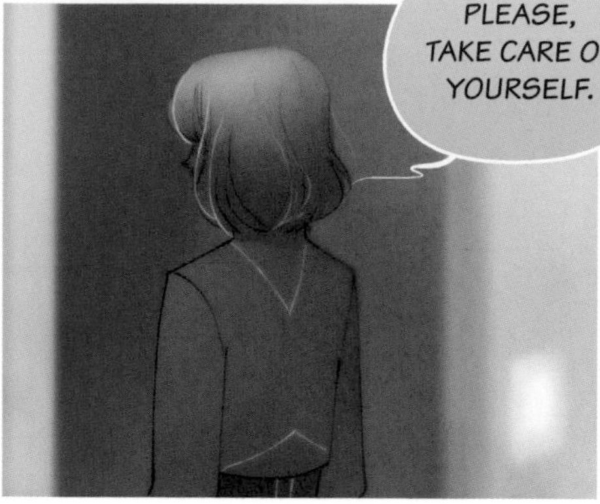
PLEASE,
TAKE CARE OF
YOURSELF.

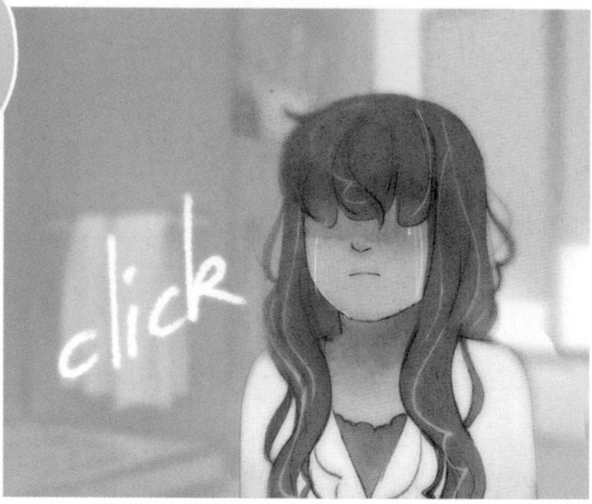
click

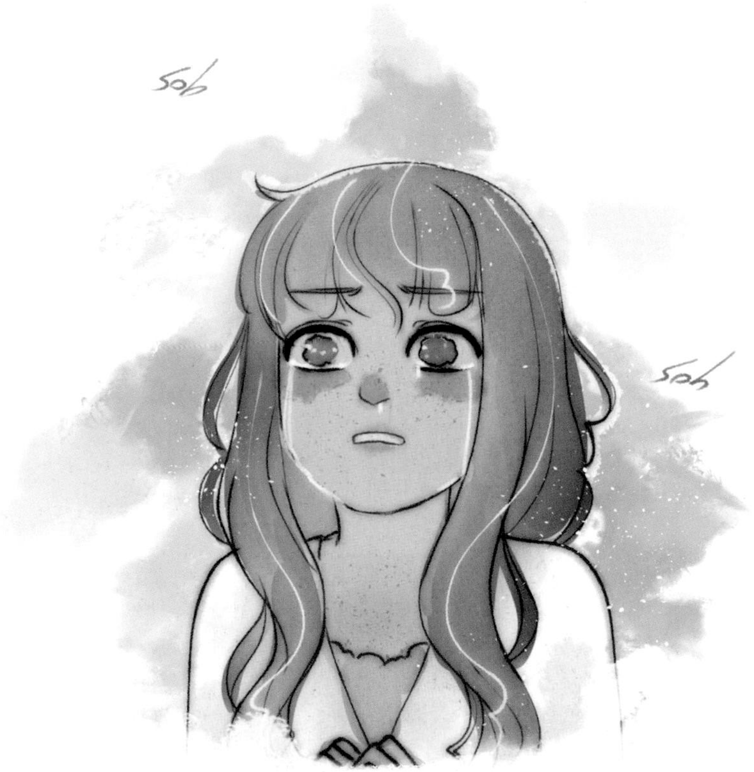
sob
sob

WHY DID I
SAY THAT?

sniff

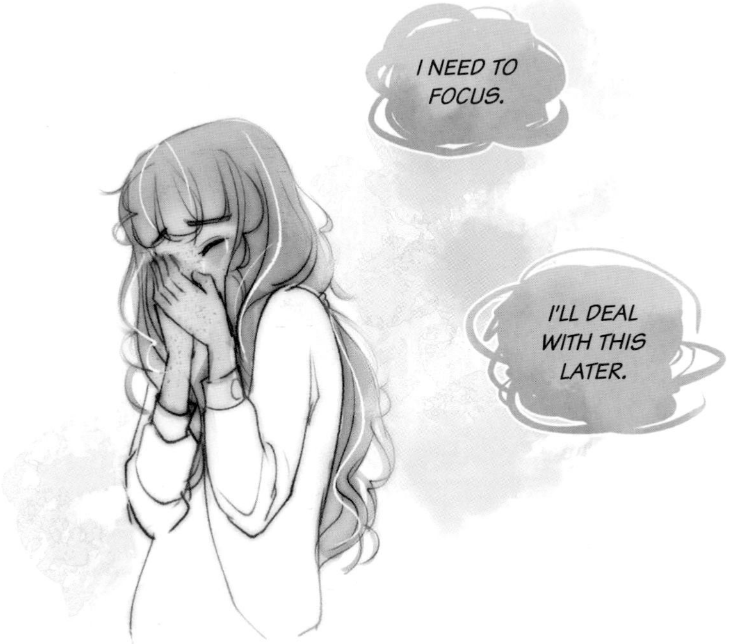
I NEED TO FOCUS.
I'LL DEAL WITH THIS LATER.

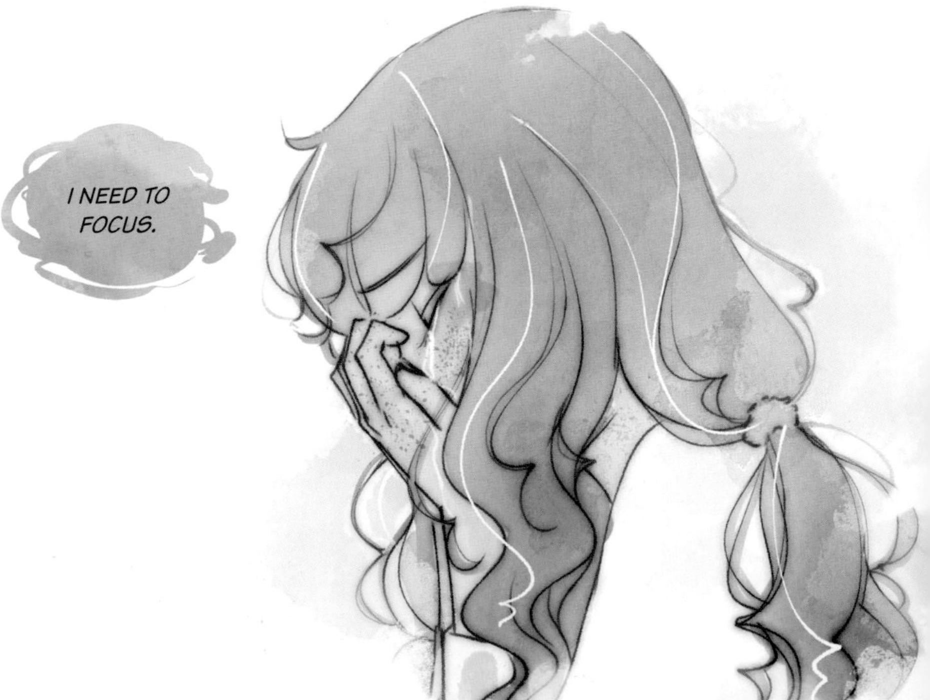
I NEED TO FOCUS.

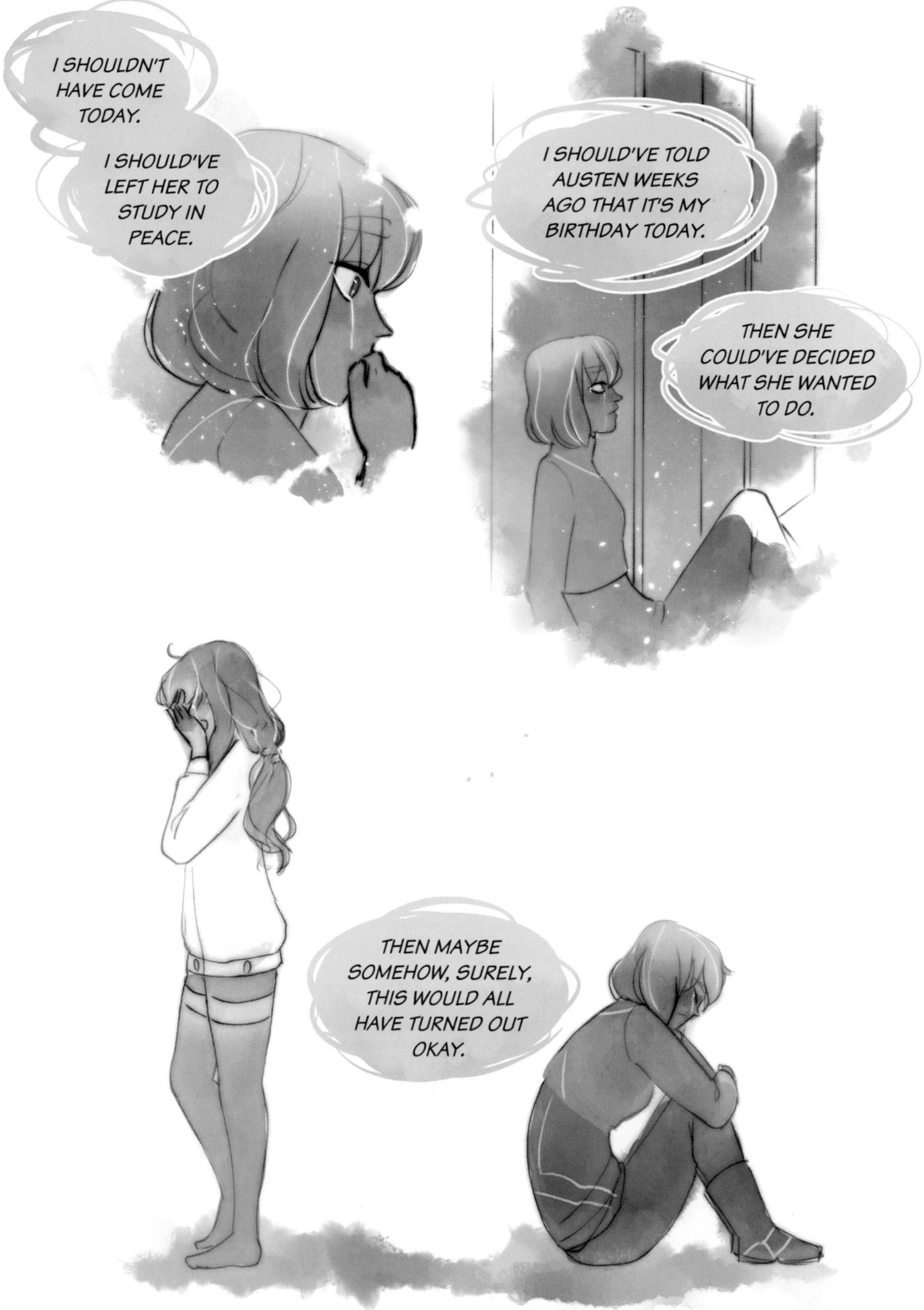
I SHOULDN'T HAVE COME TODAY.
I SHOULD'VE LEFT HER TO STUDY IN PEACE.
I SHOULD'VE TOLD AUSTEN WEEKS AGO THAT IT'S MY BIRTHDAY TODAY.
THEN SHE COULD'VE DECIDED WHAT SHE WANTED TO DO.
THEN MAYBE SOMEHOW, SURELY, THIS WOULD ALL HAVE TURNED OUT OKAY.

24 – I DON'T KNOW

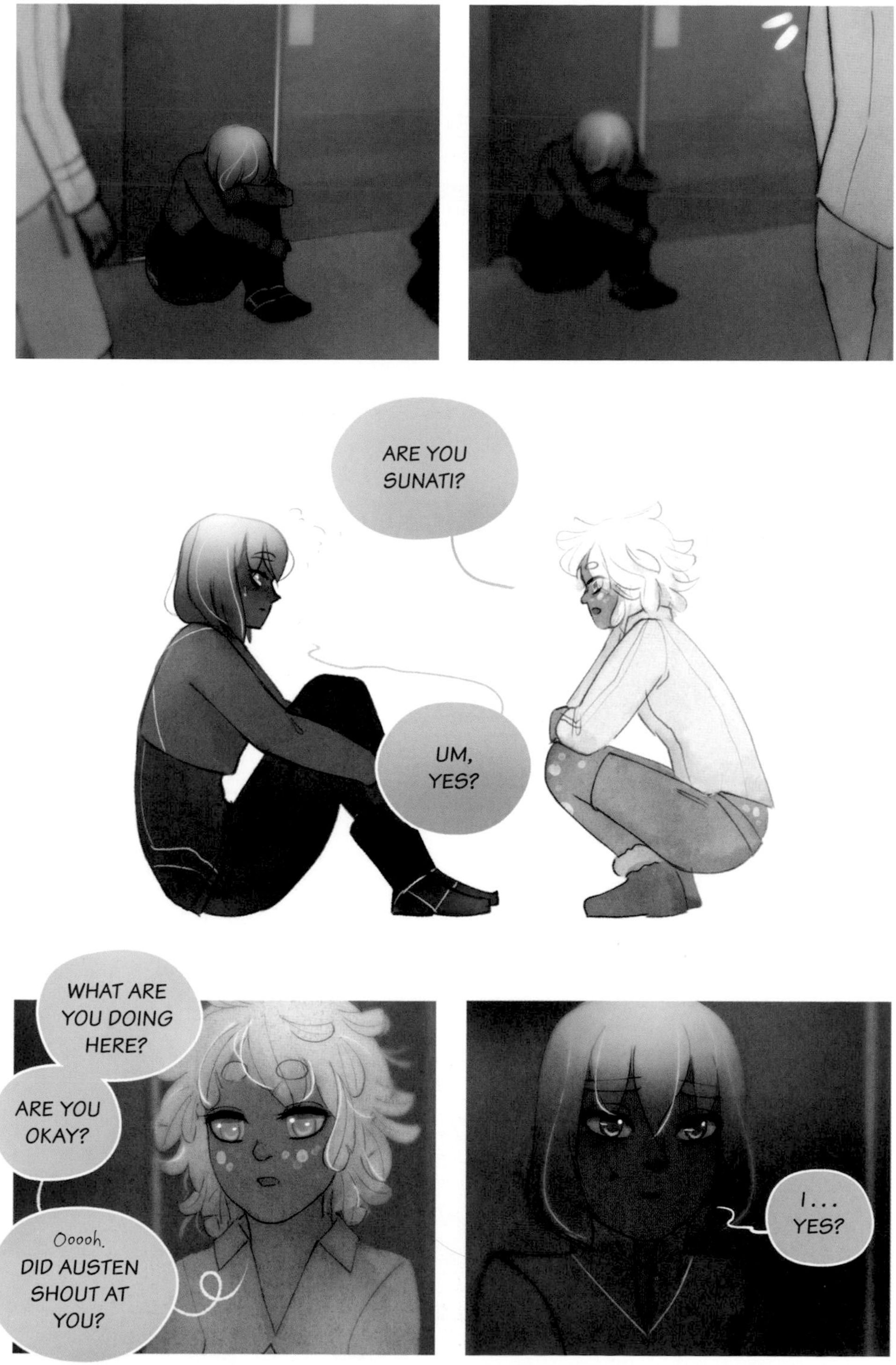
ARE YOU SUNATI?
UM, YES?
WHAT ARE YOU DOING HERE?
ARE YOU OKAY?
Ooooh. DID AUSTEN SHOUT AT YOU?
I... YES?

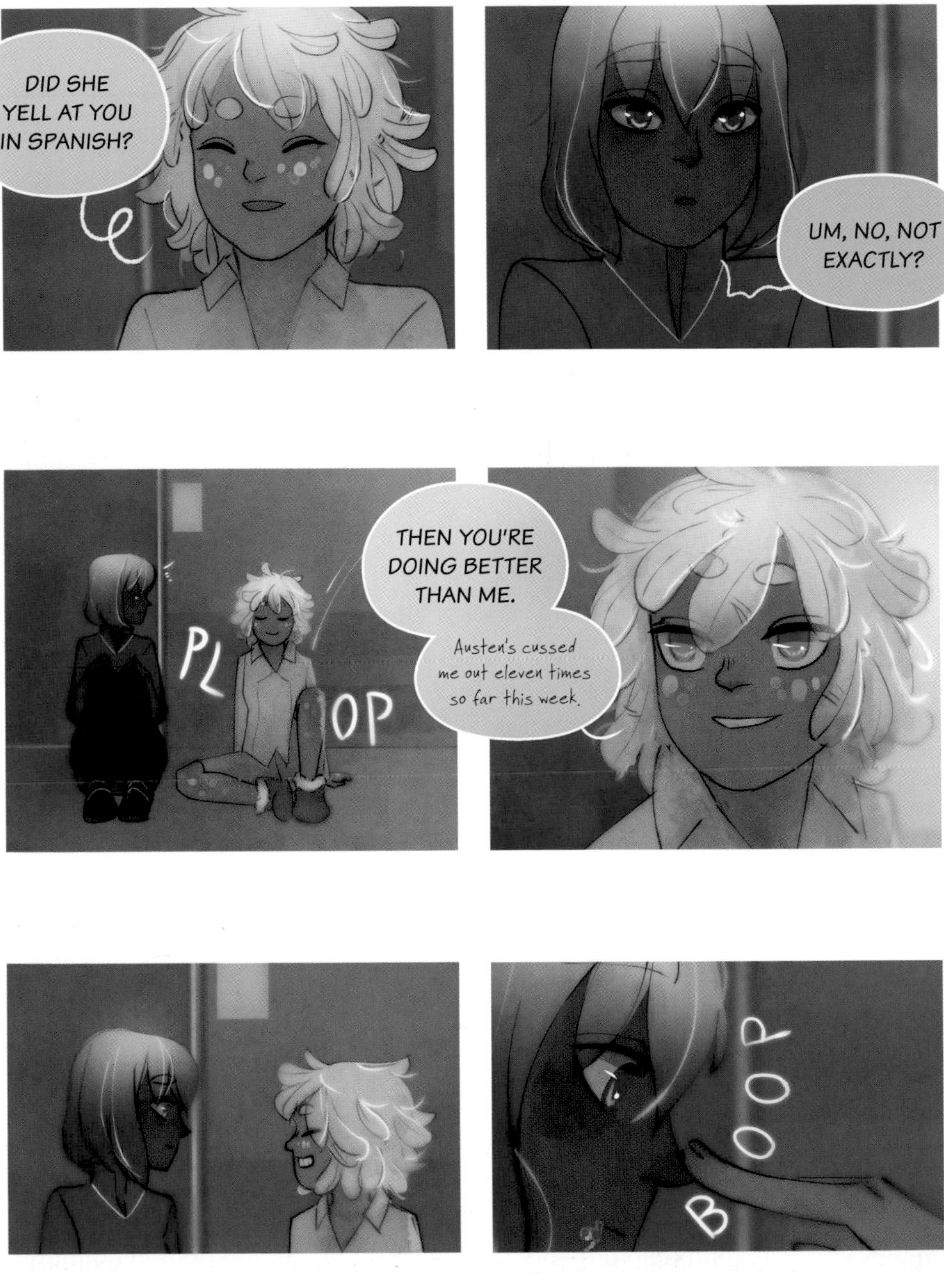
DID SHE YELL AT YOU IN SPANISH?
UM, NO, NOT EXACTLY?
PLOP
THEN YOU'RE DOING BETTER THAN ME.
Austen's cussed me out eleven times so far this week.
BOOP

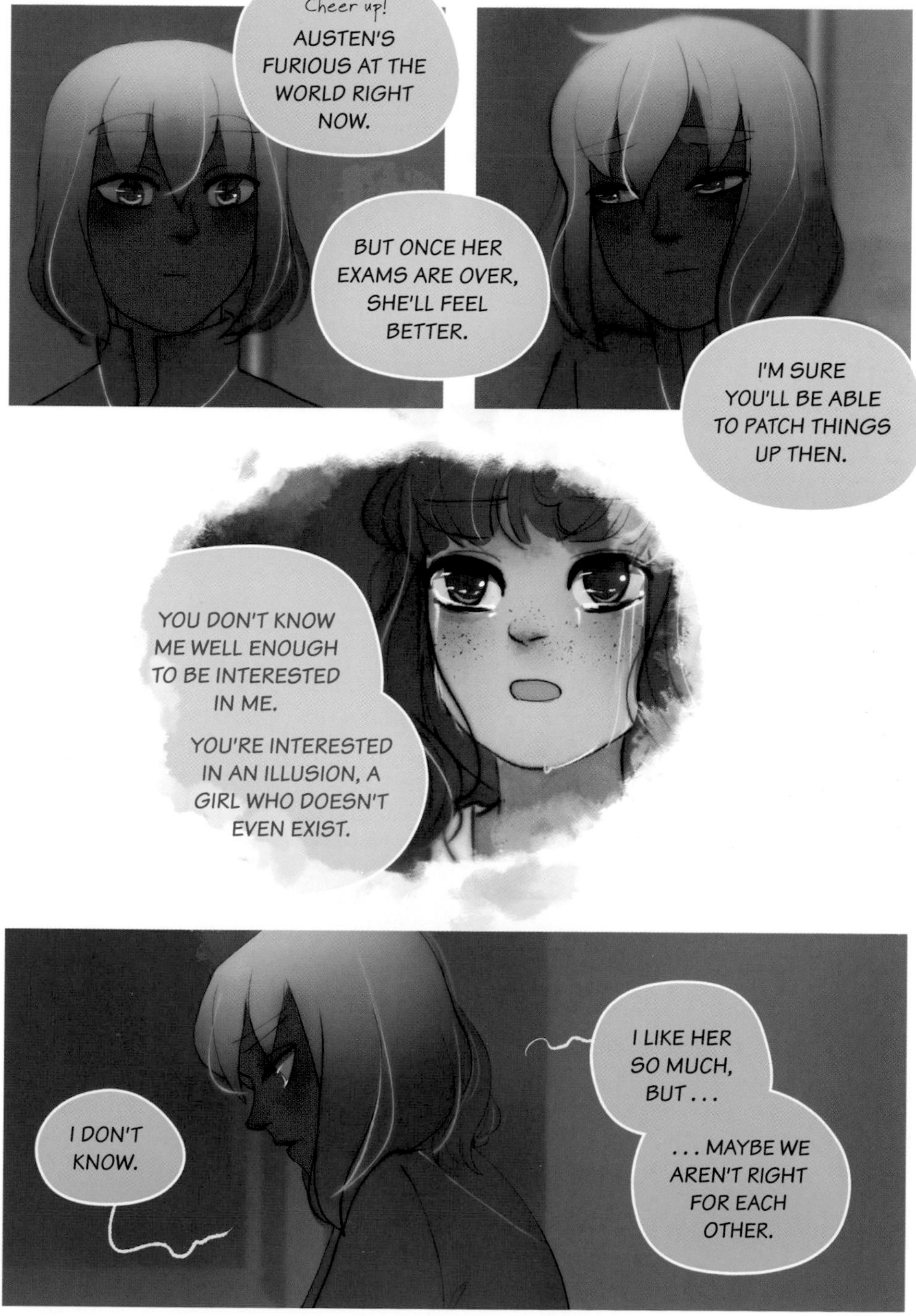
Cheer up! AUSTEN'S FURIOUS AT THE WORLD RIGHT NOW.
BUT ONCE HER EXAMS ARE OVER, SHE'LL FEEL BETTER.
I'M SURE YOU'LL BE ABLE TO PATCH THINGS UP THEN.
YOU DON'T KNOW ME WELL ENOUGH TO BE INTERESTED IN ME.
YOU'RE INTERESTED IN AN ILLUSION, A GIRL WHO DOESN'T EVEN EXIST.
I LIKE HER SO MUCH, BUT . . .
. . . MAYBE WE AREN'T RIGHT FOR EACH OTHER.
I DON'T KNOW.

THAT'S A PITY.

AUSTEN'S BEEN REALLY RELAXED THE PAST FEW WEEKS.

YOU MAKE HER HAPPY.

IT WOULD SUCK IF THE TWO OF YOU BROKE UP.

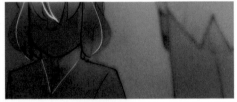

OH WELL.

DO YOU MEAN THAT?

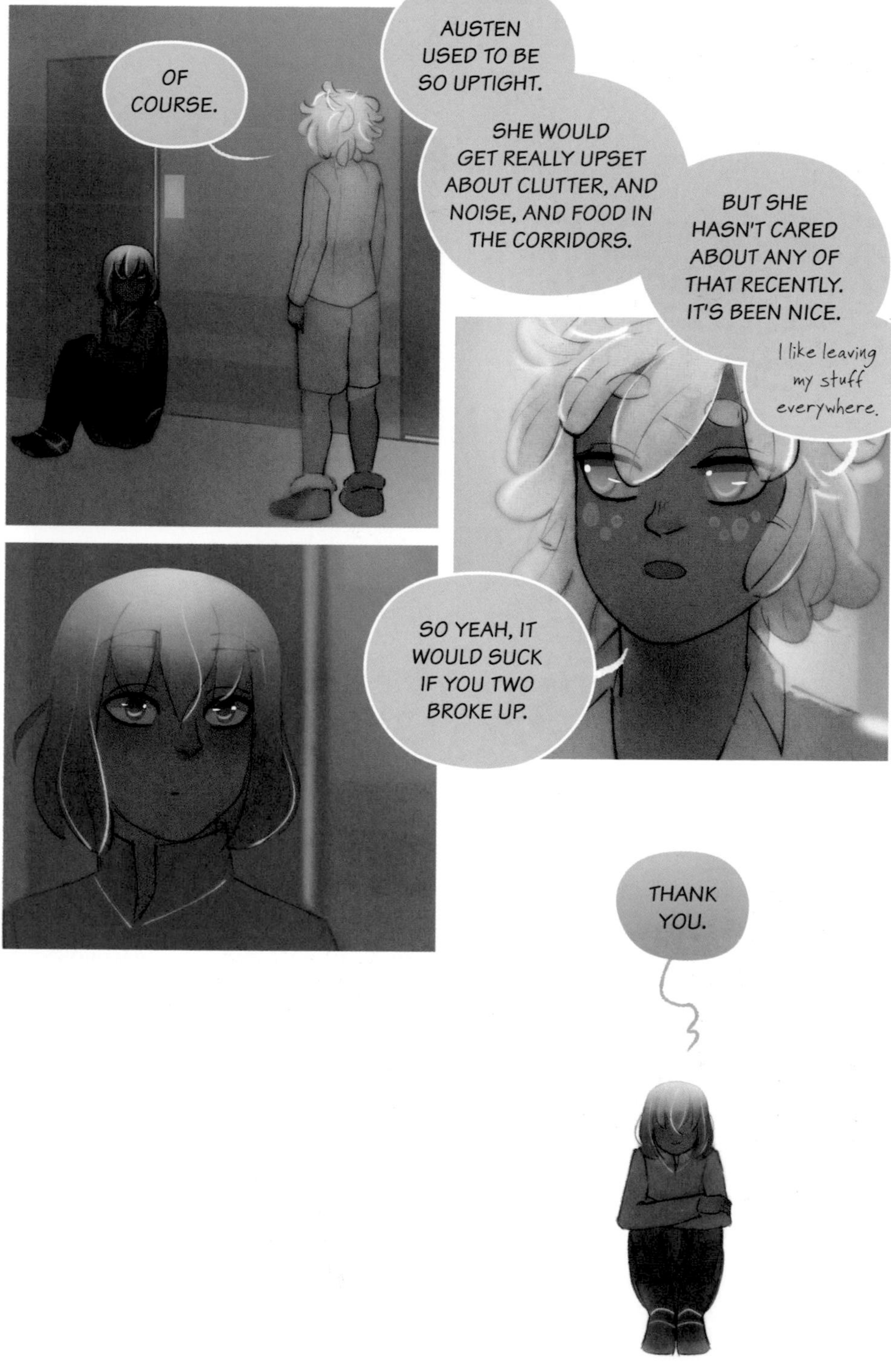
OF COURSE.
AUSTEN USED TO BE SO UPTIGHT.
SHE WOULD GET REALLY UPSET ABOUT CLUTTER, AND NOISE, AND FOOD IN THE CORRIDORS.
BUT SHE HASN'T CARED ABOUT ANY OF THAT RECENTLY. IT'S BEEN NICE.
I like leaving my stuff everywhere.
SO YEAH, IT WOULD SUCK IF YOU TWO BROKE UP.
THANK YOU.

25 - SORRY

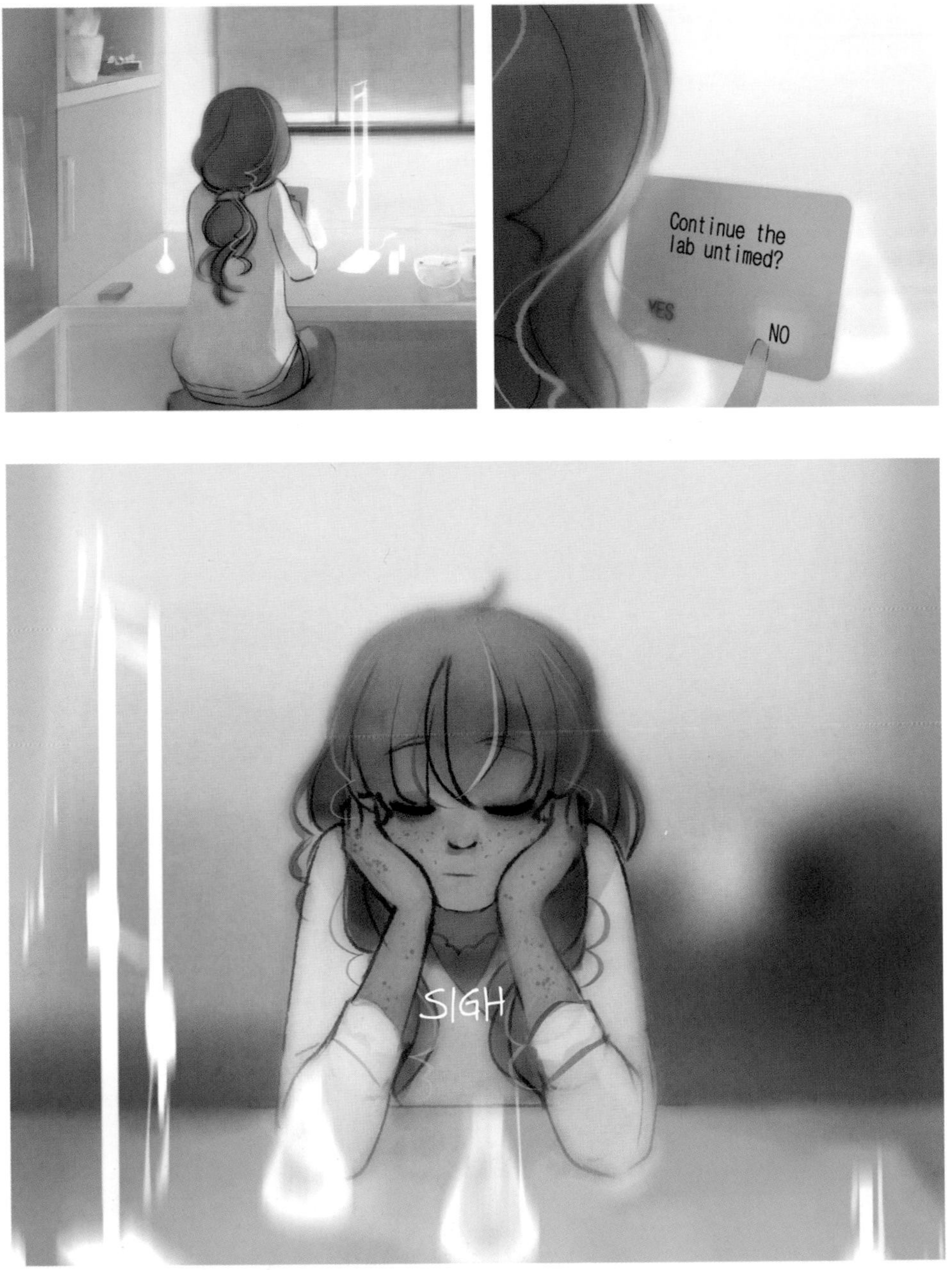
Continue the lab untimed?
YES
NO
SIGH

PLEASE, TAKE CARE OF YOURSELF.

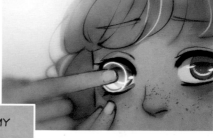

I NEED TO GIVE MY EYES A BREAK . . .

. . . AND GET SOME FRESH AIR.

AND WRITE A DRAFT OF THE WORLD'S MOST REPENTANT EMAIL.

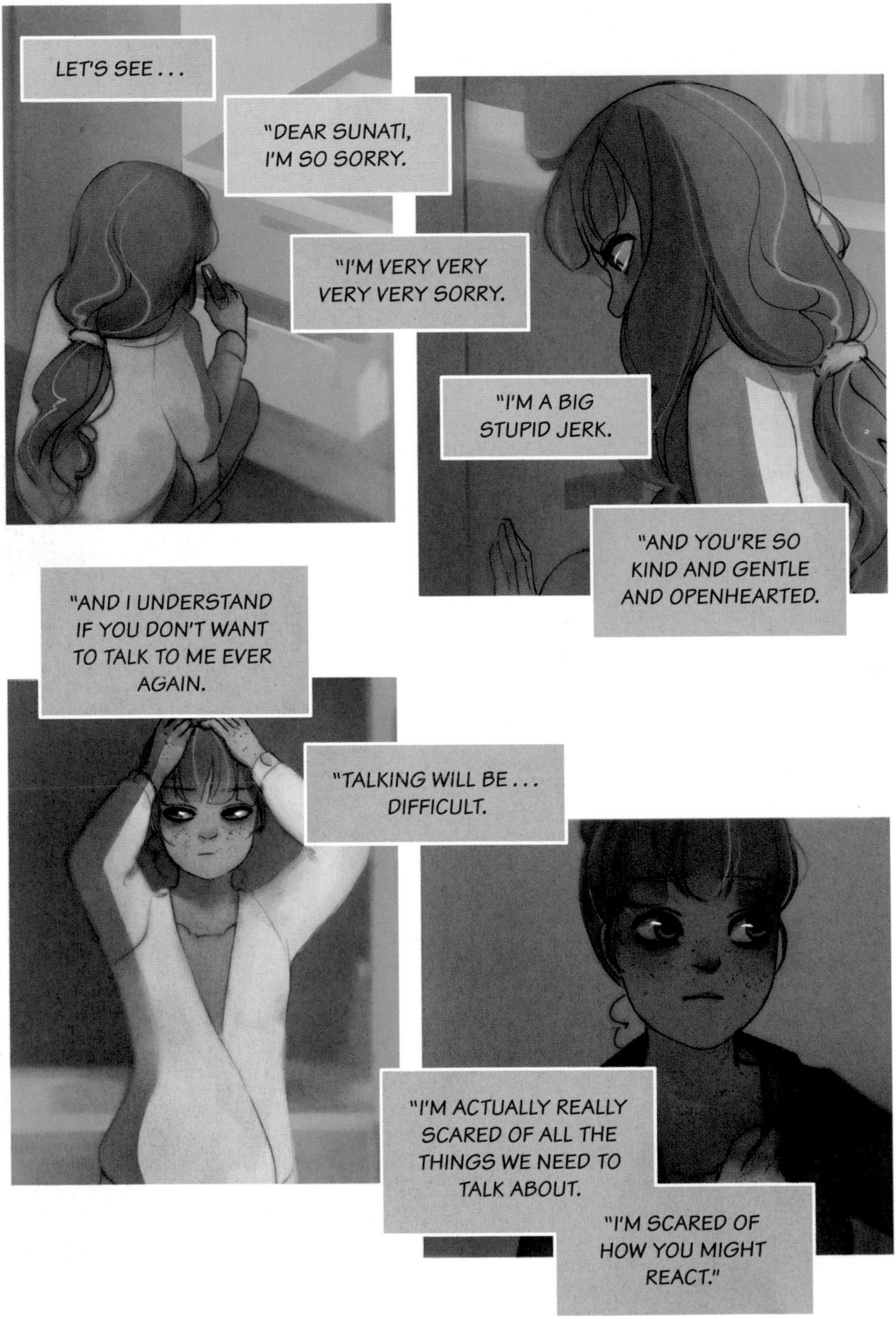
LET'S SEE . . .
"DEAR SUNATI, I'M SO SORRY.
"I'M VERY VERY VERY VERY SORRY.
"I'M A BIG STUPID JERK.
"AND YOU'RE SO KIND AND GENTLE AND OPENHEARTED.
"AND I UNDERSTAND IF YOU DON'T WANT TO TALK TO ME EVER AGAIN.
"TALKING WILL BE . . . DIFFICULT.
"I'M ACTUALLY REALLY SCARED OF ALL THE THINGS WE NEED TO TALK ABOUT.
"I'M SCARED OF HOW YOU MIGHT REACT."

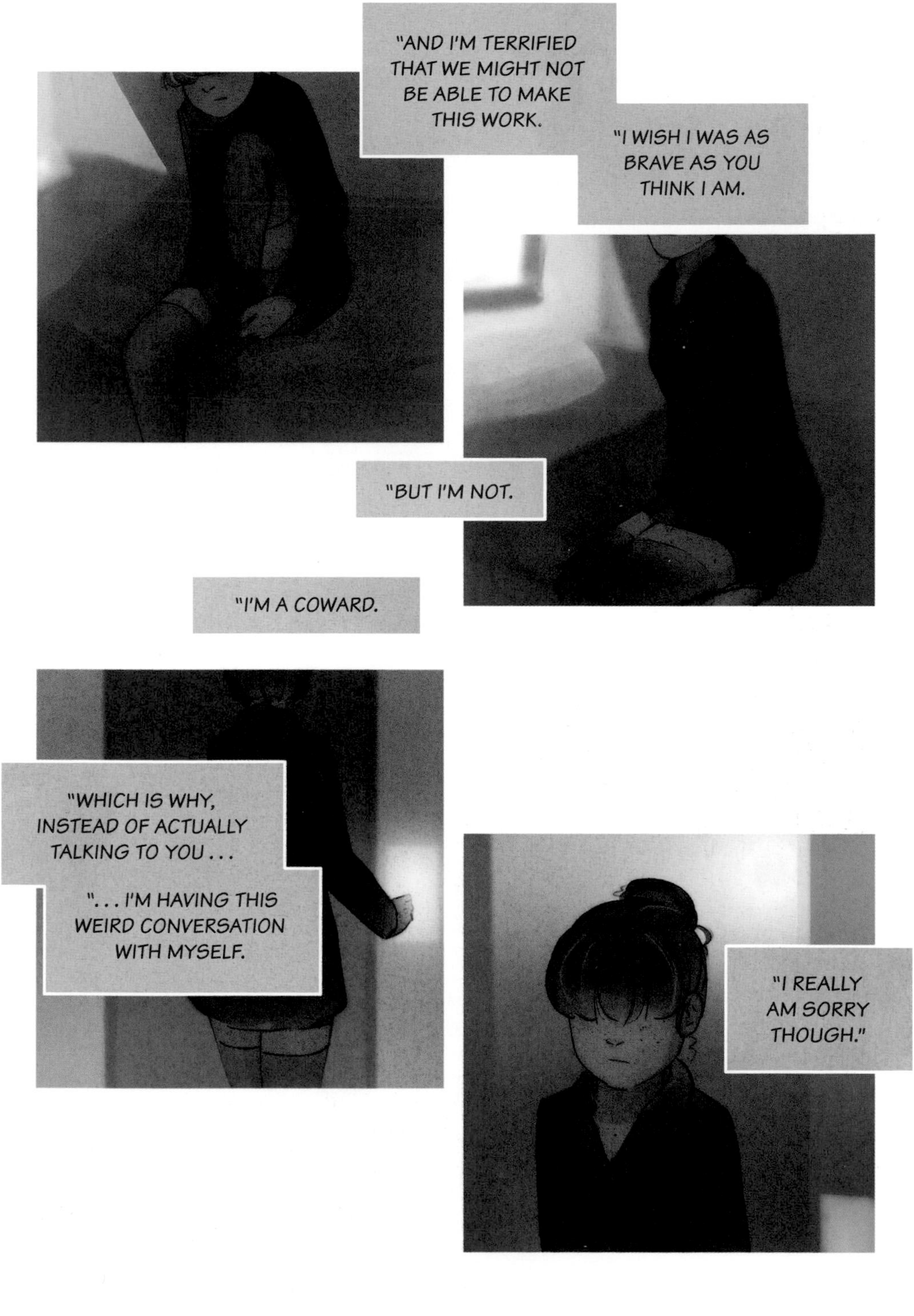
"AND I'M TERRIFIED THAT WE MIGHT NOT BE ABLE TO MAKE THIS WORK.
"I WISH I WAS AS BRAVE AS YOU THINK I AM.
"BUT I'M NOT.
"I'M A COWARD.
"WHICH IS WHY, INSTEAD OF ACTUALLY TALKING TO YOU . . .
". . . I'M HAVING THIS WEIRD CONVERSATION WITH MYSELF.
"I REALLY AM SORRY THOUGH."

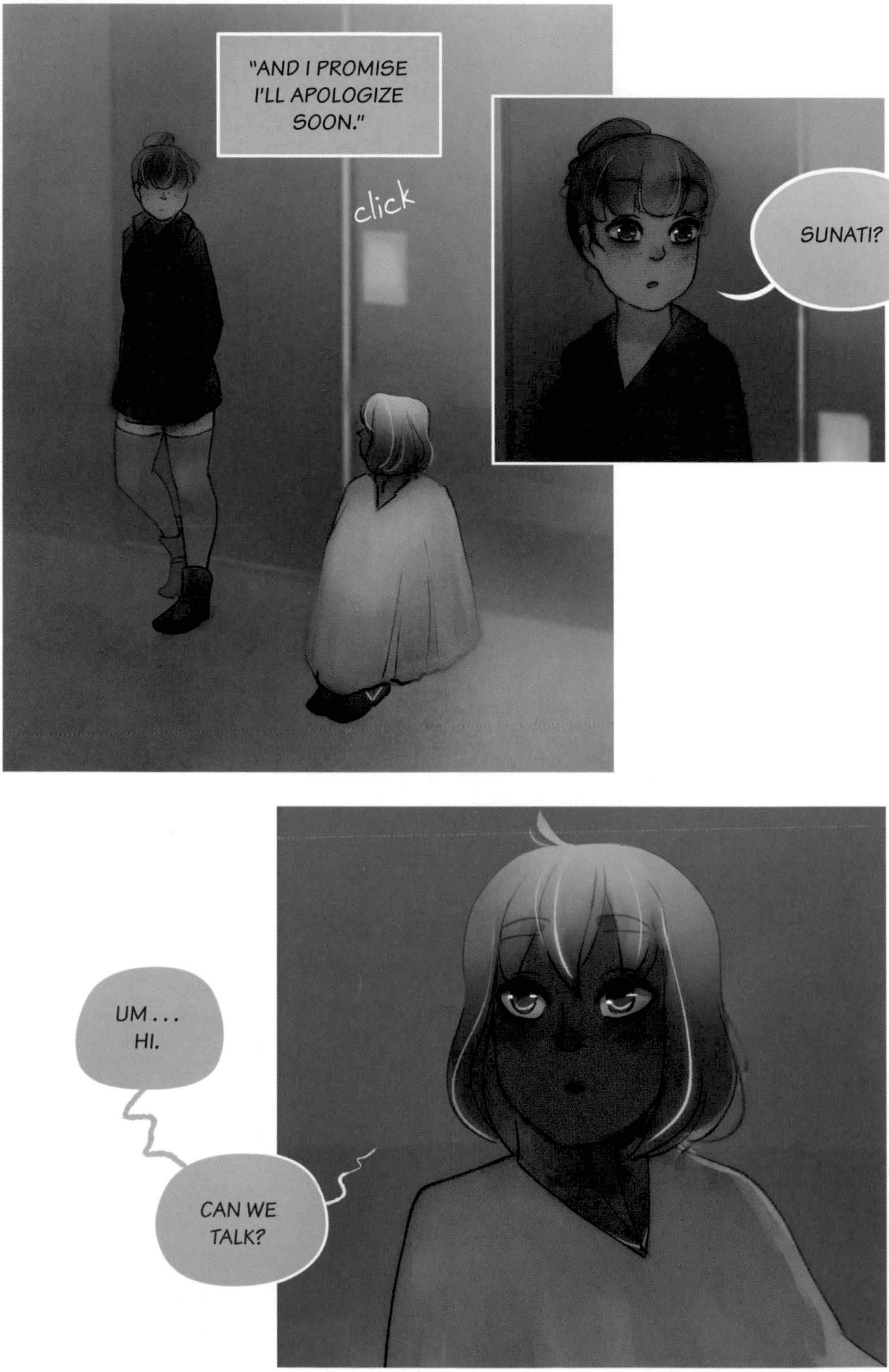
"AND I PROMISE I'LL APOLOGIZE SOON."
click
SUNATI?
UM . . . HI.
CAN WE TALK?

26 - I'M NOT PERFECT

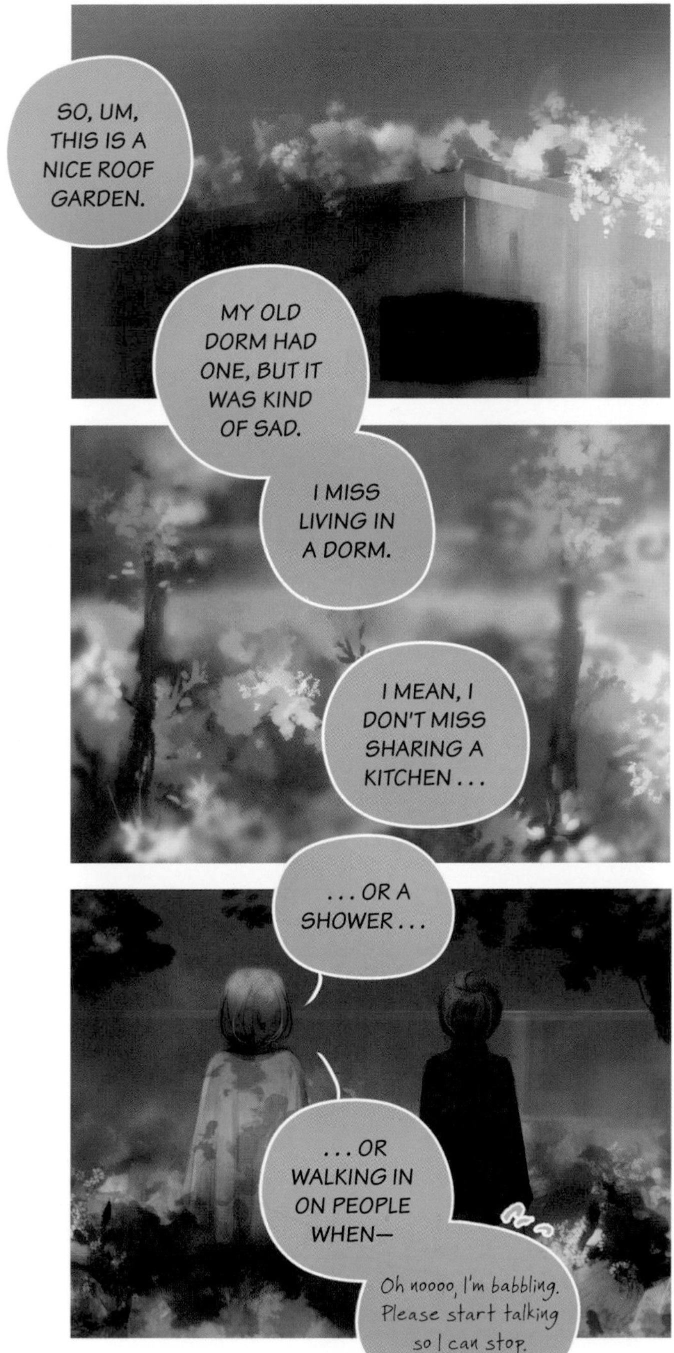
SO, UM, THIS IS A NICE ROOF GARDEN.
MY OLD DORM HAD ONE, BUT IT WAS KIND OF SAD.
I MISS LIVING IN A DORM.
I MEAN, I DON'T MISS SHARING A KITCHEN . . .
. . . OR A SHOWER . . .
. . . OR WALKING IN ON PEOPLE WHEN—
Oh noooo, I'm babbling. Please start talking so I can stop.

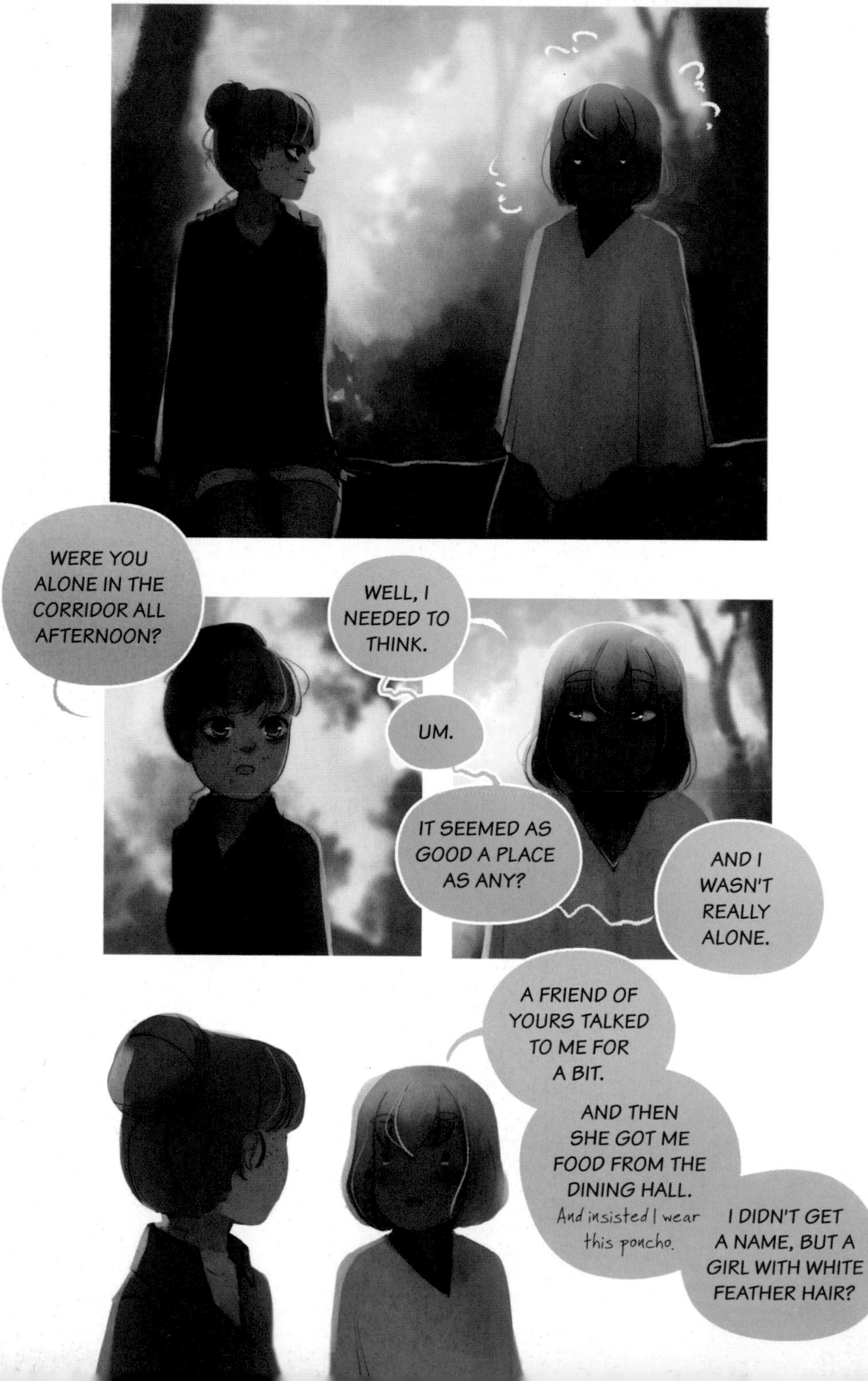
WERE YOU ALONE IN THE CORRIDOR ALL AFTERNOON?
WELL, I NEEDED TO THINK.
UM.
IT SEEMED AS GOOD A PLACE AS ANY?
AND I WASN'T REALLY ALONE.
A FRIEND OF YOURS TALKED TO ME FOR A BIT.
AND THEN SHE GOT ME FOOD FROM THE DINING HALL.
And insisted I wear this poncho.
I DIDN'T GET A NAME, BUT A GIRL WITH WHITE FEATHER HAIR?

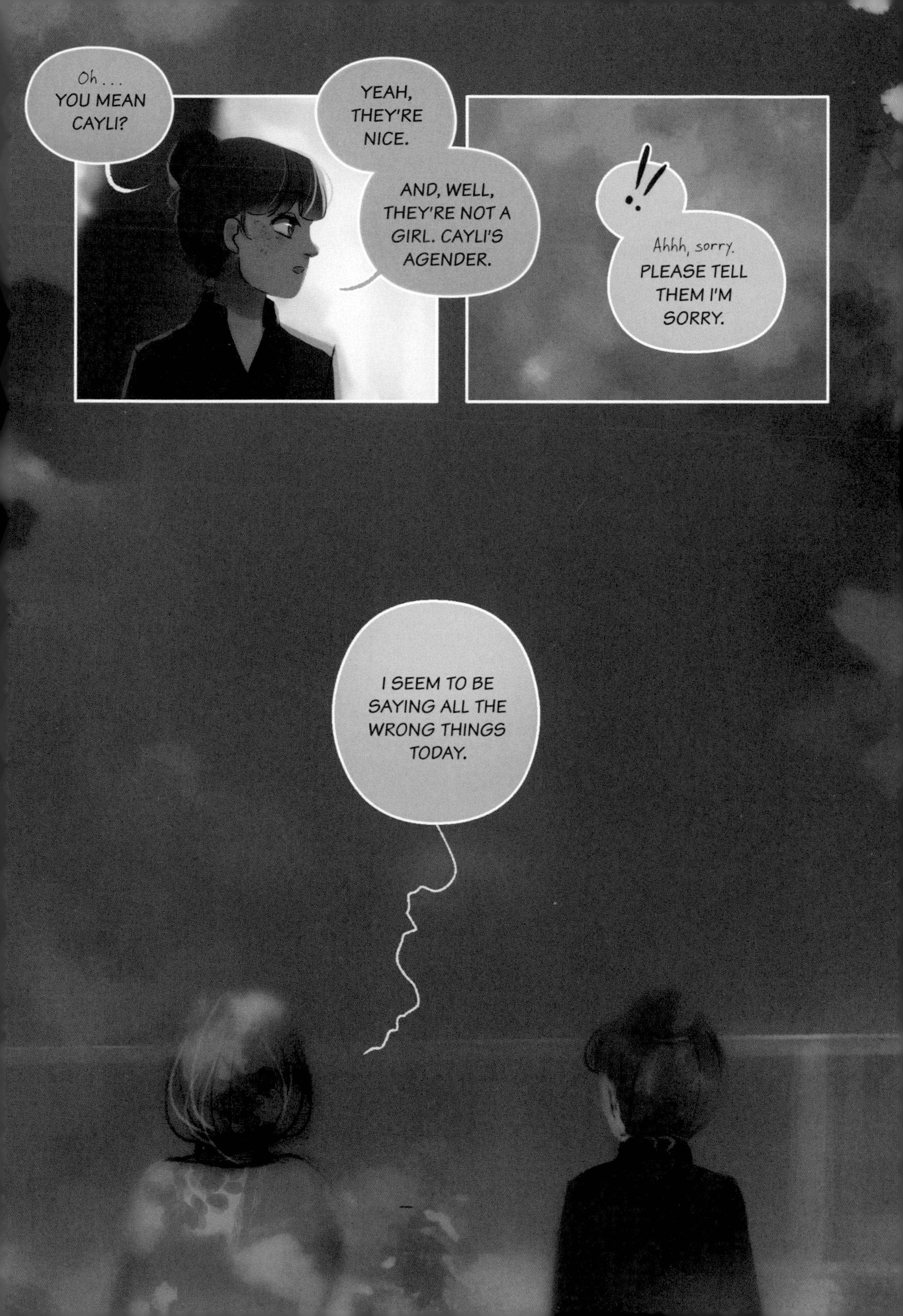
Oh . . . YOU MEAN CAYLI?
YEAH, THEY'RE NICE.
AND, WELL, THEY'RE NOT A GIRL. CAYLI'S AGENDER.
!!
Ahhh, sorry. PLEASE TELL THEM I'M SORRY.
I SEEM TO BE SAYING ALL THE WRONG THINGS TODAY.

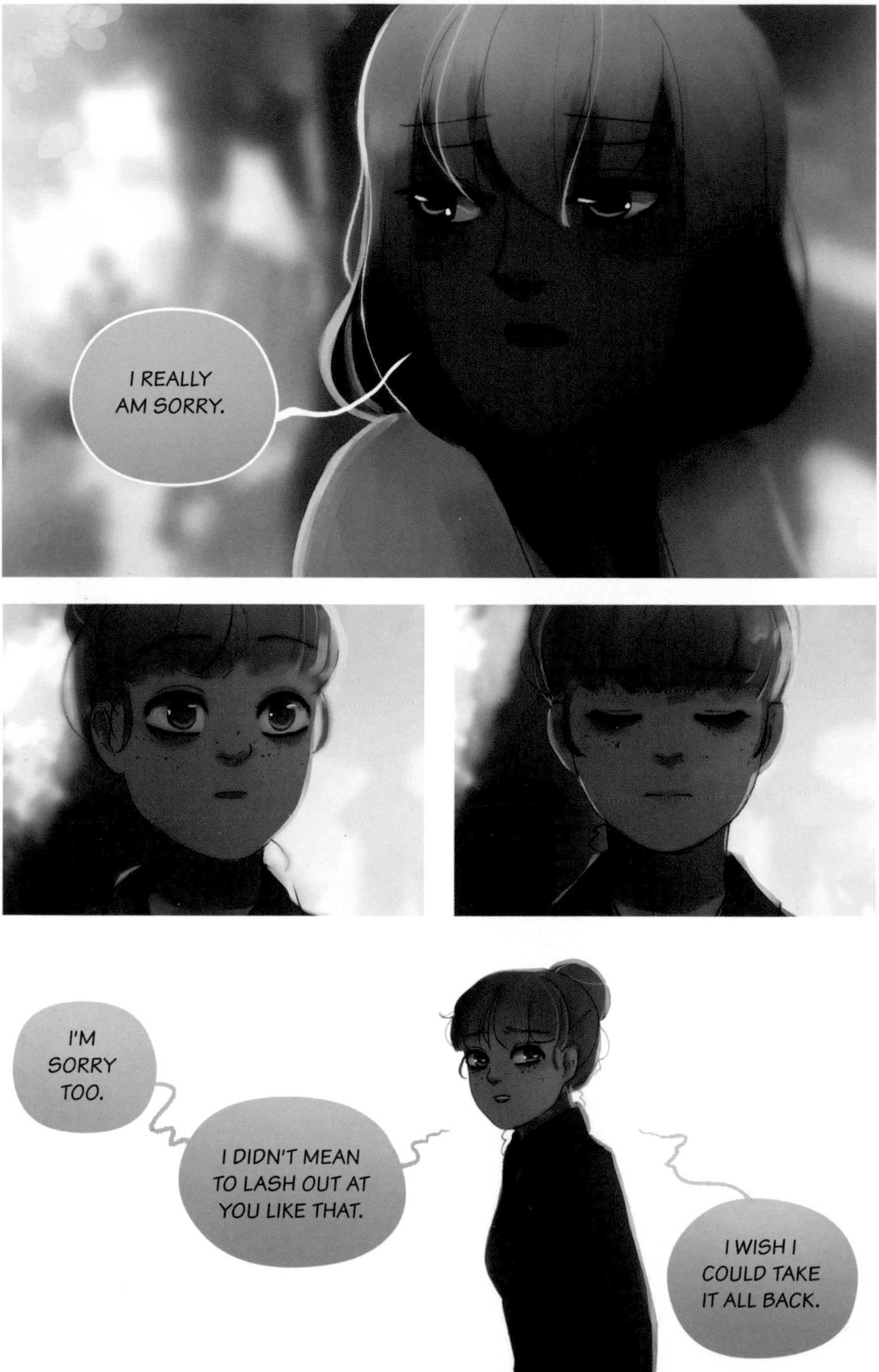
I REALLY AM SORRY.
I'M SORRY TOO.
I DIDN'T MEAN TO LASH OUT AT YOU LIKE THAT.
I WISH I COULD TAKE IT ALL BACK.

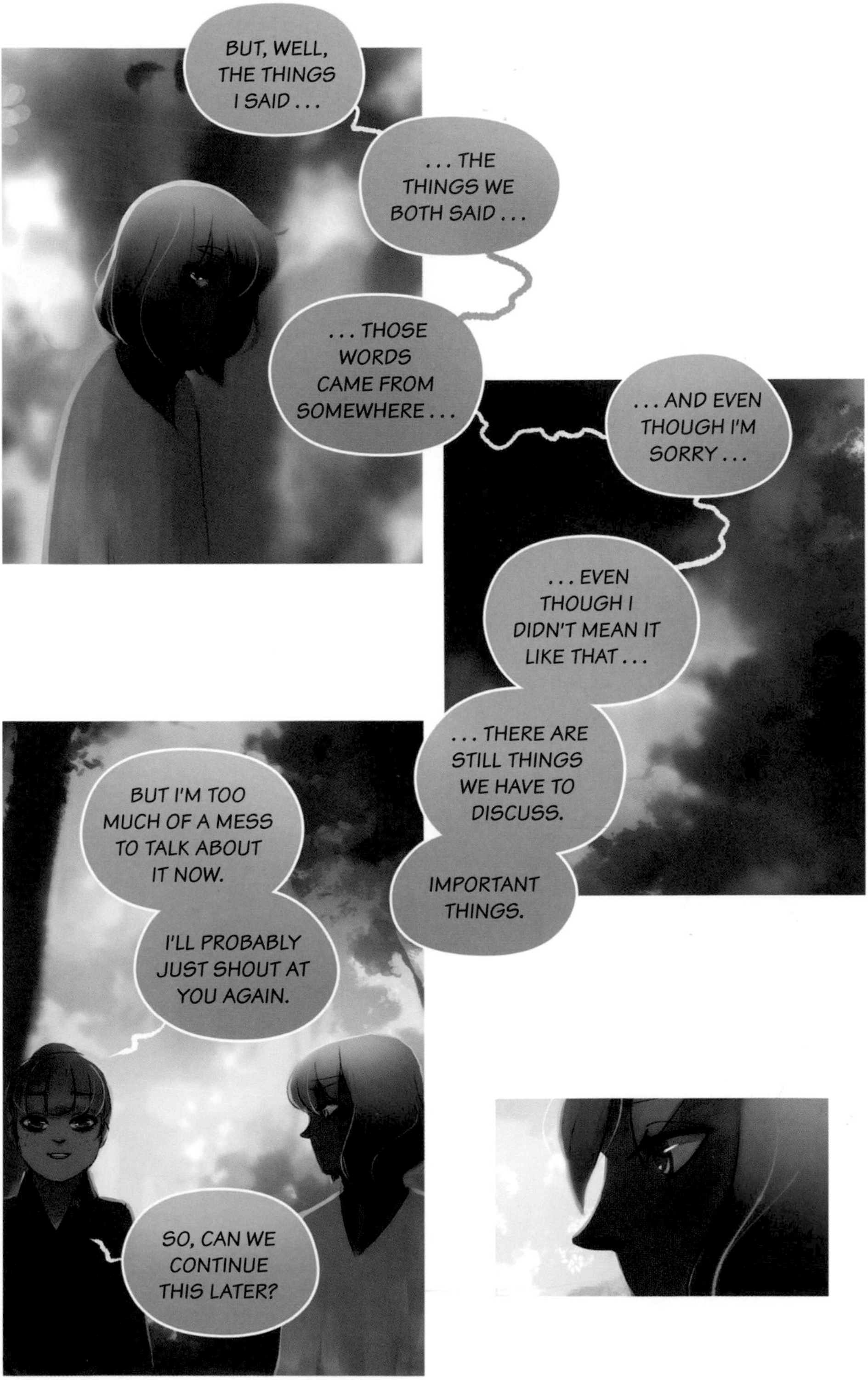
BUT, WELL, THE THINGS I SAID . . .
. . . THE THINGS WE BOTH SAID . . .
. . . THOSE WORDS CAME FROM SOMEWHERE . . .
. . . AND EVEN THOUGH I'M SORRY . . .
. . . EVEN THOUGH I DIDN'T MEAN IT LIKE THAT . . .
. . . THERE ARE STILL THINGS WE HAVE TO DISCUSS.
IMPORTANT THINGS.
BUT I'M TOO MUCH OF A MESS TO TALK ABOUT IT NOW.
I'LL PROBABLY JUST SHOUT AT YOU AGAIN.
SO, CAN WE CONTINUE THIS LATER?

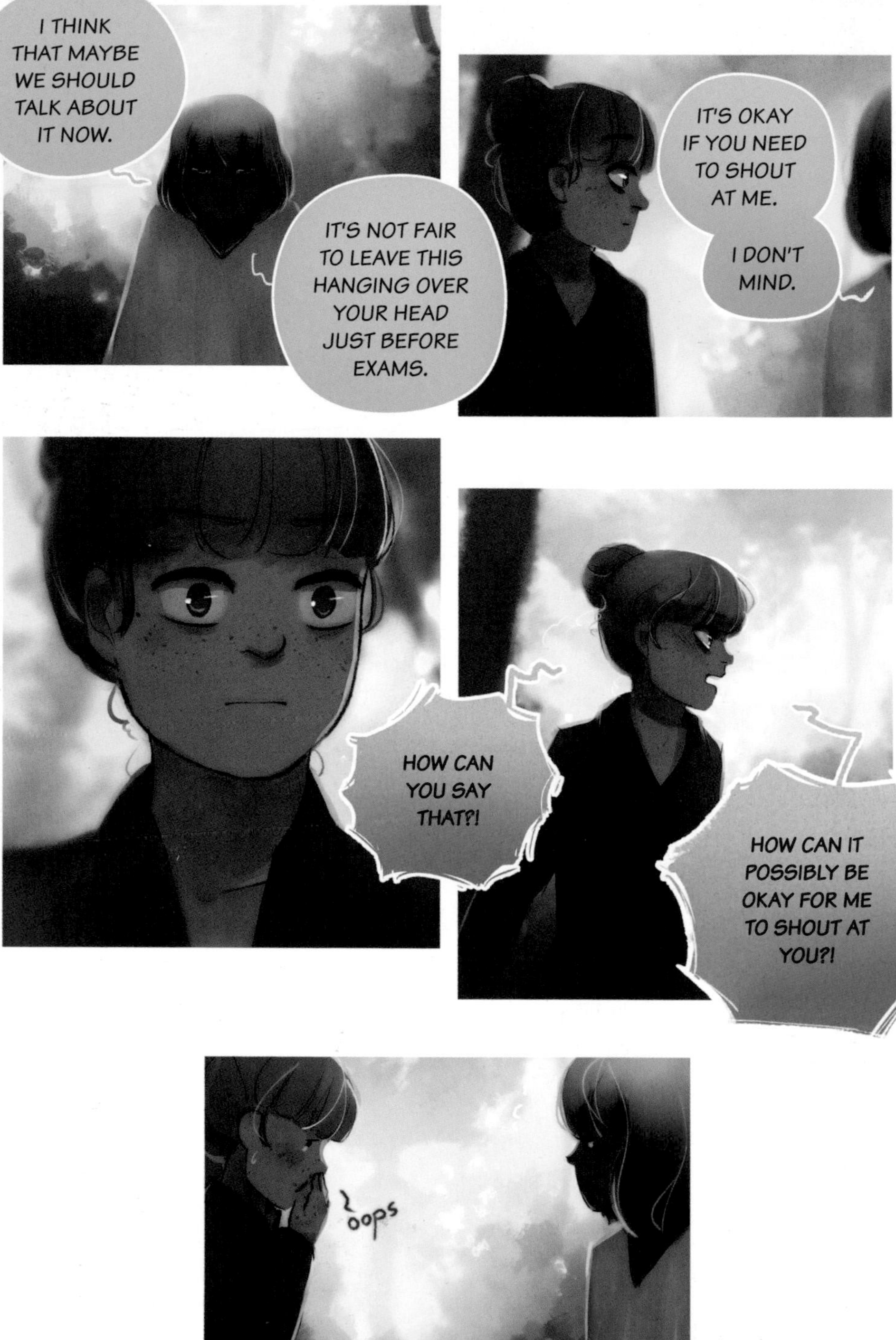
I THINK THAT MAYBE WE SHOULD TALK ABOUT IT NOW.
IT'S NOT FAIR TO LEAVE THIS HANGING OVER YOUR HEAD JUST BEFORE EXAMS.
IT'S OKAY IF YOU NEED TO SHOUT AT ME.
I DON'T MIND.
HOW CAN YOU SAY THAT?!
HOW CAN IT POSSIBLY BE OKAY FOR ME TO SHOUT AT YOU?!
oops

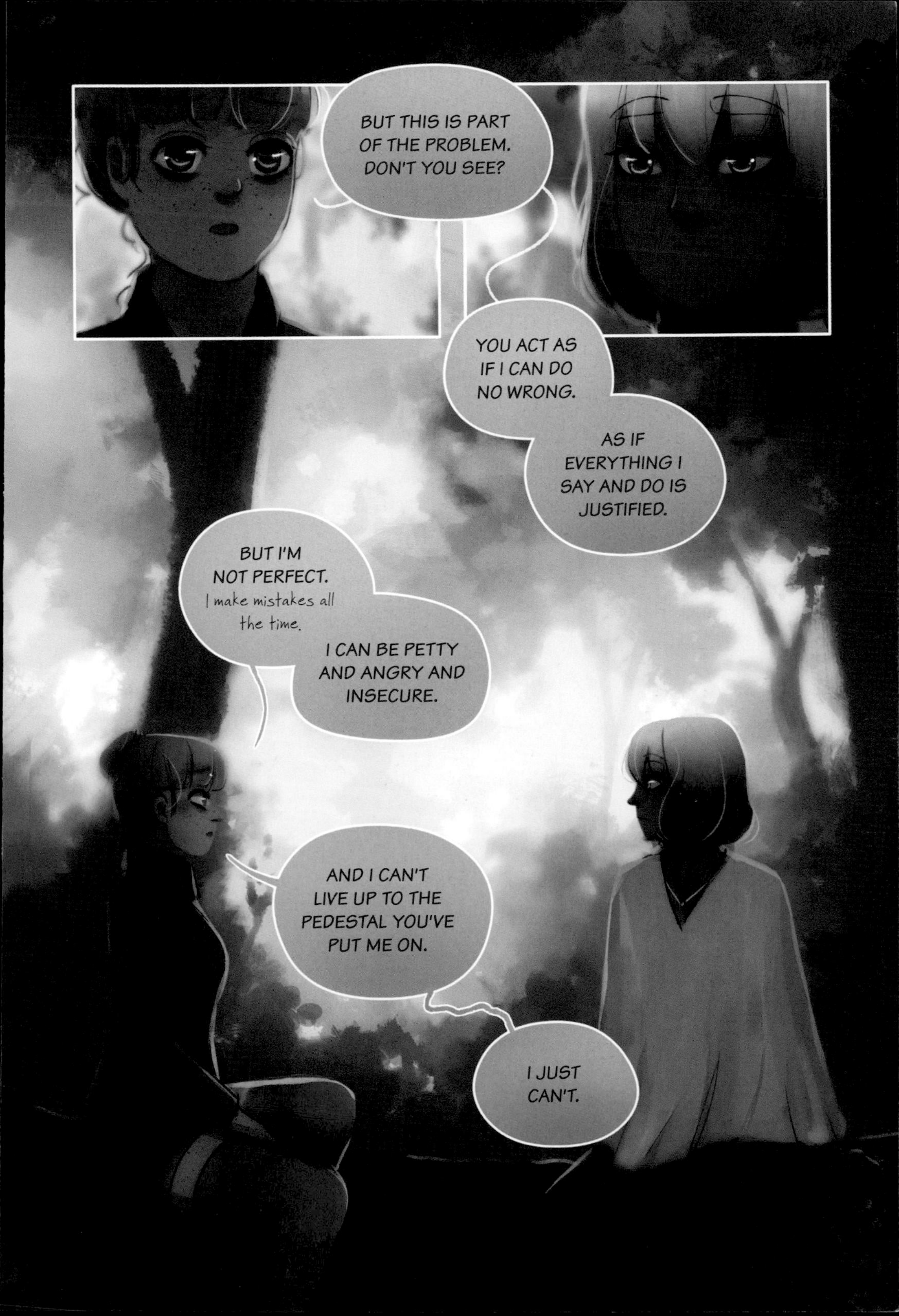
BUT THIS IS PART OF THE PROBLEM. DON'T YOU SEE?
YOU ACT AS IF I CAN DO NO WRONG.
AS IF EVERYTHING I SAY AND DO IS JUSTIFIED.
BUT I'M NOT PERFECT. I make mistakes all the time.
I CAN BE PETTY AND ANGRY AND INSECURE.
AND I CAN'T LIVE UP TO THE PEDESTAL YOU'VE PUT ME ON.
I JUST CAN'T.

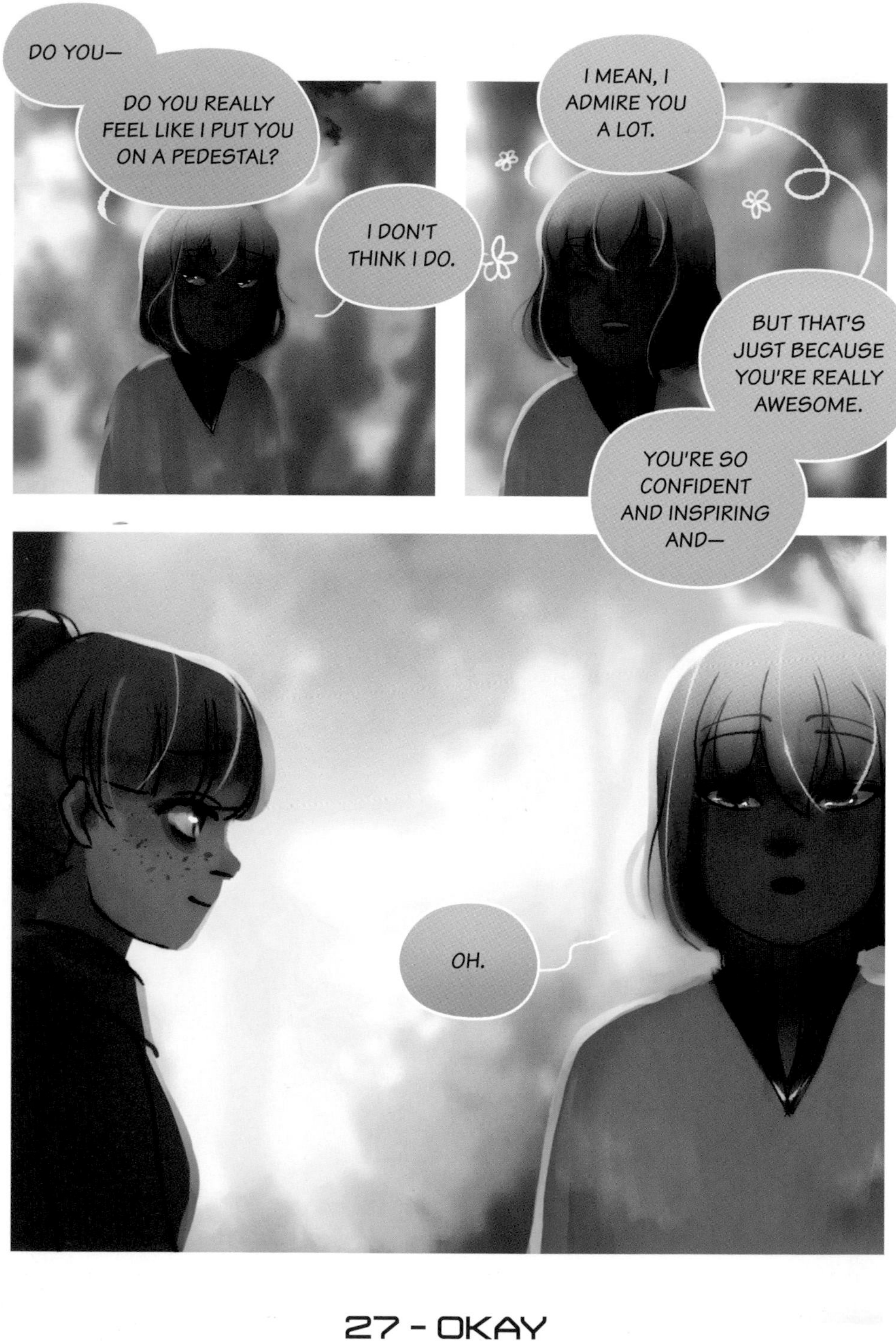
DO YOU—
DO YOU REALLY FEEL LIKE I PUT YOU ON A PEDESTAL?
I DON'T THINK I DO.
I MEAN, I ADMIRE YOU A LOT.
BUT THAT'S JUST BECAUSE YOU'RE REALLY AWESOME.
YOU'RE SO CONFIDENT AND INSPIRING AND—
OH.

27 - OKAY

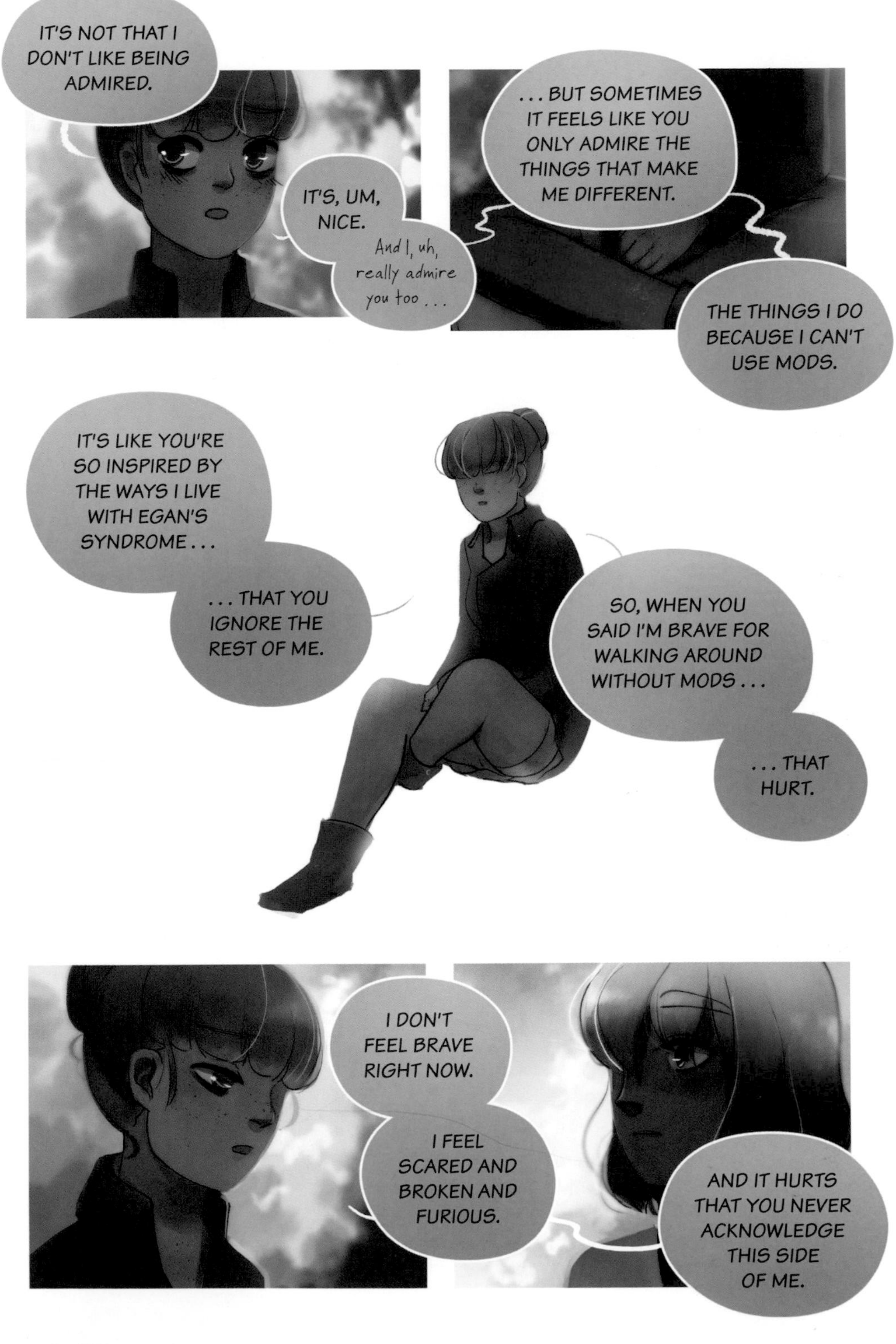
IT'S NOT THAT I DON'T LIKE BEING ADMIRED.
IT'S, UM, NICE.
And I, uh, really admire you too . . .
. . . BUT SOMETIMES IT FEELS LIKE YOU ONLY ADMIRE THE THINGS THAT MAKE ME DIFFERENT.
THE THINGS I DO BECAUSE I CAN'T USE MODS.
IT'S LIKE YOU'RE SO INSPIRED BY THE WAYS I LIVE WITH EGAN'S SYNDROME . . .
. . . THAT YOU IGNORE THE REST OF ME.
SO, WHEN YOU SAID I'M BRAVE FOR WALKING AROUND WITHOUT MODS . . .
. . . THAT HURT.
I DON'T FEEL BRAVE RIGHT NOW.
I FEEL SCARED AND BROKEN AND FURIOUS.
AND IT HURTS THAT YOU NEVER ACKNOWLEDGE THIS SIDE OF ME.

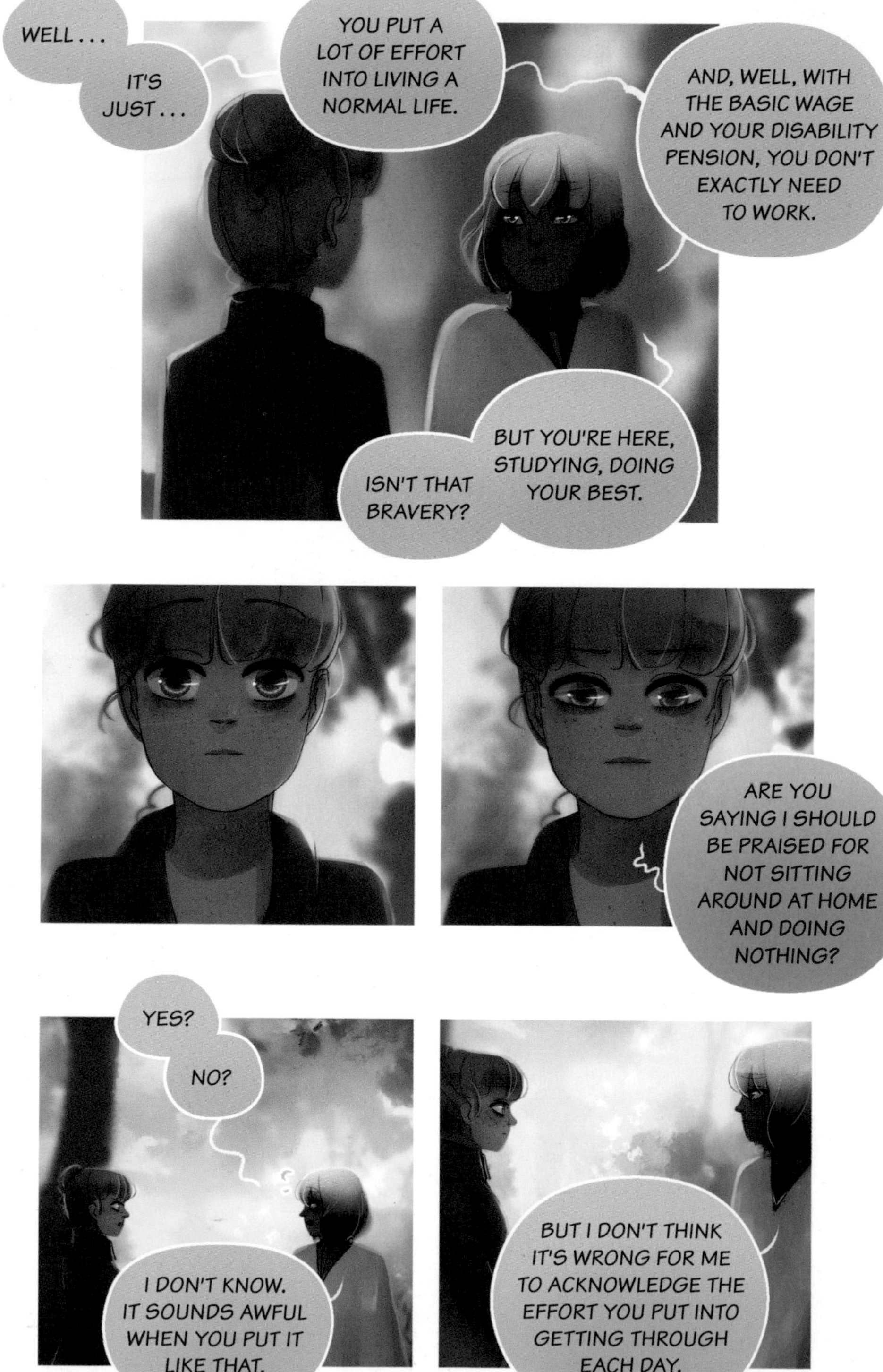
WELL . . .
IT'S JUST . . .
YOU PUT A LOT OF EFFORT INTO LIVING A NORMAL LIFE.
AND, WELL, WITH THE BASIC WAGE AND YOUR DISABILITY PENSION, YOU DON'T EXACTLY NEED TO WORK.
BUT YOU'RE HERE, STUDYING, DOING YOUR BEST.
ISN'T THAT BRAVERY?
ARE YOU SAYING I SHOULD BE PRAISED FOR NOT SITTING AROUND AT HOME AND DOING NOTHING?
YES?
NO?
I DON'T KNOW. IT SOUNDS AWFUL WHEN YOU PUT IT LIKE THAT.
BUT I DON'T THINK IT'S WRONG FOR ME TO ACKNOWLEDGE THE EFFORT YOU PUT INTO GETTING THROUGH EACH DAY.

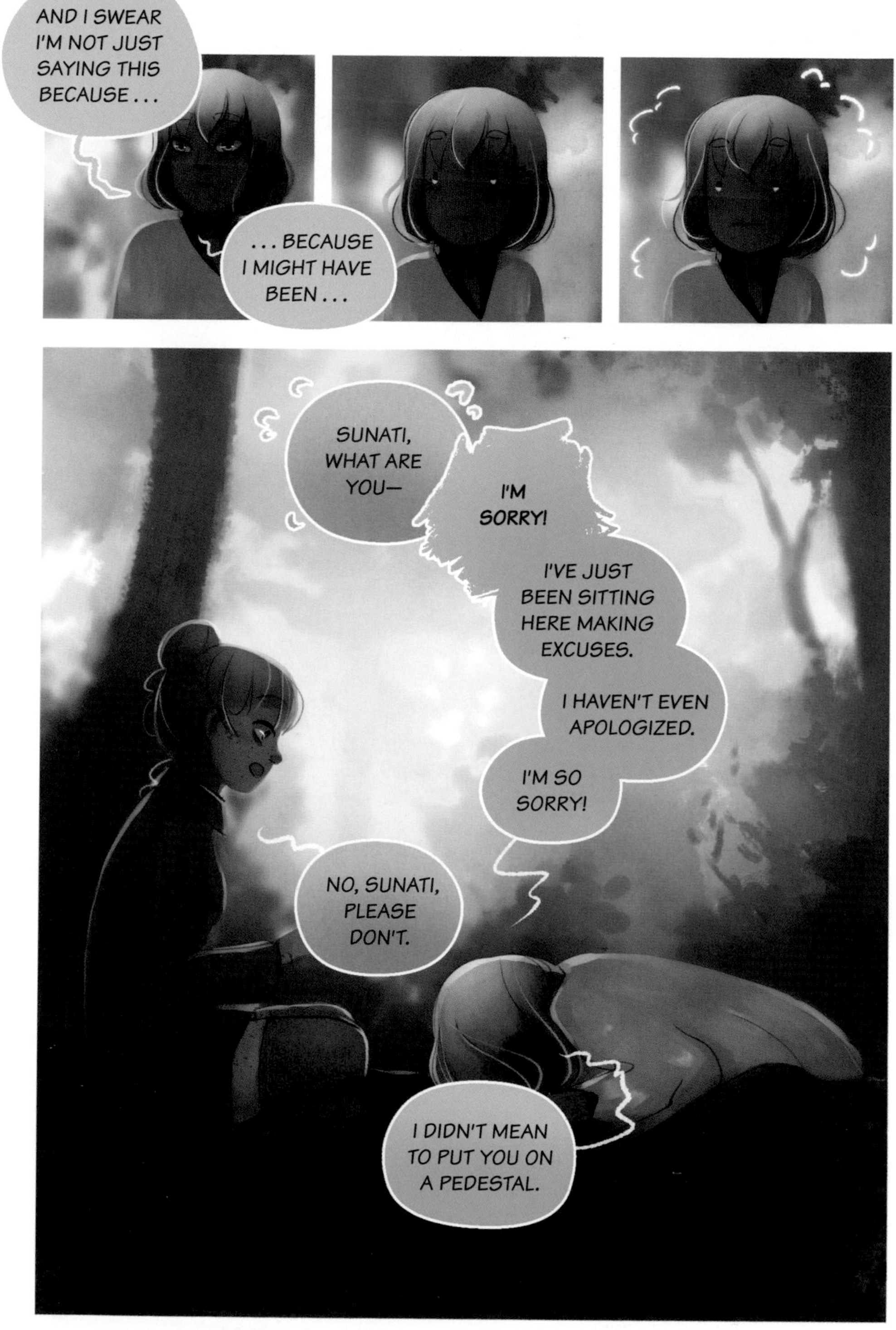
AND I SWEAR I'M NOT JUST SAYING THIS BECAUSE . . .
. . . BECAUSE I MIGHT HAVE BEEN . . .
SUNATI, WHAT ARE YOU—
I'M SORRY!
I'VE JUST BEEN SITTING HERE MAKING EXCUSES.
I HAVEN'T EVEN APOLOGIZED.
I'M SO SORRY!
NO, SUNATI, PLEASE DON'T.
I DIDN'T MEAN TO PUT YOU ON A PEDESTAL.

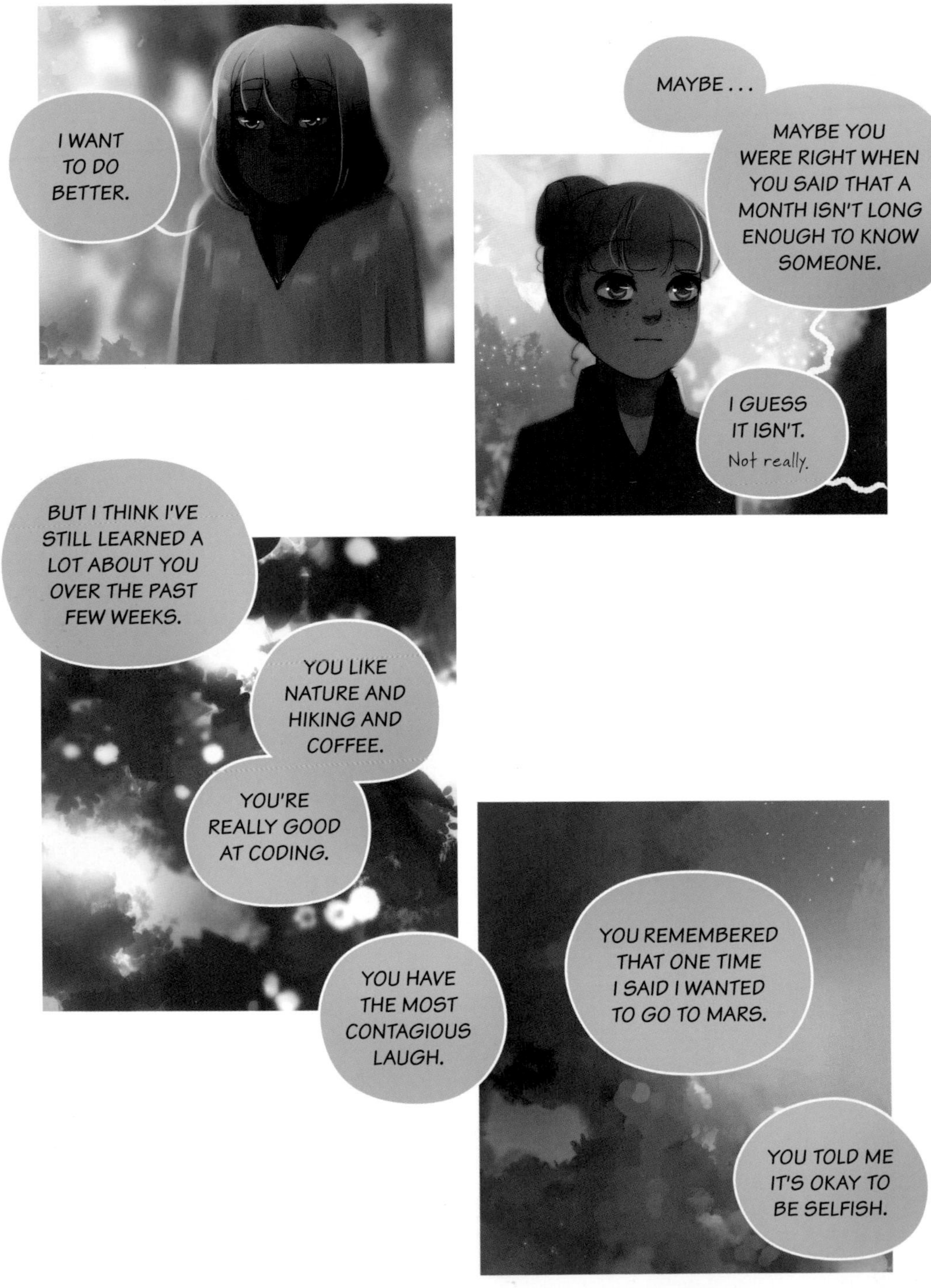
I WANT TO DO BETTER.
MAYBE . . .
MAYBE YOU WERE RIGHT WHEN YOU SAID THAT A MONTH ISN'T LONG ENOUGH TO KNOW SOMEONE.
I GUESS IT ISN'T. Not really.
BUT I THINK I'VE STILL LEARNED A LOT ABOUT YOU OVER THE PAST FEW WEEKS.
YOU LIKE NATURE AND HIKING AND COFFEE.
YOU'RE REALLY GOOD AT CODING.
YOU HAVE THE MOST CONTAGIOUS LAUGH.
YOU REMEMBERED THAT ONE TIME I SAID I WANTED TO GO TO MARS.
YOU TOLD ME IT'S OKAY TO BE SELFISH.

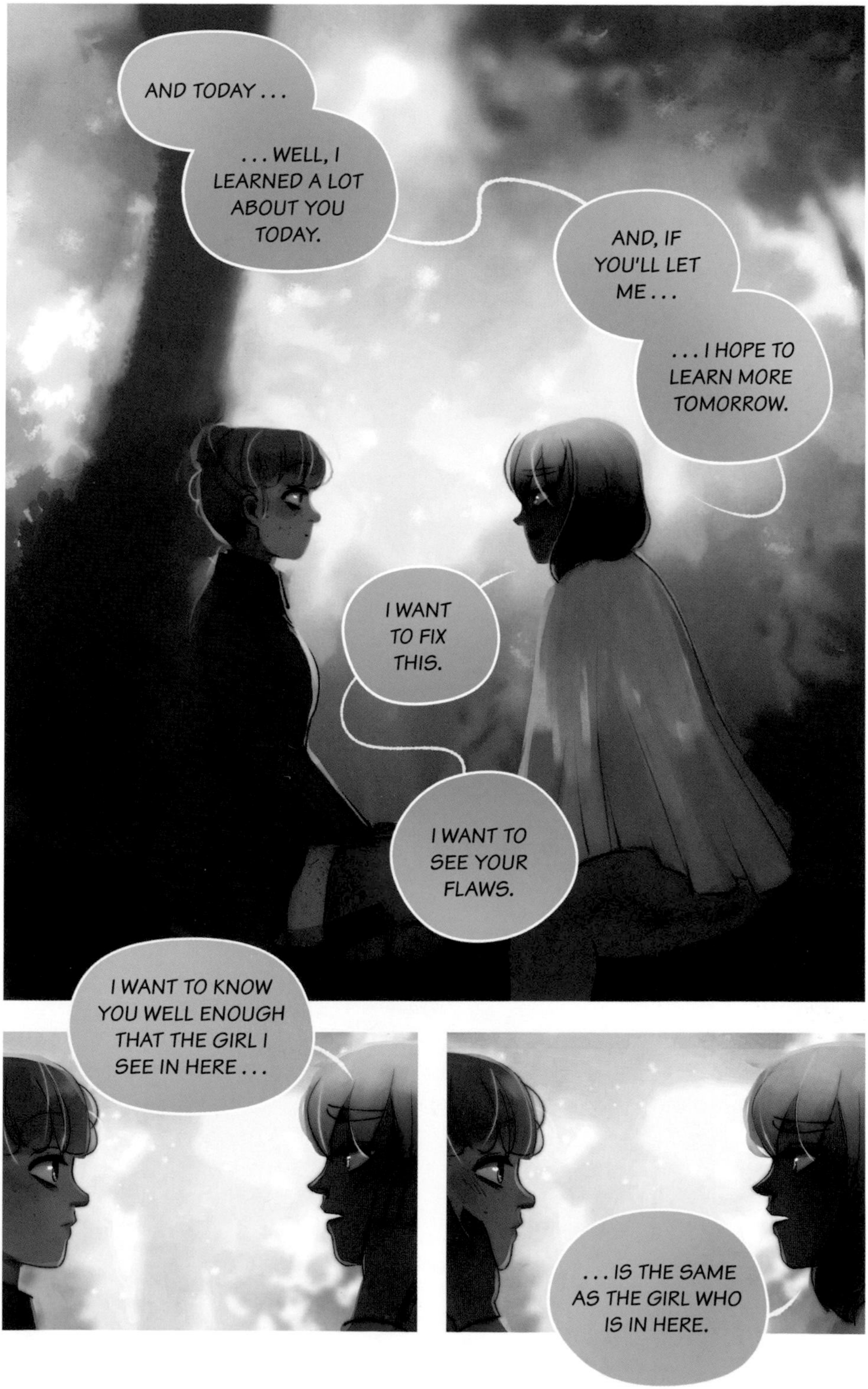
AND TODAY . . .
. . . WELL, I LEARNED A LOT ABOUT YOU TODAY.
AND, IF YOU'LL LET ME . . .
. . . I HOPE TO LEARN MORE TOMORROW.
I WANT TO FIX THIS.
I WANT TO SEE YOUR FLAWS.
I WANT TO KNOW YOU WELL ENOUGH THAT THE GIRL I SEE IN HERE . . .
. . . IS THE SAME AS THE GIRL WHO IS IN HERE.

IS THAT OKAY?

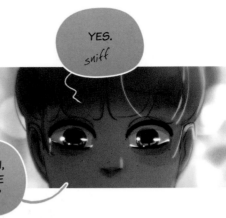

YES.

sniff

SUNATI, ARE WE OKAY?

I WANT US TO BE OKAY.

EVEN THOUGH I GET UPSET REALLY EASILY?

AND I KEEP ON CRYING WHEN YOU'RE JUST BEING NICE?

I WANT US TO BE OKAY.

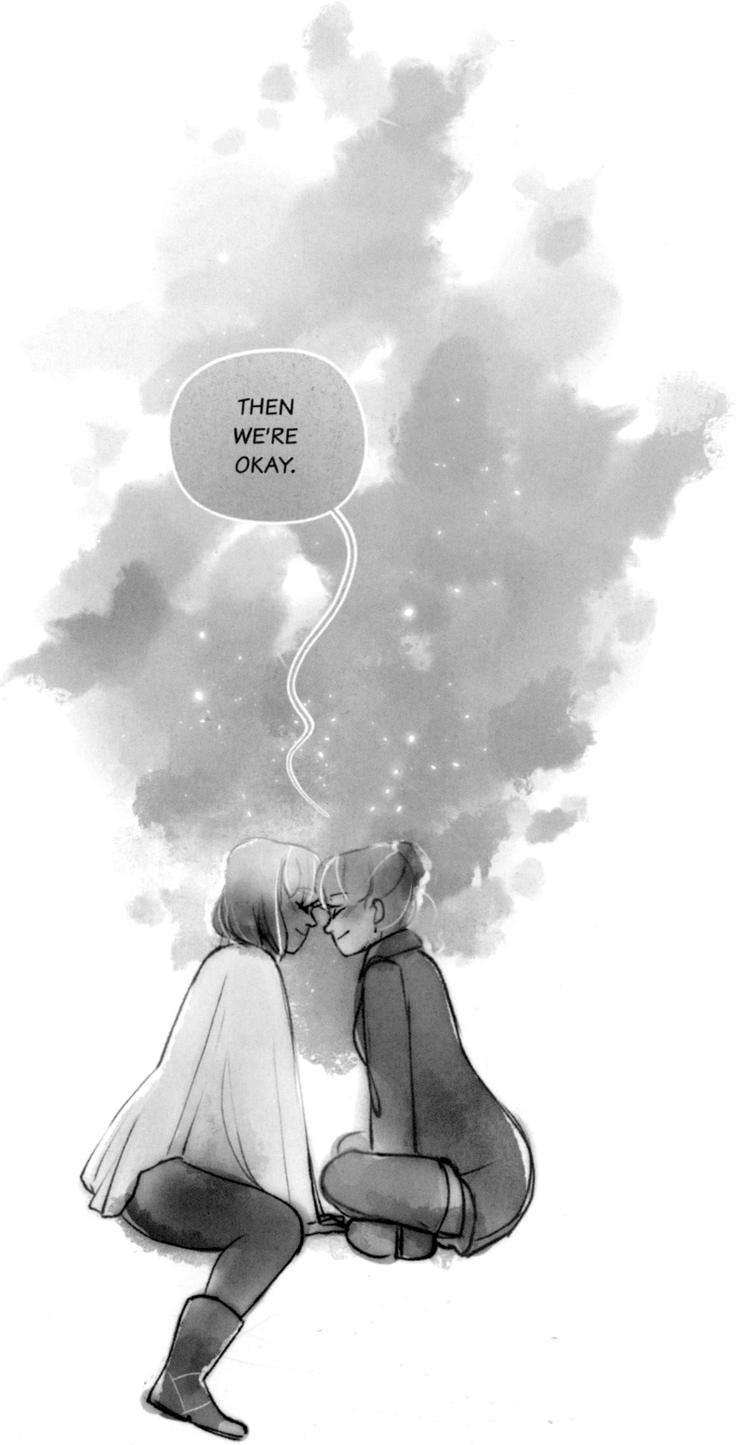
THEN WE'RE OKAY.

28 - FIRST KISS

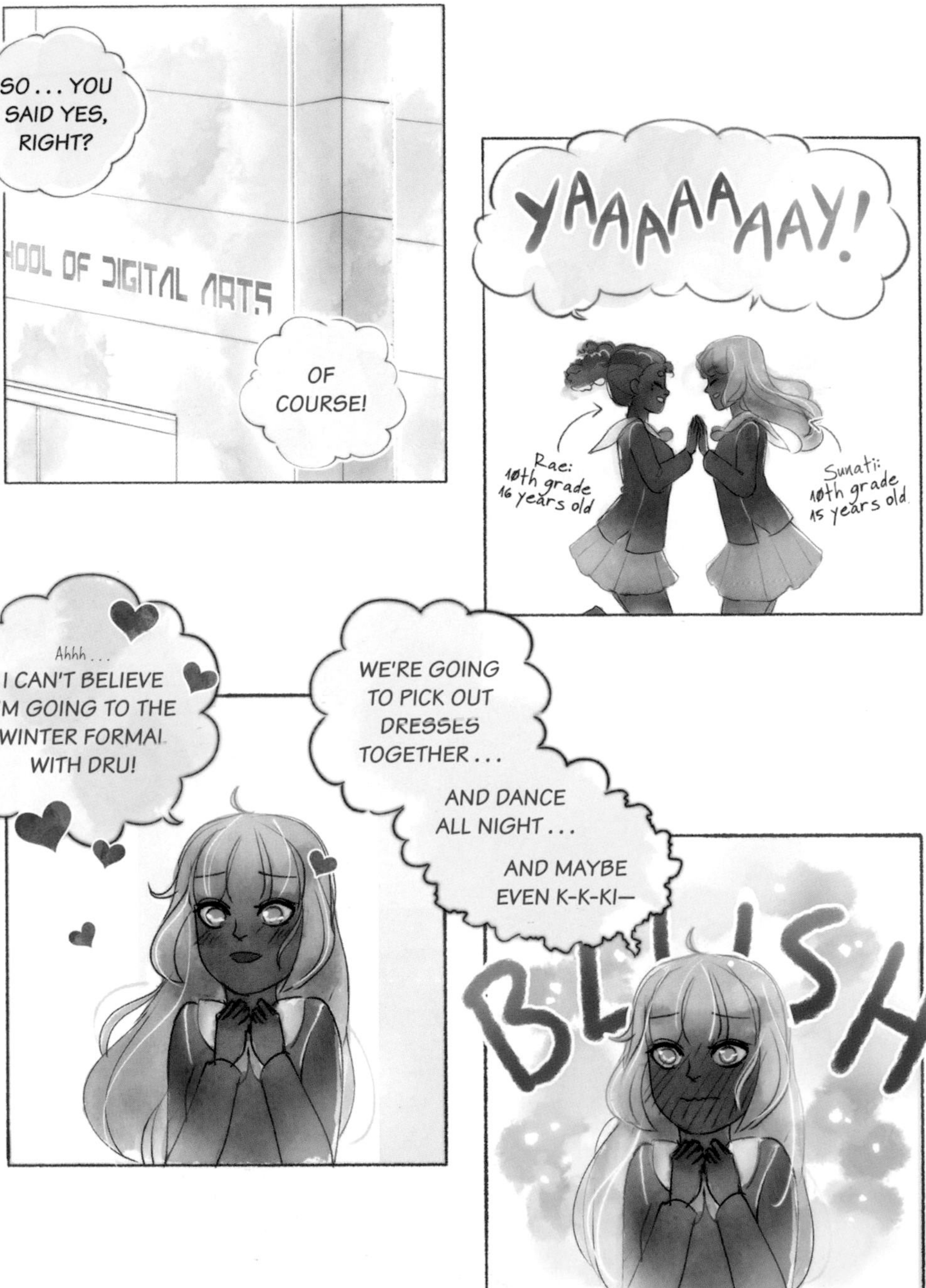
SO . . . YOU SAID YES, RIGHT?
HOOL OF DIGITAL ARTS
OF COURSE!
YAAAAAAAY!
Rae: 10th grade 16 years old
Sunati: 10th grade 15 years old
Ahhh . . . I CAN'T BELIEVE I'M GOING TO THE WINTER FORMAL WITH DRU!
WE'RE GOING TO PICK OUT DRESSES TOGETHER . . .
AND DANCE ALL NIGHT . . .
AND MAYBE EVEN K-K-KI—
BLUSH

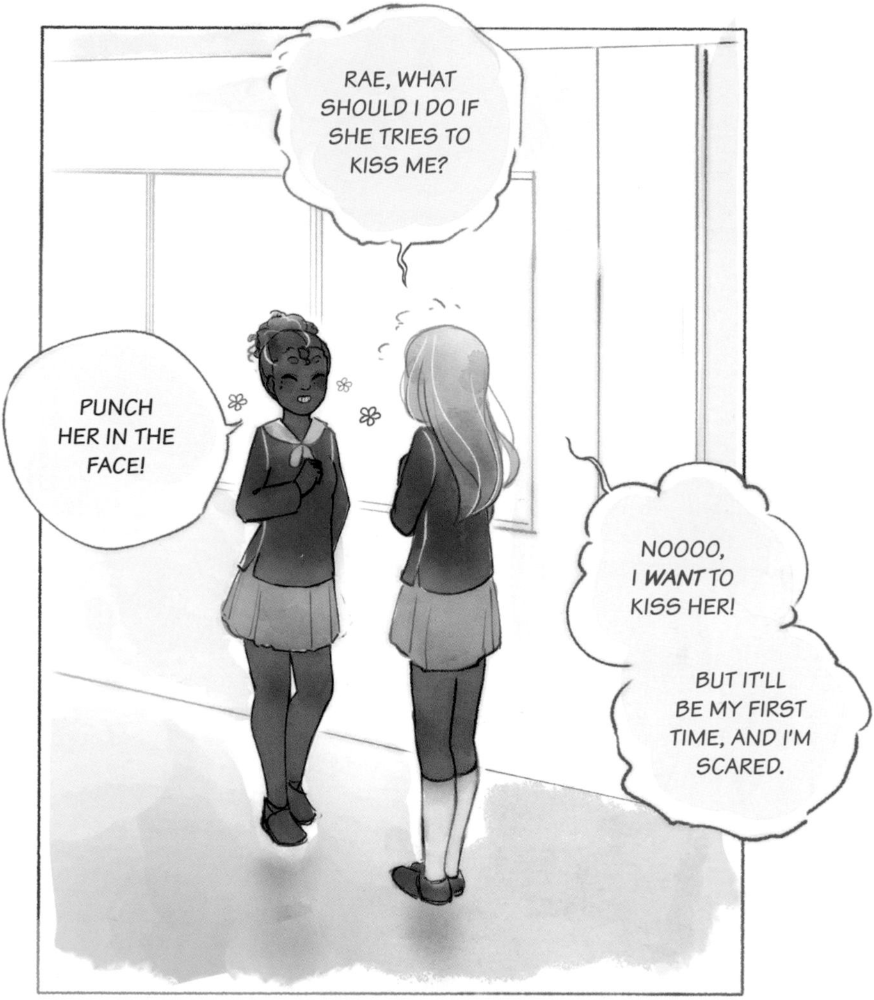
RAE, WHAT SHOULD I DO IF SHE TRIES TO KISS ME?
PUNCH HER IN THE FACE!
NOOOO, I **WANT** TO KISS HER!
BUT IT'LL BE MY FIRST TIME, AND I'M SCARED.

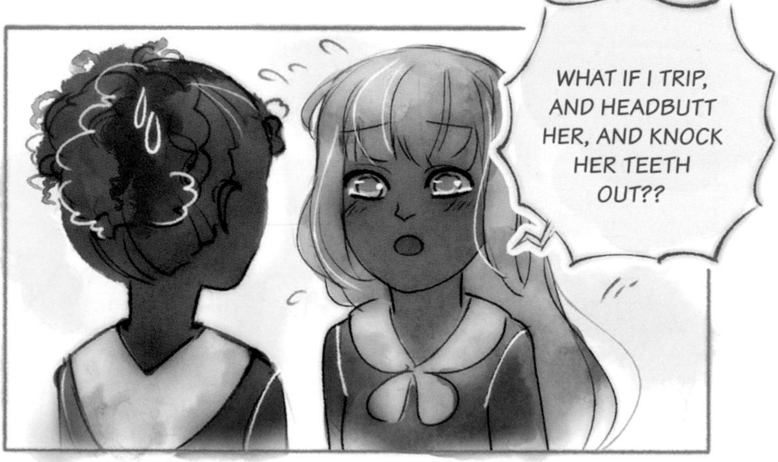
WHAT IF I TRIP, AND HEADBUTT HER, AND KNOCK HER TEETH OUT??

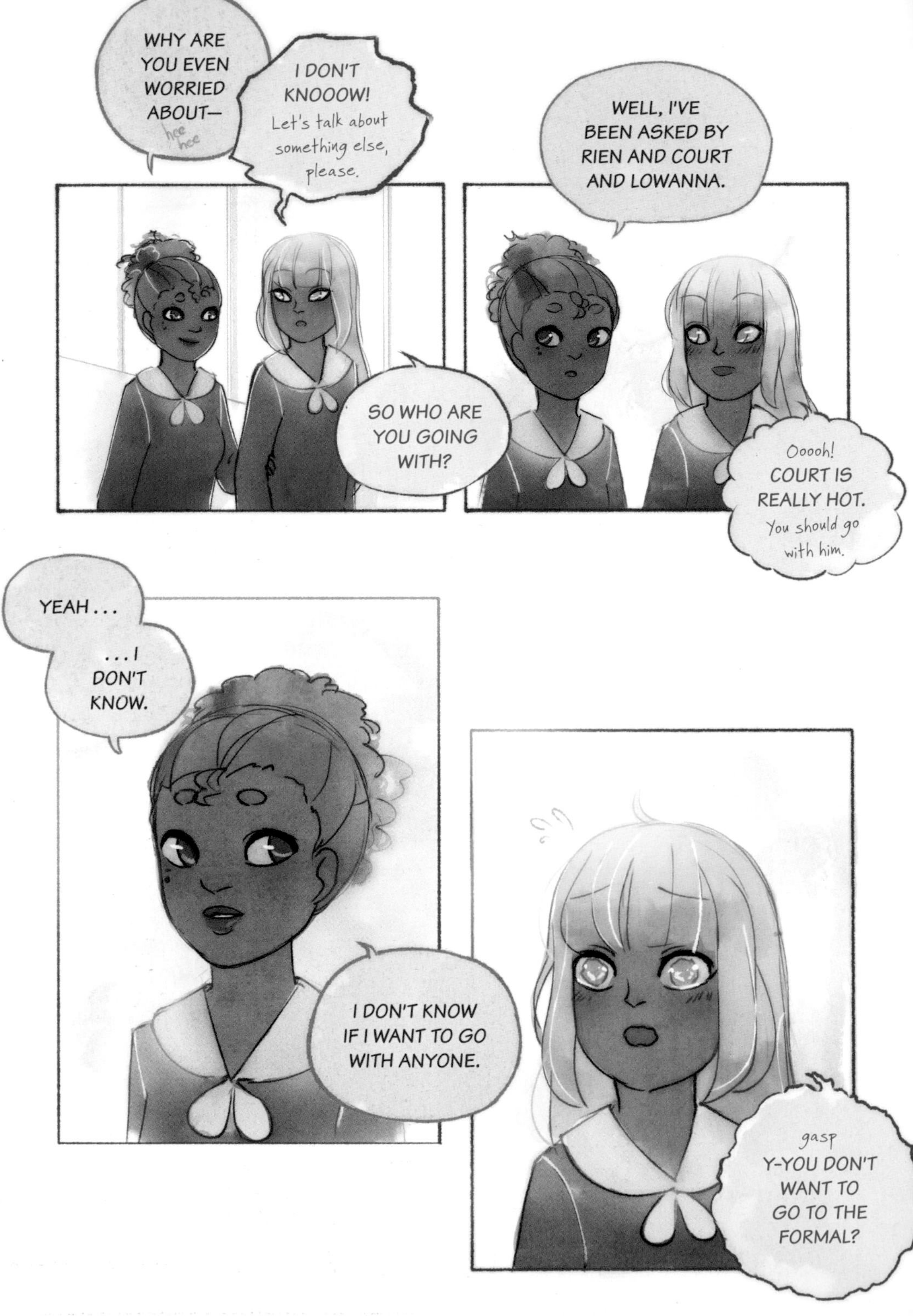
WHY ARE YOU EVEN WORRIED ABOUT—
hee hee
I DON'T KNOOOW! Let's talk about something else, please.
SO WHO ARE YOU GOING WITH?
WELL, I'VE BEEN ASKED BY RIEN AND COURT AND LOWANNA.
Ooooh! COURT IS REALLY HOT. You should go with him.
YEAH . . .
. . . I DON'T KNOW.
I DON'T KNOW IF I WANT TO GO WITH ANYONE.
gasp Y-YOU DON'T WANT TO GO TO THE FORMAL?

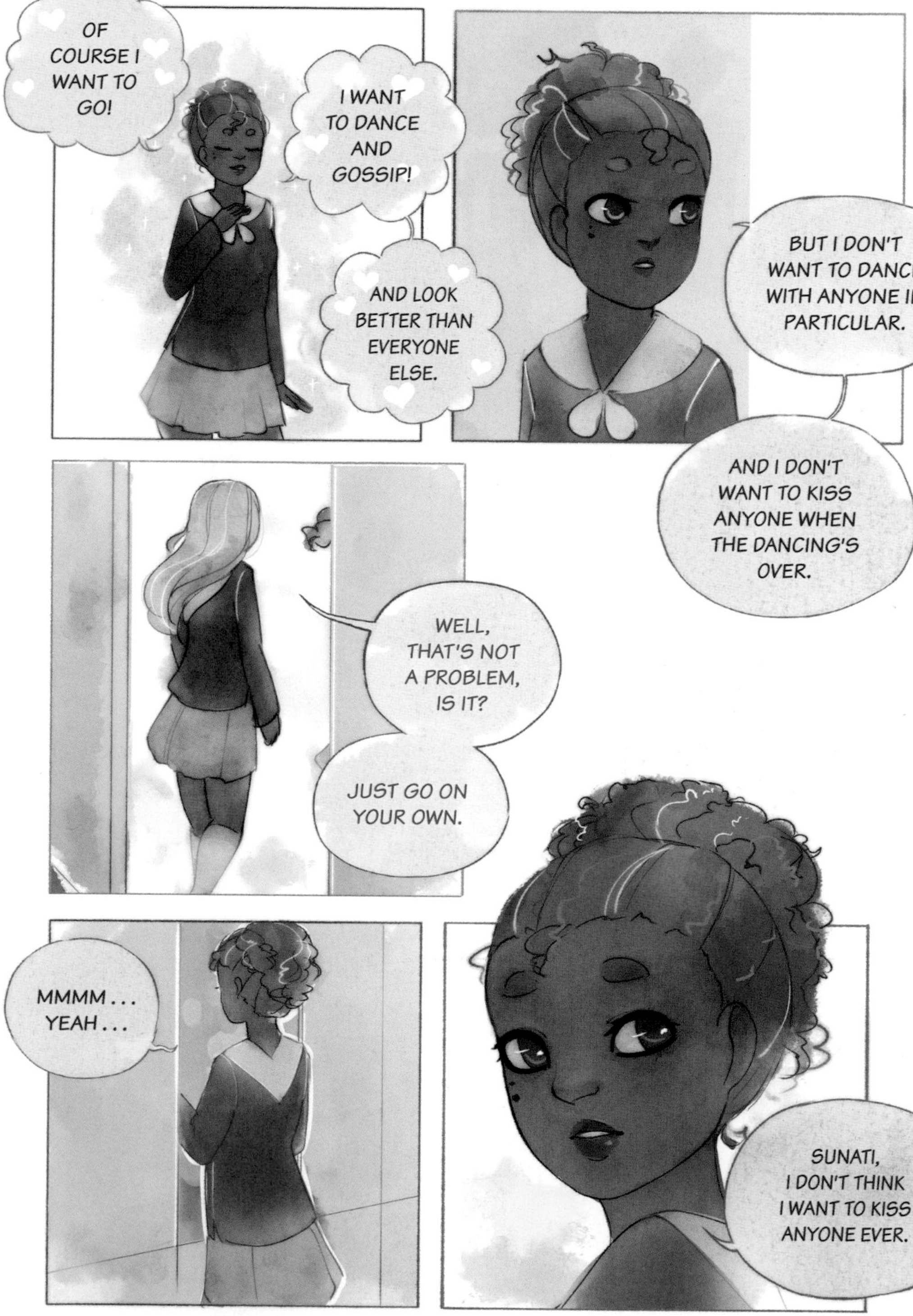
OF COURSE I WANT TO GO!
I WANT TO DANCE AND GOSSIP!
AND LOOK BETTER THAN EVERYONE ELSE.
BUT I DON'T WANT TO DANCE WITH ANYONE IN PARTICULAR.
AND I DON'T WANT TO KISS ANYONE WHEN THE DANCING'S OVER.
WELL, THAT'S NOT A PROBLEM, IS IT?
JUST GO ON YOUR OWN.
MMMM . . . YEAH . . .
SUNATI, I DON'T THINK I WANT TO KISS ANYONE EVER.

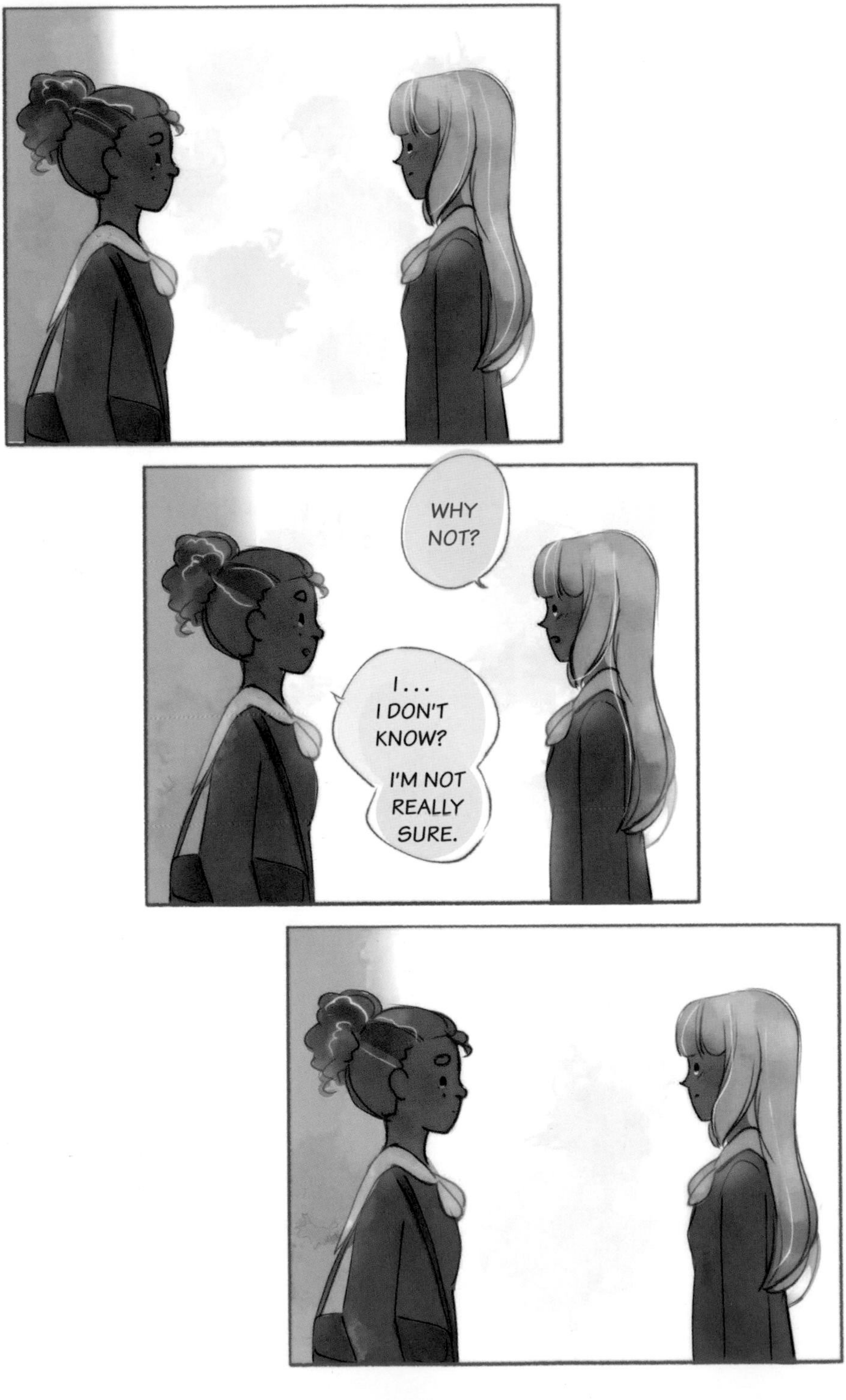
WHY NOT?
I . . . I DON'T KNOW? I'M NOT REALLY SURE.

OH!

WE SHOULD KISS!

YOU MAKE NO SENSE.

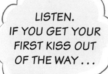

LISTEN. IF YOU GET YOUR FIRST KISS OUT OF THE WAY . . .

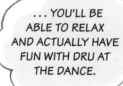

. . . YOU'LL BE ABLE TO RELAX AND ACTUALLY HAVE FUN WITH DRU AT THE DANCE.

Besides, you know I'll forgive you if you somehow knock my teeth out.

AND IT'LL HELP ME OUT TOO BECAUSE I'LL GET TO FIND OUT IF KISSING IS AS BIG A DEAL AS EVERYONE SAYS.

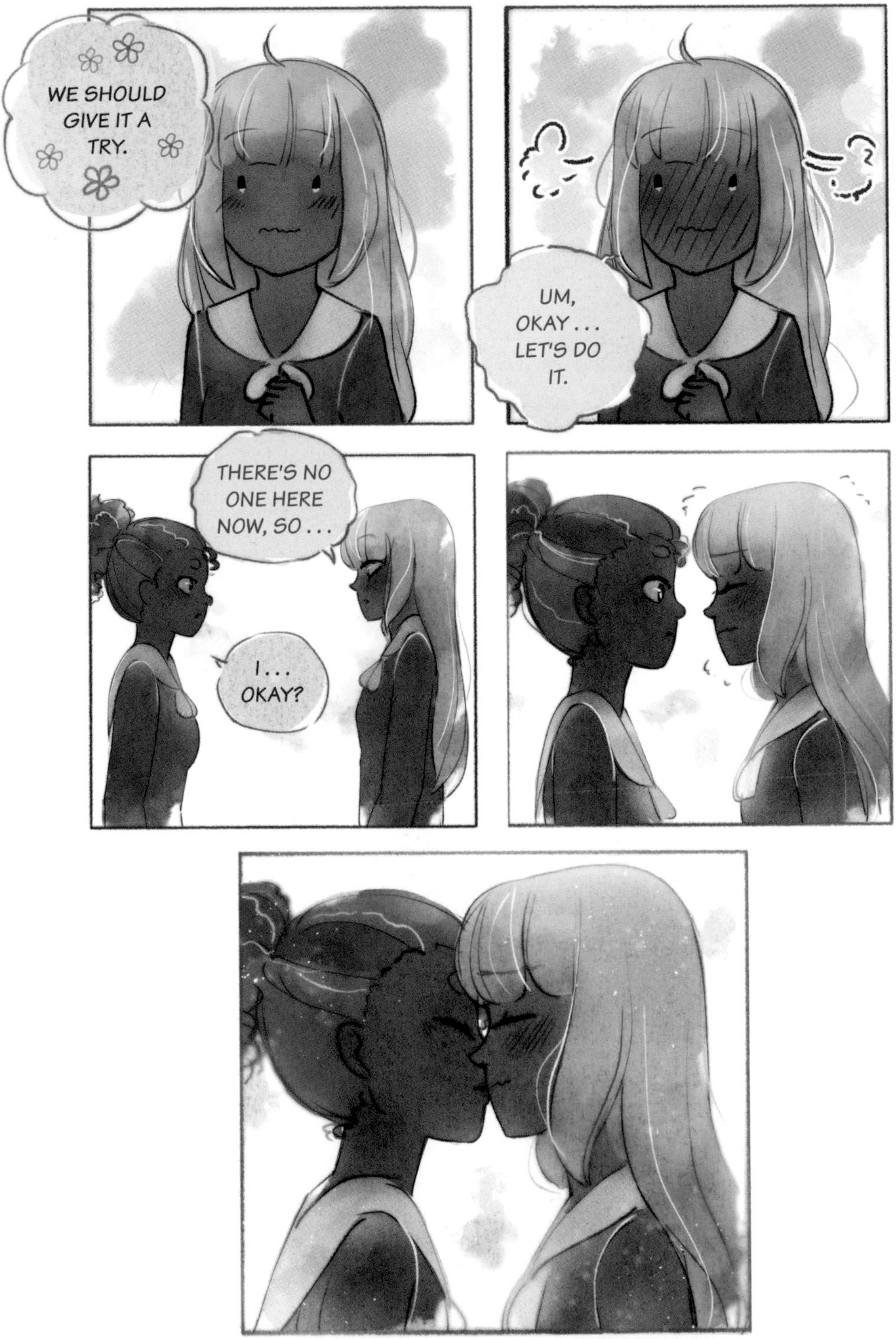
WE SHOULD GIVE IT A TRY.
UM, OKAY . . . LET'S DO IT.
THERE'S NO ONE HERE NOW, SO . . .
I . . . OKAY?

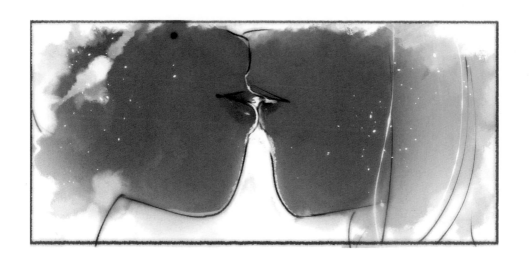

SO, WHAT
DO YOU
THINK?

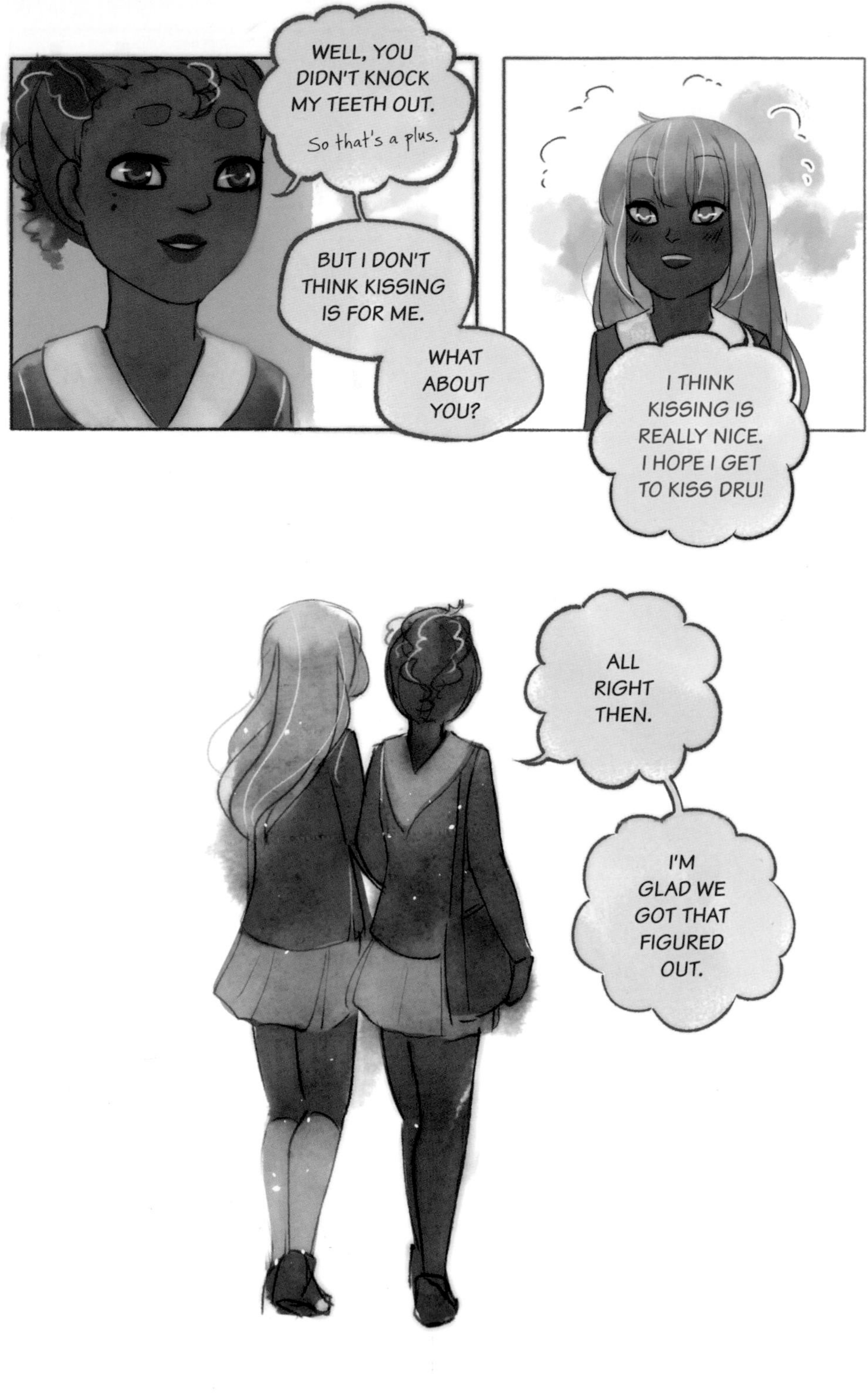
WELL, YOU DIDN'T KNOCK MY TEETH OUT.
So that's a plus.
BUT I DON'T THINK KISSING IS FOR ME.
WHAT ABOUT YOU?
I THINK KISSING IS REALLY NICE. I HOPE I GET TO KISS DRU!
ALL RIGHT THEN.
I'M GLAD WE GOT THAT FIGURED OUT.

29 - WHEN YOU'RE WAITING

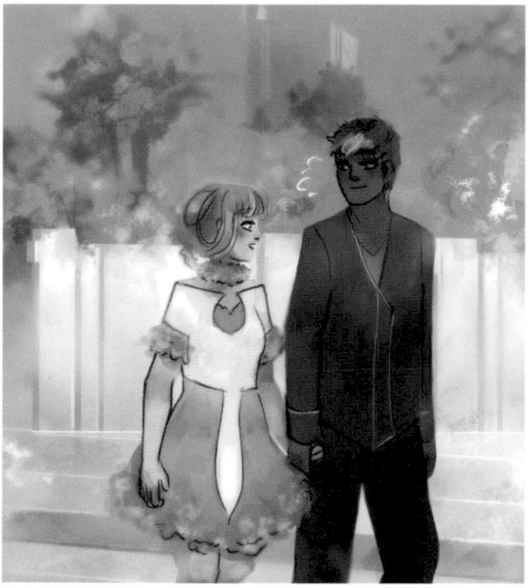

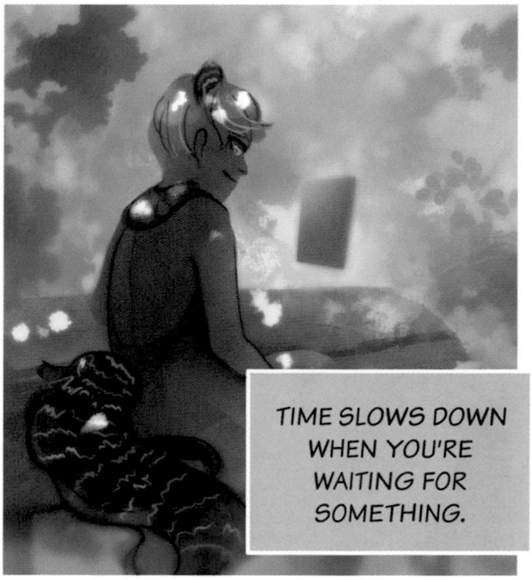
TIME SLOWS DOWN WHEN YOU'RE WAITING FOR SOMETHING.

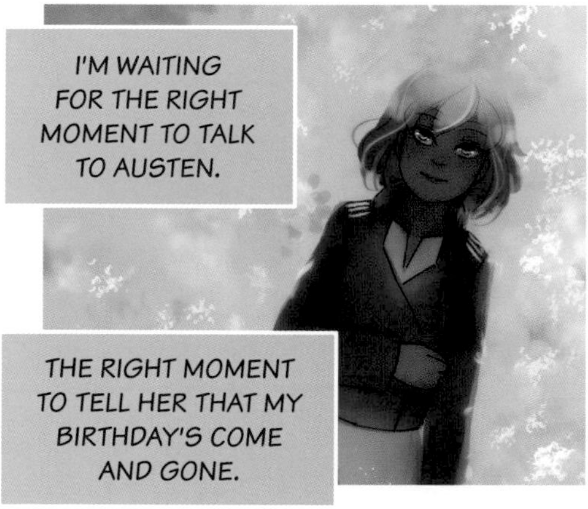
I'M WAITING FOR THE RIGHT MOMENT TO TALK TO AUSTEN.
THE RIGHT MOMENT TO TELL HER THAT MY BIRTHDAY'S COME AND GONE.

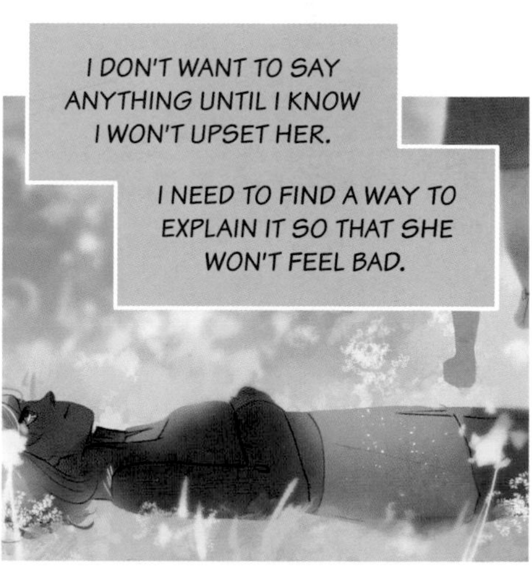
I DON'T WANT TO SAY ANYTHING UNTIL I KNOW I WON'T UPSET HER.
I NEED TO FIND A WAY TO EXPLAIN IT SO THAT SHE WON'T FEEL BAD.

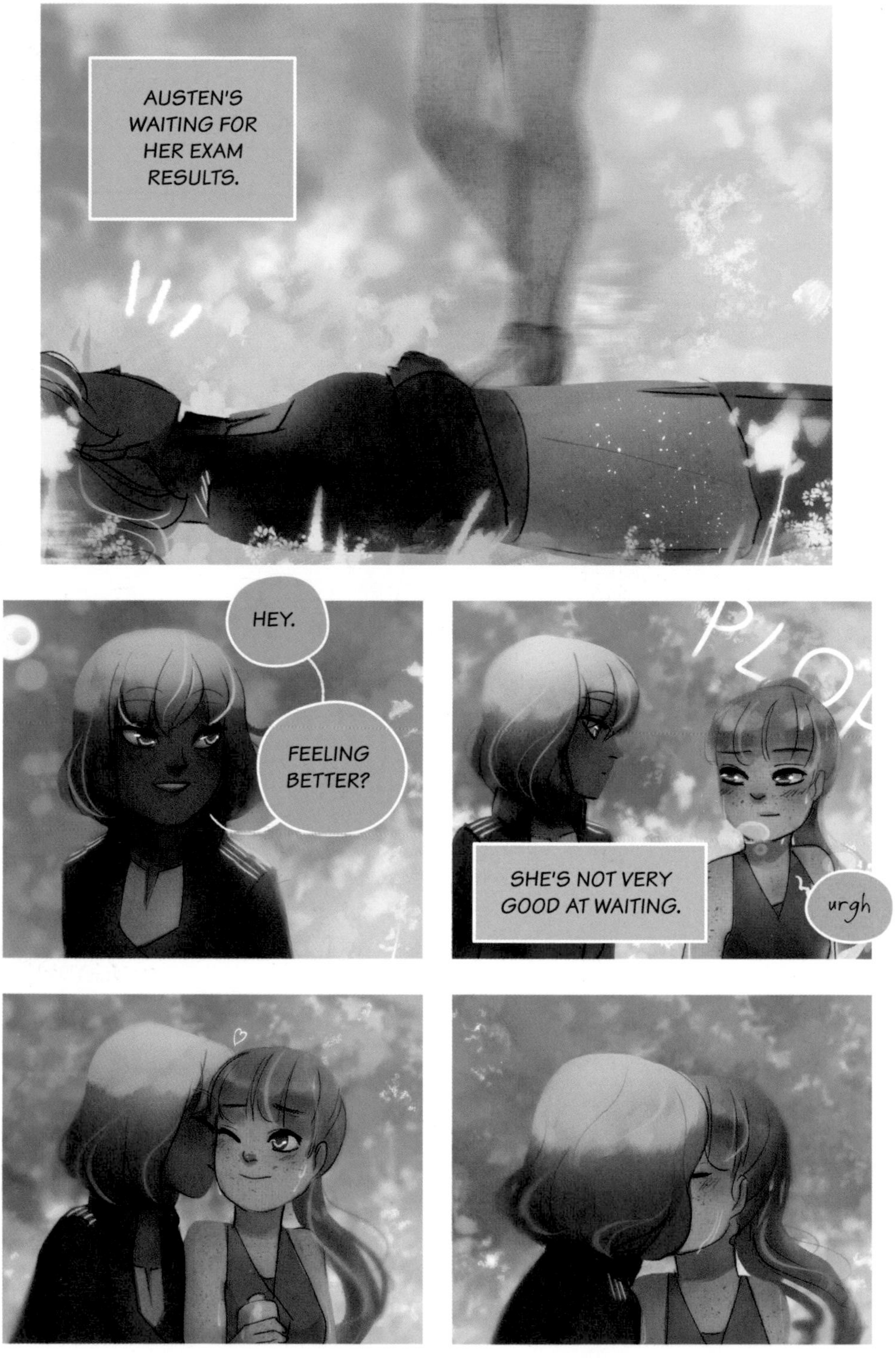
AUSTEN'S WAITING FOR HER EXAM RESULTS.
HEY.
FEELING BETTER?
SHE'S NOT VERY GOOD AT WAITING.
urgh

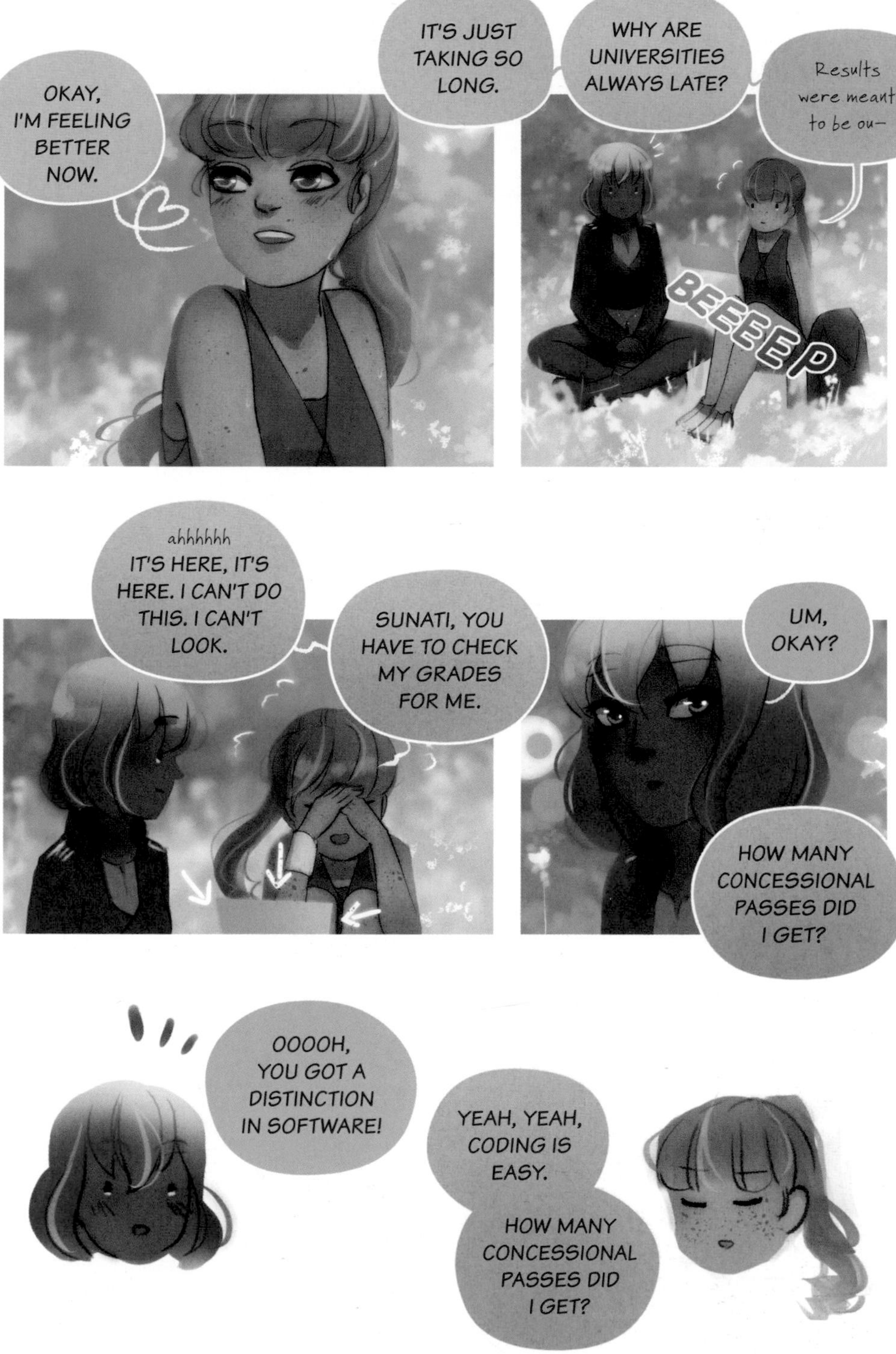
OKAY, I'M FEELING BETTER NOW.
IT'S JUST TAKING SO LONG.
WHY ARE UNIVERSITIES ALWAYS LATE?
Results were meant to be ou—
BEEEEP
ahhhhhh
IT'S HERE, IT'S HERE. I CAN'T DO THIS. I CAN'T LOOK.
SUNATI, YOU HAVE TO CHECK MY GRADES FOR ME.
UM, OKAY?
HOW MANY CONCESSIONAL PASSES DID I GET?
OOOOH, YOU GOT A DISTINCTION IN SOFTWARE!
YEAH, YEAH, CODING IS EASY.
HOW MANY CONCESSIONAL PASSES DID I GET?

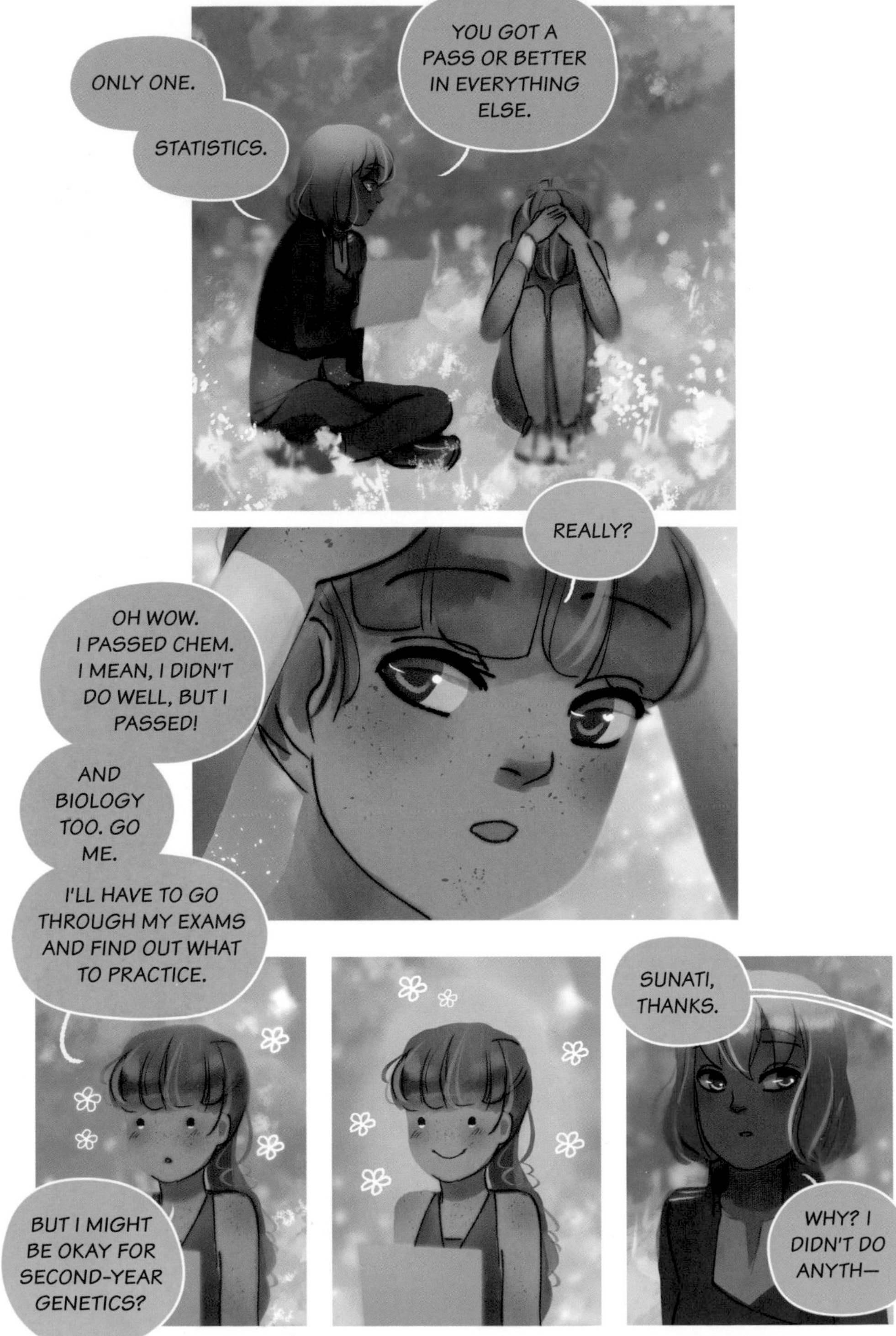
ONLY ONE.
STATISTICS.
YOU GOT A PASS OR BETTER IN EVERYTHING ELSE.
REALLY?
OH WOW. I PASSED CHEM. I MEAN, I DIDN'T DO WELL, BUT I PASSED!
AND BIOLOGY TOO. GO ME.
I'LL HAVE TO GO THROUGH MY EXAMS AND FIND OUT WHAT TO PRACTICE.
BUT I MIGHT BE OKAY FOR SECOND-YEAR GENETICS?
SUNATI, THANKS.
WHY? I DIDN'T DO ANYTH—

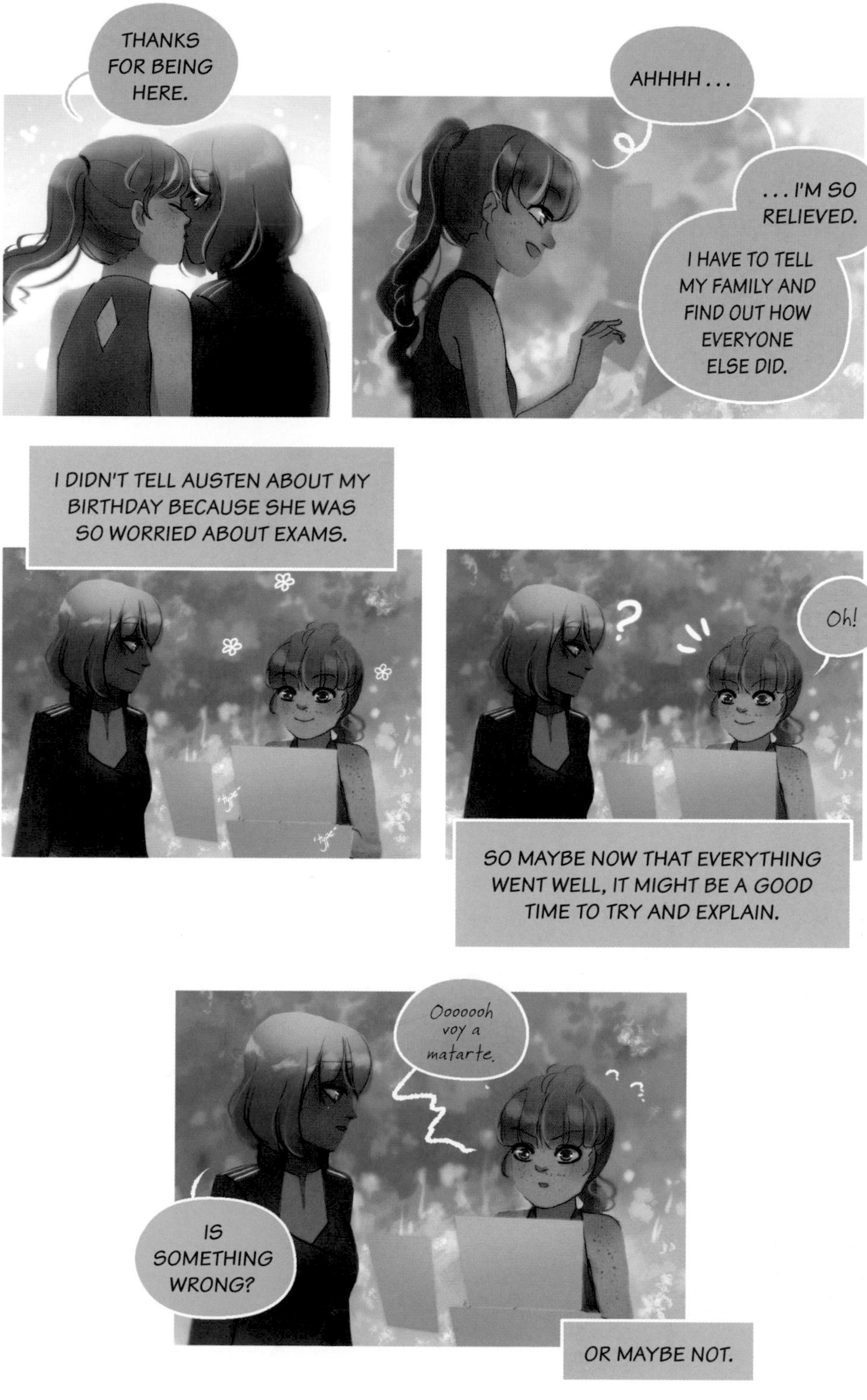
THANKS FOR BEING HERE.
AHHHH . . .
. . . I'M SO RELIEVED.
I HAVE TO TELL MY FAMILY AND FIND OUT HOW EVERYONE ELSE DID.
I DIDN'T TELL AUSTEN ABOUT MY BIRTHDAY BECAUSE SHE WAS SO WORRIED ABOUT EXAMS.
?
Oh!
SO MAYBE NOW THAT EVERYTHING WENT WELL, IT MIGHT BE A GOOD TIME TO TRY AND EXPLAIN.
Ooooooh voy a matarte.
IS SOMETHING WRONG?
OR MAYBE NOT.

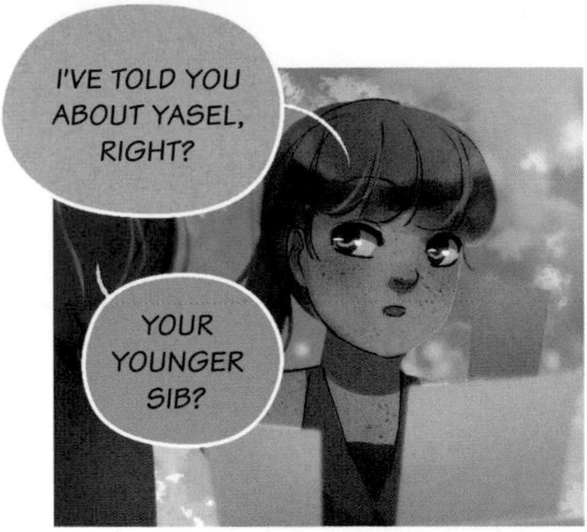
I'VE TOLD YOU ABOUT YASEL, RIGHT?
YOUR YOUNGER SIB?

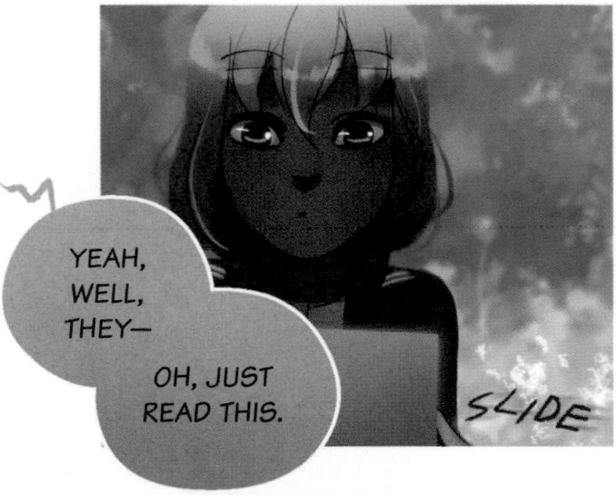
YEAH, WELL, THEY—
OH, JUST READ THIS.
SLIDE

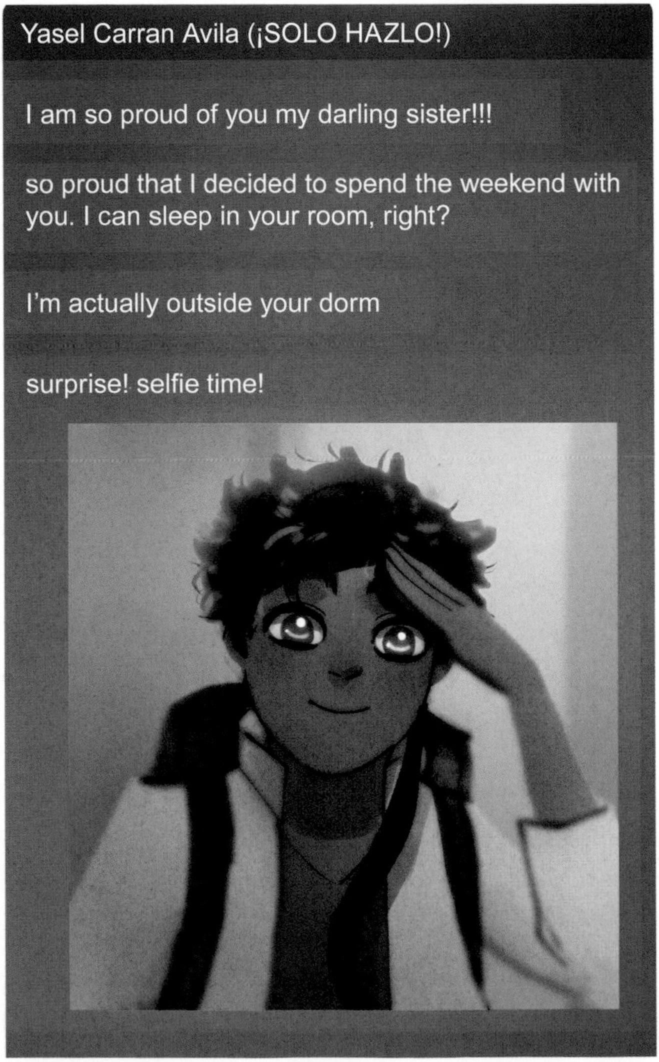
Yasel Carran Avila (¡SOLO HAZLO!)
I am so proud of you my darling sister!!!
so proud that I decided to spend the weekend with you. I can sleep in your room, right?
I'm actually outside your dorm
surprise! selfie time!

30 - YOU'RE HILARIOUS

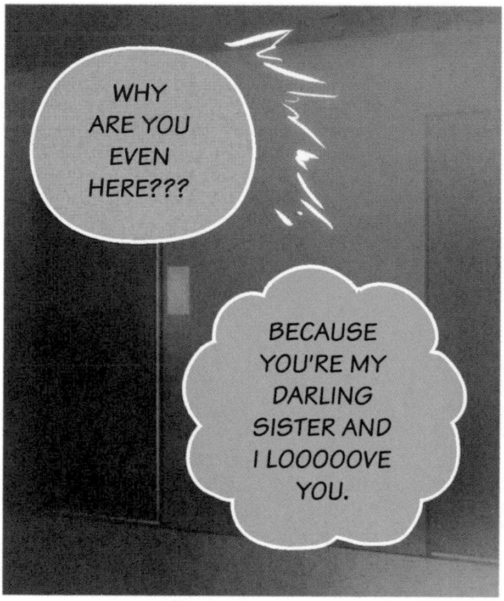
WHY ARE YOU EVEN HERE???
BECAUSE YOU'RE MY DARLING SISTER AND I LOOOOOVE YOU.

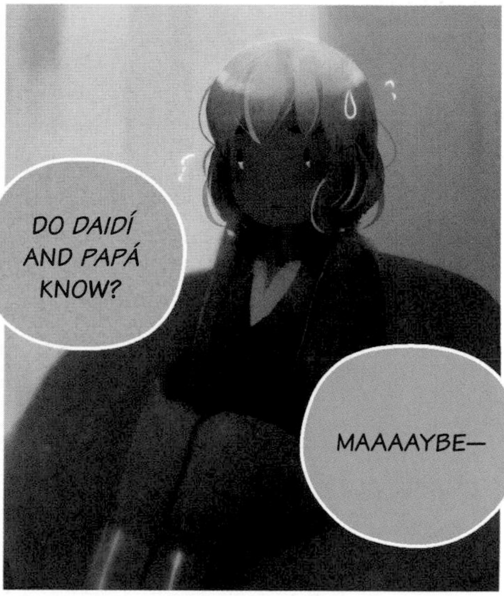
DO DAIDÍ AND PAPÁ KNOW?
MAAAAYBE—

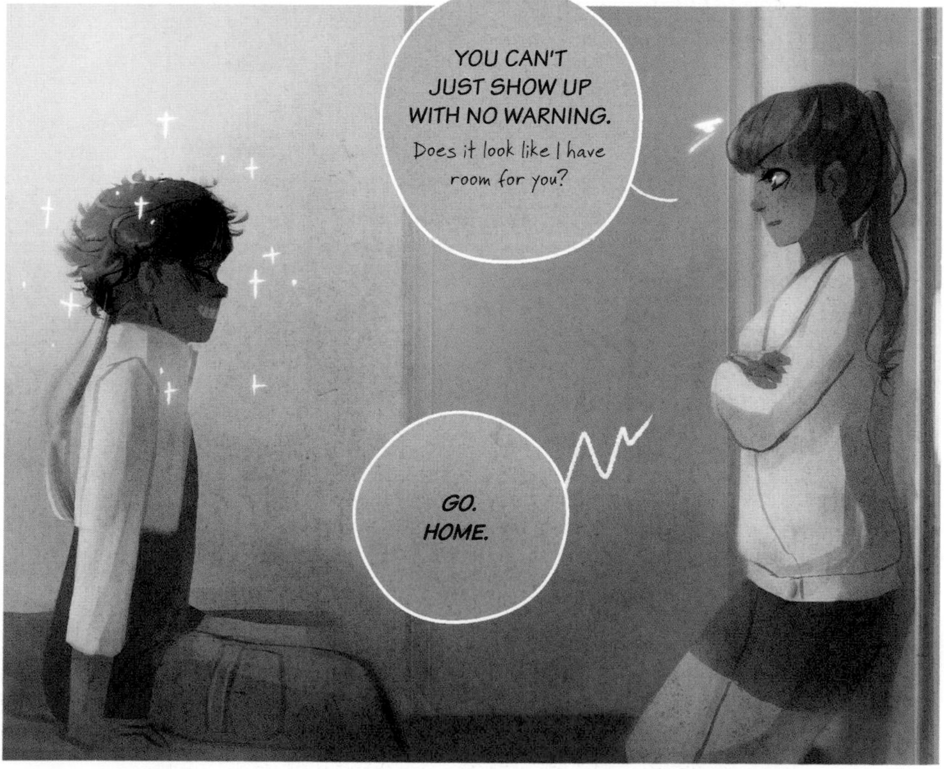
YOU CAN'T JUST SHOW UP WITH NO WARNING. Does it look like I have room for you?
GO. HOME.

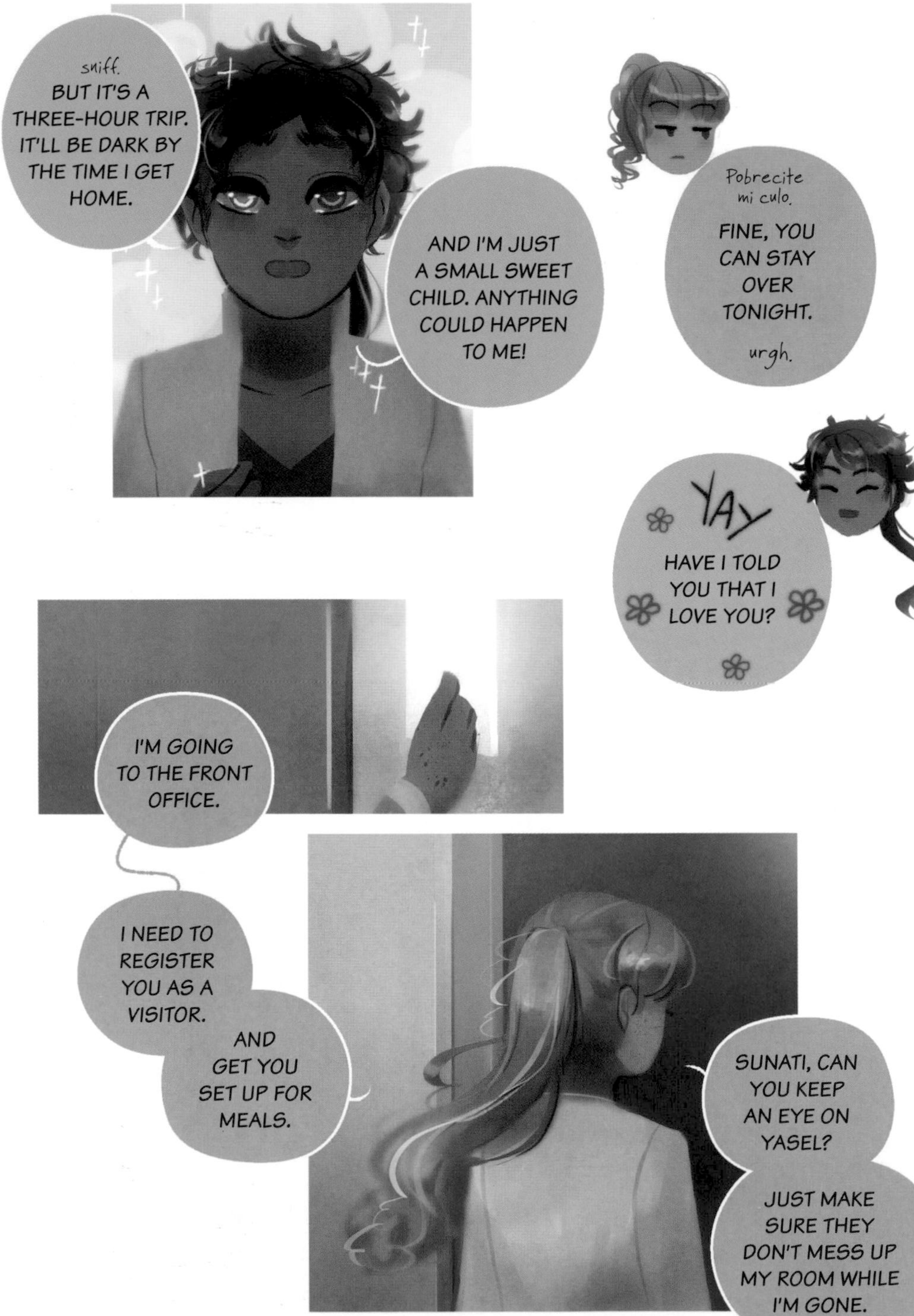
sniff.
BUT IT'S A THREE-HOUR TRIP. IT'LL BE DARK BY THE TIME I GET HOME.
AND I'M JUST A SMALL SWEET CHILD. ANYTHING COULD HAPPEN TO ME!
Pobrecite mi culo.
FINE, YOU CAN STAY OVER TONIGHT.
urgh.
YAY
HAVE I TOLD YOU THAT I LOVE YOU?
I'M GOING TO THE FRONT OFFICE.
I NEED TO REGISTER YOU AS A VISITOR.
AND GET YOU SET UP FOR MEALS.
SUNATI, CAN YOU KEEP AN EYE ON YASEL?
JUST MAKE SURE THEY DON'T MESS UP MY ROOM WHILE I'M GONE.

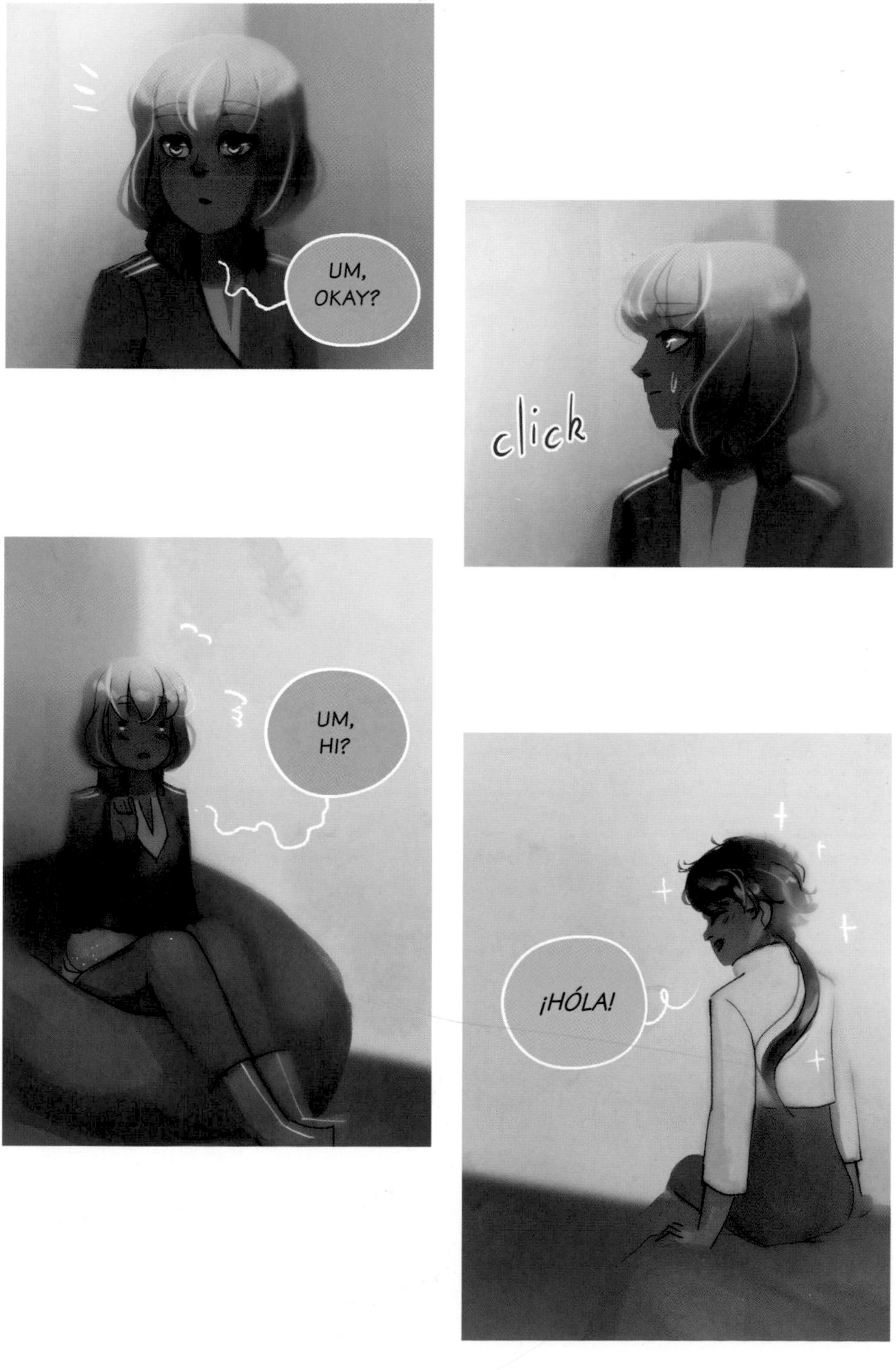
UM, OKAY?
click
UM, HI?
¡HÓLA!

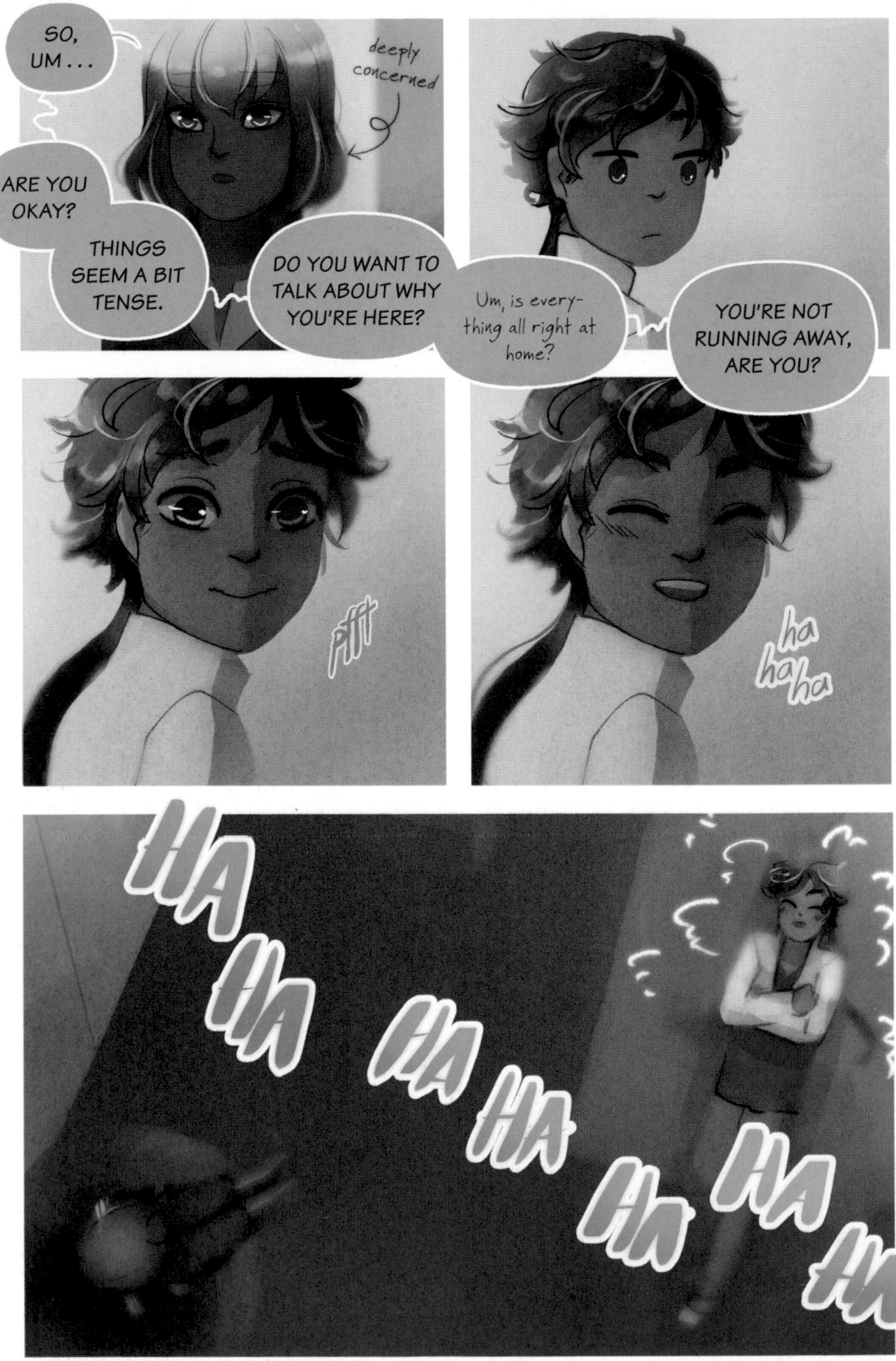
SO, UM . . .
deeply concerned
ARE YOU OKAY?
THINGS SEEM A BIT TENSE.
DO YOU WANT TO TALK ABOUT WHY YOU'RE HERE?
Um, is every-thing all right at home?
YOU'RE NOT RUNNING AWAY, ARE YOU?
pfft
ha ha ha
HA HA HA HA HA HA HA HA HA HA

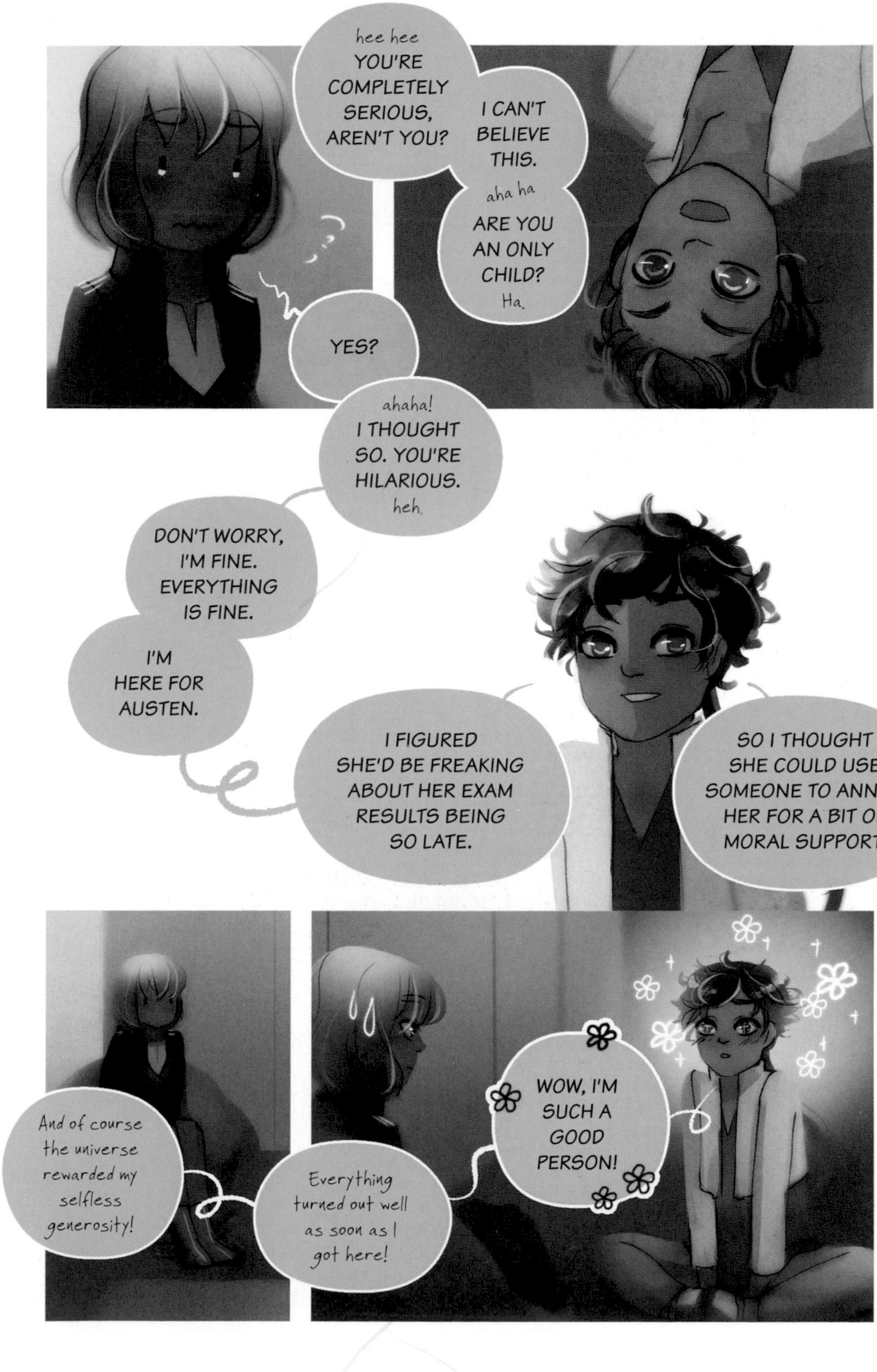
hee hee
YOU'RE COMPLETELY SERIOUS, AREN'T YOU?
I CAN'T BELIEVE THIS.
aha ha
ARE YOU AN ONLY CHILD?
Ha.
YES?
ahaha!
I THOUGHT SO. YOU'RE HILARIOUS.
heh.
DON'T WORRY, I'M FINE. EVERYTHING IS FINE.
I'M HERE FOR AUSTEN.
I FIGURED SHE'D BE FREAKING ABOUT HER EXAM RESULTS BEING SO LATE.
SO I THOUGHT SHE COULD USE SOMEONE TO ANNOY HER FOR A BIT OF MORAL SUPPORT.
WOW, I'M SUCH A GOOD PERSON!
Everything turned out well as soon as I got here!
And of course the universe rewarded my selfless generosity!

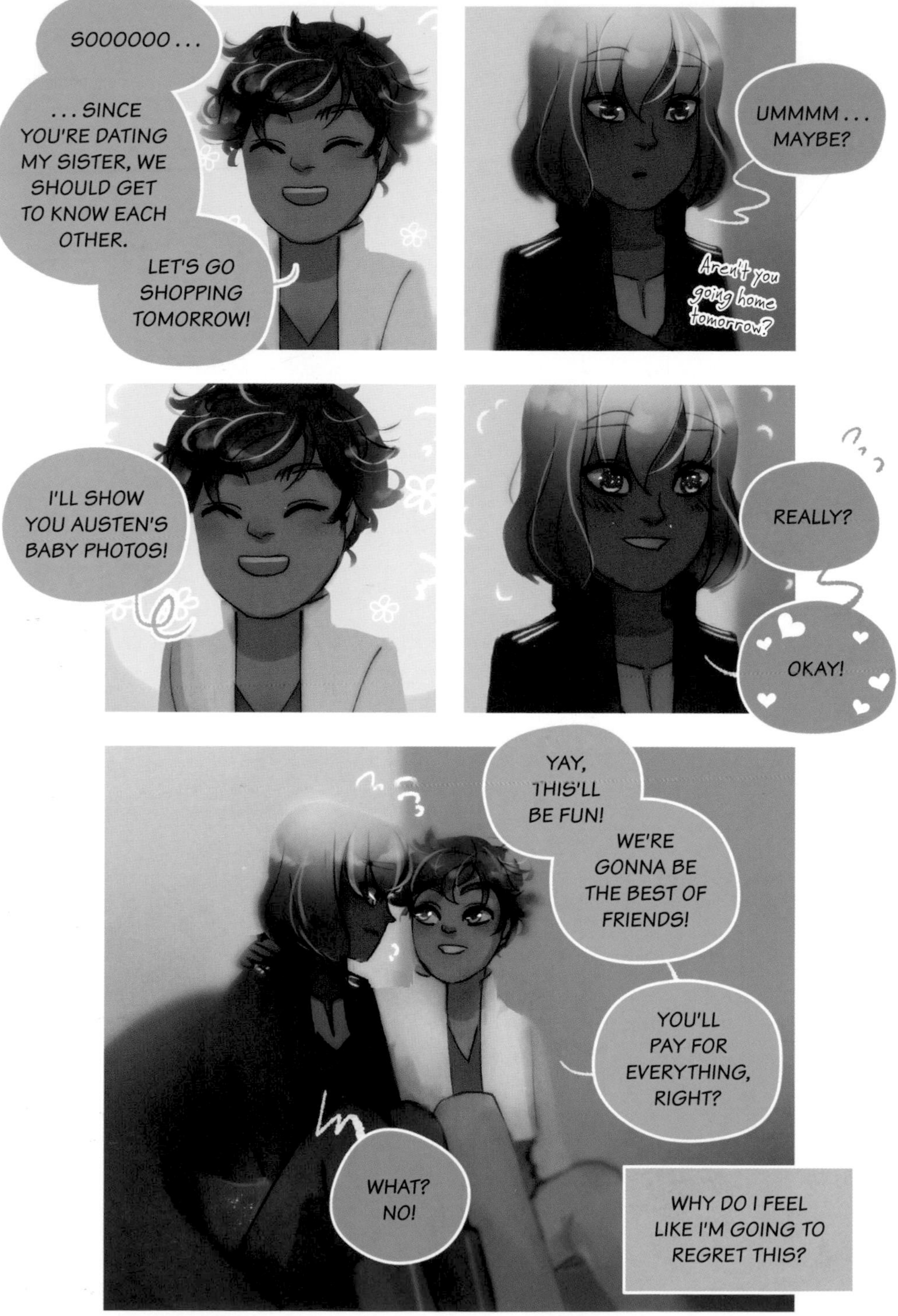
SOOOOOO . . .
. . . SINCE YOU'RE DATING MY SISTER, WE SHOULD GET TO KNOW EACH OTHER.
LET'S GO SHOPPING TOMORROW!
UMMMM . . . MAYBE?
Aren't you going home tomorrow?
I'LL SHOW YOU AUSTEN'S BABY PHOTOS!
REALLY?
OKAY!
YAY, THIS'LL BE FUN!
WE'RE GONNA BE THE BEST OF FRIENDS!
YOU'LL PAY FOR EVERYTHING, RIGHT?
WHAT? NO!
WHY DO I FEEL LIKE I'M GOING TO REGRET THIS?

31- PLEASE LET THIS TURN OUT OKAY

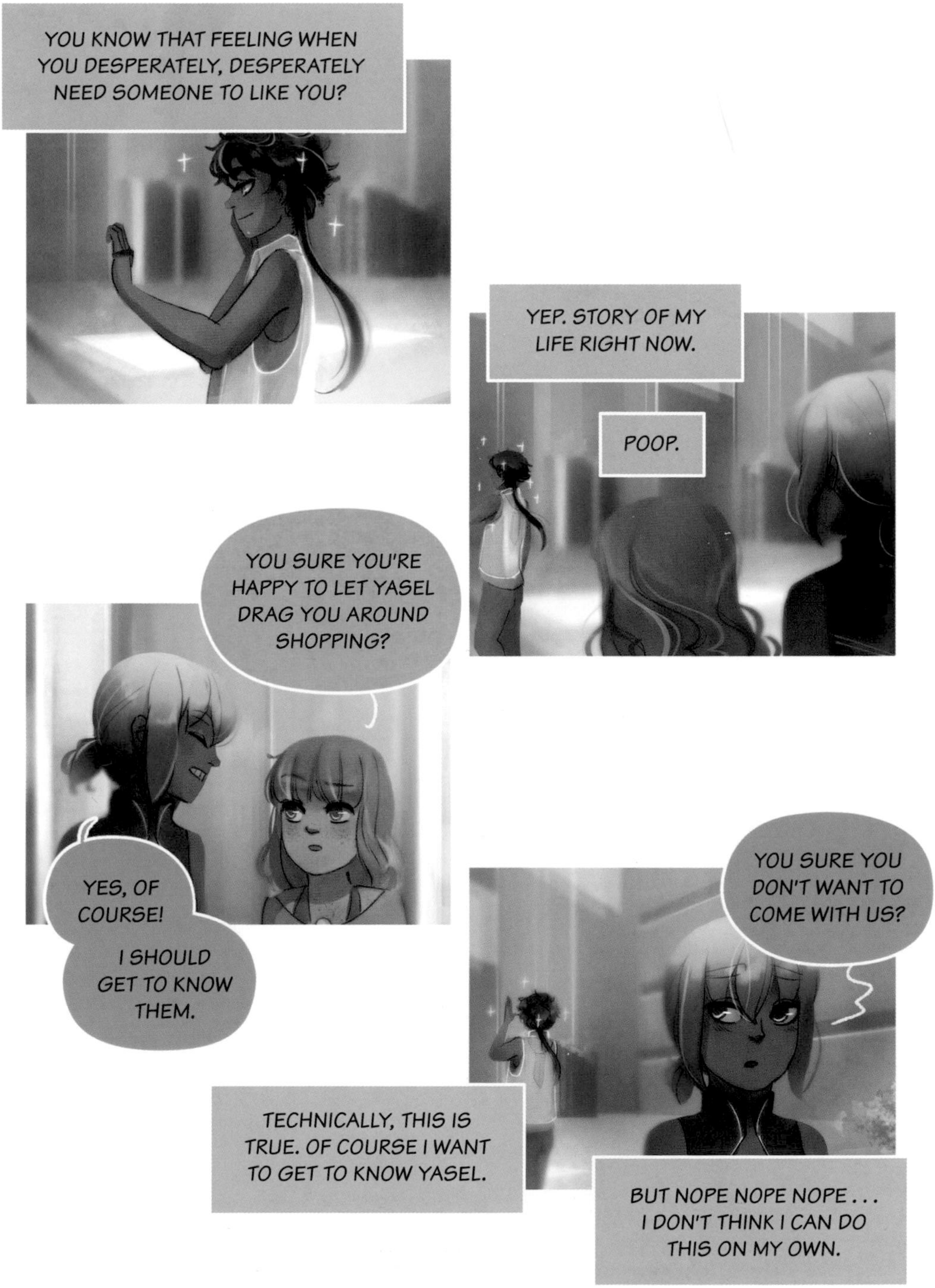
YOU KNOW THAT FEELING WHEN YOU DESPERATELY, DESPERATELY NEED SOMEONE TO LIKE YOU?
YEP. STORY OF MY LIFE RIGHT NOW.
POOP.
YOU SURE YOU'RE HAPPY TO LET YASEL DRAG YOU AROUND SHOPPING?
YES, OF COURSE!
I SHOULD GET TO KNOW THEM.
YOU SURE YOU DON'T WANT TO COME WITH US?
TECHNICALLY, THIS IS TRUE. OF COURSE I WANT TO GET TO KNOW YASEL.
BUT NOPE NOPE NOPE . . . I DON'T THINK I CAN DO THIS ON MY OWN.

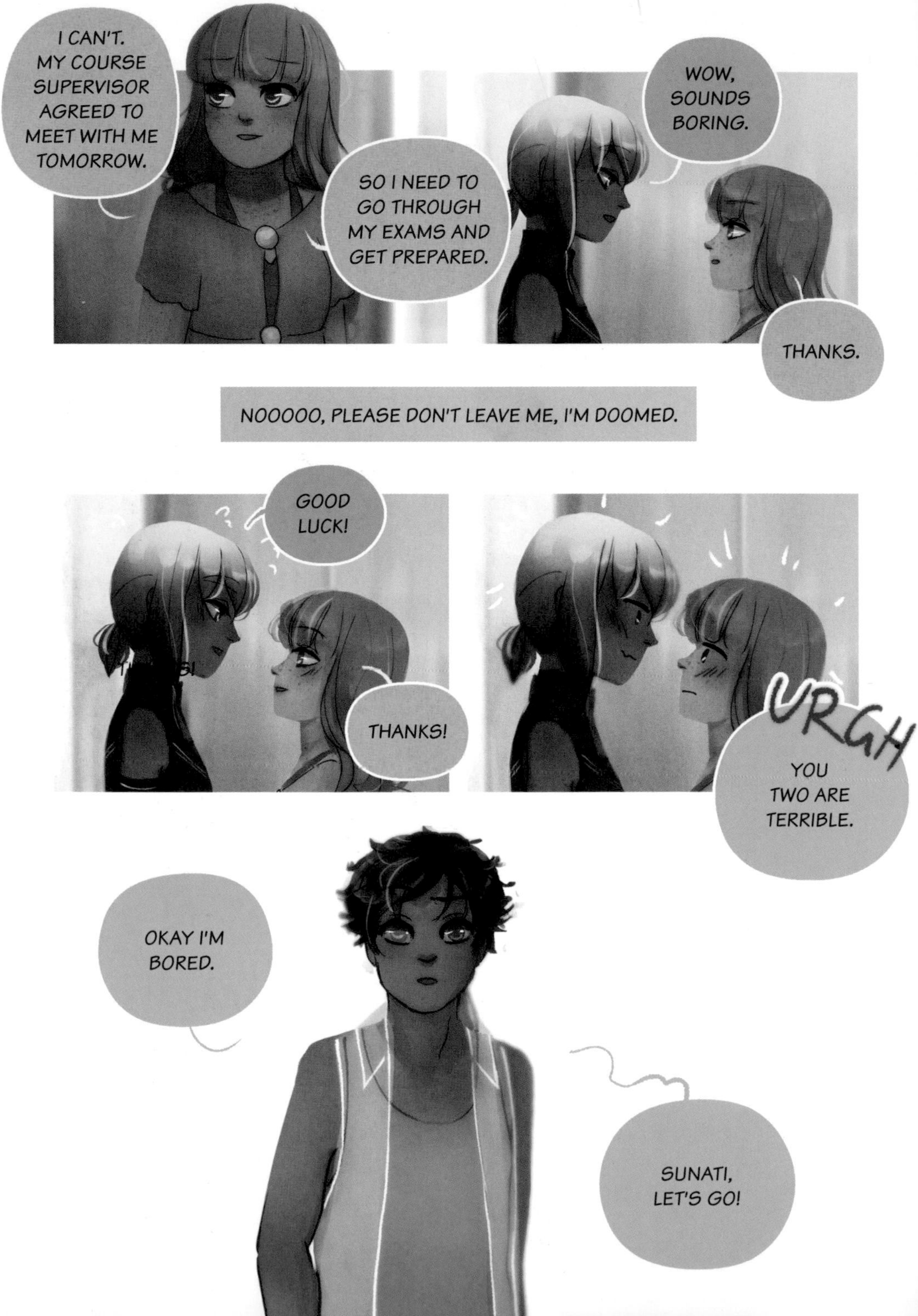
I CAN'T. MY COURSE SUPERVISOR AGREED TO MEET WITH ME TOMORROW.
SO I NEED TO GO THROUGH MY EXAMS AND GET PREPARED.
WOW, SOUNDS BORING.
THANKS.
NOOOOO, PLEASE DON'T LEAVE ME, I'M DOOMED.
GOOD LUCK!
THANKS!
URGH
YOU TWO ARE TERRIBLE.
OKAY I'M BORED.
SUNATI, LET'S GO!

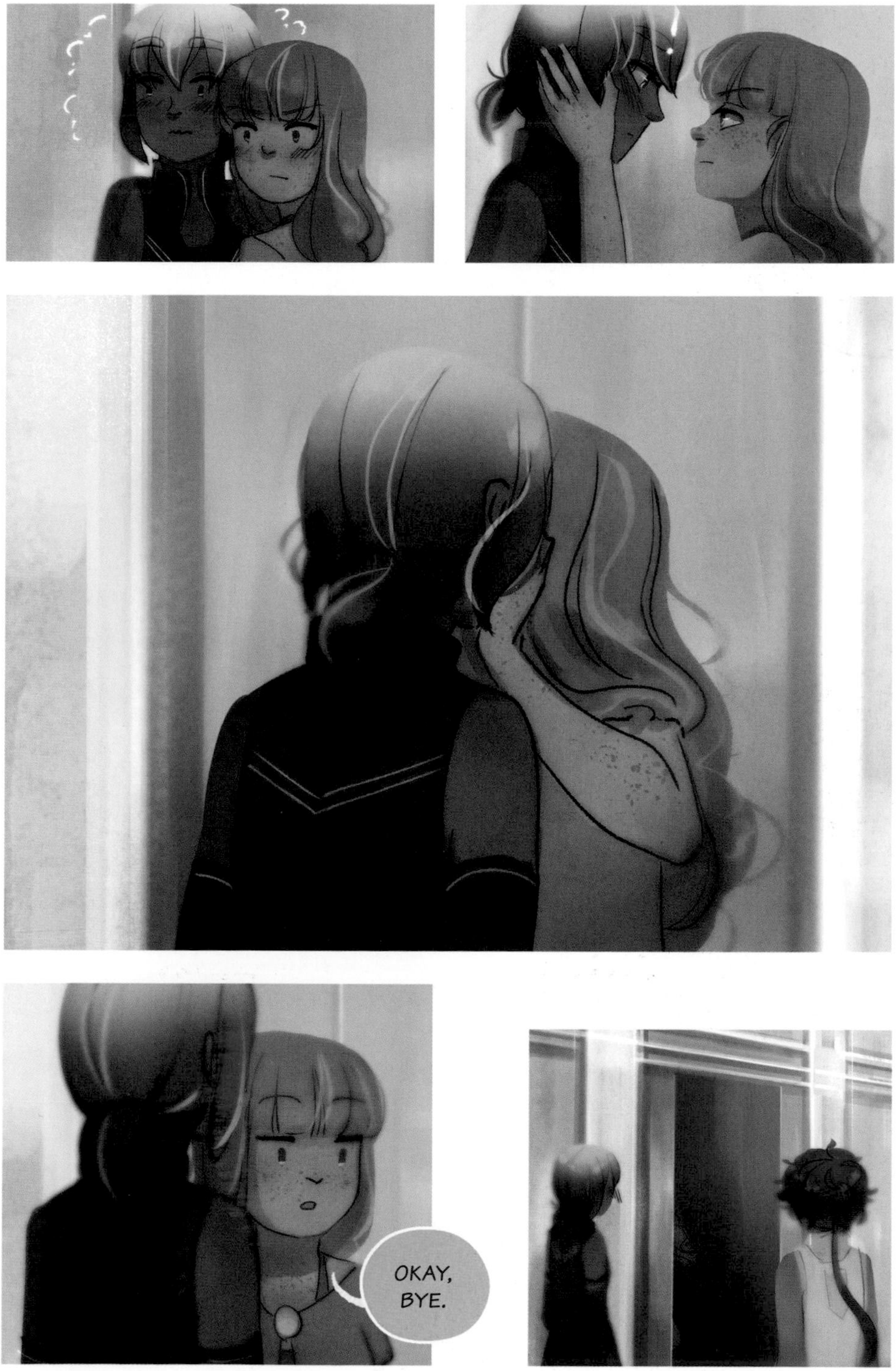
OKAY, BYE.

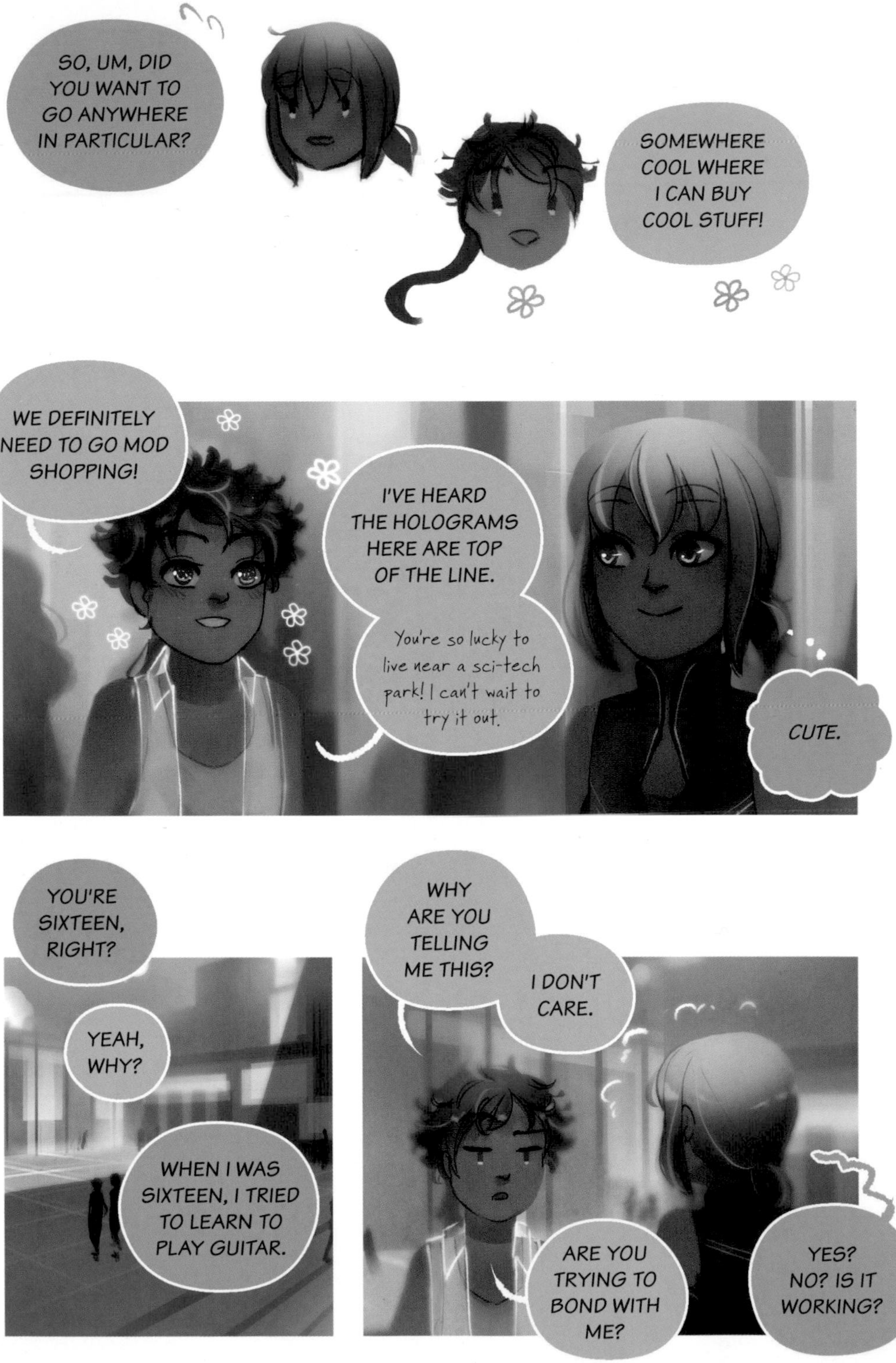
SO, UM, DID YOU WANT TO GO ANYWHERE IN PARTICULAR?
SOMEWHERE COOL WHERE I CAN BUY COOL STUFF!
WE DEFINITELY NEED TO GO MOD SHOPPING!
I'VE HEARD THE HOLOGRAMS HERE ARE TOP OF THE LINE.
You're so lucky to live near a sci-tech park! I can't wait to try it out.
CUTE.
YOU'RE SIXTEEN, RIGHT?
YEAH, WHY?
WHEN I WAS SIXTEEN, I TRIED TO LEARN TO PLAY GUITAR.
WHY ARE YOU TELLING ME THIS?
I DON'T CARE.
ARE YOU TRYING TO BOND WITH ME?
YES? NO? IS IT WORKING?

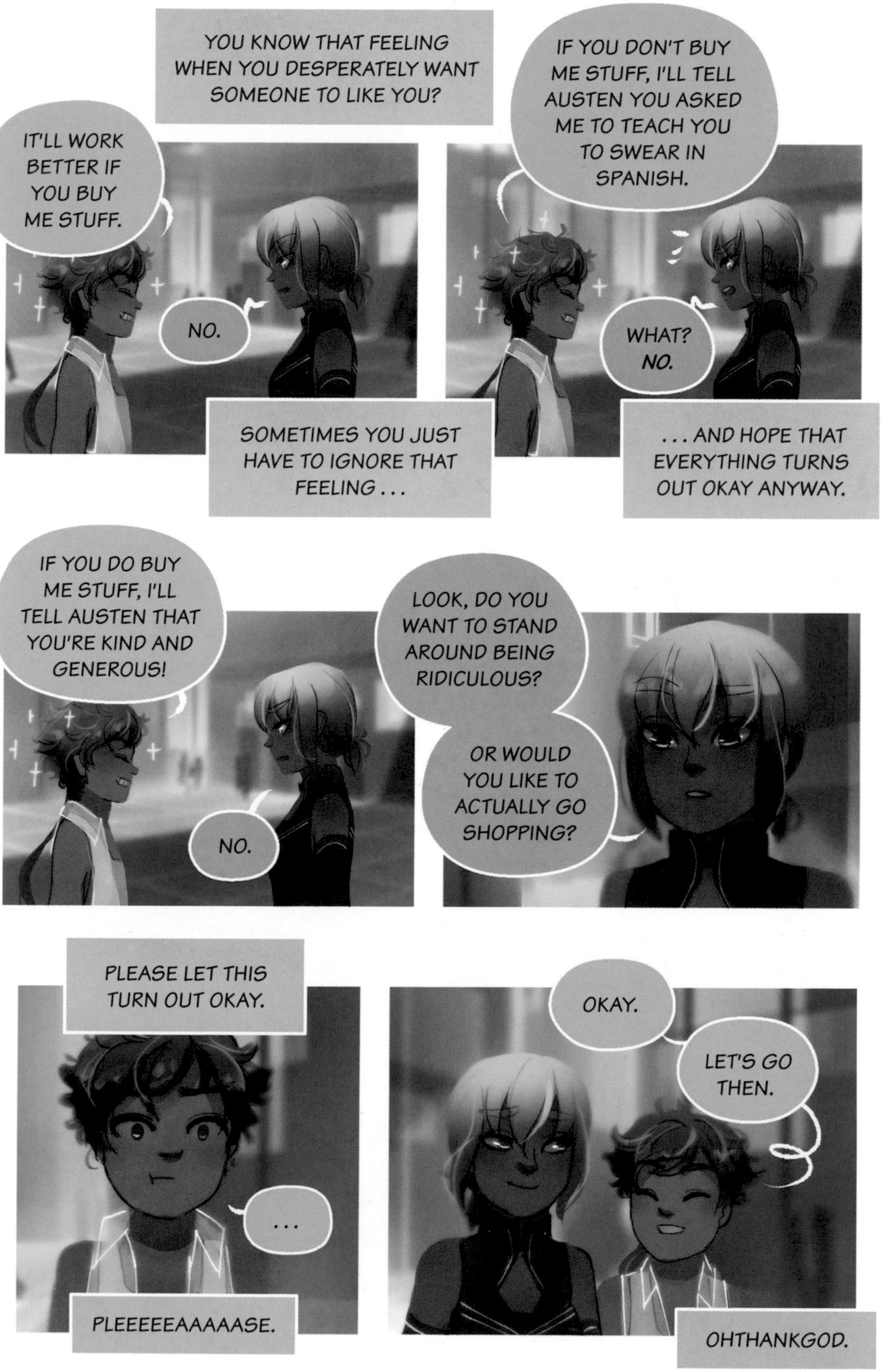
YOU KNOW THAT FEELING WHEN YOU DESPERATELY WANT SOMEONE TO LIKE YOU?
IT'LL WORK BETTER IF YOU BUY ME STUFF.
NO.
SOMETIMES YOU JUST HAVE TO IGNORE THAT FEELING . . .
IF YOU DON'T BUY ME STUFF, I'LL TELL AUSTEN YOU ASKED ME TO TEACH YOU TO SWEAR IN SPANISH.
WHAT? NO.
. . . AND HOPE THAT EVERYTHING TURNS OUT OKAY ANYWAY.
IF YOU DO BUY ME STUFF, I'LL TELL AUSTEN THAT YOU'RE KIND AND GENEROUS!
NO.
LOOK, DO YOU WANT TO STAND AROUND BEING RIDICULOUS?
OR WOULD YOU LIKE TO ACTUALLY GO SHOPPING?
PLEASE LET THIS TURN OUT OKAY.
. . .
PLEEEEEAAAAASE.
OKAY.
LET'S GO THEN.
OHTHANKGOD.

32 - YOU SHOULD BE WORRIED

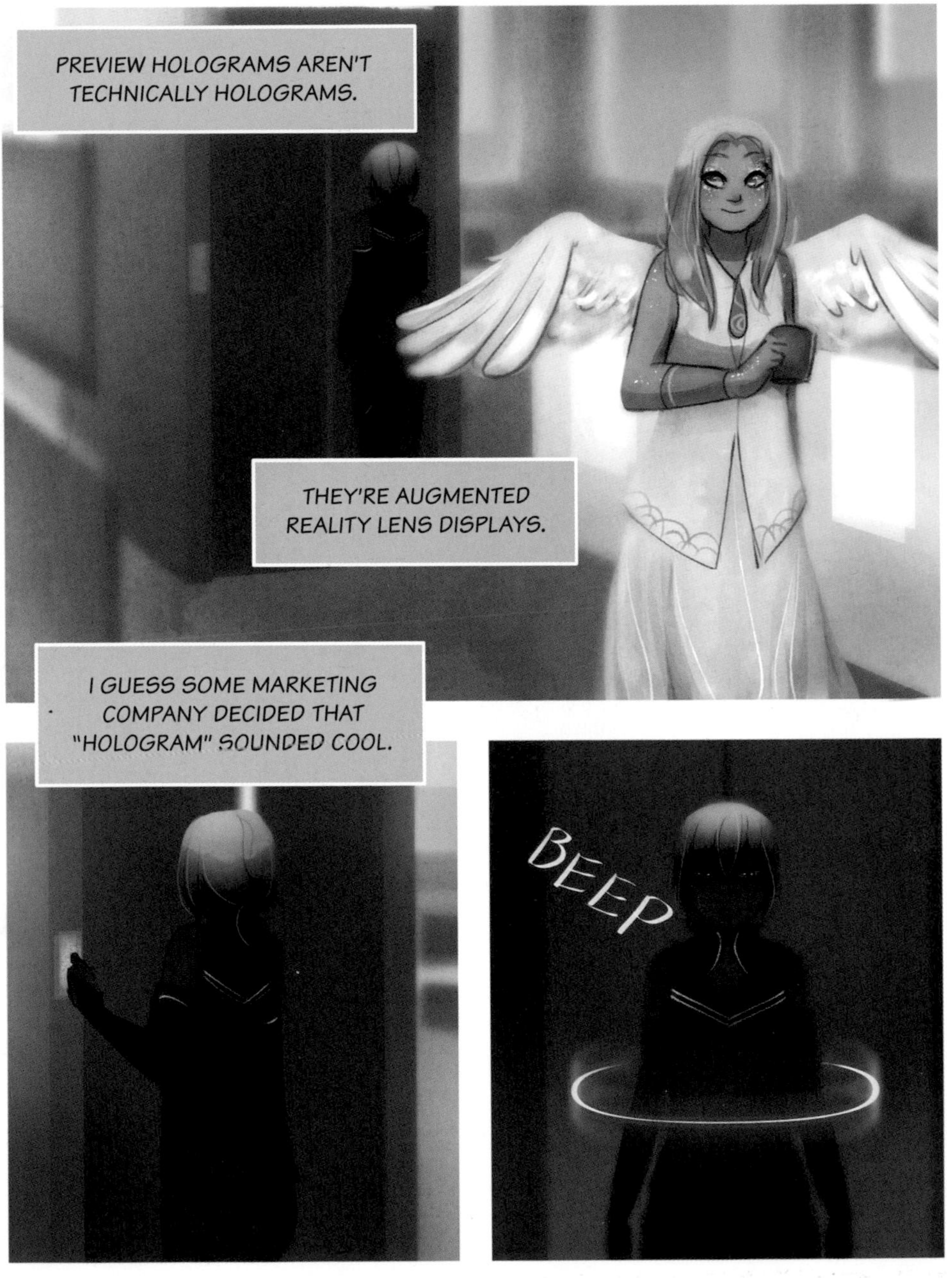
PREVIEW HOLOGRAMS AREN'T TECHNICALLY HOLOGRAMS.
THEY'RE AUGMENTED REALITY LENS DISPLAYS.
I GUESS SOME MARKETING COMPANY DECIDED THAT "HOLOGRAM" SOUNDED COOL.
BEEP

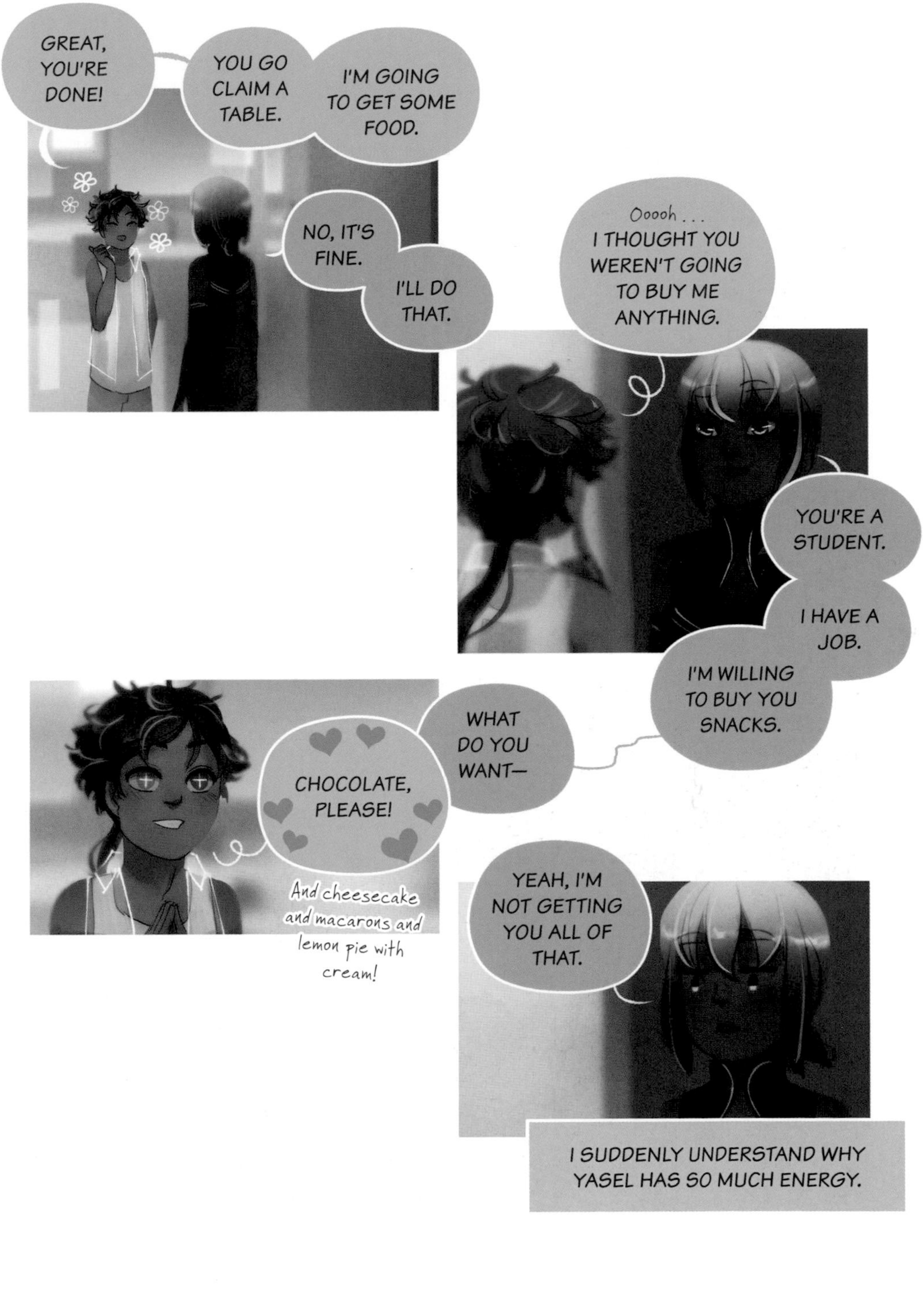
GREAT, YOU'RE DONE!
YOU GO CLAIM A TABLE.
I'M GOING TO GET SOME FOOD.
NO, IT'S FINE.
I'LL DO THAT.
Ooooh . . . I THOUGHT YOU WEREN'T GOING TO BUY ME ANYTHING.
YOU'RE A STUDENT.
I HAVE A JOB.
I'M WILLING TO BUY YOU SNACKS.
WHAT DO YOU WANT—
CHOCOLATE, PLEASE!
And cheesecake and macarons and lemon pie with cream!
YEAH, I'M NOT GETTING YOU ALL OF THAT.
I SUDDENLY UNDERSTAND WHY YASEL HAS SO MUCH ENERGY.

I USED TO SPEND HEAPS OF TIME HERE.

I LOVE TRYING DIFFERENT LOOKS.

I LOVE THE FREEDOM THAT COMES WITH BEING WHOEVER I WANT.

BUT IT'S NOT LIKE THAT WHEN YOU'RE DATING SOMEONE.

WHEN YOU'VE GOT A PARTNER, YOU NO LONGER WANT TO LOOK DIFFERENT.

YOU WANT TO LOOK LIKE THE PERSON THEY LIKE.

YOU WANT TO LOOK LIKE YOU.

AND SINCE THE PERSON I'M DATING IS AUSTEN . . .

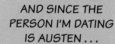

smells good

. . . WELL, IT'S HARD TO EVEN THINK ABOUT FASHION MODS WITHOUT FEELING GUILTY.

I WONDER WHY IT DOESN'T SEEM TO BOTHER YASEL?

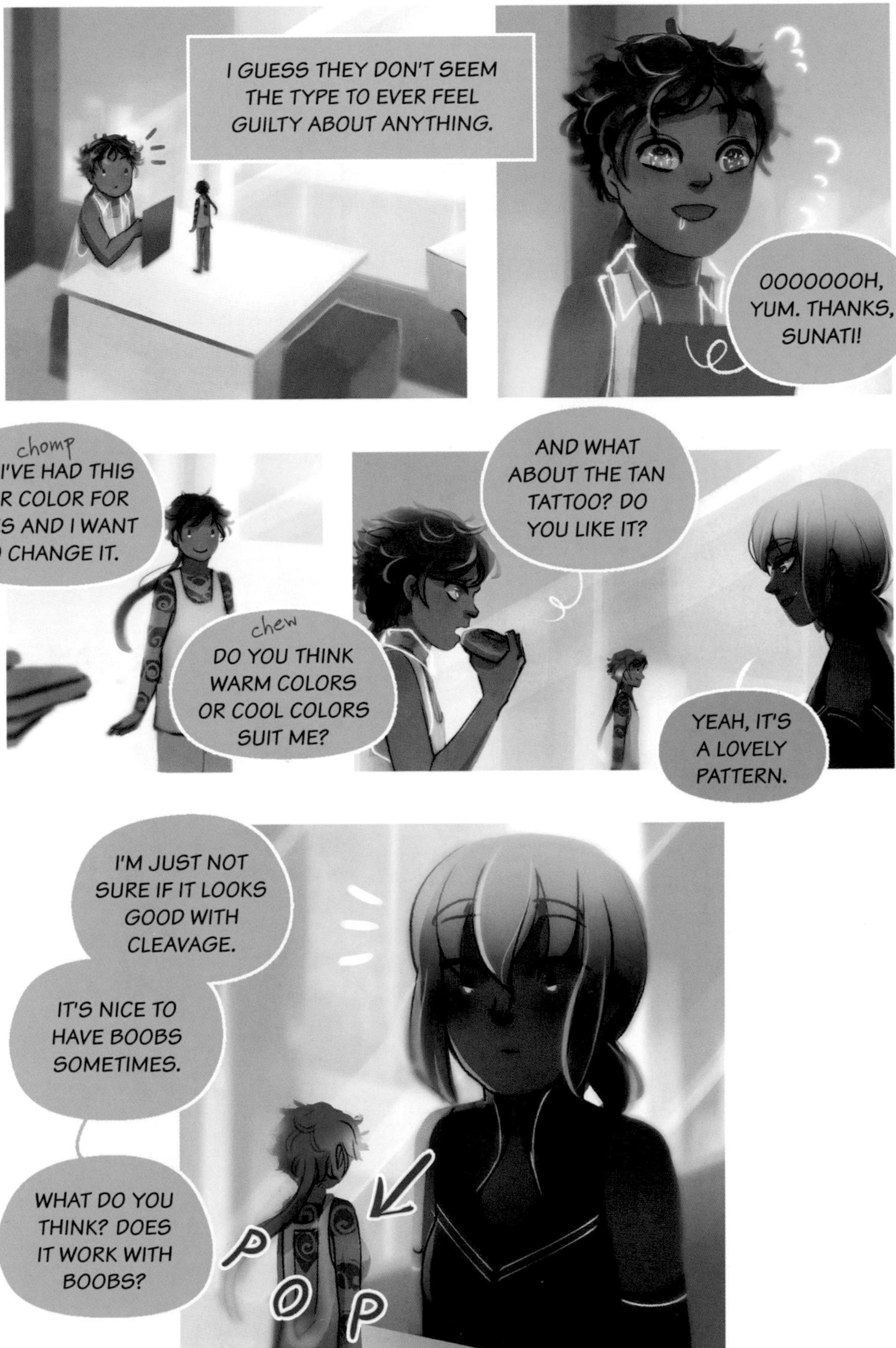
I GUESS THEY DON'T SEEM THE TYPE TO EVER FEEL GUILTY ABOUT ANYTHING.
OOOOOOOH, YUM. THANKS, SUNATI!
chomp
SO, I'VE HAD THIS HAIR COLOR FOR AGES AND I WANT TO CHANGE IT.
chew
DO YOU THINK WARM COLORS OR COOL COLORS SUIT ME?
AND WHAT ABOUT THE TAN TATTOO? DO YOU LIKE IT?
YEAH, IT'S A LOVELY PATTERN.
I'M JUST NOT SURE IF IT LOOKS GOOD WITH CLEAVAGE.
IT'S NICE TO HAVE BOOBS SOMETIMES.
WHAT DO YOU THINK? DOES IT WORK WITH BOOBS?
POP

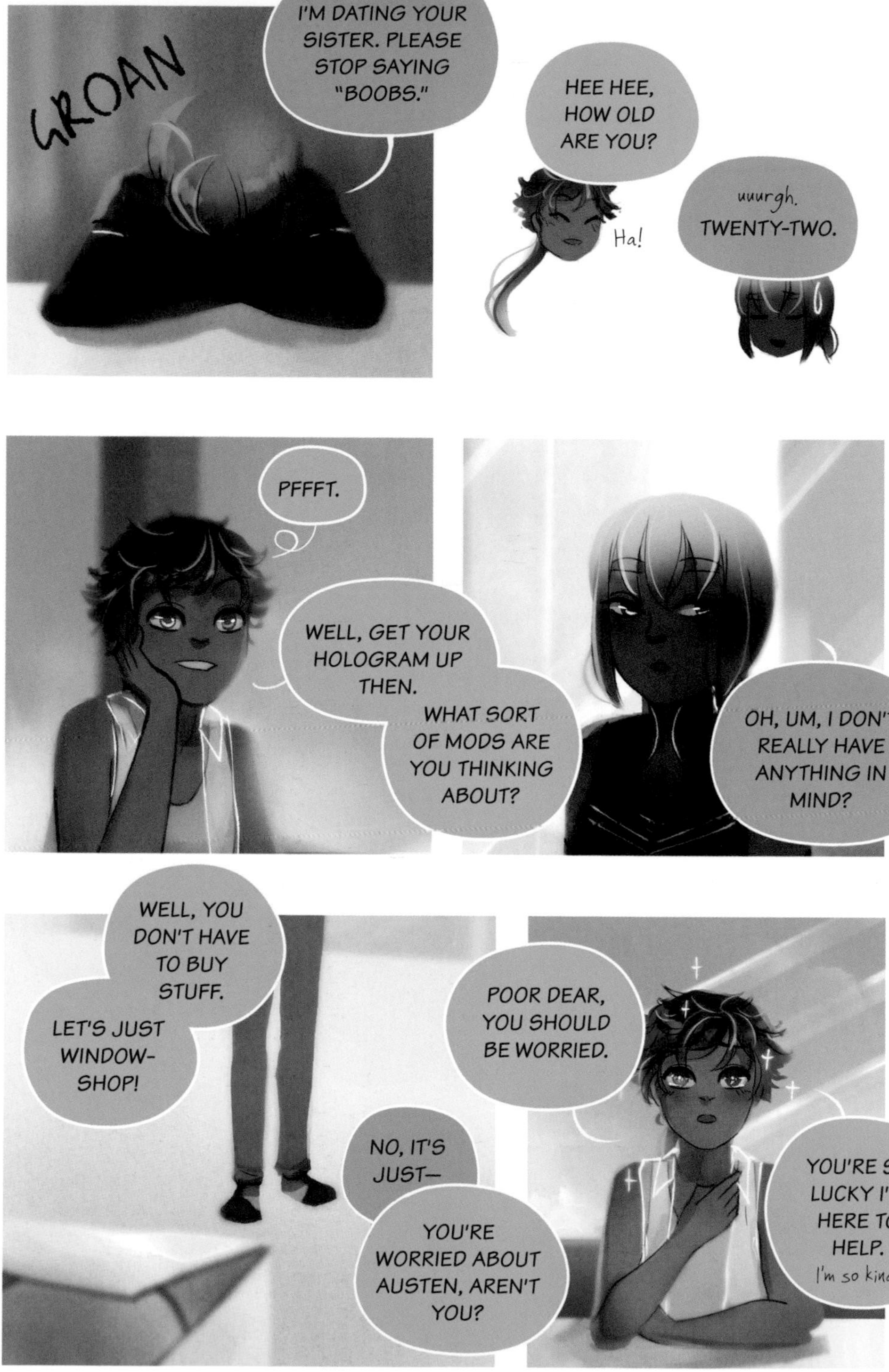
GROAN
I'M DATING YOUR SISTER. PLEASE STOP SAYING "BOOBS."
HEE HEE, HOW OLD ARE YOU?
Ha!
uuurgh.
TWENTY-TWO.
PFFFT.
WELL, GET YOUR HOLOGRAM UP THEN.
WHAT SORT OF MODS ARE YOU THINKING ABOUT?
OH, UM, I DON'T REALLY HAVE ANYTHING IN MIND?
WELL, YOU DON'T HAVE TO BUY STUFF.
LET'S JUST WINDOW-SHOP!
NO, IT'S JUST—
YOU'RE WORRIED ABOUT AUSTEN, AREN'T YOU?
POOR DEAR, YOU SHOULD BE WORRIED.
YOU'RE SO LUCKY I'M HERE TO HELP.
I'm so kind!

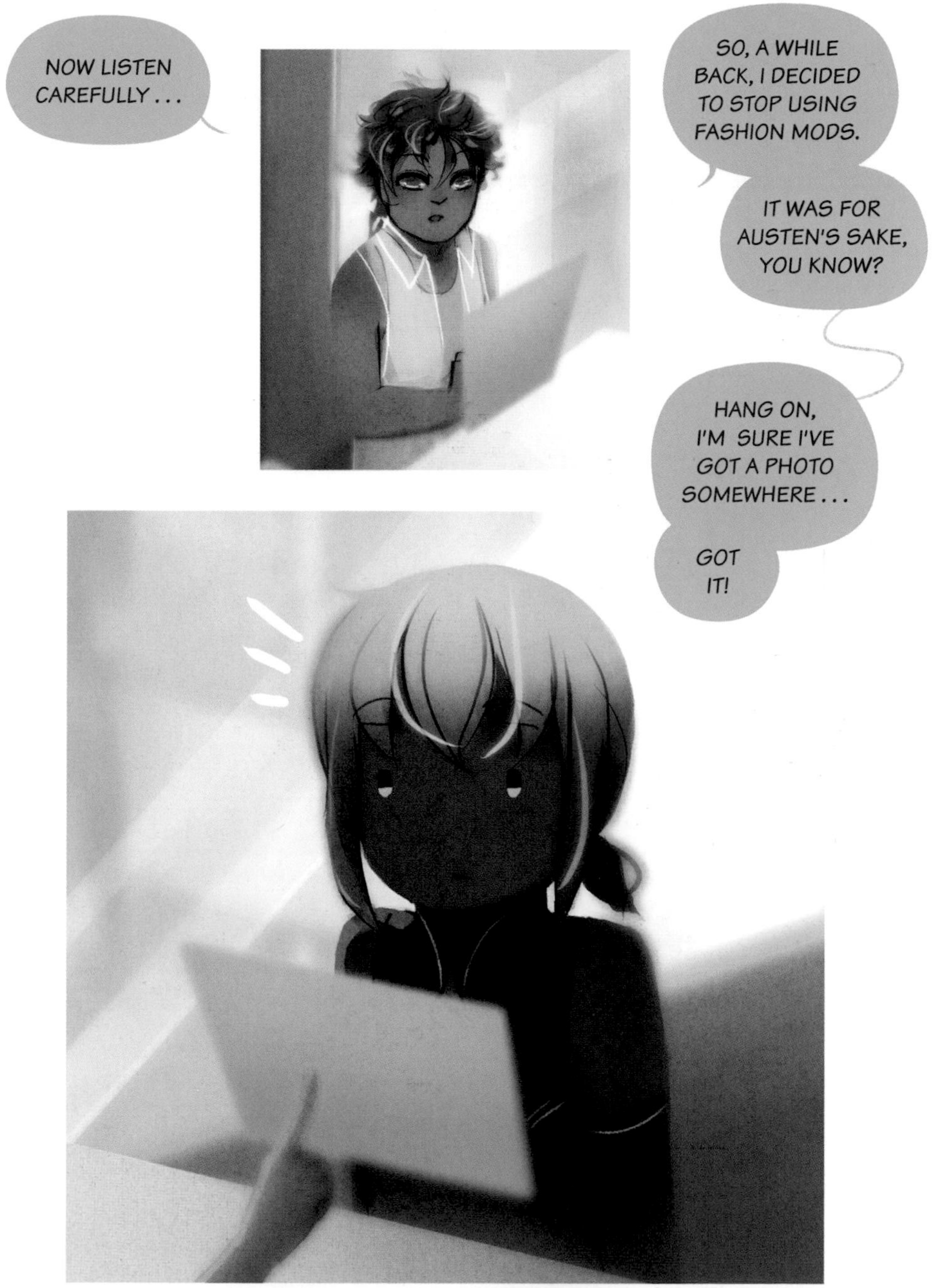
NOW LISTEN CAREFULLY . . .
SO, A WHILE BACK, I DECIDED TO STOP USING FASHION MODS.
IT WAS FOR AUSTEN'S SAKE, YOU KNOW?
HANG ON, I'M SURE I'VE GOT A PHOTO SOMEWHERE . . .
GOT IT!

33 - I KNOW THAT

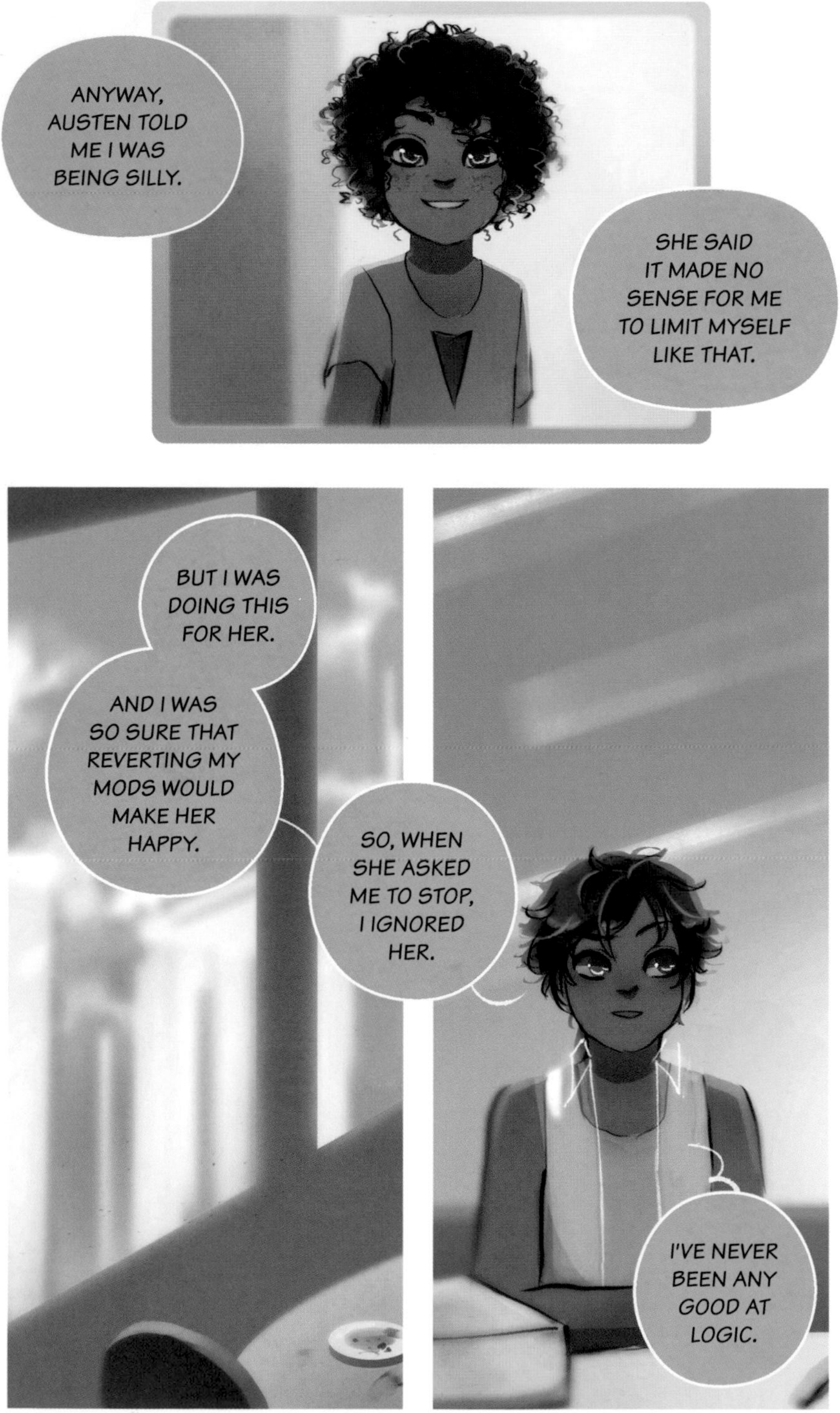
ANYWAY, AUSTEN TOLD ME I WAS BEING SILLY.
SHE SAID IT MADE NO SENSE FOR ME TO LIMIT MYSELF LIKE THAT.
BUT I WAS DOING THIS FOR HER.
AND I WAS SO SURE THAT REVERTING MY MODS WOULD MAKE HER HAPPY.
SO, WHEN SHE ASKED ME TO STOP, I IGNORED HER.
I'VE NEVER BEEN ANY GOOD AT LOGIC.

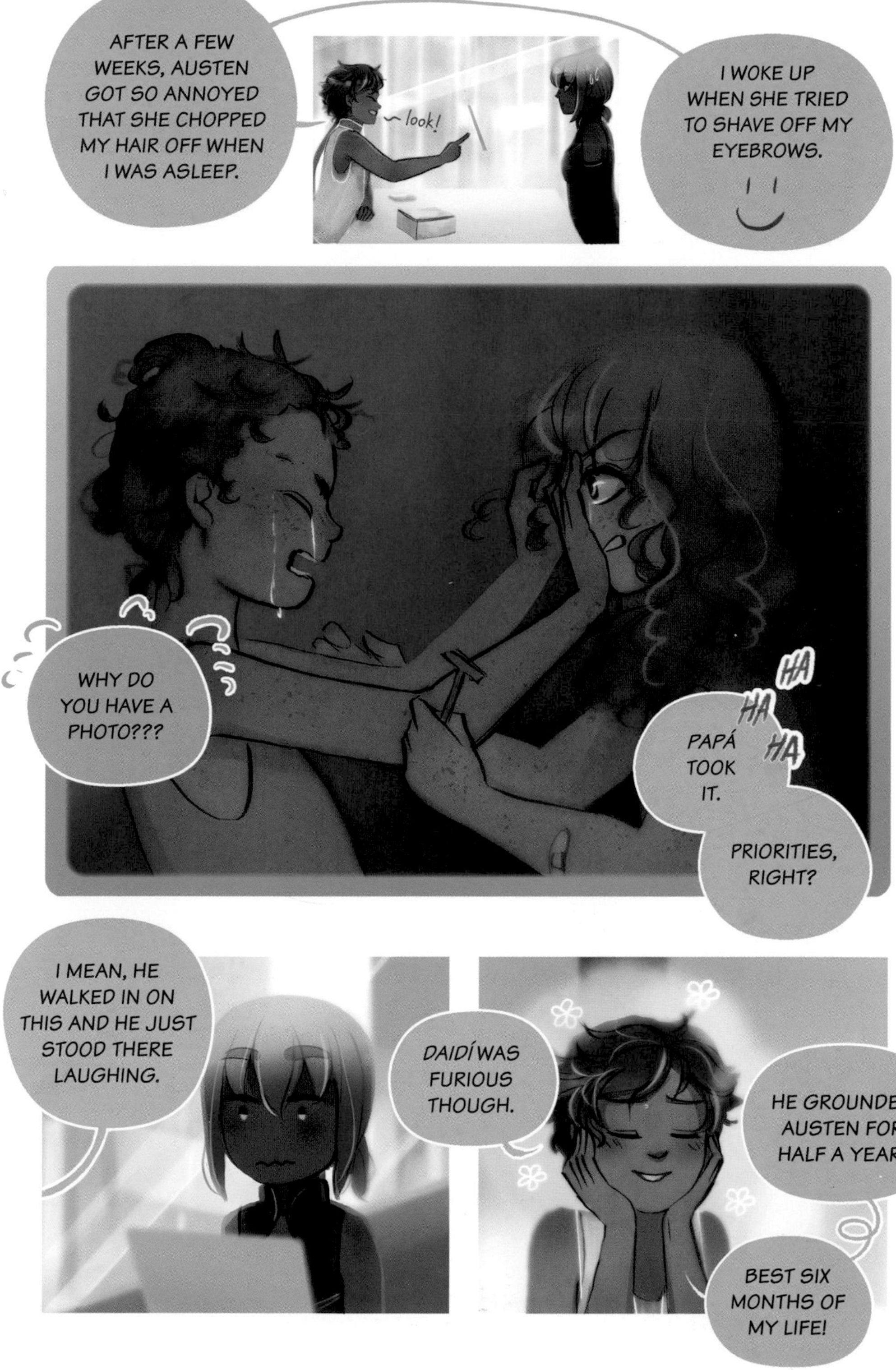

AFTER A FEW WEEKS, AUSTEN GOT SO ANNOYED THAT SHE CHOPPED MY HAIR OFF WHEN I WAS ASLEEP.
~look!
I WOKE UP WHEN SHE TRIED TO SHAVE OFF MY EYEBROWS.
WHY DO YOU HAVE A PHOTO???
HA HA HA
PAPÁ TOOK IT.
PRIORITIES, RIGHT?
I MEAN, HE WALKED IN ON THIS AND HE JUST STOOD THERE LAUGHING.
DAIDÍ WAS FURIOUS THOUGH.
HE GROUNDED AUSTEN FOR HALF A YEAR.
BEST SIX MONTHS OF MY LIFE!

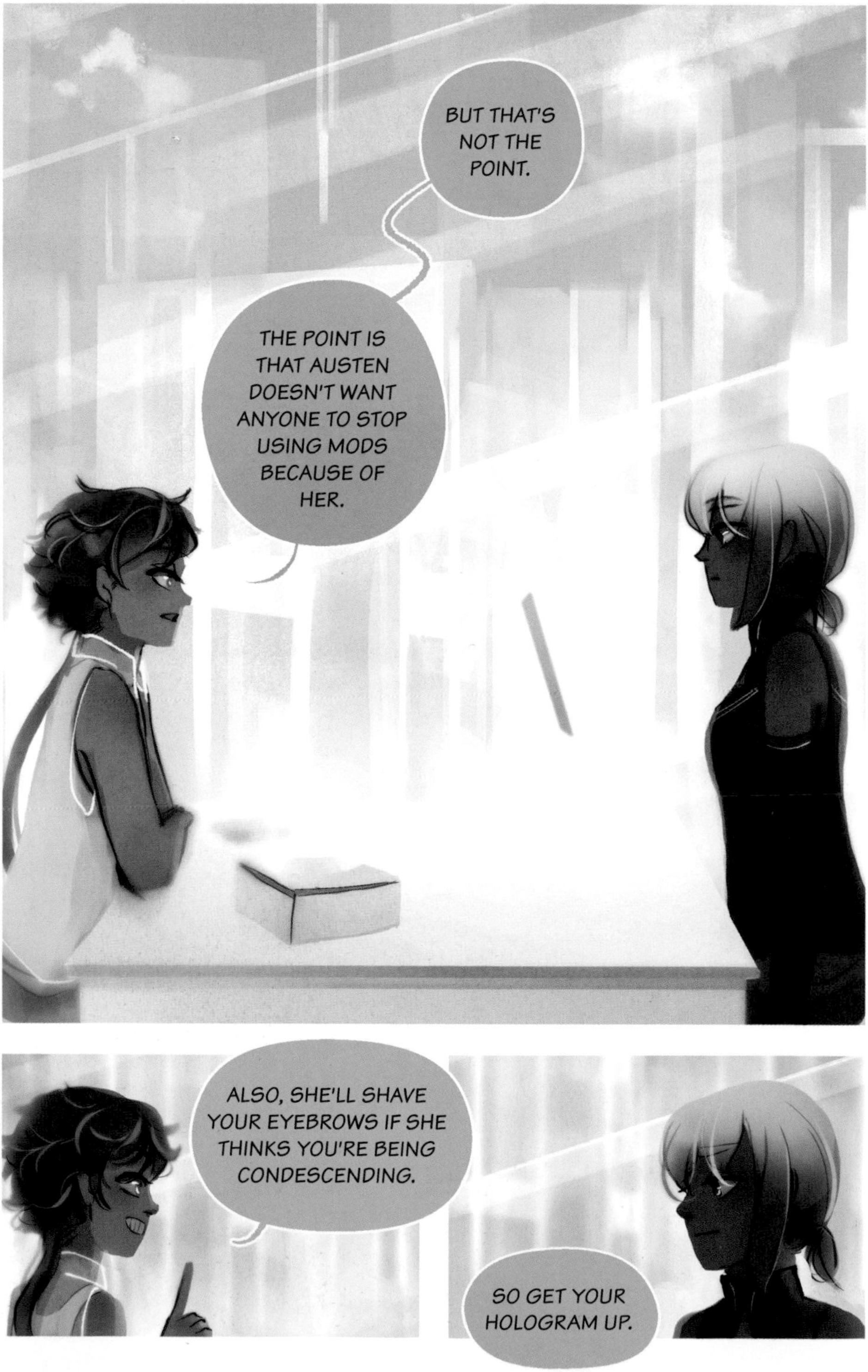
BUT THAT'S NOT THE POINT.
THE POINT IS THAT AUSTEN DOESN'T WANT ANYONE TO STOP USING MODS BECAUSE OF HER.
ALSO, SHE'LL SHAVE YOUR EYEBROWS IF SHE THINKS YOU'RE BEING CONDESCENDING.
SO GET YOUR HOLOGRAM UP.

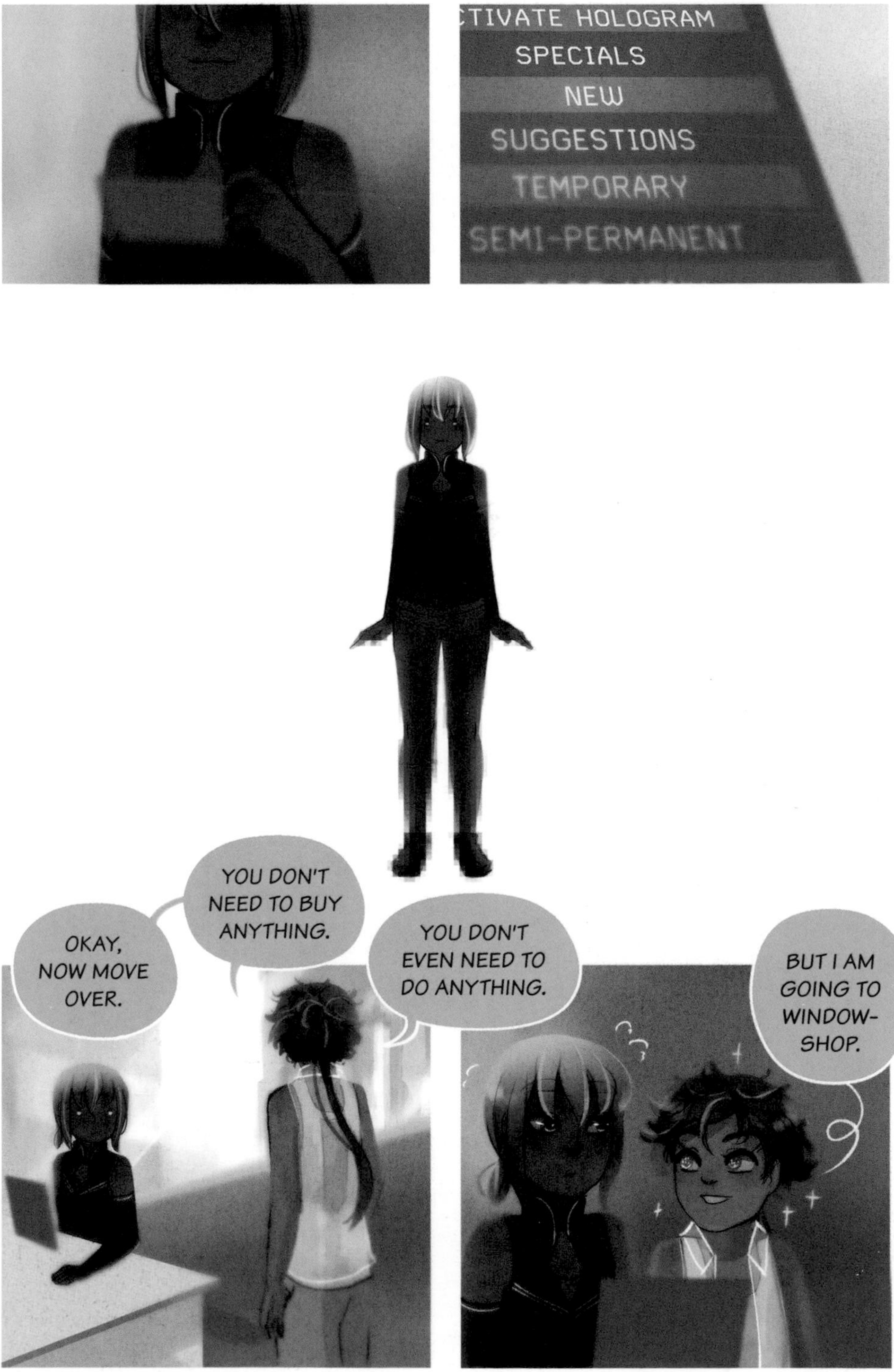
CTIVATE HOLOGRAM
SPECIALS
NEW
SUGGESTIONS
TEMPORARY
SEMI-PERMANENT
OKAY, NOW MOVE OVER.
YOU DON'T NEED TO BUY ANYTHING.
YOU DON'T EVEN NEED TO DO ANYTHING.
BUT I AM GOING TO WINDOW-SHOP.

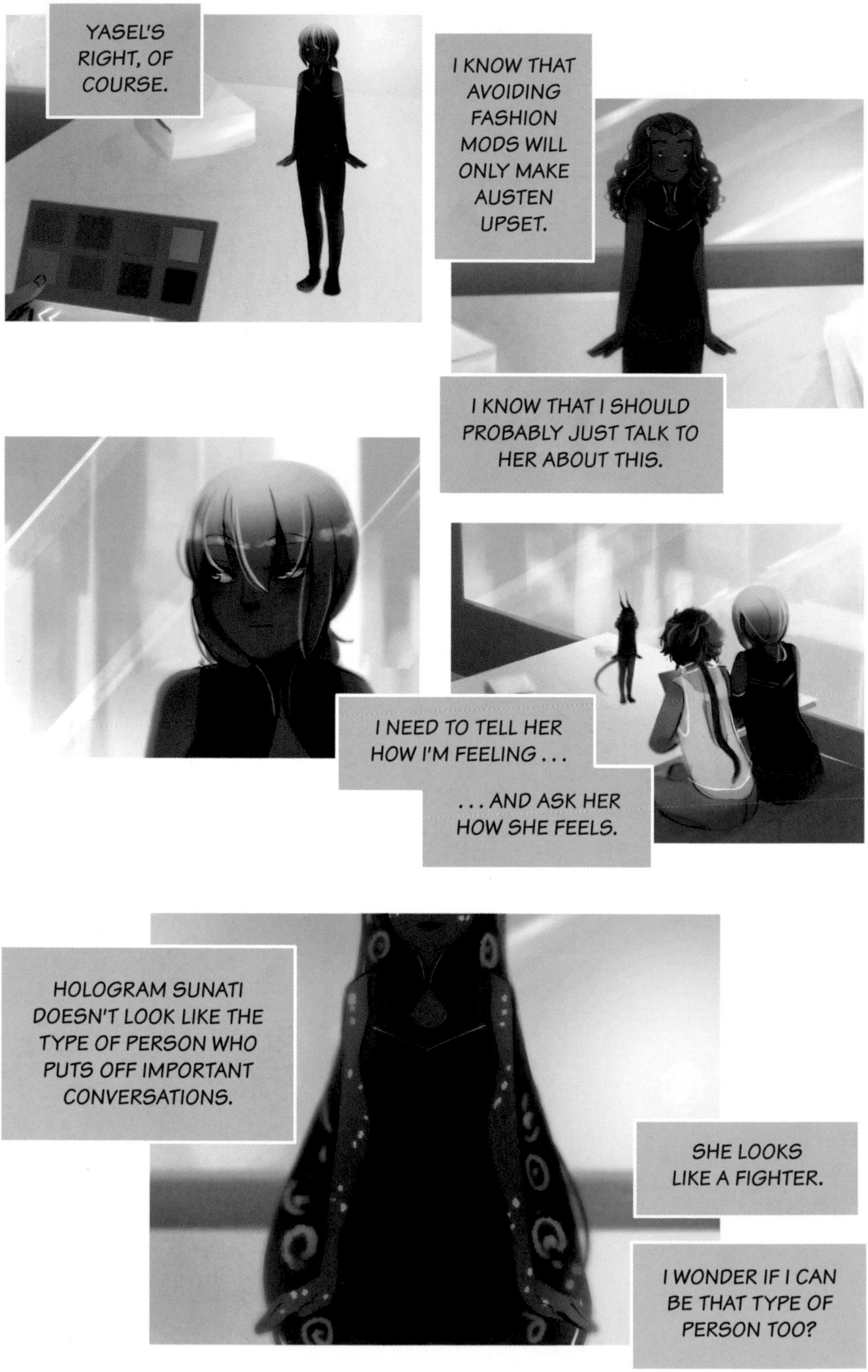
YASEL'S RIGHT, OF COURSE.
I KNOW THAT AVOIDING FASHION MODS WILL ONLY MAKE AUSTEN UPSET.
I KNOW THAT I SHOULD PROBABLY JUST TALK TO HER ABOUT THIS.
I NEED TO TELL HER HOW I'M FEELING . . .
. . . AND ASK HER HOW SHE FEELS.
HOLOGRAM SUNATI DOESN'T LOOK LIKE THE TYPE OF PERSON WHO PUTS OFF IMPORTANT CONVERSATIONS.
SHE LOOKS LIKE A FIGHTER.
I WONDER IF I CAN BE THAT TYPE OF PERSON TOO?

34 - I'M A REBEL

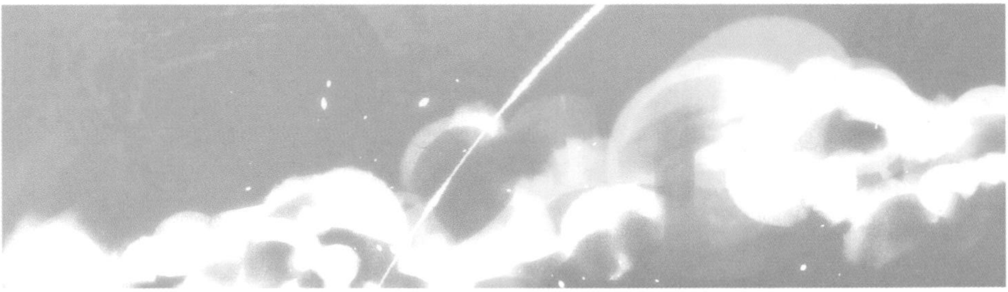

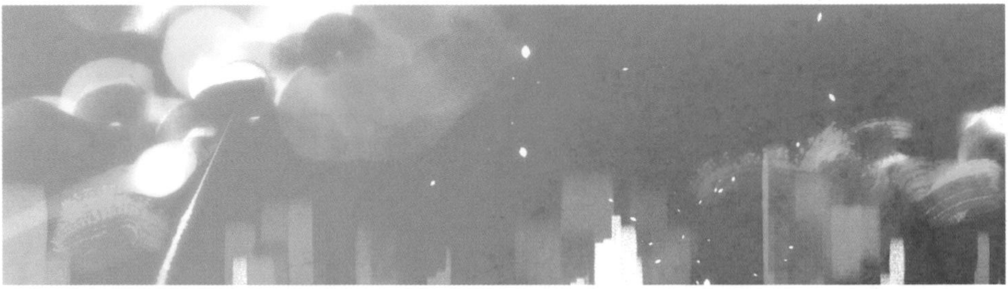

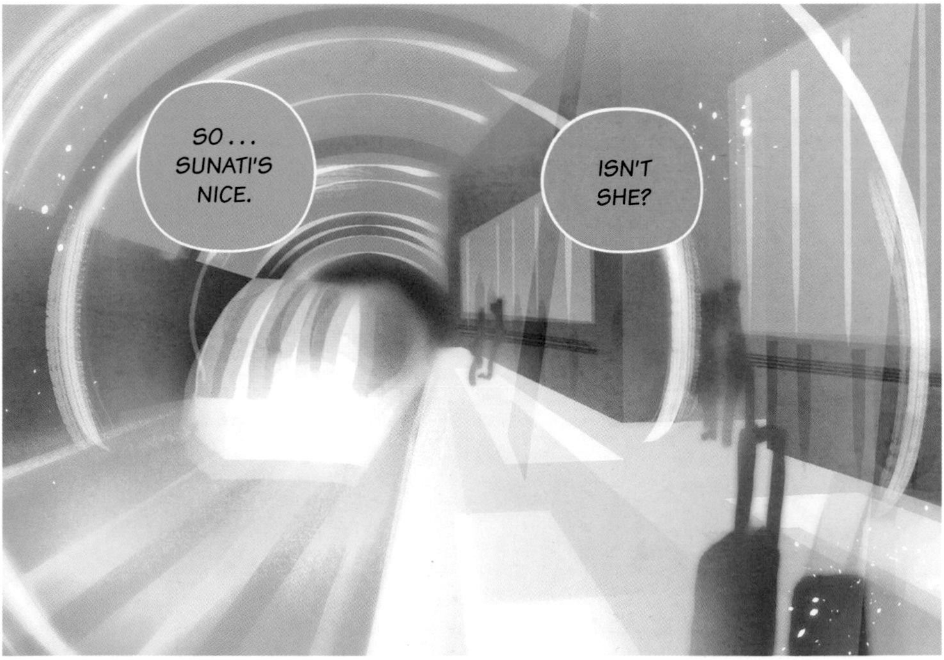
SO . . . SUNATI'S NICE.
ISN'T SHE?

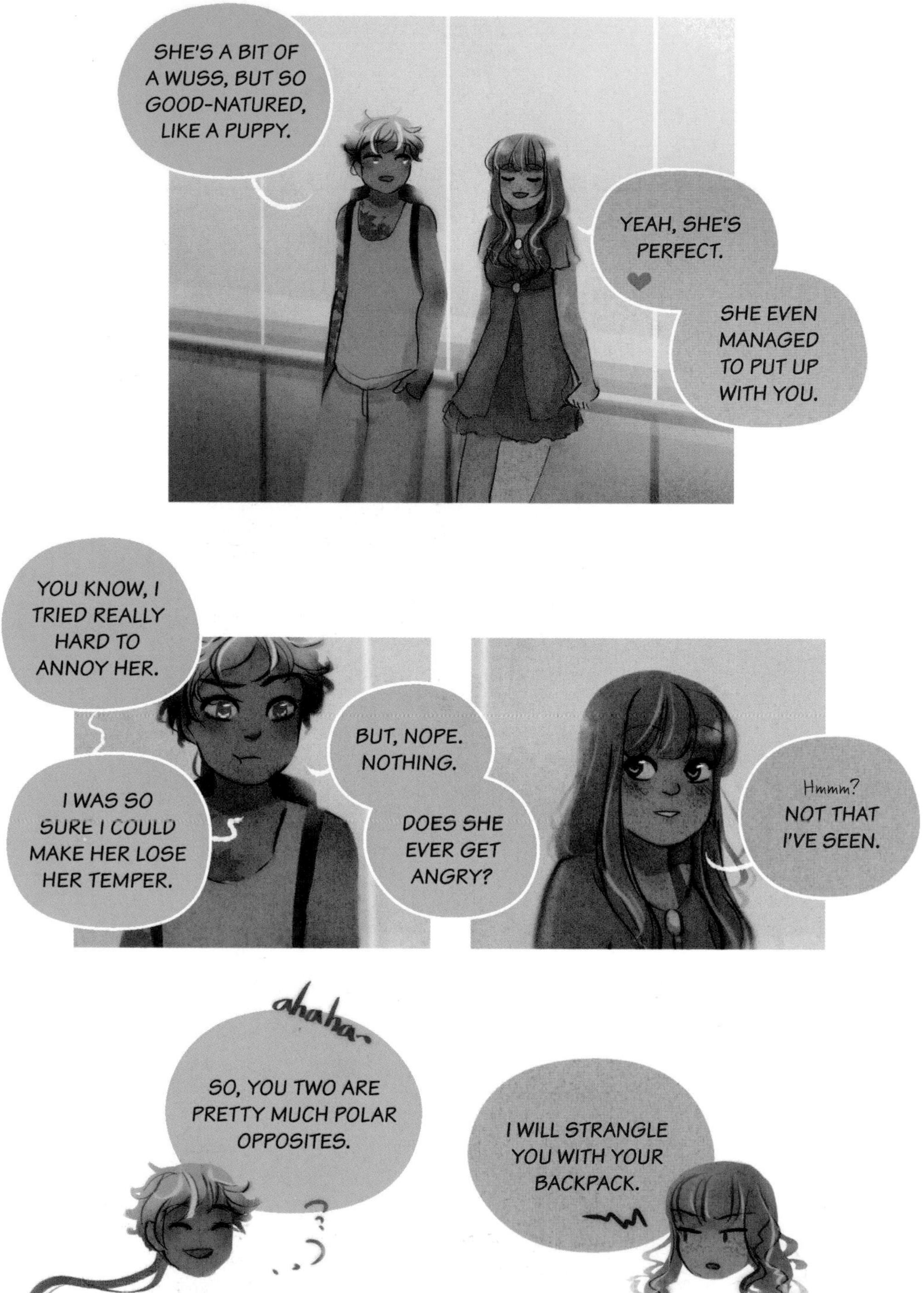

SHE'S A BIT OF A WUSS, BUT SO GOOD-NATURED, LIKE A PUPPY.
YEAH, SHE'S PERFECT.
SHE EVEN MANAGED TO PUT UP WITH YOU.
YOU KNOW, I TRIED REALLY HARD TO ANNOY HER.
I WAS SO SURE I COULD MAKE HER LOSE HER TEMPER.
BUT, NOPE. NOTHING.
DOES SHE EVER GET ANGRY?
Hmmm? NOT THAT I'VE SEEN.
ahaha
SO, YOU TWO ARE PRETTY MUCH POLAR OPPOSITES.
I WILL STRANGLE YOU WITH YOUR BACKPACK.

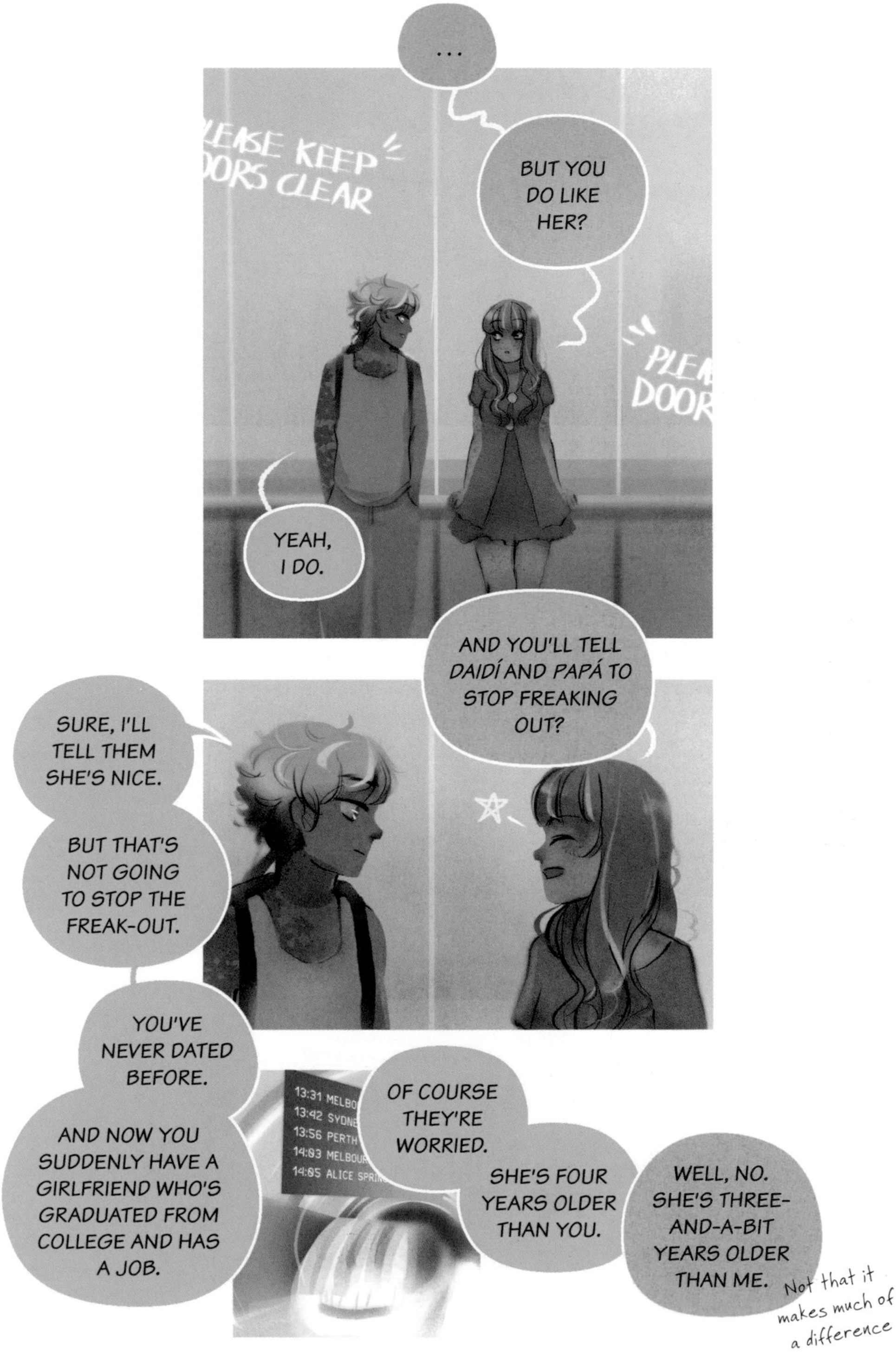
...
LEASE KEEP
OORS CLEAR
BUT YOU DO LIKE HER?
PLEA
DOOR
YEAH, I DO.
AND YOU'LL TELL *DAIDÍ* AND *PAPÁ* TO STOP FREAKING OUT?
SURE, I'LL TELL THEM SHE'S NICE.
BUT THAT'S NOT GOING TO STOP THE FREAK-OUT.
YOU'VE NEVER DATED BEFORE.
AND NOW YOU SUDDENLY HAVE A GIRLFRIEND WHO'S GRADUATED FROM COLLEGE AND HAS A JOB.
13:31 MELBO
13:42 SYDNE
13:56 PERTH
14:03 MELBOU
14:05 ALICE SPRIN
OF COURSE THEY'RE WORRIED.
SHE'S FOUR YEARS OLDER THAN YOU.
WELL, NO. SHE'S THREE-AND-A-BIT YEARS OLDER THAN ME.
Not that it makes much of a difference

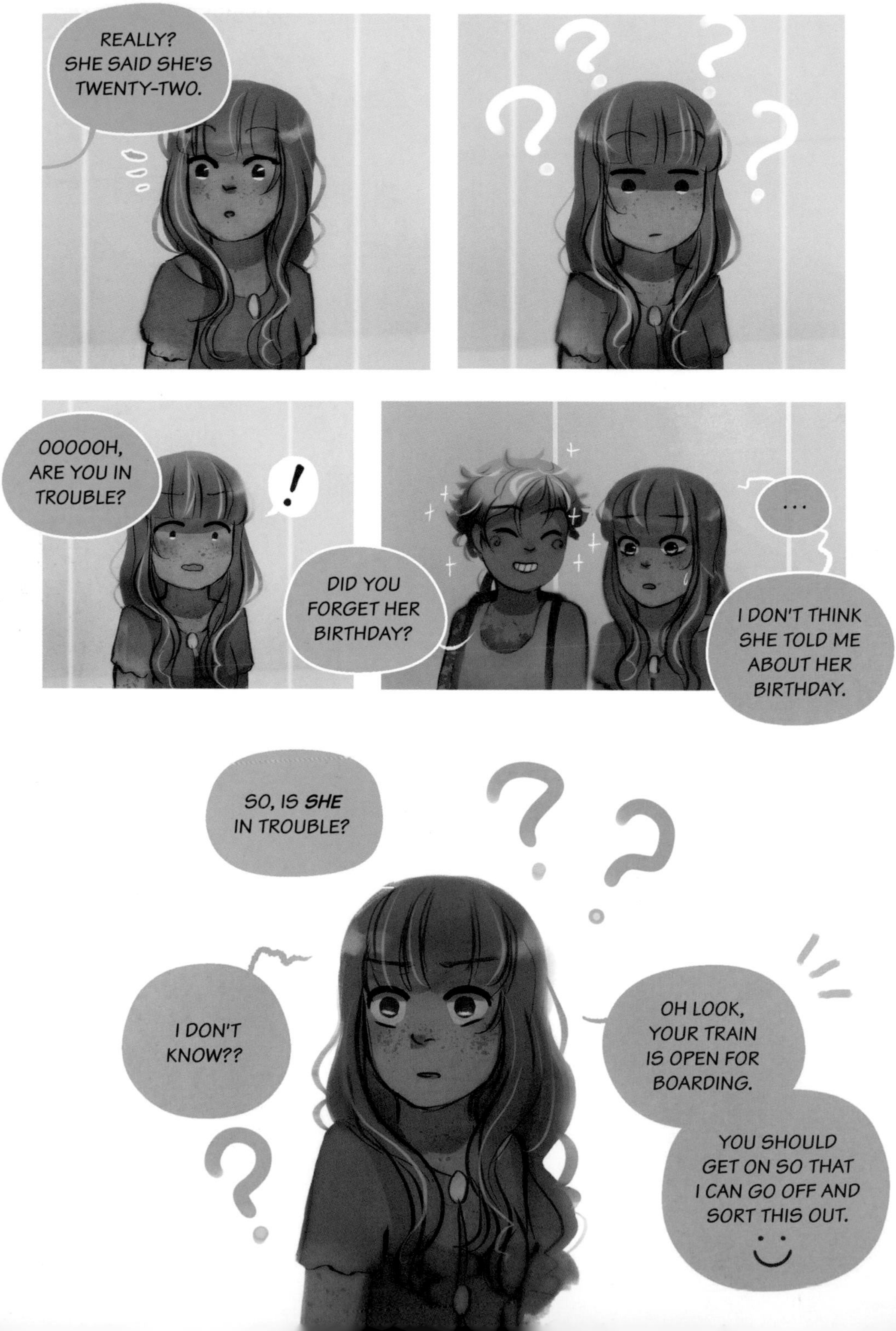
REALLY? SHE SAID SHE'S TWENTY-TWO.
OOOOOH, ARE YOU IN TROUBLE?
!
DID YOU FORGET HER BIRTHDAY?
...
I DON'T THINK SHE TOLD ME ABOUT HER BIRTHDAY.
SO, IS *SHE* IN TROUBLE?
I DON'T KNOW??
OH LOOK, YOUR TRAIN IS OPEN FOR BOARDING.
YOU SHOULD GET ON SO THAT I CAN GO OFF AND SORT THIS OUT.

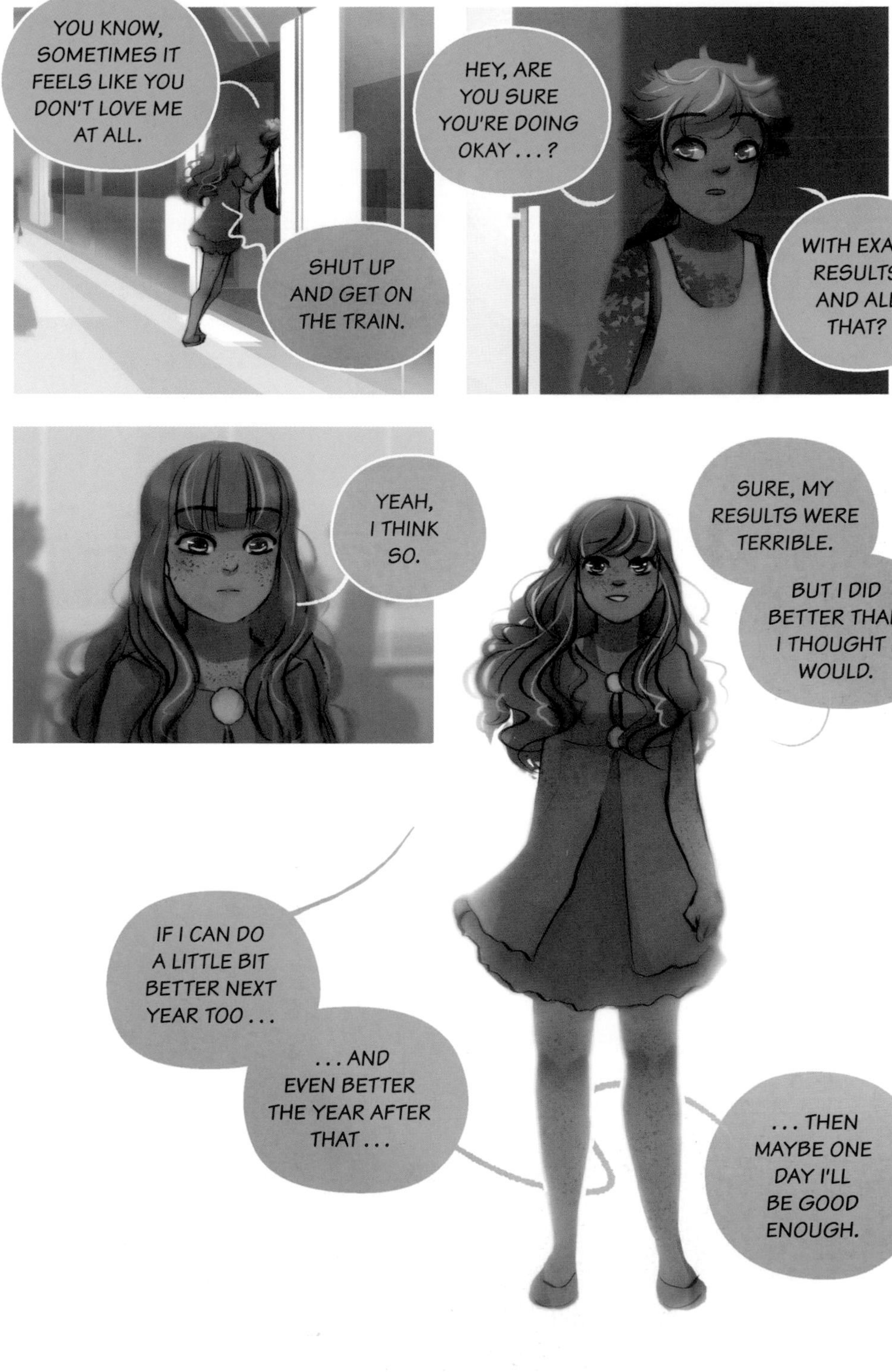
YOU KNOW, SOMETIMES IT FEELS LIKE YOU DON'T LOVE ME AT ALL.
SHUT UP AND GET ON THE TRAIN.
HEY, ARE YOU SURE YOU'RE DOING OKAY . . . ?
WITH EXAM RESULTS AND ALL THAT?
YEAH, I THINK SO.
SURE, MY RESULTS WERE TERRIBLE.
BUT I DID BETTER THAN I THOUGHT I WOULD.
IF I CAN DO A LITTLE BIT BETTER NEXT YEAR TOO . . .
. . . AND EVEN BETTER THE YEAR AFTER THAT . . .
. . . THEN MAYBE ONE DAY I'LL BE GOOD ENOUGH.

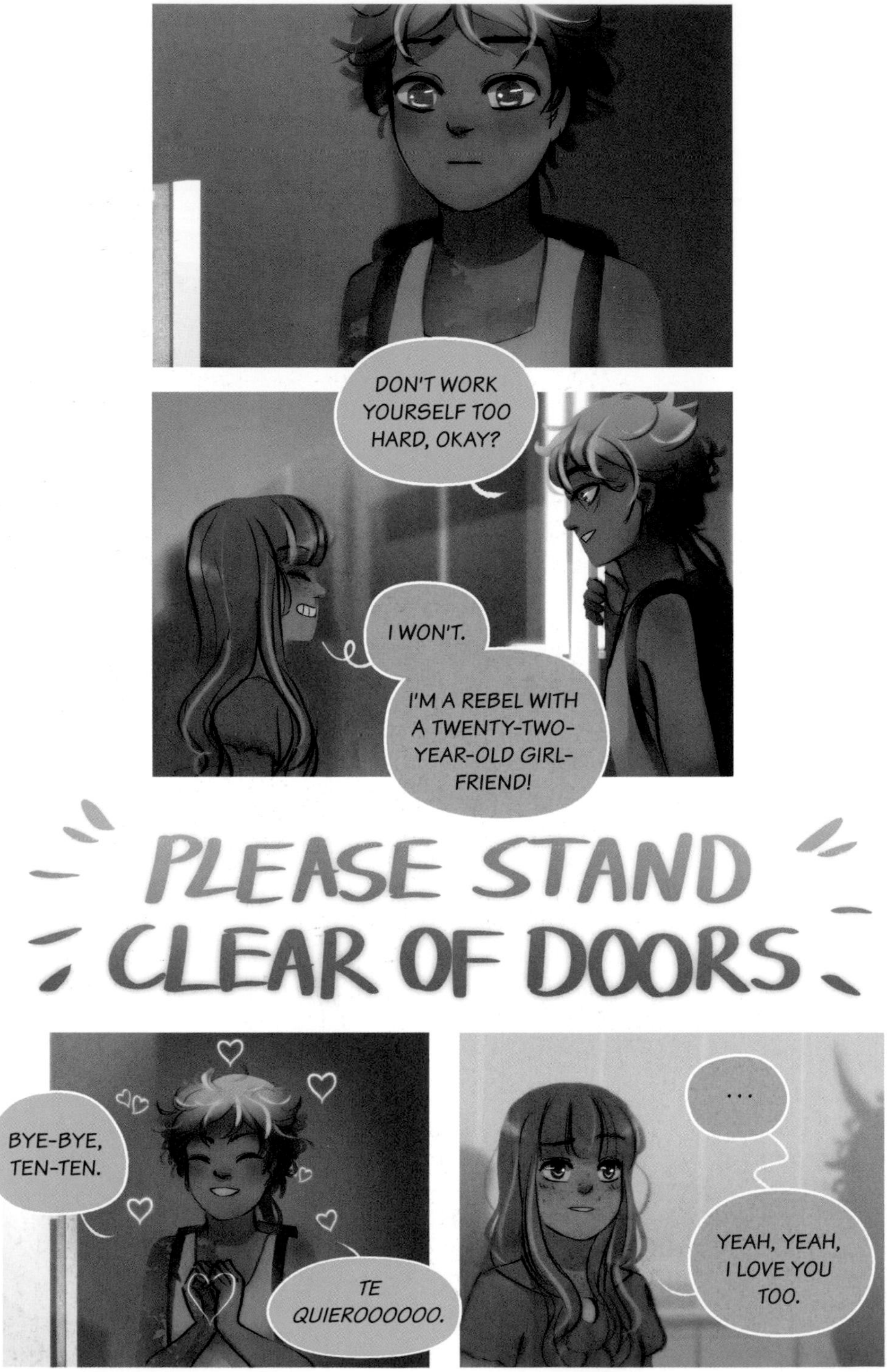
DON'T WORK YOURSELF TOO HARD, OKAY?
I WON'T.
I'M A REBEL WITH A TWENTY-TWO-YEAR-OLD GIRL-FRIEND!
PLEASE STAND CLEAR OF DOORS
BYE-BYE, TEN-TEN.
TE QUIEROOOOOO.
...
YEAH, YEAH, I LOVE YOU TOO.

35 - NO MORE SECRETS

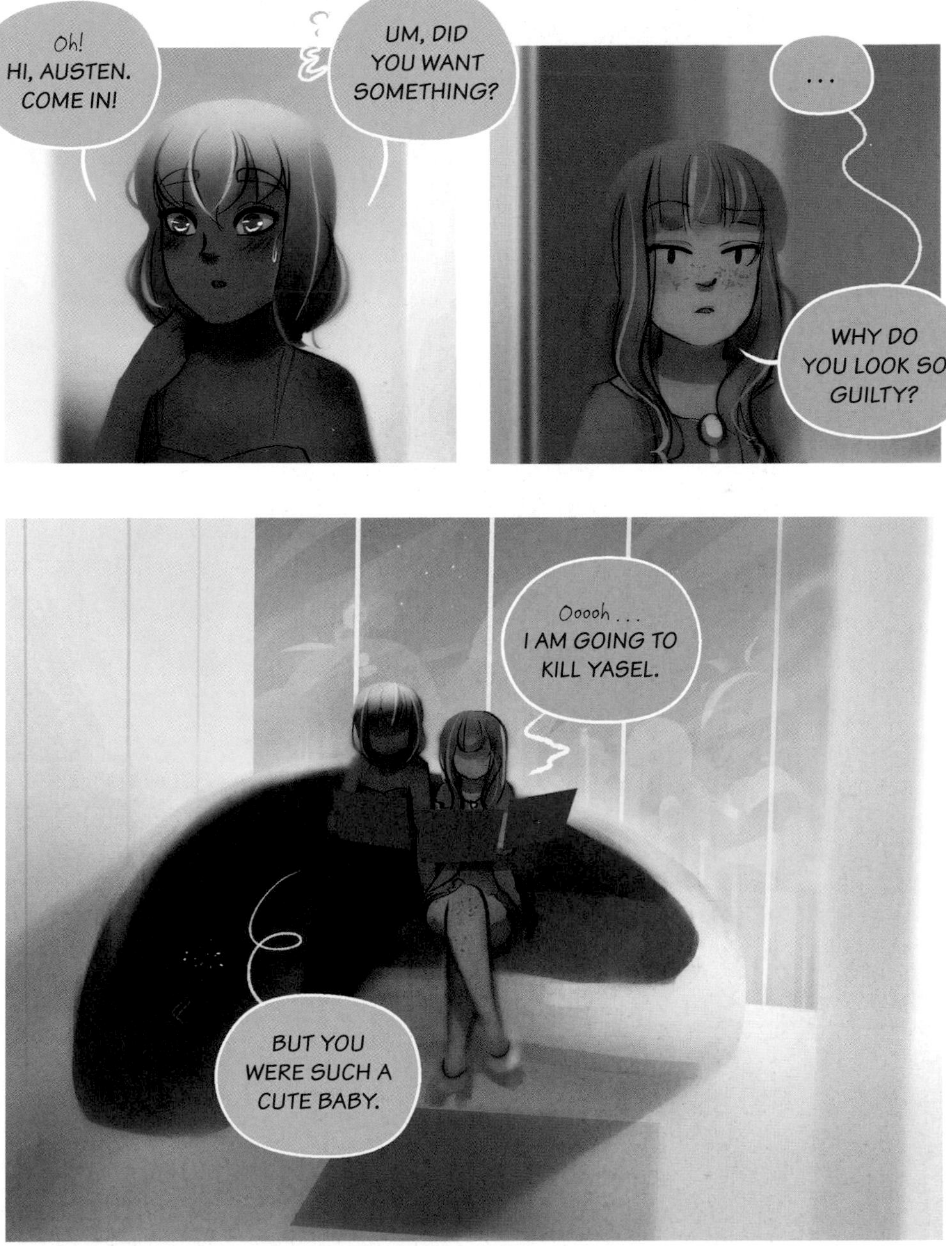
Oh!
HI, AUSTEN. COME IN!
UM, DID YOU WANT SOMETHING?
...
WHY DO YOU LOOK SO GUILTY?
Ooooh...
I AM GOING TO KILL YASEL.
BUT YOU WERE SUCH A CUTE BABY.

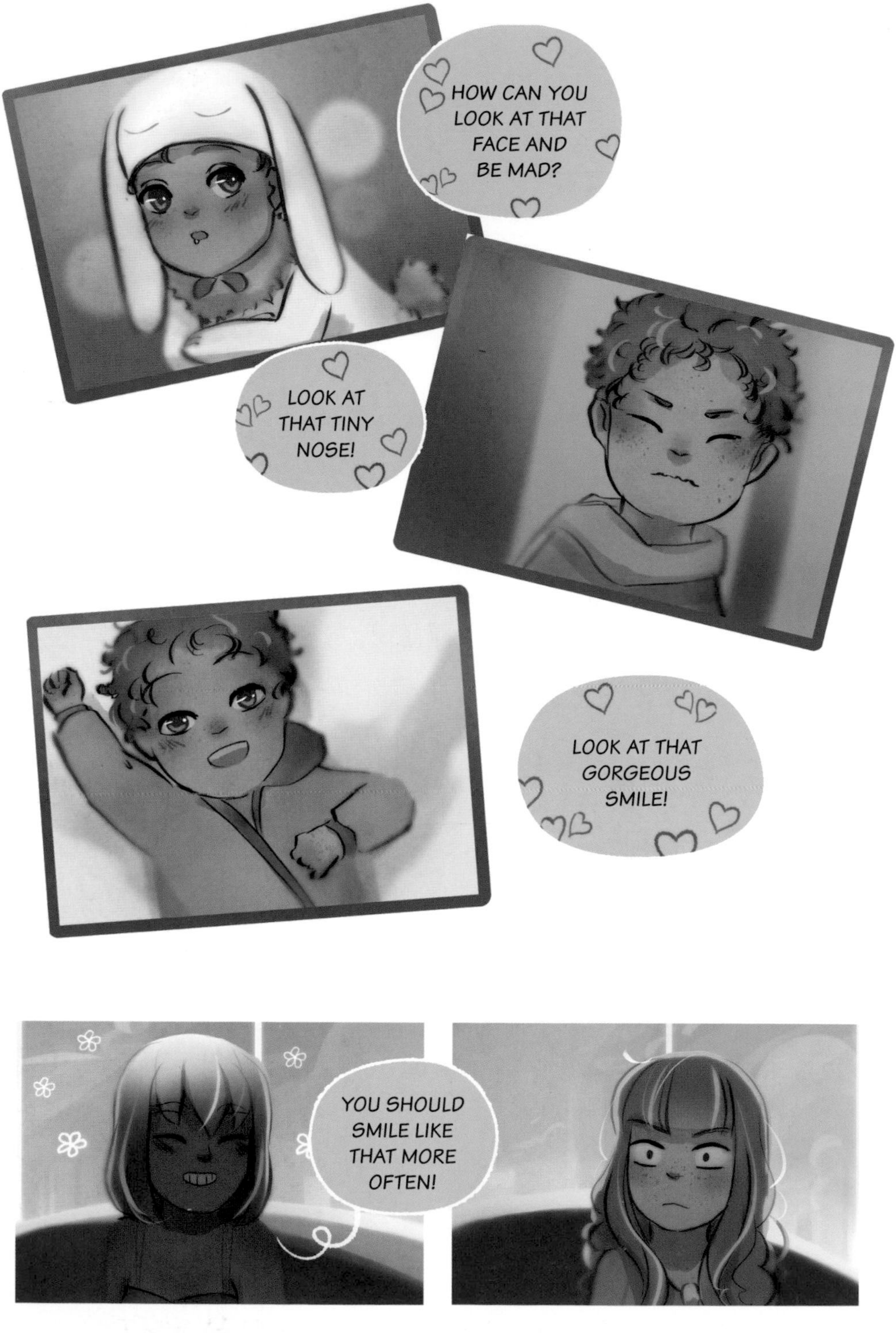
HOW CAN YOU LOOK AT THAT FACE AND BE MAD?
LOOK AT THAT TINY NOSE!
LOOK AT THAT GORGEOUS SMILE!
YOU SHOULD SMILE LIKE THAT MORE OFTEN!

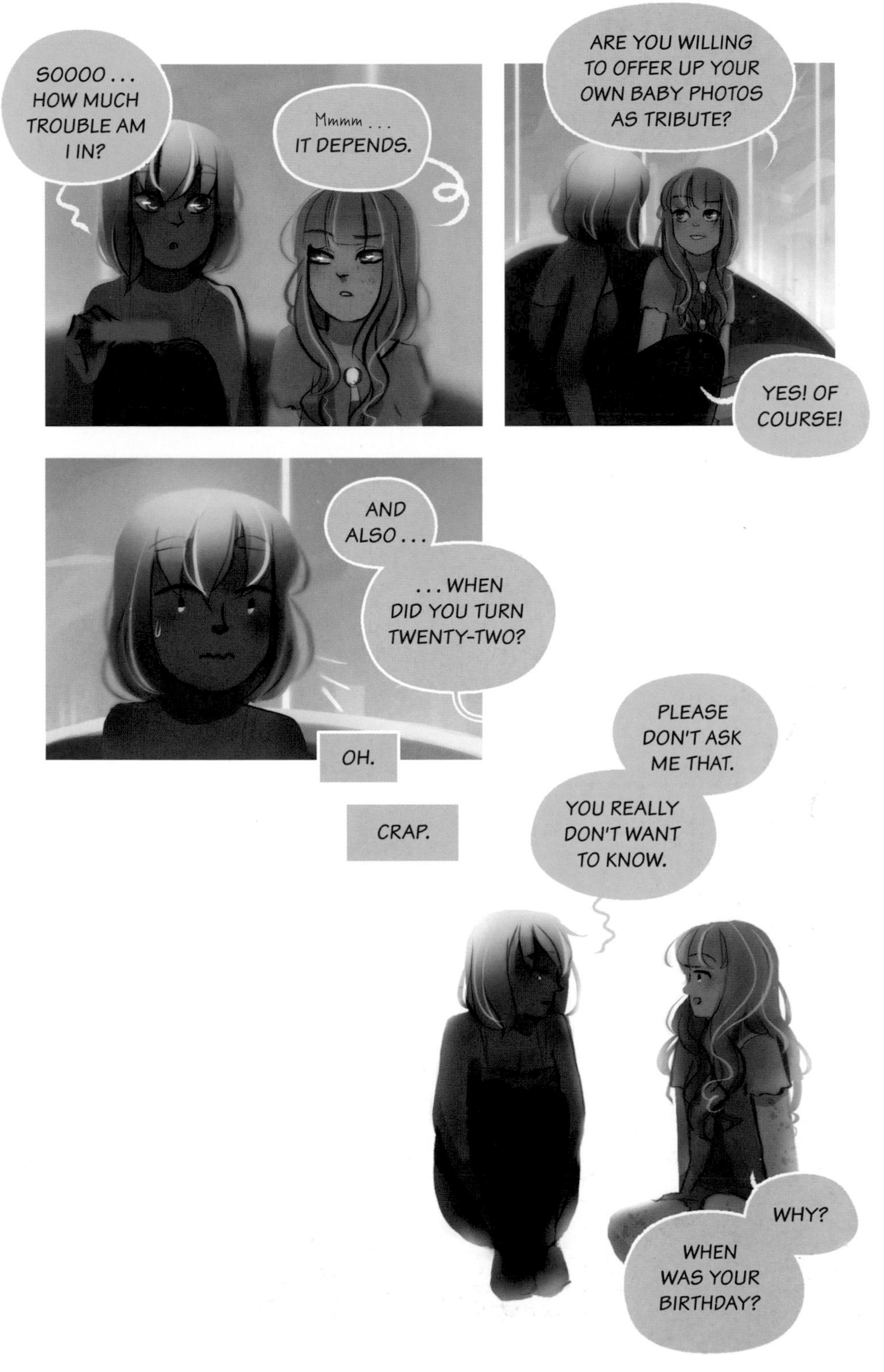
SOOOO . . . HOW MUCH TROUBLE AM I IN?
Mmmm . . . IT DEPENDS.
ARE YOU WILLING TO OFFER UP YOUR OWN BABY PHOTOS AS TRIBUTE?
YES! OF COURSE!
AND ALSO . . .
. . . WHEN DID YOU TURN TWENTY-TWO?
OH.
CRAP.
PLEASE DON'T ASK ME THAT.
YOU REALLY DON'T WANT TO KNOW.
WHY?
WHEN WAS YOUR BIRTHDAY?

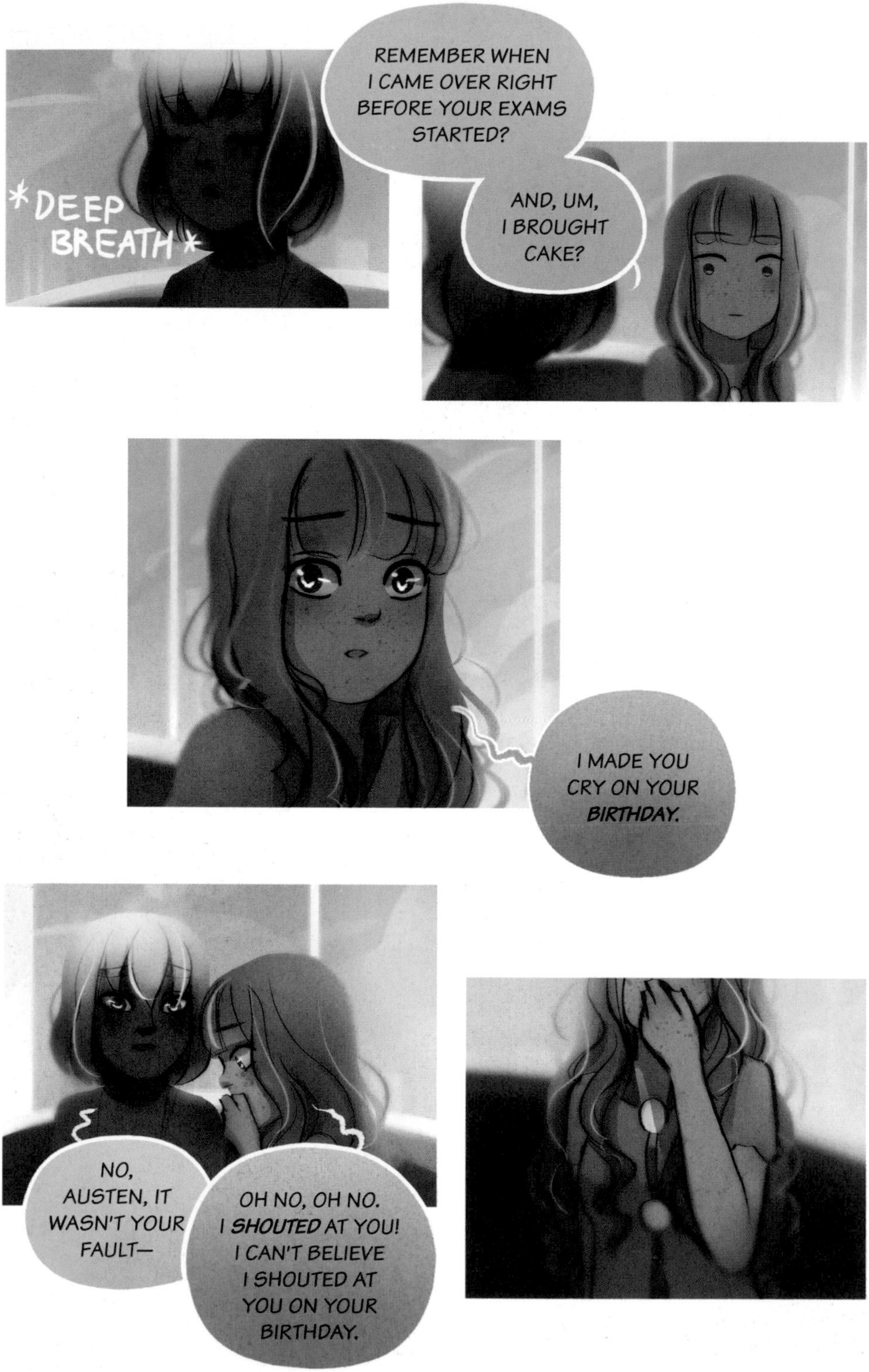
DEEP BREATH
REMEMBER WHEN I CAME OVER RIGHT BEFORE YOUR EXAMS STARTED?
AND, UM, I BROUGHT CAKE?
I MADE YOU CRY ON YOUR *BIRTHDAY.*
NO, AUSTEN, IT WASN'T YOUR FAULT—
OH NO, OH NO. I *SHOUTED* AT YOU! I CAN'T BELIEVE I SHOUTED AT YOU ON YOUR BIRTHDAY.

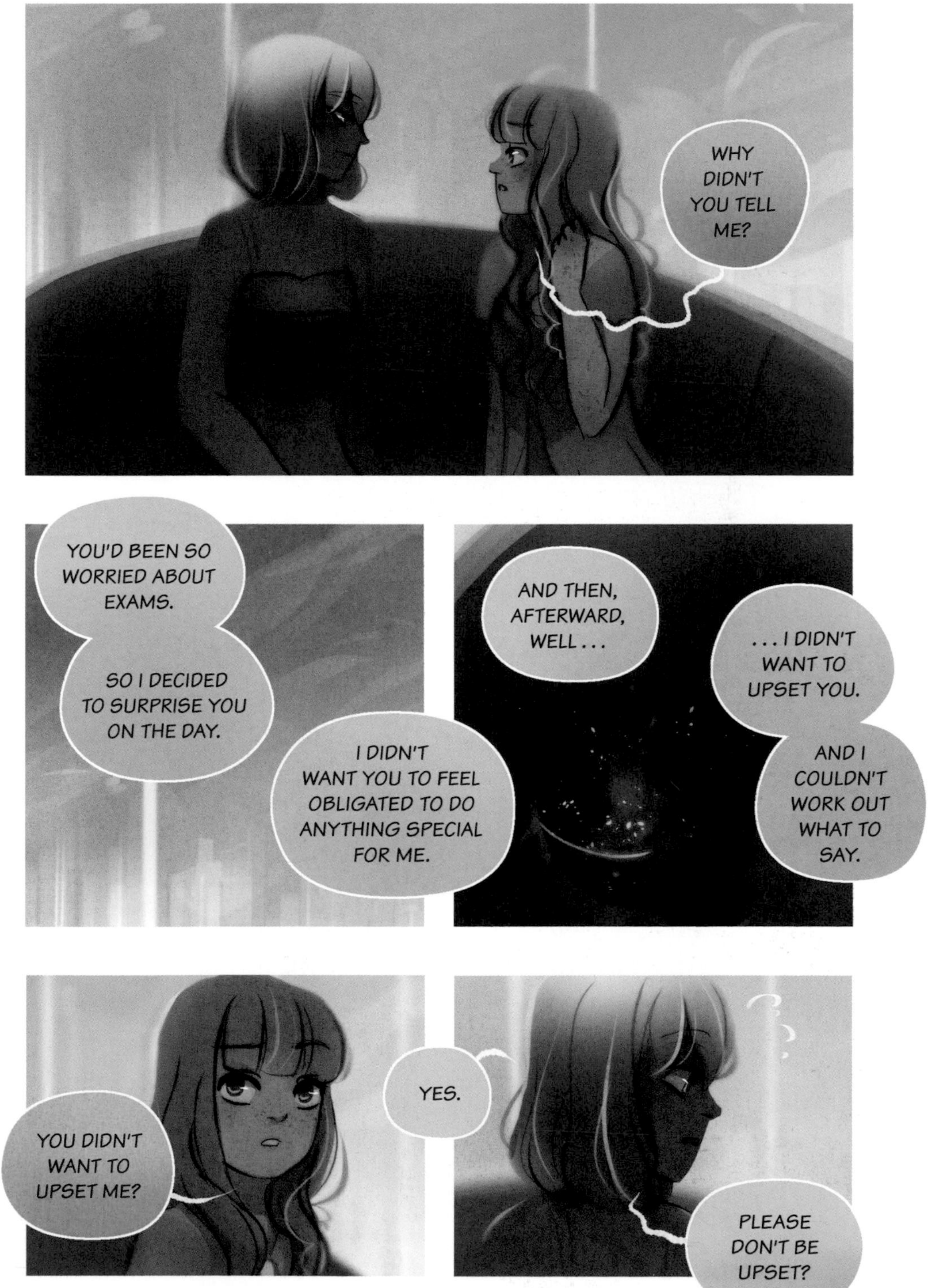
WHY DIDN'T YOU TELL ME?
YOU'D BEEN SO WORRIED ABOUT EXAMS.
SO I DECIDED TO SURPRISE YOU ON THE DAY.
I DIDN'T WANT YOU TO FEEL OBLIGATED TO DO ANYTHING SPECIAL FOR ME.
AND THEN, AFTERWARD, WELL . . .
. . . I DIDN'T WANT TO UPSET YOU.
AND I COULDN'T WORK OUT WHAT TO SAY.
YOU DIDN'T WANT TO UPSET ME?
YES.
PLEASE DON'T BE UPSET?

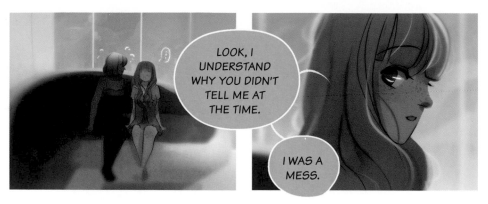

LOOK, I UNDERSTAND WHY YOU DIDN'T TELL ME AT THE TIME.

I WAS A MESS.

THANK YOU FOR LOOKING OUT FOR ME.

BUT YOUR BIRTHDAY WAS ALMOST A MONTH AGO.

AND EXAMS HAVE BEEN OVER FOR TWO WEEKS.

YOU SHOULD HAVE TOLD ME BY NOW.

I'M SORRY.

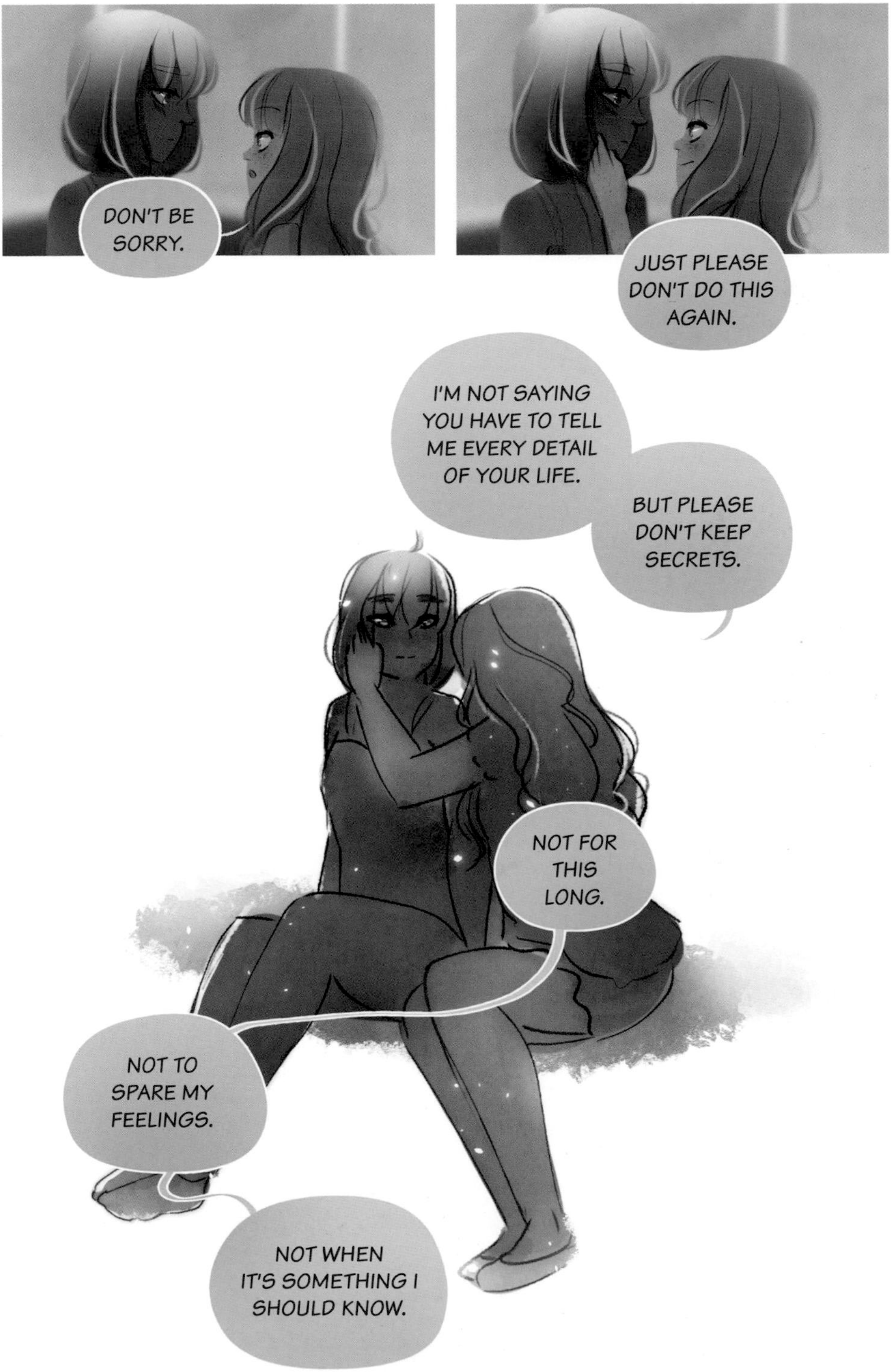
DON'T BE SORRY.
JUST PLEASE DON'T DO THIS AGAIN.
I'M NOT SAYING YOU HAVE TO TELL ME EVERY DETAIL OF YOUR LIFE.
BUT PLEASE DON'T KEEP SECRETS.
NOT FOR THIS LONG.
NOT TO SPARE MY FEELINGS.
NOT WHEN IT'S SOMETHING I SHOULD KNOW.

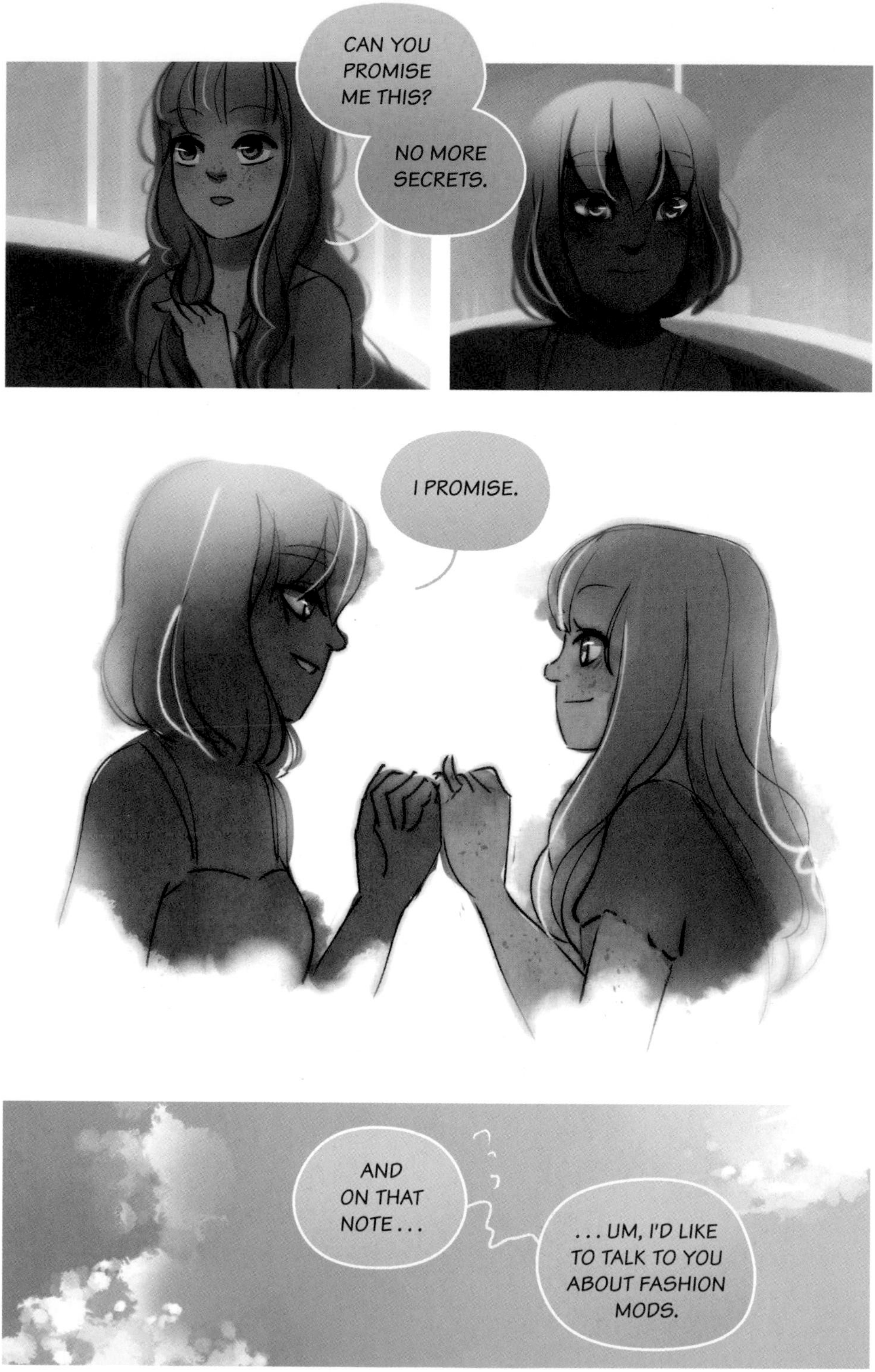
CAN YOU PROMISE ME THIS?
NO MORE SECRETS.
I PROMISE.
AND ON THAT NOTE...
...UM, I'D LIKE TO TALK TO YOU ABOUT FASHION MODS.

36 - RADIANT

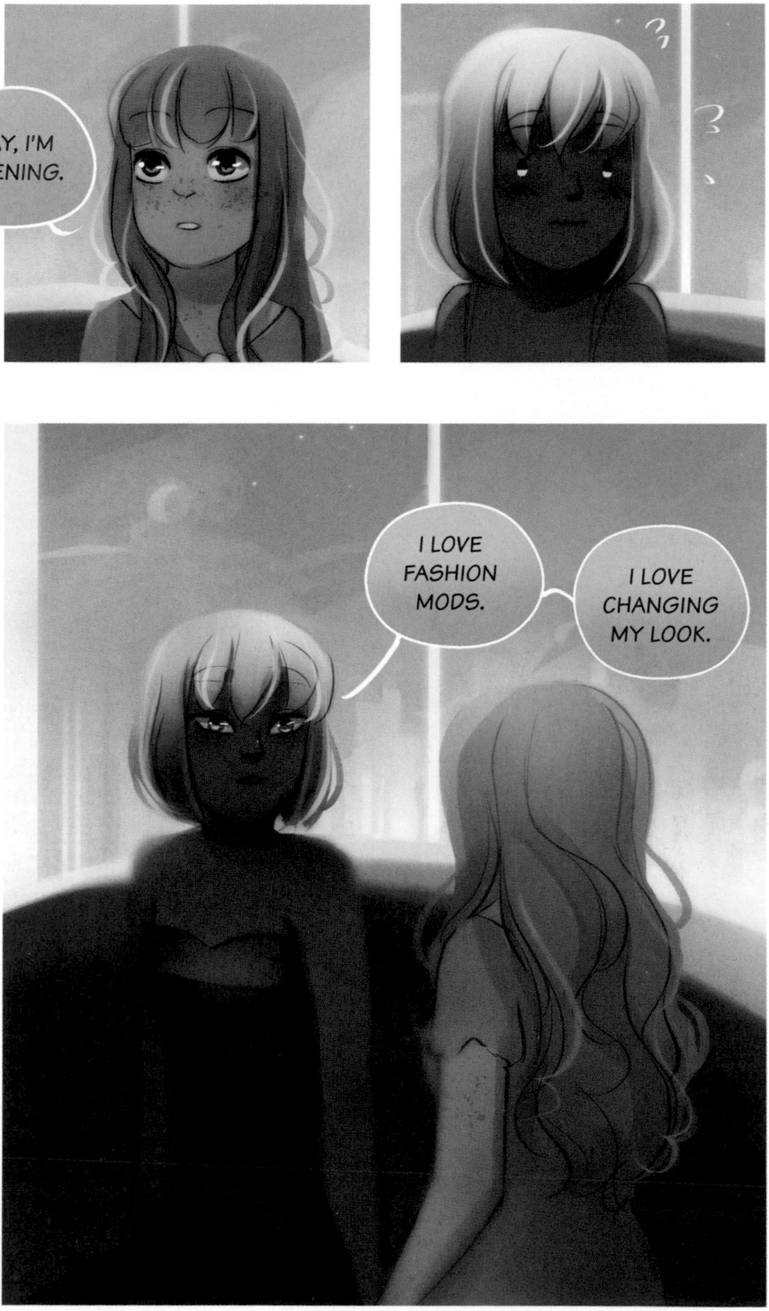
OKAY, I'M LISTENING.
I LOVE FASHION MODS.
I LOVE CHANGING MY LOOK.

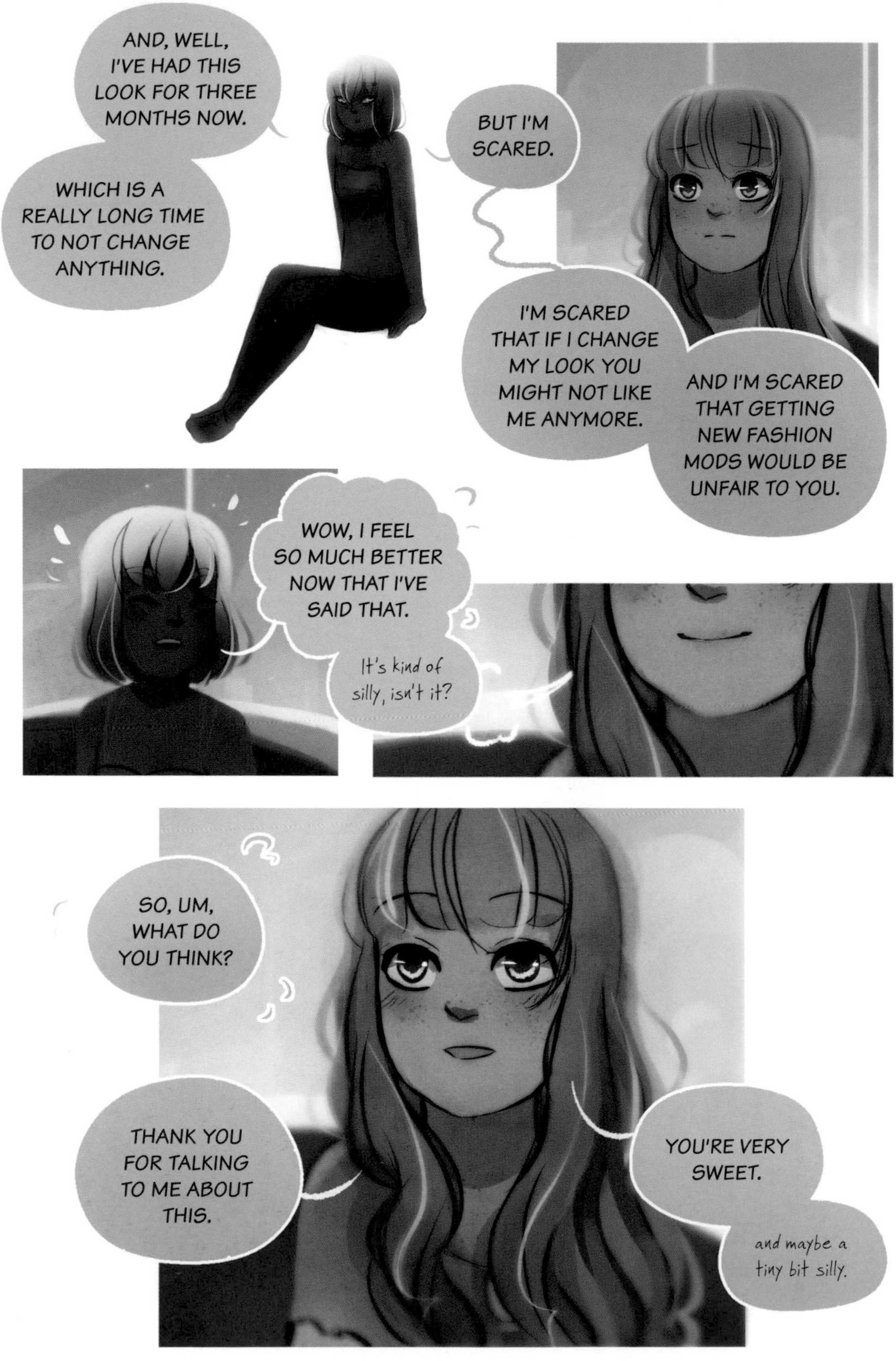
AND, WELL, I'VE HAD THIS LOOK FOR THREE MONTHS NOW.
WHICH IS A REALLY LONG TIME TO NOT CHANGE ANYTHING.
BUT I'M SCARED.
I'M SCARED THAT IF I CHANGE MY LOOK YOU MIGHT NOT LIKE ME ANYMORE.
AND I'M SCARED THAT GETTING NEW FASHION MODS WOULD BE UNFAIR TO YOU.
WOW, I FEEL SO MUCH BETTER NOW THAT I'VE SAID THAT.
It's kind of silly, isn't it?
SO, UM, WHAT DO YOU THINK?
THANK YOU FOR TALKING TO ME ABOUT THIS.
YOU'RE VERY SWEET.
and maybe a tiny bit silly.

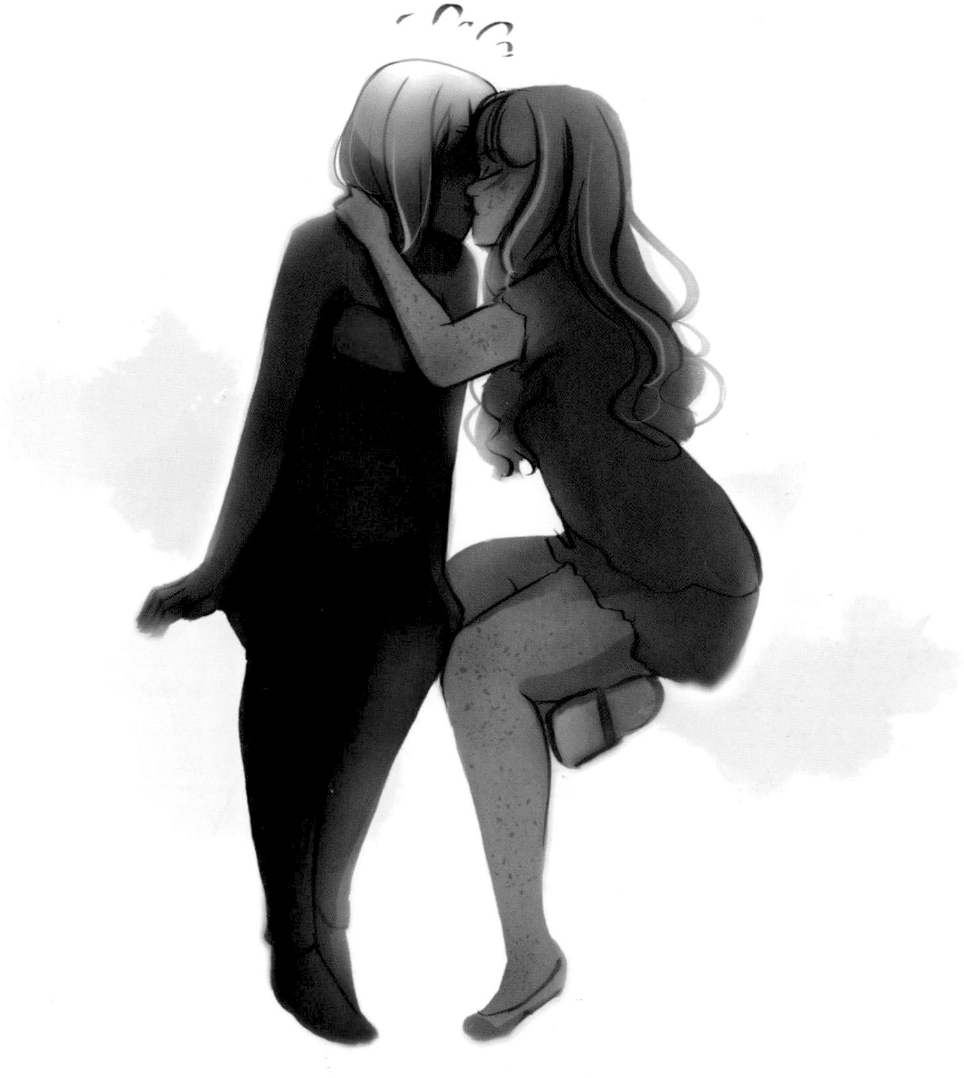

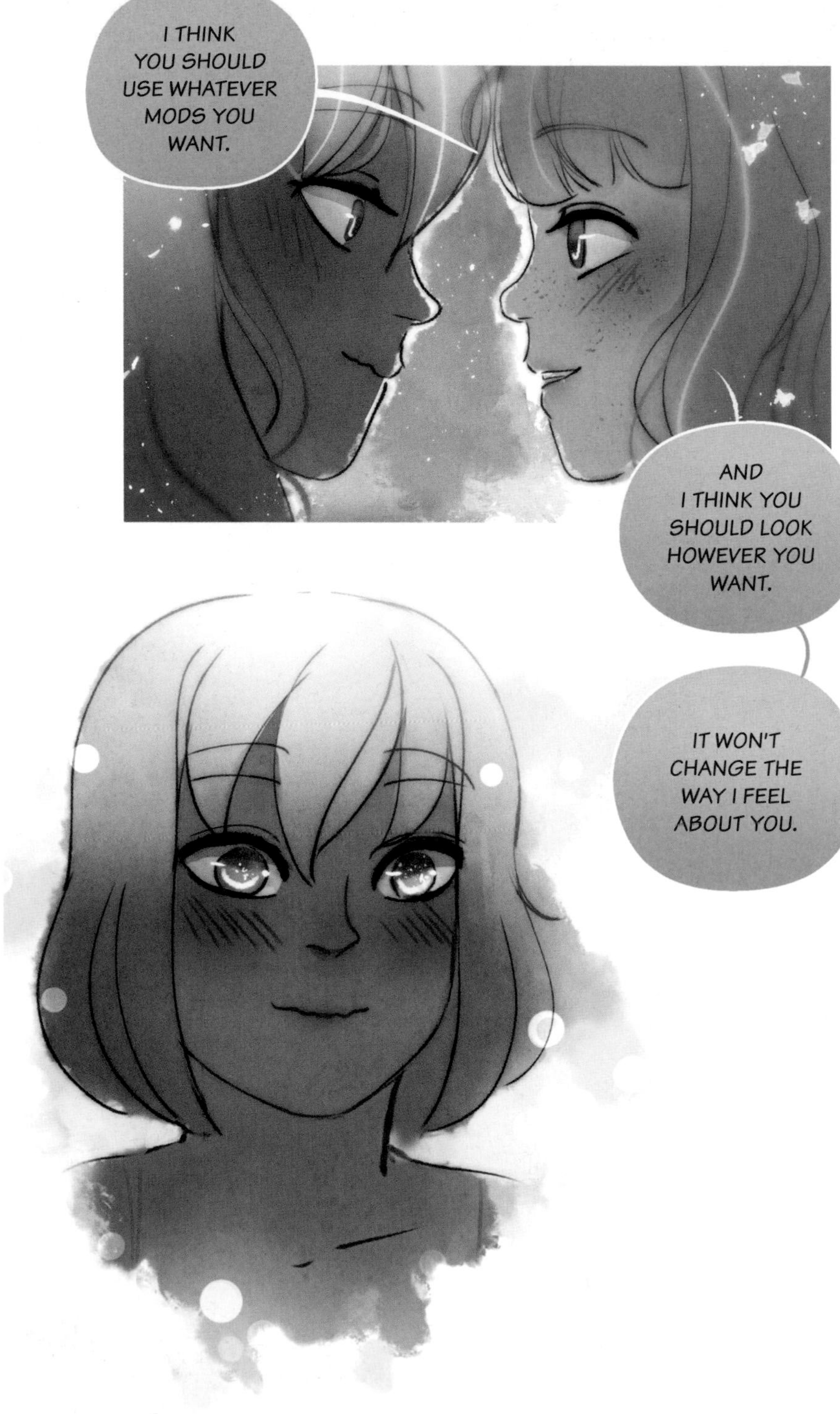
I THINK YOU SHOULD USE WHATEVER MODS YOU WANT.
AND I THINK YOU SHOULD LOOK HOWEVER YOU WANT.
IT WON'T CHANGE THE WAY I FEEL ABOUT YOU.

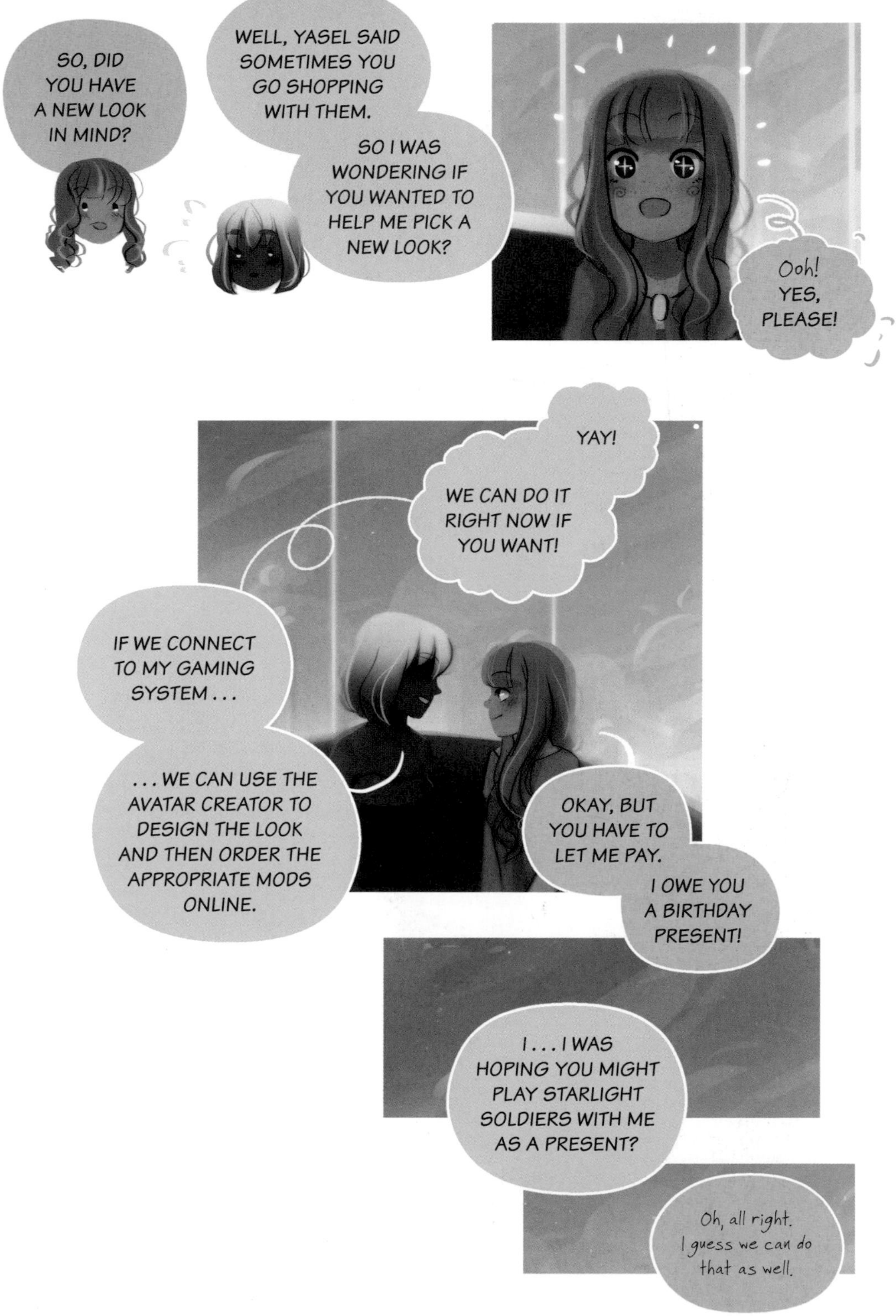
SO, DID YOU HAVE A NEW LOOK IN MIND?
WELL, YASEL SAID SOMETIMES YOU GO SHOPPING WITH THEM.
SO I WAS WONDERING IF YOU WANTED TO HELP ME PICK A NEW LOOK?
Ooh! YES, PLEASE!
YAY!
WE CAN DO IT RIGHT NOW IF YOU WANT!
IF WE CONNECT TO MY GAMING SYSTEM . . .
. . . WE CAN USE THE AVATAR CREATOR TO DESIGN THE LOOK AND THEN ORDER THE APPROPRIATE MODS ONLINE.
OKAY, BUT YOU HAVE TO LET ME PAY.
I OWE YOU A BIRTHDAY PRESENT!
I . . . I WAS HOPING YOU MIGHT PLAY STARLIGHT SOLDIERS WITH ME AS A PRESENT?
Oh, all right. I guess we can do that as well.

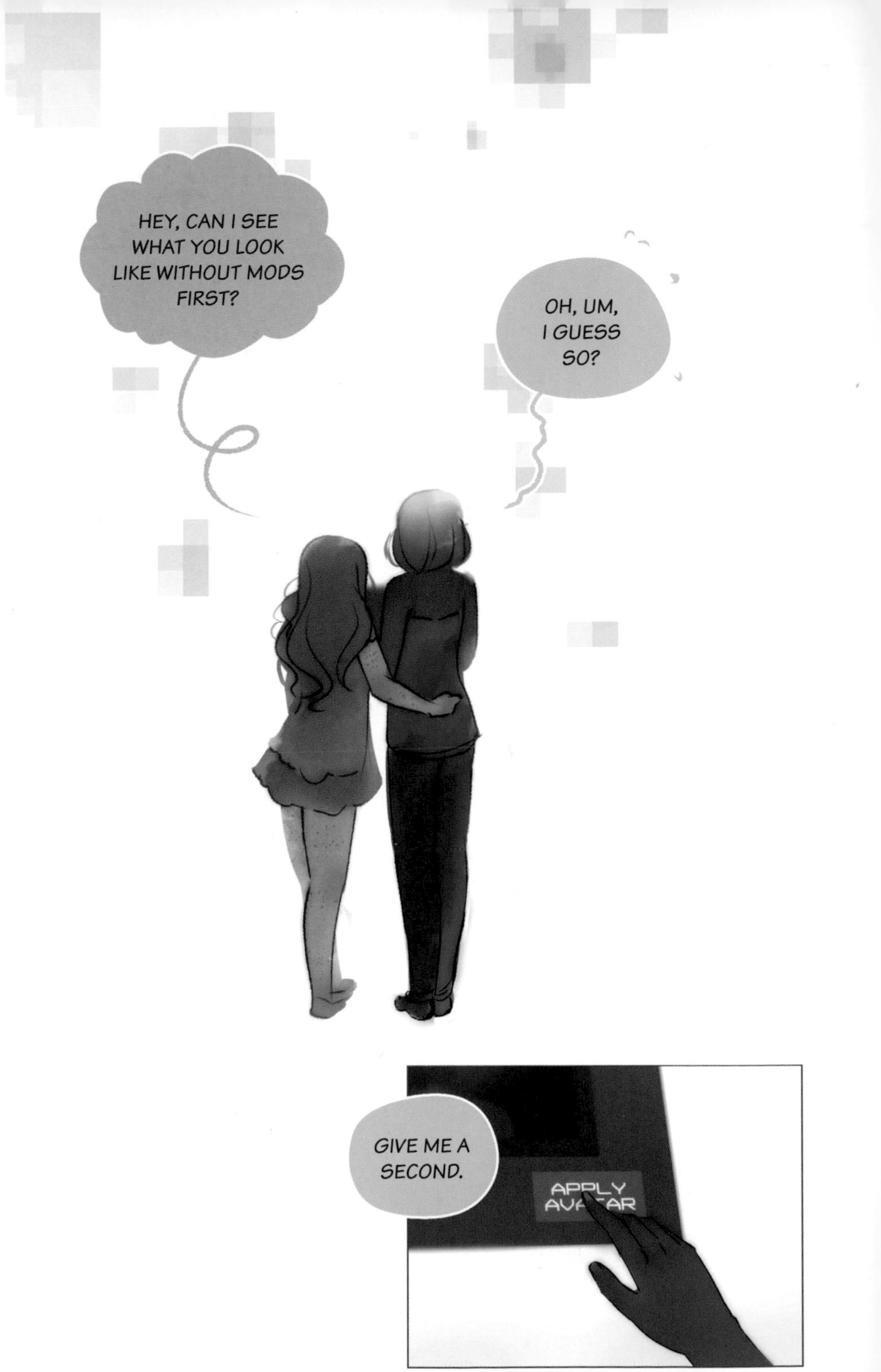
HEY, CAN I SEE WHAT YOU LOOK LIKE WITHOUT MODS FIRST?
OH, UM, I GUESS SO?
GIVE ME A SECOND.
APPLY AVATAR

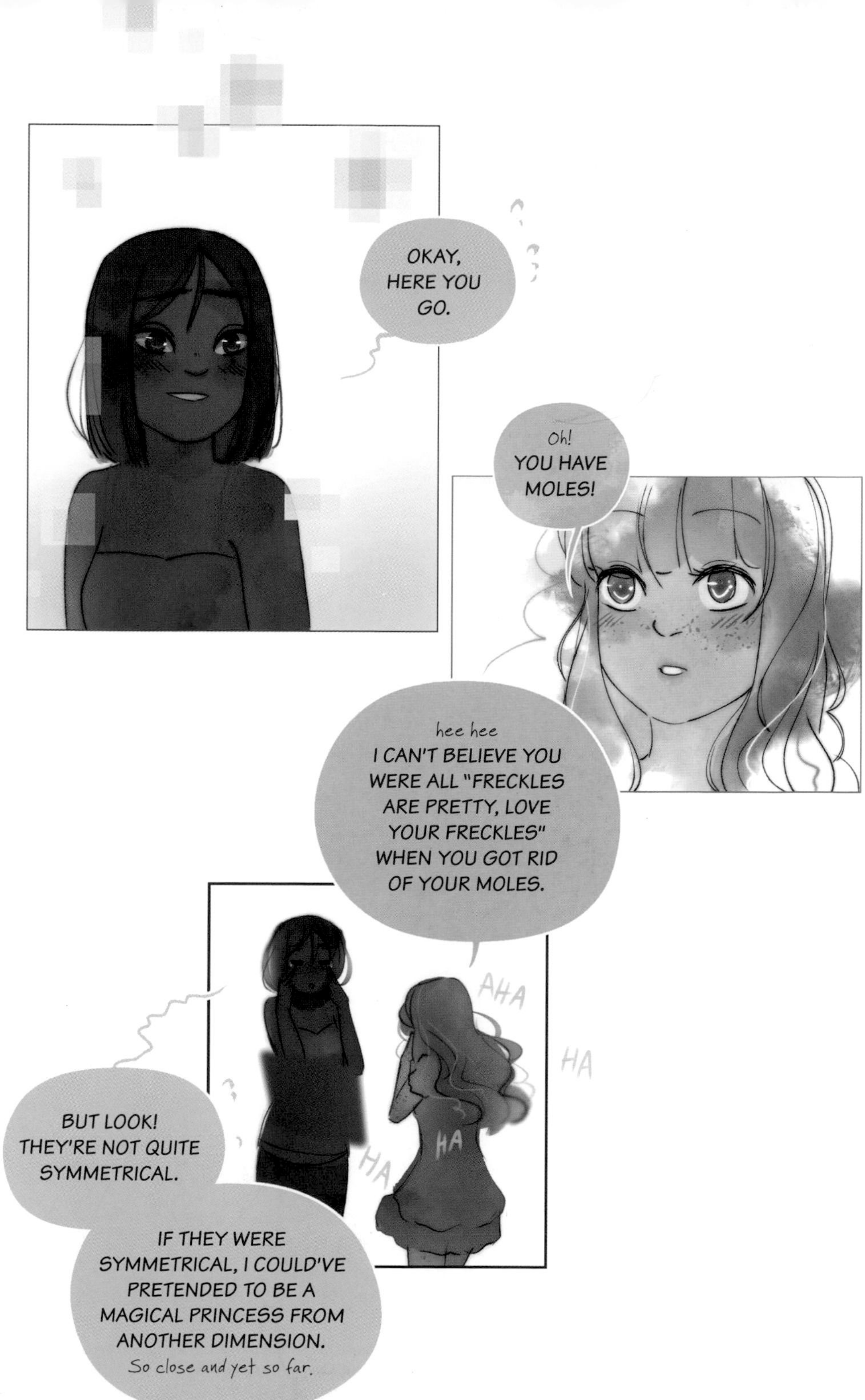
OKAY, HERE YOU GO.
Oh! YOU HAVE MOLES!
hee hee I CAN'T BELIEVE YOU WERE ALL "FRECKLES ARE PRETTY, LOVE YOUR FRECKLES" WHEN YOU GOT RID OF YOUR MOLES.
AHA
HA
HA
HA
BUT LOOK! THEY'RE NOT QUITE SYMMETRICAL.
IF THEY WERE SYMMETRICAL, I COULD'VE PRETENDED TO BE A MAGICAL PRINCESS FROM ANOTHER DIMENSION. So close and yet so far.

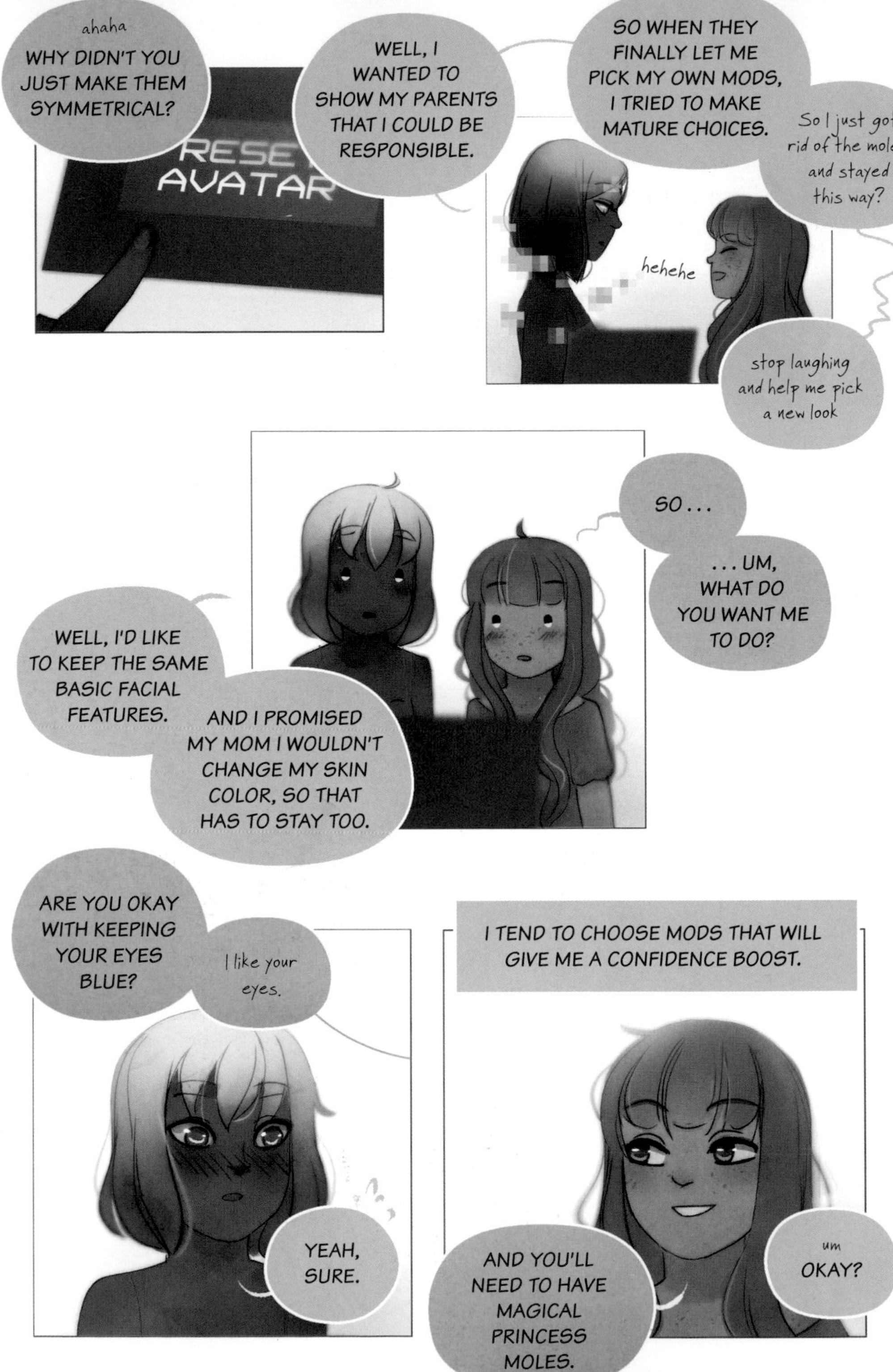
ahaha
WHY DIDN'T YOU JUST MAKE THEM SYMMETRICAL?
RESET AVATAR
WELL, I WANTED TO SHOW MY PARENTS THAT I COULD BE RESPONSIBLE.
SO WHEN THEY FINALLY LET ME PICK MY OWN MODS, I TRIED TO MAKE MATURE CHOICES.
So I just got rid of the moles and stayed this way?
hehehe
stop laughing and help me pick a new look
SO . . .
. . . UM, WHAT DO YOU WANT ME TO DO?
WELL, I'D LIKE TO KEEP THE SAME BASIC FACIAL FEATURES.
AND I PROMISED MY MOM I WOULDN'T CHANGE MY SKIN COLOR, SO THAT HAS TO STAY TOO.
ARE YOU OKAY WITH KEEPING YOUR EYES BLUE?
I like your eyes.
YEAH, SURE.
I TEND TO CHOOSE MODS THAT WILL GIVE ME A CONFIDENCE BOOST.
AND YOU'LL NEED TO HAVE MAGICAL PRINCESS MOLES.
um
OKAY?

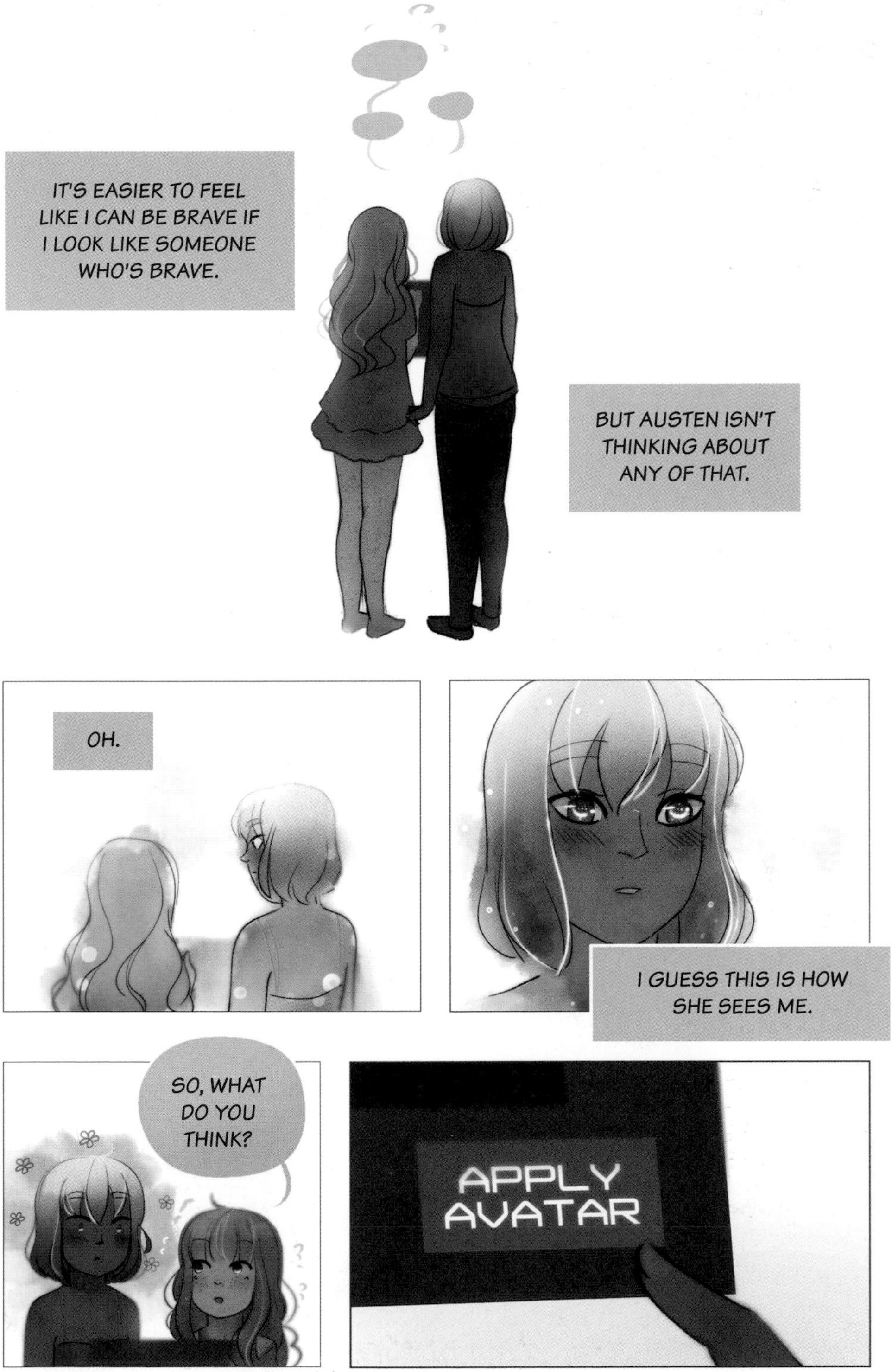
IT'S EASIER TO FEEL LIKE I CAN BE BRAVE IF I LOOK LIKE SOMEONE WHO'S BRAVE.
BUT AUSTEN ISN'T THINKING ABOUT ANY OF THAT.
OH.
I GUESS THIS IS HOW SHE SEES ME.
SO, WHAT DO YOU THINK?
APPLY AVATAR

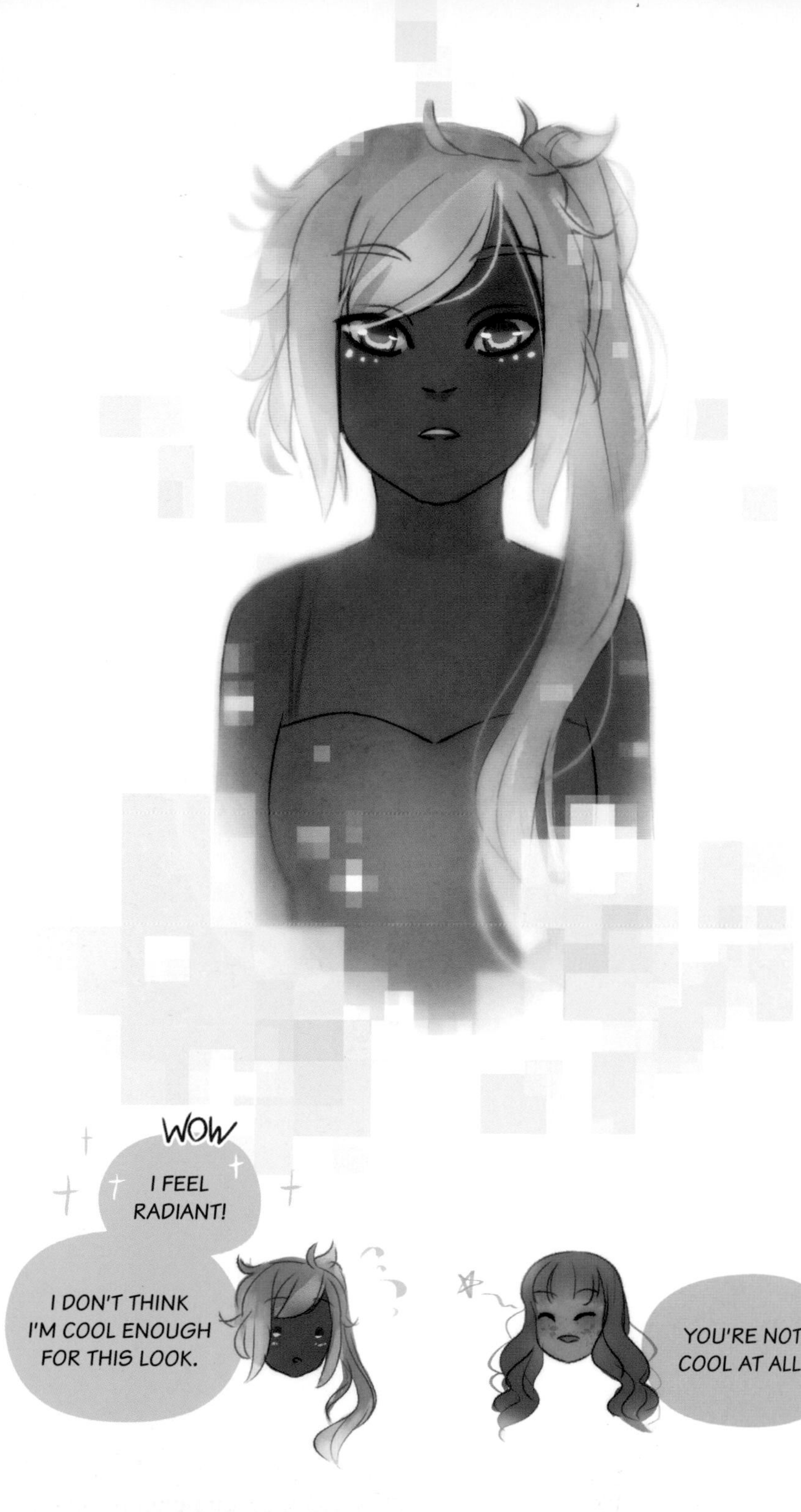
WOW
I FEEL RADIANT!
I DON'T THINK I'M COOL ENOUGH FOR THIS LOOK.
YOU'RE NOT COOL AT ALL.

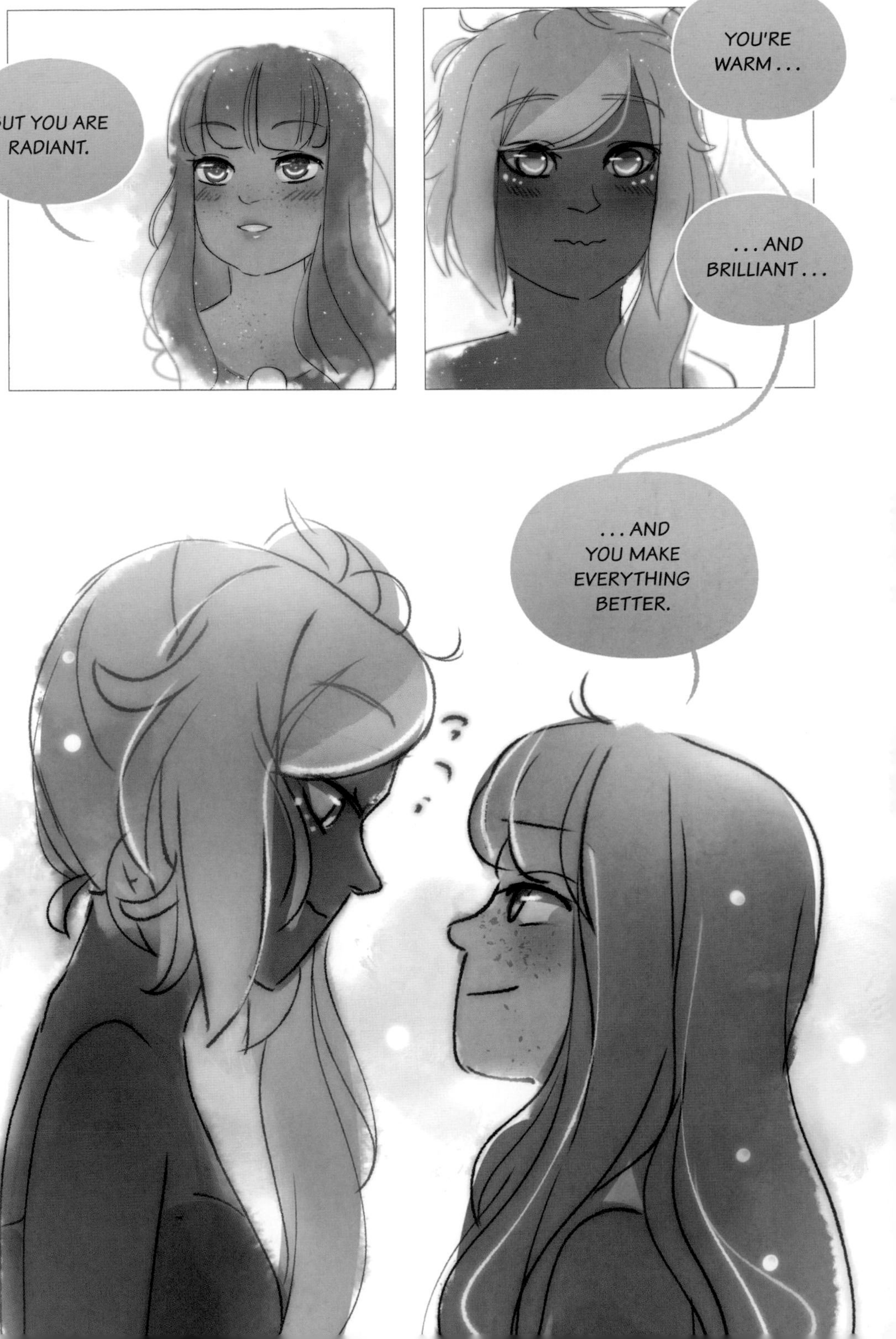
BUT YOU ARE RADIANT.
YOU'RE WARM . . .
. . . AND BRILLIANT . . .
. . . AND YOU MAKE EVERYTHING BETTER.

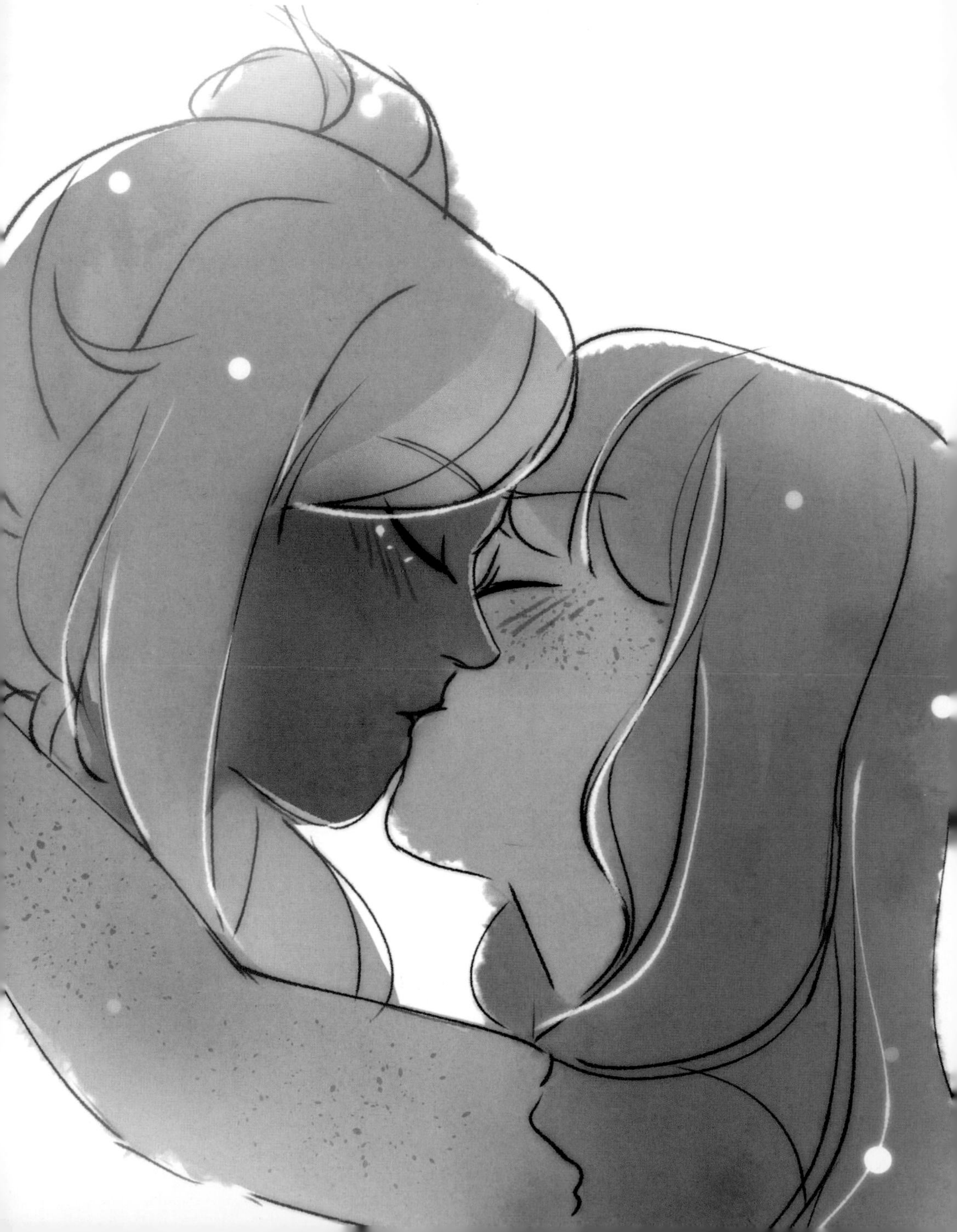

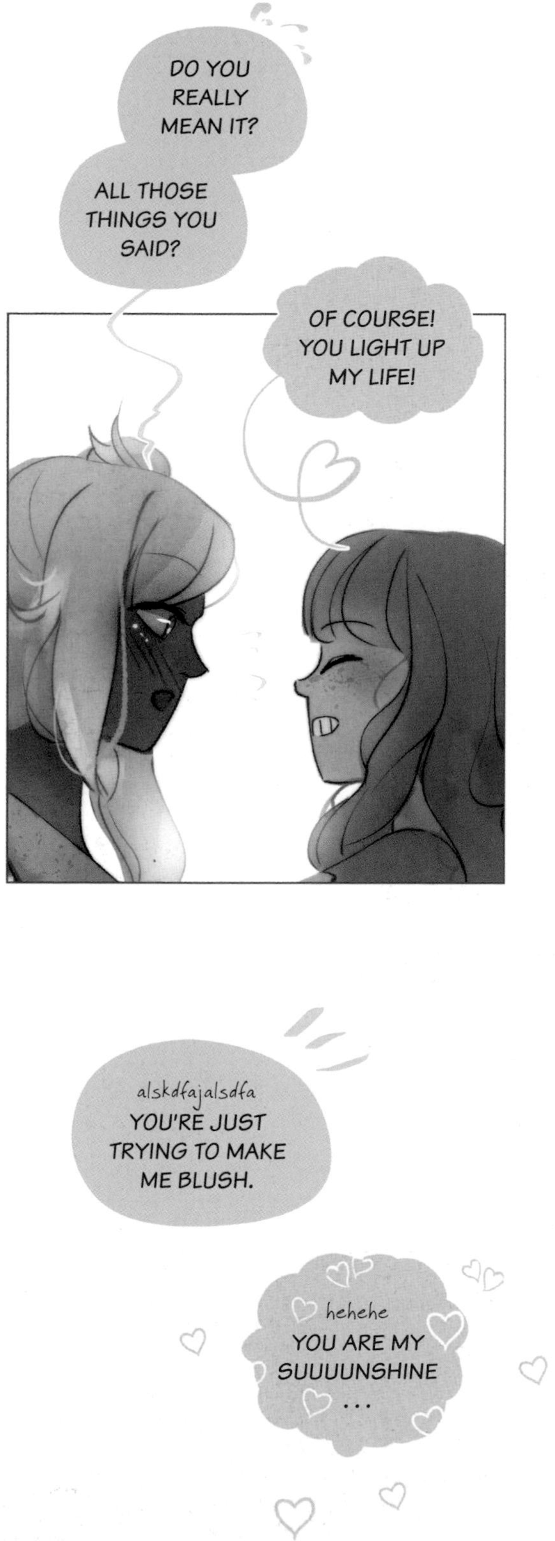
DO YOU REALLY MEAN IT?
ALL THOSE THINGS YOU SAID?
OF COURSE! YOU LIGHT UP MY LIFE!
alskdfajalsdfa YOU'RE JUST TRYING TO MAKE ME BLUSH.
hehehe YOU ARE MY SUUUUNSHINE ...

37 - STARLIGHT SOLDIERS

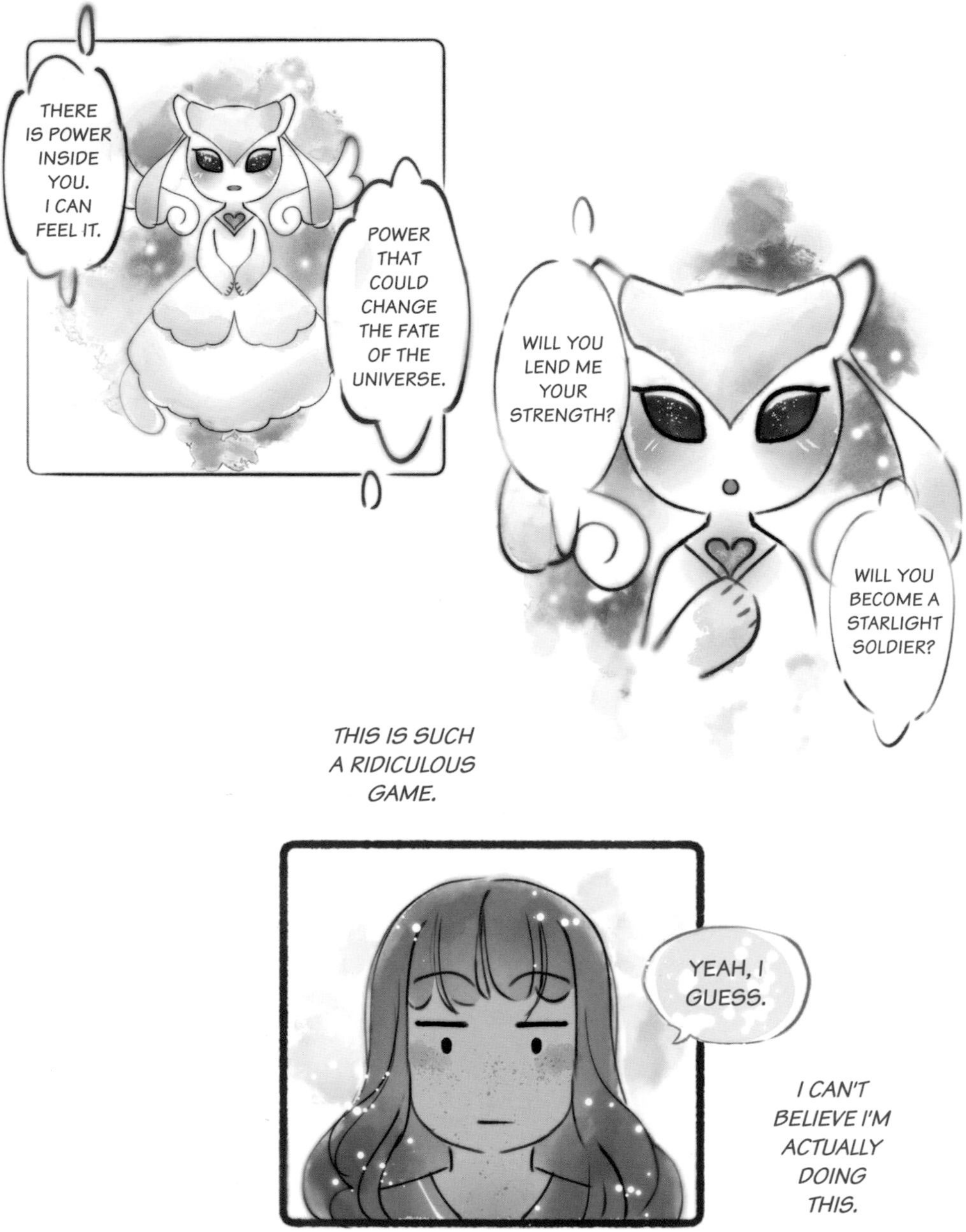

THERE IS POWER INSIDE YOU. I CAN FEEL IT.
POWER THAT COULD CHANGE THE FATE OF THE UNIVERSE.
WILL YOU LEND ME YOUR STRENGTH?
WILL YOU BECOME A STARLIGHT SOLDIER?
THIS IS SUCH A RIDICULOUS GAME.
YEAH, I GUESS.
I CAN'T BELIEVE I'M ACTUALLY DOING THIS.

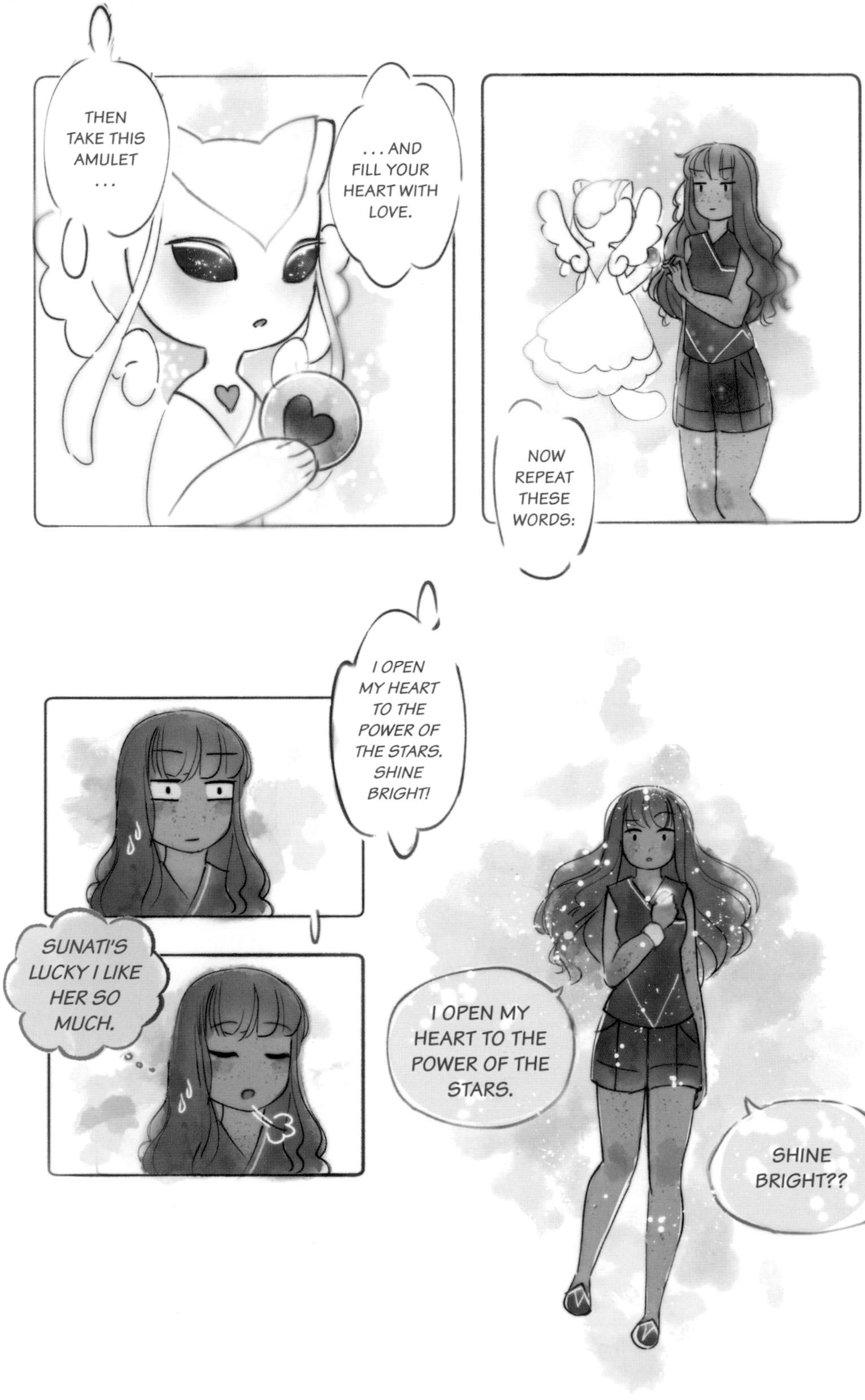

THEN TAKE THIS AMULET . . .
. . . AND FILL YOUR HEART WITH LOVE.
NOW REPEAT THESE WORDS:
I OPEN MY HEART TO THE POWER OF THE STARS. SHINE BRIGHT!
SUNATI'S LUCKY I LIKE HER SO MUCH.
I OPEN MY HEART TO THE POWER OF THE STARS.
SHINE BRIGHT??

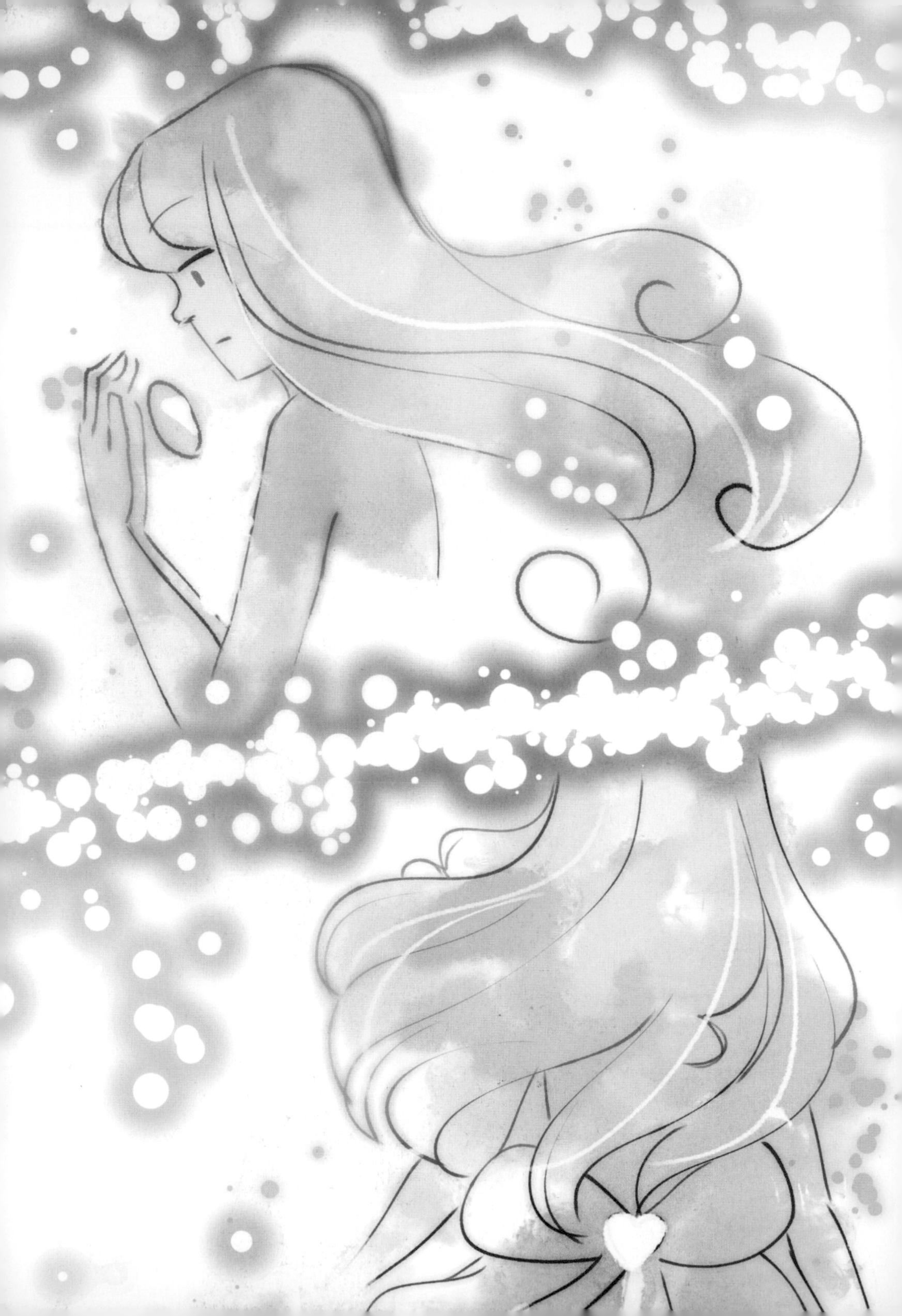

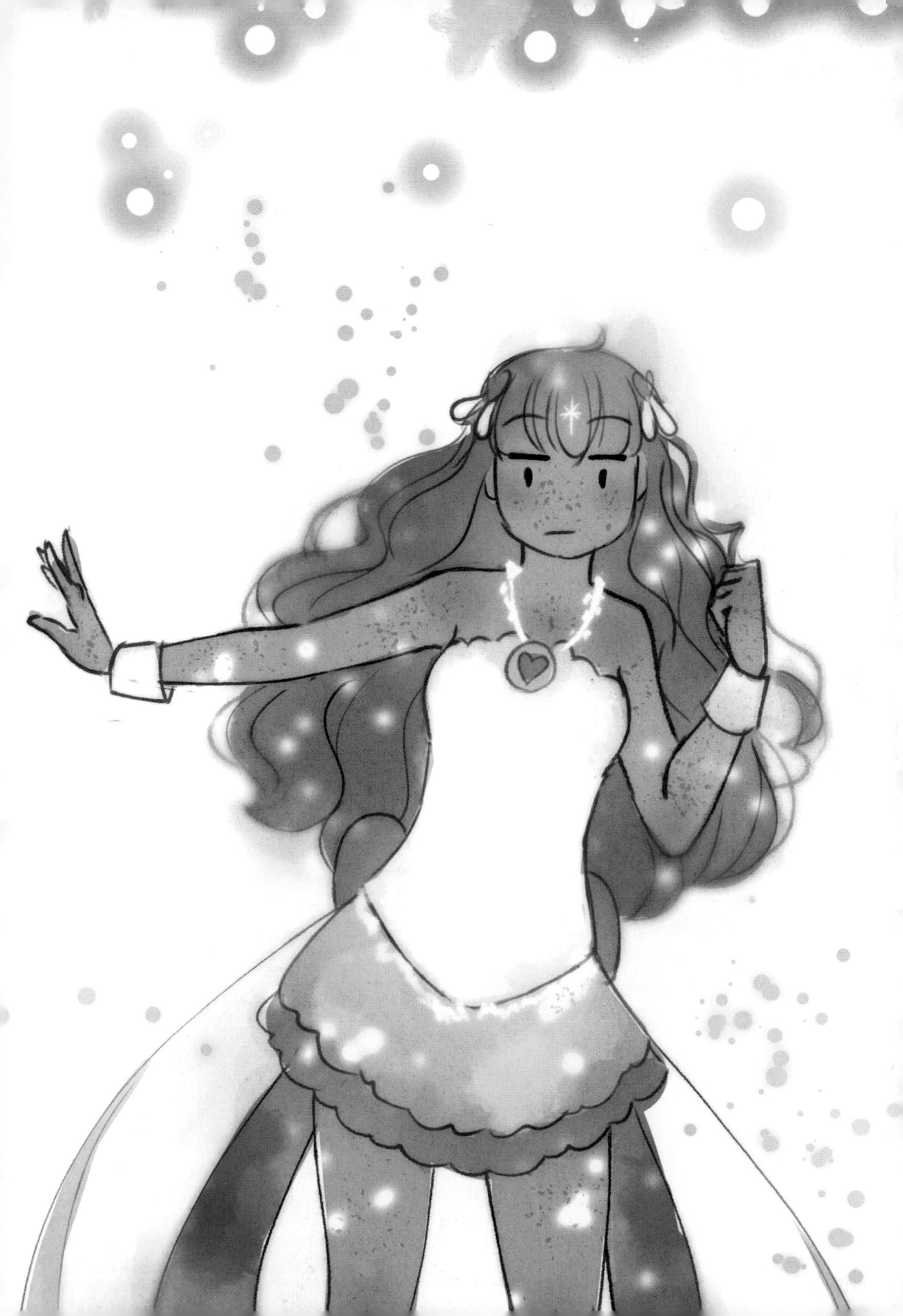

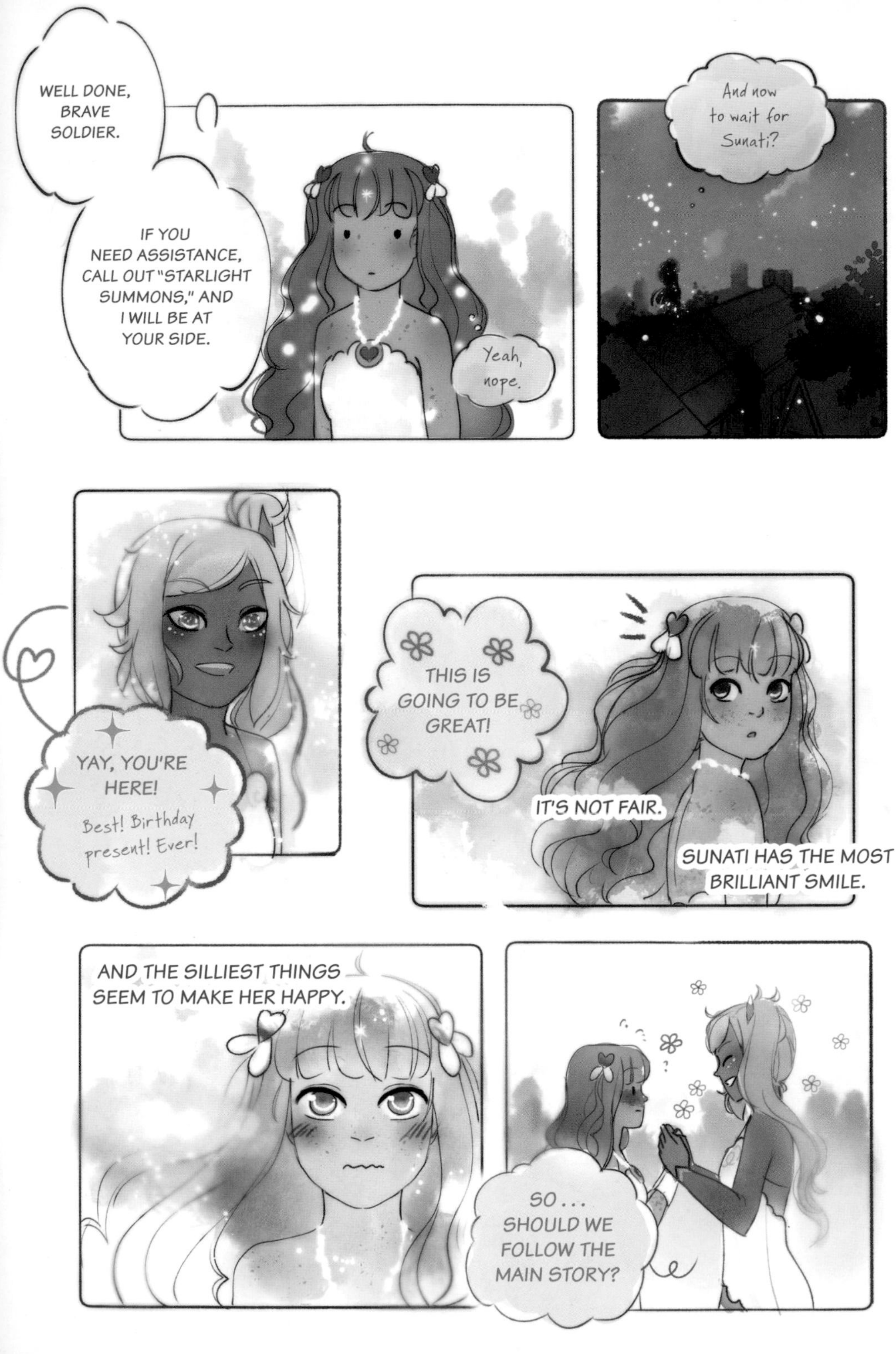
WELL DONE, BRAVE SOLDIER.
IF YOU NEED ASSISTANCE, CALL OUT "STARLIGHT SUMMONS," AND I WILL BE AT YOUR SIDE.
Yeah, nope.
And now to wait for Sunati?
YAY, YOU'RE HERE!
Best! Birthday present! Ever!
THIS IS GOING TO BE GREAT!
IT'S NOT FAIR.
SUNATI HAS THE MOST BRILLIANT SMILE.
AND THE SILLIEST THINGS SEEM TO MAKE HER HAPPY.
SO . . . SHOULD WE FOLLOW THE MAIN STORY?

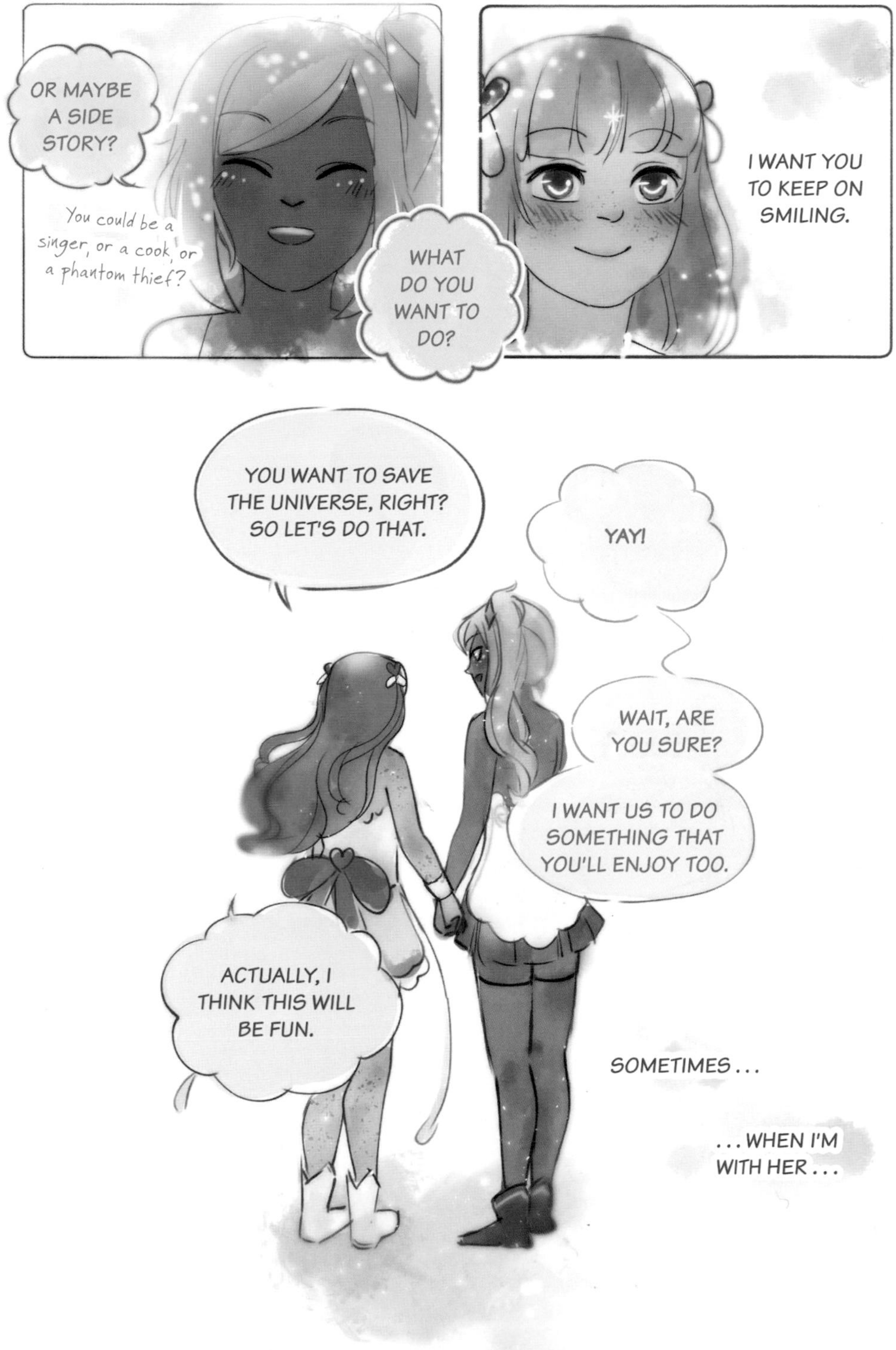
OR MAYBE A SIDE STORY?
You could be a singer, or a cook, or a phantom thief?
WHAT DO YOU WANT TO DO?
I WANT YOU TO KEEP ON SMILING.
YOU WANT TO SAVE THE UNIVERSE, RIGHT? SO LET'S DO THAT.
YAY!
WAIT, ARE YOU SURE?
I WANT US TO DO SOMETHING THAT YOU'LL ENJOY TOO.
ACTUALLY, I THINK THIS WILL BE FUN.
SOMETIMES . . .
. . . WHEN I'M WITH HER . . .

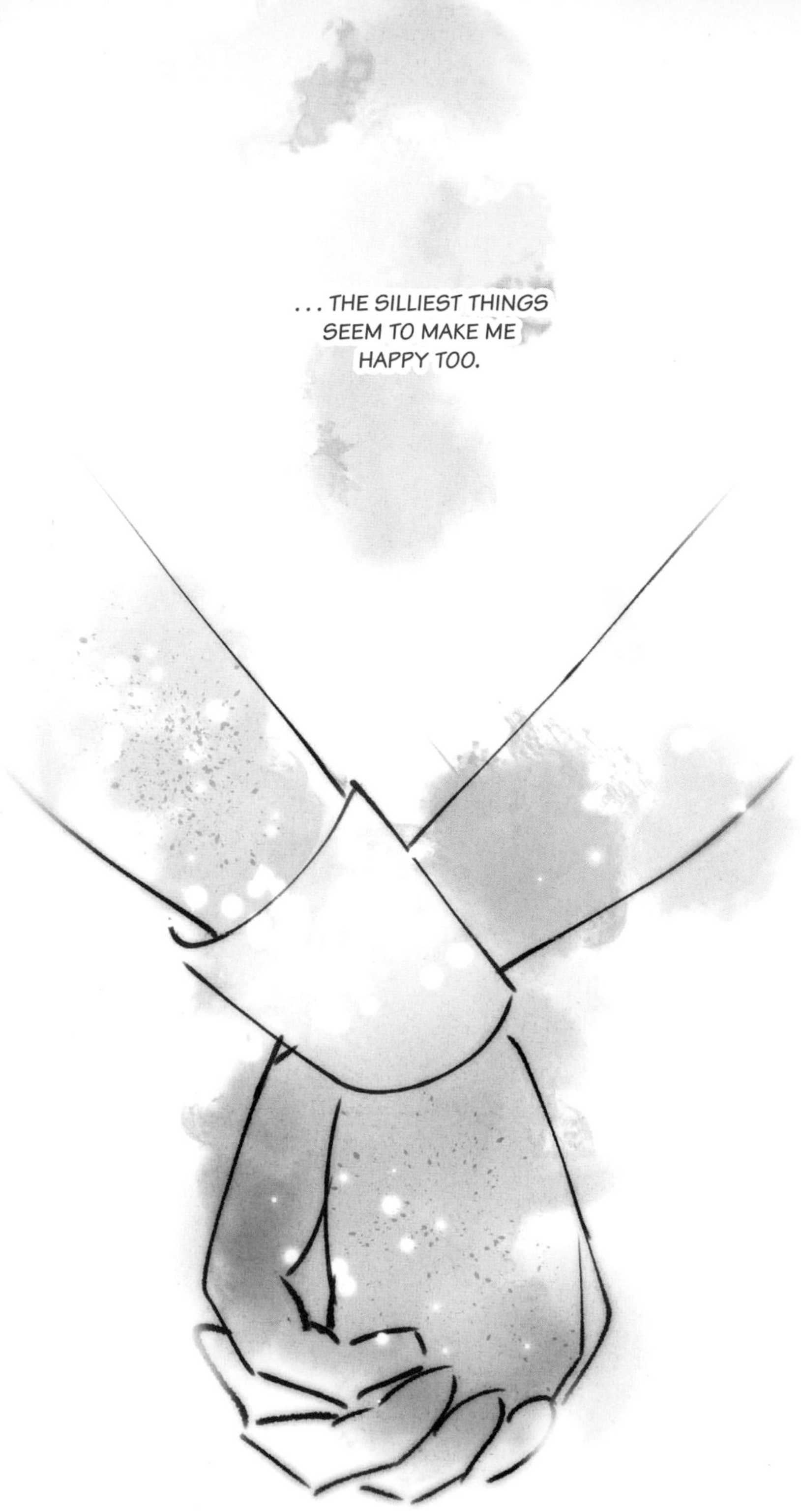
. . . THE SILLIEST THINGS SEEM TO MAKE ME HAPPY TOO.

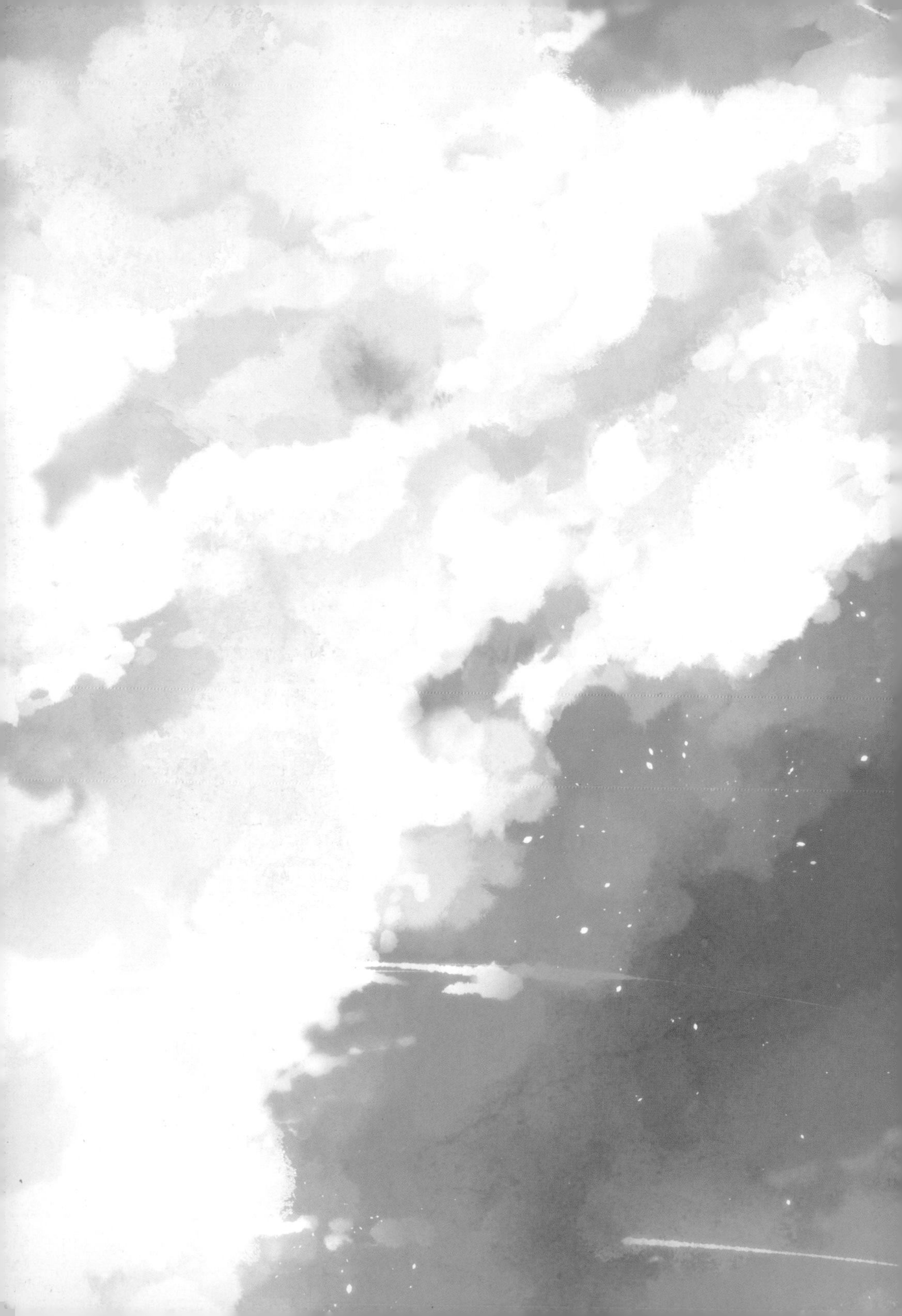

ACKNOWLEDGMENTS

Thank you to Webtoon.com for providing my very self-indulgent webcomic with a home. This comic would not exist without the sci-fi contest, and I will forever be grateful for the support and opportunity. Thank you to everyone, especially Emily. :)

Thanks to l-a-l-o-u, luciand29, forestofpaper, accioyash, catstylist, kaddy-heartstar, the-maneatingcabbage, a-very-strange-place, seoday, may12324, meganeburhapsody, and yuyuyoumu for reading the very first chapter before I posted it publicly, and giving me feedback and the confidence to share it. Thanks to everyone else who's given me feedback and confidence since. (I wish I could name you all.) Thanks for sharing *Always Human* with your friends. Thanks for saying the nicest things to me. Thanks for drawing fan art, writing fan fiction, making music, and cosplaying in bringing your creations to life. You inspire me so much!

Thank you to the incredibly generous Mari Lintz (marisketch) for helping me with Chilean Spanish (you are wonderful, and all mistakes are my own), and to Rinny Alonso (faerinny) for helping with the gender-neutral Spanish. (You are also wonderful!)

Thank you to ArtOfFlorence for being my Sapphic sci-fi webcomic buddy.

Thanks to Little Bee and GLAAD for taking a chance on my webcomic and being as excited about this as I am! Thanks to Rachel Gluckstern for championing *Always Human* and helping to make this print edition the best it can be. Thanks to Rob Wall for the hard work and magic involved in converting a mobile-formatted comic to a print-formatted comic.

Thanks to Maria Vicente, an actual angel, for answering all my questions and taking such good care of me.

Thank you to my family—my husband, my brother, my mother, and my father. If I can write about love, it is because of you. Thank you for encouraging me to be creative. Thank you for the magic paintbrush and the magic can of paint.

And thank *you* for reading this book. Stories exist in the space between the author and the reader, and I am delighted beyond words to be able to share this story with you.

ARI NORTH is a queer cartoonist who believes an entertaining story should also be full of diversity and inclusion. As a writer, artist, and musician, she wrote, drew, and composed the story and music for *Always Human*, a complete romance/sci-fi webcomic about two queer girls navigating maturity and finding happiness. She's currently working on a second webcomic, *Aerial Magic*, which is about the everyday lives of the witches who work at a broomstick repair shop. She lives in Australia with her husband.